# River into Darkness

# RIVER INTO DARKNESS

## BENEATH THE VAULTED HILLS
## THE COMPASS OF THE SOUL

## SEAN RUSSELL

**DAW BOOKS, INC.**
DONALD A. WOLLHEIM, FOUNDER
375 Hudson Street, New York, NY 10014

ELIZABETH R. WOLLHEIM
SHEILA E. GILBERT
PUBLISHERS
www.dawbooks.com

BENEATH THE VAULTED HILLS:
I'm sure that every writer, at some point, has received encouragement
and advice from kindly teachers, and in this I'm no different. This book
is dedicated to them (for teachers receive so little credit for their work),
especially the late Helen Fawcett, Chris Evans, Catharine Jones,
and Larry Kendal, wherever he is.

THE COMPASS OF THE SOUL:
For Peter Stampfel for rescuing my first book
from the slush pile,
and Besty Wollheim for patience and insight.

*The journey out through darkened lands*
*A way beneath the vaulted hill*
*The tidal years sound elder bells,*
*Though falcons cry and thrushes trill.*

# Beneath the Vaulted Hills

Men of such stature, of such undeniable greatness, cast shadows beyond our limited world.

—Halden: *Essays*

# Prologue

He sat before a window which stood slightly ajar and read by starlight. There had been a time when he'd preferred the warm light of day, but in the decades since the passing of his centenary, he'd become more inclined toward the cool illumination of the stars or even the moon. He studied the stars, of course, and one could hardly do that by daylight, but even so, he found the pale light so much more restful. Or perhaps he had just seen enough of the world.

Recently there had been a particular wandering star that he'd been observing nightly, using his improved telescope—an invention of Skye's, ironically. This star had a strange halo about it and a fiery tail. Things even the ancients did not know.

But more than anything he *felt* its passing. Felt it pull on all the heavenly bodies and, in turn, the effect this had elsewhere. Here, in the house of Eldrich, for instance.

The mage marked his place with a feather and closed the ancient book with care, placing it on a small table. He rose and walked out onto the terrace, looking up at the heavens. Eldrich had been reading Lucklow's treatise on augury—its practice and its perils. Especially its perils. The chapter on interpretation particularly fascinated him. Interpretation was the key, and it was the least certain aspect of the art.

The wandering star, for instance. It meant something—he was utterly sure of that—but try as he might, he could not understand what. And there was no one else whom he might ask.

"Do I feel lonely, being the last?" he asked the stars. He waited a moment and then decided that they could not reply. Only he knew . . . and would not say.

From beyond the garden wall he heard a wolf raise up its voice, the howl reverberating in his own breast. His familiar, off in the hills and wood, hunting as it must.

A spring night . . . still, awaiting the voices of the frogs and insects. Only the choral stars singing their ancient melodies.

He looked up and found the wandering star. *"Perhaps we have roamed long enough,"* he whispered.

Augury tempted him. He could feel it. Perhaps this time he would have a vision that was absolutely clear, and his course of action would be obvious. Obvious beyond all doubt.

"A fool's hope," he said aloud. Certainly he was too old for those.

The world was in motion. There was no doubt of that. Everyone poised to play their part, to make their sacrifice, if that was what was required. After all these many years he could not have a mistake. Not the smallest error.

Eldrich tilted back his head and gazed at the stars, wondering again if he had calculated correctly. If he could make an end of it soon.

# ⤳ One

*It is, perhaps, less than true to say it all began in a brothel, but I found Samual Hayes hiding in such an establishment and this marked the turning point if not an actual beginning. How Samual Hayes had become misfortune's whipping boy, I will never understand.*

*—The journal of Erasmus Flattery*

Hayes thought it particularly appropriate that the streets of the poor lacked public lighting of any kind. One passed out of the light of the better areas into near darkness, only dull candlelight filtering through dirty panes and casting faint shimmering rectangles on the cobbles. At night one often saw dark feet and legs passing through these rectangles of light, or if the passerby walked closer to the window, one would see a silhouetted head and shoulders floating oddly above the street. Hayes had sat in his window often enough to mark this strange anatomical parade passing by—incomplete men and women flitting into existence before each dull little window, then ceasing to be, then coming to meager life again.

Paradise Street—he wondered if the man who named it had foreseen its future—lay near the boundary between the light and darkness, an area of perpetual twilight, perhaps. Almost a border town where few seemed to make their homes permanently. Most were on their way into darkness—a handful were moving toward the light. It was a place where a young man might end up if his family had sacrificed their fortune to foolishness and keeping up appearances, as was the case with Samual Hayes.

For him Paradise Street was also a place to hide from one's creditors, as astonishing as that seemed to him—a young man who, for most of his life, had never given money a second thought.

He passed through a candlelit square of light and looked down at his hands. There he was, not gone yet. Still more or less substantial. Perhaps there was hope.

"His High and Mightiness is still among us, I see," came an old man's voice out of the shadows. Hayes stiffened, but walked on, feeling his resolve harden as well.

He would have thought his fall from grace into this world would have made him one of them, perhaps even engendered some sympathy, but for some few it made him an object of enormous disdain. *How could anyone born to privilege have fallen so far as to land in Paradise Street?* That is what they thought. Only a fool or a weakling could take such a fall. And there were moments when Hayes feared they were right. It made him all the more grateful for the kind treatment he received from some of his other neighbors.

As he came up to his rooming house, he realized that there were perhaps a dozen people gathered in the shadows across the street, but they were uncommonly quiet.

"Mr. Hayes!" said a woman who was one of the local busybodies. "There's men taking your rooms apart. Look, sir." She pointed up at his windows.

Shadows were moving in his room, though Hayes knew he'd left no lamp burning.

"Flames!" he heard himself say. He realized that everyone stood looking up, but no one made a move to interfere.

Someone laid a hand on his arm as he went to run for his door. It was an old soldier who lived down the street. "Them's navy men, Mr. Hayes," he said with distaste. "Mark my words. Navy men, whether they wear their fine uniforms or no. You'd be best to give them a wide berth, sir. That's my advice, for what it's worth."

"Navy men?" Hayes' rally to save his possessions was stopped short. "Agents of the Admiralty?" There was clearly some mistake.

"And they aren't the only ones, Mr. Hayes," the woman said. "When they arrived, they surprised others already in your rooms. Those'ns jumped out the window. My Tom saw 'em, didn't you, Tom?" she said to a boy who clutched her hand.

The boy nodded and took his fingers from his mouth. "They floated down, landin' soft as pigeons, if you please. Soft as birdies."

The woman looked back to Hayes, as though awaiting an explanation.

"But who were they?" Hayes said, asking a question instead. "Robbers? I—I have so little to steal."

"If they were robbers, Mr. Hayes, they were uncommonly well-dressed ones. 'Gentlemen,' Tom said, and the old blacksmith saw them, too. 'Gentlemen,' he said as well. I don't know what you've been up to, Mr. Hayes, but there are men around asking after you—navy men. You'd best be on your way before someone turns you in for the few coins they'll get. There are enough around that would do it, too, I'm sorry to say."

"I'll talk to them. There's some explanation, I'm sure. . . ."

The old soldier touched his arm again. "I'm sure you didn't do whatever it was they think you done, sir, but you'd best go. When authorities come bustin' down your door, they don't want to hear no explanations. The gaol is no place for the likes of you, Mr. Hayes. Find the most well-placed friend you have, sir, and go to him. That's your best hope—that and a good barrister. Be off now, before some'un turns you in, as Mrs. Osbourn said. Good luck to you, Mr. Hayes."

A group of burly men appeared around the nearby corner and in the light from a window Hayes saw someone pointing toward him, and he was sure the men he was leading weren't residents of Paradise Street.

Hayes slipped back into the shadow, making his way along the fronts of the buildings, hugging the wall. He pulled up the collar of his frock coat quickly to hide the white of his shirt and neckcloth. Fifty feet farther he broke into a lope, as quiet as he could, passing ghostlike through the rectangles of stained light.

He dodged down an alley, slowing now for lack of light, feeling his way, his heart pounding and his breath short, though he'd hardly run at all. *Fear,* he realized. *I am running in fear from the authorities.* This was how men disappeared into the darkness of the poor quarter.

There were shouts behind him and the sound of men running, then suddenly slowing. A lantern swung into the alley at his back, but it was too far away for the light to touch him.

In a hundred feet he came out into another street and turned left. His instinct was to head for the lighted streets—the safe streets—but the men chasing him were not cutthroats who kept to the dark, and in the streetlights he would be seen more easily.

But still he found himself gravitating that way, mothlike. It was the habit of a lifetime; a desire to escape, to not disappear entirely.

He continued to hear the men shouting. Hayes pushed himself on, fighting to catch his breath, not even sure if they were still following him—afraid to look back.

He was heading toward Brinsley Park, and Spring Street—the beginning of the lighted boulevards. *This is madness,* he told himself. The darkness was his ally now. The place he thought constantly of escaping, and now it sheltered him. He should cling to it, wrap it around himself, for it was all that protected him.

But if he stayed here, in the twilight quarter, someone would give him away—for he would never be anything but an outsider, here. Not safe in the darkness or the light. Better the light, then. Too many disappeared in the darkness.

Hayes took the risk of pausing before he went out onto the lit street that bordered Brinsley Park. For a moment he stood listening to the sounds down the darkened alley he was about to leave. His pursuers were likely not far behind.

Almost more than hear, Hayes sensed noise down the street, not on top of him but too close. Composing himself, he stepped out onto the lamplit street, monitoring his pace so that he would not stand out, yet making the best time he could.

Couples walked at their leisure, especially on the street's far side, which is where he wanted to be, as far from his tormentors as he could be. Weaving between carriages and tradesmen's carts, Hayes strode quickly to the opposite side, realizing that this was a mistake—because of the size of the park there were no streets leading off from that side of the avenue for a distance equal to several blocks. More than anything, he needed to make as many turns as he could to confound his hunters, and now that wasn't possible. They might think he'd scrambled over the iron fence into the park, keeping to darkness like any criminal would, but the fence was so high. . . .

He pressed on, fighting the urge to look back—a man who appeared to have pursuers would be noticed, no question of that.

Men and women passed, arm in arm, chatting and laughing. A coach clattered by, a young man leaning out its window, toasting the passersby theatrically; his drunken companions laughed and as one of them tried to fill his glass, a crimson stream of wine splashed over the cobbles.

"*Hayes?*" someone called.

Hayes looked about wildly. Bloody blood and flames, someone was announcing his name to everyone on the avenue!

"*Samual Hayes?*" the voice came again; from the carriage, he realized. "Driver! Heave to, man."

Slowing, the carriage veered toward the curb, frightening pedestrians, clearly not in perfect control. Hayes was not sure who had called to him, but he took one look back and made a dash for the still-moving carriage. As he approached, the driver set it off again, laughing inanely, for it was another young gentleman with the reins in hand. Hayes forced himself to sprint, and as the door swung open, he reached out and grabbed the carriage, feeling hands take hold of him and drag him in where he sprawled on the floor.

Half a dozen men his own age looked down at him, grinning. "Why, Samual Hayes," one of them said, "have a drink," and proceeded to pour wine all over Hayes' face.

"Hume!" Hayes managed, almost choking. He pushed himself up, fending off the bottle.

The young gentlemen were laughing madly.

"Aye, have another drink, Hayes." Hume began tilting another bottle toward Hayes, but he managed to push this one away, too.

"Flames, Hume, but you came just in time. I was being chased by footpads."

"On Spring Street?" someone said, clearly certain he was joking.

"You'd have been better off with the footpads, I'll wager," someone laughed. "We're celebrating Hume's impending demise. Marriage, that is."

Hayes struggled up into a crouch and stared out the rear window. He could see them now, a group of men at the run, but too far back to be distinguished. Too far back to catch them, that was certain.

"Blood and flames," Hume said, twisting around to look out. "You were serious."

"Let's go back and give them what-for," someone called out. "I've a rapier in here somewhere."

"No!" Hayes said quickly. "Drive on."

"Hah! Out of the frying pan into the fire, Hayesy. You're with us now and our intent is far more wicked than any footpads. Driver," the young man called, *"The brothel!"*

*"The brothel!"*

*"The brothel!"* The others took up the cry, and the carriage careened off down the street, only the fragile common sense of horses keeping the gentlemen from disaster.

The anemic light of coach lamps smeared across rain-oiled cobbles and lit the moving flanks of horses without having a noticeable effect on the overwhelming darkness. Avonel of an evening in early spring.

Erasmus Flattery stepped down from the hired coach and, with barely a nod, shook some coins out of his pocket for the driver. This was the address, he was sure. A doorman held an umbrella for him, interrupting a drizzle so fine it seemed more like a cool, falling dew, or the actual substance of darkness dribbling down from the heavens.

"Sir . . . ?" the doorman said expectantly, and Erasmus realized he was standing there as though unsure he would enter—like a young man who'd lost his nerve. In truth he had always avoided such places, though not on moral grounds. He was not a prude. But brothels were the haunts of foolish young men, and the old attempting to deny the truth of time. Either way it was a house of delusions, and, as such, repugnant to Erasmus. But then, Erasmus had come out of perverse curiosity.

Only the Marchioness of Wicklow could ever have brought off such an event, for who could refuse an invitation from Avonel's principal hostess? Only a prude or a man who had much to hide, clearly. Any woman who did not attend would unquestionably be admitting that her husband frequented such establishments and that therefore she could not bear to even enter the place herself. No, the Marchioness had weighed things out with a kind of ruthless precision and cruel irony that Erasmus thought had to be admired. Of course, as a bachelor, he was in no danger here. His wife would not be watching, wondering if any of the matron's comely employees seemed to treat him with just a bit too much familiarity.

So here gathered the cream of Avonel society, pretending to be engaged in something exciting, risque, and watching each other like predators. Erasmus thought that the Marchioness had gone a long way to expose the truth of

Avonel society this evening. He, for one, was almost certain he could smell the sweat.

Erasmus was escorted quickly up the short walk and into a well-lit lobby. Smiling young women relieved him of cloak and hat, gloves and cane.

"Lady Wicklow's party," he said, and one young woman turned to the matron who approached and, still smiling, repeated his disclaimer.

The matron was a cheerful looking woman whose age could not be disguised behind even the layers of makeup she had applied. Erasmus thought that if you took away the makeup, she would look far more like the competent wife of a particularly boring, country squire than the proprietress of such an establishment. She should have been serving tea and exaggerating the accomplishments of her children.

"Mrs. Trocket at your service. And you are . . . ?" she asked as she curtsied, surprising Erasmus with a bright look of both intelligence and humor.

"Erasmus Flattery, ma'am."

Her face changed as she heard the name, and though she held a list of guests, it was immediately forgotten. "Ah, Mr. Flattery. It is a great pleasure, I'm sure."

She motioned for him to escort her, clearly pleased to have a member of such an important family visit her establishment. The name, Erasmus thought, did occasionally prove useful—when it wasn't a curse.

"Well, you'll find we've created a place of refined entertainments for the discerning gentlemen—and lady—for we do not cater to gentlemen alone. Not at all."

All of the "ladies" Erasmus could see were clearly in the employ of the able Mrs. Trocket, and they smiled at him less than coyly as he passed. One blew him a kiss. They wore gowns that one would not see in most Avonel homes, that was certain, and several seemed to have forgotten their gowns and wore only the most exotic Entonne lingerie. He tried not to stare, but they really were the most fetching creatures. And they laughed with the gentlemen present, flirting in the most open manner. Erasmus thought suddenly that the place was a bit too warm.

The air was redolent with the smell of perfumes which did not quite mask a musky odor that pervaded the rooms. Erasmus did not have to wonder what that scent was, his body reacted to it of its own accord, and likely would have had he never encountered it before. Love had its own scent.

They passed into another room, not so different from the first, though perhaps not so well lit. Here musicians played, and the men had shed their coats or loosened neckcloths. The women seemed to have joined in the spirit, and were less encumbered by clothing as well. Some couples—or even threesomes—were dancing drunkenly, pressed close while others were locked in more passionate embraces, too drunk or too aroused to care that they were in public. On either end of a divan a naval officer sprawled, like tumbledown bookends, insensible with drink. So much for their evening with the ladies, Erasmus thought, though it would not likely stop them from boasting, all the same.

A woman put her hand on Erasmus' arm as he passed, and she did it with such familiarity, meeting his eyes so calmly, that for a moment he thought he knew her, and he was sure he looked at her with the greatest surprise. Mrs. Trocket led him through the next door.

They entered a hallway with large rooms to either side, and through the open doors he could see that several "refined entertainments" were underway. He glimpsed near-naked dancers through one set of doors, and heard singing from another. A farce, played out in elaborate and outrageous costumes, was in progress in yet another room.

"We try to have something for everyone," Mrs. Trocket said, noting his interest. "And things change often—nothing stale at Mrs. Trocket's. Amusement with wit and charm, that is our goal. A bit too . . ." She used an Entonne word that did not have an exact Farr equivalent, though its meaning lay somewhere between "racy" and "fashionable." ". . . for many of the worthies of Avonel. But for a young man such as yourself . . ." She smiled knowingly.

Erasmus was thirty—not so young by the standards of Farrland—and was, despite his name, no longer easy prey to flattery.

Up a broad flight of stairs and finally into the most eccentric library Erasmus had ever seen. It belonged in an ancient abbey or college for studies in the arcane. The room was polished oak from the floor to the very top of the shelves—some two stories up—and was all nooks and alcoves and stairways and carrels. Balconies were suspended precariously overhead, backed by cliffs of books. Sliding ladders, at odd angles to everything else, ran up to bronze railings. People stood on these ladders, surveying the crowd or holding forth to groups who gathered about their feet.

Erasmus realized that Mrs. Trocket had left him alone. Perhaps she had even bid him farewell.

The room was crowded with people, and there was such a hum of conversation that he thought of his beehives in far off Locfal. It was, to Erasmus' eye, a typical gathering of the educated classes of Avonel, though to one well-versed in such things, it might have been a more fashionable group than was common. Erasmus did not much care for such distinctions.

He noticed that everyone seemed a bit more animated than usual, as though they were trying to hide their discomfort, or perhaps they were merely thrilled to find themselves in such a place, for certainly none of the ladies had been in a brothel before. Many of the men looked distinctly uncomfortable, and Erasmus was sure it wasn't because this was their first visit—but they had unquestionably never been here in the company of their wives. They were likely terrified that some young woman was going to recognize them, though Erasmus knew that the able Mrs. Trocket would have advised her young ladies beforehand. Still, it was good sport to watch the husbands shying like nervous foals.

Scattered among the people attending the party were both servants and working girls and they talked and laughed with the guests and plied them with spirits and delicacies. The atmosphere here, in the center of the Marchioness' circle, was less bawdy and brazen than Erasmus had seen in the other chambers. Passions were well under control where one's reputation could actually suffer some damage. After all, the usual code—that one did not speak of who or what one saw in a brothel—would not be in effect this night. People would likely talk of nothing else for days.

Erasmus began searching the room for familiar faces, and though there were many that he knew by sight, he couldn't find anyone he thought might offer interesting conversation, and he saw several he knew for a fact had never said an intriguing thing in their lives. He thought the rather intense looking man across the room seemed vaguely familiar, and then realized that it was his own face in a looking glass, and this made him laugh.

*Well, he certainly won't have anything to say that I haven't heard before,* Erasmus thought.

He backed up against the wall of books, and thinking he would keep people at bay if he were engaged in some activity, he took a volume from the shelf and opened it. In two lines he realized that it was erotic fiction, and returned it to the shelf. What pleasure could such an activity provide if one could indulge it openly? All the books he could see were of the same variety, so he turned back to the gathering.

"Isn't it divinely wicked?" a young woman said to him, and he realized he was looking at a daughter of the Shackleton family, though his memory would not cooperate by supplying a name. She waved a glass of wine expansively, the look of drunken delight not varying measurably. "Only the marchioness would dare such an evening." She looked at him suddenly, her manner inquisitive if a little unfocused. "Don't I know you?"

"Erasmus Flattery," he said, and watched her expression change from drunken delight.

"Really?" she managed, remaining fairly collected. "You've been to our home, I think."

Erasmus nodded.

"I so wanted to ask if the rumors were true, but I was too shy, and my mother warned me to mind my manners. But tonight I've had enough wine. . . . Is it true you served Eldrich?"

He shook his head. "Vicious rumor. I once visited a school chum at Lord Eldrich's home—he was a great-nephew or some such thing. But it was all very ordinary, and the legendary Eldrich never appeared. Not even to my school chum, if he's to be believed."

"Too bad," she said, her look of delight fading a little more. "Too many good stories end up that way. The truth is a bit of a bore, isn't it?"

Erasmus shrugged.

"Well, that's what I've found anyway," she said resignedly, placed a hand on his chest rather clumsily, then backed away into the crowd, waving theatrically, as though she had lost all capacity for the unself-conscious gesture.

*Dora*, Erasmus thought as he watched her disappear into the crowd. Dora Shackleton, although "Simpleton" might be more appropriate.

Nearby a gathering of people swayed and bobbed, all trying to view the object of interest that lay at the very center of this movement. Drawn by what force Erasmus did not know—perhaps merely because the audience was almost entirely young ladies—he found himself looking over the heads of the watchers. Heads of lustrous swaying hair that fell to bare shoulders and beyond.

"But you see she is completely relaxed," a man was saying. "In fact, she will wake from this refreshed, as though she had slept the night through and experienced only the sweetest of dreams."

The man bent over a young woman seated in a chair. He sported both an ostentatious mustache and a monocle and looked too much like a player on the stage—the foreign count whom no one trusted, despite his charm. He laid a hand on the young woman's shoulder, but she did not stir, and kept her eyes closed. Indeed, she seemed to be asleep sitting up.

"But what will she do?" a woman asked, a little embarrassed by her question.

"Or not do," another added, and they all giggled at her boldness.

"Clara will do nothing in her present state that she would find objectionable while awake. She is mesmerized, but her morals are perfectly awake, let me assure you."

"Can you cure illnesses, then?" someone asked. "Some make such a claim."

"Some illnesses, yes. I have had encouraging results treating nervous dyspepsia, insomnia, dropsy, and brain fevers, to name but a few. Consumption, I regret to say, it will not affect, though it will take away some discomfort from the consumptive patient. Irrational fears I have treated with great success. Recurrent nightmares I have solved utterly."

"Can people really remember back to their very childhood, Doctor? To their birth, even?"

"I have seen long-lost memories surface, often, but I cannot claim perfect success. I treated the great Lord Skye, who as you know can remember nothing that took place before his childhood accident, but we were unable to recover his past. It is lost, I believe. Lost when he suffered his terrible injury."

"But his intellect was not affected . . . ?"

"Only his speech, slightly. But otherwise we do not know. Perhaps if he had not suffered his tragedy, he would have shown even greater genius. But what is a memory? Can it be weighed or measured? If one is forgotten, does the brain weigh less? How is it that we hold so many in our minds? And where are they kept?" He looked around at the gathering as though expecting answers, but when none were forthcoming, he continued. "There are those who claim the mind and the brain are not one and the same, but clearly when the brain is injured, so also is the mind. Thus Skye lost his memories—as though they were destroyed when his brain was damaged. But in an undamaged brain I believe the memories are never truly lost, but only misplaced. Memories of every event and smell and taste and emotion, all there, like perfect novels in infinite numbers. The novels of our lives. It is one of the mysteries that empiricism has yet to explain." He turned to the sleeping woman. "But let us see what Clara can remember. Perhaps she has some memories long forgotten. Clara? I want you to turn your mind to your childhood. . . . Your very earliest memory."

Erasmus drifted away. He had seen such displays before. Fascinating the first time or two, but largely quackery, he thought. This man had made more modest claims than most, who were milking the ignorant for their hard-earned coin with promises to cure all manner of illness and deformity, and much more. Which only made this man slightly less of a charlatan.

*But what is memory?*

Perhaps not an entirely foolish question, Erasmus thought, but he was more interested in knowing why one could not forget. Or how one could forget. For that he would hand over his own money, and gladly.

A young woman offered him a glass of champagne. She was wearing nothing but lingerie of black lace, sheer black stockings, and an astonishing tumble of dark curls.

"You look, sir, as though you might require some help erasing that troubled expression from your brow," she said in a lovely warm voice. Erasmus was usually easy prey for a beautiful voice.

"I cultivate looking troubled," he answered. "It keeps people at a distance."

"Ah," she said, stepping aside to let people pass and pressing herself softly against him. "Are you trying to keep me at a distance, then?"

"It's very likely, I fear." Erasmus glanced around the room. "I'm looking for friends, actually."

"Do they have names?" she asked, speaking near to his ear in a tone so intimate that Erasmus could hardly help but respond.

Erasmus hesitated. "I believe so, though they've never told them to me."

This caused her to pause for a moment, then she laughed.

"Ras! Short for rascal, I see," came a voice from behind. Erasmus felt a hand on his shoulder and turned to find Barton, an old classmate from his Merton days. "Come out for an evening of wickedness, I see?" The man was beaming at him a bit foolishly, as though overcome with delight at finding Erasmus Flattery in a brothel, of all places.

"I was invited by the marchioness," Erasmus said, not quite sure why he was trying to explain his presence.

"Oh, to be sure! As were we all." Barton laughed. "But have you seen the contortionists? Well, I tell you, it will fire your imagination. Possibilities undreamed of!" He laughed again, and snatched a glass from a passing tray. Barton's face was red; even his now completely bald pate was flushed. "You look a bit out of sorts, Ras," he said sympathetically, and then suddenly looked a little self-conscious himself, as though afraid he'd been caught in the act of frivolity. "I hear you're setting your stamp on the Society. Making quite a name for yourself," he offered, perhaps searching for some topic that would put Erasmus at ease.

It was not a good choice—Erasmus did not like to be patronized. He nodded distractedly, and the woman who still held his arm pressed against him again, calling for his attention.

Barton smiled and drained his glass. "Well, mustn't keep you from your friend," he said, nodded to the woman on Erasmus' arm and turned to go.

"But, Barton . . ." but Barton was gone.

The woman, pressing herself into Erasmus, leaned close to his ear and made a rather outrageous suggestion. Erasmus disentangled himself. "Ah, '*If it were not a phantom moon, and your affections, Lady, were but true.*'"

She looked at him, confused.

"Denis," Erasmus said. "*The Prince Alexander.*" And seeing that this information did not help, he added: "It's a play, my dear."

She released him, her look of confusion not fading, and Erasmus set out into the fray. Tight little alleys opened up in the knots of people, and he pushed his way down these, awash in the scents and sounds, the colors and shapes.

He jostled someone accidentally and a rather poorly dressed young man shot him a look.

"Erasmus?" the young man said. "Farrelle's ghost, Erasmus!"

"Samual?"

The young man put a finger to his lips. "Don't say it so loudly." He looked truly frightened, shrinking down a little so as not to be noticed.

"Hiding from a fiancée, are you?" Erasmus smiled.

"No, nothing like that. Far worse, in fact." Samual Hayes looked about him quickly. "I'm hiding from the law, Erasmus."

Erasmus almost laughed, thinking it a joke—Samual Hayes in trouble with the law!—but then he realized that the young man was completely serious. "Martyr's blood, man, what have you been up to?"

"Nothing," Hayes said quickly. "I swear. Yet I am being pursued all the same."

"Mr. Flattery?"

Erasmus turned to find a naval officer approaching, smiling. The navy men were always extremely amiable to him, not for anything Erasmus had done, but because a recent ancestor had been an admiral and something of a war hero. Odd how the accomplishments of one's family seemed to somehow rub off on a man.

"Captain Adelard James. We met once at the duke's country home. At a dinner, this two years past. . . ."

"Of course. A pleasure to see you again, Captain. You were off to Farrow, wasn't it?"

The man looked pleased that Erasmus would remember. "That's it exactly. Yes, we talked much about the island. Have you been back since we last spoke?"

Erasmus shook his head. "No, I'm afraid not." He turned to introduce Hayes, but the young man had disappeared. They talked for a moment about nothing much in particular, and then parted. Erasmus stood wondering what in the world Hayes had been on about.

Barton reappeared suddenly. "Finished with that little bit already?" he asked, speaking too loudly. "Well, never mind, there's always more here, Ras. Do you know, I've just been told that the Countess of Chilton is in attendance? Can you believe it? I'm dying for a glimpse." He raised a bushy eyebrow comically. "Come along, old man, and we'll see if the rumors are true. See if a dart of pure desire strikes right to our very hearts."

They had taken an astonishing length of time to make their way to this room, searching as they went. Hoping for a glimpse of the woman said to be the most beautiful in the known world. Barton touched Erasmus' arm suddenly, and he turned to look in the direction his friend was staring. There was someone there, no doubt, in the middle of the press of both men and women—like a queen bee surrounded by her attendants. And the similarity seemed very apt to Erasmus. It was as though they all hovered about, rubbing antennae, caught up in a collective orgy of adoration.

He could not see the woman who was the focus of this adulation, but he could see the reactions of those around. They were transported, foolish with delight at finding themselves in the company of this woman. And it was not just the men. The women seemed hardly less affected. Erasmus felt it himself, and he still had not caught a glimpse of the countess.

"Can you see her, Barton?" Erasmus asked, for Barton was a good half a foot taller and looked over virtually everyone's head.

"Almost," he answered, not shifting his gaze away from the spectacle.

Suddenly someone in the throng moved to one side and Erasmus thought he caught a glimpse of a beautiful smile.

"Now, now, gentlemen. Not polite to stare. Actually, the countess has gone, and what you see there are merely the people who were so unbelievably fortunate as to actually have spoken with her."

"Sennet," Barton said, turning to a dapper young man who looked on in vast amusement. "Do you know Erasmus Flattery?"

"No, but certainly I know your brother, the duke. Your servant, sir. And I should add that I know you by reputation. I'm not an empiricist myself, but, even so, one cannot help but hear the name of Erasmus Flattery. Not these days."

Erasmus never knew how to respond graciously to praise, and as usual changed the subject. "Were you serious?" Erasmus asked. "Are these merely the people who spoke with the countess?"

Sennet bobbed his head, his long, rather sharp nose performing a precise arc in the air. Erasmus thought the marquis—for this was undoubtedly the Marquis of Sennet—was the most oddly formed man. His chin seemed to have been drawn out too far, his forehead sloped back. Freckles of vastly differing sizes were scattered over his face, and yet all of this seemed to be offset by the most kindly eyes, large and filled with humor, with deep lines at their corners from much laughter, Erasmus suspected.

"Yes," Sennet said, his amusement apparently growing. "Isn't it wonderfully absurd? It's really a madness. A collective madness." His look became just a bit more serious, as though something in this disturbed him.

"I've never actually seen the countess myself," Erasmus said, wondering if there was as much regret in his voice as he heard. "Is she as beautiful as everyone claims?"

Sennet tilted his head to one side. "One would have to say yes, I think. It is very odd. I actually believe there are other women in Avonel just as beautiful—perhaps even in this room—but they do not have the effect of the Countess of Chilton. It is a force of personality. . . . I don't think I know a word to describe the effect, for she is more than enchanting." He shook his head and laughed. "Well, you see, I am as besotted as everyone else. Though I shall not duel with others who do not declare her the most beautiful woman who has ever lived, which apparently happened this week past."

Erasmus thought this a good thing. He seemed to remember hearing that Sennet was a formidable swordsman, and had once won a duel with the master of Avonel's principal fencing academy. A feat that had given him something of a reputation these past three years.

"No, I make it something of a rule," Sennet said. "Never risk your life over a woman who cannot remember your name. Sensible, don't you think?"

Erasmus' answer died on his lips, for he saw Samual Hayes half-hidden behind a column, trying to catch his attention.

Erasmus excused himself and made his way over to the young man.

Samual was the only son of neighbors of the Flattery family. The Hayes family were kindly if not terribly competent people, who had lost their estate not too long ago from bad investments and profligate spending. Not an uncommon story, unfortunately.

"I have to get out of here," Hayes said as Erasmus came near. "It's the navy men; they're after me." He paused, avoiding Erasmus' eyes. "But I have no place to go."

Erasmus reached out and took Hayes' arm. Better to find out what went on here. He owed it to the young man's parents. "Come along, then. You can hide at my home—at least until you've told me what's happened. Don't look so frightened, Hayes; unless you've murdered the prince royal, it's unlikely agents of the navy will try to wrest you from me without a proper warrant, and I rather doubt the officers present this evening have one in their pockets. They have other things on their minds."

Erasmus steered Hayes toward the door, wondering if he would miss anything that evening, but then decided that he had only come out of boredom. An unhealthy reason in the first place. The rescue of a family friend seemed infinitely preferable.

## ∽ Two

It was not a secret in Avonel that the Earl of Skye had a preference for a certain type of woman—petite, white-blonde, green-eyed, and young. An Entonne accent was desirable but not absolutely necessary. For a man of surpassing intellect, his tastes were hardly extraordinary.

The woman who answered the door, however, was not only a complete stranger, but she had none of the characteristics that Skye expected. In truth, he thought her a rather unusual looking woman. Not more than twenty-three, he guessed, but he had seldom seen a woman so . . . faded. Her hair, her skin, they appeared to be drained of color. The hair was red, but of such a lifeless variety. If anyone were to return from death, Skye thought they would look like this—as though part of their life had been drained away. Yet her eyes had the gleam of youth and even standing there, holding the door, he sensed a vivacity about her.

She curtsied with grace. "Lord Skye, it is an honor. Please, come in," she said pleasantly. Whoever she was, she was no one's maid servant.

He hesitated on the doorstep. "This is the right address?"

"You've come to visit Miss Finesworth?"

He nodded and she beckoned him in.

"You have me at something of a disadvantage, Miss. . . . I do not know your name."

"I am a friend," she said, and smiled as though she had been put up to this and found his reaction rather amusing. "Come up, sir," she said, not offering to take his coat or cane, nor was there any servant to do so.

It was turning into something of an odd assignation, Skye thought. Where was Miss Finesworth? She had assured him the house would be empty.

At the stair head the young woman opened a door and preceded him into the room.

"What in bloody blazes!" Skye stopped abruptly. There were three naval officers slumped so limply on chairs that Skye feared they were dead.

"They are drugged," the young woman said matter-of-factly.

Skye felt an urge to bolt, but he stood, staring, almost dumbfounded, at the scene.

"But why?" His voice came out in a whisper. "Why are they here?"

"To arrest you, I'm afraid," she said. "You see, the young woman you were to meet, Miss Finesworth, was to pretend to be an Entonne spy who had offered her allegiance to Farrland. She would claim that you had come here to give her plans for the cannon, so that Entonne could produce naval guns of their own." She waved a hand at the unconscious officers. "These gentlemen were then to take you away. To gaol, Lord Skye."

"That's . . . that's preposterous. It's . . ."

She crossed to a table and slid a large roll of papers across the smooth surface. "You will recognize these, I think?" she asked, releasing the ribbons that bound them. She spread them quickly open and looked over at Skye.

Not sure why, he went to look.

He let out a long breath. "My drawings of the naval gun. The Admiralty had them."

"Yes, and sheets of specifications. Instructions for casting. Everything one would need to produce cannon."

Skye stepped back stunned to silence. "Who are you?"

"A friend, Lord Skye. Someone who would not see you harmed." She touched his arm gently. "You needn't fear me. Without my intervention you would be on your way to gaol this moment. You have made an enemy, Lord Skye. A formidable and somewhat ruthless enemy. Moncrief, I assume, but perhaps you know already."

"Moncrief!? But he is my friend! I dine with him. I . . ." He blustered into silence.

She stared at him with what appeared to be compassion. "I would be surprised to learn that Moncrief has any friends. Lord Skye. You threaten him in some way. You are a favorite of the King and have His Majesty's ear. Perhaps too much for Moncrief's liking."

Skye leaned on the table. "It is unbelievable. Moncrief would not dare attack me."

"Moncrief dared to attack Entonne, Lord Skye. What is a mere citizen to him? Even one as influential as yourself. After all, he has brought men down before. Powerful men."

"Why have you done this?" Skye asked, stepping away from the table, eyeing this peculiar looking woman.

"You have many admirers, Lord Skye. We would not see you fall victim to . . . anyone. Trust me when I say this. We are your friends. It is best that you leave now. Tell no one you were here. Is your driver to be trusted?"

Skye nodded.

"Then you should be gone."

Skye nodded again, turning away without further urging. He was not sure what went on here, but escaping this place seemed imperative.

At the bottom of the stairs, he turned to the young woman. "If this all proves to be true, Miss, I will be in your debt."

She nodded. "So it would appear, Lord Skye. But for now . . ." She opened the door for him, and with a quick bow he went out, opening the door to the carriage himself, and sending his surprised driver on.

He slumped back in his seat, a hand over his face. Had he just escaped ruin? It didn't seem possible. Flames, but he should not wait in Avonel to find out.


## ∽ Three

*Memory is fiction, a narrative we write and rewrite to explain an ever-changing present, a story in which we are the hero, the victim, the wronged or the incomparable lover. And if memory is fiction, what then is history?*

—*Halden:* Essays


The ride to Erasmus' home passed almost entirely in silence, as though Hayes were afraid the driver might overhear them. Erasmus thought that something dire must have happened to frighten the young man so. He looked positively haunted, and this was not helped by the fact that he was rather poorly dressed and smelled of wine—though he appeared perfectly sober.

It came out that Hayes had visited the brothel only because he'd been rescued by friends who were on their way there. They were celebrating the coming marriage of one of their circle. An odd practice, Erasmus thought. Apparently the groom-to-be had been stripped naked and tied to a woman, who was also without clothing, and they would not be released until they had performed the act before the groom's so-called friends. All rather difficult in that they had been tied in such a way as to make consummation almost impossible. Somewhat more entertaining than anything Erasmus had seen, but then his exploration of the brothel had been cut rather short.

They arrived at Erasmus' town home and were let in by his manservant, Stokes, who looked askance at this young vagabond Erasmus had brought home.

After Stokes had found Hayes some clothing and let him clean up, they met in Erasmus' study on the second floor. "I will tell you, Hayes, you look like you've survived the war."

"Do excuse me, Erasmus, I—I appreciate you taking me in like this."

"Yes, well, come and sit by the fire and warm yourself." Erasmus motioned to his servant. "Brandy would seem to be in order. And coffee. Will that answer?" he asked Hayes, who nodded.

Erasmus took the second chair. "I think you should tell me what's happened, Hayes. There will be time for pleasantries later."

The young man nodded, rubbing his hands up and down his thighs as though to bring some feeling into them. He stared into the fire, martialing his thoughts.

The young Samual that Erasmus remembered was barely detectable in the man seated before him. The good-natured, apple-cheeked child was gone, and in his place was someone leaner and harder. The bones of his face showed through, as though hardship had caused his skeleton to expand and strengthen. This young man looked like he could stand up to some adversity, which no doubt he already had.

"I don't need to acquaint you with my recent family history, Erasmus. Suffice it to say that, since leaving Merton, I've been living in . . . one of the city's more picturesque quarters." Hayes shook his head as though he could not quite credit his memory. "I came home this night to find my rooms had been invaded by . . . well, my neighbors claimed they were navy men. And I was pursued by others and only managed to escape by pure luck." He looked up at Erasmus. "I really had no place to go. No friend good enough to burden with my troubles."

"Don't worry, Samual, you're both safe and welcome. There are one or two advantages to having a brother who's a duke. You haven't any notion of why these men were in your rooms, I take it?"

Hayes shook his head. "None."

"And you're sure they were men from the Admiralty? You saw uniforms?"

"No, but the people in that quarter of the city have an uncanny ability to spot the representatives of the Crown no matter what their dress. If they say they were navy men, I would wager all I have they were right. Not that it would be much of a wager, I'm afraid."

Stokes appeared just then with coffee and brandies. Erasmus wanted to reassure Hayes that his life would not always be thus, but by the time Stokes left, the moment had passed.

"Well, perhaps it is a case of mistaken identity." Erasmus stared at Hayes, who gazed fixedly down into his brandy. The silence was protracted and more than a little awkward.

"It makes little sense to come to me, Samual, and then not trust me," Erasmus said softly.

Hayes shook his head and shifted his gaze to the fire. "I have been racking my brain all evening trying to think of any reason, any reason at all, that the Admiralty would be interested in me. Interested enough to sack my rooms."

"And . . . ?"

Hayes looked up at him. "I can think of only one thing, and even it makes almost no sense."

"Out with it, Samual."

"I had been doing some research for a gentleman. Someone who wanted utter discretion. It was paid work, you see," he said, a little embarrassed.

"No shame in that. Not to my mind, anyway." Erasmus waited, his patience wearing thin, though he fought to hide it.

"Well, the gentleman has some involvement with the Admiralty. That is the only explanation I can think of. But, for the life of me, I can't imagine how the work I did could lead to naval officers searching my rooms." Hayes rose from his chair and paced two steps across the hearth, clearly troubled. He stood looking down at his hands oddly, turning them over and over before the flames.

"It is such a strange thing. . . ." He hunched down before the fire.

"Perhaps you should tell me about this work you've done, Hayes. I might notice something someone with less distance would miss."

Hayes nodded, still looking into the fire. "It is a story I want to tell you, Erasmus. You, in particular." He glanced up. "But I would have to ask for complete secrecy in this matter."

Agents of the navy were involved, Erasmus reminded himself. "If your story bears upon the security of the nation in some way, Hayes, I cannot guarantee that I'll be able to keep your confidence."

Hayes stood up quickly. "But it doesn't, Erasmus. I swear it."

Erasmus considered. It was not that he didn't want to offer Hayes some help, it was just that he didn't want to become more involved than was necessary. "You said that you particularly wanted to tell me this tale. . . ."

Hayes nodded hopefully. "Yes, for you see, the story involves a mage, or at least I think it does. That is what I hope you can tell me."

Erasmus shifted in his chair, wary now. "I will tell you honestly, Hayes, that I have little special knowledge of mages, despite what people will persist in believing."

A tight smile of polite disbelief flickered across Hayes' face. "Of course . . . I simply thought. . . ." He stopped and looked away again.

"If, as you say, the matter is innocent, I will honor your confidence. That is all I can promise."

Hayes nodded. "It all began about two years ago with a professor at Merton. You see, he called me and a classmate to his study one day and asked if we'd be interested in undertaking some research for a prominent gentleman— he would not tell us who it was, for the gentleman desired absolute discretion. We had to agree before we were told his name. Our professor did assure us that the gentleman in question was above reproach and it was all on the up and up. I agreed readily, for I would be paid, and my classmate, Kehler, agreed as well.

"We were sent off to meet our prospective employer, completely in the dark as to what we would be doing, and I dare say we would have thought it something of a lark if we hadn't known the man by reputation." He glanced up at Erasmus, clearly still impressed by this mysterious gentleman. "I can't say more than that he is a person of some standing.

"We speculated a great deal about what our task might be, but I can tell you, Erasmus, we were not even near the mark. Do you know anything about a little village called Compton Heath?"

Erasmus shrugged. "Just the name."

"And I should have said that's really all there was to know—except for this one peculiar incident that the gentleman was interested in." Hayes reached down and took a sip of his brandy. "I don't know how he ever learned the story, but his fascination with it was obvious. As he told it, he could not sit still but paced across the room speaking as though he were explaining a great discovery.

"According to our employer, a stranger appeared one day in Compton Heath: a man dressed oddly, who spoke no tongue that any recognized. He seemed more than a little disoriented and distraught, as well as a bit fearful of the people, though from all accounts they treated him kindly. A doctor was called who determined that the man suffered nervous dyspepsia and required rest and quiet.

"A priest, skilled in languages, was located and came to hear the man's strange speech. The priest confessed that he could neither name the man's language nor even from what region it might originate. Some theorized that the stranger had been shipwrecked and was the only survivor, and that he had come from a land in some unexplored part of the world where there was a rich civilization. The imagination being what it is, these people also believed the stranger was a man of importance in his own land—a prince or a wealthy adventurer. The problem with this theory, of course, was that the town of Compton Heath lay some twenty miles inland, and it seemed unlikely that this man would have traveled so far without first encountering other towns or homes and their people.

"But then the stranger was not quite right in his mind, so it was not entirely out of the question that he had wandered so far. The local officials took the man under their wing, not quite sure what should be done. He became something of a local curiosity, and men of learning traveled from neighboring towns to see him for themselves and to hear his strange tongue.

"But this situation did not last long. One evening a grand coach arrived, from where no one knew, and when it left the stranger was no longer domiciled in Compton Heath. The officials claimed the man had disappeared of his own free will, though few believed them. In fact, the town worthies were clearly frightened and did not like to speak of the matter at all. Afterward the rumor went about that a mage had sent for the stranger, though this can be neither proven nor disproven."

Erasmus was silent for a moment, and Hayes turned his attention to him, trying to read his reaction to the news of a mage's involvement. This was clearly the question he hoped Erasmus would answer, for everyone knew that Erasmus Flattery had once lived in the house of the mage.

"What year did this happen?" Erasmus asked.

"1453."

"Over sixty years ago."

Hayes nodded. "As we traveled to the village, we speculated endlessly about the gentleman's interest. It seemed extremely odd to us. The gentleman in question is of a serious bent of mind, I will tell you, yet this story seemed the kind of thing that would be taken up by people who believed in fairies and spirits. We could not quite understand, for certainly we could give no credence to such a tale ourselves."

"So that is what you discovered?" Erasmus said. "There was no truth in it?"

Hayes looked a little troubled. "We set out only to disprove it, of course, but that was to be more difficult than we expected.

"We arrived in Compton Heath more than half a century after the fact, but we could imagine no other way to begin. The incident had not happened so long ago that there would not still be a few who had been alive at the time: people who had seen the stranger and heard the man's odd tongue." Hayes' brow knit together, and his look grew more serious. "But nothing was to be as we imagined. We were not in the town long before becoming convinced that, indeed, something strange *had* occurred there on or about the dates that we had been given. Certainly the townsfolk earnestly believed it, at any rate. And though many were willing to speak to us about it, those who had been directly involved in the incident—those few still alive—would not even see us, despite all our best efforts and charm. It was utterly frustrating. Everything we learned came second- or third-hand, and though it all corroborated our employer's story, none of it came from anyone directly involved. We had been instructed to be absolutely thorough in our inquiry, but it was impossible. The people who had been directly involved, some of whom were said to have met the stranger, would not speak with us. They would not even open their doors so that we might plead our case."

Hayes sat down in his chair and leaned forward, hands on his knees. "I will tell you, Erasmus, after a week in the village we were more intrigued than ever, for the silence of the people involved seemed terribly peculiar. A bit macabre, even. We finally agreed that our last hope remained with the doctor who'd taken an interest in the stranger—the one who had diagnosed nervous dyspepsia—for he was the only man who we had not approached who might still be alive.

"We were especially interested in him because several people in Compton Heath told us that the doctor had kept notes of his observations of the stranger, and not just his medical observations. A few months after the stranger's disappearance the doctor had moved on, and there were only rumors of his whereabouts, but even so I thought we must pursue it. We feared we would find him as silent as the people of Compton Heath—if he were alive at all—but felt there was little other hope of fulfilling our obligation to our employer."

"While in Compton Heath we did find some intriguing bits of information," Hayes said, sitting back, "though, of course, much that we were told was contradictory, so it was difficult to discern what might be true. Apparently the stranger could write, not as we do, of course, but he wrote nonetheless. An old woman showed me what was alleged to be a sample of this script, and for a small fee she allowed me to copy it. I'm not sure she isn't laughing with her friends about this yet, but all the same, I paid her the money and took my copy away, as not a few others had before me, I suspect."

"Do you have that writing?"

Hayes shook his head. "I'm afraid it is being held hostage in Merton with many of my other possessions, pending the payment of some back rent."

"Ah. And that is the story?"

"Not quite," Hayes said, glancing at Erasmus, a bit of triumph in his look. "You see we eventually found the physician who had first examined the stranger.

"It was not an easy task," Hayes said, "for the man was prone to moving and not leaving a forwarding address, though this did not seem to be for the usual reasons. The good doctor appears to have been as dedicated to the payment of his debts as he was to shifting his domicile. He moved almost yearly for most of his life, before finally settling in the village of Nearbrook, on the Tollingham Canal.

"It is my guess, now, that the good doctor felt he had finally managed to outrun whatever he believed to be pursuing him—or perhaps he had just grown too old to keep running. We found Ripke, for that was his name, living in the house of his daughter and son-in-law, who was a physician as well. I regret to say that the beginnings of dementia were evident in the doctor's speech and manner, although he had not yet succumbed completely. There were times when he spoke with clarity, and his memories were not so intermingled with his delusions.

"It was the oddest meeting, Erasmus. His daughter began by assuring us that the old man would not speak to us of this matter. Indeed, that he would not speak of it even with her. We asked if we might talk with Doctor Ripke all the same in hopes that we might change his mind, and this was eventually allowed.

"And talk we did. We sat in a small garden above the canal, the old man tucked beneath an ancient, threadbare blanket, for he would use no other. He seemed something like a child who believes that once under the blankets he is safe from all the monsters hiding in the dark. The conversation ranged freely, as you might imagine, though it was not all unpleasant. At times his old self, or so I imagined, would come forth and he displayed real charm, and even some concern for others. Then, very unexpectedly he would lapse into tirades, for he believed himself a victim of terrible persecution.

"The man took a liking to me, I think, and at a sign from my partner, Kehler, I took over our inquiry, Kehler being content to sit and listen. It was some time before I could steer him round to the topic of interest to us, but finally after some cajoling, he fell into a long silence, and then said, 'Damn him, I shall not take it to the grave!' I think he had been keeping the secret so long, and living in fear, that he could no longer bear it. 'Let him take me now and be done with it,' he kept repeating, as though some terrible fiend would learn of our conversation and come for him. Occasionally he would even fall to accusing us of being agents of this thing he feared but never named.

"It was a long difficult process taking three days, and I don't think I would ever have been allowed to press my questions as I did, for obviously the interview was a detriment to the old man's already precarious state, but his daughter was clearly even more interested than I. She sat just out of the man's sight and listened carefully to every word, hardly able to believe that her father was telling the story at last." Hayes stopped to drink, his throat dry. "I learned a number of things from Ripke that our visit to Compton Heath had not uncovered. The stranger was certainly civilized, not a wild man as some claimed. He was modest regarding his body and submitted to the doctor's examination only after it was demonstrated to him that he would not be harmed. His hands bore no calluses or signs of labor. He was clearly curious, even amused at times by things he saw. The workings of a clock caused him great merriment, apparently, and he obviously understood the ways of mechanical things. Given writing implements he not only wrote in a script no one had ever seen but produced a number of sketches of objects, the purpose of which could not be readily grasped."

"Farrelle's flames!" Erasmus blurted out. "Do these drawings and script exist?"

Hayes shook his head sadly. "No, but I will come to that part of the story. The stranger began to learn Farr; quite rapidly I believe, and it soon became clear that he knew more about many things than his supposed teachers. He drew a fairly detailed anatomical drawing of the human body, and clearly had strongly held beliefs about how it functioned—Ripke was of the opinion that the man might well have been a physician in his own land. If what Ripke said was true, the stranger suggested things about the functions of the heart and lungs that are only just now being considered. For instance, Ripke is convinced that the stranger did not believe that air in the lungs cooled the heat of the blood but rather *infused* it somehow, and this enriched fluid was carried to the extremities of the body to nurture it, like fertilizer does a garden. Or so I understood him to say."

"This is what some medical men are proposing now," Erasmus said, a bit surprised.

Hayes nodded. "So it is." Though he did not seem nearly as astonished as Erasmus. "Just as Ripke and the others began to realize what a miracle they might have on their hands, a large carriage arrived in Compton Heath late in the night." Hayes took a long drink of his brandy, and seemed suddenly very sad. "Ripke was not present when the coach appeared, but as Compton Heath was a small village, he soon had word of it. He hurried to the house where the stranger was lodged and found a scene of terrible confusion. Horsemen held back the few onlookers from an ornate carriage that had pulled up in the lane, and when the doctor tried to enter the house to determine what went on, he was stopped by the horsemen, who would provide no explanation. He stood helplessly by as he saw the bewildered stranger bundled into the carriage, and as the door opened, in the darkened interior, he saw a man, or at least his silhouette, calmly waiting.

"At this point in the telling, Doctor Ripke went into a spasm of cursing and cowering that finally sent us away for the rest of that day and part of the next. When we were allowed to return, only I was able to speak with the doctor. He would see no others. I found a haggard looking Ripke waiting, for he had been awake raving all night. But he was more lucid than at any other time during our visit, as though the fit of madness had run its course and left him too exhausted to continue with such mania. I took a seat with him before the fire—for though it was a warm day, he huddled next to the hearth as though it were the worst day of winter—and he suddenly reached out and took hold of my hand. You cannot imagine the look he gave me then, as though he pleaded with me for his own life. 'Pursue this no further,' he said, his voice all but gone from his night of raving.

"When I asked why, he would not answer but curled up in his chair, drawing his ancient blanket up over his head, and from underneath I heard him muttering, and then crying pitifully. I could learn nothing more from him, and finally his daughter took pity on the man's state and sent me away."

"But what of the writing and the sketches?"

"They disappeared at the same time as the stranger."

"And no one could reproduce them?"

Hayes shook his head. "Ripke tried, but each time he put pen to paper, he would be overcome by a strange fear. A fear so great that it drove what he had seen out of his memory. And his notes, taken at the time, could not be found. His daughter thought that he hoarded them in a wooden box which he kept locked and hidden away, but when he died, a few months after our interview, her husband opened the box and found nothing but pages of gibberish. Lines that connected in no way that conveyed meaning. The artistic equivalent of a madman's ravings."

Erasmus felt a sudden chill himself, for he could almost see the poor doctor huddled up by his fire, slipping back into madness. "And who was it took the man away?"

"I was hoping you would tell me, Erasmus. This doctor was filled with a terror that he could never escape. I might dismiss this as just the dementia of one old man, but several others who were present that night suffered similarly—two much worse, in fact. They self-murdered not long after. Was this the doings of a mage? That is my question? Could one place such a terror on a man? Would they do such a terrible thing, for surely this Ripke had done nothing that could offend a mage? Unless there was some part of the story he was not telling. A stranger appeared in his village, and the doctor endeavored to learn something of the man, and did nothing to cause him harm. That is all." Hayes stared hard at Erasmus, clearly unsettled by what had happened to this poor doctor. "Could this have been the workings of a mage?"

"I fear it is entirely possible," Erasmus said quietly. "I . . . yes, they could instill such a fear in a man, and it would not likely go away with time—not in the years that men live, at least. That this man Ripke lasted as long as he did with some apparent sanity is the miracle."

"You speak with some confidence, Erasmus," Hayes said.

Erasmus glanced at him, his annoyance not hidden, but Hayes did not look at all abashed.

"Yes, well, I had an experience while I was in the house of Eldrich that left me with some special knowledge." He pressed the tips of his fingers together, staring into his past, Hayes was sure; and it was not a happy past either.

"Perhaps it is an evening for stories," Erasmus said softly, as though he spoke to himself. "I will tell you of this one incident that might give you some evidence of the mage's indifference to our ideas of what is just." Erasmus paused, as though reconsidering, but then pressed on. "The millennium was but four years off when I was taken to the house of Eldrich," he began. "To this day I have only the vaguest idea of why this was done. Some feat I had performed as a child, I would suppose, though for the life of me I can't remember what.

"My father, the duke, must have made the arrangements, though he never bothered to explain his reasoning to me—a pattern that continued through the rest of his days.

"There were three other boys in the house at the time. One was two years older, had been there longer and kept to himself; another was younger and had attached himself to a woman servant. That left Percy and me.

"Percy was three months older, several inches taller, and though quick of wit, he left it to me to lead in our friendship. His family were mildly successful shopkeepers, I understood, but even at that age I cared little for social distinctions. He was a good and true friend, and we stood by each other in a situation that, though never truly threatening, was less than hospitable and more than a little strange.

"Percy had less idea of why he was there than I did, and the fact that his family had no influence at all makes me wonder if my own family's prominence had anything at all to do with my being there. We knew that Eldrich was said to be a mage, and we were both terrified and fascinated by this. That is to say, by day we were fascinated, but once darkness fell, terror reigned. Most nights, after the lights were doused, we slipped into the same bed and clung to each other, almost paralyzed with fear, until we finally fell asleep. We were never sure what we were afraid of, though we speculated endlessly.

"For months we didn't see Eldrich himself, so we imagined that he was a hideous near-monster, or perhaps turned into one after nightfall. The one truly frightening thing we did see was Eldrich's familiar, a great wolf that roamed the halls, often by night. This beast never actually threatened us in any way, though we did much to stay distant from it, but we did on occasion hear sniffing outside our door—and there were many more times when I suspect we imagined it. This put a fear into us that cannot be truly conveyed, for there is no one so accomplished at terror as a ten-year-old.

"We were given a pleasant enough room to share and put in the charge of a tutor who was to see to our studies. He was a good-hearted old man who reeked of tobacco smoke and the fecund soil from the gardens in which he loved to dig. In the spring he also smelled of horse droppings.

"Mr. Walky, as he was called, was a man of prodigious learning—or perhaps I should say he had been a man of prodigious learning in his day. By the time Percy and I came to him, his mind had begun to ... 'decay' I think would be the right word. It was solid enough in places, and growing if not quite flourishing in others, but, overall it had begun to lose its foliage, and the trunk was sadly rotten at its center.

"Walky often called us by the names of former students, and lost track of our lessons, his mind wandering off. Very occasionally he would tell us the most wondrous tales of the past, and sometimes even tales of the doings in the house of Eldrich. To children, these seemed more like stories than history— like ghost stories, some of them—and it was difficult for us to discern those that were real from those that were fanciful.

"Had I been only a little older, I would have been wise enough to set these down in ink, but I was not yet perfectly proficient in my letters, and—to be honest—the thought never occurred to me. They seemed so much like tales from old books that I didn't for a moment imagine that they would not be recorded elsewhere. But I realize now that they weren't—at least not anywhere that could be found.

"Percy and I had a great deal of time to ourselves—too much, really—and, I confess, we got up to some mischief occasionally. For this Mr. Walky would give us extra work and refuse to tell us stories, though earning his temporary disapproval was far more injurious, for we had no other friend or ally in that strange world.

"In all the months I lived in Eldrich's house I never actually spoke with the master himself and, in fact, only saw him perhaps three times. The first I was sitting in a window seat staring out at the garden. It was a cool autumn day, windless and with an odd, thin cloud layer through which the disk of the sun was visible, though just. In the distance occasional holes in a more dense cloud layer would open and shafts of light that we then called 'mage rays' would illuminate some far-off patch of the countryside, the colors of fall appearing there like some promised treasure.

"I was supposed to be reading a book, but as I had not the habits of mind that I later developed, I was staring out the window, daydreaming. At some point I realized there was a man standing in the garden, looking down into one of the fading flowerbeds. He was a tall gentleman dressed in black but for a white shirt. On his head he wore no wig and his dark hair, curly and loose, framed his pale face which, at that distance, was hard to distinguish.

"I had about two seconds of mild curiosity before I had a sudden realization: this was the legendary Eldrich! I knew it as though I had seen him a thousand times. *This was the mage.* My heart began to pound like mad, and I leaned forward to press my forehead to the glass so that I might have a better look. At that very moment the man looked up, perhaps attracted by the movement in the window. And I swear to you that I thought my heart had actually stopped.

"The look this man fixed on me . . . ! I was sure he could read my thoughts, learn every bit of wickedness I had ever thought or done. I nearly fell out of the window seat I was so terrified. He had noticed me! And all those months I believed he was unaware of my existence, but now I knew this was not so. I could tell by the look. He knew me. Eldrich knew me!

"I flew back to my room as though pursued by the foulest murderer, and burst through the door in such a near hysteria that I alarmed Percy even more than I had been frightened myself.

"For a long moment I could not speak, but only gesticulated wildly, opening and closing my mouth to no avail; finally I managed, 'Eldrich.' And Percy, who thought I meant the mage was on his way to our room, went completely white with horror. He began to tremble uncontrollably and actually became so light-headed that he collapsed onto the bed, and his eyes threatened to roll back in their sockets.

"'What does he want with us?' he whispered when he had recovered a little.

"'He wants nothing of you,' I told him. 'At least not that I know of. But he saw me! Saw me shirking my studies. Flames, what if he turns me into a goat? Or fixes me with a stutter?'

"It sounds ridiculous, now, but at the time I had never been so terrified. We both stared at the door as though it would burst open at any moment and the mage would be carried in on a blast of wind, and we would find out at last for what terrible purpose we had been sent to this place.

"We stayed like that until a servant came to call us to supper—he must have wondered why, when he opened the door, we were clinging to each other, cowering as though we were about to be spitted, our eyes the size of saucers. Of course, Eldrich never appeared and we recovered from our fright after a few days, but we never laughed about it, nor teased each other. No, anything to do with the mage was not a laughing matter. And I will tell you honestly that I am not convinced that this fright was simply the natural result of two young boys living in strange circumstances. Can you imagine what kind of man would take amusement from so terrifying children?" Erasmus stopped, unsure if he would go on, but the memories kept flooding back.

"While I was there, the older boy tried to run away, but reappeared the next day looking decidedly sullen, and could never be convinced to speak of the matter. This proved what we suspected: we were prisoners, and though it might have been more like boys at boarding school than prisoners in gaol, a stranger boarding school I had never heard tell of.

"One of the things Walky taught us, once the weather grew fair, was the art of swimming. He scoffed at our protests that it would ruin our constitutions, and called us old wives. His own good health, he claimed, was due to regular physical labor and swimming. He even said that the mage himself swam, though we did not believe that Lord Eldrich would stoop to such a frivolous activity.

"We not only learned the art of swimming, we grew to like it and while the weather remained warm, complained if a day went by without us being allowed into the water. Walky used this as a carrot for us. 'Finish your maths, my young lions, and we shall go for a nice swim. Be about it now.'

"He often called us his 'young lions,' especially when he was pleased with us or when he was in a particularly agreeable mood. I did not know it at the time, but old half-mad Walky, as we thought of him, was a good friend to us, and concerned with our welfare.

"Sometime later in my stay at Eldrich's house, Walky's grip on reality seemed to slip a little more. Occasionally he would forget what lesson he had begun and make odd requests of us. Once he asked me to name the three herbs used to purify water, which I had to tell him was not in my course of studies. Another day when he was particularly distracted—to the point of mumbling to himself—he demanded I recite the incantation for locating springs, and when he saw the look of incomprehension on my face, he began a strange rhythmic chant in a language neither Percy nor I had ever heard. After a moment of this strange behavior, Walky faltered in mid-word, looking at us in astonishment. Quite abruptly he fled the room.

"We did not know what to say, and for a long moment sat there in stunned silence. But there was no doubt about what we had heard. It had been magic! We both felt the power of it. Walky had been performing an enchantment!

"'Do you know what I think?' I said to Percy. 'Walky must have been a teacher of mages.'

"'He'd have to be a hundred years old—maybe more,' Percy protested, always practical.

"'Nevertheless, that is what he is doing in Eldrich's house.' I was utterly sure of what I said.

"'Then he must be a mage himself,' Percy said.

"'Maybe not. He might prepare the young ones before they go to study with the mage proper.'

"There was a long silence while we considered the ramifications of this insight, neither of us wanting to actually put into words what it meant. We did not look at each other, and the silence stretched on. I remember hearing the insects buzzing outside the open window.

"'Are we to be mages, then?' Percy said, his voice very small and filled with awe.

"'No,' I said quickly. 'It can't be that.' But I was not so sure." Erasmus fell silent, lost in his memories of those days, long past.

Hayes leaned forward. "And was that it?! Was that why you were there?"

Erasmus looked up, startled. "What? No, of course not. I don't know to this day. . . ." He felt his head shake in denial, though of what he was not sure.


## ꙅ Four

The final hour of darkness held the city close, not willing to release it until touched by the burning sun. The birds that lived in the eaves and openings of houses stirred and cooed their waking songs, like men and women sleepily readying themselves for their day's toll.

Anna's carriage entered the courtyard through an arched opening and she heard the gates close behind her. By the main door, a lamp chased the darkness from that small corner of the courtyard, illuminating the wisteria vine climbing the posts of the entry porch.

*It's done*, she thought. *For better or worse, it's done.*

The door to the carriage opened, and she was handed down to the cobbles, where she stood a moment, not quite ready to go in.

Banks appeared beneath the wisteria.

"Anna?"

"Coming," she said, still not wanting to. A walk in the garden to clear her head and calm her was what she would prefer. She had never felt such elation and such anxiety at the same time. The two emotions seemed to be struggling within her, producing a nervousness that was entirely uncharacteristic.

Banks took a step toward her, and rather than have him come and lead her inside, she relented and went toward the door, sweeping past the concerned-looking young man so that he could not take her arm in his too-possessive manner.

The house was warm, the air redolent with smoke and the smells of coffee.

"Everyone is here?" she asked Banks.

He nodded. "Yes, there have been no mishaps. Your part went well, I take it?"

"Not as I expected, but well enough. We are in the library?"

"The dining room, in fact."

She set out for the dining room, where she found the others seated around the table, talking with animation despite the hour.

"Anna," Halsey said, standing, as did the others. Halsey was the oldest of the group, the leader by both seniority and acclamation.

"We've just been speculating about Skye," Kells said. "So tell us what happened."

She took the chair that Banks pulled out for her and collapsed in it, suddenly tired. The high back pressed into her skull, and she shut her eyes a moment.

"All went much as we expected. Not as well as we might have liked, but not as badly as it could have—not nearly as badly." The sound of a coffee cup arriving on the table before her brought her upright. "He . . . he was shocked, as you might imagine, but I think, on balance, the earl believed me. The unconscious sailors helped make my point. As the earl left, he owned that he was in our debt. . . ." She lifted her cup and let what she'd said sink in.

"Well," Kells said, "that is hardly bad news, though it was the least we could expect from a gentleman. We did save him from gaol, after all. From utter ruin, in truth." Kells nodded. He was always quick to judge. Quick to act. In some ways she felt closest to him for that. As usual, Halsey said nothing, weighing her words, considering every possible interpretation that might suggest disaster.

"But what will Skye do now? Did he say?" Delisle was five years older than Anna, and asked most of the questions—even the obvious ones, which was good, she'd come to realize. Many things would never have been discussed openly without him.

"I don't know, and I didn't ask. It was a delicate moment. As we agreed, the most important thing was that Skye realize and believe we had saved him—for no reason other than our admiration of him. I think he did believe that. What of your own tasks?"

Delisle glanced quickly at Banks. "I wish we could say things went so well. We were almost apprehended in Samual Hayes' rooms. A pack of navy men came up as we were there, and we had no exit but the window. I fear they are still wondering how we jumped from such a height and apparently sustained no injury. It was the worst luck, but once we were up the stairs, there was nowhere else to go."

"It never occurred to us that the Admiralty would send men to search

Hayes' rooms at the same time as they sprung their trap for Skye," Banks said. "I still can't imagine why they did it."

Halsey was shaking his head just a little, sitting back in his chair, a look of some disbelief on his face. He was not happy with what he heard.

"You had no difficulties?" Anna asked the old man, her tone quiet and deferential. He had never been entirely in favor of this endeavor and now seemed to be having his worst fears confirmed.

"Difficulties? No," he said softly. "I have always managed what must be done, even when it is murder." He shook his head again, clearly disturbed. "So, Skye did not offer to open any gates for you?" he asked, fixing Anna with a gaze. She wondered how a person made their look so hard.

"He offered nothing, not that I expected he would. Not yet. But I still do not doubt that my vision was true. He *will* open a gate for us. I'm sure of it."

"Yes, but who will wait inside? You still do not know, I collect?" Halsey's gaze didn't soften, nor did it release her.

Anna shook her head. Visions were not so easily explained, and augury was imperfectly understood, even by the ancients. Anna could recall her vision in detail if she closed her eyes, yet she still could not say who stood beyond the gate. A man who held a book and a white blossom, but as he turned toward her so that she might see his face, a light blinded her. Nothing more. Skye would open the gate to knowledge and power, that was the vision's meaning. Who held the book, she was sure was irrelevant.

"Let us not have the argument again," Kells said. "It will not come out differently. Eldrich still plans to bring an end to the arts in our time. The years of caution are past. We cannot wait Eldrich out—not now. When the mage is gone, the arts will disappear with him."

Yes, Anna thought. She had seen it. Eldrich disappearing down the corridors of a forest, leaving behind a world devoid of its former power, devoid of all magic. She shuddered at the memory. The forest had seemed so lifeless, though to most it would appear still green and growing. She could not imagine wanting to live in such a world.

"But, Anna," Banks said gently. "You've not seen what we recovered from Hayes' rooms." He slid a letter across the table. "There was much more—a journal, a sheaf of notes—but we were caught unawares and left it all behind in our panic."

Anna picked up the letter.

"It is from this other young man Skye employed," Delisle said. "Fenwick Kehler. We have wondered where he got to. It appears he has been researching in the Farrellite archive in Wooton!"

*My Dear Hayes:*

*I had begun to despair of ever accomplishing my task here, no matter how hard I searched, but recently things have changed. You would not believe what I have found, sir! All that we ever dreamed and more! The archive is a mine of knowledge lost and forgotten, one must only find the vein one seeks. I will tell you much more when next we meet. I hope to be granted a few days' leave come late spring and will travel to Avonel in all haste.*

*I hope this letter finds you well.*

*Yours always,*

*F. W. Kehler*

"It says very little," Anna said, surprised that Banks would think this so significant.

"So one would think, but we saw Hayes' journal. Pages and pages about the Stranger of Compton Heath. And much speculation about Baumgere! Assuming that Kehler is still in the employ of Skye, the letter says a great deal. One should realize that Kehler must write with extreme caution. After all, he is clearly delving into matters of which the priests would not approve—and they are likely not above monitoring the correspondence of their guest scholars. No, if read in the proper light, this letter says a great deal. Skye might open the gate, and the man standing inside could well be this young scholar, Kehler. Who can guess what he has found in Wooton? We know the priests have been hoarding knowledge for centuries, and not all of it of a religious nature."

Anna shrugged. "Do we know what has happened to Hayes? Do the Admiralty have him?"

No one answered for a second.

"We don't know," Kells said. "It is possible. Now that Skye has escaped their trap, it will not look good if they have taken this young man into custody. He is, after all, innocent of any crime. I don't know what they'll do with him. And who knows what the worthy gentlemen of the Admiralty will think if he tells them what he has been researching for Skye."

"We needn't worry about the Admiralty," Halsey said suddenly, his aged, gravelly voice sounded tired and somewhat sad. "For now we must watch for any sign of Eldrich's hand in all of this. We wait and keep our distance."

"Certainly caution has served us well all the long years," Anna heard herself say, "but those days are at an end. If we are too cautious now, we'll sacrifice everything. The arts will be lost to us forever. And Eldrich will have triumphed."

"You will learn a terrible lesson, Anna, if you persist in underestimating him," Halsey said, some frustration in his voice. "*He is a mage.* Even if Eldrich is the least skilled of mages, he is still more powerful than you can imagine. You do not begin to understand what he can do. It is entirely possible that Skye does his bidding, or that the men who attempted to ruin Skye did so on behalf of the mage, whether they were aware of it or not. And we have leaped to Skye's rescue. We have revealed ourselves. Revealed ourselves after centuries of hiding. We have been reckless enough. Now we must wait.

"It is one thing to say that the time for caution has passed and another to go running foolishly into the arms of Eldrich. I will not allow it. Imprudence now will be our ruin. Let us see what Skye will do. I don't want to find that he has opened this much vaunted gate only to discover that the man who awaits us is no man at all—but a mage."

"Perhaps Anna should attempt to see again. After all, we have contacted Skye. We have passed a way-point—a significant one." Delisle glanced a bit guiltily at Anna. "Things might be clearer, now."

Anna sat immobile. The thought of attempting augury again brought up something near to panic. She had gone down that path too often, at great cost, and more often than not there was nothing to show for it. Halsey had begun to protect her from it recently, protect her from the others who saw augury as the solution to all doubt, despite the fact that it never was. She waited for the old man to come to her rescue so that she would not have to start making excuses . . . start showing her fear.

*It draws the life out of me*, she thought. *Can't you see that?*

Halsey did not look at her, but suddenly nodded his head, the smallest motion. "Can you bear it?" he asked looking up at her, the sadness he had nurtured all evening suddenly manifest, like the scream of a newborn.

"Of course," she heard herself say. There was no other answer. She was no less dedicated than the others who would do anything to keep Eldrich from accomplishing his purpose.

*But why is he doing it?* she asked herself again. She did not know. The mages were selfish and willful. They needed no more reason than that.

They are taking the magic with them . . . somewhere.

She saw the image of Eldrich, disappearing down a corridor of the forest. Saw the world left beind. A world where augury would no longer be possible. A world where her talent had even less chance of blossoming than it did now. No chance, in fact.

She pushed back from the table, not waiting for the others. Better to lead than follow. She was the one born to talent. She was the one who would lead one day, if all went as they hoped.

She went out into the garden, into the starlight, listening to the night as she walked. Forcing her heart to be still, her mind to become calm.

*I cannot be afraid*, she chanted over and over again. There was a difference between not showing fear and not being afraid, and simply not showing fear would not pass here. It could even bring her to . . . well, she did not like to think about that.

They went to a small pool among the trees. Anna stopped here and breathed in the night, drew the darkness into her lungs, the starlight, the shadows. Still, they were so still. She listened for the songs of the stars—the choral stars.

They appeared before her as she closed her eyes, wavering, and then holding steady. She began a whispered chant, bending quickly to make a mark in the earth, to draw a figure of pale light.

When it held steady, she rose and stepped into the pattern, not needing to open her eyes, for the lines burned in her mind, burned so that she could feel them.

*It is not pain*, she told herself, though she longed to shut out the glowing lines, longed to scream.

*It is not pain*. She repeated the lie, knowing it was the only way to survive.

A burning heat searing her nerves like fire, like the coldest ice. Pain so terrible in its intensity that it did not seem human. Mankind could not feel such agony. Like birthing a child and then experiencing your own horrible death as the child howled.

Anna screamed, opening her eyes suddenly. Staring down into the dark sky of the pool, where the stars hung like points of white hot fire.

*I'm looking into my own mind*, she thought, and then stiffly tossed a pebble into the water. The stars wavered, swaying back and forth and she felt herself falling. But still she stared, waiting. Waiting. Opening herself to the emptiness, to the agony, but only for an instant. It was all she could bear. All anyone could bear. And then she shut her eyes, feeling the earth beneath her knees, hands taking hold of her.

She had seen nothing. *Nothing.*

## ↬ Five

This particular visitor always arrived unannounced and, somehow, unexpected. Considering the amount of time that Sir John dedicated to contemplating this gentleman, and the dread he felt whenever Bryce actually appeared, it was impressive that the man invariably seemed to arrive when Sir John's guard was down. The maid thought it very peculiar, and Sir John was sure that his own reaction made her even more suspicious. There was, however, nothing he could do about it. These visits were not a matter he controlled or even had influence upon—and not many things transpired in Avonel that Sir John could not influence.

It was understood that Sir John never kept this visitor waiting, no matter the hour or circumstances. He looked at the clock again in disbelief. Not even half-five—still dark, and only morning by the most liberal interpretation of the term. He bent over and stirred the coals of the fire, carefully arranging dry kindling. Mornings were cool, though that would soon change, but a fire was still a pleasure if not an absolute necessity. There was a crack from the cedar, and a thin thread of smoke streamed up. Flame erupted with a sigh.

Sir John was still dressed in his nightclothes, and felt strangely vulnerable, not that he usually felt any less vulnerable when Mr. Bryce came to call, no matter what the circumstances.

"Congratulations on your baronetcy, Sir John." Bryce stood at the door to the drawing room. No apology for arriving at such an hour, not that Sir John expected any.

"May I?" Bryce gestured toward a chair.

"Please. Brandy? Wine? I have a fine claret from the southern slopes of Farrow." Sir John insisted on pretending it was late at night rather than obscenely early in the morning. It made it all easier to deal with, somehow.

"Claret, please."

Sir John poured them each a glass and took a seat by the fire. Bryce was, without a doubt, the most self-assured man Sir John had ever met—not arrogant or full of himself, but apparently without self-doubt. And the effect of this confidence on others was profound. Sir John was quite sure the King himself would defer to the man.

The odd thing about it was that Sir John, who prided himself on his ability to understand his fellow man, could not quite explain how Bryce managed to convey this degree of confidence, nor what lay at its center.

The truth was that Bryce was invariably extremely polite, even sensitive; things that Sir John did not associate with this kind of self-assurance. Power was what he thought of when he met a man with confidence, and Bryce was not typical of men who possessed power.

Sir John thought Bryce almost inhumanly precise. His dress was impeccable, his speech exact and explicit, as though it conveyed his thought perfectly and without effort. Sir John had never spoken to a man who did not occasionally grope for a word, or use some term that was less than exact—except for Bryce. The man was meticulous in every way—disturbingly so. Sir John could not escape the feeling that he was dealing with someone who had passed beyond normal human functioning.

Sir John could not imagine Bryce ever making a mistake, needing sleep. He was certain the man did not sweat. Bryce existed on some other plane and descended only occasionally to the muddled world of men, who must seem only slightly more organized and thoughful than beasts to him.

Bryce sat regarding him for a moment, sipping his wine. "I suspect the seeds you've sown have begun to bear fruit, Sir John."

As a political animal Sir John had spent many years learning to keep his feelings and reactions to himself, but he was under no illusion that he could hide such things from Bryce, so no doubt what Bryce saw was the flash of fear that Sir John had just experienced.

"What has happened?" Sir John asked. Who had fallen? Moncrief or Skye?

"That is what I hope you will be able to tell me. I suggest you pay a visit to your friends in the Admiralty. Bring every little detail you gather to me. I will weigh them, Sir John. Do not presume to know what is significant yourself. Only I can decide that. Do you understand?"

Sir John nodded. This little lecture was unnecessary, for he was well aware that he had not the slightest insight into the man's intentions. At Bryce's instructions, Sir John had nurtured this feud between Moncrief and the Earl of Skye—though feud was hardly the right word; Moncrief never let his vendettas become public. It was one of the reasons the man was so feared. He would go about knifing you in the back and all the while you would have not the slightest sign of what was about to befall you. But by any name, Sir John had encouraged Moncrief's jealousy and loathing of Skye. Not a task he had taken on with great joy. Sir John might not understand all the discoveries Skye had made, but he had no doubt that the man was a genius, a genius and largely benign. Benign in a society where Moncrief was the most voracious of predators, but where predators were not in the least uncommon.

"I will visit you again this night. That will give you ample time. . . ."

This was most definitely not a question, and a day would certainly not be anything like the time Sir John needed. "I . . . yes, that will be adequate."

"Good." Bryce looked at Sir John and attempted something like a smile. Like all other human emotions, pleasure and joy seemed beneath him, and any attempt at imitating them was doomed to sad failure—though Sir John certainly never found any amusement in such attempts.

"You do not look pleased, Sir John. Were my assurances that we intend no harm to Skye not enough?"

"More than adequate, but I suppose I still worry. Setting Moncrief against someone . . . I don't know if there is any animal so vicious as the King's Man."

"Yes, it is a wonder . . . the way he walks through civilized society, as though he were actually part of it. . . ." Bryce shrugged. He was not given to philosophizing about mankind. "You admire Skye."

"Yes," Sir John said quickly. "Yes, I do. But not for the reasons he is admired by everyone in the nation."

Bryce did not say anything, but waited patiently.

"I admire him for his convictions. It is no secret that Skye has had great misgivings about the use of his invention. The cannon is the deadliest weapon in the history of warfare, after all. Some say we have hardly begun to understand its uses. And look what has happened already. The battle off Cloud's End was pressed too far, many think. It is said that the admiral of the Entonne fleet tried to surrender, but even so his ships were destroyed. They have taken poor Admiral Stewart to task for this, but it was policy. I have no doubt of it. The goal was to destroy the Entonne fleet to the last ship." Sir John shook his head. "Barbaric, really. And so many seamen lost. It did not matter what flag they sailed under, they should have been allowed to surrender. It was nothing short of murder.

"Lord Skye is not pleased with the way the Farr government has used this advantage he has given them, and I dare say he would be less willing to give them such a weapon again."

Bryce actually raised an eyebrow at these words. "A man of conscience," he said, and Sir John nodded. Bryce seemed to consider this for a moment and then his focus returned, his gaze fixing on Sir John.

"Well, you needn't worry about this moral dilemma much longer. You see the Entonne now have the ability to produce cannon and gunpowder on their own. In fact, they have been engaged in this activity for some months."

Sir John sat forward in his chair. "How in the world . . . ? Was it Skye?"

Bryce shrugged. "I don't know how they discovered this. It was apparently not so difficult to manage, really, not once the cannon had been invented. Even the Admiralty must have realized their advantage would be brief. No doubt that played a part in their decision to destroy the Entonne fleet—press their advantage while they still had it."

*The Entonne had the cannon?!*

"You look rather surprised, Sir John. It was inevitable. And will the world be different when Entonne has the cannon? No, it will be the same as it was for the last three hundred years: neither country having an advantage. Better to have balance."

"But my government should be informed."

Bryce's manner seemed to indicate that he thought this a matter of little consequence.

"If you think it's important. I suppose it might profit you to be the first with the news. So you see? Do I not act with your best interests at heart? Was that not always our arrangement? Have you not been granted a baronetcy as a result of my efforts?"

"Are you suggesting that I'm not worthy of this honor?" Sir John said, the words out of his mouth before he realized what he said.

Bryce only smiled. "You are thrice worthy, my dear Sir John, but worth has little to do with the granting of titles, as you well know. You have long been worthy, but never influential—at least not influential enough."

"But whose purpose does this baronetcy suit, I often ask myself."

"My employer's, Sir John, make no mistake of that. My employer's. But will it not benefit you as well? Do you not have the joy of it? Does it not gratify you to be addressed as 'Sir John'? Speak honestly."

"You know it does," he said quietly, feeling a little overwhelmed.

"And I know your fear, Sir John. You worry that you will be asked to compromise your principles. Or that my employer will demand something of you that will bring about your ruin or the ruin of your good name. Is this not so?" He did not wait for an answer, as though he didn't require confirmation of another's thoughts. "But rest assured; my employer does not wish you ill. You're a good and loyal servant, Sir John. Why would he endanger one such as yourself? When one has a champion race horse, only a fool would demand it run to the hounds. My employer, Sir John, is the least foolish of men, let me assure you."

Sir John felt himself nod. One could not disbelieve Bryce. As with so many things, he was likely above lying. If he did not want Sir John to know something, he merely did not tell him. He had no qualms about that. There was always an insidious logic to any claim Bryce made. Sir John often wondered if he were not merely under the man's influence, bespelled by his superior logic and overwhelming self-confidence. Was he losing sight of his own principles, or merely learning to see the world more clearly, tutored by this stranger who came to him at all hours?

Bryce waited patiently, almost watching Sir John's thought processes.

"I will find out what I can," Sir John said.

"My employer also needs to know where Skye is now."

Sir John nodded, not at all sure he could find him.

Bryce showed no acknowledgment, but reached into his coat and removed an envelope. "There is a venture you will find interesting, Sir John. A short canal to join the Singe and the Trent Rivers, undertaken by reliable men. All the details are here." He handed the envelope to Sir John, who took it quickly. Mr. Bryce actually smiled at him. "In a few months your debts will be discharged, Sir John. I think you can indulge in a manservant now. Next year you shall have a carriage, the year after a larger home. You have been following your budget assiduously, I trust?"

"To the letter . . . or number in this case." And I have not been out to gamble, not once. Bryce had been right; the desire had faded. Even though he had failed to master it for more decades than he cared to count, it had disappeared. And even more remarkable, his debt, which he had previously thought insurmountable, was nearly paid.

Bryce did not even bother to smile politely at this weak jest. "It is a profitable arrangement, is it not?"

Sir John nodded.

Bryce rose, "I shall let you get on with your valuable work, Sir John. No, please, I will let myself out."

*But who is his employer?* Sir John asked himself.

Sir John went to the window, though he hung back a little so that he would not be seen. Bryce emerged onto the street below, into the light of the still glowing street-lamps and the pale luminescence of approaching dawn. There was no carriage waiting, not even a hired hack. Mr. Bryce crossed the street with a determined air, like a man on his way to an appointment, and just as he stepped up onto the curb, he stopped, and looked directly up at Sir John, and nodded.

Involuntarily Sir John stepped back from the window. *Surely he could not have actually seen me up here*, he thought. Surprisingly unnerved, he sat down heavily in a chair.

*How could he have known I watched?*

## ⤳ Six

She hated confessions. She did not care to listen to other people bare their souls, and she cared even less to hear her own voice speaking in that pathetic, too-intimate tone. Yet here she was, standing before the fire, the portrait of her late husband staring down upon her sternly—though he had never, in real life, turned such a look upon her—and she was revealing things that embarrassed her deeply. Confessing things she would much rather keep to herself, and she did not know why. And to Marianne Edden, of all people!

"I thought he showed signs of interest," Lady Chilton said, annoyed by the meek little voice that escaped her lips.

Silence. A blessed moment of silence. Perhaps she had finished. May Farrelle help her retain some dignity.

"I am impressed. You seem to have found the one man in all of Farrland who is immune to your charms," Marianne said dryly, rather unaffected by the countess' plight. "But you rate genius rather too high, I think. I myself know several men of undeniable brilliance, and I must tell you that I think them the greatest bores in the nation. I would as soon hear a mother talk of her children than listen to these 'men of brilliance.' There is no one so self-absorbed as a man convinced of his own lofty intellect—a condition that far too many suffer from, I must say. But if he is the only man among the hordes who are smitten with you, well. . . ."

"All right, Marianne, I will stop feeling sorry for myself. You have made your point." The countess shook her head. There was no room for melodrama around Marianne Edden. She was a novelist and had the novelist's eye for such things.

And then the countess found herself speaking again. "The most humiliating part," she said, unable to stop, "was that I attended the marchioness' evening only in hopes that I might see him. I went to a *brothel* because I had dropped a hint that I would be there, and he did not even bother to show his face! A brothel! And what did I hear people discussing but his latest passion, and she's hardly more than a child. . . ." She put a hand on the mantle and leaned against it. There, it was out. Perhaps now she could stop.

"Is that not like a man?! A beautiful and accomplished woman pursues him, and he chases after a doll. Now there is *genius* for you! A genius at making a perfect ass of himself!"

The countess did not answer. Oh, it was good to hear Marianne offering her support, but it had little effect on how she was feeling. *Shake yourself out of this*, she thought. *You of all people should not complain because you are not being madly pursued by a gentleman.* The thought caused a different feeling of distress. There was a madness that whirled around her, and had for many years, and she could not control it except by staying out of society, which she could not do entirely. She could not hide herself away.

The countess was a widow, it was true, but she was still young. Certainly she could not be condemned to living out her life alone, or worse, with a partner who was only vaguely satisfying. Men pursued her with a kind of ferocity that other woman almost never experienced; surely one of these countless men would be the match she sought. The wall against loneliness.

"When will you show me these paintings he is so interested in?" Marianne asked.

The countess felt a tiny shudder at the mention of the paintings. "I will have them removed from their cases for the gentleman who is to authenticate them. What was his name?"

"Kent. Averil Kent."

"Yes. So you might see them this afternoon, if you like."

"This day I shall be otherwise engaged, but I should like to see them at some point. What is Skye's fascination with them, do you think? Have you ever found out? He hardly seems the kind of man to be interested in things mystic."

The countess ran her hand along the mantlepiece and looked up at the portrait of her late husband—even with his disapproving look, she found more comfort in this painting than in the pieces by Pelier.

"So one would think. I don't really know what it is about Pelier that so fascinates him. He is not an open man, Skye." She shook her head, thinking that she meant that he was not emotionally open, for about most subjects he would happily speak at length—but about his interest in the Peliers he was very close. She suspected that, about this one thing, he was embarrassed.

"There is something more to his interest than mere art. Perhaps now that I have them in my possession, I will discover what it is that so intrigues him."

"Perhaps, though I fear you will not tell me," Marianne said. "You are rather unfair, I must say. I share all my gossip with you, and it is not just gossip but gossip of the very first rank, and you . . . well, you are positively *discreet*." She said the word with impressive disdain. "Hardly ladylike. You are only supposed to be discreet in the company of others—not with your dearest friends, of which I presume I am one."

"You most definitely are, Marianne, but I have so little to tell you. It is terribly unfair, I agree, but do I not introduce you to everyone you could ever want to meet? Do you not gather reams of material for your novels from the people you meet through me? There is some return, I think."

Marianne nodded a little reluctantly. "I suppose I cannot deny that entirely." She looked up at the clock on the mantlepiece. "I fear I must be going. My public awaits me."

The two women said their good-byes, and the countess was left alone. She settled herself in the chair so recently vacated by Marianne and stared at a still life across the room. It was hardly a remarkable work, merely competent, but it soothed her all the same. The Peliers, on the other hand, she found unsettling, to say the least. There was something about them. . . . Like looking at another's dreams—or nightmares perhaps. Not that they were horrific, just disturbing and oddly unreal. They seemed more the result of delirium—the fever dream—than of a normal imagination.

Why was Skye so fascinated by them? It was almost unseemly that an empiricist would be so captivated by a man like Pelier, who was said to paint "visions," some of which later, it was claimed, came true.

"Foolishness," she said aloud. Yet Skye was hardly foolish. Oh, he was a little vain, and took too much pleasure from his great reputation, but he was not foolish—not yet at any rate.

The countess was surprised not to have heard from the earl. She had sent him a note as soon as the paintings had arrived the previous afternoon and had expected a reply almost immediately. He might not be in thrall to the Countess of Chilton, as so many others were, but she expected the Peliers would bring him at a run.

Very odd.

*Why does he not care for me?* she wondered. *Why, when so many others are driven to foolishness?* The mere thought disturbed her. Two men had dueled over her recently. She turned red with embarrassment and distress. Dueled over her, and she had never met either of them! Strangers. . . . And one had been wounded fairly seriously. What if he'd been killed? Did they never think of her? How would she live with that?

*I will be driven to hiding myself away*, she thought. *But not yet. I need to be sure that there is not the least chance of interesting Skye. Not the least chance.*

Kent sat in the parlor, waiting as patiently as a man could to meet the most beautiful woman in Farrland, and very likely beyond. He sat in a chair across the room from a looking glass, staring at the poor, anxious wretch who looked back at him so guardedly.

*Take hold of yourself, man*, he chided himself. *It's not as bad as you think.*

His head knew this to be true; after all, Kent was something of a favorite of the ladies of Avonel. Oh, he knew he was not an outstandingly handsome man, but he had his good qualities. He gazed at the man in the looking glass and willed him to appear more at his ease.

*That's better*, he thought. *Yes, sit up as though you were vital and confident— no matter what the truth might be at the moment.*

No, he was not so difficult to look at. His brow was high and smooth, his eyebrows well formed. If he were looking at his ideal portrait, he would certainly repaint the nose if he had the chance, for it was a bit larger than he would like. And his chin could be a bit more in proportion—not quite so strong. His eyes, of course, were very fine—a grayish blue that changed with the light. He'd worn a blue frock coat that brought out the color of his eyes. He had always known how to dress—had even become something of trend setter this last while. Yes, the man sitting across from him would do. Many a woman would be happy with less. Oh, taller. He would like to be a bit taller, but he wasn't short by any means, and his form was perfectly acceptable. No, many a lovely woman had settled for men no easier to look at. Even the countess' first husband was said to have been a rather ordinary man, in the physical sense.

Footsteps sounded in the hallway outside and he rose in anticipation, his mouth a bit dry, but the sound passed on and faded, leaving Kent feeling a disturbing sense of loss. He was so unsettled that he went to the mantlepiece to examine a miniature portrait, as though he would hide the fact that he had risen nervously in expectation, only to have no one arrive. *But no one is watching*, he told himself. Still, he felt he had looked foolish.

He hardly registered the subject of the portrait; a man like many another. His mind was on the woman. Kent had seen the countess on more than one occasion—his recent success had brought him entrance to such circles—but he had never actually been introduced. Which meant that in many ways he was still on the outside. Yet, here he was, invited to the countess' Avonel home, even if it was in a professional capacity.

He dearly hoped that the countess would buy one of his paintings. It would set the rest of the aristocracy scrambling to follow suit, and would send the prices up. This thought produced a bit of anxiety. But not as much as the idea that the countess would take a disliking to him. That was his great fear. Not only would it likely ruin his career, but such a humiliation was not to be recovered from. He would be forced to leave the country.

*I do not expect her to fall into my arms at first sight,* he told himself. *I'm not such a fool as that. But if she could find my conversation pleasant, and be at least a little charmed by my wit. . . . If I could enter her circle—even its outer rings—so that she would invite me to her home on occasion and acknowledge me at the theater, then I would feel at least that I am not a complete buffoon.*

Kent knew a little about the countess, as did almost everyone in Farrland. She was said to be very bright, easily bored, literate, artistic, aloof in her manner. The men who managed invitations to her famous salons were all of the first rank, known for their personal charm and sophistication. Mere physical beauty did not qualify one for invitations to the home of the countess—a woman renowned for physical beauty. Nor did a title seem to much impress her, for several of her favorites were not of particularly notable families.

*I am almost there,* Kent told himself. Recently his paintings of nature had gained him entrance to the Empiricist Society—an achievement of which he was justifiably proud. And his landscapes would soon have him made a Fellow of the Royal Society for the Arts. Averil Kent, F.E.S., F.R.S.A.

By accomplishments alone he was almost ready to step into the countess' world. But accomplishments were not enough. The countess must meet him and judge him worthy.

"My late husband, the Earl of Chilton," a woman said in a voice so warm and full of color that it melted into Kent's very heart. He turned to find the countess standing just inside the door. "Or perhaps you were more interested in the artist? Montpelier, I believe."

Kent bowed a bit awkwardly, unsettled by her sudden appearance. "It is a lovely little piece, Lady Chilton," he managed. "Lord Chilton was a striking man."

"Do you think so?" she said, a very slightly mocking smile appearing on her lovely mouth.

Kent nodded. What was it about her? Why did she drive men to utter foolishness? He fought the urge to stare.

"I never really thought of him as striking, not even as handsome. But he was kind beyond measure, and deft in politics, and fair, and considerate. And he seized life like no other. Though his life was cut short, I am sure Lord Chilton lived more than many whose spans tripled his own." She looked over at the small painting in its silver frame with a look of great affection and some sadness.

The countess held out her hand suddenly. "And you are Mr. Kent, I take it."

"Averil Kent, Lady Chilton. Your servant." Kent touched his lips to the offered hand, and realized as he did so that he blushed, though the countess gave no indication that she noticed.

She gestured to a chair and Kent gladly sat while tea was called for.

It struck Kent that the countess did not possess the ideal feminine figure, for in truth she was too tall and slim. Almost willowy, he thought. Too girlish and not womanly enough, and this surprised him, for no one would hear the slightest suggestion that she was less than perfect. Her dark hair, nearly black, was perhaps perfect, for it was thick and fell in lustrous curls about her heart-shaped face.

With his painter's eye Kent quickly noted her features. Large blue eyes set too wide apart and slightly elongated, which was unusual and gave her face an exotic appearance. He realized that there was a mole hidden in her right eyebrow, though no one would likely notice. Her lips were full and complemented the shape of her eyes. Kent thought the structure of her face very fine. Unquestionably she was a beautiful woman but not really so striking as to cause the furor that she did.

And if that were true, why was he responding as he did? He hadn't felt so nervous since he had first begun to court. It was her voice, he realized. It was so rich with color—he could almost see it. A palette of the most vibrant hues. When she spoke, her voice penetrated into his very center and something there began to vibrate as though in harmonic empathy. When she spoke, he wanted to close his eyes and just feel the effect, as though he were being caressed.

"My friend, the Marchioness of Wicklow, has a very fine landscape you did of the Whye Valley, Mr. Kent. I admire it greatly. Have you done others?"

"Of the valley?" he said, almost unable to hear the words for the warmth of her tone.

"No, landscapes."

"Ah. Yes," he said trying to pull himself together. "The countryside has been my principal subject these past few years, though the natural world has also drawn my attention."

She smiled. Kent got the distinct impression that he was talking to a woman who was unhappy. Something about her features—slightly frozen—as though she were tired of keeping up the facade. "And this is what gained you entrance to the Empiricist Society?"

Kent nodded. "I'm surprised Lady Chilton would know."

"You are thought to be an artist with a considerable future, Mr. Kent. And I am an admirer of the arts and a friend to the artist."

Kent felt a slight shiver as she said this, as though she had inferred that she admired him. Tea arrived, interrupting the conversation and giving Kent a chance to try to collect himself. He hoped his blush had disappeared, though his face felt warm yet.

"I'm given to understand, Mr. Kent, that you are an expert on Pelier."

"I must say, in all modesty, Lady Chilton, that this is precisely true."

She laughed, which he found gratifying. "But I think you are being too humble, sir." She gestured with her teacup to the doors behind Kent.

"Would you be so kind as to give me your opinion of these pieces?" She rose, taking up her cup and saucer, and led Kent through the adjoining chamber and then into the room beyond. He thought she walked a little stiffly, as though undertaking some task she found distasteful.

The paintings were not hanging but resting on a side table and leaning against the wall. Though Kent had a longstanding interest in Pelier and his work, he realized that focusing his mind on anything other than the countess at that moment would take an act of extreme will. For her part the countess stood back from the paintings, an odd look on her face.

"As you will see, they are signed Pelier, but there seems to be some doubt as to the veracity of the claim."

Kent set down his cup and moved closer to look. The first was a typically ambiguous piece: three figures gathered about a marble crypt. If it had meaning, it was impenetrable, as was the case with many of Pelier's works. They were reinterpreted regularly to fit events. The second was even odder. A man, dressed unconventionally, his back to the viewer, crossed a bridge over a stream, but the bridge changed its form from one end to the other, as though two different designs flowed together in the center. On one bank of the river it was morning, the light pouring down upon the flowering trees of a spring day. The other bank was neither spring nor morning, but depicted a fall afternoon. In the background Kent could see the ruin of an ancient cathedral, and then he realized that there was an old-fashioned carriage drawn up in the shade of the trees. It seemed to be waiting.

"How very odd," Kent said. "Do you see the way the river flows in two directions? As though the bridge were downstream from either side." Kent shook his head and smiled: the wonderful ambiguity always made him do both of these things.

"Do you have a lens?" he asked.

The countess rang for a servant who quickly fetched a lens. Kent bent closer to the canvas, examining the signature, the technique, the brush strokes, the palette.

The inscription on the tomb was not in any script that Kent knew, he realized, making it likely a Moravian painting. Pelier had almost unquestionably been a member of this secret society. It might be a message for fellow Moravians. But there was something about this painting. . . .

"I believe, Lady Chilton, that this one, at least, is a very skilled forgery. I am sorry to say it. Was it sold to you as a Pelier?"

"It was a gift, Mr. Kent, and the kind soul who gave it me did not claim with certainty that it was genuine. What is it that makes you so certain that it is not a Pelier?"

Kent gestured with a hand. "Do you see the white in the marble of the tomb, and here in the gentleman's shirt? It was not made from lead, I'm sure. Pelier used only white made from lead. And the brush strokes, though a very close imitation, are not quite as I would expect. Pelier had a very light touch that is particularly difficult to imitate. The signature is astonishing. I should have believed it to be real if not for these other things." Finally Kent pointed to the area of sky. "But this is the true error in the painting. I have often thought that Pelier's handling of cloud and light in the sky was unparalleled. This is only competent. No doubt about it, Lady Chilton. A wonderful forgery, but a forgery all the same."

The countess shrugged and smiled. "Oh, well, it was a gift given in kindness and that is what matters. It is rather ironic that I have it at all. I pretended to admire these paintings at someone's home—out of politeness, you see—and the next day they arrived at my door." She stepped back and looked at the painting. "And they are forgeries, to boot."

"Oh, no, Lady Chilton. This first is a forgery. But the man crossing the bridge. This is a Pelier. I'm quite sure of it. Look at this tremendous sky! If he had painted nothing but skies, I would have counted him a master all the same. No, this one is quite genuine, and more than that, I have never heard tell of it. It happens, now and then—a real Pelier is found. It will set the art world abuzz—not to mention those who spend their time interpreting and reinterpreting Pelier's work."

"How exciting for all concerned," she said, looking at the painting and wrinkling up her nose.

"The countess is not an admirer, I collect?"

"Oh, I suppose there is nothing wrong with Pelier, but . . ." She made a face. "Do you believe Pelier was a seer, Mr. Kent? Or was it all a terrible ruse?"

Kent considered a moment. Somehow he felt his answer to this question was "the test." His fate hung on his reply.

"Well, I will say without hesitation that Pelier was no charlatan, which is to say that he believed that his paintings were inspired and prophetic, though he did not claim to know what they meant. Whether he was a seer . . . ? It depends on whose interpretation you read. I think there is little doubt that he predicted the great earthquake of 1378. If you look at the two paintings that deal with this incident—Have you seen them, Lady Chilton?"

She shook her head.

"One shows the ruin of the city of Brasa, so much like the actual ruin after the disaster that it cannot be mistaken. Thirteen doves fly overhead against the perfect clouds and sky. The number 78 can be seen on a fallen house, and there is a cherry tree in blossom, which would make the scene February—exactly when the tragedy occurred. A young girl runs naked down the street, obviously a victim of burns, as so many were. And a team of gray horses still in harness can be seen running wildly across the distant hillside, their carriage lost." Kent met the countess' eyes, wondering if she thought him a fool. "I think it is clearly a case of prophesy. I cannot explain it any other way."

"I see. And did Pelier really paint in a trance with his eyes closed?"

"I very much doubt that his eyes were closed, but he would not allow anyone in the room as he worked, so we will never know. Pelier did say that he did not know what the painting would be when he set brush to canvas and that he was 'inspired' as he liked to explain it. He made very few claims for himself, Lady Chilton, it was only those who gathered around him toward the end. They were responsible for his myth—these men and those who came after."

"It is a fascinating story," she said looking at the paintings again. "I am a little sorry that only one is genuine," she said, but Kent was sure she did not mean it. She still stood back unnaturally far, and everything in her manner spoke of great discomfort. These paintings unsettled her in some way.

Kent looked back at the paintings. "But the other could easily be a copy—perhaps even a very faithful one. Many were made, and there is no precise catalogue of Pelier's works. Once a canvas was complete, he did not much care what happened to it. He was simply driven to make the painting. I tend to agree with those who believe there were some forty paintings that were never recorded. Sold for near to nothing or given away. Lost now these many years. A genuine Pelier, like this, turns up every decade or so, and there are any number that might merely be imitations made for gain, or actual copies done by his various devotees."

"You do not subscribe to the school that tries to find meaning in every element of his paintings, do you?"

Kent shook his head. "No, I tend to think that is a bit off the mark, nor do I believe that an event must be found for every painting. Some, however, I think were genuine acts of prophesy, and although this runs against my beliefs, I can't think of any other explanation." Kent shrugged, a bit embarrassed. He had told the truth when it might have been better to have lied. But it was done now.

"Well, Mr. Kent, I certainly agree that there is more to life than we perceive daily, that is certain. After all, there is still a mage alive in this very land, and one cannot deny all the acts of the mages, augury among them. That a man painted pictures that alluded to events in the future is not impossible, I think."

"I agree entirely, Lady Chilton," Kent said, his enthusiasm, and perhaps relief, obvious. "That is what I have long said. . . ."

"Lady Chilton?"

Kent and the countess turned to find a maid standing in the door. "Pardon me, ma'am. There is a letter. . . ."

There was an odd second of hesitation. Kent thought he saw a hint of annoyance flit across the countess' face, and then her manner changed. "Oh," she said, then turned to Kent. "Would you excuse me for a moment, Mr. Kent?"

"Certainly."

The countess swept out, leaving Kent to watch her go, more graceful than a dancer, he thought. He could hear quiet voices outside, for the door had been left slightly ajar. Kent found himself gravitating toward the door, straining to hear, not really sure why. Perhaps the countess would say something about him, give him some hint as to how he had been judged.

But the whispering fell silent, making him wonder if he'd been heard. *That would finish your chances*, Kent thought. *Sit down, man!* But he stayed where he was, straining to hear.

A rustling of paper. "Castlebough," the countess said. "Have things ready. I will leave today if it is possible. The morning at the latest."

Kent stepped away from the door and pretended to examine another painting.

"Not another forgery, I hope," the countess said, but Kent could see her manner had changed. The letter had erased the discomfort caused by the Peliers, though she did not seem utterly sure and joyful, as though she had heard from a lover. In fact she still seemed rather sad.

"No, not that I can tell," Kent tried to smile but found the countess' manner distressed him, as though he could hardly bear to see her unhappy—a complete stranger.

"More tea?" the countess asked, clearly prepared to continue their visit in all politeness.

"I think Lady Chilton has other matters more pressing. Please, don't let me detain you."

She stopped, looking at him, her manner very solemn. "You are very kind, Mr. Kent. Yes, I am called away. Perhaps we might try this again? I was so looking forward to getting to know you a little better."

Kent was touched by the apparent sincerity in her voice. "Nothing would please me more. I will be away from Avonel briefly—a painting expedition—but when I return. . . ."

"Then we shall indeed meet again." She seemed to have a thought. "Do you do portraits?"

"I'm afraid I don't, Lady Chilton."

"Unfortunate. But perhaps I could visit you in your studio? I would very much like to possess an Averil Kent and want to be certain not to get an imitation."

"It would be an honor, Lady Chilton," Kent said, bowing his head.

"Hardly," she said, "but for some strange reason my influence in Avonel society is entirely out of proportion to my actual accomplishments. I might increase the demand for your work, Mr. Kent. Unless you are a man of independent means and disdain the making of money from your art?"

Kent met her eyes briefly, shaking his head almost imperceptibly.

"Good. I despise dabblers. Real artists who must make their living by their own hand—these are the men and women who have made Farr art what it is. Not the Lord Dinseys and Sir Gerrard Bainbridges." She paused and fixed him with a pensive look. "If we are to be friends, Mr. Kent," she said, her rich voice dropping to a tone so intimate that Kent almost forgot himself. "I must tell you that I cannot bear to be treated like . . . Well, as though I am something other than human. Do you understand?" Her manner was most sincere, her last words almost a plea.

Kent nodded, feeling suddenly a deep sense of loneliness from this, the most desired woman in all of Farrland.

"Until we meet again, Mr. Kent," she said, offering her hand.

Kent touched his lips to her perfect skin, and found himself out on the street, walking in the wrong direction. The tiny glimpse he had of the woman behind the persona of the Countess of Chilton had left him utterly confused. Was she lonely? Could a woman in her position have a life that was less than perfect? Did she have doubts? Or dream of life being other than it was? What was it that called her away on a moment's notice?

He stopped on the street, looking around as though lost in a foreign city. After a second—as though recovering from a mental lapse—he realized where he was.

"What are you thinking?" he said quietly. "You would be seen as a fool, certainly." But he went off down the street wondering how many days it would take to reach Castlebough, and whether they might meet along the way, so that he would not have to wait so long to hear that voice again.

## ↩ Seven

To call it an uneasy alliance would be something of an understatement, but the compact between Moncrief and Admiral Sir Joseph Brookes had survived a decade and continued to totter along as precariously as could any alliance between two men whose ambitions were not entirely mutually exclusive.

Brookes was the older of the two by some fourteen or fifteen years, placing him in his middle sixties, though he appeared to be much older than that. Not that he was fragile or frail in any way, for he was a vital man, hale and strong yet, but he was gray and wrinkled from his years at sea as were few men who lived even to their eighth decade on the land.

Like most navy men, Brookes was highly conscious of his appearance and groomed and dressed himself with a kind of self-awareness that was usually the prerogative of a dandy—yet he was not in the least vain. It was merely a habit required by the service—a point of pride that had almost nothing to do with narcissism.

Despite its fragility, the alliance was founded on rather solid foundations. Sir Joseph Brookes had become Sea Lord largely, though not exclusively, through the efforts of Moncrief. Not that he lacked qualifications—that was certainly not the case. Brookes was an efficient and even somewhat imaginative leader. But one did not rise in the service of the King without well-placed patrons.

In return for Moncrief's continuing support, Sir Joseph put at the disposal of the Kings' Man the intelligence-gathering organ of the Admiralty. Of course the palace had agents of its own, but they were forced to operate under the scrutiny of the government—a situation that Moncrief found . . . inconvenient.

The Admiralty, however, was almost an independent principality—and the Sea Lord was the prince of this not so tiny nation within a nation. One of the reasons Sir Joseph had lasted as long as he had in the position was his political acumen. Like the sovereign of any small nation, he had developed an unparalleled deftness for balancing the needs of his own principality against those of his more powerful neighbor—in this case the King and government of Farrland. He was a master at disguising his own plans as actions for the benefit of Farrland—and sometimes they even were.

"We've found the woman," was the first thing Brookes said as Moncrief entered.

The King's Man had taken one of the leather chairs in the Sea Lord's office. He leaned on his cane and stared at Brookes, making his displeasure known, and though he felt some relief at this news, he did not allow it to show. "So we know who it was put her up to this betrayal?"

"The hell of it is, we don't." Brookes was not a man to be easily intimidated. When one has faced both battles and storms at sea, even a King's Man does not look so frightening—but all the same, he did not look comfortable. "She was discovered this morning floating in the harbor—drowned."

Even Moncrief could not keep his face entirely impassive at the news. "Surely Skye would never have done such a thing," Moncrief said. "Was she in the employ of the Entonne all along, then? The plans for the cannon are missing, I take it?"

Brookes nodded. "Yes, unfortunately, they are. Whether she was an Entonne agent . . ." He shrugged, maddeningly.

The plans for the cannon were missing! It had to have been the Entonne. Farrelle's flames! Had he and Brookes given away Farrland's military advantage in their attempt to bring down Skye? Moncrief felt a little ill, suddenly, and sat back in his chair leaning heavily on one arm.

"I suppose I should hear what happened," he said at last, his mouth dry.

Brookes took a long breath. "It is a little difficult to be certain. Our people were in place in the house, just as we had arranged. The doorbell rang, and Mary went down to answer it, and that is all the officers can tell. They awoke some six hours later. Both Mary and the plans had disappeared. And that might have been the end of the story if we had not found Mary this morning, as I have said."

"That is it? That's all we know?"

Brookes shook his head. "Almost. All we know for certain, at least, but there are a few other small details. Two of the men present swear they had neither food nor drink while they were in the house, nor for several hours before, yet they all seem to have fallen unconscious at precisely the same time."

Moncrief snorted. "Well, clearly, they're lying. I'll wager they were all drinking and are afraid to say it. Who admits dereliction of duty, after all?"

"So one would assume," the Sea Lord said, "but I spoke with the men myself, and I tend to believe they were telling the truth—or at least most of it."

Moncrief was surprised to hear that Brookes would actually speak with men involved in such an action. Best to keep oneself a step removed. That was always Moncrief's policy.

"But they were obviously drugged. . . ."

"So one would think. But how do we explain the men who took no refreshment?"

"If they are not lying, then they must be mistaken," Moncrief said. "Liars or fools—take your choice."

Brookes did not look convinced of this.

"If you will indulge me for a moment, Lord Moncrief, I will bring in two witnesses to an event you might find edifying."

Moncrief was a little shocked at the suggestion. He did not want to get too closely involved—as Brookes clearly had. "If you think it absolutely necessary," he said, making sure his reluctance was clear.

Sir Joseph nodded, seemingly unaware or unconcerned. He tugged on a tasseled bellpull, and his secretary's pockmarked, but rather dignified face appeared in the open door. "Sir?"

"Send them in, will you."

The secretary made a motion that resembled a bow and disappeared. A moment later the door opened, and two individuals came reluctantly in with heads bowed and taking small, timid steps. One was a seaman, who held his straw hat in hand, and the other was a woman—a harlot, Moncrief was sure.

"This is Abel Ransom, purser on His Majesty's Ship *Prince Kori*. And Miss Eliza Blount—*seamstress*," Brookes said. "Would you be so kind, Mr. Ransom, as to tell us what you saw last night."

The seaman nodded, his eyes only flitting up occasionally. Moncrief wondered if a man of so little rank had ever entered this office before—unless it was to scrub the floor.

"If it please you, sir, I was on the dock by Halls and Hale, sail-makers, late this night past when a carriage drew up along the quay." He glanced up apprehensively, as though he did not expect to be believed. For a moment he struggled, fear apparently having driven all memories from his head.

"Well, go on, Ransom," Brookes said, none too patiently.

"Yes, sir. Two gentlemen and a lady disembarked from the carriage, sir. I couldn't see them clear for the light was poorly, but one gentleman was older, sir. Older and a bit cranked, sir."

"Bent," Brookes translated for Moncrief.

"Yes, sir, bent and not so spry. He was speaking to the lady, though we could not hear what was said. We was in the shadow of the door . . . talking, you know.

"The woman left the gentlemen, walking a bit stiffly toward the quay's edge, but she didn't stop, sir. I swear. She just walked right in. Didn't jump, sir, but walked in as though she didn't see the water. The two gentlemen went to the edge, sir, and watched for a few moments, doing nothing to help her, as though she were in no difficulty. And then they loaded themselves back in their carriage and set off." He looked up, his apprehension changing to defensiveness "We went to see what had happened, sir. But the tide was at full ebb, and she was not to be found. Drownt, I'll wager."

Brookes looked over at Moncrief, raising his eyebrows.

"And you did nothing to help?" Moncrief asked.

The man glanced at the woman. "Well, sir, we didn't realize she was in trouble, you see. The two gentlemen stood by so calmly, we didn't know what to make of it. 'Perhaps she can swim,' thought I. These folk do the oddest things for sport, sir, if you don't mind me saying. They'll row a boat for pleasure, sir. And some are said to swim, though I've never seen it myself. It was all so peculiar that I just didn't think clear."

"And you, Miss?" Sir Joseph said. "Do you agree with Mr. Ransom's tale?"

She nodded quickly, clearly hoping to not have to speak at all. Moncrief realized that under the makeup hid a girl of perhaps sixteen or seventeen. Older than some, perhaps, but still too young. Having daughters himself, Moncrief was both appalled and filled with pity.

"Speak up when you're spoken to, girl," Brookes said.

"Yes, sir," the girl managed, her voice coming out as a whisper. "Just as Abel tells it, sir. If it please you, sir."

"Very little pleases me," Brookes said, though he was not really talking to the girl. "Have you any questions, Lord Moncrief?"

"I suppose I need not ask who the woman in question was?" Moncrief said quietly to Brookes, who nodded. "Can they identify the men?"

"Can you?" Sir Joseph asked the pair.

"I'm sorry, sir. It was very dark."

"I'm sure," Brookes said. "Have you anything more to ask?" he said to Moncrief.

The King's Man shook his head.

"I will have them kept close by in case they can offer anything more," Brookes said as the man and woman were led out. "But do you see what I mean? Is it not an odd story?"

It was Moncrief's turn to shrug. "The woman was threatened. It was either into the harbor or some terrible violence would be done her: a choice we might have made ourselves."

"Yes, I suppose, but both Ransom and the girl are sure there was no threat. Only quiet conversation. When the woman went into the harbor, they were completely taken off guard. No wonder they thought it innocent—some lark of the gentry, though no one was laughing, I will wager."

"So how do you explain it?"

"I can't explain it, but it was damnedly peculiar, don't you think?"

"To say the least." Moncrief was not at all sure what to make of it.

"But do you see, there is a pattern of a kind?" Sir Joseph said. "Two of the men waiting for Skye swear they touched neither food nor drink, yet they fell as insensible as their mates who had. Then this odd occurrence at the harbor. Now let me add something more. The officers sent to look into the rooms of one of these young men that Skye employed encountered others who arrived before them with the same intentions." He paused for a second. "These gentlemen vacated the rooms by the only means available—they leaped from the window. This seemed peculiar enough, as the window was quite high, but they apparently landed without harm and disappeared into the darkness. The officers who were present assure me that they would have been badly hurt if they had performed this same leap—and naval officers see men fall from the rigging often enough to know."

Brookes raised his bushy gray eyebrows—like great storm waves, Moncrief thought. Raised them as though what he had just said made some sense.

"And your point, Sir Joseph?"

"Men fell asleep as though drugged when they had ingested neither food nor drink. A woman walked calmly into the harbor and drowned. She did not cry out or plead for her life, but simply went into the water as though nothing would come of it. And finally, men jumped from a great height to escape our men, and landed so easily that they were able to *run* off. Landed so softly that the men who chased them out barely heard a sound. These things are all more than peculiar, they are . . . well, I fear they are not natural. . . ."

If anyone but Sir Joseph Brookes had made this statement, Moncrief would have laughed aloud, but the Sea Lord had an uncanny intuition and had been proven right too often for Moncrief to scoff, no matter how outrageous the proposal.

"Do you think it's Eldrich? Is that what you're suggesting? Flames, Joseph, the mage has not left his estate in . . . decades. The rumors are that he is not long for this world."

"Yes, the rumors always abound where the mage is concerned. He makes very certain that no truth ever escapes from his own lands—unless it serves him. No, we cannot be sure the mage is anywhere near death, I think. Nor can I say with assurance that Eldrich was either involved or not involved, I only know that something happened in the city last night that was not quite as it should have been, and it all centered around Skye. Perhaps the King is not his only protector."

The two men sat brooding for a few moments, as though the idea was so far beyond their usual experience that they could not even begin to imagine what it might mean, or what they should do. And then Moncrief interrupted the silence. "What has become of Skye?"

"We don't know."

Moncrief shook his head. "I have done everything I can to insure that he doesn't reach the King, or even send His Majesty a message, but this can't be kept up forever. A few days at most. . . . We must assume that Skye knows who was behind his attempted ruin?"

"Not necessarily. Surely Mary suspected but had no proof, and the officers involved I trust utterly. No, we are safe from prosecution at least—how else we might suffer I cannot say. If the King were to believe Skye over us . . ." Sir Joseph rubbed one of his eyes gently and Moncrief realized that the man had not slept this last night. "But I have a feeling, Lord Moncrief, that Skye and the King are the least of our worries. Something else is afoot. Something very odd. If we assume that the men who jumped from the window on Paradise Street and the men who sent the woman to drown in the harbor were not the same gentlemen—for they would have had to have been in two places almost at once—then there would appear to be more than one man who has at least some knowledge of the arts. That leaves us with two possibilities. They are servants of the mage," he paused, as though surprised by his own words, "or they are some group of whom we know nothing at all."

"The former seems much more likely to me."

"I would have to agree, but let me tell you something else. The officers who went to search Samual Hayes' rooms came back with a journal and a number of interesting letters. Most from his friend Kehler who has been studying at the Farrellite archive in Wooton. You will not believe what they've been up to. It seems Skye employed them to delve into this matter of the so-called Stranger of Compton Heath. Have you heard of this?"

"Something, yes. Some kind of a lunatic who appeared in the town, and the locals made claim that he was from an unknown land. Wasn't that it?"

"More or less. But the odd thing is Hayes and Kehler came away convinced that the man was not mad at all. They also seem to believe that it was a mage who took the man away."

Moncrief was at a loss for words, and unsettled by how out of his depth he suddenly felt. Moncrief who controlled the government and much of the kingdom, besides. "Joseph, I haven't even the beginning of a notion as to what goes on. Have you?"

"I can't claim that I do, Lord Moncrief, but no matter how absurd it might seem, it begins to look as if Skye has some interest and perhaps even some involvement in the arts. Whether it is Eldrich or some other, I cannot say. But it seems to me that we should know if the arts have come to life again around the Entide Sea."

Moncrief also wanted to know what went on here, but if a mage were involved. . . . "I question the wisdom of interfering with Eldrich. He will not look kindly on us meddling in his affairs. I don't care how old or infirm Eldrich has become—he is still a mage."

Brookes nodded. "Yes, but I would never advocate interference. Observation is all I am suggesting. If there is some other who practices the arts, we should know his purpose—or at least be reassured that he means us no harm. If it turns out to be Eldrich, then we will break off our operation. If we are reasonably sure it is not Eldrich, then I would think it advisable to inform the mage."

"It is still a risk, but I agree, however reluctantly." Moncrief stopped as he began to rise. "But, Brookes, we should be sure your best people are involved and that they understand how important it is for them to keep their distance. We must limit the risks as much as possible."

"Certainly, Lord Moncrief. Leave that to me."

Moncrief rose, but had a sudden realization—clearly the surprising turn the conversation had taken had reduced his capacity to reason. "How will you begin, Brookes? You lost track of Skye."

Brookes had risen to his feet as well. "Yes, but only temporarily, I think. If Skye reappears in Avonel, we will know, for we still have one of the earl's servants in our pay. But I don't think it will be so difficult to find Skye. He had these young men looking into the story of Baumgere, and I am all but sure that interest will give him away. I will wager that Lord Skye has retreated to the village of Castlebough—a town conveniently near the Entonne border should he need to quit Farrland altogether. I'm sure he has only temporarily dropped from sight, for the earl is far too well known to be able to hide for long. We will soon know his whereabouts, and then we'll see what goes on in our kingdom. Something very odd, I think. Something very odd indeed."

## ∾ Eight

The sound was rhythmic and syllabic but too low to be distinguished. Chanting, Erasmus was sure. He could almost make out the words, though they did not seem to be Farr. Anxiety began to grow in him. The day was clear and warm, but here, among the green hallways of the wood, it was cool, the sunlight filtered to muted greens. Smoke; he could smell the smoke. It seemed to burn his nostrils, but then there was a hiss, and it turned sweet and aromatic. Leaves had been tossed onto the fire. Luckwort leaves, but they did not calm him as they should. Knowing what came next, he wanted to shout, but try as he might, he could produce no sound.

He pushed aside a branch, hurrying now, feeling the horror of what was about to happen drive him. But something was wrong; he seemed to be gliding so slowly, like a bird hanging on the wind, making little progress.

And then the scream. He stopped, standing on the pathway between the trees and the angled trunks of falling light. More than anything he wanted to look away, close his eyes to it, but he could not. Not quite. And then the child appeared, engulfed in flame, mouth open in a silent scream of unimaginable agony. Every nerve shrieking in anguish. The child stumbled toward him, arms out as though begging for help, to be held. And then it stumbled, looking at him still, the recrimination clear.

*Why? Why did you do this to me?*

The burning child toppled forward, and the last thing Erasmus saw was its face. *His* face. He was burning. Not some other. He was aflame.

Erasmus woke from the dream, covered in sweat. He stumbled up from the divan where he had fallen asleep and made his way to the doors looking down into his garden. He sucked in the cool air, almost sobbing. Alive. He was alive and unharmed. It had not been he who burned. Thank Farrelle. Not him.

The dream was never easy to drive from his mind, and Erasmus was grateful that it came infrequently. He paced back and forth across his study, unable to sit, running his hand back through his hair over and over.

"Blood and flames. Bloody blood and flames."

He often wondered what caused the dream to return, but, as always, he could not say. Perhaps nothing caused it. It just would not let him be. His penance.

"We did not know," he said aloud. "How could we?"

He tried to think of something else: his conversation with Hayes, but Stokes arrived with Erasmus' wash water. The servant wore an odd, pensive look that was not quite in character.

"You look either troubled or ill this morning, Stokes. Now which would it be?"

"Never ill, sir," he said quickly. "Nor particularly troubled . . . but your young man has been up since I don't know when, pacing, sir. Back and forth across the library. Across the main hall. He seemed to be considering leaving, sir, or so I thought."

"He's here now, I hope?"

"Oh, yes, sir. He's had a pot of coffee all to himself and is vibrating like a harp string. He seems anxious to speak with you, sir. Keeps asking when you might be up."

"I'll be down directly. Don't let him leave before I've spoken with him."

Erasmus continued with his toilet, not letting Hayes' impatience ruin his morning ritual. Stokes came back a few moments later to shave him, and lay out his clothes, and with the warmed steel scraping across his face, Erasmus again considered the conversation of the night before.

The tale of the Stranger would have seemed nothing more than folklore if it hadn't been for Hayes' encounter with this physician, Ripke. That had a ring of authenticity to it that Erasmus was not about to deny. And Erasmus' intuition told him that the man who'd come in the carriage to collect the Stranger was no man—not in the sense that he understood the word. It was a mage, and Erasmus thought he might even be able to supply the mage's name. If a mage was interested in this Stranger, then Erasmus was interested, too. So Hayes had better be prepared to reveal a little more—the name of the gentleman who had employed him would be a good start.

As he went down the stairs, Erasmus wondered what the Admiralty's part was in this affair. Unless they really did believe the Stranger was from an undiscovered land, for certainly most of the vast globe remained a mystery. Perhaps they'd learned something on a recent voyage. . . .

Hayes was sitting at a small table in the breakfast room, looking out into the garden. As Erasmus entered, he jumped up, obviously relieved to see him. There was a certain anxiety in the young man's manner that did not disappear, however.

"Ah, Erasmus. I can't thank you enough for your help and generosity, but I've decided that I must get messages to both Kehler and our employer as soon as possible."

"Not before you've eaten, I hope." Erasmus took a seat at the table and dropped a napkin into his lap, reaching for the coffee pot. "Sit down, Hayes. I've been thinking as well."

Hayes took his seat slowly, as though he were ready to run out the door without any further discussion.

"The agents of the Admiralty might well be looking for you yet, so I'm not sure I like the idea of you racing around the city on your own. If they've come after you because of your link with this gentleman who employed you, they're likely after him as well."

Hayes shook his head. "I've thought about that and decided it's very unlikely. You see, my patron is beyond . . . well, not beyond the law, but certainly even agents of the Admiralty would not dare apprehend him without . . ." He hesitated. "Let me just say that the man is not unknown to the King."

Erasmus stopped with his cup in the air. *Are you telling me that it is Skye?* Erasmus could hardly credit this idea, but who else could Hayes mean? A man of great reputation and standing who had some involvement with the Admiralty. An intimate of the King, a man whose interests wouldn't lead one to believe he would be interested in stories of mysterious strangers. An empiricist, obviously. *Skye.* It could be no other.

Hayes hesitated, chagrin obvious on his rather tired countenance. "I'm not telling you . . . at least not intentionally," he added quietly.

Erasmus sat back in his chair and stared at his friend. If he had been told the man in question was his own brother, he would have been less shocked.

"What possible interest could Skye have in such a tale?" he asked finally.

Hayes shrugged, reaching down and picking up his spoon as though suddenly interested in silverware. "Erasmus, I hope you understand that the earl does not want his name connected with our inquiry—he was most adamant."

Erasmus nodded dumbly. "But why is he interested?"

Hayes turned the spoon over and dropped it so that it rattled off the floor. Erasmus bent down quickly and retrieved it, reaching out and taking hold of Hayes' wrist so that the young man would look at him.

"Why?" he said quietly.

Hayes shook his head. "I don't know. It . . . I don't know. We speculated endlessly about this, but you must know that one does not ask the Earl of Skye impertinent questions."

Erasmus nodded. The earl had a reputation for impatience with anyone who presumed too much of their friendship. "Well, I agree that a message should be taken to him directly. And this young man, Kehler . . . what's become of him?"

"He has continued in the employ of Lord Skye, though not here in Avonel. I'm not at liberty to say more."

"Do you intend to see him in person—Kehler, that is?"

"No, I'll have to write him."

"Well, eat, and we'll pay a call on the Earl. I think, given the circumstances, we can risk doing so without warning him."

"You'll come with me? But, Erasmus, he'll know I've told you."

"Yes, well, that is a problem because I'm not sure you should appear at his door, not with the Admiralty looking for you." Erasmus thought a moment. "We'll approach it like this. You write a letter to the earl, and we'll take a carriage to his home where I'll deliver it. You can stay in the carriage unless the earl is there and wishes to speak with you. I'll claim to be merely a loyal friend helping without explanation. Skye and I are both members of the Society and I'm known not to be one of the gossips. Will that answer?"

Hayes looked enormously relieved to have an ally and went immediately to write the note, not having touched his food.

The ride to Skye's town home was not so long, as it turned out he did not live far from Erasmus. Hayes stayed in the hired carriage, as planned, while Erasmus rang the bell.

As he stood on the step, he turned around to survey the street. If Skye's home was being kept under surveillance, it was being done with some discretion. An old woman stared down from a window across the way, but she didn't have the look of an Admiralty agent to Erasmus' mind—a busybody was more likely.

The door opened and a manservant nodded respectfully as Erasmus handed him a calling card. "Erasmus Flattery. It is imperative that I speak with Lord Skye. I have a letter that I must deliver."

"I'm terribly sorry, Mr. Flattery, but Lord Skye is not at home. I'll certainly see that the letter is delivered safely, however." He reached out a hand, which Erasmus ignored.

"I've been charged to place it in the hand of Lord Skye and no one else."

"I am sorry, sir, but that isn't possible at the moment. . . ."

The servant looked up at the sound of the carriage door opening.

"Mr. Hayes!"

Hayes ran quickly up the steps. "Yes, is the earl not at home? I desperately need to speak with him."

The servant shook his head, apparently pleased to see Samual. "No, sir. Lord Skye set out early this morning and didn't say where. It was most peculiar. You don't know where he'd have gone, do you, Mr. Hayes?"

"I'm afraid I don't. You haven't had men from the Admiralty about asking after your master, have you?"

"Not a one, sir, though your colleague, Mr. Kehler, was by this morning. He left a letter as well."

Hayes shook his head in worry, looking at Erasmus as though unsure what to do. "Kehler didn't say where he was staying, I don't suppose?"

"I'm afraid not, sir. Will you leave your letter with me, Mr. Hayes?"

Hayes was about to say yes when Erasmus stepped in, pocketing the letter quickly. "No, but thank you. If Lord Skye does return, would you ask him to contact me?"

The servant eyed Erasmus oddly, as though he were a little offended that Erasmus did not seem to trust him. "As you wish, sir."

Erasmus steered Hayes down the stairs and into the carriage.

"Whatever led you to do that?" Hayes asked. "We don't know when Skye might return or if he is even actually away. It would be better if he had my note at the soonest possible opportunity."

Erasmus nodded. "Perhaps, but did you not think that servant was more curious than was polite?"

Hayes was brought up short by this. "But he knows me, and was likely concerned about his employer."

"Perhaps so, but it is the practice of the agents of the Admiralty to pay servants for information about their employers. I would rather err on the side of caution." Erasmus tapped on the ceiling to have the driver move on. "It seems your colleague is in Avonel. What's his name? Kehler?"

Hayes nodded, thinking. "Yes, but where, that is the question. Under normal circumstances he would be my guest. As things stand, however, he could be rooming anywhere."

The little window between the driver and the carriage slid open. "I'm not sure where I'm to go, sir," the man said.

"Nor am I. Hold your course for a moment while we decide." He turned back to Hayes. "I assume Kehler has some friends in the city? Besides yourself, that is?"

"Emin, primarily, but he's abroad till midsummer." Hayes considered a moment. "We could try the Belch."

"Of course," Erasmus said. "The old Gulch and Swallow."

They pressed on to the inn where Hayes thought they might find Kehler, a place well known to Erasmus, though he had not been there in years.

The Gulch and Swallow Inn was called "House Hopeful" by many of its patrons for the simple reason that budding empiricists gathered there, both for organized discussion, and for discourse that could only be described as unruly. The truth was that, beyond their various interests, the patrons spent an inordinate amount of time gossiping about the doings of the *Society for Empirical Studies* and its fellows, for House Hopeful (also referred to as the "Belch and Swallow") was filled with young men who longed to become fellows of that august Society.

They spent uncounted hours discussing how one would best go about bringing one's efforts to the notice of the Society, as well as dissecting the tactics of every successful candidate.

Of course House Hopeful also provided a stage for the conquering hero, for who could resist returning to the "old neighborhood." And no matter how gracious the newly appointed fellow was in victory, or how much he assured the others that their turn would come, there was always a little triumph there, and a bit of jealousy as well.

Erasmus thought that these young men could speed their fellowship considerably by simply using the time spent in the Gulch and Swallow to further their original studies, not that he hadn't squandered his own fair share of hours in this very establishment. Youth, it seemed, had an undeniable need of company. It was rather like misery in that regard.

Neither of them spoke as they rode. The measured clip-clop of hooves on paving stones was hypnotic, lulling Erasmus into a contemplative state. The dream came back to him, but he pushed it out of his mind—much easier to do in broad daylight. They were not long in coming to their destination.

Erasmus followed Hayes through the door and stood for a moment, letting his eyes adjust to the darkness of the room. There was a faltering of the conversation as many of the young men present noted that one of the gods had descended to walk among them. Though perhaps Erasmus' reputation was not yet so large as to strike awe into the hearts of young empiricists. He might have been considered a mere demigod.

Hayes surveyed the young men present, acknowledging the occasional nod, and then he waved to someone, and crossed the room to him, Erasmus in his wake.

"Pleasures of the day to you, Dandish. Have you seen Fenwick Kehler?"

Dandish almost vaulted out of his chair, glancing nervously at Erasmus. "Yesterday. He was in here for an hour or more, asking after you, too, as I remember. He was talking to Ribbon most of the time." Realizing that Hayes didn't intend to introduce him, the young man turned to Erasmus. "Sanfield

Dandish at your service, Mr. Flattery. I'm a great admirer of your work in horticulture and botany, sir."

Erasmus offered the young man his hand and a tight smile, never comfortable with even genuine praise. "Kind of you," he said.

"You might try old Sam," Dandish suggested. "He likely spoke with Kehler."

Hayes ordered ale and left Erasmus at a table while he spoke with the tapman. He was back in a trice. "Sam's not sure where Kehler's found lodging, but likely in this quarter. There are a number of rooming houses that cater to visiting students and scholars. I'm sure I'll find him." Hayes picked up his ale and sipped it, staring at Erasmus. "Look, Erasmus, it doesn't seem that agents of the Admiralty are out in force searching for me. They haven't been in here, apparently, and this is a spot they'd likely not miss. I see no need for you to spend your day searching out Kehler. Leave me to it, and I'll bring you any news I might gather; that is, if you don't mind having me as a guest another night. I still feel a little trepidation at the idea of returning to my rooms."

"You are thrice welcome, Hayes, but see if you can bring Kehler back with you. I'm curious to hear his story as well. I could have Stokes put another room to rights and put you both up, if you'd like."

Hayes brightened at the offer. "You're too kind, Erasmus. I'll see if I can find Kehler, and we'll see what he's discovered in the archives of Wooton. I'm a little surprised that he's in Avonel so early in the year. It makes me a bit suspicious. If I'm not at your home by eight, it will mean the Admiralty have me. I trust you'll know what to do, for I certainly don't."

"Leave it to me, Hayes, but stay alert and be careful who you give your name to."

Erasmus spent the afternoon puzzling over the story that Hayes had told him. It had brought unfamiliar emotions to the surface. He had even spoken of his time in the house of Eldrich, which he almost never did. No, it was all very odd. The worst of it was that Erasmus was certain he could feel the hand of the mage in the story of Compton Heath. The unseen hand.

*"He does not sleep,"* Erasmus whispered to the window. *"Not yet."*

Erasmus was quite sure the rumors that Eldrich neared his end were not true—at least not in the way that others interpreted them. Eldrich, Erasmus was quite certain, would not pass through until he felt his time had come. But the idea that the mage was lying on his deathbed, aged and feeble, was simply not possible. Eldrich would likely remain hale and vital up until his last hours in this world. People simply did not understand mages—not these days, anyway.

Erasmus went out onto a small balcony, which looked down into his garden. Unlike most people of stature in Avonel, his home did not provide him a view of the sea. He found that the vast, open horizon begged too many questions and he felt that enough questions plagued him as it was. No, Erasmus much preferred his small garden. It gave rest to his soul in a way that the expanse of ocean never could. A garden whispered no questions.

The onset of twilight released the spell over the shadows dwelling beneath the shrubs and trees so that they began to swell, flowing slowly out into the open. A distinct demarcation between light and shadow began to climb the foliage of an ancient oak, and the corner of the house cast a shadow in dark relief on the lawn. Soon all of reality would blend in darkness, and everything would lose definition. Erasmus would dream and lose definition himself.

*The world when Eldrich is gone*, Erasmus thought. *A commonplace world.*

A hard tap made him start, and his manservant, Stokes, appeared. He opened his mouth and then stopped, a bit surprised. "Would you not like a lamp, sir?"

"Please," Erasmus said, trying to calm his heart, feeling much as he had when a boy, expecting Eldrich to sweep in on a blast of wind.

Stokes lit a lamp, and then lit another on Erasmus' desk. The light seemed to have a calming effect—like oil on stormy seas.

"Most unusual, sir. There is a Farrellite priest at our door asking to speak with you."

"Does he want money? Can you not tell him we are not of his faith?"

"It seems he has not come asking money, sir, but wishes to speak with you, though he'd not say why." Stokes looked a bit out of sorts. Though not a believer himself, Erasmus was, like most people in Farrland, respectful of the priests, if only as a concession to good manners.

"I am half-inclined to send him away," Erasmus said, thinking aloud. "Could he not take the time to send me a note telling me the purpose of his visit? These priests . . .!" He looked back out into his garden, which was slowly being consumed by darkness. "Oh, bring him up. I suppose I shall find out what he wants."

Stokes bobbed his head and went out, leaving the door slightly ajar so that his employer might hear the guest approaching.

A moment later Stokes opened the door and let in a small man dressed in the robes of the Farrellite faith. "Deacon Rose, Mr. Flattery."

Erasmus extended both his hands as was expected, though he disliked doing it. He tried to remember where a deacon fit in the Farrellite hierarchy. Above a parish priest, he thought, though the old root of the word was servant—servant of the martyr in this case. Certainly not servant of the parishioners.

"Mr. Flattery," the man said softly, his manner very humble, which annoyed Erasmus even more—falsely humble, he was sure. The deacon grasped both of his hands and said a quick blessing in Old Farr. "Thank you for seeing me without prior notice, Mr. Flattery. I apologize. It is not a habit of mine to burst in upon people unannounced, I assure you."

"Don't apologize, Deacon. Will you take wine or brandy? Coffee or tea?" Erasmus gestured toward two chairs.

"Brandy would be very welcome, I must admit. I have been traveling for the last three days and only came to Avonel this morning."

"Well, then, you need a brandy, Deacon." Erasmus was about to ask if the man had eaten, but stopped himself. He had never been too friendly with the priests of Farrelle, for he believed them to be a cynical, self-serving group that did much to slow progress in Farrland.

The priest collected up his robes and sat, smiling at Erasmus in a way that was kindly but not too familiar. Deacon Rose was a small man, his shape well disguised by robes. His hair, both gray and black, was cut short in the common style of the priests and he wore the round, crimson skull cap that denoted his rank. Rose might not have been a particularly handsome man, but he had a face that exuded a great deal of charm and humor, and his eyes suggested real kindness, although there was a trace of great determination there as well.

Erasmus was about to begin the small talk that was expected on such occasions—comments on the weather, etc.—but decided that the unexpected visit was hardly polite and so went right to the heart of it.

"What is it that I might do for you, Deacon Rose?"

The priest gave an odd smile that was half a grimace, as though he was hurt by the lack of politeness, but such was the burden of bearing the one truth. "And well you may ask, Mr. Flattery. But let me assure you, to begin, that you need do nothing for me. I have come regarding a mutual friend for whom I have great regard and concern. It is for his sake entirely that I am here.

"You see, after my arrival in Avonel earlier today, I went seeking this young man, and though I was not fortunate enough to find him, I was told in one establishment where the young gather that someone fitting his description and answering to his name had visited earlier, and, to my great surprise, I was not the first man who had come seeking him this day. Only an hour before the notable Erasmus Flattery had been asking after the same young man."

Stokes arrived with brandies and lit another lamp before leaving. Erasmus should not have been surprised that this visit had something to do with Hayes and his friend Kehler, but somehow he had been caught off guard.

"Erasmus Flattery was a name I knew well because of my own interests, and this brought me here. You see, Fenwick Kehler is a student at my college and, I have to say, such a student as we see only once a decade, if that. Mr. Kehler has the makings of an exceptional historian, perhaps even a great one. That is why I'm so concerned."

Cynical though Erasmus believed the priests to be, this one seemed genuinely worried about his student.

"The problem, Mr. Flattery, if I might come right to the point, is that young Kehler has been searching into the archives. I fear he has poked into matters the church considers to be private. Things that, strictly speaking, he was not to have had access to." For a second the man looked embarrassed. He began rubbing his hands together slowly, and then turned the single ring that he wore. "Yes, I know, many people think we are hiding things in Wooton, but that is not precisely true, or at least is not what they likely think." He looked up at Erasmus suddenly, and there was a keen intelligence in that look. "Perhaps Mr. Kehler has spoken to you of this . . . ?"

Erasmus said nothing, but gazed coolly at the priest.

"Of course, that is your affair and not really my business," the priest hurried to add. "But let me only say that Mr. Kehler has looked into documents that would give him merely part of a story."

Erasmus almost interrupted to plead ignorance to the subject, but the priest began to speak again, turning his gaze out the window and continuing to toy with his ring. "The whole affair of Honare Baumgere is a grave embarrassment and something of a mystery to us. And all of this speculation . . ." He looked back at Erasmus. "It's such utter foolishness.

"But that is not my real concern. You see, Mr. Kehler's making free with our archives has caused quite a stir. He was granted great trust, and did . . . well, did what he did, unfortunately, and now he is in grave danger of expulsion. Not the end of the world, you are no doubt thinking, but the worst of it is that our young Kehler is from a family of extremely modest means. He is entirely dependent upon the good graces of the Farrellite Church for his tuition and other expenses. Oh, he does some work in the library in return, but not enough to recompense, and now, you see, he has put his situation in grave danger. He has not the means to return to Merton, or even some lesser university. I fear that we are about to see the end of an exceptionally promising career, Mr. Flattery." He shook his head. "I am not quite sure what to do, for you see he will not face up to the consequences of his actions. As soon as it was learned that he had broken his word to us, Mr. Kehler slipped out of the monastery and away. Now a man of his age and learning should have the mettle to own up to his wrongdoing and, at the very least, apologize. Yet he ran off like a child, to the disappointment of many who had done much to further his studies and who had esteemed and trusted him."

He reached out and touched Erasmus' wrist. "That is why I have come to you. If he does not return and take responsibility for his actions, he will certainly be expelled, which would be a terrible loss to the world of scholarship, not to mention the effect it will have on his life. I'm sure he has great regard for you, Mr. Flattery. You are a fellow of the Society, as all young men wish to be these days. Can you not speak with him? I assure you there is no great mystery to be uncovered in the archives of Wooten. He is throwing his career away for nothing." He spread his hands. "Nothing." The deacon looked up at him, anxiety overcoming his facade of peace and charm.

Erasmus was affected by the man's concern, though it was against his better judgment. "Let me explain, Deacon, it would be something of an exaggeration to say that Mr. Kehler and I were acquaintances. I suspect I would have less influence on him than you hope."

Deacon Rose looked a bit surprised. "I did not realize. I thought perhaps it was a relationship of long standing. In a way it would make sense that Mr. Kehler would cultivate your friendship. Did he ask you about mages, Mr. Flattery?"

Erasmus was a little taken aback by this. "I really feel any conversations I've had with Mr. Kehler were private matters, Deacon. I'm sure you understand."

"Quite so. But even if you have not been long acquainted, you could do the young man a good turn. Could you not have a word with him, Mr. Flattery? I suspect he would respect your advice. Think of poor Kehler. What will become of him? He has no trade, no family connections. We are talking about a great career being cut short over mere stubbornness. And that is a tragedy. *Youth*, Mr. Flattery. Only a young man could be so impetuous. Only a young man could fail to see the consequences of his decision. The future, no doubt, seems infinitely bright to him, but we both know that much can happen in the course of a few short years. I fear he will live to regret this decision. Regret it most terribly."

Erasmus wondered what Kehler was up to in the Farrellite archives. He was still in the employ of Skye, and Skye was proving to have some very peculiar interests.

Scholars had long believed that a great deal of Farr history was hidden in the archives of Wooton. Perhaps a great deal of information about the mages. "I'm not sure where Kehler has gotten to, but if he can be found, I'll speak with him. I can promise no more than that. I have no faith that he will heed my council."

The priest reached out and took both Erasmus' hands. "Thank you, Mr. Flattery. May Farrelle bless you for your good heart. And Kehler will thank you as well, one day." He muttered another blessing in Old Farr.

The priest sat back in his chair, taking up his brandy, and looking at Erasmus as though he were a particularly prized student. "As I said earlier, Mr. Flattery, we have a common interest: viticulture. Years ago, now, I held a position in the south countries, and at the abbey there we cultivated the vine—oh, and made wine as well—but my love was the vine and the grape. To work in the fields beneath the sun of high summer, to see the clusters swell upon the vine . . . I miss it terribly. I have a few vines growing at Wooton, but it is too far north—though I am finding some better results these last few years. Certainly you haven't done all your work up in Locfal?"

"Some of it, but I have a small holding on the island of Farrow."

The priest reacted as though Erasmus had mentioned the name of the man's lost love—the loss that had sent him into the priesthood. "Oh, how fortunate you are, Mr. Flattery. I have traveled to Farrow only once, and for far too short a time, but there can be few places better suited to viticulture, I think. Have you seen the famous Ruin?"

Erasmus nodded.

"Is it not marvelous? Astonishing really. Life is filled with mysteries, Mr. Flattery, and I am glad of it. I'm much saddened by these young empiricists who wish to explain everything. Contemplating the mysteries is a worthy meditation, in my view. It teaches humility and fills us with proper awe for this world we have been blessed with. Don't you agree?"

Erasmus shrugged. "I thought it was the business of the church to explain mysteries."

The priest did not look at all ruffled, his amiable manner not changing in the least. In fact, he seemed almost pleased that Erasmus might dispute with him. "The Farrellite Church is not monolithic, Mr. Flattery. There are schools of thought—many of them—and though we agree on the central issues, there are many more on which there are differing views. This is very healthy, I think.

"Perhaps I'm something of a mystic. I believe there are mysteries that were not meant to be comprehended by men. Not in this life at least. But these mysteries are there to fill us with awe. To instruct us in ways we cannot explain. They are like the best art in that regard. Their contemplation opens doors within our own thoughts. We see things we would not otherwise have seen. And they fill us with joy at their beauty. Those who study the words of Farrelle in an attempt to comprehend the mind of the martyr are entirely misguided in my view. These writings were never meant to be understood, but were created to stimulate the minds of his followers. They were not meant to be the basis of doctrine but of inspiration." The man paused, a bit embarrassed perhaps, but clearly this was a subject near to his heart. "May I tell you my view of mysticism?"

Erasmus nodded his consent, interested, in spite of himself, by what the man was saying.

"Imagine that you were trained as a dancer, and for many years that was your calling. But then you realized that it was necessary to your art to learn greater mental focus, and so you took up the meditative discipline of the Belthamite Hermits and pursued this for some time. When you had completed your study, you discovered that there was much to be expressed by the hands and the motion of the arms and so traveled to Doorn to work with a master there.

And then, perhaps some time later, you returned to Avonel and one day, for no particular reason, picked up a fencing foil only to discover that all of your years of training had made you a great fencer, yet none of the specific disciplines you studied seemed to be in any way connected to fencing. This is mysticism. You read the teachings of Farrelle. Meditate on the ways of a running stream. Labor in a public garden to feed the poor. And if you do all of these things mindfully, one day you have an epiphany that has somehow grown from all of these things, yet does not seem to be made up of them in any recognizable way. All of these things lead to a greater understanding. Yet understanding is an inadequate word, for it is not an 'understanding' that you can explain. It is more like a blossom opening inside you. It is beautiful and awe inspiring and teaches you greater compassion and might allow you to accomplish much in the world. But can you give it a name? No. That is the way of the mystic, Mr. Flattery, and one does not have to be a believer in mysticism to experience it." A sudden grin creased his much-lined face.

"Now you see what I have done? Began talking about viticulture, a subject dear to both of our hearts, and end up lecturing you about mysticism. I do apologize. I am carried away by my own enthusiasms. It is a great weakness and has turned me into something of a bore, I'm afraid. Do forgive me." The priest rose suddenly.

"But I have taken up enough of your valuable time, Mr. Flattery. I thank you again for agreeing to speak with Mr. Kehler. It is noble of you, and I'm sure that Kehler will one day thank you for it."

Deacon Rose was still thanking Erasmus as he passed out the door to the street. Erasmus stood for a moment before the door, lost in wonder, and then realized that he looked like a man performing his devotions before an altar, and this sent something of a shiver through him.

He turned and went back up the stairs. This priest was not so charming as he thought—or at least not so cunning. Fenwick Kehler had discovered something in Merton that had the church very worried. Erasmus had no doubt of that. Something to do with Strangers, perhaps. Strangers and mages.

## ᴄ Nine

Avonel had dozens of private clubs of varying degrees of exclusivity. The most exclusive, and therefore the most private, were the clubs that bore no markings to distinguish them in any way from the surrounding buildings. Some of these did not even have public names, and were referred to by their members simply as "the club."

Every club had a purpose, though it was not always the purpose inscribed in the association's charter. For instance, the club that Sir John had come to this night was ostensibly a gaming club, but its actual purpose was to put certain of its members in such debt that they would, for the foreseeable future, owe their allegiance to the "club." Sir John had once been so far in debt to this particular organization that he expected to do its bidding for the rest of his career—furthering the interests of its members at great cost to his own credibility as a minister of the government. That was before he met Bryce.

Now he expended effort to further the interests of Bryce's mysterious employer, though this had not brought him into conflict with his conscience nearly so regularly. Still, more than anything else, Sir John longed to be free. To owe allegiance to no man but his King, and to his country. That was why he had gone into government service in the first place: idealism. He shook his head. Hard to believe he had once been idealistic when you saw how things had turned out.

Sir John wondered if his news of the Entonne development of the cannon had leaked out yet. It could not be kept secret forever, that was certain. He was only afraid that the first the navy would hear of it would be when an Entonne man of war opened fire on a Farr ship. He could not allow that, but before it happened, he planned to make some political coin from his knowledge. It was, after all, a commodity like gold or grain; a value could be placed on it and it could be traded, and that was precisely what Sir John intended to do.

"Sir John! How good to see you. We've not had the pleasure of your company in a good long while."

It was one of the senior members of the club. A man Sir John had once done many favors for.

"No, not for some time," Sir John said.

"Feeling lucky tonight?"

"Indeed I am." Sir John felt so incredibly fortunate that he did not intend to gamble a single coin.

The man touched his arm, smiling widely. "Well, you know your credit is always good here."

Sir John looked down, nodding. The man's smile caused such a surge of anger and resentment. He knew what it really meant: We knew you'd be back. *I am back,* Sir John thought, *but I am changed. Now I can resist. I don't quite know how or why, but I can resist.*

He moved on through the rooms, nodding to a man here or there. Feeling a little let down by this encounter. *They thought me so weak, so in thrall to my demons.* The realization undermined his confidence a little.

He remembered well his conversations with Bryce, as he had come to know the man. Bryce had once said, daring insult: "I will tell you what it is, for it is no mystery to me. You believe you are a man blessed: intelligent, of good family, first of your class, healthy and vigorous, and handsome to the ladies. You believe so completely in your good fortune that you cannot accept your luck would desert you at the tables. How could it? And so you go back, to prove your good fortune is no accident, as though you cannot accept this failure. Your luck will win out—it must. And so you have lost a fortune, thrice over."

Bryce, almost a stranger then, had been so utterly right. Sir John had known it the moment Bryce had uttered the words. A man so blessed should not lose at something so trivial as cards or dice. Really. It was absurd. But he did, repeatedly.

And then he had come to his agreement with Bryce—his deal with the devil. Bryce would clear his debt to the club, though not his other debts—those that had been accrued because gaming took all his money—Sir John would have to deal with those himself. And so it had happened. Bryce had accompanied him to the club one night, they had sat down at a table with the men who owned Sir John's debt, and they had played at cards. And Sir John had won! He had won as he always believed he should.

And then, when his debt was cleared, Bryce had stood up, and announced it was time to go. Sir John had never felt such frustration. Go!? But the look Bryce fixed on him told him that there was no arguing. When Bryce left the table, Sir John's luck would go with him.

He asked Bryce how he had done it—this was before he realized that one did not ask questions of Bryce—but the man would say nothing. Sir John was left with the impression that Bryce must be the sharpest of players, handling cards so deftly that no man could see what he was doing. Sir John did not care that he had won by cheating, for he always suspected he had been cheated anyway.

But the most incredible thing was, after that night he had no urge to gamble. None whatsoever. He did not even come down to the club to socialize. The desire was gone. He no longer felt that he had to test himself—test his good fortune. In fact it seemed a foolish pastime now. He could barely understand how he had been trapped in such folly.

He went into the largest room, searching among the faces, hoping to find the right gentlemen in attendance this evening. Few of the men at the tables looked up—intent on their cards. A wine tasting was underway in the next room, with a number of men from both the dragoons and the navy seriously engaged. One, the scion of the Palle family, raised a glass to him as he passed. Sir John smiled.

Ten minutes later he found one of the men he looked for; the Marquis of Sennet. The marquis leaned back against a wall with his thumbs tucked into his waistband and, with a rather bored air, watched several men playing a game called skittles on a pocketless billiard table.

"Lord Sennet," Sir John said, leaning a shoulder against the wall.

"Lord? We are being formal tonight, aren't we? Have you come back to lord it over certain gentlemen?" he asked, and Sir John laughed. "Tell me, Sir John, how did you do it? It has been the subject of endless speculation around these rooms for twelve months past."

"Well, I sacrificed a ram and painted pentagrams on my chest in its blood. I went to the ruin of the old abbey on the city's edge and sold my soul to a dark spirit. . . ."

"The usual, then?"

"Well, I sacrificed no virgins, not even symbolically."

"I see." Sennet looked back to the game as everyone groaned.

"I have a bit of news that might interest you," Sir John said, lowering his voice. "In fact, I'm sure it will"

"Do you?"

"We should speak more privately."

"In the library?"

Sir John nodded, setting off for the stairs. In this club one could usually rely on the library being vacant. It was not the literary set that came to gamble.

Sir John cast a glance back at the gaming room, and all the men intent on their fortunes. It seemed a rather pathetic scene to him. He shook his head, not without some sense of moral superiority, he realized, and continued on.

The library was indeed deserted. He found a copy of the day's news and made himself comfortable by the cold hearth. A few moments later Sennet appeared, his curiosity well in check.

He slouched into one of the chairs and stared at Sir John as though he did not believe for a moment that he could tell him anything of interest.

"I have some news about the Entonne—not even a rumor yet."

"News of the Entonne is always intriguing."

"And I'm very interested in knowing what goes on with Skye. There have been some rumors. . . ."

"I might be able to help you there." The one thing about Sennet was that he could be trusted to return an equal measure of information. It was one of the things Sir John liked about the man.

"My friends in Entonne tell me that their countrymen are casting cannon, and producing gunpowder as we speak. In two months, perhaps fewer, they will have armed ships."

Sennet sat up in his chair, his look changing completely. Sir John almost smiled. It was hard to catch Sennet unawares.

"You've told the King's Man?"

"Not yet."

"Martyr's blood," Sennet said, his agile mind running over all the implications of this news. "We all knew it would happen, but not so quickly." He looked up at Sir John, clearly impressed. "You shan't make Moncrief happy with such news—not one bit."

Sir John said nothing. No one in Farrland would be happy at this news—except, perhaps Skye.

Sennet broke into a grin. "Well, you caught me looking at the wrong hand, Sir John. Well done. But then you've long been a better conjurer than most." He tipped an imaginary hat to Sir John. "You must have the finest of friends in Entonne. Very well placed." Sennet looked at him with a little admiration, his mind clearly trying to divine the names of these sources. "But your question—" His look became more serious. "I don't know if you realize what a hornets' nest you've broken open. Flames, but Moncrief is playing a dangerous game.

"I am not sure what you've heard, but I have a friend in the Admiralty. . . ." Sennet let the sentence die. "This night past Skye had gone to meet a woman. Though it was unknown to him, she was once an Entonne agent now likely in the employ of the Admiralty." He tilted his head at Sir John, who did not catch the inference.

What in the world was Sennet suggesting? And then it struck him. Moncrief's jealousy had run out of control! "They were trying to entrap him," he said, not needing confirmation. That would be Moncrief's approach. Ruin Skye by destroying his reputation. It would not be so hard. Have a woman who was reputed to be an Entonne agent claim that Skye was bringing her the design of the ship's gun, then have agents of the Admiralty apprehend them in the act. Treason. Even the King would not be able to save Skye from that.

But Sir John, and now Sennet, knew that the Entonne already possessed the cannon! They needed nothing from Skye. If this got out, Moncrief's plot against Skye would explode in his face.

"What happened exactly, do you know?" Sir John asked.

"Not in detail, but I'm sure you can guess. It went awry somehow. Moncrief actually visited the Sea Lord—went to the Admiralty building! They're more than distressed. No one knows where Skye is at the moment, and I'm sure that Moncrief and the Sea Lord are living in terror that he will appear in the palace, lunching with the King. If it gets back to His Majesty that Moncrief and Brookes plotted against Skye . . . well, there will be no saving them."

"Did Skye realize what was afoot and escape?"

"I don't know. Perhaps. But there is more. This morning a woman who fit the description of this former Entonne agent was found floating facedown in the harbor."

Sir John shook his head, realizing suddenly that he had underestimated Moncrief's jealousy. The man was less balanced, and now more desperate, than he had suspected.

Sennet smoothed his frock coat with exaggerated care.

"I sense there is something else, Lord Sennet."

"I don't know what to make of it. I'm even a little embarrassed to tell you."

Bryce's warning came back to him. Bring everything you learn back to me, and I will judge it.

"Please, Lord Sennet, put aside your reticence. I will pass judgment on the information only, not on its source."

Sennet nodded. "Something very odd has happened. My friend in the Admiralty, even he is not certain what it is. But it seems there is some hint of . . . well, the arcane." He looked up at Sir John, a bit defensive, but interested in his reaction, too. "Does that make any sense to you?"

Sir John shrugged, suddenly feeling as though he had been set adrift. *The arts?* Is that what he was suggesting? "Perhaps. Can you say more?"

"Not really. My friend was not very clear. You might delve into the death of this woman—the one found in the harbor." He shook his head. "I was told that Brookes and Moncrief both looked as though they had seen ghosts. And they interviewed some sailor and a trollop. My friend believed they knew something about the woman's death. Bloody peculiar."

"So it seems." Sir John shifted in his chair, anxious to leave. Anxious to relay what he'd learned to Bryce—to see the man's reaction.

"You had best be careful who you tell about the Entonne and their naval gun, Sir John," Sennet said, sensing that his friend was about to leave. "Moncrief will not want that information to get out too soon, I should think."

"No, I'm sure he wouldn't, though there can't be many who know about his plot against Skye and therefore could put two and two together." He stared at Sennet, who shook his head.

"I'm sure that's true. Still . . . if Skye knows what was planned, then he will likely not keep it secret, though accusing Moncrief without evidence would be a mistake. Especially as it is well known the two men dislike each other. It might seem merely an attempt to slander the King's Man, and that would be foolish. I can't imagine Skye acting rashly."

"No." Sir John had thought his own news of great value, but Sennet had repaid him with coin to spare, if for no other reason than he was now on his guard against Moncrief. He would likely have gone to Moncrief with his news of the Entonne and the cannon. And where would that have led?

Sennet had discharged his debt, that was certain, but Sir John was willing to trade on his credit a little.

"You don't know where Skye has disappeared to?"

Sennet shook his head. "It is a mystery. Is it idle curiosity or do you need to know?"

"I need to speak with him. I have information that he must have."

Sennet considered this request, gazing at Sir John as though weighing his ability to pay. "It has come to my attention recently that the Countess of Chilton has a certain regard for Lord Skye. She would not likely give him away intentionally, but . . ."

"The countess? Really? I should have taken up empirical studies."

Sennet smiled politely.

Sir John was willing to make one more withdrawal against his credit. "I have a last request. Have you ever had dealings with a man named Bryce or heard tell of him?"

"Bryce? What is his given name?"

"I—I don't know," Sir John admitted, a bit embarrassed. "He is a mystery to me. Tall man, dark, very sure of himself. Extremely fastidious. Precise in his speech. I cannot really tell you more."

"But aren't you describing the stranger who sat at the gaming table with you the night of your phenomenal luck?"

Sir John nodded.

"But everyone believes he was a friend of yours. A . . ." He did not want to say "sharp." "You really didn't know him?"

Sir John shook his head. A small lie, only. He barely knew Bryce.

"Well, that is interesting. I don't know if I can learn anything with so little to get me started. You can't tell me anything more? Is he a gentleman of leisure, or does he follow some profession? What schools? I suppose you know nothing of his family?"

"I can tell you nothing more. No, that is not precisely true. He has a head for figures, especially where money is concerned, and is a shrewd investor."

"Ah, there you go. If he is an investor, then he can be found."

"Well, that might or might not be true. I am not absolutely sure he invests himself. . . . Though one would think he must."

Sennet took out the smallest pocket watch Sir John had ever seen. "I will do my best, Sir John."

"I will be in your debt," Sir John said, meaning it more than figuratively.

"Hardly." Sennet turned to him, very serious suddenly. "Do be careful with what you know about the Entonne. I would not like to see Moncrief hush it up because it could potentially hurt him. Some innocent Farr sailors might die to learn what is already known. I suggest you find some other way to send that information to the King, and not through the Admiralty, that is certain."

"Moncrief is my superior. I can't bypass him and go directly to the King myself." He fixed a look of appeal on Sennet. "You could take this information to the King for me, and Moncrief would know nothing of its source. If anyone could manage that, you could."

Sennet nodded. "Very likely, but aren't you afraid that you'll lose credit for your discovery?"

So, there would be a greater cost for this interchange than he'd anticipated. "It's immaterial who receives the credit. Better Moncrief not know it came from me, and you're absolutely right—the King must know immediately. Can you manage it?"

Sennet nodded. "Leave it to me, and if there comes a time when it is propitious to do so, I will share the credit with you. Is that acceptable?"

"More than acceptable," Sir John said, feeling his peerage slip away.

"Then I will be about our business, Sir John. Good luck with locating Skye. If I learn anything more, I will send you word immediately."

*Yes, no doubt you will. You're about to receive all manner of honors for the information that I have given you.* Sir John realized that he felt a little more amused than resentful. He had discovered what Bryce wanted to know, and that was what mattered, for good or ill.

Sir John wandered down through the club in something of a daze, barely acknowledging the men who spoke to him. The thought that it was he who had started this entire affair—setting Moncrief up to be ridiculed by Skye—was finally making its significance felt. He had known that Moncrief would never let such an insult go unanswered. Had Bryce been out to bring down Moncrief all along? Was that his purpose? Astonishing. Who Bryce's mysterious employer was suddenly took on more meaning. Moncrief had enemies, that was without doubt, but which one of them employed Mr. Bryce?

But there was something else in his conversation with Sennet that stood out—for its strangeness if for nothing else. *"There was some hint of the arcane."* Was this why Bryce had cautioned him to relay everything he heard to him? Sir John shook his head. What was he caught up in?

Sir John stepped out the front door of the club and was about to ask the doorman to find him a hack when the door of a large carriage opened and a man leaned out.

"Sir John?"

It was Bryce, waiting at the curb.

Sir John stepped up into the carriage and settled into a seat, more than a little surprised.

"What in the world brought you to be here at this hour?" Sir John asked.

"You might call it a hunch," Bryce said, smiling only slightly. "Have you found Skye? Do we know what happened?"

"I have the name of someone who might know Lord Skye's whereabouts, or so I hope. Whether she will help us or not remains to be seen. As to what happened, it seems that Moncrief, in a fit of jealousy, tried to entrap Skye." He told Bryce what he had learned from Sennet, holding back only the last piece of information.

Bryce merely nodded. "And that's it? That's what you learned?"

"No, there is one more thing. . . ." Sir John watched this mysterious man very carefully, though he didn't expect to be able to read Bryce's reaction—he never could. "My friend tells me that there was some hint of the arcane in this matter. Perhaps something to do with how the woman died."

To Sir John's amazement, Bryce smiled. Not a smile of mockery or disbelief, but one of great satisfaction. As though he'd been told that the woman he desired most in the world was mad for him.

"Well," he said, and no more.

"Does it have some significance?" Sir John asked, unable to stop himself.

"That is for my employer to decide," Bryce said, though he still looked pleased, and not annoyed as he always did when Sir John asked questions.

This made Sir John suddenly bolder. "So you will bring down Moncrief. Is that what you've planned all along?"

Bryce looked surprised. *"Moncrief?"* he said as though hearing the name for the first time. "Sir John, Moncrief is no concern of ours. None whatsoever." And with those words he folded his arms and turned to look out the window.

## ꙮ Ten

It was some time after dinner that Hayes returned to Erasmus' home. He looked as though he'd run across the entire town on his own two legs, he was so red in the face and out of breath.

Stokes led him into the study, his manner toward this young waif considerably softened.

"Ah, Hayes. Without your friend Kehler, I see." Erasmus paused. "Is something wrong?" It appeared that Hayes was more than just red in the face, he was unsettled. "Nothing ill has befallen your friend, I hope?"

"No. Not that I'm aware of. But I just had the strangest encounter. As I came up to your door—I was just lifting the knocker—someone called out Kehler's name. I turned around to find this little man hurrying across the street. He came to the bottom of the stair and realized I wasn't Kehler at all. Then he mumbled an apology and scurried off. The strange thing was that he was a Farrellite priest and Kehler has been studying at their college in Wooton."

"Deacon Rose."

"You know him?"

"Only since this afternoon. He came here looking for Kehler. He had been by the Belch and learned that I was in there asking after him. He came here hoping I would help him find your friend. It seems Kehler has been delving into things he was not meant to find, and this has the church in rather an uproar. This man Rose claimed that Kehler had betrayed their trust, and now was in danger of expulsion, which would ruin his career, for he was dependent upon the church for his tuition."

Hayes snorted. "I've never heard such rubbish. Kehler's people aren't wealthy, but they're certainly able to pay his school fees. No, I don't think the Farrellites are searching for Kehler for charitable reasons." Hayes reached into his jacket and pulled out a letter. "Kehler left this with a friend." He started to offer it to Erasmus, appeared to change his mind, and then pushed it into Erasmus' hand.

Erasmus slipped the letter from the envelope—a single page written in an appalling hand.

*My dear Hayes:*

*I've instructed Colghan not to trust this letter to anyone but you. I do hope it finds you. I tried to see you while I was in Avonel, but you'd fled your rooms and there were all kinds of rumors as to what had happened.*

*I've been on the run as well; from my good teachers. It seems they have not properly appreciated my search for the truth. Well, be that as it may, I have found some things that would amaze you. I dare not say more in a letter, but hope to be able to tell all in person. I've chosen the road of honor, I'm sure you will understand.*

*I am leaving you this one line of text which is a complete mystery to me. Can you find someone at Merton who might be able to read it?*

There followed a single line of characters which caused Erasmus to sit down abruptly.

"Erasmus?" Hayes sounded worried. "Are you well? You've turned white as a ghost. Shall I call Stokes?"

Erasmus looked up at Hayes, who stared at him with great concern. "He found this text in the archives?"

"So I would assume. Can you read it?"

Erasmus shook his head. "No. No one can read it. No man at least. It is the writing of the mages. . . . I saw it—in the house of Eldrich." Erasmus raised the letter again, still unsettled and oddly saddened. "Where is Kehler now, do you think?" he asked, his voice very soft, as though he had just learned of a friend's death.

Hayes did not answer, and Erasmus looked up.

"I think it would be better if you told me, Hayes. I'm beginning to suspect that your friend Kehler has involved himself in matters he does not clearly understand. And we mustn't forget that the Admiralty searched your rooms—perhaps they have some interest in this matter, as well."

Hayes took a seat, clearly struggling with promises he'd made to Skye and Kehler. "Kehler wrote that he'd taken the road of honor," he said, his voice very subdued. "It is a reference to a priest. A man who died years ago. Honare Baumgere. Do you know to whom I refer?"

Erasmus shook his head. "No, but the priest mentioned his name—almost in passing—as though he wanted to see my reaction to it."

Hayes raised his eyebrows. "Baumgere was someone Skye was interested in. I mentioned that in Compton Heath they sent for a priest learned in languages? That priest was Honare Baumgere." Hayes took a long breath, and let it out slowly, his gaze fixed on some point well beyond the room. "Later—many years later—Baumgere excavated a . . . structure near the town of Castlebough in the Caledon Hills."

"I've heard something of that. Wasn't it a crypt?"

"That's how it's known, though there is no reason to believe it was really a crypt other than the fact that it vaguely resembles one. But it is a puzzling piece of architecture. Some say it is as unique as the Ruin on Farrow, for we don't know who built it or when, or even its purpose."

"And Skye has some interest in this? It connects to the Stranger in some way?"

Hayes nodded stiffly.

"Samual," Erasmus waved the letter at him, "this is the script of the mages and though it might one day become a matter of academic interest, I can assure you that while Eldrich lives, it is still a jealously guarded secret. If the priests are keeping texts in this language in Wooton and Kehler has found them, then it is no wonder they are searching for him. Eldrich will be in a blind rage if he discovers the church has been hoarding texts dealing with the arts.

"You see, when the Farrellites lost their war against the mages, they swore they would never practice the arts again, for they had used the mages' own arts against them. All of the texts they had gathered were to have been surrendered to the mages. If they have held some back, or even discovered a text since that they've hidden, Eldrich will not be merciful. I can assure you of that. The worst of it is, your friend Kehler might end up suffering as much as the priests. Remember, mages are not known for being just or fair. I think it best that you tell me what you know and then we set out to locate Kehler. I only hope we can find him before he does something foolish. What say you, Hayes, will you trust me with the rest of your story?"

Hayes thought for a moment, his boyish face very serious, which mysteriously made him look even younger. Then he nodded quickly, pulling his waistcoat down. For a moment he was very still. "Baumgere was a scholar of some note," he began, "who, for many years, was an archivist at Wooton. Sometime in his middle years he was struck by the urge for a more pastoral life and was granted the living of the church in Castlebough. Do you know Castlebough? It is not far from the famous Bluehawk Lake. I think it the most beautiful country. Right in the heart of the Caledon Hills. The village is not as well known now as it was—oh, fifty years ago—when it was the fashion to take the waters there, but people still travel to Castlebough for their health.

"Baumgere had always been a scholar—had likely never given a sermon in all his days—but he was apparently a respected man within the church, and if that was what he wanted, then his superiors were happy to oblige. After a scant three years in Castlebough, Baumgere left the church, odd enough in itself, but then he discovered the buried 'crypt' near the castle.

"He began to wander the hills, as though still searching for something. People would see him occasionally, in the company of his servant—a massive man who was both deaf and dumb. They were said to have excavated other locations in the area, but if they found anything, no one saw.

"Baumgere purchased a manor house outside the town, proving he had a bit of money, though he had always claimed that he did not come from a moneyed background, not that he made many claims for himself, for he was a secretive man.

"There are any number of rumors from this point in the story. The ones Kehler seems to believe—and he knows much more about this than I—have to do with writing on the crypt. It was said the edifice bore a significant script, though Baumgere had this writing eradicated as soon as it was discovered, which must have taken some labor. Apparently you can see where the work was done. No one knows why.

"There is another odd fact. . . . Baumgere apparently owned a painting of the crypt, by Pelier, no less—which means it was done over two hundred years before Baumgere discovered the crypt. Everything that Kehler could find indicated that the crypt was unknown in that time—still buried, in fact.

"The painting is typical of Pelier's oracular style, complete with symbols and portents. Unlike most of Pelier's paintings, his interpreters did not have an explanation for this one. If it foretold some event in the future, no one seemed able to suggest what that might be.

"The painting apparently showed the tomb with the writing still intact, and three individuals paying their respects or perhaps examining the tomb, it is difficult to say. There was supposed to be a gentleman, a somewhat grotesque man thought to be a servant, and a veiled lady dressed entirely in black. Oh, and there might or might not have been a dark figure hidden in the shadow of the door. In the background one can see the old keep that sits above Castlebough, and Kehler believes that Baumgere used this to locate the crypt.

"Apparently Skye had been looking for some time for the Peliers that Baumgere owned. He had spoken of them to Kehler almost at their first meeting, and this had influenced Kehler's decision to attend Wooton. Many thought that Baumgere's effects were taken by the church, including the Peliers and whatever writings the man might have left behind."

Hayes rose from his chair and went to the window, closing it to within an inch, for the night was growing a little chill. He leaned forward cautiously and looked down into the street.

"Is he there?" Erasmus asked, almost whispering.

Hayes shook his head. "I can't tell." He picked up his story, not relaxing his vigil. "I find it odd that the Farrellite Church appeared to take no interest in their former priest, but then I suppose he did nothing to interest the church—not until later on." Hayes sat on the window ledge now where the lamplight threw odd shadows on his face; creasing it with lines of worry. "It is said that when Baumgere was on his deathbed, the priest who was his replacement came to administer last rites. But upon hearing Baumgere's confession, he refused to perform the absolution, storming from the house in a passion and leaving the man to die the true death—an astonishing event in the history of the Farrellite Church, even if he was no longer a priest. So Baumgere passed through like any man who had not found the faith. And then, oddly, not long after, the priest who refused him the absolution was found hanged from a tree in the forest. Self-murder! A mortal sin according to the teachings of the Farrellite Church. And that is more or less the end of the tale.

"Baumgere left no money to any individual nor to his church, and no one knew his story unless he confessed it on his deathbed, which is what everyone believes. Whether the priest who heard his confession ever passed the story along is not known." Hayes stood up and smiled at Erasmus. "So you see, it is fertile ground for speculation."

"I should say so. Do we assume this script that Kehler sent you has some connection to Baumgere?"

"It's quite likely, but he didn't say, as you saw."

Hayes turned to look down into the street again. Erasmus could just make out his reflection in the dark glass. "One can never be sure what Kehler is up to. His interests are . . . peculiar."

"Such as?"

"Lost knowledge. Secret histories. Things he believes the church has long known but kept hidden from the lay public. One can never be sure with Kehler. He very much keeps his own counsel—rather like you, Erasmus. The story of the Compton Heath Stranger sent him off on a completely new direction. Before that, his interests had been very academic and rather respectable. Skye opened up a world of mystery for him. An area that academia ignored. You cannot imagine his excitement. He hoped to find something about the Stranger of Compton Heath in the archives. He thought Baumgere might have written something that would be found there."

Erasmus considered for a moment. There were pieces missing from this story—entire chapters, he was sure. "Is there some connection between the Stranger of Compton Heath and the structure that Baumgere found?"

Hayes made an odd motion—almost a shrug. Almost a lie, Erasmus thought. "Anything is possible."

"I imagine Kehler must have a theory about Baumgere and what he searched for?"

"Yes, I think he does." The same reticence. Lying did not come easily to young Hayes—at least not lying to friends. Perhaps he felt he'd said too much already.

"But you cannot say, I collect?"

A long moment of hesitation, as he looked down into the street, or stared at his own reflection. "Perhaps if we find Kehler, he will tell you more. That is all I know. Oh, there is one more thing. . . . Apparently Baumgere's own gravestone has a line of characters inscribed on it that can't be read. Perhaps Baumgere's final word, or merely a black jest by the headstone carver; no one knows." Erasmus nodded, staring hard at Hayes, who gazed down into the darkened street. The hollow *clip-clop* of a passing horse drifted up to them; a log in the fire shifted.

"You are thinking that you should travel to Castlebough to aid your friend—and to warn him," Erasmus said softly. "And I do not think your concern is misplaced. If the church has texts in the language of the mages. . . ." Hayes glanced at him, his look of helplessness lifting a little. "It seems imperative that Kehler know what he has stirred up. I can arrange my affairs to leave by noon. What of you, Samual? Will you come with me?"

For a moment Hayes only stared at Erasmus, and then he stood up, almost shaking himself, shaking off the lethargy and helplessness that was the legacy of Paradise Street. Then a thought came to him, and the light that had ignited inside him dimmed. "But Erasmus, I must tell you I haven't. . . ."

Erasmus held up his hand. "Don't even speak of it. We are talking about Kehler's well-being here. He is potentially in danger from both the church and Eldrich. No, let us not quibble about money. My father, bless him, left me enough that I might live in complete idleness. Rescuing Kehler is far better use than I would otherwise put it to."

When Hayes finally took himself off to bed, he left the letter from Kehler behind. Erasmus took it up, and for a long time stared at the line of foreign script. Just the sight of this writing brought up old memories and the accompanying turmoil. Yet he could not put the letter down. For a moment he thought of throwing it in the fire, but the idea of it bursting into flame was unsettling.

"*He has escaped from memory,*" Erasmus read aloud. *Escaped from memory.*

# ∽ Eleven

The Caledon Hills crowded up against the western border where they grew to near mountain status, before falling away to a high plateau just inside Entonne.

Sparse population and rugged geography meant that only a few roads managed to find their way through the twisting valleys and gorges. The geology of the area was dominated by a thick stratum of whitestone that current thinking said was formed at the bottom of a shallow sea, millennia ago, though it now resided high above sea level.

The pale stone had been worn and broken by the long ages and left irregular hills standing, sometimes quite rounded but often steep sided and angular. Rivers wound through valleys and plunged between high cliffs into gorges where the water roiled and foamed and then fell in precipitous drops into deep turquoise pools.

An ancient forest spread its branches over most of the Caledon Hills and here one could find species of oak, beech, and walnut that were not common to any other area of Farrland. A particularly fragrant pine, called the Camden Pine, grew on the north sides of hills at higher altitudes, and the rose family had spread a few of its species—from bitter apples and hawthorns to flowering rosebushes—across the hillsides and valleys.

Long known for the abundance of game, the hunting lodges of the aristocracy were scattered among the hills, and here and there a fertile valley provided a patch of farmland. Deep, clear lakes became the destination of travelers drawn to the lonely beauty, and in particularly picturesque locations towns catering to such travelers sprang up.

Hayes looked out over the valley below and then toward the northern hills. They had stopped the carriage at this point, not just to rest the horses after the climb but because it was a well-known viewing point, and the fact that they were not the first to find it did not reduce the pleasure.

In the distance Hayes was sure he could see the remains of a large structure, though, when built of the same stone as the surrounding hills, it was sometimes difficult to tell—limestone had a tendency to break into blocks that looked surprisingly man-made.

Erasmus was slowly sweeping a field glass across the scene.

"Is that an old lodge there, on the hill to the right?" Hayes asked.

Erasmus focused his glass and then shook his head. "A tower. Perhaps even a small castle."

It was the other thing the Caledon Hills were famous for; the ruins of castles and other defensive structures. In the long years of warfare that had plagued the nations around the Entide Sea, the hills had seen more than their share of battles, and castles had been built and torn down and built again for over a thousand years. No doubt there were several under construction at that very moment, though closer to the present border in the great passes between the high hills. It was difficult to move a large army any other way—in fact, it had so far proved impossible.

Erasmus took a few steps to the right and leaned against a low stone wall so that he could look west along an arm of the valley. A small lake lay there, reflecting the colors of the late afternoon, the image of a cloud floating white and ghostlike in its center.

"There," Erasmus said. "That will be Castlebough, I think. Do you see?" He handed Hayes his glass.

It took Hayes' eye a second to adjust, but then he saw, at the lake's end on top of an angular hill, a town huddled around the ruins of an old citadel. "True to its name, there is a castle, or at least the remains of one."

"A keep of the Knights of Glamoar," Erasmus said, surprising Hayes by knowing anything of the history of such an obscure little village. "The place where this man Baumgere discovered a mysterious crypt. And the place where our good Kehler is likely pursuing his obsessions, as you call them. Let us hope that we are here before the agents of the Admiralty, and that the agent of the church has not guessed where Kehler might be."

Hayes swept the glass up the valley. A hawk hanging above the lake suddenly let go of its perch on the sky and plunged toward the water. He lost sight of it before it struck, as though it had vanished into the clear air.

"Look! Erasmus! A wolf, by the lake." He handed Erasmus the glass. "Halfway along the left shore. Do you see?"

Erasmus swept the glass along the lake's edge, then back. "No . . ." he said, his voice oddly tentative. "No. It seems to have gone." He lowered the glass, his look utterly changed. As though he had seen something that had unsettled him. "We should be on our way." Erasmus motioned Hayes to precede him toward the carriage, but when Hayes looked over his shoulder, he saw that Erasmus was looking back, his manner very grim.

He must be reminded of the wolf he said prowled the home of Eldrich, Hayes thought, and felt a wave of pity for the child Erasmus. He could not imagine such a strange experience—so unlike his own rather carefree boyhood.

They traveled on, Erasmus even less communicative. He sat very still, staring out the window by the hour, his chin supported on his hand, looking like a man bereaved. He didn't know why, but somehow Hayes thought that

Erasmus mourned for his lost childhood and for the terrible legacy of memory which haunted him still.

Sir John stood on the edge of the road, which dropped several hundred feet into the gorge. He glanced down and then quickly up again. The sight of the roiling waters—white and impossibly porcelain green—caused all his muscles to tense. He stood there on the cliff edge like a stick man—unbending, awkward, utterly discomfited.

In contrast, Bryce hovered on the cliff edge as though he had not noticed that a step to his right would send him into the sky, briefly, before drowning him in the river below. He might have been a bird for the amount of concern he displayed. A mere instant of loss of balance and either of them would see their life end.

Bryce pointed suddenly. "There—do you see them?"

Sir John squinted, leaning slightly and then pulling himself back abruptly. A field glass was what was needed here. But then perhaps he did see something move. Perhaps a yellow carriage. They had been told at the last inn that the countess was not far ahead of them, and at the pace they had been traveling, it was no wonder. Sir John half expected them to arrive before her.

"I'm sure you're right, though I'm surprised that the countess travels with such a small retinue. Two carriages only." For a second Sir John thought he'd lost his balance, and stepped quickly back from the edge, his heart pounding.

Bryce looked at him closely and then smiled—half from amusement, half from pity. "I think we should let them travel on for a bit. I'd rather not be seen." He turned his head suddenly, his look intent. "Do you hear that?"

Sir John listened, but could hear only the river, the sound of the breeze bending the trees, and the poor trees uttering their complaints. A raven called.

The horses had pricked up their ears, suddenly excited.

"Is someone coming?"

"Yes. Let us wait and see who it is. If your Admiralty men are still chasing after Skye, I want to know." Bryce bent down suddenly and retrieved a pinecone, throwing it over the precipice. Like a school boy he stood and watched it fall, veering to one side suddenly as it neared the water, caught by a current of wind gusting through the gorge. Then there was the smallest splash. Bryce stood for a moment as though watching the cone's progress, and then he turned to look down the road just as a two-horse team appeared around the corner, pulling a trap.

The only occupant of the carriage sat a bit taller in his seat as he approached, obviously peering at the two men on the road. And then, as he came closer, he raised his arm and waved.

"Sir John?" he called as he pulled his team up.

"Why, Kent, what a surprise. Where are you off to?"

"Castlebough," Kent said. "And yourself?"

Sir John hesitated, not sure if Bryce would want their destination known, but then Bryce spoke up. "The same. You must be the illustrious Averil Kent. . . . Percival Bryce, your servant, sir."

"And I am yours, Mr. Bryce," Kent said. Sir John did not know Kent well, but even so, he thought the young man looked a bit uncomfortable, almost as though he had been caught doing something he'd rather others knew nothing about. There was an awkward silence for a moment, and then Kent tipped his hat.

"Perhaps we'll meet in Castlebough, then," Kent said. "Pleasures of the day to you, gentlemen."

Sir John and Bryce followed Kent's progress for a moment.

"Odd to meet Kent here," Sir John said as Kent disappeared around a bend. "He must be on one of his painting jaunts."

Bryce laughed. "He is pursuing the countess, Sir John. Could you not see it?"

Sir John looked at his companion in surprise. "How can you be certain?"

"Oh, it was written in his manner. In the tilt of his head. His slight embarrassment at meeting someone he knew. Did you not see the way he peered ahead so hopefully when he saw our carriage, and then the disappointment when he saw who it was—or who it was not, I should say. Do not doubt it. The poor man is here in pursuit of the Countess of Chilton, like any sad hound chasing a bitch in heat. I pity him; he is in for a bad time of it, I think. Let us hope he is not fool enough to end up in a duel over such a woman."

"Such a woman, indeed!" Sir John said. "Do you disparage her, then?"

Bryce turned to him rather sharply. "I meant only that she is a woman who draws men to her even when she does not mean to, Sir John. Do I disparage her? No. On the contrary. I pity her. More even than poor Kent." Bryce looked off down the valley. "I pity her utterly."

## ✑ Twelve

*A man may either move westward through life, following the light, or eastward toward the gathering darkness. It is a kind of orientation of temperament that is set in our earliest years; an emotional compass. One either pursues one's dreams or one's memories, and it is an exceptional man who, once his compass has been set, can alter it even a point or two.*

*—Halden: Essays*

When Hayes came down to break his fast in the morning, he discovered that
Erasmus had been gone over two hours. Hayes cursed himself for a lazy fool
and considered going out after his companion, but then decided that this would
invariably lead to Erasmus returning while Hayes was out, and so on, so he
decided on food and staying in one place.

Around the site of Castlebough were several hot springs, the waters of
which were said to be healthful, and these almost more than anything ac-
counted for the town's survival. Certainly the terraced gardens and small pas-
tures he had seen on the slope below the town did not provide commerce, and
the few travelers who stopped there on their way elsewhere would not support
anything but the smallest inn.

But Castlebough boasted nine good-sized inns, and these catered almost
exclusively to people coming to take the waters. To Hayes' satisfaction Erasmus had chosen one of the better establishments, the *Springs*, and here he had
found them each a room on the same floor. As Hayes had no worries about
finances on this journey (Erasmus insisted on paying) he felt something like
a gentleman of means again. He had never realized what a great sense of freedom one felt at being able to spend money without concern—not until he had
been forced to count every penny.

Imagine, he thought, going into an inn and having to ask the cost of a meal
before ordering! It had never even occurred to him to do such a thing before,
and though he had become used to it in time, at first he had found the experience rather humiliating.

*Well, I have been humbled enough to last a lifetime now,* he thought. *I shall
never worry about growing arrogant or vain, that is certain.*

Now, if they could only find Kehler. Hayes wondered, not for the first time,
what his friend was up to, for Kehler was secretive even with him, and Hayes
was very likely his closest friend in the world.

*May we find him before he gets himself in too much trouble,* Hayes thought,
though he realized that, more than anything, he wanted to know what Kehler
had discovered. His curiosity was burning.

The dining room was not half-filled with people, all of whom appeared to
be taking their leisure—not residents of Castlebough, that was certain. There
were a few elderly people who might actually suffer infirmities, but most he
saw were hardly old—in their thirties or forties—nor did they look to be suffering from any illness. If anything, they seemed to be on a holiday. He could
hear some of them discussing plans for the day: a boat trip down the river
which would actually take them through a cave; a sail on Blue Hawk Lake; an
excursion to various ruins. Hayes felt a bit jealous of their leisure, supported
as it obviously was by resources he did not have.

"Ah, Hayes. . . . You've finally managed to face the day," Erasmus said as he found his companion. "Have you been here long?"

"No, not at all. Just long enough to overhear the plans of our fellow guests, and to begin to feel a bit sorry for myself. You have come along just in time to save me from that particular emotional quagmire."

Erasmus pulled up a chair and ordered coffee. "Well, I have been out to look at our town and to check the other inns. None seem to have a Mr. Kehler in their care, nor anyone who fits his description, so I hope we have not come so far to find he has already been and gone."

"But he was two days ahead of us! I can't imagine that he has already left." Hayes was a bit distressed by the idea that he might have brought Erasmus Flattery so far, on an errand of mercy, and found it was only a fool's errand, after all.

"Well, I'm told there are any number of residences in Castlebough that are owned by people from the lowlands. Some of these are let out by the week, and others are lent to family friends. You don't know if Kehler has friends who might keep a home here?"

Hayes shook his head.

Coffee arrived, and Erasmus took it up without cream or sugar. "Then I suggest we go have a look at this mysterious crypt, then perhaps at the house that Baumgere owned. I have been asking the staff for directions—not so uncommon it seems. Baumgere and his mysterious excavations have drawn any number of people before us, apparently. Kehler might find his mystery well picked over. I wonder what he hopes to discover?"

Hayes shrugged.

Erasmus fixed an odd look on his companion, and the younger man turned his attention to his food, realizing that Erasmus believed he was holding back information. It was always difficult to know where one stood with Erasmus, for the man seemed to have made up his own mind about which of society's strictures he would obey and which he would blatantly ignore.

"As soon as you're ready," Erasmus said, having bolted his coffee. He rose from his chair. "I'll be in my room."

Forty minutes later the two gentlemen were walking up one of the steep streets of Castlebough. It was a typical town of its type, built of local stone, the main street jagging back and forth up the hillside with numerous alleys and stairways joining the levels. A spring somewhere high up had been tapped for the village water supply and this ran down among the houses on a circuitous route, appearing here and there and could often be heard whispering beneath the paving stones. Hayes thought it a picturesque little town, trim and neat, and no doubt kept in this state for the visitors.

As they emerged above the last houses of the town proper, they found the old stair they had been directed to and headed up. The graveyard they wanted was on the hilltop behind the old castle, and though one could reach it by road, the stairway led to a shorter, if slightly more adventurous path.

Conversation soon ceased as they saved their wind for the climb. The stair ended at a path that wound up into the wood, then suddenly set off up a steep gully. Here stones had been set as steps occasionally and in one place a rusted chain acted as a hand rail; they pulled themselves up on this with some effort. Eventually they found stairs again, then a ledge, a final staircase, and then they emerged on the top.

Both Erasmus and Hayes threw themselves down on a stone bench to catch their breath. Before them spread a wondrous view, out over the town and down to the lake. To the north they could see the hills lifting up like seas toward an indistinct horizon that seemed impossibly distant and mysterious. If Hayes stared hard, he was certain that he could see another mountain beyond those he had thought were the farthest, and then others beyond that.

In the west the high hills lifted up to a jagged meeting with the cold sky, and here there was still snow to be seen, bright and pure in the morning sun.

"If Kehler proves not to be here, I will feel we've been amply rewarded just by this view," Erasmus said, making Hayes feel a bit better, for he was worried that Kehler was gone, or worse—the priests had found him first.

They sat for a moment more, not speaking, but absorbed by the scene. Then Erasmus got to his feet, and Hayes followed. Reluctantly they turned away.

The castle had been greatly reduced by the villagers taking away cartload after cartload of stone to enlarge the town below, but even so there were still the remains of some high walls and towers. Hayes could see the blue sky through some of the openings, and tufts of dry grass and small yellow flowers sprouted from cracks and ledges.

A vine of morning glories had taken hold on the west wall, and these were open now, nodding in the light breeze. Behind some wild berry bushes they found an old graveyard. The most magnificent hornbeam Hayes had ever seen presided over the site, its trunk nearly three feet thick and its branches twisted and gnarled as such trees tended to be.

There were perhaps a dozen headstones half-obscured by brush and tall, golden grasses. Hayes bent over the stones and began to examine them closely. After a moment he called out, "Look! Baumgere's grave, but only his name remains. The inscription has been obliterated." He bent close, running his fingers over the few discernable lines. "Was this vandalism, do you think? Or could it have been erased for some other reason?"

Erasmus shook his head, but offered no opinion. There were a few bits of what might once have been a design or parts of an inscription left, and Erasmus looked long at these before taking out a pen and ink and copying them into a little notebook.

"And will you make sense of the remains, Mr. Flattery, where so many others have resorted to mere fantasy?"

Both Hayes and Erasmus turned to find the source of this strange, high-pitched voice, and there, a dozen feet away, stood an outlandishly dressed man who could not have been four feet tall. They were both so surprised by the sight that they stared dumbly.

"Randall Spencer Emanual Clarendon, at your service," the dwarf said, making a sweeping bow. "And you are the illustrious Erasmus Flattery, I take it?"

"At your service, sir, and my particular friend, Mr. Samual Hayes."

"Your servant, sir," Hayes said, offering a hand to the man who reached up his own small hand to meet it.

Randall Spencer Emanual Clarendon was impeccably dressed in expensive and elaborate clothing of bright colors, and carried at his side a short rapier in a beautifully tooled scabbard. His high boots bore enormous silver buckles and his shirt studs glittered with pale stones that Hayes believed were diamonds. He wore no wig and tied his fringe of gray hair in a tail with a bright blue ribbon. His pate was bald and colored by the sun, his eyes the blue of mountain lakes, and beneath a magnificent white mustache, his full mouth smiled as though he enjoyed the reaction of the men before him, for certainly they stared like country boys with their first view of a noble.

"You know who I am," Erasmus said.

"Yes, forgive me. It is a small village, and the news quickly spread that Erasmus Flattery was domiciled among us. Your studies of the noble grape are well known to those of us who are dedicatees. There is, you see, quite a large vintners' society here. Some of the most successful oenologists and viticulturists spend part of their year in Castlebough, and you might imagine what the talk is among them." He smiled winningly, showing a gold-capped tooth. "I hope you will have time to come to our meeting, Mr. Flattery, and your companion as well. Are you a horticulturalist also, Mr. Hayes?"

"I'm afraid not, though I admire a decent bottle of wine." Hayes felt there was a hint of pity in the look this statement elicited.

"Well, you might find it of interest all the same. We have converted more than a few gentlemen to our cause in the past. But, Mr. Flattery, there is more of a connection between yourself and the village of Castlebough. The famed Admiral Vinzen Flattery kept a house here for a number of years, and came often with his wife to take the waters."

"I had no idea," Erasmus said. "The admiral was not known to me, unfortunately, though still alive, I think, when I was born. I shall have to see this house."

"And I would be happy to show it to you. But I've come looking for you because I'd heard you had been asking questions about our mysterious Baumgere. I thought I should find you before those who would try to sell you copies of the inscription, or maps that lead to supposed treasure or what not. Not that you would be taken in by them, I'm sure, but they will waste a gentleman's time. I once took an interest in Baumgere and his story and would be pleased to put my small knowledge at your disposal and act as your local guide, if you will permit me."

Hayes and Erasmus looked at each other, their decision clear. "We would be delighted," Erasmus said.

Suddenly something erupted out of the grass, causing Hayes to spin around. A massive wolfhound darted past him and came panting up to Clarendon, who was obviously its master.

"This is Dusk, my particular friend," he said. "Put out your hands and let him sniff you. I hope neither of you wish me harm, for he will attack if you do. He can sense things men cannot and will not be persuaded that a man who does not like me should be allowed to go happily about his business. Fortunately I am not widely disliked, or I fear poor Dusk might have met his end by sword before now. Ah, there, you see, he has found you worthy, and that is a judgment worth more than many a man's, I will tell you." He stroked the dog behind the ears, barely having to reach down to do so, for Dusk came almost to Clarendon's shoulder.

"As Castlebough is so small, Mr. Clarendon, perhaps you have heard of a friend of ours. We were hoping to meet him here. A young man named Fenwick Kehler?"

"Kehler? No. . . . I know no one of that name, but I will ask. And please, call me Randall." The dwarf gestured toward some nearby trees. "Baumgere's discovery lies back here. You are trying to discern the remains of the mysterious inscriptions . . . ?"

"Did they really exist?" Erasmus asked.

"Oh, indeed they did, though not for many years now. The inscription was erased during the time of Baumgere, as you have no doubt learned, though whether this was done by Baumgere is not known. The story, you see, has been . . . *embroidered* over the years, and the unfortunate truth is that the factual evidence—what is indisputably known—is very slim." He took a deep breath, and looked at the headstones, an air of sadness settling over him. "That Baumgere chose Castlebough for his home has fueled the fire of speculation, for there are few regions around the Entide Sea as fertile for such theorizing as the Caledon Hills, with its uncommon history and many real mysteries. And perhaps the story of Father Baumgere *did* have its beginnings long ago, in some event that took place here in these hills. That is what many say." He motioned again to the trees. "If you have the time, I will show you the mysterious 'crypt,' as it is called, and we can sit for a while and I will tell you what I can remember."

Randall led them into the bower of silver-barked beeches, then down stone steps between lilac trees. The path circled around and then emerged in what almost seemed a small quarry.

There before them, carved into the whitestone, stood the facade of a small structure. Four pillars stood proud from the stone, the heavy eaves of the roof facade appearing to rest on them. A doorway had been cut into the stone, and a bronze door hung from heavy pins. This door stood ajar and slightly askew, as though it had been forced open and damaged in the effort. Hayes was quite astonished by what he saw, for though it was not large, the tomb projected a sense of grandeur.

"There was an inscription over the door, as well as on the lintel," Randall said. "All gone now, as you can see." He turned to the others. "You look surprised, Mr. Flattery?"

Erasmus did not take his eyes from the structure. "It is not quite what I expected. It is . . . well, humble in its scale, yet grand in its design, as though merely a model for the real thing."

Randall turned back to the tomb, gazing at it for a moment. "That is precisely true. And what did the designer mean to convey by this contradiction? That the person buried here was more than others realized? That his or her true greatness was not recognized?" He stood a moment longer and then sat down on the stairs, his eyes still fixed on the facade.

"I have sat here like this often, and therefore the building, if it can be called that, is extremely familiar to me, yet it seems more a mystery each time. Perhaps this is what happens when the truth of an object eludes you—it seems somehow to be resisting your efforts." He shook his head and smiled. "But it is just a facade cut into the rock, empty inside, as you will see if you venture in. A chamber not twelve feet square carved into the bones of the cliff. No secret doors or hidden chambers. Perfectly solid rock. The body or ashes long ago moved elsewhere, or perhaps it was never meant to be a crypt at all. Who can say, for it is only known as such for its vague resemblance to such structures. It might have served some other purpose entirely." Randall looked at each of the others, and then down at the stone he tested with his hand.

"As you no doubt remember from your days at school," he began, "the Caledon Hills have not always been part of the Kingdom of Farrland. Once they were claimed by what is today Entonne, and at other times they were autonomous or semiautonomous. Seven hundred years ago this was the Duchy of Atreche, and only nominally under the control of Farrland. Early followers of Farrelle hid here from their persecutors, and more than one mage has chosen to make his home among these enchanted hills. Great feats of chivalry were performed here—in this very spot as well as a thousand others. And the hills have witnessed tragedies, too. It is a harsh land, really. Agriculture is difficult; whitestone offers no metals to be mined. Only the forester and the huntsman can live to profit here. But despite that, the hills have a beauty that I think incomparable, and many before me have thought the same, so they were drawn here to find a life, and often had to fight to preserve the lives they made.

"The Order of Farrellite Knights, called the Knights of Glamoar, raised their great citadels here, eradicating the Tautistian Heresy which had taken root among people who had fled Entonne and Doorn. And then the knights themselves were branded heretics, and fell finally to the army raised by the Bishop of Nearl during the great turmoil.

"Many think the Knights of Glamoar left a treasure hidden among the hills, for certainly they had wealth enough, and this treasure some believe was the source of Baumgere's wealth. And perhaps it was, but it is hard to imagine that Baumgere found the directions to this treasure among the Farrellite archives. Although it is said that a great deal of Farr history has been devoured by the church." Dusk had wandered off, sniffing the ground and the air, and suddenly he came bounding back again, checking on his master and eyeing the strangers.

"But what do we know of this man for certain?" Clarendon continued, sounding like a lecturer. "Baumgere did appear to come into at least a little wealth after he left the service of the church, and there is no obvious source for this. That is all true. I will show you his home on the edge of the village and you will see what I mean. It is not only large and ostentatious, but it is an architectural oddity as well. The home of a true eccentric.

"Undoubtedly Baumgere had done something that made the local priest, who by the way was his friend and admirer, refuse him absolution. Now there are only certain varieties of sin that will see a man denied absolution, and they are well known: heresy, though what constitutes heresy changes over time; sacrilege, of course—robbing a grave, for instance is sacrilege. Murder, oddly, will not see you denied absolution, as long as you seek forgiveness from the church and repent of your sin.

"But if you are a priest of the church, there are a number of other things that can damn you and leave you wandering in the netherworld. Treachery during the religious wars would have seen a man denied absolution. Betrayal of a mystery of the church will have the same result. And so will acquiring knowledge beyond one's station—a parish priest cannot have certain knowledge possessed by a bishop, you see.

"I have long said that much of the speculation about the source of Baumgere's wealth could be repudiated by merely considering the possibilities laid out for us by the refusal of absolution. If we eliminate betrayal of the church in time of war, we are left with heresy, sacrilege, betrayal of a mystery of the church, acquiring knowledge beyond one's station."

"You seem quite sure that this denial of absolution related to Baumgere's acquisition of wealth or to his discoveries, Randall," Erasmus said.

"Ah, that is true." Clarendon smiled, as though pleased to find that Erasmus had not gained his reputation without reason. "But I set out only to tell you what was known to be utterly true, not to subject you to either my own opinions or the speculation of others. Forgive me, for you are obviously correct: these things are not necessarily connected as cause and effect. As difficult as it is, I will try to stay with what is known, although resisting the desire to speculate in this particular instance is almost impossible." The small man ran his hand over the stone again, as though he searched for something there. "Father Joseph, the priest who refused Baumgere his absolution, self-murdered within a week of Baumgere's death. Utter disillusionment? Loss of faith? Or perhaps melancholia that was in no way related to Baumgere and his secret—for certainly Baumgere *had* a secret. Of that even I am certain. But one must believe strongly in coincidence to accept that these two things were not related, just as one must believe strongly to deny a connection between Baumgere's mysterious discovery and the denial of absolution; or Baumgere's years in the Farrellite archives, his unexpected departure from the service of the church and his sudden wealth." Clarendon laughed.

"You see, I cannot confine myself to the particulars! Do forgive me, gentlemen. I am doing my best." He appeared to focus his will. "Baumgere was an interesting person. He never rose far within the hierarchy of the church though he was said to have been an excellent scholar—something admired by the Farrellites. But perhaps he was not a political animal, which one must be to rise in the church of the martyr—it is like government or the court in that regard.

"Baumgere had few friends and kept his affairs to himself. I therefore suspect this was apocryphal, but a prominent citizen once claimed that Baumgere had answered his inquiry about the source of his wealth by saying, 'Why is no one concerned with my true riches? My real wealth is in my knowledge,' he said, 'the years I spent immersed in the study of our history. These are the basis of real riches, and no one seems to be at all interested.'

"As I say, I don't believe this story to be true but mention it only because it has become an integral part of the myth. Baumgere might not have been so rich as people thought."

"And the headstone, and the ruined inscription on the tomb: where do they fit in?" Hayes asked.

"Ah. An excellent question, Mr. Hayes, for where things 'fit in' as you say is certainly the crux of the matter. There was an inscription on the headstone that did disappear, though whether this was an act of vandals or done for some other reason cannot actually be proven. The inscription on the crypt, however, was unquestionably eradicated—and almost certainly by Baumgere.

"I have only one thing to add to this particular instance—and I have shared it with very few. But, Mr. Flattery, I will make this knowledge available to you, for it is possible you might have something to add to the matter." The small man stared at Erasmus as he spoke, then he stood. "Come. Let me show you."

Clarendon crossed to the tomb again. He put one knee on the ground and bent to point out something in the design carved there. "You see, this is a floral motif circling the column."

Hayes bent closer to look at what was a very common design—a vine and flowers in high relief.

"This is said to be wisteria, and though it is clearly stylized, I have often wondered if the clumps of flowers are flowers at all but bunches of grapes. You are a botanist and horticulturist, Mr. Flattery, what would you say?"

"That is the grape vine, Randall. You are absolutely correct."

Clarendon brightened. "Ah," he said with some satisfaction. "Now," he said rising and pointing to the lintel above the columns. "Look there. It is the only break in the pattern. What do you make of that, Mr. Flattery?"

Hayes could see three flowers carved there, their stems intersecting.

Erasmus leaned back and looked up. "The two outer flowers are almost certainly roses, but the other flower I cannot name. I have not seen it before."

"Exactly. One flower is unknown and the others are roses. Vale roses, I am told, by a man who has a great knowledge of roses."

Erasmus stepped back abruptly, suddenly quite guarded.

Clarendon looked up at Erasmus. "I see you know what this symbol means, Mr. Flattery."

Erasmus shook his head, though it was not a strong denial.

*"Teller,"* Clarendon said, and nothing more, but he stared at Erasmus who met his gaze.

Hayes looked from one man to the other, wondering what in the world they meant. Teller? "Who was Teller?" Hayes heard himself ask.

Clarendon did not take his eyes from Erasmus. "He was a man who once apprenticed to a mage: Lapin being the most likely candidate. But he did not complete his apprenticeship, for his mentor died." Clarendon's gaze seemed to become even more intent as he said this. "There is a possibility that Teller assisted the Farrellites in their war against the mages. We do not know what happened to him after that, though he may have lived for some good number of years. Some believe that Teller started a secret society dedicated to learning the arts of the mages—those he did not already possess. During the Winter War the mages destroyed what was left of Teller's society—or so historians believe. The token of Teller, and later his society, consisted of three vale roses arranged as you see the blossoms here."

"But there are only two roses here," Erasmus said quickly.

"That is true, Mr. Flattery, but I am content that it is Teller's token all the same."

"But this crypt is certainly not five hundred years old," Erasmus protested.

"It is difficult to say. Authorities believe it might be much older, but it has been buried and not subject to the usual weathering, so it cannot be dated with certainty. It might have been built long after Teller's death, and his ashes moved here."

"But if Teller's society somehow survived beyond the Winter War, why would they do anything to call attention to themselves? It would have been foolish of them to build a tomb," Erasmus protested. "The mages had tried to eradicate them once. Why do anything that might bring down the wrath of the mages? It makes no sense."

Clarendon shrugged. "This tomb sat undisturbed and unknown until the time of Baumgere. It is only in the last century that Castlebough has become of interest to the outside world. Perhaps it was not such a great risk. Or perhaps the world had changed enough that they did not think it would matter. But it is interesting, don't you think?" He placed his back against one of the pillars. "But you began an apprenticeship with Eldrich, Mr. Flattery, and did not complete it. . . . Perhaps you might shed some light on what happened so long ago to Teller?"

Erasmus shook his head. "I began no apprenticeship, I assure you. . . ." Erasmus' denial was interrupted by a wild barking and snarling.

"*Dusk!*" Clarendon called, and immediately began to run in the direction of the noise.

The barking came from inside the castle ruin. Hayes and Erasmus followed Clarendon, though he was slower due to age and size, but neither of them wanted to find the apparently enraged wolfhound before his master.

After a moment of searching through the ruin, they rounded a corner to find Dusk staring up at a wall, snarling and taking the occasional leap, trying to scale the steep stone, and snapping his powerful jaws at some invisible foe.

"What have you treed, Dusk?" Clarendon called, trying to catch his breath. "Come out of it now."

Hayes followed Clarendon, who took hold of his dog, and looking up found a man balanced in a niche in the wall looking quite terrified.

"*Kehler!*" Hayes exclaimed, completely surprised.

"Please, Hayes, call him off. I cannot hold myself here a second longer."

And indeed Hayes thought that this was true. Poor Kehler was red with exertion and his arms were beginning to tremble.

"You may come down, sir," Clarendon said, pulling back the still growling dog. "I have him."

Kehler hesitated, perhaps comparing the relative sizes of man and straining dog, but then his body decided for him and he slipped, falling awkwardly onto the soft grass below.

Hayes helped him to rise, unable to hold back his laughter, and Kehler came up brushing at his clothing.

"I hope you are not injured, sir?" Clarendon inquired, not letting go of Dusk.

"No, only frightened half out of my wits. Martyr's blood, but that is a fearsome beast," Kehler said, eyeing the dog.

"But he will not hurt you now, Mr. Kehler. Have no fear. He means only to protect me, and was unsure of your intentions." He turned his attention to the still growling wolfhound. "Now, Dusk, that will be enough. This is a friend."

The dog and Kehler were properly introduced, though neither looked as though they would trust the other immediately.

Kehler collapsed onto a grassy bank, looking up at the two men and the astonishing little man they accompanied.

"I cannot tell you how surprised I am to find you here," Kehler said.

"Nor can we tell you how happy we are to find you," Hayes answered. "Where are you staying? We tried all the inns."

This seemed to unsettle Kehler a little. "I'm not staying in the village. Have you been asking for me by name?"

"And how else would we inquire about you?" Hayes asked. "By reputation? Your accomplishments aren't yet so grand, I'm sorry to tell you."

"And these gentlemen are not the only ones searching for you, Mr. Kehler," Clarendon said, his manner very serious. "A Deacon Rose has been asking about town for you."

"Demon Rose!" Kehler said. "Farrelle's flames! Do not give me away, please," he pleaded, his face contorting in fear.

## ∽ Thirteen

*Memory is nothing more than a receptacle of our past; the future a fabric of dreams. And the much vaunted present, that which we are all to seize with a passion, is but the smallest measure of an instant, the single tick of a clock, a medium for translating the future into the past, dreams into memory.*

*—Marianne Edden: A Reflection on the Death of Michael Valpy*

The evenings were cooler in the highlands, and the countess stood at the closed door looking out over the balcony into the valley. Dusk seemed to alter the distances so that the farthest hills appeared not so much to be disappearing as slipping away. A moment more and they would be out of sight.

A light flickered to life behind the countess, casting her reflection back off the glass. She almost stared, as though a stranger had appeared before her. An unhappy stranger.

"And do you see him there?" came the voice of her companion.

The countess shook her head.

"I never thought I would see the day when the most desired woman in the kingdom would chase after a man like a lovesick girl. And even more astonishing, he would seem to be running. Are you certain that he likes women?"

What had she been told? That all of his women had looked the same—petite and very blond. The countess was neither of these. She touched her forehead to the cool glass. Did he think of her as only a friend—the way she thought of several men who were mad for her? Did those poor souls feel as tortured as she?

"*Elaural?*"

"Excuse me, Marianne. Yes, he likes women. What is in doubt are his feelings for this particular woman."

"He must be playing at indifference. The oldest ploy. Introduce him to me, and I will soon have an answer for you."

The countess did not doubt that. Marianne Edden, she believed, was the most perceptive woman in Farrland. This insight into others had gained her great fame. No, that was not precisely true, and Marianne could not bear inaccuracy. It was her ability to put these perceptions into words that had gained her fame, for Marianne was the finest social novelist of her day.

"Well, come away from the window and try to take your mind off the damn fool. I will even play at cards with you, if you like, as much as I detest the activity. Anything to not see you pining away like a lady in a bad novel. It is undignified."

The countess turned to her friend. "I thought you felt dignity was a foolish concern."

"Dignity? No. I am entirely in favor of dignity—it is this exaggerated pomposity of the aristocracy that I cannot bear. Pomposity is not dignity—it is not even *dignified*. It is an ass' attempt to hide his own mediocrity. A dignified shopkeeper—there is someone worthy of respect. Someone who does not believe he has a special place in society, yet bears himself with self-possession and grace—and not without humor. A shopkeeper who believes that he fulfills his role in the world to the best of his ability. Who is honest and fair because he believes in honesty and fairness—not just when he thinks others are looking. A man who suffers the setbacks and humiliations of life without constant complaint. Dignity."

Marianne bent over and thrust a dry stick into the fire until its end began to smoke and glow. She used this to light a pipe, and then rose up in a great cloud of smoke, puffing like a beast of burden.

This was the portrait of Marianne Edden that needed to be painted, the countess thought: all but obscured by a cloud of bittersweet-smelling smoke, as though she had risen from the flames like a demon . . . or a martyr, and cast her all-seeing eye on the weaknesses and foibles of the mortals scattered about her. The countess smiled for the first time that evening.

"I'm sure I do not suffer setbacks and humiliations with quite the fortitude of your noble shopkeeper, but I shall try not to complain, as a woman in my position has no right to do, I'm sure."

Marianne settled her large frame into a chair, a look of distraction on her face. The countess always imagined that Marianne Edden was a woman who had mistakenly been raised as a farm boy—the mistake only discovered when she was twenty, and the attempts to correct what had been done only partially successful. To call Marianne masculine was not accurate. Oh, she was certainly not "ladylike," as the term was used. One could not imagine Marianne suffering the vapors. Or suffering fools, something Farr women seemed to have been bred to do.

Marianne had once paid some medical students to allow her to be present at the dissection of a corpse—saying that she needed to know more about the substance of man to write the truth about him—and not only had she failed to suffer as the more sensitive sex should, but she went around to people's parlors appalling their guests with graphic descriptions of what she'd seen!

"She is not your average . . . citizen," the countess had once heard her described, which had made her laugh. Even for understated Farr society, that was an understatement.

"What is it, precisely, that you see in this man?" Marianne asked, as though it were not a personal question at all. As though it were something that caused her great confusion and perhaps the countess could set her straight.

The countess could not help but smile at this innocence. "Well, he is a genius. . . ."

"*I'm* a genius, and I don't have the most beautiful man in the kingdom pursuing me. In fact, in my case intelligence appears to have the opposite effect. But go on. Clearly this faculty has more attraction for you than most."

"But he is guarded, as though there were things he must hide. He almost never makes an effort to impress with his wit and conversation, as others do. As though it is merely a game that he cannot be bothered with. As though he would not put his gifts to such use. When he speaks, he is very sincere, choosing his words with great care. And when he pronounces, for he is not known for making long speeches, everything he says is worth listening to with the utmost care. Although it is infrequent, I have seen Lord Skye refute the arguments of every man present with only a few well-chosen words, and no one could gainsay him. As though his own thoughts were unassailable."

"A man not in love with the sound of his own voice seems very unnatural," Marianne mused, as though the thought disturbed her.

The countess was suddenly overwhelmed with her inability to say what she felt. She had not the powers of her companion and that was certain.

"Should we not have some tea?" she asked suddenly.

"Ale would be more to my liking," Marianne said, looking at the countess with some distaste, obviously appalled by the idea of tea. It was dark, after all.

"Then I shall call for ale," the countess said. She rang for a servant, asking for both ale and tea, not quite ready to join Marianne in her passion for working man's tastes.

A bubbling mustache appeared on the satisfied face of the novelist as, a moment later, she lowered her glass. "You should try this, Elaural," she said, using the countess' given name, her love for things working class not allowing titles— at least not in certain circumstances. The countess smiled sweetly, she hoped.

Marianne leaned forward to poke at the fire, her short hair swaying in the lamplight.

*She would have such pretty hair were she to let it grow*, the countess found herself thinking. *But she will not be admired for her appearance, but only for her mind—why it would be wrong to be admired for both, I cannot fathom.*

But in some way the countess admired the stand Marianne Edden had taken. It was courageous if a little eccentric. The countess believed it natural for men and women to admire each other. To flirt and court. Did not the very animals do the same? Natural. But then it was easy for her to be sanguine about such a thing—she had not been born with crooked teeth or a hideous nose. Men admired her—too much for her liking. But to be ignored. . . . She couldn't imagine how painful that might be. *Will be*, she reminded herself. Age would see to that. She would have the experience soon enough, and the thought disturbed her as it always did.

"Will you consent to my seeing these portraits now?" Marianne asked suddenly.

The countess felt a small shiver run through her. "If you like, though they are not portraits." The Peliers were still in their cases, where she had purposely left them. The truth was that, as much as she wanted to be rid of these paintings, she feared that once they were gone she would never see Skye again.

Reluctantly, the countess went to the wooden case in which the paintings had been transported. "Could you lend a hand? The frames are not light."

The two women lifted the first painting from the case and unwrapped it carefully, and then the second. They leaned them against the wall on a side table and shifted the light so they could be clearly seen. For a long moment they stood there, gazing at the paintings by lamplight, which, the countess thought, made them, if anything, more eerie.

"What is it about these paintings that disturbs you, Elaural?" Marianne asked softly.

The countess shook her head. "I don't know," she whispered, not even attempting to deny the truth.

"But are you drawn to them, as well?"

The countess nodded, as much as she would have liked to have disagreed.

Marianne turned her attention back to the paintings. "And this man of yours has an obsession with these?" the novelist said flatly.

"I would not say that, but he believes they are significant in the larger mystery."

"This is the story you told me as we traveled? What was the man's name?"

"Baumgere."

"But one painting is a forgery, you say?"

The countess nodded. "Though it might be an accurate forgery—an exact copy. That, at least, is what Mr. Kent believes."

Marianne leaned closer to look at the signature.

"There is something peculiar about these paintings. I feel it myself. And this man." She gestured to the figure crossing the bridge. He looks like a man going to the gallows. Look at his face. He knows his fate has been decided and continues only because there is no alternative. Something or someone awaits him, and he cannot turn back. Now here is a character to be pitied. This is the Stranger Skye spoke of?"

"That is what he believes. The spire in the background belonged to a church that burned years ago in the village of Compton Heath."

"But what became of the man?"

The countess shook her head. "He was taken off in a carriage, though by whom, no one knows. The story has it that it was a mage—but then that makes for a better story, doesn't it?"

"Yes, it does," Marianne said. "I wish you were not involved in this matter, Elaural. Skye . . . Skye has his own obsessions. You would be best to involve yourself no further. You don't even know what he is seeking—or do you?"

The countess shook her head. She didn't. Something more than he was telling her, that was certain. It was not just curiosity. It *was* an obsession.

Where had the Stranger come from, and what was it that this priest sought? Was that what drew Skye? Did he know what Baumgere was searching for?

"What does the writing on the crypt say? Does Skye know?"

"No. Apparently it cannot be read, or so Skye says."

"And I understand one may not gainsay the great Skye?"

"You may, but at your peril."

"I will warn you only this one time, Elaural. I am famous for my intuition, and I do not have a good feeling about this matter. There, I've said my piece." The slightest pause. "It would be different if this man was mad for you. . . ."

"I thought you'd said your piece?"

"I have." She turned away and went into the other room.

A moment later the countess followed, shutting the door tightly between them and the Peliers.

Marianne looked up, her face still somewhat grim, as though the paintings had left her feeling ill. "This crypt is nearby?" she said, forcing her voice to sound normal.

The countess nodded.

"Then we should at least see it while we're here. I hope this genius of yours will contact us soon. It does seem a bit inconsiderate."

"He is not my genius, and I am sure there are reasons for what he is doing. I would like to see the structure myself—I do not know if it can be properly called a crypt. Apparently it is one of the sights around Castlebough."

"Well, we cannot miss the sights. We should have something for our trouble after traveling so far. Perhaps a ghost will rise from the crypt and answer all our questions."

The countess shook her head, trying to force the feelings caused by the paintings to subside. "I don't think you're taking this as seriously as you should, Marianne. I think tomorrow it will be time for you to go back to your work. I am going to keep my word on this. You will be locked into a room with pen and paper every morning at ten sharp, and not let out until you have slipped three pages under the door for me to judge."

"I was being facetious, Elaural. I will show you the word in my dictionary: *facetious*." But it was banter by rote—neither of them laughed.

## ✐ Fourteen

*A memory is a dream turned to disappointment.*

—*Halden*

"I was something of a prodigy of the local Farrellite School, but my father, who was more shrewd than his lot in life would indicate, took me out of the clutches of the priests." Clarendon lifted a glass of wine. "He realized there was a possibility of making money from my talents, and money was the one thing that had always eluded the poor man." He paused to taste his wine. "Do you find the finish bitter?" he asked Erasmus.

They had come down from the ruin late in the afternoon to Clarendon's house. Kehler had insisted on coming later, after darkness fell, and had arrived looking more than a little apprehensive. He still would say nothing, and the others gave up asking, hoping he would come to it in his own time.

Erasmus thought there was quite a contrast between the lad-next-door looks of Hayes and his sharp-featured friend. Kehler's motions were all quick, and he held his head lowered at the neck in such a way as to leave the impression that he was ready, at an instant, to duck out of sight. The two were about the same age, but Kehler already showed gray at the temples and crow's feet pressed into the corners of his eyes. But there was also something between these two young men, some commonality despite their divergent appearances. They were both a bit haunted, perhaps for vastly different reasons, but it was unmistakable.

Erasmus tasted the wine again, his focus entirely inward. "Bitter? Very slightly so, perhaps. I almost think I enjoy it. There is an odd aftertaste, like slightly burned apple."

Clarendon tasted his own wine again, inclined his head to one side, and closed his eyes. "Yes. Yes, I see what you mean. You must meet the others, Mr. Flattery, they will make you most welcome." He looked up at a painting on the wall—a circus troupe under the light of torches and great lanterns, and then seemed to remember that he had been telling a story. "Originally I would perform arithmetical calculations in my head—problems posed by people who came to see the show, for we had joined a traveling show: General Albert W. Payne's Traveling Company. Unfortunately the 'General' took most of the money, and my father squandered what was left on fine clothing, women, and drink. He was not a very original man, I'm afraid," he said, as though apologizing.

"Many feats were performed. I memorized enormous blocks of text in one reading and parroted them back without mistake, or merely glanced at a thirty digit number and then wrote it down. I once sat the final examinations in mathematics at Merton making not one error and halving the previous record for time. I was at that time three months shy of my tenth birthday. I gained quite a reputation, and made even more money for the owner of our traveling company. Not long after this my father died—choked on his own gorge while insensible with drink. There was a struggle between several of my relatives, people I hardly knew, and the General, to decide who would be my legal guardian. In the end, one of the women in the show, whom I had always called 'aunt,' produced a signed certificate of marriage proving that she and my father had been joined in sacred matrimony—when he was drunk beyond knowing, I'm sure.

"It was something of a scandal, really, but finally my 'aunt' managed to outbid my dear family and the General, who only offered the judge money. Aunt Liz, who was a stunning young woman, managed to offer the judge something he did not already have, and perhaps had never possessed—the apparent adoration of a beautiful young woman, however briefly it lasted.

"My life changed on that day. Aunt Liz and I left the company immediately. She had been a dancer and tumbler in the show, which was lewd in the extreme, and perhaps she had even worked in the tents when the show was over, I don't know, but she was as shrewd a businesswoman as ever palmed a coin, I can tell you that. She took what money she had managed to save, which would indicate she really was working on the side, and hired tutors. A retired professor from Merton to teach me higher maths. An elocution instructor. My crooked working-class accent was hammered straight, and I was also allowed to read as much as I wanted—and I wanted to read all the time. Very soon Aunt Liz had Farrland's most respected scholars vying with each other to instruct me, for I have a flawless memory and an ability to perform calculations that would take other men hours or even days, though they might take me only a few moments."

Hayes watched the small man's face, utterly entranced by the story, but sensing a sadness in Clarendon as he exposed these memories.

"Soon all the performances I did were in the private homes of Farrland's wealthiest citizens, or in grand halls. Once, I was invited to be a guest of the Society, where they posed the most difficult questions of all, though I acquitted myself well. I began to feel like less of a spectacle, less of a freak, though the old feelings were not entirely gone. I was called The Petite Professor, or the Dwarf Savant. Professor Memory. All manner of appellations. And among all the educated people I even made a few real friends. And I also made money. Lizzy saw to that. She was my guardian goddess, and I loved her hopelessly." He swiveled as though to look out the darkened window, raising a hand to his face, but turning the movement into a mere gesture, placing the hand beneath his chin.

"When I was seventeen, my darling Lizzy fell victim to a cad. A Colonel Winslow Petry. They were too quickly married. . . ." His voice trailed off. And then he resettled himself in his chair, straightening his small back. "And so I was forced to begin again. For the second time in my short life I had lost everything. Lizzy and the money, too. But fortunately I had a head for figures, and in one sense that's all money is—numbers, marks on a page. I knew what to do to make it, even if it gave me little joy, and the lesson of my father taught me to preserve what I acquired.

"Lizzy and her colonel went off, spending the money we had made. To this day I can't think of it without the deepest sadness. She was the one person I had trusted utterly. . . . After that I traveled continuously for six years. Through Doorn and Entonne. To every corner of the lands around the Entide Sea. Everywhere I went, I moved in society. I learned to play the pianum, though I am not so skilled at that as I am at other things I have turned my hand to. I became a devotee of the arts and met many artists and writers. And it was through this that I was saved." He looked up at his guests, his face brightening a little.

"I was so fortunate, after all my years of travel, to meet the Haywood family—do you know them?"

"The porcelain people?" Hayes asked.

"The very ones. I was invited to their home to give one of my demonstrations, and I almost did not leave. Such open-hearted people, such complete joy in life, I had never encountered. I was captivated by them in a way that you cannot imagine. You see, they invited me into the fold, as it were, as they did a select few they took a genuine liking to. They rescued me . . . from cynicism, bitterness, resentment, all the ugly, unworthy things that had become lodged in my heart. And I cast all of these things out, like demons, and made myself anew. Through the Haywoods I learned that my gifts were to be treasured, and that I was no more a freak than a man who sits before a pianum and holds the audience in his hand, playing upon their emotions with his own given skill. I was gifted, perhaps supremely so. As for my small stature . . . well, in their home it did not matter."

"You see, I had never thought of myself as an intellectual, but only as someone who could perform tricks, tricks of the mind to be sure, but tricks all the same. In my own view I was no different from the performing animals in General Payne's traveling show, or from the other freaks whose physical deformities were a source of fascination and horror to the general population. But the Haywoods made me realize that this was not true, that in fact I was the equal of a professor at Merton—even more so, for I disremember nothing and can perform calculations in my head that others can never equal.

"Through them I actually taught for a year, higher mathematics at the University in Belgard. It will sound odd to you, but the Haywoods humanized me, for I was always an outsider in my own mind—a near-human. A dwarf; different in both mind and body." He smiled almost beneficently. "And so you see before you a man, small in stature, yes, but large in mental abilities. A true man of parts, as they say. And through the good graces and efforts of the Haywoods, I was even able to develop my other sensibilities." He raised his glass as though toasting his benefactors. "And that, more or less, is my story. I have made enough money that I no longer perform as I did, but devote myself to my interests and my many friends, for as you know people born with my particular physical characteristics often do not live a normal span of years, and I want to be sure to waste as little time as possible." He drank from his glass.

"And so here we all are, having lived our separate lives, followed our separate journeys, yet somehow we have all arrived here at this exact moment. If, like me, you have grown suspicious of coincidence, you might think that there is some reason for this. Why have we all come to this place tonight?"

Hayes was not sure the question was rhetorical. He even found himself wondering the same thing. What were they all doing there?

"But you have an interest in the mages, Randall," Erasmus said, "and you know something of Teller, and this is truly arcane knowledge. Has this long been an interest?"

Randall looked down at the table, and Hayes thought the man was trying to decide what he would tell Erasmus, for though it was obvious that the dwarf was an admirer, Erasmus was still a near stranger.

"I came by this interest accidentally. You see, I discovered Castlebough through a physician who attended me. He suggested I come here for the cure, which I did, and for me, at least, it worked. During that visit I fell in love with the village and the surrounding countryside. It is a healthful environment, I think. Clean air, salubrious water, exercise, and few of the aggravations of the city.

"I come here in the spring and usually stay for the entire summer. In the winter I travel. This winter last I visited Farrow." He stood suddenly in his place, but it was only to lean forward to fill Kehler's glass. "I am naturally curious and thought to learn something of the history of my new home. And what a history it has! The citadel above saw some of the most terrible battles of the Wars of Heresy." He shook his head, the sadness coming back. "And, of course, there was the mystery of Baumgere, which has intrigued the village for years. Unlike the inhabitants of Castlebough, however, I had an enormous advantage during my research. In my travels I have had occasion to meet men of great knowledge, and I have looked into private libraries to which few have been granted access.

"It is astonishing the way knowledge is scattered around our world," he said suddenly. "Some written in books of which only one copy remains extant. Much passed down by word of mouth, and very temporarily stored in the minds of the most unlikely people in the most out of the way places. And then there are the great libraries and the innumerable attics of the known world. . . . The things people confide in their correspondence! So, yes, it began with an interest in this local legend—the crypt of Baumgere and the denial of absolution—and led me to this man named Teller, and then to the mages." Clarendon looked up at the others, his manner almost defensive.

Hayes could see that Kehler was staring raptly at his host, listening to every word, and to all that was suggested but never stated. It was a wonder that Kehler managed to contain himself.

"The society that Teller founded was almost certainly destroyed during the Winter War—about 1415—almost five centuries after Teller. Five centuries! What did they learn in that time?" He looked at each of his guests, as though sure they were keeping the answer to the question from him. "I do not know," he said, dropping his gaze. "I do not know. But enough that the mages felt they must hunt them down and destroy them. Destroy them after they had managed to keep themselves secret for five hundred years."

"The mages had no need of hunting them down," Erasmus said, surprising everyone.

Clarendon looked up, his eyes suddenly alive with interest.

Erasmus met no one's eye, but stared at the empty chair across from him, as though he addressed someone seated there. "The Tellerites—and I use this term for lack of any other; what the society called themselves is unknown, and the mages would not speak their name—the Tellerites were caught—trapped, I think—all together. Trapped and destroyed."

"How?" Kehler asked quietly.

"I don't know, though it seems likely they had gathered to perform an important ritual. I haven't been able to learn more. I can't even say where this happened nor, with any certainty, when, though Randall's date of 1415 is probably very close."

"But what do you make of the crypt and the gravestone by the citadel?" Clarendon asked.

Erasmus shook his head. "I don't know. If some remnant of the society had survived the purge . . . well, I think it unlikely they would do anything to draw attention to themselves. Is that the tomb of Teller? I very much doubt it. What purpose it served is a mystery. As to the gravestones . . . well, you said yourself that it is only rumor that connects them to Baumgere."

Kehler leaned forward in his chair, barely suppressing his excitement. "But where? Where were the Tellerites destroyed? Could it have been here, in Castlebough? Could that explain the grave?"

"No," Erasmus said. "I don't know where it occurred, but I am more certain about where it did not, and I can say almost without doubt that it did not happen here. There is a very old song that originated among the Cary minstrels, and is as ambiguous as all their works." Erasmus sat forward in his chair, and softly he began to sing in a thin, though expressive voice.

"*A shepherd, a maiden, an orphan of ten*

*A night 'neath a kint in fragrant spring*
*Seven men came walking by torchlight and star*
*And low by moonlight were heard to sing,*
*A delro, a delro*
*Ai kombi aré.*
*We have come to the gate,*
*The gate of Faery.*
*Five passed through the moonlight more ghostly than men*
*Singing by starlight in tongues unknown*
*Passed by the orphan, the maiden, the man*
*Down into the labyrinth, to the mouth of stone.*
*A delro, a delro*
*Ai kombi aré.*
*We have come to the gate,*
*The gate of Faery.*
*The darkness ascended, devouring the sky*
*And wind cried in fury and toppled the tower*
*The heavens were scarred with letters of fire*
*Shattering stone with words of power.*
*A delro, a delro*
*Ai kombi aré*
*The sun would not rise at its appointed hour*
*And the stars wandered, lost, across the sea of the sky*
*Five men slowly walking in sullen power*
*Past orphan, and maiden, and the one devoured.*
*A delro, a delro*
*Ai kombi aré,*
*We have come to the gate,*
*The gate to Faery.*
*A delro, a delro*
*Ai kombi aré.*"

Erasmus sat back in his chair, staring unseeing at the others. No one spoke for a moment, and then a breeze moved the curtains, causing Hayes to start. He laughed nervously, the sound dying like a pinched-off flame. A moth came in from the night and fluttered wildly over the heat of a lamp, unable to resist the light.

"But what could it mean?" Hayes asked.

"The destruction of Teller," Randall said firmly.

Erasmus nodded.

"And the language . . . ? It is the mage tongue?"

Erasmus shrugged. "Perhaps. I don't know. The song is partly fancy, certainly. '*We have come to the gate, the gate of Faery.*' But there is something there, as there usually is in the minstrels' songs. A buried truth. Seven men passed in the moonlight. Five came behind, 'more ghostly than men.' Five mages. A great spell was cast, or a series of them. Five men returned 'in sullen power,' past the witnesses, one of whom was devoured—went mad, I think. Mad with fear. That is the story."

"But you know something more, Mr. Flattery, for you would hardly make such an assumption from so little evidence." Randall fixed his gaze on Erasmus again, though this time Erasmus did not even look up to meet his eye.

"You will not say." Randall smiled kindly. It was not a question. A long silence. "Not now, perhaps," the dwarf said, "but when you know me better. . . ." Randall stood and filled Erasmus' glass with wine, then did the same for the others. He raised his glass, and his guests stood as well. "To mysteries, gentlemen, for they keep me alive. To unexpected meetings, for they, too, are mysterious. And to coincidence, which I believe in not at all."

## ᴗ Fifteen

Hayes sat in a chair in his room and watched Kehler pace back and forth across the small square of carpet. Occasionally he would go to the window and twitch the curtain aside just enough to peer down into the dimly lit courtyard. For a moment he would stare, perhaps searching for malevolent forms in the shadows, and then he would return to his pacing.

"Deacon Rose is a lot more dangerous than you realize. Certainly more dangerous than Erasmus believes." He stopped and made a visible effort to calm himself, taking long, slow breaths. "No, Deacon Rose is to be avoided at all costs." He looked over at Hayes in a way that was uncharacteristically measuring. "But where is our much vaunted employer?"

"I agree with Erasmus; I think Skye would come here," Hayes said, trying to ignore the gaze that was cast upon him. "Though I can't imagine the famous Lord Skye could be long in Castlebough without everyone knowing."

Kehler resumed his pacing, went two steps, and then stopped, looking at Hayes in some surprise. "What in Farrelle's name were agents of the Admiralty doing in your rooms?" he said, going back to an earlier part of the conversation. "They can't be interested in this matter we've been chasing . . . can they?"

Hayes lifted his hands in a gesture of helplessness. "I wouldn't think so. No, it must have something to do with the naval gun. Perhaps they're afraid Entonne agents were trying to steal the plans from Skye. Would they not begin to look at all of his acquaintances, then? And here I am, in terrible financial distress, recently applying for a position in the foreign department. Do I not look like the perfect person for the Entonne to enlist? That is my guess, at least. I do hope Skye will exonerate me, I don't much like living as a fugitive. Things have gotten so bad that I'm acutely aware of the nearness of the border. I've even made a plan for slipping across into Entonne if it becomes necessary." A short, sad laugh escaped him, and he shook his head.

"I'm quite sure it won't come to that, Hayes. You have Erasmus on your side, which means the Duke of Blackwater will stand behind you. And certainly Skye will vouch for you—for us. I'm one of the earl's associates, too, don't forget. At worst we'll be exiles together."

This almost brought a smile to Hayes, but not quite. "Yes, well, that is some comfort, but at the moment I am rather adrift. I'm sure my landlord in Avonel will have sold off my few belongings by now, and here I am, entirely dependent on the good graces of Erasmus Flattery." The sadness pulled at his face, pinching it so that his eyes almost glistened. "I have seldom had less hope for my future than I do now."

"I don't think you need to worry overly about your future, Hayes," Kehler said, a sudden smugness very poorly disguised.

Hearing this, Hayes looked up at his friend with some hope. "Why do I have a feeling you're about make me a devil's offer?"

"Nothing of the sort, my dear Hayes. Well, not too much of the sort." The words might have been jocular, but Kehler's manner had become very serious. "To be candid, Hayes, I am not completely satisfied with my relations with our employer. Perhaps it is the perennial grievance of assistants, but I feel I have done the lion's share of the work and see Skye taking all the profit." He stopped to think. "The truth is I don't understand what it is that Skye hopes to learn or do with what I've found, but I suspect he will not put it to any use but his own." He looked directly at Hayes. "I've made some discoveries in Wooton that will leave you a little breathless, I think."

"And I'm anxious to hear about them, but, Kehler, you undertook this matter for Lord Skye. Does that mean nothing to you?"

"Indeed, it does. I delivered a letter to the earl's home outlining several of my discoveries and have heard nothing from him. Hardly a fair return for my efforts. But I promised Lord Skye that I would deliver my information, and keep the earl's confidence—by which I meant that I would not reveal his part in the matter. But what *I* do with my findings is another thing entirely. Now, what would you say if I told you that we could satisfy both our curiosity, make what I hope will be a major discovery, and net you a substantial sum of money into the bargain?"

"I would say, bully for Kehler, of course, but you must know—considerations of Skye aside—Erasmus seems to think that you're involving yourself in matters that could well be dangerous. If the Farrellites have been hiding knowledge from the mages, Erasmus believes they will go to almost any length to keep it from Eldrich. Thus the priest is pursuing you, or so I assume. Perhaps you should tell me precisely what you have discovered."

"All in good time, Hayes. All in good time. Our first order of business is to slip away from all concerned—agents of the Admiralty, priests, friends, and well-wishers, all. I've collected the gear we'll need." Kehler gestured toward the door.

"But where are we going?"

"To complete what Baumgere began, but grew too old to finish. To make our names in the world. Come along while there is time, for I can assure you of this, Hayes—it is an opportunity which shall not call twice."

## ✑ Sixteen

There was something about Skye that Marianne Edden could not quite grasp. Possessing an intuitive faculty that she thought justifiably celebrated, it was difficult to accept that someone could so completely elude her. Skye shifted slightly in his chair, and she watched his every move, hoping somehow that this meditation on him would help. She had even placed her chair so that she could watch him unobtrusively.

Her eye wandered for a second to the countess—who, compared to Skye Elaural, was as easy to read as a child. She could hide nothing, not from her friend at least. But Skye. . . .

Marianne had never met him before, and she was not unaware that there were people who would consider this evening of historic importance. The meeting of two of the great minds of their time—one scientific, the other literary. It was lucky that none of these people were present; they would have been exceedingly disappointed.

Skye sat staring at the Pelier paintings, only occasionally breaking away to attempt polite conversation. His mind was clearly not on his hostesses—and most pointedly not on the admiring countess.

*Alone in a room with the most brilliant novelist and the most celebrated beauty of his time, and he hardly seems aware of us,* she thought, not entirely immodestly—it was not, after all, Marianne who went about proclaiming her brilliance, at least not usually.

"Have you learned anything of the script?" the countess asked, her voice very small. She was obviously aware that Skye barely noticed her.

He turned to her with a confused look, and then her question registered.

"Oh. . . ." He went back to the painting, his gaze not even lingering on the face that other men could hardly tear their eyes from. "Nothing useful. It has been suggested that it bears some similarity to the writing found on the Ruin of Farrow, which is an intriguing idea. There is also some evidence that it might be a very old Farr language, one not spoken for some centuries, though perhaps known to the mages far more recently. Unfortunately the two men who might be able to tell me the truth of this are not inclined to be helpful."

"Who might they be, pray?" the countess asked, obviously making an attempt to capture his attention, something she managed effortlessly with other men.

The way Skye shifted in his chair . . . there was something not quite right here, Marianne was sure of it.

"Well, Eldrich, obviously, and the other is Erasmus Flattery. Do you know the man? He is a brother to the Duke of Blackwater, I think."

"No," the countess answered, clearly feeling a sense of failure. "No, I'm afraid not. But is this Erasmus Flattery not an empiricist? A colleague of yours in the Society?"

Skye nodded, a slight grimace appearing. "Yes, though he seldom attends, and is not well known to any fellow at the Society. Something of an eccentric, this Flattery." He paused uncomfortably, then went on. "He lived in the house of Eldrich when he was a boy. Did you know that?"

"Well, I knew it was a rumor, but I have never given it much credit. Have you, Marianne?"

"I confess that I have not formed an opinion on the matter of Erasmus Flattery's boyhood."

The countess cast her a look of mild annoyance, but Marianne could not resist. The situation seemed so patently false and strained to her. Why did Elaural continue to humiliate herself with this man?

"Well, it is quite true," Skye said quickly. "Flattery spent some three years in the house of Eldrich, if you can imagine. But he will not speak of it, avoiding all questions with some energy. Too much energy, many people think." A long awkward pause followed, and Marianne braced herself mentally for what would follow. Did the countess not see what was happening here? Did her usual instincts abandon her in this man's presence? Farrelle help her, Marianne thought, it must be love.

Skye cleared his throat quietly. "The great irony is," he began, trying to force a casual tone, "Erasmus Flattery might actually be in Castlebough—at least there is a rumor to that effect." He stared hard at the paintings, careful not to look at either of the women. "It is an odd coincidence that Flattery is here at this time." He glanced quickly at the countess, then back to the painting. "Imagine having spent time in the house of a mage and never saying a word of it. The man is keeping a small part of our most fascinating history to himself. It seems so odd that I have heard some suggest that Flattery is bespelled and cannot speak of it." Skye snorted. "Apparently he also spent some time studying the Ruin on Farrow and says little of that either, though he has claimed that he discovered nothing new. I wonder if that is true." He leaned forward to gaze at the inscription on the tomb. "Can he tell me what tongue this is? Can he, perhaps, read it?"

"What makes you think the mages knew this language?" Marianne asked, hoping to deflect what was coming.

The earl hesitated. "I have seen a note—written by one of the mages—Lucklow, to be precise. Not a very remarkable note really, considering its source, but beneath his signature letter L, there is a line of characters astonishingly similar to the characters we see here. I admit it is unlikely that Erasmus could answer my question, but who else might have such knowledge? No one that I'm aware of."

"But what would that mean?" the countess said, sounding genuine for the first time that evening. The news had excited her interest. "How would Pelier have known such a script, if, as you suggest, it is the script of the mages? And why would one find the same script on Farrow? The discovery of the island is comparatively recent—in the last four hundred years."

Skye raised a finger, his face brightened at the countess' interest. "Exactly. How would Pelier have been familiar with this writing? Either he was truly gifted with the sight and merely reproduced his vision, having no more idea what it meant than we do ourselves, or he somehow had knowledge that only the mages possessed.

"It is well known that Pelier was a member of various arcane societies, though there has been so much speculation about this that the truth is certainly beyond retrieving now. Perhaps he belonged to some group that had knowledge of this script. There are rumors of such cabals: men who had some knowledge of the ways of the mages. I am convinced that at least one of these groups actually existed, though it was destroyed years ago."

"But why do you care?" Marianne asked, and she watched Skye's face change, his manner suddenly suspicious, vaguely hostile.

"It is the great mystery," he said easily. "The fascination of every man in Farrland, and every woman, too, I dare say. The mages and their arts. Men who lived twice or thrice our span of years, and could perform feats that were far beyond our own meager powers. That is reason enough for such a fascination."

"But what of this Stranger and the priest, Baumgere? What have they to do with your great mystery?"

Skye shrugged. "That is what I hope to learn, Miss Edden. Where did this Stranger come from?"

"You don't think it a hoax, then?" Marianne said, pushing Skye more than was polite.

The great empiricist shrugged. "I cannot prove that either way, but if it was a hoax it was managed with astonishing cunning, for some very astute men were taken in."

"But was he from another land—a civilized nation yet undiscovered?" Marianne could almost sense Skye closing down, becoming more and more reluctant to answer her questions.

"He was from some other place," Skye said, clearly becoming uncomfortable.

"But what does that mean, 'some other place'?"

Skye shrugged, guarded now.

"Really, Marianne," the countess interrupted, sounding a bit anxious. "You are being difficult this evening. We all have our interests. I venture that you are seldom required to justify your own."

Marianne bowed her head. "Do forgive me, Lord Skye," she said smiling at the countess' rebuke. "I have been told that I have no tact at all, and apparently it is true."

"No need, Miss Edden," Skye said solicitously, relaxing visibly now that her inquisition was over. "No need." He said nothing more, and they turned their attention back to the paintings again, no one sure what to say to save the moment.

"Do you really think there is some possibility that Erasmus Flattery can read this script?" the countess asked quietly.

Skye shrugged. "It's not impossible."

The countess took a deep breath. "Well, if you send him to me, I will find the truth for you," she said.

Skye turned to her, his eyes bright with . . . what? Smugness, Marianne realized. It was what he had hoped for all along.

"Do you really think you could?" he asked.

"Have no doubt of it," the countess said, clearly happy to have his full attention finally. "Some men find me difficult to refuse."

Skye almost leaped to his feet. "Then I will find him within the hour. Write a note, and I will see it delivered to him this night." He turned to Marianne in his joy, and realized she was not so enthusiastic as he. But this did not cause him to reconsider.

Erasmus heard the note being slipped under his door, and after a moment rose from his bed to see what it was. Sleep after all, was not so easily found that night. There was enough starlight and moonlight in his room that he found the envelope easily—a rectangle of gray against the dark wooden door.

For a moment he stood by the window trying to make out the hand by the poor light—was it from Clarendon? Hayes? Perhaps even Deacon Rose? Finding a candle, he lit it from the coals of his fire and slit the note with a pocket knife.

*My Dear Mr. Flattery:*

*I have just been informed that you are also visiting Castlebough (the joys of small towns) and wonder if I might entice you to visit. I have long wanted to make your acquaintance, and will confess that I have a very small favor to ask. I look forward to our meeting.*

It was signed by the Countess of Chilton.

"Indeed," Erasmus said to the room. "What in the round world does the countess want with me?" Erasmus slumped into a chair. There was no question of him having suddenly become an object of interest to the smart set in Avonel. That was not possible. No, it was this "small favor" that had occasioned the sudden interest. And if that were the case, it had either to do with botany or the ways of the mages, and somehow Erasmus did not think it had anything to do with botany, though he was not sure why. Even so, one did not pass up an opportunity to meet the Countess of Chilton. It was the kind of thing that would intrigue people a decade hence. "*You actually met the countess?*" "*Yes, but none of the rumors are true. We were nothing more than acquaintances.*"

Lost in thought, he sat by the window until his head suddenly rolled to one side, and he forced himself to take to his bed.

*No report had been exaggerated.*

That was Erasmus' first thought upon meeting the countess. She was, if anything, more lovely than he had imagined—and his imagination was usually unrivaled in this regard. He found he was hardly able to take his gaze away from those exquisite eyes, that perfect face. *Certainly,* he thought, *no man can look at those beautiful lips without wondering what it would be like to kiss them.*

The morning sun cast elongated rectangles on the floor and turned the border of the countess' tresses into a flaming nimbus about her heart-shaped face.

*I should have worn my blade,* Erasmus thought, *I am prepared to fight a duel for her already. It is no wonder that men are driven to foolishness around her.*

"It is very kind of you to come, Mr. Flattery. And on such short notice. I am honored."

"It was the summons I'm sure every man in Farrland dreams of, Lady Chilton. I would have come on a moment's notice."

"Well, you are not letting down the family name, I see." She smiled charmingly to let him know that she teased and motioned to a divan set in the light of the windows.

Erasmus took his seat stiffly, and Lady Chilton sat at ease near him.

"You are known to be a man of some genius, Mr. Flattery," she said, perhaps not to be outdone, "so I will not patronize you. I was speaking truthfully when I said I had long wished to make your acquaintance, but as I wrote, there is a small favor I will ask, if you will allow it."

"Lady Chilton, certainly any favor you ask will be too small. Please, do not hesitate." Erasmus was glad that she did not indulge in an hour of aimless chitchat before coming to the point. Glad and a little disappointed. One did not want a visit to the countess to end any sooner than it must.

She turned her attention to two paintings that Erasmus had not even registered, though he had walked right past them.

He felt a certain disorientation looking at the paintings, though he could not say why. There seemed to be subtle breaking of the rules of perspective, and a hyperrealism, as though the painting were really part of a fever dream. And then he realized that the crypt in one painting was the same as he had seen above Castlebough. *These were the Peliers Skye had found!* He turned back to the countess, his manner guarded.

"It is the inscription on the tomb that I am interested in," the countess said.

"Lord Skye has put you up to this, I see," he said, his voice colder than he meant it to be.

The countess averted her gaze a little. "I rather put myself up to it," she said softly.

Erasmus stared at her, feeling sorry that he might have caused her discomfort. One could hardly look at this woman and want to cause her anything but pleasure.

"But you are correct in your assumption," she said. "How did you know?"

"I . . . I had heard a rumor that Skye found the paintings once owned by Baumgere." He inclined his head toward the paintings.

"I see. And can you read this text? Skye believes it might have been a language used by the mages. He also wonders if it bears some passing resemblance to the writing on the Ruin of Farrow. I understand, Mr. Flattery, that you are an authority on the Ruin, among a great many other things." She turned her gaze back to him, her look a mixture of defiance and guilt.

The countess could see by his face and the stiffness of his posture that Erasmus Flattery was not pleased with this development, and she was not so happy herself to be using him so. There was something in his manner that also told her Erasmus was hiding more than most realized. She wondered if Skye was right—Erasmus *could* read the writing.

"It is a mystery to me," he said firmly.

The countess looked down at her fingers worrying the cushion's edge. "Have I offended you, Mr. Flattery? It seemed an innocent enough request to me." She looked up again, meeting his eyes fully, watching the effect this had. Yes, this man, at least, was not indifferent to her charms.

"Offended me? No," he said, though obviously she had unsettled him.

"Does this have to do with your service to Eldrich? I understand that you mislike speaking of it."

"In no way." He hesitated, looking down for an instant, but he could not keep his eyes from hers. "Do not apologize, Lady Chilton. It is I who am sorry that I have no answer to your question."

"Oh." She blew air through her lips in dismissal of his apology. She favored him with her most charming smile. "There are some who say that you were bespelled by Eldrich and cannot speak of those years. . . ."

He laughed.

She had managed to save the moment.

"I am not bespelled, Lady Chilton. My brief time in the house of Eldrich was so utterly without incident that I refuse to bore people with the tale. I was a boy. I was sent to the house of the mage where I lived for three years almost to the day. During that time I was under the guardianship of a tutor who was so ancient that at the end of three years he still occasionally got my name wrong. I studied the things every schoolboy studies. I stole sweet-tarts from the kitchen. I confess I missed my mother and family. And then I was sent home, and at no time was I offered an explanation—either then or since. Oh, and I forgot to say; I never met the mage himself. I did, however, see him, or so I believe, on more than one occasion, though never close to. A tall man with black hair and a stiff gait. And from this rather odd experience, people think I learned the secrets of the mages." He shrugged and smiled a bit helplessly.

"I see what you mean. Tea, Mr. Flattery?" She motioned for the servant to come in, realizing that Erasmus was more than relieved. He was hiding the real story, she was certain. She wondered what it would take to pry it out of him.

She sent the servant off and poured the tea herself.

Erasmus Flattery, she decided, was not a bad looking man. Oh, he was not fashionable, though certainly well enough dressed, but his entire manner was not what was currently acceptable in Avonel society. No, Erasmus Flattery committed the unforgivable sin of allowing his passion to show. He was a man of great intensity, and did nothing to hide it, unlike the fashionable gentlemen of Avonel who feigned boredom in almost any situation. Farrelle help them, they were so indifferent (except to her, it seemed). She found Erasmus' manner rather refreshing.

Erasmus exhibited none of the openness and naivete that characterized many empiricists and scholars. Instead he seemed guarded, like a man who had seen a great deal and not all of it pleasant. She had seen men who had been in battles who wore this same look.

"I understand there is a move afoot, Mr. Flattery, to allow ladies to attend some of the lectures at the Society," she said, turning to small talk, though small talk of his own world.

"There is, though I will tell you that I have little hope of its success. The old men are still very much in control there."

"Are these the gentlemen known affectionately as the 'fossils'?"

Erasmus laughed. "Very affectionately, I assure you!" He tasted his tea. "There is a plan to offer lectures to the public for some very small fee. Not on the Society premises or under its auspices, but most, if not all, of the lectures heard at the Society meetings might be offered. It would be a good thing, I think. The best we can manage until the old men step down."

"Well then, may the fossils soon pass on into the collections of the cosmic museum."

"Hear, hear."

"Tell me about this ruin on Farrow, Mr. Flattery. It is rather romantic, don't you think? This great mystery sitting there all these centuries, its purpose unknown, its builders long passed from history. What on earth could it have been for?"

Erasmus shrugged. "I don't actually know, though I fear it might be something less than romantic. My best guess is it was a kind of calendar. Almost an instrument used to calibrate the movement of stars and planets, to gauge the exact moments of certain celestial events. The longest day of summer, the shortest of winter. It likely had ceremonial purposes as well, though what those were is anyone's guess."

"But it is sitting there nearly intact, and has been for who knows how long, and yet all the other ruins on the island are buried beneath the earth, the walls fallen to foundations. How is that?"

Erasmus sipped his tea. "The other ruins bear no resemblance to the Ruin of Farrow. They are of different stone, and not built in the same style. I think they predate the Farrow Ruin by some time. Perhaps centuries."

"Astonishing," she said. "I must make a trip there. I don't know why I haven't." Her own voice sounded so false to her that the countess could not believe that Erasmus was not offended by her manner.

*Look what I do here*, she thought. *This poor man has secrets he wants to keep, perhaps for good reason, and I have set out to charm them from him.* A wave of self-revulsion swept over her. She thought of Skye jumping up from his chair like a boy when she assured him she could get the information he wanted from Erasmus Flattery.

*How little he cares for me that he would use me so,* she thought, and felt a sadness near to tears. And now I will use this good man equally poorly. She looked over at Erasmus and felt that they were both victims in this.

"I must ask—though please don't let me pry—are you not haunted by what happened to you in your youth? If such a thing had happened to me, I'm sure I would think of nothing else. Your good father never offered an explanation?"

"The duke was not in the habit of explaining himself to anyone." Erasmus looked up, reacting to the sympathy on her face. "And yes, I do wonder." He looked down into his cup for a moment. "I'm sure there was a reason. I mean there must have been. It seems very likely that I performed some feat in my youth that brought me to the attention of Eldrich. It has long been known that mages required some kind of native talent that allowed them to be trained in the arts—just as a singer must have a voice. Perhaps I showed some signs of this, but either was found wanting, or more likely, the mage held faith with the others of his kind, and trained no apprentice."

"But if he did not intend to train you, why on earth were you taken into his home?"

Erasmus looked out the window. "Perhaps Eldrich was not absolutely sure that he would not take an apprentice. No one knows for certain why the mages have stopped the practice of training the next generation. It is a mystery that will likely never be solved. But Eldrich may have reconsidered. Or perhaps true talent, in the measure needed to become a mage, has become very rare."

"Overwhelmed by reason, perhaps?" the countess said.

Erasmus smiled. "Perhaps." He met her eyes for a second then looked away, obviously unsettled by his own hopes, his feelings.

The countess felt badly for him. She was, after all, attempting to raise those hopes—not too much, just enough to get what she wanted.

*What a truly awful woman I have become,* she thought.

"Tell me, Mr. Flattery, how have you enjoyed becoming the 'illustrious Erasmus Flattery'? Has it given you great pleasure, I hope?"

Suddenly, Erasmus sat very straight and met her eyes, his manner no longer congenial, or so eager to please. "The script, Lady Chilton," he said more coolly than men commonly spoke to her, "is not the same as that found on the Ruin of Farrow, though a few characters have enough similarities that I would venture they are not so distantly related. I can't tell you how Pelier could have written it, nor can I read it. Is that what you wanted to hear?"

The countess felt herself shrink inside. "You do me disservice, sir," she protested softly.

"Do I, indeed? Then please accept my humble apology." He set his cup on the table and looked as though he were about to rise.

She reached out and placed a hand on his arm. "No. It is I who should apologize. I. . . ." She searched for the right thing to say, but everything suddenly seemed false. "I should not have misused you so, Mr. Flattery. I hope you will forgive me. You see . . . I have found these last few years that . . . I am not always satisfied with my conduct . . ." She looked down at her hands which made small movements that seemed rather helpless at the moment.

"The attention you receive, Lady Chilton," Erasmus said softly. "It cannot be easy."

"It is not," she said quickly. "Though it is no excuse for my behavior, and I have no right to complain. Some women have no suitors at all. Imagine the pain of that? No, I must not complain. But . . . I am really not so charming." She smiled painfully.

*Look at the effect of this on him*, she thought. *Farrelle help me, I have tried to be honest for once, and I think I have melted his heart.*

"What is Skye's interest in this?" he asked with some difficulty. "These are the Peliers Baumgere possessed?"

After what she had just done, she felt that she had no choice but to answer. "I believe they are, though I have been informed that one—the painting of the tomb—is not a Pelier. Skye believes it to be a close copy—including the inscription that you see on the tomb—of an original, but I am not sure why he thinks that."

Erasmus turned his attention back to the painting. She wondered what he was thinking at that moment, for his look was very dark and serious.

"Is it not remarkable, Mr. Flattery, that Pelier would paint such a thing—and then this man Baumgere would dig up the very crypt depicted?"

"Most remarkable, Lady Chilton." Erasmus shook his head as though baffled, and then turned back to his hostess. "I'm sure I have taken enough of Lady Chilton's time. It has been a great pleasure."

She was certain her mouth dropped open. Men never volunteered to leave her presence. More often than not she had trouble ridding herself of them.

"It—it was very kind of you to come, Mr. Flattery, and I hope you will do so again."

They both rose at the same time.

The countess could hardly remember such feelings of confusion. Look what she had been reduced to! Skye had her performing seductions for his own ends, and even if they were emotional seductions only, even so. . . . She felt such a sense of emptiness at her center when she thought of what Skye had her do.

*You did offer,* she reminded herself. But he did not protest, as a gentleman should.

And here was this poor man, Flattery, who had never done her harm, nor any other that she knew of, and she had used him so badly. And insulted him in the bargain. Treated him as though he were a fool.

She could almost feel his pain at this experience. Invited to tea with the Countess of Chilton for no reason but this information that he did not want to share. Terrible.

Anger toward Skye boiled up in her. Helpless anger, for she knew she could never let it show before him. He did not care for her that much. He might simply walk away, and she would never see him again. Was this anger focused on him, or upon herself for her weakness?

She accompanied Erasmus to the door, so lost in these thoughts that she could not even attempt polite conversation. The silence walked with them, like another, a ghost in their company that they could feel but not see.

At the door they stopped, both wary. She thought they circled each other, unsure if they would fight or embrace.

Erasmus bowed stiffly. "Lady Chilton."

"Mr. Flattery," she said the last syllable disappearing from her lips unexpectedly. An awkward second, then Erasmus reached for the door, but she snatched his hand away and did not release it.

"If you ask me not to repeat what you have told me, I will swear to keep it to myself." She realized she stood close to him now, holding his hand in both of hers, almost clasping it to her.

"It . . . it does not matter," Erasmus said.

She searched his eyes unself-consciously. "Then I will keep this secret, at least. I know you can read what was written on the painting. No. Do not deny it. I know. And I know there is more to your story of Eldrich. But that, too, I will not tell."

Erasmus held her hand tightly now, almost causing her pain. And he stared at her, his look unreadable. She thought he would either explode in fury or take her in his arms, she could not tell which.

He managed to open the door a crack with his free hand. Then she stood on tiptoe and bussed his cheek before he went out the door, saying only her name as he took his leave.

She watched him make his way to the gate, not looking back, and then he turned onto the street and was lost from sight. Still the countess did not close the door, but stayed drinking in great draughts of the cool highland air.

"What has come over me?" she said aloud but could find no answer in the confusion of feelings that seemed to be whirling inside her. Why had she suddenly felt such guilt at the way she used this man? It was not the first time she had applied her charm for some specific end—nor was it the hundredth.

*Because now I know how it feels*, she thought.

"Poor man," she whispered to the street, though she was not entirely sure which man she meant.

## ᔐ Seventeen

Erasmus sat at a table on the terrace on the warmest morning that had been seen yet that year. His mind was on his meeting with the countess, which troubled him more than he had expected. Had she not warned him that her interest was his knowledge? Why then did he feel such a sense of dejection and emptiness?

Erasmus had also begun to wonder what had happened to Hayes. On his way out that morning he'd left the young man a note saying that he had been briefly called away and would find Hayes here at noon. They were to meet Kehler within the hour.

Erasmus was hoping they would get some explanation for Kehler's flight to this place—more than he had heard from Hayes, at any rate.

What had Kehler learned in the archives of Wooton? Could he have made the same discovery as Baumgere? If so, were the priests pursuing Kehler to offer him money for his silence, as, apparently, some thought they had Baumgere?

Erasmus took his timepiece from his pocket and cursed silently. Almost one! Was this Hayes' idea of a reasonable hour to rise? Erasmus could not be more patient. Draining his coffee he jogged up the steps to Hayes' room and pounded ungently on the door.

Nothing. No sound of movement within. No voice calling out. Again he hammered on the door so that it shook on its hinges. Nothing. He went back down the steps two at a time, looking for the manager.

In five minutes they returned with a key for the room, finding it empty, the bed made as though it had never been slept in, and most of Hayes' belongings gone.

"I do not care for this," Erasmus muttered.

"The young are impetuous, not to mention intemperate, Mr. Flattery," the manager said soothingly. "I'm sure nothing dire has befallen your charge."

"You are, are you?" Erasmus said, annoyed by the man's tone. "Ah. . . ." A folded note was pinned to the wardrobe door.

"There will be your explanation," the manager said, as though proven right.

Erasmus jerked the note free and opened it.

*My dear Erasmus:*

*I have gone with Kehler to look into the cavern called the Mirror Lake Cave. He believes that it was here that Baumgere searched and failed. Perhaps it is mere optimism, but Kehler believes there is still a great discovery to be made there. I have been sworn to secrecy, but only a fool would go into such a place without alerting others. Do not come after us immediately, but if we are not returned five days hence, you might confidently mount a search. It is our intention to look beyond the Fairy Galleries. I will mark our way with the letter H. Apologies for this, but Kehler would take no others.*

*Your servant,*

*Samual Hayes*

"All is right with the world, I take it?" the manager asked.

Erasmus glared at the fool of a man and then swept out the door without a word.

Clarendon unrolled the survey across the table, placing weights on each corner.

"There you are, Mr. Flattery," Clarendon said, "just as I told you."

Erasmus had never seen anything like it. He was looking at a "map" of a cave system, and it was truly labyrinthine. Passages crossed over and under each other, or even paralleled each other only feet apart. He tried to compare the plan view and side view and was soon confused. The complexity was staggering.

"There must be miles of passages here," Erasmus said, dismayed.

"More than thirty, apparently, and likely even more that have not been explored or yet discovered. There might be a more current survey than this. I will find out." Clarendon put his finger on a chamber. "Here are the Fairy Galleries, so called. I have not been in this section myself, though I know men who have. We can certainly speak with them, but perhaps we should wait the five days the letter suggests before we gather the men for a search."

"I don't want to gather men for a search. I want no one to know of this at all—at least not until we are absolutely certain they are lost. No, I will take this map, or the more recent one if it exists, and go immediately to the cave entrance. If they have not emerged in a day or two, I will go in after them."

"Yourself, alone?"

Erasmus nodded.

"Well, I cannot allow that. It is more treacherous than this map might indicate. You must take me, at least, Mr. Flattery. You would be imprudent not to."

Erasmus began to protest, but Clarendon raised his hand, his mustache bobbing oddly; a sign of determination, Erasmus thought. "I am far more vital than you guess, and in a cave, where passages can often grow very tight, the smaller man may perform the greater deeds. And you forget—I have been in the caves before." He paused to consider. "We should not go unprepared, that would be dangerous, Mr. Flattery. But preparations take time. Let us plan to leave the day after tomorrow." He looked down at the survey, then raised his head and met Erasmus' eye, a sly smile appearing. "Tonight there is little we can do and I have promised to deliver Erasmus Flattery to a gathering of devotees of the grape. Tomorrow I will put my staff to work on the preparations, and the next day we shall set out well rested. I will tell you honestly, Mr. Flattery, that we stand little chance of catching up with these young men even if we were only hours behind them. They are younger than we and have the fires of both youth and curiosity. We will not catch them up until they have slowed their pace, and that will be in the Fairy Galleries—two days' hard push into the cave. They are young but hardly foolhardy, I think, so I do not worry that they will come to grief; at least it would be very unlikely. Be of good heart, sir, we will find them safe, I'm sure."

Erasmus and Clarendon walked to the meeting, for Castlebough was small and the evening pleasant. This night the gathering was to take place at the home of a man who, like most of the Society's fellows, did not reside year round in the town.

As a result of all the comings and goings, the society had a constantly changing membership, and one never knew who might be present, though Clarendon assured him that several men Erasmus knew at least by reputation would be there. Erasmus had agreed to speak briefly about his own work, and to answer questions.

The two men made their way through the streets and down stairways by the light of stars, the glow of the occasional street-lamp, and what illumination leaked from unshuttered windows. They were like two shadows moving, one elongated by a low source of light, the other made short by light from above.

The house they went to was very pleasant, built in the general style of the town with much dark wood inside, all carefully polished. The gentlemen were welcoming and gracious to Erasmus, and if he did not feel he'd found his place in the world here with these men, he at least felt highly appreciated. Odd that so many people he had never met held him in such high esteem.

Clarendon introduced him to the man who had surveyed the great cave, who had brought along the current survey at Clarendon's request. Although the man had reached an age where he no longer went into the cave himself, he consoled himself by meticulously recording the advances of others.

"I once thought I should complete the picture, Mr. Flattery," the man said. "Explore every last tunnel and chamber, but it was bigger than me, I fear. Nature's energies far exceeded my own. Sometimes I look at the still-growing plan and think we must be near the end, but then remember that I thought the same thing twenty years ago when only half what we now know had been discovered.

"Layel, the famous geologist, walked over miles of hillside around the cave, examining the drainage patterns and finding any number of sink holes, most of them choked closed, and he told me he would not be surprised if we eventually found ourselves linking to another system of caves as large again as this. Can you imagine? It would be one of the natural wonders of the world, I should think. As it stands now, there is much to admire inside. Stalactites and columns, curtains, and delicate crystal straws hollow in their cores and as thin as the stems of fine wineglasses. I know where there are ceilings covered in them, and they are astonishingly beautiful. And there are helectites as well—crystal straws, but twisted about as though gravity had changed as they formed, for they do not hang downward as the other formations do but contort into the most astounding shapes."

"Can one still become lost inside? Surely this map has eliminated that problem?" Erasmus asked.

"I wish that were so, Mr. Flattery, but I fear it is nothing like the truth. I sometimes think our efforts to chart the passages have done more harm than good in that matter. People who venture in armed with the survey are too confident, I think. They don't realize the real dangers, for there are some very precipitous climbs and descents required to get into the less frequented regions. Those who seek to open up new areas are the most often injured. But you can become lost even in the more frequented areas. It is more confusing than you might imagine. And I venture there are still many undiscovered passages, even in the parts that are fairly well known." He put his finger on the drawing. "You see this passage here? People walked by it for twenty years before it was discovered, for it is high up and difficult to see. I'm still not sure what caused anyone to notice it. But look! It opens up fully one quarter of the cave and eventually led us to find the third entrance: a tight little squeeze high up on a cliff. Twenty years that went undiscovered. Who knows how many such passages exist? No, if you go into the cave, Mr. Flattery, don't assume this survey will keep you safe. Only common sense will do that, though I am certain you have no lack of that."

Erasmus continued to examine the survey. Every so often there were ancillary drawings with lines pointing to a passage. "What are these?"

"Cross sections of the cave at that point." The man looked at Randall. "It is a bit early yet to go far into the cave. It will likely be wet in places. Take good oiled cotton bags, Randall, and try to keep as much dry as you can. It is dangerous to go wet in the cave for long. I have seen men begin to lose their reason from this. They become lethargic and refuse to go on. I'm sure they would have died, too, had we not warmed them with our own heat."

"But surely the cave is not cold?" Erasmus said.

"No, Mr. Flattery, not overly, though the water is quite chill, especially this time of year. But the cave is not what you would call warm either and a man soaked through, unless he is very hardy, soon loses the natural heat of his body. Take my advice and keep as dry as you can. But perhaps it will not be so bad, and Randall has been in before and knows what to expect. You will be in good hands. Have no fear."

The meeting proper was convened then, Clarendon taking up the speaker's place at the front of a large room that had been fitted out with chairs for all the company.

"As many of you have already heard," the small man began, "the illustrious Erasmus Flattery, Fellow of the Empiricist Society, is among us this evening and has consented to speak on the subject of grafting to wild root stocks. I would venture to say that there is no greater authority on the subject. We are also fortunate to have visiting us Delford Simon, proprietor of Simon and Dean Wineries—a man well known to many of us, I'm sure. I would also welcome Deacon Rose of Wooton, a grower of great skill. Mr. Flattery, if you are ready. . . ."

Erasmus was so taken aback by the discovery that Deacon Rose was there that he did not start well. He found the priest seated in the middle of the audience, apparently in the company of two gentlemen not of the cloth.

It took a few moments for Erasmus to get over his surprise and warm to his subject, but then he managed to gain the attention of his audience, and held it for the duration of his speech. Discussion followed, and Erasmus had seldom found such a knowledgeable audience, even within the Society itself. Two hours went quickly by, and then the meeting broke up for the evening's real activity—the tasting of wines.

Erasmus was just swirling a particularly fine claret around in his mouth when the Farrellite priest found him.

"Well, Mr. Flattery, I did not imagine meeting you in Castlebough. I assume we have come pursuing the same matter?"

"You have come to take the waters as well?" Erasmus asked innocently.

"I was referring to our mutual friend, young Mr. Kehler," the priest said, his look of pious concern never slipping.

"Why would you think he was in Castlebough, Deacon Rose?"

The priest looked away for a moment, as though controlling his temper—not something Erasmus had seen in the man before.

"Perhaps we might speak more privately, Mr. Flattery?"

Erasmus took a second sip of his claret, considered a moment, and then nodded for the priest to lead the way. They went out into a walled garden awash in the fecund scents of early spring.

"Have you spoken to Mr. Kehler?" Rose asked. "Is he here?"

Erasmus looked at the man for a moment. "Since our last conversation, Deacon, I have learned that Mr. Kehler is not particularly destitute, as you suggested." Erasmus was about to ask how long Rose had watched his town home waiting for Kehler to appear but held back, to see what the priest would say.

Rose turned away stiffly, his eyes unfocused in the light streaming from the windows. "I will confess, Mr. Flattery, that I was less than forthcoming when last we spoke, but I assure you my concern for Mr. Kehler is quite genuine. He has taken something from our archives at Wooton that is of . . . great concern to us. I would even say that he is in some danger."

"From whom, Deacon?"

The priest hesitated, then turned his intelligent gaze on Erasmus. "You do not trust me, Mr. Flattery."

"I do not, that is true. Until you are willing to tell me more, I don't think that will change."

The priest stared down at the dark ground and nodded. "You were making inquiries this evening about the Cave of the Mirror Lake. . . . I assume that Mr. Kehler is seeking something there?"

Erasmus did not react—not even a shrug.

"If I camp before the entrance, I assume I will be able to speak with Mr. Kehler, for speak with him is all I wish to do."

Erasmus did not offer to confirm this.

The priest's manner changed, becoming suddenly very earnest. "You will not help me, then? Even though the young man's safety might depend upon my intervention?"

"I'm afraid I can't," Erasmus said quietly, suddenly afraid that the man might be speaking the truth. Who had invaded Hayes' rooms and chased him through the streets? Could these men have been agents of the church? Or even of Eldrich himself? Could Eldrich know about Kehler's discovery?

"Are you going into the cave after Kehler? Tell me that, at least."

"I'm sorry, Deacon, but I will tell you nothing until you give me reason to."

The man reached out and put his hand gently on Erasmus' arm. "Let me accompany you, and then you can see yourself that I mean him no harm." Rose looked out over the garden wall to the stars and the hills. "I will tell you my fear, Mr. Flattery; I fear that I am already too late." He turned his gaze back to Erasmus. "When you spoke with Kehler, did he ask you about a man named Teller?"

Erasmus must not have hidden his surprise well.

"I see that he did. Perhaps he then told you what he found? If that is so, you realize why I must speak with him. It is true that I was not entirely candid with you on our first interview. I confess it, but certainly you can see that I could not be. You must see that? You lived in the house of Eldrich. I do not know what that might mean, but the mages and the church have long had an uneasy truce. We fear them, Mr. Flattery—even Eldrich in his waning years." Rose stopped, clearly unsettled to be saying these things aloud to someone outside the church. "Let me assure you, Mr. Flattery, in case you still have commerce with the mage, what happened was not of our doing. As soon as we became aware, we moved quickly to . . . cleanse our house of the disease. We have kept our pact all these long years and will continue to do so at any cost." The priest searched Erasmus' face, perhaps looking for some sign of understanding, but Erasmus was not willing to accept the position of emissary to Eldrich, or to refuse it. Better to let the priest wonder.

"Kehler came to you with questions that he hoped you might answer," the priest went on. "Did he tell you what he hoped to do?"

Erasmus did not answer, but the priest would not speak further.

"No," Erasmus said after a moment, "Kehler told me nothing, but I am hoping you will remedy that, Deacon. Why has he gone into the cave? What is he looking for?"

Deacon Rose turned and looked back at the house, then out over the garden at the sky. "Something that might not even exist. Something that certainly should not exist."

"If you want my cooperation, Deacon, you will have to do better than that."

Rose continued to stare off at the stars, but he nodded vaguely. "Do you know, Mr. Flattery, that there is within the cave an area called the Fairy Galleries. It was named for its reputed resemblance to a mythical place—or perhaps the place was merely literary."

"'The Journey of Tomas,'" Erasmus said, realizing suddenly what the priest was saying.

"Yes. 'The Journey of Tomas.' It is an ancient lay, older than the Cary Minstrels' rendering, that is certain. The story of a man lost in a great cave who emerges into the starlight finally, almost starved, but he recognizes no constellations. When the sun rises, he finds he is in another land, similar but not the same as his own, and peopled by a different race. He lived there some time, learning their ways and their tongue. But finally he began to miss his wife and wonder about his small children, so he ventured back into the cave again. What happened there is a story unto itself, but eventually he emerged. And what did he find? His children grown, his wife dead and in the grave for many years, though he had been gone only two years by his reckoning. No one knew him, and his world was changed.

"After a brief time among his own people, he went back into the cave to seek the way back to Faery. There are different endings to the song: he finds his way back, he dies in the cave, or he almost dies when the people of Faery come and bear him through by their secret way. One may choose the ending one prefers—unlike life."

"What are you saying? That Kehler is seeking the way to Faery?" Erasmus laughed but this did not seem to affect the priest or his mood.

"The song is just a song, no more. I am only saying that men go seeking the objects of their desire. Perhaps even the creations of that desire. But what they find is invariably different than they imagined or hoped. This strange propensity in mankind is what makes us children—it is also what makes us great.

"What does Mr. Kehler seek? I am not absolutely certain, Mr. Flattery, though knowing him as I do, I would say he seeks knowledge. But what he will find, I fear, might be quite different."

Clarendon laughed as he and Erasmus walked through the village, returning from the gathering of vinophiles.

"'The Ballad of Tomas.' I do know it." He chuckled again. "Though I think most could say the same. You see, when the cave was discovered, it was given an entirely different name, and then some local worthy—a mayor, I think—got the idea to rename it for the cave in the old song. There is a fairly large lake within it and other features that are similar enough, though most large caves would have many of these. It draws the tourists, for in the summer many of the town's visitors tour the caves, the Cave of the Mirror Lake chief among them, for, you see, the plan worked." Clarendon laughed again. "This priest, what is he up to, do you think?"

"I wish I knew, Randall. I dearly wish I knew."

"Well, at least I think he spoke the truth when he said that men go seeking their desires and often find something quite unexpected. He failed to say, however, that these are among mankind's greatest discoveries—both for good and ill."

## ⤳ Eighteen

Kehler held aloft the lantern, illuminating the opening.

"I think we should go in tonight, at least some way, in case we're pursued."

"Do you think it's wise to go on in darkness?" Hayes asked.

"It's always night in the underworld, Samual."

Hayes could hear his companion's smile in the words. "Yes, of course, but . . ." He let the protest die. "All right, if you think it's best."

They climbed back up the path among the firs and found their guide unloading the horses. "We can make a camp here," the man said.

"We thought we'd go in tonight," Kehler said, not at all self-conscious.

The man stopped what he was doing. "Tonight? You might be better rested in the morning." He paused and looked at each of the gentlemen. "But suit yourselves." He set one of their bags on the ground. "I would caution you to be most careful in your explorations, gentlemen. You cannot imagine the difficulties of carrying a man back to the surface again. There are some tight places in the cave, and getting an injured man through such can be near to impossible. I have had to do it myself and never want to be so employed again. I urge you, be mindful as you go."

Kehler and Hayes divided their effects into sturdy canvas packs of the type used by foot soldiers.

"It seems an enormous amount of gear," Hayes said hefting his pack.

"We must have it, though. A spare lantern is a necessity, and lamp oil, and ropes. We must have food and a change of clothing, a compass, candles, and the survey. I have left everything out that I felt we could possibly do without. Feel fortunate that we do not have to carry water, for there is water enough in the cave." Kehler took a last look at their bags. "We will leave some food and a few other things just inside the cave to await our return, but the rest I'm afraid we must shoulder. Let me just fill the lantern, and we shall be ready."

A moment later Kehler resealed the fuel tin and hoisted his pack to his back. "Into the netherworld, my friend." He went to thank their guide, but the man was rolled in a blanket and already snoring.

They descended along the path to the cave mouth. At this elevation and among such massive trees the underwood was very sparse, and the earth was often carpeted in mosses. Hayes felt as though they were leaving a soft, green world for one hard, gray, and lifeless, for very little lived out of sight of the sun. He could not help feeling that the darkness emanated from this opening into the earth, exhaled like a dark breath each night. He didn't really want to go on, and hesitated at the very lip of the cave.

Kehler looked over at him. "It will be the discovery of a lifetime," he said simply. "And we shall write an account of it that will be seen by every reading man, woman, and child in all the nations around the Entide Sea. You will not want for money ever again, Hayes, I can assure you."

"It would come down to money," Hayes said peevishly. "Lead on, Kehler, I'm dreadfully tired of hiding from my creditors."

Kehler gave him a hint of a concerned smile, and went resolutely into the mouth of the cave. The lantern illuminated a floor of dried mud, caked and flaking, and convoluted walls worn by years of water erosion, now broken here and there and not so smooth as they were.

"You're sure this cave is . . . solid," Hayes said, his voice echoing in the small entrance chamber.

"There are some areas of breakdown marked on the survey, but for the most part the cave is utterly solid and not to be worried about. I can't believe you didn't read the pamphlet, Hayes."

"You read most of it to me," he reminded his friend.

Some enterprising individual in Castlebough had published a small pamphlet on the cave, and though its aim was to draw visitors out to see this natural wonder, there was some useful information as well. But even so, Hayes was not convinced that a survey and the information contained in some hack's pamphlet could really be considered adequate preparation for their expedition. But Kehler absolutely refused to take a local guide other than the man who brought them to the entrance. Whatever it was he hoped to find, Kehler was to be certain that he shared it with no one but Hayes—and Hayes was not sure that he would have been included if Kehler had felt he could have undertaken the matter alone. But apparently even the driven Kehler was not willing to go into the bowels of the earth on his own.

"You promised to tell me what you had learned once we were underground," Hayes said as they made their way into a narrowing passage.

"When we stop to rest," Kehler said. "You will not be disappointed, Samual."

*No, but I will likely be too far along to turn back if I am.*

The passage was high, disappearing from the lamplight at a dozen feet and varied in width as they went from three yards to places where the two could not walk abreast. The walls were uneven, appearing almost fluted in places, as though over the great expanse of geological time water had run here at different levels, and slowly eaten away at the softer whitestone so that the surfaces were uneven. The cave twisted unexpectedly, and then began to descend so that they were soon climbing down drops of four and five feet, like erratic stairs.

They went on like this for an hour or more, Kehler leading the way and holding the lantern for Hayes. They were young and hale, and even Hayes soon forgot his fears and began to enjoy meeting the challenge. They heard no sound but their own breathing and the scrape of their feet over stone, the sound of the packs rubbing against the walls of the cave as they squeezed through some narrower part. And then Kehler stopped, holding up his hand, obviously listening.

"Do you hear water running?"

Hayes listened. "There is something. . . . It must be water. Does your survey show it?"

"Yes, but I did not think to come upon it so soon. We are making better time than I guessed."

Heartened by this, they pushed on, hurrying where the cave would allow it. At one point the passage narrowed at its bottom, forcing them to climb higher, bridging their arms and legs to either side and picking their footholds with care. An hour later they were able to take to the floor again, but they had been slowed appreciably by this section.

The air changed, becoming suddenly damp and a bit refreshing, for they had been working hard and were both hot and sweating. In another twenty minutes they came to the lip of a drop, and there at the bottom lay a pool of water fed by a small falls. The water swirled in a swift whirlpool and then plunged down into the cave, sounding unnaturally loud in the hard world of stone.

Kehler handed the lamp to Hayes and peeled off his pack, setting it down with a theatrical groan. "I think we can easily climb down, but we should lower the lantern and the packs separately." He dug out one of their ropes, flaking it down onto the rock, and formed a loop at its midpoint. "When I get down, throw me the end, then tie the lantern to the loop. Feed it out to me, and I will endeavor to keep it clear of the rocks."

Carefully, but apparently without trepidation, Kehler climbed the thirteen or fourteen feet down to the edge of the pool.

"All right," he said, and Hayes threw him the other end.

The lantern was lowered down without mishap, and then the packs, one at a time. Hayes followed his friend, though with less confidence. Kehler held the lantern high and gave his friend instructions as to the best footholds. In a moment they were both standing beside the small pool, their relieved laughter echoing with the water sounds.

"Where does this go?" Hayes asked, waving a hand at the passage from which the water flowed.

"It goes a few hundred yards, and then chokes off, I think. Only a hole big enough for the stream."

They both drank and then sat for a moment. The chamber they were in was almost perfectly circular, rising fairly evenly to a dome overhead.

"It is remarkable, isn't it?" Hayes said, surprised by his reaction to the place.

Kehler agreed. "But we haven't come anywhere near the true wonders of the cave. There are chambers decorated with stalactites and curtains and flowing moonstone. There is a falls almost a hundred feet high and even a small lake, or so the survey shows."

"How far have we descended?"

"I don't think we've gone down a hundred feet yet, which leaves quite a lot of cave below us, for we started about three thousand feet above Blue Hawk Lake, which lies at the cave's bottom. Unfortunately we will have to climb up again, for the entrances at the lake are under water until the dry summer months."

They sat quietly, watching the water swirl into the pool, a bit awed by what nature had carved around them.

Kehler filled the lamp again, checking his watch. "We may have to kill the flame when we stop to sleep," he said. "I'm not sure we have enough fuel to keep it alive for the entire time otherwise."

"But we have candles," Hayes said.

"Yes, though I hope we'll not need them. A lamp is so much more convenient and casts much more light. Imagine trying to keep a candle alight and make good time in here?"

There was a moment's silence, and perhaps sensing that Hayes was again about to ask the purpose of their expedition, Kehler jumped up and hefted his pack into place.

"Take the lantern and the lead, Hayes. I will follow blindly for a while."

They followed the course of the water, which ran swiftly down, its voice echoing in the dark tunnel. Where the passage narrowed, and there was no dry footing, they at first tried to keep their boots dry, climbing up and bridging again, but soon enough they had both slipped in one place or another and after that they simply plunged into the water, accepting the ruination of their footwear.

In half an hour they came to a short drop where the water course deviated into a fissure in the floor which left only a little room on one side where they might pass. They went carefully by this opening, afraid to slip into it, both imagining being swept down into a dark, water-filled tunnel devoid of both light and air.

"I did not care much for that!" Hayes said, slumping up against the cave wall once they were past.

"Nor did I. Fortunately we have clear sailing now for a while." Kehler filled their single water bottle here, and then they set off again.

"In a little over an hour we should reach a splitting of the way," Kehler said. "We can go either left or right, for both ways join again. After that, I think we will be an hour from the great junction where four passages meet. Can you go on till then? Are you game?"

Hayes thought he was. Kehler took the lead now, pushing on as though driven to complete their journey that very night, though it looked more likely that they would require two days or even a bit more. It all depended on their ease of going. The passage was presently running along quite evenly, and they were making excellent time though that could quickly change. The next time they stopped, Hayes wanted to have a look at the survey. His memory of it was getting muddled already.

Hayes was not quite certain how he had gotten drawn into this, aside from the obvious reasons: money and bloody curiosity. He felt like he had betrayed Erasmus, slipping away without a word, but Kehler had insisted.

*"It will be the discovery of our lifetime,"* Kehler had said, his eyes almost shining with his excitement. *"And your name will be attached to it forever."* Kehler realized how much his pride had been damaged by his fall in society. *Erasmus will never forgive me*, he thought. *I do not know exactly what Kehler expects to find, but with the similarities between his interests and Erasmus', I have little doubt that Erasmus will wish he were with us.* And there was also Erasmus' stated concern: that Kehler was pursuing matters that could be dangerous to him—matters that Hayes was pursuing as well.

The roof of the passage had begun to dip, forcing Hayes and Kehler to crouch as they went. But soon their packs were dragging on the rock, and they were forced to their knees. Packs were shed with some difficulty, and they proceeded, pushing the packs ahead as they went. The ceiling continued to drop until they were slithering along on their bellies, though the width of their tunnel remained six or seven feet.

"I hope it is not all like this," Hayes said, "or we shall be in here forever."

Ahead of him Kehler cursed. "Yes, I would say our pace has slowed to the proverbial crawl. Flames! I shall have no knees left at this rate!"

Hayes laughed, the sound echoing oddly in the darkness. They crawled on, saving their breath for their effort, though that did not stop an occasional curse. Hayes began to think of the tons of rock above him, and the tunnel seemed to press down, as though the roof of the cave were bending under the immeasurable weight. He struggled with a growing panic. What if the tunnel became smaller yet? What if they became trapped, unable to move? The thought caused him such anguish that he pushed it from his mind.

*Concentrate on moving forward*, he encouraged himself. He fought to lift his pack over an edge that snagged it, shoved it on in frustration, and then crawled after. He was not getting much light from the lantern, and Kehler, who could see perfectly, no doubt, was getting farther and farther ahead. At this rate Hayes thought he would soon be in complete darkness. To make matters worse, he was certain the tunnel was narrowing. And he had to struggle with his panic again.

He did not know how long they proceeded in this fashion, but it seemed hours. Hayes felt that his existence was shrinking as the tunnel became smaller. He was reduced to a crawling beast, fighting his fears, pushing his pack a foot, then dragging himself forward, pushing his pack . . . again and again.

And then the light appeared to grow; he thrust his pack through a hole into an open area and light flooded in. Hayes squeezed through and lay catching his breath. Kehler was sitting with his back against the rock wall, and he tried to smile.

"Do you know the hour? I have managed to smash my timepiece."

Hayes fished in a pocket and found his own watch unscathed, though he made note to place it securely in his pack.

"Two minutes beyond midnight."

Kehler nodded. "Six hours we have been at it. Three perhaps in this last section. Our progress is less than I expected."

"Perhaps this walking upright has its drawbacks after all. I'm sure our distant relatives, the ape men, would have managed much better than we."

Kehler produced the water bottle, and they both drank deeply. The survey was spread out in the lamplight, and the two bent over it.

"I would venture that we have just passed through the section known as the 'Slug's Race Course,' and I no longer wonder why it was so named. I wonder how far it is to this splitting of the ways?" He tapped the drawing. "Shall we go on, or call it a night?"

Hayes took a look around. He was feeling decidedly tired, but he was not certain that he could sleep. The claustrophobia of the last hours still touched him.

"I think we should go on. We have almost emptied the water bottle, and it would be good to be nearer water in the morning."

Kehler nodded. "You're right. Let's go to the place where the four ways meet. From there it can't be more than two hours to the resurgence."

They clambered on, relieved by the size of the passage, which was ten feet high and roughly round, though it quickly began to vary, and twist as it went. Their spirits rose, as often happens after an ordeal, and they talked as they went, buoyed by a sense of adventure.

In the world above, people slumbered, secure in their homes and the routine of their lives, while here, far beneath the surface, Hayes and Kehler went seeking secrets long hidden. Hayes thought that he felt more alive at that moment than he had in several years.

Sooner than expected, they found the Y in the tunnel and, for no particular reason, elected to take the left passage. In twenty minutes the passages joined again and they pressed on. A series of short drops, none more than ten feet, slowed them only a little, and an hour more brought them to the place where the four ways joined. Here they found a small alcove off the side of one passage and, calling it the "sleeping chamber," threw down their packs.

Hayes impressed Kehler by using the lantern as a stove. He removed the glass chimney and, using one of their tin cups and the lamp's handle, managed if not to boil water at least to heat it. Taking a small package from his pack, he brewed something resembling tea and this they shared quietly by the lamplight.

Kehler produced the survey again and hunched over it, examining it minutely. "If we take the southern passage, we will be forced to use ropes to negotiate some rather large drops, but there are no significant squeezes on this route. The northern way has a long crawl, perhaps longer than the one we have just survived."

"Let us go by the south, then, Kehler. I fear heights less than the tight spots."

Kehler looked over at him, his gaze resting on his friend with some concern. "I will tell you honestly, Hayes, that we have not really entered a tight passage yet. Some tunnels we might meet are just large enough to let a determined man pass and no more." Perhaps he saw the distress this caused, and he quickly added. "But I am smaller than you and will do most of the real exploration. Your job will be to pull me out by my ankles should I get stuck."

Hayes took the tea from his friend and sipped it. "You said you would tell me the story once we stopped."

Kehler laid his head back against the rock and closed his eyes. Hayes thought he would claim exhaustion and put the moment off again, but without opening his eyes Kehler began.

"In my time at Wooton I managed to gain the trust of a number of the priests who worked in the archives, although I will confess that I planned to abuse that trust right from the beginning. Like many historians in Farrland, I was of the belief that the church hid much of our history in their records. If they had so cheated us, I was prepared to do the same to them. I make no more excuse than that.

"The archives at Wooton house what is, perhaps, the most important collection in all Farrland. There are some documents there of astonishing age! Many of the priests who do their scholarly work there maintain exhausting hours, appearing to need no more than a few hours' sleep each day. This is part of the surrender of their will to the church, I think. I came to see it as a form of self-abasement, really. But it meant that the archives were open at all hours. I began to work long hours myself and gained the trust of a number of the priests this way, for I think they were impressed by my monk-like capacity for work. I was not one of them, but I was, at least, like them in habits.

"I soon learned that there were rooms in the buildings that were not open to any but the most senior priests or scholars, and then only with consent from on high. The keys for most of the rooms were in the possession of the senior archivist, an ancient and kindly priest. I gained his trust by offering my services to him, for he did not get around as he once did. Through this action, I managed to gain occasional access to his keys. The poor man, he trusted me far too much, and I do regret this one betrayal, for I'm sure he has been retired in shame for what happened.

"I traced his keys one at a time, and then filed duplicates out of brass. It was a laborious process, I can tell you, and it did not always produce results, but eventually I had keys for most of the locked chambers. The first I entered

documented the struggle of the church to influence government, and was astonishing enough, I'm sure, but it was not what interested me. I was a while
finding what I looked for and, in fact, began to despair of ever discovering
what I sought.

"And then fortune found me. I could only gain access to the rooms at
certain times of the night, when those few priests who were in the archives
were engaged elsewhere, and during vespers. I was expected to attend though
occasionally I did not and was seldom missed, but everyone else attended,
leaving the archives protected only by their ancient locks.

Kehler opened his eyes and fixed them on his friend. "I will tell you truthfully, Hayes, there is an archive at Wooton that deals almost exclusively with
the Farrellite Church's struggle against the mages. It is an astonishing history!
I hadn't time to read it all, of course, or even a hundredth part of it, but even
so—the things I found! It was Althons, the mage King, who preserved the
vestiges of the Farrellite Church after the war between the church and the
mages. And the church leaders did not know why! It was as though the mages
had some use for the church, perhaps far in the future, but would say nothing
of it. The church fathers suspected that augury had led to this decision. The
mages had seen something in one of their visions that had led them to spare
the church, and the priests had no idea what it might be.

"But the information I sought was more elusive and took me months of
subterfuge to find. All the while I expected discovery and expulsion—at the
very least! And then one day I found a letter from Baumgere himself—a letter
to the senior bishop of the Farrellite Church, no less. Although it was written
with all apparent deference, and was clearly a response to a letter from the senior bishop, it contained a threat that was only very slightly veiled. 'I should not
want to contemplate the reaction of the mages,' Baumgere wrote, 'were they to
learn that you concealed their enemy all these years.'"

Kehler leaned forward and blew out the flame, plunging the chamber into
a darkness such as Hayes had never known. There was not a trace of light. No
shadow or area darker than another. Uniform blackness, and then odd visions,
shades of color, seemed to appear before his eyes, though they were not light
but only the eye's reaction to its absence. He heard his own breath indrawn.
And then Kehler's voice came out of the blackness.

"I had learned about Teller by then, though at first I didn't make the connection. It was not until I found a record of an inquisition within the church
carried out with utter secrecy that I began to realize what had happened. A
hundred and sixty years ago the Farrellites found that the society the mages
believed they had destroyed was still alive, and living like a parasite within the
bosom of the church! The society of Teller had somehow survived. And where
better to take refuge than within the defeated church? The church that no

longer posed a threat to the mages; that did not dare to pose a threat! A priest speaking out from the pulpit against the mages would have been summarily excommunicated for endangering the church. And this was almost without question what Baumgere was referring to. He must have learned of it in his studies.

"Of course, by Baumgere's time, the society of Teller had been rooted out, though I was not able to learn what their fate had been. But still, the mages were not known to be just, and the fathers of the church were, with good reason, terrified that the mages might one day learn the truth. What if this had been their sole function, the reason the mages had allowed the church to survive? To destroy the vestiges of Teller's society? Would the mages have no more use for them if they were to find out? And Baumgere blackmailed them with this information—blackmailed his own church, though for what gain was unclear. No wonder he was denied absolution!

"So hearing Erasmus and Clarendon speak of Teller did not surprise me." Kehler paused a moment. "The priest came to the Caledon Hills seeking something, and he was clearly not doing so at the behest of his church. People would see him out roaming the hills with his deaf-mute servant, silent, as always, about his business. In any number of places there were excavations attributed to Baumgere. Then, when I had begun to lose hope, I found some of Baumgere's papers. Nothing like I'd hoped—no journal containing all the answers to my questions—but a few odd things that were likely deemed of no importance by whomever had filed Baumgere's papers away in this forgotten room. A deed to his home. A map of the vicinity to the west of Blue Hawk Lake marked here and there with intriguing circles and lines. A meticulous catalogue of everything he read. In a crate, I even found some of Baumgere's books—all of which were entered in the catalogue. And something that seemed very odd at the time—a number of cave surveys, all annotated in his wispy hand. It seemed from what he wrote that he had been engaged in carefully eliminating every section of each cave, though by what criteria could not be ascertained. On each survey there was a date and a brief entry; usually something like, 'nothing here' or 'not this one', but this cave—the Cavern of the Mirror Lake—this one he did not complete his work in. Something stopped him. Stopped him just when his hopes were rising, for on one section of the cave were written the words: 'Here, the way by darkness into light.'"

"And that means something to you?" Hayes said, surprised at the weight Kehler seemed to attribute to the inscription.

"I confess, at the time it meant nothing. But as I studied Baumgere's effects, these few scraps that proved the man had passed through this world, I was provided an answer. Among the books that Baumgere owned, I found that several contained the same lyric, and each was much underlined and written over, which was very anomalous, for he had not written in his books in any other place. It was an old lyric called the 'Ballad of Tomas' that interested him. You've likely heard it sung. . . ." Kehler then proceeded to sing, off-key, a line or two.

"Remarkably, I actually do recognize it, which is saying a great deal as you entirely missed the tune, like a blind carpenter after a nail."

"Well, I make no claims as a singer. But the line, 'the way, by darkness, into light,' is from the ballad."

"I'm waiting for you to enlighten me," Hayes said.

"Well, clearly Baumgere had a romantic or poetical nature and a particular affection for that lyric. The way by darkness into light was the tunnel that To-mas used to reach Faery. The one tunnel in a vast cave. So you see, he used this line to mark the spot where he believed lay whatever it was he looked for. It is also a metaphor, obviously. Perhaps, given his religion, he would have interpreted it to mean the way to eternal life through death. Or the way to knowledge through struggle."

"Well," Hayes said, "I'm glad we have come down here on such concrete evidence. '*The way by darkness into light.*' Why didn't you just say so earlier? No more explanation would have been necessary. I would have plunged into darkness ready to do battle with all the creatures of the underworld, both real and metaphorical. Farrelle's flames, Kehler! Is that why we're crawling along on our bellies through utter darkness? Because Baumgere wrote that particularly edifying line on a cave survey?"

"There is more, Hayes, if you'll just bear with me."

"Well, I'm glad to hear that, but just for your information, I'm fixing you with a devastatingly skeptical look at this moment."

"I can actually feel it." Kehler paused only to draw breath. "I kept searching and began to take greater risks, going to the rooms when it was not really safe to do so. But by this time I was obsessed. I felt I was so close to such astonishing secrets. I kept digging, just as Baumgere had.

"And then I heard from Skye, a rather cryptic note, for he was concerned that my correspondence might be monitored. I gathered, though, that he had found the Peliers, which was news indeed. I assumed they were in the possession of the church. I spoke to one of the monks who was a resident expert on art and, fortunately, a man without a trace of suspicion in his rather narrow character. To my surprise I learned that there were Peliers in Wooton, stored away with a great deal of other art that is not on daily display.

"I managed to get access to these storage rooms as well, and was more than surprised by what I found, for there, carefully covered and leaning against a wall in a stack of other art, I found one of the Peliers that Skye described, and two other paintings as well."

"But if Skye had it, how could it have been found in Wooton as well?"

"An interesting question. I assume one or the other is a copy. Be that as it may, I found the painting of the crypt that you saw above Castlebough, the same painting that was owned by Baumgere, and a second painting of a man in priestly robes standing in a grape arbor. But his hair was too long, and he held a book that at first I thought was scripture, but upon closer examination turned out to be a book of the arcane, for it had upon it strange symbols and writing that I could not read—a book of the arts.

"Flames, Kehler! Pelier knew that Teller's people hid within the church?!" Hayes exclaimed increduously.

"I don't think you can say that he knew, but he had a vision that this was so. Perhaps he predicted it. Either way the church was forewarned, for Pelier lived before the discovery of the Tellerites within the church. The third painting was even more obscure. . . . It shows a gate pushed open, leading into what might be a courtyard or perhaps a garden. Inside stands a man, smiling oddly, almost gloating, and like the figure in the other painting, he holds a book inscribed with arcane symbols and a strange script. He also holds a leafed stem bearing a pair of small white blossoms. The background is difficult to discern, but the odd thing about this painting is that the man bears an uncanny resemblance to Erasmus."

"You aren't serious?! Erasmus Flattery?"

"None other."

"Martyr's balls, Kehler! Erasmus? Does the church know this? Do they realize it is Erasmus?"

"I would think they must, now. Deacon Rose will not have missed that when he visited Erasmus, and I am almost certain he will have known of the painting."

"But what does it mean?" Hayes asked, still trying to grasp the idea that someone had painted his friend, Erasmus, hundreds of years before he was born!

"I am not sure. As I said, the figure bears a striking resemblance to Erasmus—too near for it to be coincidence, I'm sure. I think it means that Erasmus knows more of the mages than he claims, or at least so I would surmise. So you see, it began with Baumgere being called to Compton Heath to listen to the Stranger's peculiar tongue. I don't know how he came across the Pelier that showed the stranger crossing the bridge, but he did, and from there a growing interest in the work of the artist would explain how he came across the Pelier that showed the crypt in Castlebough—and then the last painting that shows Erasmus."

"But that can have meant nothing to him. Erasmus was not even born when Baumgere was alive."

"No, that's true, but there is writing on the book that Erasmus held, and I haven't even the slightest idea of what it might mean. But then we're forgetting something. . . . We don't know that Baumgere knew anything about this last Pelier."

"But this still does not explain why we are here. What is it we hope to find?"

Kehler did not answer for a long moment, and Hayes was about to repeat his question when his friend finally spoke. "We are here because Baumgere searched for something in this cave. Something that had some connection to Teller and the remains of his society that was destroyed by the church. If you ask me to theorize, I will tell you this. I think the crypt Baumgere uncovered might have been the burying place of Teller himself, laid to rest by his followers, who then concealed the place. I think the painting of Erasmus indicates hidden knowledge—that is what Baumgere was looking for. Why he believed it to be here is not clear, but you must remember that Baumgere was a very accomplished scholar. He would not have been searching here if he did not have reason. I think he was seeking knowledge of the arts—knowledge that was hidden long ago, by the followers of Teller."

"But why was Erasmus the subject of a painting? What has he to do with this?"

Hayes could hear Kehler shake his head. "I don't know, Hayes. I don't know. Unless Erasmus was meant to find this knowledge . . . and somehow it has fallen to us. Or perhaps it meant that Erasmus would be the guardian of the arts, in some way. I can't say. All I know is that Baumgere believed what he sought was here."

They fell silent in the darkness. From somewhere Hayes could hear the slow drip of water punctuating the silence. Hayes' mind was racing to take in the story—a terribly incomplete story. What was Kehler keeping back? Something, Hayes was sure. Kehler would hardly have made such an expedition because of an obscure line of poetry scribbled on a survey. He was too thorough a scholar for that.

"It seems very slim evidence," Hayes said. "Hardly enough to bring us down into this particular netherworld. What is it you're not telling me?"

The silence was protracted this time.

"There was another letter," Kehler admitted with such reticence that Hayes suddenly felt apprehensive. The distant sound of water measured Kehler's reluctance.

"Yes . . ." Hayes softly prompted.

He heard his friend shift in the darkness, his clothing rasping against hard stone. "Atreche, the priest who refused Baumgere absolution, wrote a last missive to the church. Baumgere had been searching the cave, looking for what, the priest did not know, but he had employed two young orphans in this endeavor—brothers ten and twelve years. Beyond the section of the cave known as the Fairy Galleries . . ." Kehler stopped and drew a long breath, "one of these boys met a very untimely end." He paused again. "The letter did not say how. The brothers were not from Castlebough, and so the boy was never missed. Baumgere kept it secret, somehow." Kehler cleared his throat, trying to force the emotion from his voice. "The priest who refused Baumgere absolution, killed himself not far from one of the lower entrances to the cave, after performing last rites, it would seem."

"For the dead child."

"That is what I think."

"But why did he self-murder?" Hayes could hear Kehler's breathing in the darkness, short breaths. This was not a subject he liked to speak of.

"It is difficult to say, though he was responsible for putting the two boys into Baumgere's care. It would seem likely that he felt culpable. Perhaps he knew that Baumgere planned to use the boys in a dangerous endeavor."

"And this is where we are going, beyond the Fairy Galleries?"

"Yes."

"I can see why you didn't want to tell me this before. Why did Baumgere seek this knowledge?"

"The seeking after knowledge is, as you know, simply in man's nature—some men far more than others. But if there was some reason beyond that, it might be found in the story of Baumgere's hero—Tomas. He sought truth, and though he paid dearly for it, he also saw things no other had seen, and lived far beyond the years of men. That is enough reason to seek the knowledge of Teller."

"And this knowledge is guarded by the ghost of a dead boy?"

Kehler did not answer.

"Sacrificed for what gain, I wonder?"

No response from the darkness, only the slow drip, drip of water, measuring the passing years in this sunless world.

## ᔐ Nineteen

The countess was not sure what had roused her. A sound? Had someone been whispering her name over and over? Almost a chant.

"A dream," she told herself. Even so, she got out of bed, agitated. It had seemed so real. Elauralelauralel. . . . She pulled a robe over her sleeping gown and went out into the hallway. Had Marianne called her? Perhaps called out in her sleep? She went to the door of her companion's sleeping chamber but decided that the voice had not been Marianne's and passed by.

Certainly it had not come from this floor. She went down the stairs and into the entryway, where she stood completely bemused, not quite sure what she was doing there.

"I am still half asleep," she muttered.

"*Lady Chilton?*"

This time there was no mistake. Someone had whispered her name. The handle of the door rattled.

*It is Skye*, she thought, and quickly drew the bolt, throwing open the door. On the threshold stood a small, round man, bowing awkwardly, his manner so sincere and so inept that she had to smile.

"He awaits you, m'lady," the man said, keeping his voice low. "You mustn't keep him waiting longer."

"Who? Who awaits me?" she said, still utterly confused, though, strangely, she did not feel frightened. "Skye?"

The little man bobbed his head, smiling encouragingly. He gestured behind, and she realized a carriage stood in the darkened street.

"But I am not even dressed."

"It does not matter. You must come as you are. Quickly," the man said. He extended a hand and she felt herself reach out and take it.

"But who are you?" she said, allowing herself to be lead down the few stairs.

"Walky, m'lady," he said, handing her up into the carriage. "There is a goose down for your comfort, m'lady. We've not far to go."

I'm dreaming, the countess realized and felt some relief wash through her. She almost laughed.

"Wake up," she said aloud, but still she remained in the carriage, moving through the streets of Castlebough. And it was cold! She reached over and pulled the goose down close around her. *I do hope I wake soon*, she thought. *This is most unsettling.* But then, if it was a dream in which she went to meet Skye, perhaps she should not try to wake, but keep this fantasy assignation.

Up they went through the town, the team laboring to pull the great carriage. It was a large coach she realized; large and quite old-fashioned. She could not remember Skye owning such a carriage.

*It does not matter*, she told herself, *it is a dream.* Certainly she felt as bemused as she did when dreaming. Nothing seemed quite real—not the little man who had come to her door, or the too-large coach, or even the moonlight which appeared too fair and bright.

Her thoughts seemed to drift, but when she pulled herself back to consciousness she still rode in the back of the carriage. Shaking her head did not clear it.

*Should I not be frightened?* Certainly she would be if she were awake, so that proved it was a dream. *I will shut my eyes and wake up in my bed*, she decided, and did exactly that, except that when she woke, she found the same small man leaning in the open door of the coach, shaking her gently.

"M'lady? We've arrived. Let me assist you." He handed her down onto the cobbles. They were beneath the roof of a large coach entrance, though the door lamps were not lit.

"He awaits you inside, m'lady, if you please."

"Who?"

"I thought you knew."

"Skye."

"Well, come along, and you will see."

"But who are you?"

"Walky, m'lady."

They went into the darkened house where, to her relief, a candle burned in a niche. Walky took it up and led her on. Down a wide hallway with old suits of armor standing guard, and weapons mounted on the walls. Martyrs and gargoyles were carved into the capitals of responds and looked down at her passing, alternately benevolent and ghoulish.

A dream, the countess told herself. Only a dream.

They passed through two massive doors into a rotunda.

"Here you are, m'lady. Wait but a moment."

And he was gone, taking the candle with him. Yet there was light. She looked up and realized she stood beneath a dome of stained glass. Through the clear panes, she could see stars and moonlight, which fell in a broken pattern on the stone floor around her, like weak sunlight falling through the forest.

Columns stood in a circle, like the great boles of trees supporting the canopy of the forest above. A dozen feet behind, lay a dark wall.

The countess waited in the center of this room, where the light was brightest and where she could see if anyone or anything approached.

Silence. Only the sound of her own breathing, her heart.

*Awake*, she willed herself. *I am becoming frightened. Awake!*

And then she heard the noise of someone moving, clothing rustling, but no footsteps.

"Who's there?" she snapped.

"Who indeed," came a voice from behind.

She whirled around and there, just near a pillar and slightly back of it, she saw a dark form.

"Who are you?"

"A question many have asked, my dear, though few have had an answer." The voice was musical, soft; not malevolent but nor was it kind. Mocking—it seemed to be mocking her.

"What . . . what do you want of me?"

"That is why you are here—so that I might decide." He came forth from the shadow, but still she could not make him out—as though the shadow moved with him. He began to walk slowly about her. "No, stay as you are," he commanded as she moved to keep him in view.

The countess was not sure why, but she did as she was bid. Very slowly he went, as though she were a mare to be bought—and bred, she feared.

"It is dark," she said. "I cannot see you."

"But I can see you. Perfectly."

Again she shook her head, trying to clear it, afraid that this fog that clouded her senses would bring her to grief. *I am in danger*, she told herself, but she did not feel it.

"Who are you, sir?"

"You don't know?"

"No. My mind is . . . it is in a fog."

"And would you have it cleared? You may be happier as you are."

"I would like my mind to be clear." She felt a stab of fear, and she drew a great breath, her senses returned. *"Eldrich . . . !"* she said.

"*Lord* Eldrich, Lady Chilton. You should respect your elders, at least."

She began to turn and shrink away from him, and suddenly she no longer controlled her muscles, but stood firmly rooted.

"Are you happy now?" he asked, his voice still gently mocking.

"I am far from happy. You abduct me from my home, and bring me here, wearing my night clothes. What gentleman would act so?"

"No gentleman, I would imagine. But I am a mage, the last of my kind, Lady Chilton. And you . . . well, you are not what men think."

"And what is that supposed to mean?"

"Perhaps you are not aware that it is the prerogative of a mage to speak in hints and riddles. Have you not read the histories?"

She did not answer, but stood, fighting to have command of her own muscles.

"Do not struggle, Lady Chilton. It is futile. Remove your robe," he said.

"I will not!"

He laughed. "What is it they always say in novels? 'I like a woman with spirit'?"

The countess realized that she was obeying his command. Her robe slipped to the floor from stiff fingers. Eldrich continued his circuit—he was beside her now.

He laughed again, as though genuinely amused. "I will tell you, Lady Chilton, you are the most amazing creation I have ever witnessed. I tip my hat to those responsible."

"My parents would be so pleased," she said, trying to control the anger she felt.

He laughed again. "Would they, indeed?" and this seemed to amuse him. "I am sorely tempted, Lady Chilton, even with what I know and as old as I am."

"Tempted by what?" she said, not liking the sound of this.

"By you, my dear."

"I will be the least cooperative partner you will ever have known."

"Oh, hardly," he said, clearly amused by this as well. "Some of the women I have known—" He took another step and came back into her line of vision, but still he was in shadow. "In days past people had more respect for mages." He almost sang a string of syllables, and perhaps moved his hand, and suddenly the countess felt such a wave of desire that her knees almost gave way beneath her. Not just a wave of desire, but desire for this man. It was an ache beyond enduring . . . and then, just as quickly it was gone.

"The most unwilling partner I've ever known? I don't think so." A hand reached out and moved the hair away from her cheek, pushing it back over her shoulder so that he could see her profile.

"I'm cold," she said quietly.

"Then come and sit by the fire," Eldrich said, and he turned and walked away.

The countess found that she could move again. The thought of running was quickly put aside. Clearly one could not run from a mage. Beyond the pillars a large hearth stood against the wall, and here a fire had burned to embers. As Eldrich came near, it flickered to life again, and then suddenly burst into flame—glorious, hot flames. The countess pulled on her robe and went toward the fire, trying to control her fear. Always best to show no fear—it gave the other person the impression that they were in control.

The mage had taken a seat in a high-backed chair, facing partly away from the fire. Only a cushioned footstool remained. She stood looking at it for a moment, and then remembered that he had said he was no gentleman.

Cold to the bone, she took the seat expected, though not without some anger. *I am almost sitting at his feet*, she thought. *And I'm sure he is enjoying it thoroughly.*

They sat in silence for a long moment. The countess could almost make out his features, but not quite, for he was still in shadow.

"Have you decided what you will do with me?" she asked suddenly, unable to bear his silent brooding on her a moment longer.

"It is not so simple as you might think. What is your purpose? That is what I must discover."

"My purpose? What in the world . . . ? I assure you that whatever my purpose might be, it has nothing to do with you, sir."

The mage did not respond. Silence stretched on until the countess could not stand it. She opened her mouth to speak.

"Be still," the mage said.

She realized that she sat with hands in her lap, like a schoolgirl, and she felt an anger burn up at this man before her.

"It is a great risk," the mage said softly.

"Pardon me?"

Eldrich rose suddenly and walked away from the fire out into the darkness. She could see him silhouetted in the light falling from above, though none of it seemed to reach him. He made no sound as he went. Slowly he paced in a small circle, like a man deep in contemplation, and occasionally he would stop and raise his head. The countess was sure that he looked at her at those moments. And then he began to mutter, words she had never heard, and a cold light moved across the floor in a precise line, following him as he walked.

Suddenly she was standing in the center of the rotunda, up on the balls of her feet, reaching toward the dome. Around her a pattern of lines and curves seemed to glow like the embers of a fire. She watched as they dimmed and died away, her mind so clouded that she could not remember how she got there, or what had happened.

"A work of astonishing craft," a musical voice said.

Suddenly she felt all her muscles relax, and she almost collapsed to the floor. The countess looked for the sound of the voice, and as her arms came about her in a natural gesture of protection, she realized she wore nothing at all.

"I cannot tell if they have underestimated me, or taken my measure exactly," Eldrich said, apparently speaking to himself. "Who in the world did this? Certainly not Medwar. It is the greatest mystery."

"If you have finished misusing me, perhaps I might have my clothes," the countess said bitterly.

"Are you cold?"

She realized that she was not. In fact, she was astonishingly warm. She almost glowed with warmth.

"Have you no concern for my modesty?"

"None. It is a strange vanity, I find."

The countess realized that her gown lay at her feet and she snatched it up. As she slid it over her head, she noticed that Eldrich stood, watching, and she tried to ignore him.

"Mr. Walky?" the mage said, and almost immediately footsteps echoed in the hall.

"Sir?"

"You may return her."

The little man came toward the countess, his manner very deferential, as though he would make up for his master's treatment of her.

The countess took a step and then stopped, turning to find the retreating form of Eldrich. "I do not think my friends will be much impressed with your manners when I tell them of our visit, Lord Eldrich."

The figure stopped. "I rather doubt you will tell them, Lady Chilton. The pleasures of the evening to you." He bowed deeply, and turned away.

"M'lady, you must come with me," the small man said.

"But who are you?"

"Walky, m'lady. Please, I'm to take you home."

"Are you not cold?"

Marianne found the countess seated by the large windows in the library. She was curled up in a chair, watching the morning light find its way into the small garden.

"Cold? No." The countess looked over at her friend and saw great concern on her face.

"You look perfectly awful," Marianne said disapprovingly. "I will tell you, Elaural, Skye is not worth this." She waved a hand at her friend. "Have you not slept at all?"

"It is very odd, Marianne. I woke here, yet I have no memory of coming down at all."

Marianne shook her head, her lips pressed tightly together in concern.

"And I think I had the most unsettling dreams, though I cannot quite recall them." She turned back to the garden for a moment, as though searching into her memory. "No, they are gone, though I have been left with the . . . feelings. And even those I cannot put a name to." She shivered involuntarily.

"You are cold."

"Not at all. Is it cool in here? I do not feel it."

"Perhaps you are coming down with a fever. The only time I recall walking in my sleep I was terribly fevered and delirious."

The countess smiled. "Well, I am neither fevered nor delirious. I feel perfectly hale, in fact." She stretched her arms over her head. "Is this unladylike?" she asked, her mood seeming to change.

"Entirely." Marianne rang for a servant and took a seat near the countess. "Is Skye coming to hear the results of your interview with Mr. Flattery?"

"I would think."

"But what did you learn? You are being a bit secretive about this."

"I learned only that Mr. Flattery agrees with Lord Skye. He thinks the writing on the Pelier is a script and language known to the mages. It also bears some resemblance to the writing on the Ruin of Farrow. He claims to know no more."

"And do you believe him?"

The countess shrugged.

"Now Elaural, I cannot imagine that he would keep anything from you if you exercised your charm on him."

"Then perhaps he really can't read it."

Marianne looked away. "I hope you will not perform such a service for Lord Skye again. I was rather shocked that he would ask it."

"I offered, Marianne."

"Well, he should have refused."

"For a woman who has rejected so many of our social values, I think you are rather old-fashioned occasionally."

Marianne shook her head in denial. "Oh, it is not this thing of gentlemen should or should not do this or that. But to ask you to be duplicitous . . . I will tell you, I thought it rather reprehensible."

"Well, I was not nearly so cunning. I was completely forthcoming with Mr. Flattery. I told him what I wanted of him and even that it was Skye had put me up to it. So you see, there was very little duplicity involved."

Marianne looked at her oddly. "Where is all this going, Elaural?" she said softly.

"Whatever do you mean?" the countess asked, though she was afraid she knew very well what was meant.

## ⌐ Twenty

Captain James looked into his brandy snifter, then back to his cards. "I think I shall have to resign," he said to his companion.

"Resign? And not give me a chance to retrieve my losses? Is that sporting?" Wilkes was a little inebriated, slurring his words noticeably, though he showed very little sign of his state beyond that.

"There is always tomorrow, Wilkes."

"So they say, though I've known men who've proved that wrong, not that they lived to brag about it."

James smiled. "Not an accomplishment that I personally aspire to." He tossed his cards down on the table and pulled out his timepiece. It was almost midnight, not late, really, though these past few years it had begun to seem so.

Wilkes sloshed more brandy into their snifters, and though his hand was not perfectly steady, his concentration was such that he did not spill a drop. "The King's health," he said, raising his glass.

"We've already drunk His Majesty's health twice this night."

"Well then, to our health. Damn the King."

"Ah, there's a toast for you."

Wilkes replaced his glass heavily on the table. "Can you imagine having such a woman pursuing you and choosing to sleep alone?" Wilkes said, shaking his head in disgust. "'Tis not fair."

It was the litany of the evening. Skye had gone off to the house in which he stayed, not even visiting the Countess of Chilton. James wondered if it was possible that the information from the countess' maid was not accurate. Wilkes had applied some of his abundant charm and a handful of coins to the problem and managed to learn much from the countess' servant. Most astonishing of all was that the countess was in love with the Earl of Skye, who seemed hardly aware of her.

James shook his head. *Savants*, he thought. *They live too much in the rarified world of the intellect. Poor bastards.*

"I will relieve Lieutenant Darby tonight," James said. "I cannot sleep."

"Are you sure? 'Tis my watch."

"I'm sure." He stretched. "The excitement of taking all your money will not let me sleep. I must plan what I will do with such a fortune."

"Well, that's all right, then," Wilkes said, pulling a chair over and putting his feet up, clearly ready for leisure. "I'll relieve you at eight bells. You know where to find me if I'm needed. I'll tell you, if I were the earl, you'd know where to find me—in the sleeping chamber of a certain lady, make no mistake." He thought a moment. "How in Farrelle's name can he be considered such a great genius?"

"The laws of motion, the invention of the cannon, various arithmetical discoveries that I don't understand, the alloying of metals, improvements to the telescope. He even invented a better water closet. And that is only a partial list of his accomplishments. Perhaps the earl simply does not fancy the countess. He has certainly been with other women, by all accounts."

"Well, I think he's the greatest fool of a genius who ever lived!" Wilkes pronounced. "And I think this is all a fool's errand we're on. The man is a loyal subject of the King. There is no doubt of it. We should be at sea, James. Not stuck in this fool's town where the rich come with their pissing little complaints. Flames, but I hate this duty."

James shrugged and broke into a grin. "It is for the betterment of your character, Wilkes. And to keep you from trouble while you are landbound." He rose suddenly. "I must be off. Poor Darby will be asleep at the wheel by now. Till eight bells, then." He pulled on his great coat, checking the pocket for his gloves, for it was cool in the hills yet.

Darby was standing in the shadows of a small common across from the house where Skye stayed.

"All's well, sir," the lieutenant reported. "No lights, no one has come or gone. Where's Wilkes? I thought he had the next watch?"

"We've traded." James looked at the house across the street. "There has been a light in that window all evening?"

"Yes, sir, though there is no sign of movement within. A night light, I think."

James nodded. "All right, lieutenant. You're relieved."

"Pleasures of the evening to you, sir."

"And to you, Darby."

James took up his place in the shadow, leaning against the tree. He was mostly screened from the street by shrubbery, but he still worried about being seen. It was a small town, and it would soon get around if anyone realized that Lord Skye's house was being watched. But they could not let a room or even a house that afforded a view of the earl's home, so this was all they could do: stand in the dark and hope not to be seen.

There was little doubt in James' mind that they would eventually arouse suspicions in such a town—where everyone was interested in everyone else's business, for there was hardly another form of amusement.

James rocked from foot to foot, wishing that he could sit down at least. He would begin to pace soon; he could not help it. He was as impatient with this duty as Wilkes, though he did more to hide it. Unlike his friend, he had more information about what had gone on. Better Wilkes did not know. Sailors, even officers, were a superstitious lot, and any mention of mages would have driven Wilkes to the bottle with greater frequency than he visited it now. No, better to keep quiet about the admiral's real concerns.

*Let this have nothing to do with Eldrich*, James prayed silently, *or the arts in any way.*

He stared up at the windows and sighed unintentionally.

The truth was that he would have preferred to be as innocent of the truth as Wilkes and Darby. Unfortunately he had been one of the first to speak with Abel Ransom and the harlot. The worst of it was he believed they were telling the truth, and so did the Sea Lord.

Something damned odd was going on, that was certain.

"And what does the great Skye do that so interests you?" a woman's voice came from behind.

James whirled around. "What's that?" He could just make out the form of a woman standing in the shadows.

"I asked what the great Skye does that so interests you?" she said again, a little laughter in her voice. She did not seem the least uncomfortable standing here in the darkness with a strange man.

"I am merely taking the air, ma'am."

"As was your friend before you, and the gentleman before that. But that was you, wasn't it? Let me see, that would mean that Wilkes is in his cups and you have replaced him. Very dedicated of you, Captain James. The Admiralty will no doubt be grateful."

"I seem to be at a disadvantage, ma'am, for you know my name and business, but I do not know yours."

She took a step in his direction, enabling him to just make out her long coat and hat. She was dressed as a lady and certainly spoke like one.

"It is I who am at a disadvantage, sir, alone with you in the darkness. I'm sure if I cried out, no one would hear."

James did not quite know what to answer and she laughed at his awkwardness.

"You may call me Miss Fielding, Captain James, if you wish."

"Miss Fielding. What is it you want here?"

"Well, that is difficult to explain. I suppose the truth is that I wish answers to a few simple questions, but then you might take that wrongly."

He thought he heard her whisper, and in the shadow she seemed to be moving her hands, as though she wound a ball of invisible yarn.

"But I do think it would be a good idea if you were to come away from that tree. You're rather too close to the road and can be seen."

"I'm standing in complete darkness. No one can see me, I assure you."

"Well, that is not entirely true. I can see you perfectly. But indulge me, come back into the park a little farther. I give you my word that I will not harm you."

James heard himself snort. It was an old trick; send a woman to lure a man back into an alley and then—but this woman was a lady, not the usual sort to indulge in such behavior. What in the world was she doing here? Watching Skye as he was? The thought that she might be a servant of Eldrich occurred to him, and he froze in place. No, impossible, she was a barely more than a girl. Some admirer of Skye was more likely.

"I am happy here, I think," he said.

This answer did not please her, and she fell silent, perhaps wondering what she could say to convince him. "Were you among the gentlemen who invaded the rooms of Samual Hayes in Paradise Street?"

"I don't know to what you refer," he said evenly, deciding that this situation was not at all to his liking. She could not be so at ease and be alone. He glanced quickly back to the street, but it remained empty.

"In fact, you do. It is very difficult to lie to me, Captain James." She paused and he thought he heard her sigh. "What is said of the men who were surprised there?"

"What is it you want of me, Miss?" James countered.

He could almost feel her gaze on him in the darkness, as though she contemplated him. "I am not actually sure. You see, I fear you have information that might endanger me and what I do. I would rather that did not happen. What to do with you is what concerns me now."

She stepped forward suddenly, into the moonlight, and James saw that she was young, but faded, somehow, as though she had survived trials that had aged her terribly. He felt an unexpected wave of pity for her.

"Come away from the street, please. I do not have large, pugilistic men hidden in the shrubbery. If anything, I should be afraid of you. But I am willing to trust you if you will do the same."

"What is Skye to you?" James asked.

She sighed, looking off down the street and then toward the house. "It is a tale too long to be told now. Let me say that my purpose is not in conflict with your own. Please." She reached out and took his arm.

"I'm afraid, Miss Fielding, that I cannot cooperate." He took hold of her wrist. "But you will answer my questions, or you will find yourself in a situation not to your liking. What is Skye to you, and why do you care about the men found in Paradise Street?"

James heard her mumble something and reach out toward his face with her free hand. His vision clouded oddly, and he wavered. The park went suddenly dark and he felt himself falling. Someone caught him, someone soft who smelled of perfume.

"It was necessary," the woman said. "As you know there are limits to what I can do in a given situation."

James felt a cool hand on his forehead.

"I think it was a mistake," a masculine voice said. "We should do nothing more that might draw any attention. We have taken too many chances as it is. Far too many."

There were several people in the room, James thought. Mostly men. He could smell tobacco from their clothing and wine on their breath.

"What will we do with him now?" It was a third voice, another man. This one spoke very slowly.

There was no answer immediately, and James did not like the sound of that.

"Captain James?" the woman who had called herself Miss Fielding said. "You are conscious—it is obvious."

"I cannot see."

"You are in a darkened room, Captain James, but you are unharmed. There are four of you watching Skye, is that correct?"

"Yes," he answered though he had not meant to. Certainly this kind woman meant him no harm. There was no reason to keep secrets from her.

"Do you know why you have been assigned this duty? Was it the Sea Lord sent you?"

"Yes, Sir Joseph. He thinks that someone practices the arts openly once again."

A protracted silence. James heard the scraping of feet on wood as people shifted slightly.

"And who does he think this practitioner of the arts might be?"

"Eldrich," James said. "Though he has not ruled out . . . other possibilities."

"Meaning?"

"There is another mage of whom nothing is known."

Someone cursed under their breath.

"Who has set out to ruin Skye?" the old man asked. "Certainly Brookes did not do this on his own."

"Moncrief," James said without hesitation. "Moncrief hates Skye."

"And your only reason for being here is to watch Lord Skye?"

"No. . . . We are on the lookout for others."

"Who? Speak up, man."

"Two young men named Kehler and Hayes . . . and Erasmus Flattery."

No sound again. Someone cleared his throat.

"What has led Sir Joseph to believe the arts are involved?" Miss Fielding asked.

"I—I was not present, but it is said that the officers who searched for Samual Hayes surprised some others there before them, and these men leaped from the window, apparently coming to no harm."

"And who were these people?" the one with the old voice asked.

"No one knows."

"Well, we have that to be thankful for," a younger man said.

"Is there anything else that has made the Sea Lord suspicious?"

"A sailor and his girl saw two gentlemen bring a woman to the harbor. Without coercion or a word of protest she leaped into the water and drowned."

James heard the sounds of people shifting again. It occurred to him that he should not be answering questions as he was, but they seemed so kind, so trustworthy.

"It is worse than I'd hoped," the old man said, his voice trembling with fear or anger. "Far worse. Anthing we do now to disguise our involvement can only make matters worse."

James heard the woman draw in a sharp breath. Fear. He could sense fear in this room.

"What do we do with this one?"

"He is a danger to us," the old man said, his voice slow and devoid of warmth.

"It's too late to do anything about that. This goes up to the Sea Lord and Moncrief. Too late to put a stop to it with the likes of Captain James. No, send him back to his duty, that is all we can do."

"We could put him to work for us, at least," Miss Fielding said.

"No," the old man said. "It is out of the question. Eldrich would see our marks upon him in an instant. Even this is too much. If Eldrich finds him, he will know immediately."

"It is too late to worry about that. We must trust the vision now. But I was not intending to use those arts upon him. No, leave the good captain to me. Better he watches these others than we do it ourselves." She touched him; he was certain it must be her. A light hand on his head. "We are gathering here— all the players—and each will have a part. That is what our visions have taught us. Everyone will have a purpose. Perhaps even this poor sailor. Perhaps even these two boys who follow Skye so blindly."

## ⌀ Twenty-One

Kehler climbed slowly down the drop, trying to stay clear of the spray from the falls, while Hayes leaned out as far as he dared, holding the lantern to try to give his companion light.

"It is not so difficult—if one could but see," Kehler called up.

They were in a large passage, almost round and fifty feet in diameter, that sloped down noticeably. Occasionally the floor almost leveled and then dropped a few feet, though never more than seven or eight and usually less.

Hayes leaned out a little farther, holding the lantern in a rapidly tiring arm, and fought to ignore the muscles' complaints. He was stiff and sore as he could not remember being in years. His knees were tender from the long crawl, and his arms and shoulders ached so badly that it hurt terribly to carry his pack. Yet he did not really seem to mind. The cave was so incredible, so unlike anything he had ever seen, that he barely complained, and when he did, it was with a bit of laughter.

Suddenly there was a scraping of boots on stone, and Kehler shot down, landing and rolling backward.

"Are you hurt?" Hayes asked as his friend came to rest on his back.

"Oh, hardly," Kehler said with apparent disgust. "Ass over tea kettle, I think that particular drill is called. Very gymnastic, didn't you think?" He rolled over and pushed himself up stiffly, pulling off his pack and letting it fall to the rock. Bending over the stream of running water, he washed his now red face.

"Send me down the lantern," he said, "and your pack as well."

A moment later Hayes was standing beside his companion and they both hoisted their packs.

"I don't think it can be far now, though I am not so sure that the distances on our survey are really in proportion to reality. I think these passages were measured by men with vastly differing strides, that is what I believe."

They set off again, climbing down beside the falling stream, which followed its own meandering channel more or less in the center of the passage. Here and there they were forced to cross over to find dry rock on which to walk, and invariably this led to one of them soaking a boot yet again. They hardly cared now. Their clothing was soiled and torn, the leather of their boots scuffed and soaked through, and they were both in need of a bath, but it did not matter. It would not have been an adventure otherwise.

"One cannot adventure from one's easy chair," Kehler had said, and they had laughed, saying of the less difficult sections, "a veritable easy chair, that."

"I think the passage is opening a bit," Hayes offered, and in a few minutes he was proven right.

Suddenly they stepped out into a vast chamber, larger than any they had so far seen. Before them lay the dark waters of a lake. The lantern lit the far reaches of the cavern only dimly, but even so Hayes could see great stalactites and columns and formations called curtains, as well as moonstone, the flowing white substance from which the decorations in whitestone caves were formed.

The hollow sound of water tumbling into the lake seemed unnaturally loud and clear. Even though Hayes knew they were far from being the first to discover this place, it still seemed a deep wonder, hidden away, here, far beneath the surface of the world. *A lake*, at once familiar and strangely alien.

"The chamber of the mirror," Kehler said, taking up the lantern and going to the water's edge. Hayes joined him, and they both stared down at their murky reflections in the dark water. Two unkempt young men, their faces ruddy from exertion and adventure.

"I can't believe you forgot the shaving kit," Kehler said.

"Or the servants to tend our clothes and groom our wigs. Yours looks a bit shabby, I will tell you."

As if to reinforce the strangeness of the place, Hayes realized there was a bright blue skiff perched awkwardly on the rocks thirty feet away.

"Where in the world did that come from?"

Kehler laughed. "I thought that might surprise you. I'm relieved it's here. Some enterprising individuals brought it down here in pieces and built it in place, if you can believe it. In fact, there are two of them, one at the lake's far end, or so I hope. It is understood that we will take this to the far end, then use the other to return it, thus always keeping a skiff at either extreme of the lake."

Hayes lowered his pack to the cavern's floor and sat down on it, having realized that it was much softer than even the most malleable rock. "Do we go by boat, then?"

"Only a short way, and then I'm afraid it's back to our poor battered limbs— all four of them in places."

"Well, I thought it had become a bit easy. Don't want to grow soft, do we?"

They sat staring at the scene in wonder, pointing out the formations that caught their eye. Hayes trimmed the lantern wick and turned it up as high as he could, casting light out over the lake, though it did not reach the far shore.

"Pelier didn't paint this, I take it?" Hayes asked, and received a shake of the head in reply. He had begun to wonder if Kehler was right in his assertion that what lay ahead to be discovered would bring them fame and, even better, fortune. It seemed entirely possible that he was merely helping Kehler pursue his obsession, though he had to admit that so far it had been an experience well worth the effort, although he shuddered when he thought of the claustrophobia of the crawl. Occasionally he felt some anxiety when he remembered that he would have to pass back through that terrible passage.

"Do you still feel as confident of finding what we seek, now that you've seen the complexity of this cavern?"

Kehler nodded his head. "We must find it," he said quietly. Then he stood up quickly. "Well, help me with this skiff, and we will see if it still floats. I can't imagine who would leave it high and dry like this. The seams are bound to be open, at least a little."

They shifted the tiny craft down the rocks, careful not to scrape or bang it, for the boat was so lightly constructed that it would not stand misuse.

"I hardly think a boat this small will float the two of us," Hayes said, "it is barely as long as I am tall."

They loaded their two packs in, released the oars from their ties and stepped gingerly aboard. When they took their places on the seats at either end, the boat sank in the water until only a few inches of freeboard remained.

Hayes shipped the oars, careful not to make any movement that would unbalance them. "I hope a wind doesn't come up. Our ship will hardly stand any kind of sea."

He dug the oars into the still water and turned the cockleshell boat out into the subterranean lake. With Kehler in the bow holding the lantern aloft, and occasionally bailing, Hayes rowed fisherman style, facing the direction they traveled, and gazed in wonder at the cave.

The decorations were astounding and some of the columns and curtains were on a grand scale—thirty and forty feet tall from floor to ceiling—rising up like fantastic castles of ice. The dome of the chamber itself was lost in the darkness, though from the slope of the ceiling at the edges Hayes guessed it to be sixty feet.

Kehler waved the lantern at one of the largest columns. "Imagine how long it took for that to form. Thousands of years, certainly. Long before men came to Farrland, this great column might have already spanned from floor to ceiling."

"How old does that make the cavern, I wonder?" Hayes answered. They rowed on, their eyes feasting on the wonders of the chamber of the mirror: moonstone, like glacial milk, flowing over the surface of the parent rock, almost translucent, glistening in the lamplight.

"Surely it was worth all of our efforts and the ruin of our clothing to see this," Kehler said.

"Yes. I wish I were an artist, for I haven't the skill with words to describe it."

A small stream appeared from a side passage and added its water to the mirror. The lake opened up so that, for a time, they could see no shoreline, and small headlands began to appear, like the great capes of the world seen from afar. When the shore appeared again, they noted several passages of differing sizes in the walls, and, in one place, a ribbon of water fell from an opening in the ceiling. They rowed once around this in astonishment before continuing on.

Hayes could not believe the length of the chamber, but when they came to what they thought was the end, it proved to be only a narrowing. From either side a small peninsula jutted out, creating a pass no more than a dozen feet in breadth. On one headland a rock incisor was topped by a white column perhaps three feet across its base with a fine tracery of flowing drape running down from the sloping ceiling.

"Magical," Kehler whispered. "I feel like we have entered the kingdom of men who dwell beneath the mountain. A race that have chiseled and inscribed and sculpted for millennia, though now they are gone and their dark world lies abandoned."

They quickly crossed this final arm of the lake, which was more like a small bay, and found the second boat pulled up onto a shelf of stone. The stream disappeared into a passage here, and the sound of water falling could be heard.

They managed to land without tipping and Kehler immediately began dragging the boat up behind them.

"We have to return that to the lake's end," Hayes reminded him.

His friend stood up, his manner suddenly serious. "I have been thinking that we should leave this skiff here. Do you remember that Clarendon said Demon Rose was asking after me in Castlebough? And the guide who brought us here will certainly not keep our presence a secret, especially if he is offered a few coins. I don't want to suddenly find we have company on our quest."

"But is that safe?" Hayes asked, looking back out over the dark water. "What if we are injured or lost?"

"With a little luck we'll be back before anyone becomes concerned. The Farrellites are not pleased with me, Samual. I can't imagine that Rose is going to come down here after me, but the church has long been skilled at using others. I don't think that it is a great risk to keep this boat here for the next day or two. The cave is not visited often until the lower entrances open in summer when the water level is lower. Anyone else venturing in here now would be after us, I fear."

Hayes nodded. He was tempted to admit that he had left a note for Erasmus, but decided against it. Kehler would likely be furious, afraid somehow that Erasmus would reveal this knowledge to Deacon Rose, though clearly that was unlikely.

"Let's eat a bite and then go on. At our present speed we might be at our destination yet this day. Is it past noon?"

Hayes found his watch. "Good guess. Twenty past."

They made a silent dinner on the shore of the lake. Hayes felt a little guilty that he had betrayed Kehler's trust by telling Erasmus, and at the same time he was annoyed that Kehler would not return one boat to the far shore. If some misfortune befell them, reaching them would be difficult in the extreme.

After their silent meal they took to the new passage, leaving the chamber of the mirror with great regret, and followed the underground river that drained the lake. The flow of water was strong here and had cut a deep channel in a soft vein of rock. The going was comparatively easy, and they made good time, saving their breath for their efforts.

Hayes wondered what Kehler was thinking. Was his mind completely focused on their goal, or was he really worried about the priest who apparently pursued him? Hayes could not shake the feeling that Kehler had not yet told him the whole story, as though afraid that he might not continue if he knew the truth. And Hayes was not sure that his friend wasn't right in this. What were they searching for? Kehler's belief that it was lost knowledge was, at best, a guess.

Whenever Hayes asked himself this question, he thought of a small boy, trapped in a tiny hole in the stone, impossibly far from any comfort—and that small boy was somehow Hayes.

The passage proceeded to drop and twist its way down, like a bowel, Hayes thought. After an hour the sound of falling water grew to the point where they would have needed to shout to be heard, had they talked.

Finally they were forced to wade into the rushing water, though the stream had widened and was barely two feet deep. They moved slowly, placing their feet with care, and finally came to the lip of a falls. A small dike of rocks, like jagged teeth, raked the water as it plunged out of sight. Warily they moved to the very edge, holding the lantern out so that they could look down. A chaos of white water disappeared down a large well, twenty feet across, but they could see no bottom. Hayes felt the pull of the water's movement, drawn mysteriously to the darkness.

*The way, by darkness, into light.*

"How far is it?" Hayes asked, stepping back, a little breathless.

"To the bottom? I forget what I read. A hundred and fifty feet? Something on that order. Farther than one would want to fall, that is certain."

"But where do we go?"

Kehler pointed out over the falls, and up the right-hand wall Hayes could see only a dark shadow on the stone.

"That is a passage?"

Kehler nodded.

"But how do we get there?" Hayes looked down again, a sudden feeling that the motion of frigid, coursing water flowed through him.

"It is not so hard as it looks, apparently. There is supposed to be good footing, and as they always say, the trick is not to look down. We will use the rope. I will try it first, if you like."

"No," Hayes said quickly. "You have gone first too often. I will take my turn." He felt a chill run through him as he spoke, a sudden weakening of both his will and his limbs. He glanced down again, wondering how many men had stared into their own, freshly-dug grave.

Kehler balanced the lantern on a high shelf, so that both of his hands were free, and then tied the rope around his waist, making a loop of one end and throwing this over a tooth of rock at the fall's edge. The other end was made fast around Hayes' middle, then Kehler fed the rope out slowly, snugging it around his own waist in the way of mountaineers.

"Have you climbed at all?" Kehler asked.

Hayes shook his head, looking out at the route he must take.

"Nor have I, but I have a friend who is something of a fanatic about it. He told me that the trick is to keep your body away from the rock wall. You must maintain your weight over your feet. Do you see what I mean? If you lean into the cliff like this, you force your feet out and they can slip much more easily. Are you ready?"

"No. But I shall not become so with time. Weight out over my feet," he repeated, and went to the edge. His leather soles would be impossibly slippery, he realized, and elected to remove his boots and go on in stocking feet.

Balancing on the corner of the falls, Hayes looked down for the briefest second and felt his balance waver. Automatically he grabbed the wall for balance.

"Flames," he heard himself whisper.

"Easy on, Hayes," Kehler said.

Gathering his resolve, Hayes stared out at the rock and tried to pick his route to the opening. He stepped out onto a foothold and found to his relief that it was quite large and the wall was not as vertical as it looked.

The sound of the falls changed as he moved, and he could hear the frightening cascade falling into the dark well beneath him. He tried not to think about what a slip would mean. Another step onto a smaller foothold.

"Keep your weight out, Hayes," Kehler reminded him, and he tried to comply, though he felt that he was leaning out dangerously far and feared the weight of his pack might suddenly drag him back.

He searched for another place to move his foot, and for hand-holds, reaching out and testing the rock, which all seemed sound, if a bit too smooth. He took a larger step this time, up and out to his left, pulling on a good handhold. And there he stood, looking for a way to go on. A small platform a foot or so square was not far off, but he certainly could not reach it in one step, and perhaps not even in two.

"Can you see the route?" Kehler called over the sound of the falls.

Hayes shook his head. "There are no handholds and the foot-holds seem too small—barely toeholds, in fact." He felt panic begin to grow in him, and he glanced back. He seemed already to have come impossibly far. The safety of the lip of the falls seemed too far away; he was not sure he could get back without falling.

Hayes felt his leg begin to quiver, perched as he was on such a tiny hold, the muscles rigid. Suddenly the rock all looked impossibly smooth and slippery. The sound of tumbling water seemed to grow louder, reverberating inside his chest, as though making him part of it.

"Hayes? Either come back or go on, but don't stand there! Your leg is trembling, I can see it. Come back and let me try."

"Martyr's blood, there is nowhere for me to go." Hayes looked back but could not see the footholds he had used to get this far. His fingers began to cramp where he clung to the stone, and he realized that in a few seconds he would fall.

"Take hold of yourself, Hayes!" Kehler said, his voice rising.

Hayes saw Kehler sit down in the rushing water and brace his feet against the rock, readying himself for the coming fall.

*I cannot fall*, Hayes said to himself. *If I fall, even if the rope holds me, I don't know how I will ever get back up again. I must not fall!*

He looked desperately at the small platform that seemed so far away. There were two impossibly small toeholds between where he was and the comparative safety of the platform, but he could see nowhere for his hands. If he could only land on the toeholds lightly and pass on, perhaps. . . .

"Give me slack, Kehler," he called out, and felt the rope release its pressure.

Realizing that his shaking legs were about to fail, Hayes focused on the possible holds, forced his legs to be still, and then stepped quickly onward. One toehold came under foot, and he brought his other foot onto it, feeling the tiny ledge with only three of his toes. His hands found no purchase and he could use them only for balance. He moved again, setting his left foot on a hold equally precarious. He brought his other foot inside this, and passed on, almost leaping onto the platform.

It seemed a dance floor when he stood there. Impossibly large. He felt he could perform a jig there without fear of falling.

"Well done!" Kehler called out.

Hayes stood, catching his breath, nodding to acknowledge his friend's support, unable to speak.

He glanced up at the opening. Ten feet to go, but the way looked comparatively easy—almost a staircase.

"Are you all right there?" Kehler called.

"Yes. . . . Yes. I'll go on in a moment. The way looks easier now." He felt himself smile with relief.

A moment of rest and relative security helped him immeasurably, and his confidence was somewhat restored by what he had done. He caught his breath, and then examined the rock before him.

"I'm ready to go on," Hayes alerted his friend, and then went deliberately out, picking his footing carefully, feeling the cold rock beneath his stocking feet. Three or four minutes of intense concentration, thinking of nothing but where to place his feet and hands, and how to move, and he pulled himself up into the passageway. The light was not good here, but he felt around and found a place for his pack. Kehler sent the lantern over, and to his dismay discovered that he now had very poor light for climbing.

After a moment of standing and shivering, he found a candle in his pack which he could not light with a flint, and so the lantern was sent out over the falls again, swinging on the rope. Kehler lit his candle and sent the lantern back yet again. They managed to bash it into the rock as it came near to Hayes, but miraculously the glass chimney did not shatter.

Holding the stub of the candle in his mouth so that the flame wavered six inches before his face, Kehler stepped out onto the stone.

Hayes had tied himself to a horn of rock and kept a tight rein on his companion, but even so he worried. He was not sure that he could hold Kehler should he fall.

Fortunately, Kehler seemed more confident than Hayes had, no doubt helped by seeing that the climb could be done, but he was shivering visibly from having sat down in the icy waters. Even at a distance Hayes could see his hands shaking as he tried to grip the rock.

"Keep the rope snug," Kehler called out suddenly, his words distorted by the candle in his mouth. He had come to the place where Hayes had nearly lost his nerve altogether. Here he paused, too, though perhaps more to draw on his physical reserves. He shifted his weight to one side and accidently stubbed out the candle against the rock.

"Martyr's blood!" he swore around the candle, then spit it out, letting it fall into the void below.

"Can you see at all?" Hayes called out over the chaos of the waterfall.

"Barely, and if I stand here and let my eyes adjust to the darkness, I shall certainly fall. I'm trembling like a leaf in the wind as it is." A silence ensued in which Hayes could feel the fear growing.

"Hayes? Can you tie the rope off? I can't go on without light. You'll have to tie the rope off and hold the light out so I can see. Can you do that?"

Hayes did not like the sound of that. If he tied the rope as it was, Kehler would create slack when he moved on. If he did fall, he would hit the end of this slack and almost certainly part the rope.

"I'm not so sure this is a good idea, Kehler. Can't you see at all?"

"No. I must have light, and quickly. My legs are shaking so violently that I'm sure to fall at any moment. Please, Hayes, do as I ask!"

Reluctantly Hayes tied the rope over the horn of rock, but kept his own line about his waist so that he could lean out as far as possible with the light in his hand.

He swept up the light and crawled to the very lip of the passage. Taking hold of the rope in his free hand, he leaned out over the abyss and stretched the lantern out precariously. The sound of water was suddenly very loud.

"Flames!" he heard himself say. "Bloody blood and flames."

Feeling utterly helpless, he watched his friend who stood shaking on the rock. Hayes was almost certain that Kehler would fall, when suddenly he reached out with a hand, and then swung his foot onto a toehold. Just as he positioned his weight over his foot he slipped, and for a second clung to the rock with his hands, flailing for a foothold, and then, mercifully, he was back on the rock, gasping like a consumptive, though it was from fear.

Hayes could hear him muttering, cursing under his breath.

"Keep your body away from the rock, Kehler, or that will happen again."

He saw his companion nod, then push himself out a bit, though still not far enough, Hayes thought. Kehler took a second to collect himself and then moved on, with exaggerated care this time. Another step, and then he was on the platform.

"'Tis child's play from there," Hayes called out. "A regular easy chair of a climb, I would call it."

Kehler could not even manage a smile in response. His face was drawn and white, his whole manner grim, though more determined now. A moment more and he joined a relieved Hayes in the mouth of the passage.

"Are you shaking from fright or cold?"

"Both, I confess," Kehler said. "I must find some dry clothes immediately."

Hayes had to help his friend into dry clothes, for his hands were not functioning properly, and he also made Kehler take his coat, which was warm from his own body's heat. Using his previous trick, he made something resembling tea over the lantern flame and this seemed to help. Even so it was a good hour before Kehler was warmed sufficiently.

They ate there, on their balcony overlooking the falls, and drank a second cup of the warmed tea.

"I think we must go on," Kehler said. He had stopped trembling and regained some of the color in his face, though he hardly looked well. Hayes was sure that Kehler needed a night's sleep in a warm bed, and then a day's rest. But nothing even remotely like that was possible here. They could either go on or go back: those were their choices.

Hayes helped his friend shoulder his pack, and then raised his own. Taking the lantern, he set off, keeping his pace moderate. The passage they were in now suffered from a low ceiling, and in places they had to crouch, but it was ten feet wide and Hayes was relieved when it did not seem inclined to shrink any more.

"We are going up," Hayes said suddenly. After descending since entering the cave, they were suddenly ascending.

"Yes, this part of the cave drains down this passage when the water is high, and down into several other passages the rest of the year. It is almost a separate system. As far as anyone knows, this is the only link between the two sections of the cave, and another entrance has yet to be found. We are into the remote parts of the cave now. Few venture beyond the falls, for that traverse we just managed stops all but the brave and the foolish."

"We are the latter, I take it?"

"Well, I certainly was not feeling terribly brave, hanging out there over the falls. I could think of nothing but falling into that pit, and being swept down into the deep channels below the mountain. I think I shall have nightmares of it for the rest of my days."

A trickle of water ran in this passage, and occasionally they would find small pools of perfectly clear water. In one place they were forced to climb up a fifteen-foot face, but this hardly slowed them after what they had just managed.

"I should think that any fear you have of Deacon Rose sending his minions after you should be put to rest now. They would have to walk across the lake of the mirror and brave the traverse above the falls. I think we can safely say we are beyond their reach now."

Kehler nodded, but he did not respond. Obviously he was not as confident as his friend, which surprised him a little.

## ⌒ Twenty-Two

Erasmus awoke to a sound, not sure what it was. A scratching at the door and sniffing.

*The dream*, he thought. *The wolf at the door.* He rolled over and closed his eyes, bringing up a mental picture of the countess: something to drive the feelings of the dream away.

A soft knock.

Erasmus sat up.

A knock again.

*Who in this round world?* he thought, but got quickly out of bed. Perhaps it was someone with word of Hayes and Kehler. Blood and flames, he hoped they had not met with misadventure.

He threw on a robe and unbolted the door, opening it a crack. There in the dim hallway stood a small, round man, unfamiliar at first, but there was something about him. . . .

"Martyr's blood! Mr. Walky?"

"Ah, you've not forgotten me, my young lion," the man whispered. "Now, let me in, if you please."

Erasmus threw open the door, and Walky entered the room, almost an apparition in the starlight.

"I have never been more surprised by a visitor in my life," Erasmus began, both overjoyed to see the man, and apprehensive. Why, after all these years, would Eldrich's servant appear? Perhaps the question was written clearly on his face.

"I have come to fetch you," Walky said, a bit of apology in his voice.

"Ah." Erasmus felt something like dread growing in him. "What does he want, Mr. Walky?" he asked, his mouth quickly drying.

The little man shrugged. "Only the mage knows," he said, and tried to smile reassuringly. "Dress quickly, he has not grown in patience since your last meeting."

Erasmus nodded and began to pull on clothes.

A carriage awaited them in the street, drawn up in the shadow of a building.

After traveling a block in silence. Erasmus spoke. "You are well, I hope?" though it was not the question he wanted to ask.

"Yes, of course. How could I not be?"

The old man, who must be very old now, hardly seemed to have aged. His hair, what little there was of it, had been white those twenty years ago, and in the poor light his face did not appear more creased. Twenty years. . . .

"Do you still teach the young gentlemen?" Erasmus asked, trying to think of some way of hinting toward the events of the past, perhaps to see if Walky shied away from the subject.

"There have been no young gentlemen since your day, sir. I tend the garden now, and do the mage's bidding."

The slow clatter of iron-shod wheels and horses' hooves echoed among the houses—the hard sounds unable to penetrate stone.

"I don't think he means you harm, sir," Walky said suddenly, his manner reassuring.

"No? No, I suppose he wouldn't."

The carriage rattled on, climbing slowly up the switchback road. Erasmus shut his eyes for a moment and saw his last meeting with Eldrich, and Percy. Exerting all his considerable will, he tried to force the image from his mind. *Percy. . . .*

"We are almost there, sir," Walky said, pulling Erasmus from his thoughts. "Mr. Flattery? I know you have grown and become a man among men. . . . But to the earl, the greatest man in Farrland does not impress him overly. It would be best to remember that. He has no tolerance for pride among men."

Good old Walky. Even after all these years he was concerned for his charges. Had this concern only manifested itself a little more effectively all those years ago. . . .

They pulled up under the roof of a carriage entrance, and a silent footman lowered the step.

"Where are we?"

"You don't know? This is the house of the priest, Baumgere. He is waiting here."

Walky led Erasmus into the old mansion, and as they passed through the dimly lit entrance way, Erasmus realized another man emerged just behind them, led out to the waiting carriage.

*It could not have been*, Erasmus thought. It must have been a trick of starlight, for he thought he had seen a head of silver hair—like Skye—but it could not have been.

They made their way down hallways lit only occasionally by candles and finally into a rotunda, beneath a dome of stained glass, Erasmus thought, for a pattern seemed to fall upon the floor, like the imprint of wet leaves on a walkway.

When he looked down again, he realized that Walky had retreated back through the door. The room was almost entirely dark, and Erasmus felt his apprehension grow.

"You have nothing to fear," came the voice that he would never forget—musical yet entirely lacking in human warmth. Not the voice of a man at all.

"Lord Eldrich?"

"Yes, come forward, man. If I'd meant you harm I would have done it long ago."

*But you did*, Erasmus thought. He stepped forward, his hand out before him like a blind man. A fire flared up across the room, causing him to step back. He thought he heard a chuckle in the darkness.

Remembering Walky's warning, he went forward quickly. He found Lord Eldrich sprawled in a chair near the hearth. Erasmus had forgotten how tall the mage was.

He had also forgotten the man's presence. There was not a lord who could equal it. Eldrich was a man who knew his place, utterly. There was no mistake. Nor was there any mistaking what Eldrich thought of others: mere men, hardly worth his time.

"Sit down, Erasmus," Eldrich said, his voice almost soft, though still devoid of warmth. "So this is what became of you. . . ." He fixed a disinterested gaze on his former charge.

Erasmus could just make out the man, his dark hair framing a thin face, always terribly white as though he did not care for the sun. Thin lips, and a sharp nose—almost raptorlike, Erasmus thought. A hunting falcon, with all-seeing eyes and no remorse.

"It has been how long?"

"About twenty years, sir."

"Really. Time . . . it speaks to me so little. Servants die. I hear rumors that there is a new King. Friends . . . they've been gone these many years now." He shook his head a little sadly, a little confused, as though not sure how these things had come to pass. "And you have grown to manhood, and some prominence, I understand. Walky takes great pride in your accomplishments." He smiled, though it was not a smile of affection—more of amusement, Erasmus thought. Eldrich appeared to regard him for a moment, his gaze not hostile though neither was it friendly.

"What is it that I might do for you, Lord Eldrich?" Erasmus asked, suddenly losing his patience, annoyed that this man would treat him so.

Eldrich's smile was derisive. "You play your part, Erasmus, do not be concerned. I want to know if you have been contacted by certain people that are of interest to me."

"Which people?"

"Well, that is difficult to answer, for I do not know their names. You see, they have gone to great lengths to be sure that I do not know of their existence—but they have not been entirely successful. And now they are growing positively bold. Desperate even. So much so that I expect they have approached you. The only one I can describe is a woman—slim, hair of reddish-blonde, but faded. 'Drained' was the word one used to describe her. She uses divers names."

"I have no knowledge of such a woman." Erasmus was surprised to find Eldrich at all interested in the affairs of men.

The mage shifted in his chair, turning his head sharply, looking into the darkness. *Thought overlain by sadness.* That was what Erasmus saw, if one even dared to imagine what a mage felt. What they might think was an utter mystery.

"You had seen this text on the Pelier before meeting the countess, I collect?"

Erasmus was surprised. Did Eldrich keep such close track of him? Had he done so all these years? "A friend, Samual Hayes, had shown it to me. A friend of his had unearthed it in the Farrellite archives in Wooton and sent it on to him."

This seemed to focus Eldrich's attention. "You know these young men."

Erasmus nodded.

"And they are here, in Castlebough?"

"Yes. Or rather they were. They appear to have gone down into one of the caves, searching for what I cannot say."

"The Mirror Lake Cave."

"Yes."

Eldrich rose from his chair and paced out into the dappled darkness of the rotunda, pausing as though forgetting where he went or why. He turned back to Erasmus.

"Have the priests come seeking this young man? What is his name?"

"Kehler. There is a priest here—a Deacon Rose—who is pursuing him. The priest told me that Kehler is in some danger, though he would not say more. He also told me that if I were ever to see you, sir, to assure you that the Farrellites have kept faith with the mages. He seemed very concerned that this be understood."

"And well he should be," Eldrich said, and then walked another three paces, a hand to his brow, Erasmus thought, though it was hard to tell in the poor light.

The mage stopped in the rotunda center and looked up at the dome overhead, standing a moment with his arms thrown oddly out, and then he came back and stood by the fire.

"You have been busy these past years, Erasmus. No doubt you have heard of Teller in your researches?"

"I—I have."

"Do you know what became of the society the man thrust upon the world?"

"I believe it was destroyed. Five mages conspired to trap them and put an end to their efforts."

"An end was put to more than their efforts," Eldrich said emphatically, "though it was not an easy thing, for the followers of Teller had grown cunning and knew how to avoid coming to the attention of the mages. And the years have not made them less skilled in this matter, that is certain. But they think I am near to my end, my powers waning, and that is making them rash. They also sense what is coming, and they grow desperate."

"Are you saying that the Tellerites still exist?"

"Do you not listen when I speak?" Eldrich said, his temper flaring. He walked away again, out into the center of the rotunda. After a moment of pacing he turned and gazed intently at Erasmus.

*"Erasmus?"*

He felt himself falling through darkness, and then he struck something hard, though he felt no pain.

*"Erasmus?"*

He opened his eyes and saw what appeared to be low flame rippling before his eyes. His vision began to clear and he realized that it was not flame, though it was fading so quickly he could not put a name to it.

"You can get up now. You're perfectly whole."

Erasmus realized that Walky stood over him, holding something draped over his arm.

"I have your clothes, sir."

Erasmus sat up suddenly, his mind still not clear. "What has he done to me?"

"Only looked into you a little; to be sure that you had not been contacted and your memory fogged."

"What?"

"Come along, sir. I can help you if you aren't able. Daylight is not far off. We should get you back, sir."

Erasmus realized that there was a little gray seeping down from the dome above. He felt a bit of light was finding its way into his brain as well.

"What part am I to play in this, Walky?"

Even in the poor light he could see the man shrug his round shoulders. "Only the mage knows," he said.


## ◆ Twenty-Three

Skye pulled on a plain white waistcoat, checked the hour on his timepiece, and slipped it into a pocket. Still a few minutes left. He walked over to the window and stared out over the town of Castlebough down to the lake, which glittered hypnotically in the sun. The note from the countess had hardly been warm—it had been rather curt, in truth. Unusual, he thought, then shrugged. There was no understanding women, especially this countess. She seemed alternately overanimated, almost girlish, in his company, or sullen and petulant. He simply did not understand.

Perhaps the fact that she turned the head of every man in Farrland had made her a bit odd, but then this was something that was lost on him. Oh, she was an attractive woman, there was no doubt of that, but there were others he found far more lovely, and they did not act so strangely around him. As though he'd made them some promise that he had not kept.

His eye came slowly back from the lake, just visible over the slate roofs of the houses. Skye wondered what the countess had learned from Flattery; certainly her note gave no clue. Perhaps Flattery had been unpleasant to her and that explained her manner—she was angry at Flattery, not him.

His eye came to rest on the small park across the street from the house he let. Nannies watched over playing children and gossiped among themselves as they did handcrafts, apparently without devoting any part of their awareness to the activity.

On one of the benches a man sat reading a book, one of the men who always seemed to be in the park—leaving only when Skye left his house. Agents of the Farr government, he was sure, and felt the fear that seemed always to tighten around his bowel.

"They would have arrested me by now," he muttered. Certainly they had no evidence. Their attempt to compromise him had failed, thanks to an unknown woman and her friends. He thought of her often, fearing that she had somehow fallen into the hands of the Admiralty. Who in this round world was she, and how had she gotten wind of Moncrief's plot? Meeting her had been one of the oddest experiences of his life. Thank Farrelle she had been there or he would likely be in the gaol, now.

"They cannot touch you," Skye said, squaring his shoulders. They had tried and failed. And now he was on his guard. The King was still an admirer.

Moncrief would get what he deserved for this travesty, in time. Let him sweat a while.

The man in the park appeared not to notice when Skye emerged onto the street, but Skye knew he was there. Half a block behind, perhaps on the street's opposite side, but he was there.

*Put him from your mind,* he told himself. *There is nothing the man can do now but follow.* Follow rather impotently.

As it was a fine day, he decided to walk the short distance to the house where the countess was staying.

So absorbed in thought was the countess that she had lost all awareness of her surroundings. She sat on a small terrace, the warming sun touching her, protected from the small breeze by a stone wall. Though there was increasing warmth in the sun, the air still bore the cold of the recent winter, which lingered in the shaded valleys and on hilltops.

"The pleasures of the day to you, Lady Chilton," Skye said, startling the countess from her thoughts.

She rose immediately and curtsied, wondering if her manner was as guarded as it felt. Skye, of course, showed no sensitivity to her mood, as she had come to expect. "Please, Lord Skye, sit. Be at your ease." She took her own seat and faced him, silent for a moment, wondering if he would ask about her meeting with Erasmus or if he would pretend that visiting her was more important than anything she might have learned. When he did not speak, she began to feel foolish.

"Your paintings are ready. Shall I have them taken to your carriage?"

"I walked, in fact, Lady Chilton."

"Then I shall have them delivered to your place of residence, if you will but give directions to my servants."

He nodded his thanks.

"You would like to hear of my meeting with Erasmus Flattery," she said.

"You have met with him already?" he said as though the thought had not occurred to him. As if he had come here merely to stare at her in anticipation.

"Mr. Flattery was kind enough to visit me." She met his eye suddenly. "I had not realized he was a man of such charm." Her gaze dropped to her hands. "I showed him your paintings. He divined immediately that I was your agent . . . I'm not sure how." She looked up at him as though he might explain, but he only shrugged. "I managed to charm a few things from him, all the same. He admitted that the script on the Pelier, or rather the copy, was likely known to the mages and might even be similar to the script on the Ruin of Farrow, as you expected." She looked up to see Skye's reaction to this news, and though he sat perfectly still, she could see the excitement on his face. "He claimed not to be able to read the script, however." She felt herself shrug. She had almost blurted out the truth. Anything to please him. A shudder of revulsion ran through her at what she would do to attract this man.

"But can he? Did you sense he was telling the truth?" Skye had leaned forward in his seat, staring at her intently.

She shrugged again, feeling that she looked at him a bit hopelessly, trying to hide the excitement she felt in his presence. If he would only look at her so for the proper reasons. . . .

Skye turned suddenly in his seat, and stared off at the view. "But if it is the script of the mages . . . ? How could Pelier have known?"

"He did not merely adapt it from the script on the Ruin, I collect?"

"No, I don't think so. Flattery would know better than I, but no, I think it has come from some other source. Perhaps from 'inspiration' as Pelier claimed." Skye ran his right hand back into his thick silver hair, as she had noted he did when deep in thought.

"But why does this interest you so?" she asked softly.

Skye looked down on her as though surprised by the question. "It is difficult to explain."

"I have no pressing appointments. Take all day if you like. In fact, I think I will be free tomorrow, as well, if a story could take so long."

He seemed to measure her for a moment, with that gaze that never looked upon her warmly. Then he shifted in his chair, as though to speak with her more intimately, but still he said nothing. The countess remained silent, waiting, afraid to push now. The slightest misstep and he would decide to say nothing—all chance of intimacy would be gone.

Twice he turned his attention to her, and drew a breath as though to speak, but both times his resolve failed or he could not find the words, and he looked away.

"I shall swear myself to silence, if that is a concern," the countess said softly, hardly daring to utter a word.

Then she saw his face change, the tension draining from it, and he nodded unconvincingly. "The story of the Stranger of Compton Heath has intrigued me since the day I first heard it, and the more I learned the more fascinated I became. You see, I don't believe it was merely a local myth, as do many, nor do I think it was a hoax. The priest, Baumgere, met the Stranger, and I think there can hardly have been a shrewder man than this priest. No, his knowledge of languages was far too deep for anyone to deceive him. The Stranger unquestionably spoke a tongue that Baumgere had not encountered before.

"So where did this Stranger come from? Some unexplored part of the world is the accepted explanation, and one can hardly imagine a more convincing answer, but I have reason for doubt. You see, there have been other such occurrences in history, all thought to be hoaxes for one reason or another, and likely some were. Of course one would have to ask what purpose they served other than gaining the impostor some brief notoriety. But some are of such a nature that I wonder if, indeed, they were hoaxes.

"A boy was discovered in Doorn, nearly frozen on a winter's day, and he soon succumbed to his ordeal. But he, too, spoke a strange tongue and was dressed oddly and found his surroundings unfamiliar. He seemed altogether foreign to the people who found him.

"Seventy years ago a woman dwelt in the mountains of Entonne, a hermit who was said to sing songs in an unknown tongue and had knowledge of healing that others did not. She was a little mad, some thought, for she always claimed that she had been spirited here from another place—a place one could not reach by land or sea. And a boy of about twelve appeared near Tremont Abbey. A shepherd and his son found the child, wandering the hills, frightened, speaking a language the man had never heard. They took him to a physician in the town, and as happened at Compton Heath, a carriage came late at night, and the boy was never seen again."

"And last, and strangest of all, the case of the Milbrook children. You must know it? The three children and the nanny all disappeared from a room while others were outside. It was a great mystery seventy-five years ago, and rewards were offered for the nanny, who was thought to have abducted the poor children. But they were never found, nor could anyone ever explain how they had disappeared from the room without anyone seeing. The laughter of the children stopped, and the parents thought they had fallen asleep, or listened raptly to a story. But when they opened the door later, there were no children to be found. Gone. Impossibly gone." He fell silent.

"They could not have disappeared into the air," the countess said, strangely affected by this story of lost children.

"Not into the air, no." Skye paused, thinking. "In ancient times there was a belief among a group of scholars—they called themselves the 'lunarians,' for it was their habit to meet at the full moon—thus the terms 'fool's moon' and 'lunatic' were born—and they had many strange ideas about the nature of the world and the heavens, and have been much scorned by men of learning ever since. But even so, they were some of the earliest to believe that the earth was a sphere, and even calculated its circumference very close to our present value. They also believed that the netherworld was a real place. They believed it lay within our world, which they hypothesized was hollow at its center. To this end they explored some very deep caves and even tried to enter a marginally active volcano, with near disastrous results. This belief that another world lay within was part of a larger cosmology—if one can call it that—a hypothesis that there were other worlds 'infinitely distant, yet near at hand.' It was their belief that these worlds were, at times, so close that people could pass from one to another, and that sometimes, though not by design, they did." He gave her an odd defensive look as though he expected her to laugh, but when she did not he continued.

"It sounds foolish, I know, but where did the Stranger of Compton Heath come from? And where did the Milbrook children go? Somewhere. Somewhere that is not explained by our present description of the heavens. I am a practitioner of natural philosophy, and it is my belief that we will one day come to understand the laws of nature in all of their vast intricacy. I am also an empiricist and believe only in knowledge that can be confirmed by empirical methods—but what if our perception of the world is . . . incomplete? What if there are worlds 'infinitely distant, yet near at hand' that we cannot detect by any method yet devised? If this were possible, then our entire view of the cosmos would be ludicrously narrow. If such a thing were possible, then we must begin rewriting the few natural laws we have recorded—my own laws of gravity among them."

He stopped, gazing at her, judging the effect of what he'd said.

"It is . . . astonishing. I hardly know what to say. If such a thing could be proven, it would stand all orthodox theory on its head. Are there others who share this view?"

"This is the worst of it," he said, his face twisting in anguish. "The only men who give voice to such beliefs are charlatans and fools. Not real empiricists at all, but buffoons who believe in fairies and spirits. Table knockers who claim to receive messages from the dead, who conduct spirit readings and perform trumped-up 'rituals' at midnight on the solstice." He shook his head, his face turning a bright red. "That is why I keep my interest to myself and tell no one. I would become a laughing stock. I cannot think what cruelty I would meet. No, you are the first I have told."

"I am honored that you would trust me with this confidence, but what will you do? Will you keep such thoughts to yourself forever?"

"Yes, unless I can find proof. Thus my interest in this priest Baumgere. He met the Stranger in Compton Heath and, I believe, spent his life trying to discover where the man had come from. He had access to all the books and documents collected by the Farrellite Church, and I believe he found evidence there. Some information that brought him here to Castlebough where he spent the rest of his life in this pursuit. I had hoped to find this information—I still hope to find it." His manner changed, and he blinked several times quickly, turning slightly away from her.

The countess could not miss his distress. "What is it?" she blurted out, unable to stop herself.

"Nothing, I . . . I have not been sleeping well. My thoughts will not leave me alone. I sometimes think that they will drive me . . . to utter distraction."

"If you will permit me to say," the countess pitched her voice to its warmest most compassionate tone, "I think you spend too much time alone with your own thoughts, and though this may produce much for the good of the world, I cannot think it is best for the Earl of Skye, and it is he that I am concerned with. You should spend more time in society—oh, it need not be with the crowds, which I know you dislike. But with your friends who care for you."

He nodded, pulling himself up, almost reanimating himself after looking so dejected. "I'm sure what you say it true."

"I have been invited to a dinner this evening—at the home of one of Castlebough's leading families. I thought I might accept. Would you care to accompany me? It could be the beginning of your new policy."

"This evening? I—I would dearly love to, but I have foolishly committed myself elsewhere. I am sorry."

"Oh, well, not to worry. I only thought . . ."

A clock chimed in the village, and he rose suddenly. "You must forgive me, Lady Chilton, but I am called elsewhere. I cannot thank you enough for your efforts with Mr. Flattery—and for listening to my rambling. You are too kind."

When Skye had gone, the countess stood on the terrace staring at the door. He had run out on her. After what she had offered, intimacy, friendship . . . more. After what she had done for him, pumping poor Erasmus Flattery, she expected at least a little gratitude. At the very least, politeness.

"I have never been treated so . . ." She could not find a word, nor could she find words to express the pain and confusion she felt. "Perhaps he is mad."

"It is unsigned," Marianne said. "Your admirer does not want to be known—he even keeps the identity of the painter he engaged secret so that you will not find him out. You think it's Skye, no doubt?" Marianne and the countess stood looking at a painting, which had been delivered to their abode without so much as a card. It was a portrait of the countess sitting upon a divan, and Marianne had already said she thought the artist was more than a little in love with his subject.

"I don't know who it is from, though I am almost certain that it is not from the earl." She hoped her voice remained neutral, but Marianne cast a quick glance her way all the same.

"Well, whoever it is, they are likely in Castlebough. I can't imagine that anyone would find you here to deliver such a gift, but would simply send it to your Avonel home."

"I suppose."

"Well, it is a painter of some skill, and therefore he will not be unknown. We'll take it along to dinner tonight. It will be the parlor game—name the artist."

"Oh, that would be unkind!" the countess protested.

"Nonsense. If the man has not the courage to declare himself, then he deserves nothing less. I wouldn't be surprised to find he's married, for Farrelle's sake. But if we can find the artist, we will know his employer soon enough. No, no. Do not protest."

## ᔷ Twenty-Four

The house was perhaps the oldest house of any size in Castlebough, and was suitably dark in its decor, with small windows, and floors of ancient tile and deeply polished walnut. Erasmus did not want to be there. In fact, he was becoming a little frantic with inactivity. At least everything was ready for their departure early the next morning, or so Clarendon claimed. They would set out in search of Kehler and Hayes at last.

The two men had come to dinner at the Baron of Glenock's home, and though Erasmus was not usually overly enthusiastic about such events, the baron was a member of Clarendon's vintners group, and as such had applied pressure to the little man to bring Erasmus along. If he was honest with himself, Erasmus had to admit that his real reason for attending was the possibility of meeting the countess again.

*Now that she's learned what she wanted from you, the countess will likely not pay you the slightest attention*, he thought. *But I will hang back and if she does not appear to recognize me, I won't make a fool of myself by pursuing her.*

He was not quite sure why he was doing this. Certainly she was not interested in him. The Countess of Chilton was likely desired by every man of station in Farrland and beyond. Still, she had taken his hand at her door, and kissed his cheek, and for a few seconds he had felt that something passed between them. Something. . . .

The servant opened the doors to the great hall, and there Erasmus found the thirty or so dinner guests gathered in a half circle, their attention entirely taken up with something. Flames, was this how the countess was treated? People simply collected about her and stared?

"Well, it isn't a Sir Geofry Sandler, that is certain," someone offered. "The subject appears to be alive."

There was general laughter.

"Vita Corning," someone else suggested.

"No, it was done by a man, clearly. You can see the artist was enamored of his subject."

"Exactly! Vita Corning."

This brought much knowing laughter.

Erasmus came up to the edge of the group unnoticed.

"Obviously a Warton," a man said emphatically.

"Oh, don't be perfectly ridiculous. It was done by someone with talent."

Erasmus Flattery found a shoulder he could peer over and there, at the center of this gathering stood a framed painting on an easel. A painting of the Countess of Chilton which, he thought, came near to conveying the mysterious allure of the woman's beauty. Erasmus found himself staring at it raptly for a moment and then realized the head full of curls before the painting must belong to the countess herself. Suddenly he was nervous with anticipation. Would she acknowledge him? Would there be the slightest hint of what had transpired between them?

"It is a self-portrait, and the countess is hiding her talent from us?"

Such fawning was too much even for this gathering and was met with various sounds, none of which could be described as overly kind.

"There aren't a dozen good portraitists around the Entide Sea. Certainly it can't be too hard to find the artist when there are so few to choose among."

This comment was met with general agreement.

"Mr. Kent?" the countess said, "I can't believe you won't venture an opinion. Are you protecting one of your brothers in art?"

Erasmus noticed Averil Kent hanging back behind the others, looking a little sheepish, he thought.

"I fear that my own areas of interest don't include portraiture, Lady Chilton, so I am of little use in this matter."

Erasmus looked back to the painting again. The pattern of the fabric that covered the divan was striking. New world warblers of bright yellow on leafed branches of some unknown tree, likely an oak, also not an old world variety.

Erasmus leaned nearer to Kent and said quietly, "Do you know the pattern in the divan? Is that *Quercus lyrata*, do you think?"

Kent hesitated, looking back at the painting. "Perhaps *stellata*, though I'm not sure."

Erasmus nodded. *Well*, he thought, *you have not fooled quite everyone, Mr. Kent*. A quick jealousy flamed up in him, but he forced it down, smiling at his own folly. It was likely that neither the talented Kent nor the supposedly "renowned" Erasmus Flattery would stand a chance in the competition for the favors of the countess. Hardly worth a fit of jealousy.

Another painter was suggested, this one prompting even more laughter. The countess looked over her shoulder to see the originator of this suggestion and noticed Erasmus. The smile was replaced by a wavering look of uncertainty, which Erasmus did not understand. She nodded just perceptibly and then turned back to the painting.

He found the uncertainty of that look infected him, worked its way into his blood and left him ill with doubt. He forced his attention back to the painting.

Perhaps it was just the moment, but Erasmus thought the painter had captured something of that uncertainty in his portrait. The countess gazed out from the canvas with a look at once intelligent and extremely guarded, though almost masked by the beauty and by the ease with which she inhabited that near-perfect form. It was, Erasmus had to admit, a brilliant portrait.

He glanced over at Kent. The man's manner spoke very clearly to Erasmus: the painter was overwhelmed by both a sense of hopelessness, and of fervent hope. Hopelessness because his head told him that he stood no chance with the countess, yet hopeful because his heart believed that this offering of his art would make her realize the depth of his feeling for her. Somehow, Erasmus realized, Kent had convinced himself that the countess would look at the painting and recognize that such depth of true feeling could come from no one but Kent himself and this would open her eyes to him and what he offered. In a world where all men desired her, only Kent's feelings were true and noble.

*You poor bastard*, Erasmus thought. He wondered if the countess had done anything at all to encourage the painter. Clearly she knew who he was, but was there anything more to it than that?

Erasmus turned his attention back to the painting, reminding himself that looking at Kent might be more like staring into a mirror than he could bear. Best not to let a foolish obsession with the countess take hold of him, especially when it was so unlikely.

He turned away from the group, but when he did, a vision of the countess standing near to him at the door of her home appeared in his mind. Her manner, so earnest and vulnerable, pierced right to his heart. He must have looked near to falling, for Kent reached out and took hold of his shoulder.

"Are you well, Mr. Flattery?"

"Yes, perfectly." He looked over at Kent and tried to smile, for they were brothers in misery.

To his astonishment Erasmus found that he had been seated near to the head of the long table, and next to the countess. The baron sat at the table's head getting quietly drunk in his own jolly way, and his wife sat to his right. To his left was the Countess of Chilton, and next to her, Erasmus.

The baron looked like a man who had discovered that he'd died and gone to heaven. Servants continually delivered him exquisite food and drink, while to his left sat the most beautiful woman he had ever seen. He was too blissful even to talk but merely sat there filling his face and glowing. Erasmus thought he had never seen a man who so much resembled a baby—though a giant one. He wondered if the baron would have to be burped after the meal.

Kent, sadly, sat near the table's farthest end and looked like a man exiled to the provinces.

"Did you see my mystery portrait?" the countess asked when the baroness' attention was elsewhere. "From a secret admirer, apparently. Have you a guess as to the man's identity?"

Erasmus hesitated. Would she be impressed if he were to name the artist? The thought of poor Kent hanging back behind the crowd made him hesitate. "I . . . no, I don't know who it could be."

"Now, Mr. Flattery, I saw you hesitate. Do you know? Tell me."

Erasmus shook his head, leaning a little closer. "I could be wrong, and if I am not, I would rather not embarrass the man, who is, in fact, a gentleman of some sensitivity."

The countess pulled back to examine him for a second. "Was it you who had the painting done?" she said so that no other might hear. "Is that what you're telling me?"

She did not look displeased, he realized, and he felt the urge to lie, to at least give the impression that it had been him. "Me. Oh, no, Lady Chilton. Not me. Though if I had such talent, I cannot think of a subject I would rather undertake."

"Ah, live by the name, die by the name. Though I am not sure I believe you." She lifted her wineglass and smiled at him. "To flattering portraits—can one ever have too many?"

Erasmus laughed. "I have been waiting to have just one."

"Is this a private conversation?" the baroness asked.

"Not at all, Lady Bingham. We were just speculating again about my portrait."

A deep, even breathing caught their attention and they turned to find the baron asleep in his chair.

The baroness looked more amused than embarrassed. "It is the effect of the wine. Half a bottle and he cannot stay awake. Once, at a ball, he leaned against a pillar, and, I swear, he went to sleep on his feet. I roused him, somewhat, when he began to slide to the floor and managed to steer him into our carriage, though I don't think he was awake the entire time. Walked out to the carriage in his sleep, I am convinced of it. And the next day he had no memory of what had transpired. Denies it still." She shook her head, rolling her eyes a little.

"It is interesting that you would say that," the countess said, her tone more serious. "I awoke this morning in the parlor downstairs, dressed in my sleeping gown and a robe. I have not the slightest memory of rising or descending the stairs, nor do I know how long I was there before I awoke. It was the oddest thing, and I've never done anything like it before."

Erasmus stopped eating. "Why, last night I awoke while in the midst of undressing. I was sitting on my bed taking off my shirt. The odd thing is that I had gone to bed earlier, and I have no memory of rising and dressing, and wonder what in the world I was doing."

The baroness laughed. "There is an epidemic of sleepwalking apparently. Perhaps there are some at this table eating in their sleep, even conversing. Somehow, I sense that there are."

With the baron asleep, Erasmus received much of the countess' attention that evening, and he could not remember being happier. And it seemed to him that the countess took pleasure from his company.

Far too quickly, the evening was over and Erasmus found himself stalling near the door, hoping to at least say good night to the countess. Clarendon came up. "We have the kind offer of a ride home, Mr. Flattery."

"Well, that is very thoughtful. . . ." Erasmus began, trying to hide his annoyance, but he did not finish, for the countess appeared in the entry hall. He almost cursed aloud. How could he escape Clarendon and his untimely kindness?

"Ah, Mr. Flattery." It was the countess. "You have not forgotten your promise to escort me home, I hope?"

"Forgotten? Of course not. May I present, Randall Spencer Emanual Clarendon, Lady Chilton."

Clarendon bowed deeply, and the countess looked immensely charmed. "Mr. Clarendon, it is a great pleasure. Are you a resident of this lovely village or a visitor, like the rest of us?"

"I have a house here, Lady Chilton, though I confess I retreat to warmer climes once the snow begins to fall."

"Well, perhaps we shall meet again, then, as I will be here a bit longer. I'm rather charmed with Castlebough, I must admit. The pleasures of the evening to you, Mr. Clarendon."

A moment later Erasmus was handing the countess up into her carriage and then taking his place beside her, certain he was the envy of every man present. And there they were riding through moonlit Castlebough, and he was not really sure what he had done to be so fortunate.

They rolled on in silence for a moment, leaving Erasmus to wonder what would happen when they came to the door of the countess' home. The town was so small, however, that they arrived at the house before Erasmus had decided upon which tack he would sail.

"Would you like to come in and meet Marianne Edden, Mr. Flattery? She is always sitting up at this hour, and though she could not be convinced to go to dinner, she will require a complete report of the evening's events."

"I would be delighted."

Erasmus felt both let down and relieved. If there was another present, then there would be no question of how the evening would proceed. At least he would not be able to make a fool of himself if he misread the situation completely.

Servants took his hat and Lady Chilton's cloak and he was ushered into a small withdrawing room where he was left alone. A fire burned in the hearth, but Erasmus found he was drawn to the window, which looked out over the valley below. In the distance he could see the lake, silvered by moonlight and starlight, shimmering in the distance. A breeze moved in the branches of the pines, and even inside, he thought he could smell their sweet scent.

He heard a noise behind and turned to find the countess seating herself by the fire, gazing at him intently, as though there were some weighty question she was about to pose.

"It is unprecedented, but Marianne seems to have retired for the evening," she said. "I wonder if she is entirely well?" A servant poured wine and slipped away silently.

Erasmus came and sat by the fire. The countess was subdued, perhaps tired, or burdened with something, with some knowledge. He wondered if it was Skye. She had pumped Erasmus for the great empiricist, so there was clearly some connection between them. Like everyone else, Skye was probably enamored of her.

*And what are my accomplishments compared with his?* Erasmus thought.

"Have you heard this odd tale of the man they call the Stranger of Compton Heath?" the countess asked suddenly, looking up at him as though she expected ridicule.

Erasmus nodded. "I have. Yes. Most peculiar."

"Where in the world do you think he came from?"

Erasmus shrugged. "It is a mystery, though I will say that I think it was no ruse, and there seem to have been other cases."

"You give it credence, then?"

"Certainly I can neither prove nor disprove the story. I am convinced that the man did appear, and that he was genuinely lost and confused. Whether he was merely a lunatic, as some have suggested—I cannot say." Erasmus paused. "I know a man who interviewed the doctor who was first called to see this stranger. He, at least, believed the doctor's story, and he also believed the Stranger was no fraud, nor was he mad."

"You have an interest in this matter?" she asked, surprised and perhaps relieved.

"The people of Compton Heath believed a mage came and took the stranger away."

"And you are interested in the mages. . . ."

He nodded and sipped his wine.

"Do you ever feel that we are at an end of a chapter of history, Mr. Flattery, and that the world as it existed before was so much more alive with marvels? I almost feel this stranger was somehow left from that period. Like lizards are the tiny remnants of the great beasts that disappeared. And now we are left with this world of reason that we are building, and it will be an infinitely ordered and predictable world devoid of such wonders as mages and strangers who have come from we know not where. Not to mention wondrous beasts. Do you know that there were said to be white deer in these hills long ago?"

Erasmus nodded. "Yes. I have seen the hide of one. They were true and real, just as this man who appeared in Compton Heath was real, but I would not be too concerned. I think there are wonders enough in this world, to last our lifetimes at least." Erasmus could not help himself, he had to ask. "How did Skye respond to my verdict on the script?"

He wanted to see her reaction to Skye coming up in the conversation.

She did not brighten at the sound of the man's name. In fact, she turned away slightly to stare into the fire. Erasmus was not sure how to interpret this.

"It is always difficult to say with the earl. . . . Can you read the writing?" she said suddenly. "I ask this only of my own curiosity. I will say nothing."

Erasmus sipped his wine, then rose from his chair, almost without meaning to. For a moment he stood with his arm resting on the high mantle. "During my time in the house of Eldrich I was under the tutelage of a man—Walky was his name. He taught all the things that schoolboys are to learn—Old Farr, Entonne, arithmetic, grammar, history. Nothing that other boys in far more common circumstances did not learn. But old Walky was beginning to suffer the disabilities that plague the old. Not that he wasn't strong and healthy—he seemed to have these qualities in abundance—but his mind was not what it once had been. His memory was in decline. Often he would call us by the names of former students, or he would begin to teach us things that he had not meant to. On more than one occasion he asked us to repeat things that we had not been taught. Arcane things. He even occasionally addressed us in a language we could not name." He heard the countess draw in a quick breath. She stared at him in fascination, but almost, he thought, he saw some pity there.

"He once left a book on a shelf of the room in which we commonly pursued our studies. It sat there for two days before I realized that it was not a book in any common language. When I first opened it, I slammed it closed immediately. Although we never met Eldrich, as small boys we lived in mortal dread of the mage. I was certain that I would suffer some terrible magical retribution for merely opening the book. But I did not. Two days later I looked again. By the fourth day, Percy—the other boy my age who lived there—Percy and I were sure that Walky had forgotten the book altogether and we took it to our room to examine.

"We were more frightened than you can imagine, but we were also utterly fascinated, and as small boys often are, we were heedless to the effects of our action.

"The book was completely undecipherable to us. Filled with strange writing and odd diagrams." Erasmus stopped, unable to continue the story.

"What happened?" the countess asked, her voice nearly a whisper.

"We were discovered . . . and punished," Erasmus said, keeping his tone carefully neutral.

"Oh," the countess said, not quite sure what this might have entailed. "And the writing?"

"I believe it was the same script found in the painting."

"And how were you made to suffer for this transgression?"

"We . . ." Erasmus felt himself try to swallow in a suddenly dry mouth. "We were punished," he said again.

"And you will not say more?"

He shook his head.

"And this is what I have driven you to tell me?" she said, rising from her chair. She took both his hands. "I'm sorry, Erasmus. I am truly sorry. I have no business delving into your secrets. Things that disturb you. I did not bring you here to pry secrets from you, for myself or anyone else."

"Why did you bring me here?"

She paused looking up into his face, measuring, perhaps. "Because I owe you an apology. I misused you when I invited you here so that I could pry for—"

"For Skye," he finished the sentence for her. "What is Skye to you?" he asked suddenly, though he had no right to.

"Oh, do not talk to me of Skye," she said, looking down. "No, it is a terrible thing to use another for one's own ends. To play with their hopes, with their feelings, and then to dash them without regard. It is shameful. No one should be treated thus."

Erasmus was about to protest, when she looked up again, meeting his gaze, her eyes glistening. He could not help himself; he bent and kissed her. At once, he thought he had made a terrible mistake, for she responded not at all. And then suddenly her lips softened and met his.

When they pulled apart, she looked at him in surprise and wonder.

"Mr. Flattery, you forget yourself."

"Yes," he said, hardly able to catch his breath, and kissed her again.

Erasmus would have been convinced he was dreaming, if he had ever known a dream so fair, so overwhelming of the senses. He pulled a divan up before the fire, and here began a slow exploration. Each lace released was a revelation, each kiss more wondrous than the last. Erasmus felt that he had fallen into another world, a world of the senses, where one's thoughts were driven out and replaced with wonder and pleasure. A world in which he was the stranger.

## ⤳ Twenty-Five

Hayes dropped his pack to the cave floor and stretched his back. "Not what I imagined," he said to Kehler.

Kehler shed his own pack and dug out the cave survey, unfolding it near to their lamp.

In the poor light Hayes could just make out the Fairy Galleries above them. The formation of the room did give the impression of a gallery above, and here he could see elaborate decorations. Stalagmites like melting candles projecting up from the floor, a myriad of crystal straws hanging from the ceiling, shimmering even in the poor light. Hayes thought that if he sang the perfect tone, the entire ceiling would resonate in brittle harmony.

"We are in the right chamber," Kehler said after a moment. "Disappointed?"

"Not at all. It is magnificent. Beautiful, really, but not what I expected. Where do we go from here?"

"Up." Kehler pointed up into the gallery. "There is a good-sized passage there. But we should eat first, then I, for one, need at least a few hours' sleep before we go on." They were losing the rhythm of the sun, and sleeping when they felt the need, eating when hungry. Hayes still wound his watch and consulted it occasionally to see just how long they had been down here, but it no longer dictated their schedule.

Hayes had learned to put his battered jacket down for a seat and then lean against his pack, which insulated from the cold hard rock. They sat thus, their packs propped against a wall, the lantern between them, and ate their meal, unsure if it was supper, dinner, or even breakfast.

They ate quietly, then warmed more water over the flame to make their "netherworld tea." Afterward, they put out the flame in order to preserve their precious supply of oil.

In the darkness, questions would not leave Hayes alone. He wondered why he had come. Yes, Kehler had promised him there was a discovery to be made that would pay them handsomely, and that reason was as valid now as it had been at the beginning. But even so, there were moments when the risks, or at least the fears, outweighed the possible gains. And the fears were real and tangible, while the rewards were yet to materialize, if they ever would.

Worry could not keep exhaustion at bay indefinitely, and finally Hayes slipped into an unsettled sleep.

Fleeting dreams haunted him, like images floating swiftly past—clouds borne on the wind. And then he settled into a single dream. A woman's voice was calling him, echoing from far off, like someone whispering into a well. He crawled down a passage that was almost entirely dark. Again the voice called him, and he struggled on, pushing himself through places so tight that he knew he would never return.

"Hayes?"

He woke to the sounds of Kehler striking his flint. A moment later a piece of paper caught and he saw fingers pick it up and tease the lamp wick, reminding him of the squares of light on Paradise Street. An age ago that seemed.

The wick adopted the flame, and a sad light illuminated their chamber.

"Ah, you're awake."

"Only partly."

"Time to go on," Kehler said, though there was no excitement or anticipation in his voice, which was uncharacteristically subdued.

Hayes heard himself sigh. "I suppose."

While Hayes packed by lamplight, Kehler retreated down a passage to fill their water bottle. When he returned he seemed to fuss unduly with his pack.

"I'm ready to have you reveal this great mystery," Hayes said, forcing his tone to be light. "Lead on, my friend."

"Yes. Let us hope . . ." Kehler muttered, shouldering his pack and setting off, an uncomfortable silence falling between them.

Climbing up to the gallery proved easier than they'd thought, and once there, as the survey showed, there was but one passage leading on. As Kehler went ahead, Hayes used a candle to mark a letter H in wax beside the entrance. Then, with a little trepidation, he followed his companion in. Thoughts of the death of a small boy haunted him. What kind of beast had this priest been to use children so?

The passage curved gradually to the right, and maintained a fairly constant angle down. To Hayes' relief it also maintained its size, more or less, so that he only occasionally had to duck his head, something he was becoming adept at, having nearly rendered himself senseless several times early on.

When half of the hour had passed, they met a second passage and followed this. It ran along almost level toward the west.

"How far have we to go?" Hayes asked. Kehler always seemed to put the cave survey away before he had given Hayes a chance to examine it thoroughly—an annoying habit, Hayes found.

"Not far," Kehler called back, though he did not seem terribly excited. An hour later they came to a small chamber, perhaps twenty feet long, but quite high and a dozen feet across.

"Where now?" Hayes asked, stretching his back and shoulders.

Kehler pointed down into a dark corner. "It goes there," he said.

They dropped their packs, glad to be rid of them at last, at least for a while. Kehler busied himself with filling the lamp, giving Hayes the impression that there was something he was avoiding saying. Just as Hayes was about to ask what this might be, Kehler shook the oil tin.

"We haven't long to find what we seek. If we're here longer than half a day, I fear we shall have to find our way out by candlelight."

"Then we should be about our business," Hayes said, the moment passing.

The hole in the corner turned out to be about three feet around and they crawled in on bruised knees and blistered hands, Kehler ahead with the lantern, his shadow thrown back toward Hayes, and moving oddly on the floor and stone walls, like some lumbering beast of the underworld.

Hayes found this view of his friend disturbing, as though he had somehow found entrance to a world not meant for men. His knees were swollen and scraped, but he'd learned that if he could force himself beyond the initial torment, it would subside somewhat and become almost tolerable.

For a hundred yards he followed the shadow of the creature that led him, and then, to his relief, the passage opened up a little and they could actually stand if they were careful to duck their heads now and then. Not much farther on, the passage turned abruptly to the right and died in a small pool.

"What is this?" he said coming up beside Kehler.

"A pool," Kehler said, stating the obvious.

"But where does the passage go?" Hayes slumped down on his pack, his gaze darting about the walls, searching.

Kehler was staring at the pool. "The survey ends here," he mumbled.

"What? Ends? Are you telling me we've come all this way to find this?"

"No. We've come seeking something more, I'm just not quite sure where it is, though I have an idea." He spread the now-tattered survey of the cave out on the floor. "If you look here, you'll see what I mean." He put his finger on the Fairy Galleries, and the passage leading away from it toward the west. It came to a pool and stopped—clearly where they were now.

"I thought you knew of another passage. Some secret way that Baumgere had found."

"Well, there is one, I'm sure of it. 'The way, by darkness, into light' Baumgere wrote, and something else. In one of his several versions of the 'Ballad of Tomas' he had marked a passage with an exclamation point and the phrase 'How could I have missed this?'" Kehler sat back and looked at him. "In the song Tomas was looking at his reflection in the Mirror Lake—or, in some versions, a pool—when he slipped and fell. Strong currents swept him away, and when he surfaced, he was in another world. Or at least in passages that led to that world."

Hayes looked at him, stunned. "What are you telling me? That if we leap into this pool we will surface in some other place? Kehler, did you bring me all the way down here to play a cruel jest on me?"

Kehler shook his head. "No, I think Baumgere followed the instructions in the lyric and discovered another part of the cave. He passed through this pool."

Hayes stared at the calm, impenetrable surface of the water and then back to Kehler as though the man had lost his mind. "You aren't talking sense," he said firmly.

Kehler began pulling off his boots and hose. "Perhaps not. But I have come this far, I will not go back out of fear of looking foolish." Kehler stepped gingerly into the pool, and in six strides had reached the wall.

Hayes laughed. "Well, it does not seem to have worked, Kehler. You're still very much here." He could not help it; the entire situation was so absurd. They had put such effort into getting here, and for what?

Kehler bent down, his face near to the surface, staring intently into the dark water.

"Do you see your reflection?" Hayes asked, still laughing. "One mustn't dive in unless one sees a reflection!"

Kehler came out of the pool scowling at his friend. "Well, I am willing to try it."

"What? You'll smash your rather addled brain on the bottom."

"No, look. This is what I think." He fetched pen and ink from his pack and turned the survey over, drawing quickly on the back. "Imagine that this pool is but a low spot in a passage—we've seen plenty of those—and water collects here." He pointed up to the shimmering wall, which was clearly wet and dripping. "So a pool forms, but if one crawls through it, there is a passage on the other side."

Hayes felt his jaw drop open. "You can't be serious! Crawl through a passage filled with water? What if there isn't another side? What if one becomes jammed? Farrelle's blood, Kehler, you would be dead in a moment. A moment! This is too much of a risk. Think, man. Even if you're right, the water level now might be quite different from the time of Baumgere. It could be a hundred feet to air. It could be a mile."

Kehler looked from his drawing to the pool as though somehow gauging its capacity for treachery. "I'm willing to try it."

"You *are* mad. Whatever might be down here, it can't be worth dying over. Seriously, Kehler. Give it up. So we don't find this great mystery and gain fame and wealth. I would rather have my life."

Kehler stood and began to shuck his clothes. "Let us just do an experiment."

"Kehler, I will not let you go into some water-filled passage. You're clearly not rational enough to make sane decisions." Hayes put himself between the pool and his friend.

"I promise, I will not go in. Let us just see if there is a passage, as I guess. That would prove something. If it is merely a wall of rock . . . I will give it up, and we can go back, or search elsewhere."

"You give me your word that you will do nothing rash?"

"My solemn word. I have no more desire to drown than you. Be sure of that."

"Then what exactly are you going to do?"

"I'm going to lie down in this absurdly cold water and see if I can sound the passage with my foot. I promise, I will keep my head above water the entire time. Now get out of my way, Hayes. I'm freezing here and would like to get this over with."

Hayes moved reluctantly aside, and Kehler went resolutely into the water. He sat down near the wall, cursing the cold, and pushed his foot forward.

"You see! There is a hole—just as I said." He almost lay in the water, now, only his head and shoulders showing, more than half his body disappearing under the stone wall.

"Is there another side?" Hayes asked, amazed. "Can you feel it?"

Kehler pushed himself in so that only his face was dry. "No. . . . No, I can't feel anything. It does not seem to get too much tighter, though, which is something." He pulled himself back out, shivering.

"Look, I'm in here freezing as it is. Let me just duck in for a moment. You come in and be prepared to drag me out by my feet. Come on, Hayes, I'm turning to ice."

Hayes stripped off his boots and hose and went into the water, which was colder than he'd imagined.

Kehler took a number of deep breaths, then ducked himself under, flailing forward, his head and shoulders disappearing. In a second he was gone to the waist, then the knees, his absurdly white body being drawn into the dark waters.

Hayes reached down to take hold of a foot, but Kehler shook him off, pushing even farther in.

"Kehler!" Hayes called. "Don't be a fool!"

But Kehler was gone. Hayes knelt down and reached in under the rock as far as he could, but there was no Kehler there to grab.

"Bloody blood and flames! *Keh-ler!*"

What to do? Had Kehler found the other side? Or was he starving for air, and pressing on foolishly, too far in to return?

"You bloody fool! What if it's a hundred feet through! What if there's no other side at all?" He forced himself to be still, listening. The water in the pool had gone calm suddenly, as though Kehler was no longer moving.

"Damn you!" Hayes said, and took three long breaths, but as he was about to duck under in search of his companion, a hand grabbed him about the ankle, and Kehler pushed past, shooting out of the water, gasping, spitting up water and coughing horribly.

"Farrelle's balls, Kehler, you've scared me half out of my wits." Hayes began to pound his friend on the back.

Kehler nodded, drawing in long breaths, unable to speak. His coughing subsided.

"It's there," he managed after a moment. "Not far. Ten, twelve feet."

"You've gone right through?"

Kehler nodded.

"And there is a passage beyond? A passage with air?"

"Yes." He looked up at Hayes. "I had only the poorest light filtering through the water from our lamp, but I could see. . . . There is a room, at least."

"How tight is it?"

"A foot and the half, I think. Not bad. One takes a deep breath and then pulls oneself through. It is not as difficult as you might imagine. It just takes some nerve."

"I should say so! Come get out of this water and dry." He took Kehler's arm and helped him out of the water. "Even if we can get through, we'll be positively soaked. And what of our lantern and gear?"

Kehler pulled on his clothing, huddling close to the tiny flame of their lantern. "I've brought the oiled bags recommended by our guide. They'll keep our clothing at least somewhat dry for the few seconds we will be underwater. We'll extinguish the lantern and wrap it in our clothes. We've got candles as well."

"I'm not sure I can do this," Hayes said, imagining himself stuck in the small passage and dark waters.

"It is not really so difficult," Kehler said. "If one does not let one's imagination get the upper hand. You can hold your breath and crawl a dozen feet. That's all this is. One just has to ignore the water."

"And the possibility of getting stuck and drowning in a teacup."

Kehler smiled. "As I said, one must not allow the imagination a free hand."

Kehler took a candle out of his pack and lit it from the lamp. Dripping a little wax onto a ledge in the rock, he set the candle out of harm's way, then blew out the lantern to let it cool.

By the light of a single candle they began packing their things into the oiled bags.

"It will take more than one trip to bring all this," Hayes said.

"I will make all the crossings necessary, Hayes. You just get yourself through."

Hayes felt fear taking hold of him. A vague panic that was more than just mental. His stomach and bowel complained audibly, and his motions had become stiff and vaguely disconnected, as though he watched but had only imperfect control over his limbs. The stress and strain of their two days in this strange place wore on him, and their lack of sleep did not help. "I don't want to do this," he said suddenly.

Kehler sat down and looked at him. "You don't have to, Hayes. You have done much coming so far. I would hardly have dared it without you. Stay here, if you will. But I can't come this far and abandon it." He looked over at the pool. "Though I will say again that the danger is more imagined than real. I don't think you could get stuck in so large a passage. But suit yourself. . . ." He smiled. "I will still share whatever profit might come of it."

Hayes felt terribly craven, balking at this final test, but he did not swim, and the thought of dying without air—*without air to breathe*—frightened him more than anything he could name.

Kehler tested the lantern again, found it had cooled sufficiently, and in the confined passage began removing his clothes. He wrapped the lantern in these and put the bundle into an oiled cotton bag. This he sealed with a cord and then placed it inside a second bag.

"Wish me luck," he said, shivering a little.

"You have a flint and paper to light the lantern?"

Kehler nodded.

"Then good luck."

Kehler slipped into the water awkwardly, caught his breath and ducked under, propelling himself into the submerged passage. Hayes saw his feet kick and disappear, the water surging back and forth in the pool, and then after a moment it was still.

"Farrelle preserve him," he whispered to the now much emptier passage.

He waited for some sign that his friend was safe on the other side, but there was none.

"Mustn't let the imagination range freely," he muttered.

The candlelight fell upon the dark pool as it undulated slowly—like oil, Hayes thought. And then the faintest glow, like iridescence in the night sea, filtered through the watery tunnel.

Hayes felt himself relax a little.

"Oh, Farrelle's bloody ghost!" he said, and began wrapping food in a shirt and stuffing it all into one of the oiled bags. By the time Kehler reappeared, he had two bags ready and had begun to pull off his shirt.

"Hayes. . . . Are you considering a bath? I must tell you, it is past due."

"I'm sure I can't sit here with my guttering little candle while you go off to make the discovery of our age. I can't guarantee that I can do this more than once in and once to come back."

"No matter. Bring yourself. That will be enough. I'm used to it now. Except for the bloody cold. But be quick. The quicker we're through and dry, the better."

Hayes stumbled into the pool, the cold nearly taking his breath away. He stuck an arm into the hole beneath the rock, testing the way forward. At least there was some light to go toward.

"All right, Samual," he said aloud. "In we go." He took a deep breath and plunged in, clawing along the rock ceiling, panic gripping him immediately. He battered his heels and knees against the rock as he went, and immediately he became desperate for air.

He could not be sure how far he had gone. He cracked his head and then his elbow against hard stone. He was about to turn back, sure that it was much farther than Kehler had guessed, when he realized his face was in air and light.

"Thank Farrelle!" he muttered, scrambling out of the water, huddling near the lamp rather pathetically.

A moment later Kehler appeared, tossing a bag to Hayes and then a second. "Get your clothes on. I'll be back in a moment." He ducked under and disappeared back into the tunnel.

As Hayes pulled on his damp clothing, Kehler reappeared, carrying two more bags.

"One more trip, I think. Empty those bags. . . . Ah, good. Thank you." He disappeared again, clearly anxious to get the ordeal over with.

Kehler appeared again a moment later bearing the last bags and both their empty packs. He came unsteadily out of the water, grabbing up his clothing in trembling hands and pulling it on awkwardly. The two of them sat there, shivering, water streaming from their hair and eyes.

Kehler laughed. "You look like a half-drowned hound."

Hayes laughed as well. "You look much the same."

"It wasn't so bad, really—was it?"

"Yes, it was," Hayes said, and laughed. "Martyr's balls, but I don't look forward to going back."

Kehler shrugged. "It will be easier next time."

"Did you snuff the candle?"

"No. I didn't think. It's still burning. Well, we can't afford to lose any, but . . . I don't think either of us is ready to go back for the sake of saving a candle. Let's go on before we're too cold."

They repacked their bags, drank a cup of netherworld tea, and set off down the passage, which soon became large enough for them to walk upright.

In no time the passage changed. Openings began to appear on one side, most small but some seemed almost large enough for a man. The rock was riddled with them, as though it had been attacked by enormous, boring worms. Fifty feet farther the larger passage ended.

Kehler and Hayes stood looking around, and then at each other.

"There must be a hundred openings here," Hayes said. "And look at them! They are tiny!"

"Just the size of a child," Kehler said dully.

They stood staring at the endless number of openings. Openings that seemed like speechless mouths. Mouths that knew how to keep secrets.

## ⤳ Twenty-Six

Sir John Dalrymple was not asleep when the knock came. Indeed, he could not remember when he had last slept well. In concession to the idea of sleep he had gone through the motions of going to bed, where he then lay in the darkness listening for the sound of nightingales, which he thought he had heard earlier.

His first reaction was to ignore the banging, but when it seemed apparent that whomever it was would not soon stop, he roused himself slowly. A sudden fear struck him and he threw his robe on. *Bryce*, he thought, and hurried to light a lamp.

His accommodations were an odd arrangement, over a carriage house attached to a larger home. A stairway led from his room down to a door into the courtyard or a second door into the main house, where he could take his meals. It was more comfortable than an inn, and relatively inexpensive.

He opened the tiny window in the door and found his fears made real.

"Mr. Bryce! I was asleep. I do apologize," he said, wondering why he apologized for sleeping in the middle of the night!

The man said nothing, but stood waiting impatiently for the door to be opened.

Still without speaking, he led the way up the stairs, forcing Sir John to hurry after, trying to light the way, struggling for breath almost immediately. When they entered the upper room, Bryce turned on him.

"There are agents of the Admiralty, here in Castlebough, watching Skye," Bryce said.

"Ah, I should have thought Moncrief would have been warned off. . . ." He looked at Bryce, wondering why it was of particular concern. If Bryce was not out to bring down Moncrief, as Sir John had once believed, then what were his intentions? "I assume you haven't wakened me just to give me this news?"

"No," Bryce continued to stand, frustrating Sir John, who felt a great need to sit. "I have a task for you, of course. I must speak with this Admiralty man—Captain James is his name—it is an absolute necessity. You will have to arrange it."

"I suppose it would be out of the question for you to simply approach the captain yourself."

Bryce glared at him. The man had no sense of humor at all.

"I thought not. You would like this meeting arranged as soon as possible, I collect?"

Bryce nodded.

"Let me dress, then. I won't be a moment."

Kent was more than embarrassed by what he was doing—he was ashamed. The gate seemed to be barred, but the wall was not high, and there was a convenient barrel meant to catch rain.

He hoped there were no dogs nearby, for though he was as silent as possible, he was only quiet by human standards. In a moment he was over and in a lane between the house and garden wall. He stole along in the faint light of the stars, feeling before him as he went, listening for the sounds of discovery.

If he were caught doing this it would mean his ruin. "*Fool*," he hissed without meaning to. He had barely missed ruin once that evening, and he was still not out of the woods on that one. Not in his wildest dreams had he imagined the countess displaying his painting to everyone and starting a game to see who could name the artist. What a buffoon he would look if someone discovered the truth!

But that was nothing compared to what he would suffer if he were discovered now.

"*Go back*," he urged, but he was past listening to the voice of wisdom. Kent seemed to be divided in half. Part of him, the sensible part, was aghast at his actions but unable to do anything to stop them. He was being ruled by something else. Not his heart, he hoped, for he had always hoped his heart was more noble.

*It is a madness*, he thought. *I will be fighting duels next, and I have not spent as much as an hour in her company.*

He came to the corner of the house and peeked out to see what was there. A terrace, doors and windows, all closed. There seemed to be light coming from one room. For a moment he stood in the shadow, certain that he was alone, hoping that somehow his common sense would gain the upper hand—to no avail.

He bent low and went under the first window, and then came to the one from which light escaped. It was slightly ajar, and as he came to it heard unmistakably a woman moan. For a second Kent froze in place, almost reeling.

It was his absolute worst fear. It could not be the countess. She had left with Erasmus Flattery, for Farrelle's sake. The man was brilliant, no doubt, but he was hardly an object of fascination to the women of Avonel. No, this must be some maid and her buck. The sounds of love became more insistent.

Ever so slowly Kent raised his head. Before the fireplace a man and woman lay on a divan. A trill of laughter, then a moan. Then suddenly the woman rose, astride her lover, her face hidden by dark tendrils of hair. She moved over her partner more urgently now. With a quick motion she threw her head back, revealing her face, her naked torso.

Kent closed his eyes and let his head rest against the window ledge. It was she. As he stayed thus, he listened to her cry out, unable to contain her pleasure.

He opened his eyes again, watching her move over her lover. Drawing up the man's hands she pressed them tight to her breasts.

When her climax came, she collapsed over her lover, burying him in the dark avalanche of her hair.

"Mr. Flattery!" she teased, her voice filled with pleasure. "You have taken liberties with me, sir! As penance you shall be flogged . . . with my hair—fifty lashes. And you shall have to stay and pleasure me until the light of day."

Kent heard the unmistakable sound of Erasmus Flattery's laughter. The countess rose up again, and Kent did not even attempt to hide, she was so beautiful. The firelight played upon her perfect form, turning her skin the color of copper.

Kent was sure he had never felt such exquisite agony, and at the same time his heart was pounding at what he had just seen. The Countess of Chilton in the act of love. He had heard her cries of pleasure, and though it was not he in her arms, as it should have been, it was more than most men would ever know. At least he had seen her lost to passion. To his obsessed and confused mind, it seemed almost like intimacy.

Sir John waited in the small lobby of the White Hart Inn, having bribed the night clerk to tip him when Captain James came in. Not that it was likely he would mistake the man, but he knew that a bluff must be supported by something—in this case knowing the man's name and business, and very likely knowing who had sent him as well.

In his mind, he turned the possibilities over again. Moncrief and Brookes had set out to bring Skye to ruin, but surely his miraculous escape must have made them realize that this endeavor should be abandoned. So why had they men watching Skye still?

One thing was certain. The Admiralty did not continue to monitor the activities of Lord Skye without the Sea Lord's approval, though he may have distanced himself from the endeavor. Perhaps the real question was: Who in the Admiralty's intelligence department was utterly loyal to the Sea Lord, and therefore would not reveal their activities to the government? Likely Admiral Matheson, he reasoned. The man was brilliant, and utterly trustworthy. It almost had to be Matheson.

The door opened, and a tired, unshaven man appeared. He was not dressed in uniform, though his bearing was unmistakable. Sir John looked over at the clerk, who nodded.

"Captain James?"

The man stopped as Sir John rose from his chair.

"Sir?"

"Sir John Dalrymple. Foreign Ministry. I've been asked to have a word with you by a mutual friend," he said, offering his hand.

The officer's eyes narrowed as he took Sir John's hand.

"Have we met, sir? You are very familiar."

"It is likely. I'm in and out of the Admiralty offices regularly, for we have much business in common. Admiral Matheson is a particular friend, as is the Sea Lord himself."

"Ah, yes, of course." The man's eyes opened fully and he smiled. James looked tired enough to collapse where he stood, though he still held his shoulders square, even if his head seemed to bow a little.

"Can we speak more privately, Captain James? I shall not take but a moment of your time."

James retrieved a key from the clerk. "Will you come up?"

"If you don't mind, I have something to deliver to you. My lodgings are not far."

James looked at him suspiciously.

"I know it seems a bit odd, but . . ." He cast his gaze around the room. "I would like to be certain we speak in privacy. I am fulfilling the instructions of your superior. Do you understand?"

James hardly seemed less mystified, but he nodded. They stepped out into the night, and proceeded down the street and around the corner. Bryce had instructed him to bring James four blocks to a certain dark corner.

"Where are we going, Sir John?"

"But two blocks more. Not far. I do apologize for the mystery, and the lateness of the hour."

He found the carriage drawn up in the shadow of a darkened house, but it was not Bryce's carriage. It was hard to see in the dark, but it was a large, old-fashioned looking coach, drawn by a four horse team.

He thought James might balk as they approached the carriage, yet he did not seem in the least concerned.

"The carriage waits for you," Sir John said, the exact phrase Bryce had told him to use, and James nodded as though acknowledging an order.

Stopping twenty feet off, Sir John saw the door swing open and James climb unconcernedly aboard, as if it was not the most unsettling thing. The carriage moved off without a word from the driver, who hunched on the seat above, bent over his reins like a very old man.

*Well*, Sir John thought, *my involvement with Mr. Bryce becomes more and more strange.* He rather hoped no ill befell Captain James.

His head filled with questions, Sir John set out for his rooms, but soon realized that he would not sleep this night and so continued along the street, wandering about the town like a man utterly lost.

## ⤳ Twenty-Seven

It was a journey of several hours from Castlebough to the cave mouth, so Erasmus and Clarendon had left at first light. They rode a horse and a pony, while behind them followed a servant leading a packhorse that bore their gear.

On some level Erasmus was aware that the countryside they passed through was beautiful, but his attention was fixed on memories of the previous night, which he turned over and over in his mind.

*If I live to a hundred years, I shall never know a night to be its equal,* he thought.

The countess had made him no promises. In fact, her manner had left him uncertain as to their future, and this offset the incredible bliss that he felt—but only a little. Never had he imagined that he would win the favors of such a woman. Not that he had been entirely unsuccessful in his pursuit of the fairer sex, but still . . . *the Countess of Chilton.*

And here he was, entirely against his will, setting off into a cave in search of two foolish young men—and whatever it was that they had found. How he wanted to be back in Castlebough in the company of the countess. She had not quite understood why he was undertaking this expedition, and he did not really feel he could explain it all to her. Not that he completely understood himself. What, exactly, did Kehler expect to find in this cave? Certainly whatever it was, it had the Farrellite Church concerned, and this as much as anything drew Erasmus.

"You look alternately troubled, then happy beyond one's dreams, Mr. Flattery," Clarendon said suddenly. There hadn't been much conversation since leaving the road for the simple reason that the trail through the trees forced them to ride in single file, but they were crossing a wide meadow now and Clarendon had dropped back to ride beside his companion.

"I am worried about these young gentlemen," Erasmus said, not commenting on his alternate mood.

Clarendon smiled at him. "They do not seem like impetuous young men, Mr. Flattery. I'm certain we shall find them perfectly well; at the worst they might suffer a bit from disappointment."

"You don't think they'll find whatever it is they're seeking?"

Clarendon shook his head. "The cave has been explored by some very dedicated men over the years, men who were a bit obsessed by their endeavor, and nothing but natural miracles have been reported. These men had a great deal more experience than your young friends, as clever as they might be. No, I think they will be disappointed, but nevertheless, we shall go in and find them if that is what you wish."

"My concern, Randall, is that Kehler had some information that the more experienced explorers did not, and that might lead them into unknown dangers."

"But Hayes would never say what this information was?"

Erasmus shook his head.

"Though certainly it related to Baumgere's search. Perhaps they will find the source of the priest's wealth. From what you have said, Mr. Hayes, at least, would not be hurt by such a find."

They rode into the trees again where the narrowness of the path allowed no further conversation.

The trail went up and after an hour of climbing they came to an indentation in the mountainside. Here, in a hollow, they found two men sitting on moss-covered rocks and talking quietly. It took Erasmus a moment to realize that the older of the two was Deacon Rose, for he had abandoned his priestly robes in favor of a huntsman's garb.

"Ah, Mr. Flattery, you have come at last," the priest said, rising from his seat. "I was beginning to think you had changed your mind."

"Changed my mind?" Erasmus said. "I don't remember making a decision to meet you. Deacon Rose."

"Nor do I suggest you did, but nevertheless, here you are, and if I cannot accompany you, then I shall merely follow. I assume you will not stop a man from going into the cave if that is his wish?"

Erasmus swung a leg over his horse's back and dropped to the soft ground. For a moment he stood staring at the priest, and then he glanced up at Clarendon, who remained on his pony. The small man raised his eyebrows, his mustache almost twitching.

Erasmus was not sure how he should respond. Certainly he wasn't prepared to stop the priest from entering the cave. What was he to do? Tie up Rose and his companion?

Yet he did not trust *Demon Rose*, as Kehler named him. The man was not telling the truth about what he knew, that was certain, and his intentions toward Kehler were not clear. The church bred a certain kind of arrogance in its priests, and they did not hold much respect for the sovereign rights of mere citizens.

"I might be more inclined to take you with us, Deacon, if you were to tell me what you, and what Kehler, expect to find here."

The priest stood looking at Erasmus for a moment, considering, then he inclined his head to one side. "Let us speak more privately, Mr. Flattery."

Erasmus handed the reins to Clarendon's servant and motioned for his companion to follow. They walked beyond the hearing of Rose's guide, into the dappled sunlight of the pines, and a view opened up before them. Far below they could see a lake, and for the first time Erasmus noticed the fragrance of the trees.

"I am sworn to secrecy, Mr. Flattery, and a priest does not break such an oath easily, but I feel that your request is eminently reasonable, so I will break my covenant this time." The man stopped and drew a breath, considering where to begin. "I am not absolutely certain what Kehler discovered in Wooton, and I say this in complete truth. He disappeared before we could question him and discover the extent of his betrayal—which is what it was," he said, showing a little pain. "A betrayal of trust." He paused again. "I have been sent here to be sure that this betrayal does not bring my church into conflict with Lord Eldrich. In this matter I am hoping for your assistance, Mr. Flattery. It is my greatest hope to stop Mr. Kehler in his endeavor before he draws the attention of the mage."

"But what is his endeavor?" Erasmus said quickly, his impatience taking control.

Rose nodded, realizing perhaps that he could no longer answer Erasmus with vagaries. "It is likely that what Kehler found in Wooton was a painting by Pelier; a painting and perhaps a letter from the priest who refused last rites to Baumgere."

Erasmus could see that Rose suddenly had Clarendon's full attention.

"Mr. Kehler likely learned that Baumgere spent a great deal of time searching the cave. And the painting . . . the painting showed someone offering knowledge. Not just knowledge but knowledge of the arts of the mages. Forbidden knowledge, Mr. Flattery. I'm sure that is what Baumgere sought, and what, in turn, Mr. Kehler hopes to find."

"The other night you suggested this all had something to do with Teller," Erasmus said.

The priest nodded again. "It is possible."

"He hid records in the cave. Is that what you think?"

"I don't know, Mr. Flattery. Pelier's painting, like all of his work, is open to interpretation. But it seems likely that Mr. Kehler believes something is hidden here, and likely Baumgere did as well, though he never found it."

"And if that is so, why are you here?" Erasmus asked. "Even if Kehler finds some records or texts, it is, as you suggest, Mr. Kehler who will bear the brunt of Eldrich's anger, if the mage even finds out."

"I am here because we have a pact with the mage. If Mr. Kehler has found his information in our archives, it is more than likely that Eldrich will hold us accountable. But if I can convince Kehler to abandon this quest, then perhaps I can avert the intervention of Eldrich. And if Kehler finds what he seeks, I will see it myself and be the first to report it to the mage, unless you yourself do it before me. In either case you will be a witness, Mr. Flattery, and Eldrich will know that we have not broken our pact with him. Nor will we, Mr. Flattery. Let me assure you."

Erasmus looked over at Clarendon but could not read the man's reaction.

"I will not be a burden to you, Mr. Flattery. I work almost daily in the fields and barns of our monastery, and it has long been my great joy to explore the meadows and woods, walking many miles in a day. I will not slow you or need your help as we go."

Clarendon had planted his feet far apart, hands on his hips. "You will let us consider what you have said in private, Deacon Rose." It was said with remarkable firmness, from a man who did not reach the priest's shoulder.

Erasmus followed Clarendon away a few steps.

"What do you make of this, Randall?"

"As much as I hate to admit it, I think it would be better if he accompanied us, Mr. Flattery. I will feel more comfortable if he is under our watchful eye. I still do not trust him, though what he has said has me suddenly anxious. Could this matter interest Eldrich? Are those young men doing something incredibly foolish?"

Erasmus shook his head. "I don't know, Randall. I'm not such an authority on the mage as some people think. It seems unlikely to me that Eldrich has any notion of what two rather anonymous young gentlemen are up to. But if Baumgere searched here for some hidden records of the Tellerites, then it is a matter of great concern. Hayes and Kehler might not realize how much this would interest Eldrich, and how he might react to such a discovery. Rose is right in this. Better to inform the mage of what is found and then say nothing to anyone. I can't imagine what Hayes and Kehler think they will do with this knowledge."

"Then we will take the priest and watch him closely," Clarendon said. "Are we agreed?"

Erasmus nodded. "Reluctantly, yes."

An hour was lost while they prepared themselves to enter the cave. It was decided to take two lanterns and keep one carefully packed for use in case the first should be damaged or lost. They also split an enormous bundle of candles into three smaller packages.

"We must have light and more in reserve," Clarendon said. "A hundred feet into this cave we enter a world that is beyond the reach of starlight or sun. It is a blackness you have likely never experienced before. Without light we shall come to harm, gentlemen, have no doubt of it. Light. It is about to become the most precious commodity we have. A day into the cave and you would pay gold for it. Mark my words, you would give everything you own for a spark."

After resting for a moment and eating a little, they shouldered their packs and set off down the path to the cave mouth. The opening was hung with moss and vines which covered the hard rock that extended back into the darkness. The entrance to the underworld—though it was not guarded by wolves as the myths said.

They lit their lantern in the sunlight, and then, with Clarendon in the lead, set off into the darkness. Thirty feet into the cavern, Erasmus turned and looked back at the irregular patch of green framed by the cave mouth. Sunlight tumbled through the trees onto a bed of moss and lit the swaying ferns. Erasmus thought the world looked incomparably fair and verdant. He turned back and hurried after his companions who made their way resolutely downward into a land devoid of sunlight and rain and the whispering of wind in the pines.

## ⌒ Twenty-Eight

Kells tapped a glass paperweight against the table.

Knock . . . knock . . . knock. Pause. Then repeated again. He was unaware of it, Anna knew, as were most of the others, but it had begun to drive her to distraction.

Knock . . . knock . . . knock. Pause.

"Skye remains on the surface," Kells said at last. "And if he is to open the gate, as Anna has seen, then we might be advised to stay on the surface as well."

"But it is a vision," Banks said in frustration, "and therefore requires interpretation. I think the gate *is* open . . . *now*. Look who has gone down into the cavern: both these young men Skye employed; the priest; and Flattery and Clarendon as well. They have hardly undertaken such a thing for amusement."

"I think Banks is right," Anna said. "It feels . . . true to me. The gate is open, and we sit here idly arguing. If Flattery has gone down into the cave, then it is all but certain, I think."

"But he went in the company of a priest, and not just any priest—Deacon Rose. If Erasmus Flattery still serves Eldrich . . . well, *there* is an unholy alliance for you."

"But if Flattery still served Eldrich," Anna said, "would he expend all of his energies seeking knowledge of the mages, as we all know he does?"

"Over the centuries," Halsey said, "many have served the purposes of the mages and not known. Erasmus Flattery could very easily be one of these." The old man shifted in his chair, lost in thought. He was always uncomfortable, never quite free of pain, Anna knew. If she hadn't resented him so at that moment she was certain she would pity him his suffering.

"I fear, though, that Anna and Banks are right," Halsey said slowly. "The gate is open." He moved carefully in his chair, his eyes pressed tightly closed—the only sign of pain he showed. "I think the question is, how much risk are we willing to take? All other discussion is mere distraction. Do we go down into the cave not knowing if Erasmus Flattery still serves Eldrich? And do we go, knowing full well both the loyalties and intent of Deacon Rose?" He looked at the others around the table, holding the gaze of each of them for a moment.

Knock . . . knock . . . knock . . . pause.

Anna took a deep breath, knowing the full significance of the decision they made. "I believe Erasmus Flattery does not serve Eldrich, but pursues the knowledge of the mages of his own accord. As such, he is our natural ally. The priest is another matter. He will destroy us if he can. We cannot be misled by any lie or subterfuge he might employ. It is his sworn duty to destroy us, and therefore we must . . . do what the situation requires. And I believe we can."

Halsey stared at her for a moment, just a hint of emotion there, then turned to the others. "Kells?"

"I can't dispute Anna's vision if she feels this is the time. . . . I agree that the risk is Flattery. We simply do not know with any certainty what his loyalties are. And even if he hated Eldrich more than any man alive, that still would not mean that he did not serve the mage. Halsey is right in this; many have unwittingly served the mages." He looked down at the paperweight, hefting it as though he tapped it against an invisible surface. "But if the gate has been opened and the knowledge of Anna's vision is in the cave . . . we have little choice, I think. But—"

"Exactly so!" Banks interrupted. "There is no choice. That's what I—"

"Mr. Banks . . . !" Halsey said. "Let Kells finish. Please!"

Banks nodded, hanging his head a little. Anna felt pity for him—it was so frustrating at times.

"I was going to say that Anna must be prepared to be far more . . . merciless than she has ever been." He looked up at Anna. "Do you understand? This priest—in fact, all of these people—their mere existence could threaten us. Eldrich must never know what has been found. Never. Or he will train others."

Anna nodded, looking down. She was hardly able to find her voice. "I—I knew it might come to this. Deacon Rose, I believe, is well within my abilities. Erasmus Flattery is a risk. We all know it. If Eldrich trained him . . ."

"He has no familiar," Banks said firmly. "Flattery would have a familiar."

"It is not impossible to hide such a thing," Halsey said.

"I will do what is required to protect us. I must," Anna said. No one answered, and unable to bear the doubt-filled silence, she went on. "And there is something else. . . . Something we never discuss, for we hardly dare hope such things. In my vision the man had a blossom." She looked at Halsey. "If there is seed, then we should hold nothing back. I say risk everything for the seed."

Halsey did not respond, but only held her gaze a moment. "Then you will go down into the cave," he said quietly. "But if this knowledge you have seen is real—if you find it—then I charge you to let none of these others return to the surface, for if anyone escapes with knowledge . . . Eldrich will find us. Do not think this is just the irrational fear of an old man. Eldrich will find us, and his revenge upon us will be terrible."

## ⤳ Twenty-Nine

Holding the lantern as near to his face as he dared, Kehler pressed his finger to the rock and lifted it away, examining the ball of his finger for residue.

"Chalk, I think. Look." He held his finger out to Hayes.

"Taste it," Hayes suggested.

Kehler considered this for a second, decided there was likely no harm in trying and thrust the finger into his mouth. "Eagh!" He spat on the cavern floor. "No doubt of it. Chalk mixed with mud, I think."

"Baumgere, I suppose?"

Kehler nodded. "Unless someone else has been here before us. It would make sense to mark what you'd done. The place is a labyrinth. It would be easy to forget which passages you'd explored. We should mark them as well."

"But chalk is hardly permanent. Wouldn't it have made more sense to use something that would last?"

"Perhaps, but would you carry a pot of paint in here? It has been many years since Baumgere was here, so the marks have almost gone, but perhaps in the short time he was searching—maybe only a few months, or even weeks—the chalk would have been adequate." Kehler paused for a second. "Or maybe he didn't want to leave permanent marks. He may even have erased them himself."

They looked back at the faint smudge on the rock. Several such marks had been found, each above an opening, though they were illegible, now, if they ever had been writing. Unfortunately no signs could be seen above many of the passages and Hayes and Kehler didn't know if this meant these passages had not been explored or if the chalk had simply worn away over the years.

Hayes looked down the length of the passage. There must have been forty openings in the short distance he could see. "Would you not approach this with some kind of order?" he asked. "I would certainly start at one end and work my way to the other."

"Yes, certainly. Meaning?"

"Well, if we can find the last passage that Baumgere explored we would save ourselves a great deal of effort. Do you see what I'm saying? Even if the last passage on which we can discern a mark is not the last he explored, we could still be eliminating some of them."

"Yes, that would make sense." Kehler moved to the next passage and began searching the rock around the opening.

After several hours of effort, they finally chose the passage they believed was the last that still bore a mark, and this eliminated perhaps fifteen openings—less than half the possibilities, though Kehler was quick to point out that any number of passages could possess branches, making the number potentially greater—perhaps much greater.

They sat to eat and rest, for both of them were greatly fatigued, as well as stiff and sore. The exploration of caves was not as painless as they liked to pretend.

Kehler fell into a deep sleep in the middle of their meal, and Hayes blew out the lamp and shut his eyes. It was important to preserve fuel. Strangely, he could not sleep, though he was as deeply fatigued as he could remember being.

He lay in the dark, feeling the immeasurable tons of rock above him, imagining the layer of soil, and then the thin cover of vegetation. Above them the night would be unfolding. Somehow he was sure a soft breeze swayed through the branches and the sweet fragrance of the forest filled the night. Overhead stars sparkled in a clear sky.

The fantasy would not hold, however, for even in the darkness Hayes could feel the cave around him. It had a certain smell, not unpleasant, but, still, for him it would always be associated with darkness and the damp and the constant weight of the rock above.

Kehler began to snore softly, and Hayes pulled his collar closer around him, suddenly cold. He tried not to think of the trek out; the abyss above the

falls, the climbs, the sections where they would be forced to crawl. The cave
entrance seemed impossibly far away, as unreachable as the past.

At last he fell into a troubled sleep and began to dream that he was lost in
the tunnels of an endless cave, wandering through an eerie semidarkness,
constantly coming to brandlings and not knowing which way to turn. Occasionally he would see lights in the distance and think that he was rescued, but
run as he might he could never catch the bearers of the light, and he would be
left alone again, hearing only the distant fall of footsteps, and what sounded
like muttering.

He lay in the darkness listening to an even breathing.

*This is no nightmare*, he realized. *I am awake.*

Even though he had no idea how long he'd slept, he decided to light the
lamp and rouse his companion. They had much work to do and had not meant
to sleep at all.

They began with the initial unmarked tunnel, Kehler insisting that the
first would be his. The opening was small, almost round, and quite smooth.
Kehler pushed himself into this, his legs kicking awkwardly for a moment,
and then he disappeared, drawing the light in after him. Hayes was left in the
darkness with only the sounds of Kehler's progress for company. Every so
often he would call into the opening, checking on his friend, and he and Hayes
would share a few words, then he would find his pack in the blackness and sit
down, embarrassed by how dejected and alone he felt. Perhaps three quarters
of an hour passed and suddenly a faint glow emananted from the passage
Kehler had disappeared into. Hayes became confused as the light grew, for it
almost seemed to him that the glow came from the opening next to the one
Kehler had entered.

Anxiety gripped him; the next exploration would be his, and Hayes was
not looking forward to it.

A few moments later the light grew from a glow to its anemic best, and the
lantern swung out into the open. Hayes forced himself up and took it from his
friend's hand. "I must be in a muddle," he said, "for I would have sworn you
entered this next opening down."

Kehler's head and shoulders appeared. "You're not as addled as you think.
I began in the next passage, but it joins this one and then peters out to nothing. I was able to turn around in the join and come out this way."

Kehler stood up stiffly and let out a long breath. "Well, it wasn't so bad.
Shall I do another?"

"No, it's my turn. There is oil enough in the lamp? Then I shall be tortured next."

He sloughed off his coat, and took up the lantern. The next passage was no larger than the first two, but more importantly it was not smaller, and Hayes reached the lantern in and, with great reluctance, crawled in behind.

Once in the tube for his full length Hayes stopped. He looked down the narrow tunnel, which bent away from him and went up slightly. What he could see did not seem terribly frightening. Tight but no worse than he had done. It was what lay beyond that preyed upon his imagination. Could it become so tight that he would not be able to go either forward or back?

With great effort Hayes pushed back the fear and forced himself to go on. From previous experience he knew that his shoulders were made narrowest if he put one arm forward and one back and slithered along on his side or stomach, depending on the shape of the passage. He would move the lantern ahead a few inches then drag himself along, scrabbling for purchase with his feet, regulating his breathing so that he did not panic, for panic was the great enemy. He would have been better to have been born with a less active imagination, as it only made things worse. He could imagine the most gruesome scenarios: getting stuck in the passage; breaking the lamp and setting himself on fire in a place where he could barely move, let alone put himself out; and on and on. He shut his eyes and tried to will the images away. Best to think of nothing but moving ahead the next few inches, of moving the lantern carefully, being sure to set it where it would not fall and shatter the chimney.

To his great relief the passage did not grow tighter, nor did he set himself ablaze, so after thirty feet he began to relax a little. Suddenly the passage opened into a small room perhaps four feet square and here he sat up and rested for a few minutes, drawing deep ragged breaths.

From this room the tunnel continued on at an angle from an upper corner and he studied it for a moment, thinking it might be hard to get started unless there were some good holds inside that he could use to pull himself up. For a second he considered merely going back and telling Kehler that the passage ended, but he realized that he would not feel right about telling such a lie—and what if the secret they sought were here? No sense coming all this way and not making as thorough a search as they were able.

As he reached for the lantern to go on, he realized that a small bit of metal lay on the floor. He picked it up and found he held a copper rivet, perhaps from a belt or even a boot. This was not an unexplored passage! Someone had been here before. He looked up at the opening. If it was true that Baumgere did not find what he sought, then there was little reason to go on. Hayes felt his spirits lift.

Resolving to at least look into the tunnel, he thrust the lantern into the passage and peered in. Wedging himself in the opening, he managed to crawl in six feet, but it definitely tightened down to the size of a man's head in another length.

His energy restored by this, he crawled back out to the main passage and found Kehler wrapped in a blanket, fast asleep.

"Well, I'm glad I didn't need to call for help," he said as he shook his friend awake. "Look at this." He held the rivet out for Kehler to examine.

"You found it in there?"

"Yes. The passage burrows in for thirty feet or so to a small room. From there the passage doesn't go seven feet before shrinking down to mole size. But the rivet was on the floor."

"Farrelle's ghost. So Baumgere had explored this far."

"Assuming it was Baumgere."

Kehler nodded, continuing to stare at the bit of copper. "It is unfortunate that we are still poking into passages that our good fallen-priest already eliminated, but I can see no other method of going about this. Can you?"

Hayes shook his head.

Kehler forced himself up. "Well, my turn for the fire." He lifted the lantern and shook it slightly, listening to the sound of fuel in the reservoir. Before he entered the next opening he took a candle and marked those that they had explored with an X in wax. A moment latter he had wriggled into the rock, leaving Hayes to listen to his progress and watch the light fade to darkness.

Hayes wrapped himself in Kehler's blanket and settled on the two packs. It was hard to stay awake, but he wanted to be sure to hear his friend should he call out.

And so it went for several hours as they eliminated one passage after another. Exhaustion caught up with them and they slept. As they became more and more fatigued, Hayes found it harder to stay warm when he was not exerting himself and lay shivering in the darkness, sleeping fitfully and shifting his position often. Each time he slept, the dream returned, though he never managed to catch up with the lights and their bearers, but wandered alone in the underworld, hollow with hunger and thirst and yearning, never able to find his way out.

A rasping wakened him, and Hayes opened his eyes to a slight glow coming from the opening his friend had crawled into some unknown time ago. Hayes threw aside the blanket and stumbled as he went. From out of the hole he could hear muttering and the harsh rasp of breath. Hayes stuck his head in the hole and called out.

The sounds stopped and Hayes called out again.

"Am I almost out?" came Kehler's reply, though it was half grunted as he began to move again.

"I think so. I can hear you clearly."

"Farrelle be praised."

It was another quarter of the hour before Kehler's feet appeared and Hayes took hold and dragged his exhausted friend out. Kehler wavered as he found his feet and Hayes grabbed hold of him lest he fall.

"Sit down, Kehler."

"No, let me stand." He steadied himself on the rock wall. "Let me feel the space around me." He moved his arm and worked his cramped shoulders, gasping as though he had been under water.

"Flames," he said between breaths. "Bloody blood and flames. What a hellhole."

"What did you find?"

"Find? Nothing, only two hundred feet of passage so tight I thought I should never get out again. Farrelle's flames, I hope they're not all like that." He lowered himself to the rock and leaned his back against the wall. "How long was I gone?"

Hayes produced his timepiece. "Three hours and a bit, I think."

"Well. . . . We will be here some time if they all take such effort. Flames, I wish we knew which tunnels Baumgere eliminated. We could save ourselves days. We haven't brought nearly enough food, I fear."

"We'll have to ration, that's all."

"Yes, but all this effort has made me hungry all the time."

"Well, it is about mealtime anyway—noon in the world above." Hayes began to rummage in his pack for food. "Let's eat something, and then I'll take my turn."

Before they ate, Kehler took up a candle and made a prominent X above the opening he had just explored, as though to be absolutely sure not to have to enter it again.

They ate and drank and spoke of small things of the world above. Laughed at old stories of wilder days, and did everything they could to put the matter they pursued from their minds. Hayes had never really been convinced that they would find fame and fortune from this mad endeavor, but had accompanied his friend partly out of loyalty, partly from curiosity, and perhaps in part for lack of anything better to do. His creditors were unlikely to find him here. But now that the true cost of the exploration was becoming apparent, he wondered if it would not be more sensible to give it up. It was difficult for him to imagine that they would find anything that would make this terrible crawling into the bowels of the earth worthwhile.

"Can you bear to do another?" Kehler asked after they had both avoided the issue as long as possible.

Hayes felt the darkness reach out and touch him, the infinite cold stored in stone seeping into his beating heart. "We can't quit now," he heard himself say. He tried to control his fear. "I, for one, need the fortune you promised."

With the utmost care he filled the lantern, knowing that they could ill afford to spill a drop.

Hayes stretched his stiff muscles, took up the lantern, and went to meet the next passage. His courage failed him as he stood looking into the dark mouth that was about to consume him, but then he forced himself to go on. Leaning down, he stretched as far as he could, setting the lantern in the passage. He was surprised at how unresponsive his muscles were, as though he had driven them beyond exhaustion and now they no longer answered to his commands as they should.

He crawled awkwardly into the unyielding rock, feeling it bite into his battered knees and the heels of his hands. When his hip contacted the rock, Hayes stopped for a moment and let the pain subside.

"I feel like an old man," he muttered to himself.

"What's that?" he heard Kehler call out.

"Nothing but curses. Put on the tea, I shan't be but a moment."

He reached out and moved the lantern ahead, dragging himself after it, battering his shoulder cruelly into the rock. On he went, trying not to think about what lay ahead. He didn't even look up the passage except to move the lantern, for it hurt too much to wrench his neck around any more than he had to. A few moments passed before he began to warm from the exertion and then he broke out in a sweat that did not feel natural, as though he were falling ill as well.

The passage tightened down around him, and he contorted himself around to find a way forward, trying to maneuver his shoulder and hip around irregularities in the rock. For a moment Hayes jammed his shoulder back against a swelling and forced himself to relax, breathing deeply. He was so tired that he could hardly force himself to move.

He closed his eyes and concentrated on breathing. He knew he wasn't seriously stuck here, it was more the fatigue, he hardly had the strength it required to get himself free.

"*I can go back*," he reassured himself. "*Go back*." His voice sounded so overwhelmed with fatigue and laden with sadness that he almost thought he listened to another, and this frightened him almost more than anything. He shook himself, not sure if he had begun to fall asleep.

Forcing himself to back up a little, he managed to release his shoulder and then wriggle around to get past the projection that impeded him.

The cold sweat did not abate, as though it were not a bodily fluid at all but cold fear that flowed out of his pores.

He reached out to move the lantern, forcing himself to raise his head so as not to burn his fingers yet again, and he recoiled in horror, smashing himself hard into the stone, and hearing himself cry out. The lantern toppled, leaking oil, and immediately caught fire. And there he stuck, gasping for breath, cowering back against the stone, unable to bear the sight. Beyond the flames lay a human skull, a tiny wisp of hair still clinging to it like a spider's web. One skeletal hand reaching out toward him, toward the world of light.

*Oh, bloody flames. Farrelle save me. . . . It is a child. A poor, forsaken child.*

Without thought as to what would happen, he reached quickly into the flame, putting the lantern upright, his sleeve catching fire.

*"Nooo!"* He battered his wrist against the stone in desperation and managed to put the sleeve out before he went up in flame himself, though his hand stung insufferably from burns. He coughed from the smoke and backed away from the lantern that still sat in the center of a ball of flame.

*Flames! Let me go. It is a child. Baumgere's child. Farrelle grant him peace.*

The leaked oil burned away, and though he was nearly blind from the sting of the smoke, Hayes forced himself to move forward again, and reached out gingerly and touched the lantern's handle. Still too hot. He would have to wait.

He could see the entire skeleton now, spread out behind the skull, so small and shrunken he wondered how the child could ever have become jammed in such a passage, but he was sure that was what had happened, for it narrowed to almost nothing around the child's remains.

After the handle had cooled, he lifted the lantern with his burned hand and began a slow retreat, not taking his eyes from the horror, as though afraid it might follow.

The crawl out was painfully slow, inching along like a slug, finding his way through the narrow parts, until he emerged in the passage again. He lay on the floor while Kehler bent over him and took up the scorched lantern.

"Did you call me? I awoke to a sound, but I was not sure if it was a dream." He looked at his friend who sat up now and covered his face with his unburned hand. "Hayes? Are you all right?"

Hayes shook his head, though he kept his hand over his face, as though he could shut out the horror. "I found the child . . . Baumgere's child."

He felt Kehler's hand on his shoulder. "Wedged in the tunnel?"

Hayes nodded. "Though the skeleton is so small it is impossible to imagine how. Flames, Kehler, the man was a monster! Only a child, and he sent him into that hell. What terror the poor boy must have known. The priest was right to refuse that man absolution. I pray he is burning still."

Kehler sat on the floor beside his friend, saying nothing, but hoping perhaps that just being near would mean something. Hayes could not remember shedding tears since childhood, but he felt the sting of them now. The poor child. . . . What a horrible death. Trapped in a nightmare that had but one escape. No one deserved such a death. Except perhaps Baumgere himself.

Hayes felt a rage burn up in him toward this man. It was lucky for Baumgere that he was long dead, for Hayes was certain he would seek him out, otherwise. Refusal of absolution might seem like a terrible punishment to a Farrellite, but Hayes had a more earthly retribution in mind.

## ∽ Thirty

Erasmus stood by the lake of the mirror, holding his lantern aloft to illuminate the scene. It was haunting, as well as unreal in some way—the strange beauty of another world.

Behind him he could hear the others talking, the sound of their voices carrying down the passage like a strange mumbling in another tongue. He half expected some unknown creature of the underworld to appear.

Erasmus and his companions had soon realized that one lantern was not sufficient for three men, for the leader had to have light, and most of the time this left the last man in near-darkness. It was too dangerous to proceed in this way, so they had lit a second lantern, though they put it out whenever they stopped to rest or eat.

Erasmus shed his pack and began climbing over the nearest rock, searching, and it was just then that the others appeared, the strange rumble of their words turning into common Farr the second they emerged into the chamber.

"There should be a boat here," Clarendon called out to Erasmus. "Can you see it?"

"No. I fear it has been carried away, or Hayes and Kehler have not returned it."

"Can't we climb around?" Rose asked as Erasmus joined them.

Clarendon sat down on his pack, shaking his head, and looking a little angry. "No. That is why the boats were built. It is impossible to pass except over the water. Damn their imprudence. If they are in any trouble, we shall be of no use whatsoever."

"If one can't pass over the water we must pass through it," Erasmus said, peeling off his coat. "How far is it to the end?"

"Three hundred feet, perhaps a bit more," Clarendon said, rising as though he would protest Erasmus' proposal. "But the water is quite deep, and one cannot always find holds along the walls. It is too dangerous, Mr. Flattery. Far too dangerous."

Erasmus pulled off a boot. "But not for one who can swim, Randall, which, fortunately, I can."

"But three hundred feet, Mr. Flattery . . .!" Clarendon said, forcing Erasmus to laugh.

"I don't know exactly how far I can swim, for I haven't measured in some years, but in my youth I swam upwards of five miles at a stretch, so I think I can stay afloat for three hundred feet, even at this advanced age. The problem shall be that when I get to the lake's far end, I will have no light." He stopped pulling off his clothes and considered this. "If we put a candle in a tin bowl I shall try to carry it with me."

This was done, and with some trepidation Erasmus slipped into the icy waters. He tried floating the bowl before him but in ten feet he'd put the flame out. After returning to have it lit again he swam on his back and held the bowl and candle clear of the water. If he went slowly enough and was careful not to blow out the flame with his own breath, he might just make it to the far end.

But this was not to be, most of the way there the flame snuffed out again, and Erasmus decided to carry on, hoping the weak light from the lamps would be enough.

He was shivering when he finally came to the lake's end, and was beginning to imagine all kinds of creatures that might live in such a lake, when a faint curve, too consistent to be natural caught his eye.

He scrambled out of the water, stubbing a toe brutally, and found the two skiffs side by side in the darkness. Without further damage to either himself or the boat he managed to launch one of the craft, and shivering like it was the worst winter, he set his oars to work. In a moment he was back with his companions and pulling on clothes over his wet limbs.

"What lies at the far end?" the priest asked.

"I can't say, for I could hardly see," Erasmus answered, beating his arms across his chest and slapping his shoulders to try to gain warmth.

"Just a small shelf of rock not unlike this, though not so large. Perhaps there was an opening to a passage." Clarendon blew out the flame in one lantern. "I think we should make a meal here and then rest. We have been pressing hard, and this place is as comfortable as any we shall see for some time."

"How far into the cave have you been, Mr. Clarendon?" the priest asked.

"Some way beyond this, to a falls. Once we pass that, it will be as new to me as to you." He began taking food from his pack.

The three men made themselves as comfortable as they could and shared out their food: dried apples and cheese; bread that would soon be too stale to eat; and a bitter smoked meat.

As at their other rest stops, a silence fell over the group and Erasmus was sure that this was because attempts at polite conversation failed and the real questions that lay between them would not be asked—or if they were, would not be answered. Something about the harsh reality of the cave made social discourse seem utterly false—almost an offense to their situation.

So they ate in silence, all three of them speculating, Erasmus was sure. He wondered why Rose was really here. Was it truly fear of Eldrich? But certainly the priest suspected that Erasmus himself was a servant of the mage. There was some other explanation for the priest's presence, or at least he had not told the entire truth.

Erasmus thought the air in the chamber became more and more charged with unasked questions, like the atmosphere before a storm. He was not sure how long this charge could continue to build before it would be released. And he feared that what would be released would not be answers.

Erasmus looked at his two companions. Perhaps it was something about the cave—it was so harsh and unyielding that those who ventured into it could maintain few illusions—but Erasmus had begun to wonder about both Rose and Clarendon. It was obvious that he should not trust the priest, despite the man's very real charm, but now he even looked suspiciously at the savant. It was all so convenient, the way Clarendon found Erasmus at the Ruin, how he just happened to be an authority on Baumgere, and knew about the cave as well—had even explored it himself. Clarendon had refused to allow Erasmus to come down here alone, and it was not some younger man that he sent to guide him. No, he professed to be such an admirer of Erasmus that he must accompany him personally.

Too much coincidence, Erasmus decided, and this was a man who professed not to believe in coincidence.

Clarendon and then Rose drifted into sleep, their soft breathing comforting and somewhat familiar in this harsh place. Erasmus blew out the lantern and then closed his eyes, and though he achieved a state near to sleep, he never quite lost consciousness. His thoughts began to drift, random memories surfacing. He thought of the countess, and a warmth and excitement welled up in him. The idea of taking up a lantern and leaving this place came over him, rushing back to the surface, to this astonishing woman. How had he been so blessed as to have her bestow her favors on him?

But even thoughts of his night with the countess could not keep his focus, and other memories surfaced. His last days in the house of Eldrich, the terrible imprudence of young boys, and the carelessness of his teacher. Walky. What had ever become of the man? Certainly he would not still be alive? But somehow Erasmus felt that he was. There was some odd memory of Walky just at the edge of his consciousness, but he could not quite bring it into the light.

The countess again, stroking him, whispering in his ear, her eyes in the firelight. It was impossible that a woman should have such beautiful eyes. A sudden fear that he would never look into them again felt like a chasm opening beneath him—as though there were suddenly nothing solid in his world.

Percy, his loyal follower, easily influenced by his only friend in the lonely world of the mage's house. Percy . . . gone.

He slipped into something like sleep then, memory blending with dream. The countess sweeping her hair slowly across his chest. A tall man in the dark, and then a flame licked up.

A spark in the darkness, and Erasmus realized he was watching Clarendon relight the lamp, watching the flame shiver into existence, created from nothing—the miracle of fire. The priest stirred, and without saying anything the three men began to ready themselves to go on.

"Mr. Flattery and I should go first with our packs," Clarendon said, hoisting a pack into the tiny boat, "and that will leave only the deacon and one pack for you to bring next trip."

They lit the second lantern for the priest and gingerly Erasmus dipped the oars, pulling the skiff out onto the black water, the blades leaving tiny whirlpools at the surface.

When they were twenty feet out, Clarendon touched Erasmus' arm. "Hold our position," he said quietly, then he sat up and looked back at the Farrellite priest. "Deacon Rose?"

Erasmus turned the boat sideways so that he could see the priest, not quite sure what Clarendon wanted to say.

"I think it's time that we had the truth out in the open."

Erasmus saw that the little man had Rose's attention now.

"You believe that there are followers of Teller still alive, is that not true?"

Rose clearly did not like what was happening, but he kept his temper in check, for there was nothing he could do—a moat divided them. "I don't know what you're saying, Mr. Clarendon. I have come here out of concern for a prize student."

"No, you have come here because you fear he is a follower of Teller, and your church will have no practitioners of the arts remaining when Eldrich is gone. That is why you are here. Now it is time that we spoke plainly, Deacon Rose, or we shall simply leave you here until we return, and unless you can swim like Mr. Flattery, you . . ."

"No!" The priest put out his hands. "No. I must come with you."

Clarendon looked at Erasmus, who nodded slightly, giving him permission to continue. He was more than a little impressed with the small man's boldness.

"The only way you will join us, sir, is by satisfying us with the truth. Not before. Now tell me why you are pursuing Mr. Kehler, and be quick about it. I'm tired of your prevarication—speak now and take no time to concoct a lie."

Rose paced quickly to one side, his hands to his face.

"Row on, Erasmus, the priest cannot be trusted."

"No! You will need me if Kehler has made the discovery he hopes. I don't know if Kehler is a follower of Teller. I pray that he isn't. Nor do I know if there are such people still alive, but Mr. Clarendon is right. It is not impossible. I have been sent by my church to be certain that this heresy no longer exists, and to be sure that Eldrich does not turn his anger on us. I am sworn to preserve the church, Mr. Flattery, that is my function." He ignored Clarendon now, and addressed Erasmus as though appealing to his common sense.

Clarendon, however was not finished, or apparently satisfied. "You were trained to deal with just such a situation, is that not so? I know the church has ways of dealing with the arts—how else could you have rooted out the Teller-ites from among your own?"

Rose nodded his head stiffly. "Yes! Yes, I have been trained to perform this function. We must protect ourselves. If Eldrich were to find out that a student found his way here with information from our archive—It would not matter that we were innocent of any crime, the mage's anger would be turned on us. I cannot allow that, Mr. Flattery, I cannot."

"And what will you do when you find Kehler and Hayes?"

The priest did not answer.

"I don't care for his hesitation," Clarendon said quietly.

"I will obey the orders of my church," Clarendon said quickly.

"That is not an answer, Deacon."

"I will perform a ritual that will determine their . . . *culpability*, and if they are simply innocent young men driven to folly by their curiosity, then I will not harm them."

"But if they are not deemed innocent, you will destroy them if you can," Clarendon called out. "Is that not so?" The priest did not answer. *"Is that not so?!"* he shouted, the words reverberating in the cavern.

"I—I have no choice. If Eldrich is to discover that we have let such a thing occur . . . And think what Eldrich will do. His justice will be less compassion-ate than mine."

"And you believe I will be the witness you'll need to convince Eldrich you act in good faith?" Erasmus asked so quietly that he could see the priest strain to hear.

"Yes, Mr. Flattery, you will be my witness."

"But what if I am a follower of Teller, or what if Mr. Clarendon is?"

The priest shook his head. "Eldrich watches over you, Mr. Flattery; that is what I believe. It is almost certain that followers of Teller, if such exist, would be interested in you. Eldrich would want to know if they ever approached you. No, I do not fear that you can betray Eldrich."

"But Mr. Clarendon?"

The priest shrugged. "Mr. Clarendon is another matter."

Erasmus turned and looked at the small man in the boat with him.

Clarendon's face seemed to sag, his mustache drooping. "Do you suspect me, Mr. Flattery?" his voice very hard, almost hurt.

"I'm sorry, Randall, but I am beginning to suspect everyone, even myself."

"You think you are a tool of Eldrich?"

"It is not impossible, though I have not seen the mage since I was a child. But you change the subject, Randall. You said you do not believe in coincidences, yet there have been any number in our brief friendship."

"I said I didn't believe in coincidences, Mr. Flattery, meaning that I believed there are other reasons, other forces at work. There is a design, that is what I believe."

"And everything will work out for the best?"

Clarendon shook his head, almost sadly. "No, I feel that is very unlikely, for the design depends on men, and men are too often weak when they should stand firm and foolish when they have the greatest need of wisdom. And here we sit, accusing each other, while who knows what awaits discovery inside this cave, or what difficulties our young friends might have found."

"And who began these accusations?" the priest called from the shore. The boat had begun to drift back toward the priest, and Erasmus backed the oars to keep his distance.

"I began the accusations, priest, but I did not begin the lies," Clarendon said, his kind manner disappearing and disdain taking its place.

"Do you plan to test us all, Deacon Rose? Is that your intention?" Erasmus asked.

The priest did not answer. "Do not go alone with this man into the cave, Mr. Flattery. I cannot tell you if he is one of them or not, but we should always be on our guard."

"Ah," Clarendon said, "just like a priest to try to sow the seeds of distrust and dissension. He will turn us against each other, Mr. Flattery. It is their way."

Erasmus did not respond but turned back to the priest. "If you were to perform this trial on Mr. Clarendon, what would result if you found him to be what you most fear?"

Again the priest hesitated.

"I would not survive," Clarendon said, no doubt in his voice. "Is that not so?"

Still the priest did not answer.

"Well, Randall, what of it? Are you a follower of Teller? Speak carefully now, for if you deny it, I might well take you at your word and let the priest perform his trial."

Clarendon's mustache twitched, and Erasmus was not sure if it was from anger. The dwarf met his eyes for a long moment, and then he shook his head. "I am no follower of Teller, nor a member of any such society. No, I am merely a small man of enlarged curiosity, and concerned about these young men. And a friend to you, Mr. Flattery, though you don't seem to believe it."

These words sounded genuine to Erasmus and he felt guilty that he had betrayed this man's trust. It seemed to him that Clarendon had known enough betrayal in his life.

"I . . . I'm sorry, Randall, I'm just confused by all of this. I don't know who to trust any more."

Clarendon nodded. "I understand what you're saying, Mr. Flattery. It is one of life's greatest quandaries—who do we trust. But I vote we do not trust this priest."

"Mr. Flattery?" Rose called out upon hearing this. "There is more. You cannot know what we will find in this cave. If the Tellerites hid something here, it might be protected by the arts. Young Kehler and Hayes, if they are innocent as you think, could be in real danger. Unless you know more than you claim, I do not think you will be able to help them. In fact, you might suffer the same fate. I can detect such things and protect us from them. If you go on alone, you might not be able to return for me if you require my help. Do not leave me here."

Clarendon looked at Erasmus, raising his eyebrows.

"Is this possible?" Erasmus asked him.

The small man shrugged. "Let us row on and discuss it out of earshot."

Erasmus nodded, and called back to Rose. "We will consider what you've said." With that he dug in his oars and set them off across the underground lake.

Neither Clarendon nor Erasmus spoke for some time, nor did they seem to notice the wonders around them, but both brooded on what had been said. It was not until they'd passed through the strait between two small peninsulas that Clarendon spoke.

"What did you make of all that?"

"I don't know, Randall, I really don't. I'm getting the feeling that Rose expects to find . . . something significant in this cave. Perhaps the church has suspected for some time that something is hidden here. And I'm afraid of what he might try to do to our young friends. Whether they are followers of Teller or not matters not to me. I am no minion of Eldrich, and I don't believe it is the place of either the church or the mage to pass judgment on them. Unfortunately, we shall not stop Eldrich if he finds out, and I fear that this priest would not hesitate to inform the mage if he believed it would deflect Eldrich's anger from the church. For that reason I am reluctant to bring him with us. Even if he does no direct harm to our young friends, he might well do greater harm by informing Eldrich."

Clarendon considered for a moment. "But what if his claims are true? Could the followers of Teller have left some kind of charm or spell that could cause us harm? Is that possible, do you think?"

Erasmus nodded. "From the little I know, I would say that it is, though such things fade with time. Still, a well-wrought work of the mage's art can last many decades, perhaps even longer. It is possible. If Hayes and Kehler have encountered such a thing, I don't know what we shall do."

"So, though we may need him, we cannot trust him," Clarendon said.

"That seems to be true."

They came to the end of the lake and brought their boat gently to the shore. They disembarked and unloaded their packs, neither making comment on their dilemma.

The dwarf sat on his pack. "If we could only bind him to his word. . . ." He considered a moment. "We could make him swear an oath to Farrelle."

Erasmus shook his head. "If it came to protecting his church, I think our good Deacon would burn for eternity before he'd put it in danger."

"Then you're saying we cannot trust him to live by his word, so we should go on," Clarendon declared, not sounding so sure of himself, despite his earlier opposition to the priest. "I suppose that if we found need of his services we could come back for him—though he may no longer be waiting."

Erasmus nodded. "We are, of course, doing the same thing as our young friends, and making it difficult if not impossible for anyone to follow. We must hope we don't require rescue."

Having exhausted the argument they sat, still unwilling to make the decision to go on. Suddenly there was a splash and a distant call for help that echoed eerily in the cavern.

"What in Farrelle's name?" Erasmus leaped up and pushed the tiny boat back into the water, climbing quickly aboard. Clarendon set the lantern on the aft seat as Erasmus dropped the oars into their sockets and then swept out into the lake. Another half-muffled call for help and then his name, followed by more frantic thrashing of the water.

Erasmus pulled his little skiff through the narrow pass and quickly found Rose, in the water, clinging to the wall of the cavern. Just as Erasmus spotted him, the priest's grip slipped and he went under, flailing ineffectually. He managed to get a hand on the stone but only pushed himself away from the wall. Erasmus thought he would have to leap in and rescue the man, but somehow the priest's flailing kept him on the surface until Erasmus came near.

But just out of reach Erasmus brought his skiff to a stop.

"Listen to me now. If you upset the boat, we will both be in the water. Take hold of the transom gently, and do not try to pull yourself up. Just hold your head out of the water, and I will tow you to shore. Do you hear me?"

The priest nodded desperately, trying to take a grip on his own fear. Erasmus backed the oars and brought the stern up to Rose. To his relief the priest did as he was instructed.

Erasmus towed the priest back to the place from which he had started and they were joined by Clarendon who had launched the second skiff.

Rose crawled wretchedly up on the rock, looking like a half-drowned dog. "I will swear not to harm Hayes and Kehler," he said between coughing. "I will swear by my church, and my sacred oath." He tried to catch his breath. "But if you do not take me with you, I will be forced to try to make my way across the lake again, for I will not be left behind. I will not."

Erasmus glanced over at Clarendon, who looked on with some concern. The little man nodded and Erasmus stepped ashore to assist the priest, not at all sure they were making the right choice.

## ⌥ Thirty-One

Over the years Eldrich had used entrails, bones, mirrors, cards, even tea leaves, but water and its variations remained his favorite medium. He was not a master of augury, though in the present world he was almost certainly without equal. This did not, however, allow him to forget that compared to practitioners of the past he was not particularly skilled.

The mage also knew the folly of making all one's decisions based on augury—even in the hands of a master, it was, at best, an inexact art. No, one must focus on the so-called "real world," the here and now. But even so, he could not resist the occasional attempt to see into the future, though lately these attempts were more than occasional.

*Everything is so clouded*, he worried. *Nothing is clear.*

He knew that events were building to a crisis, but the closer this point came, the less certain were the signs. But perhaps one more attempt. . . .

He had collected a double-handful of white cherry blossoms, and crouched before the pond, waiting for a cloud to reveal the moon. Starlight would do, if it were pure, but if there was a moon, one had to use it. He heard the sounds of his familiar in the copse nearby. It watched him, a little apprehensive though it did not understand what he was about to do.

*Instinct*, Eldrich thought. *It is a creature of almost pure instinct.*

He looked up at the sky. The moon illuminated a cloud so regular in shape that it looked like a white, translucent stone worn smooth by the endless flow of years. The night resonated inside of him: the movement of the stars and planets. The mage could feel the earth hurtling through the cosmos. He could actually feel it.

For a second he shut his eyes, and experienced himself falling, tumbling through the darkness among the stars.

He looked down into the pond and watched the reflection of the moon emerge from behind its pebble cloud, and at that precise instant he cast the cherry blossoms into the air and watched them fall upon the water. They rippled the surface, creating patterns, and Eldrich focused on them, opening himself to the cosmos for a split second, letting the great void flow into him through this pattern on the water. And a second was all he could bear.

He shut his eyes, reeling back from the water's edge, staggering. He felt his wolf pass near him, felt its uneasiness. He staggered a step or two and dropped to his knees, trying to grasp the kernel of knowledge, nurture it.

A woman riding an armored steed, her hair flowing back, a sword raised. But the steed was a massive wolf, its fur tipped with silver, its eyes impossibly light, like the cloud illuminated by the moon. His vision changed, and he saw a skeleton aflame and heard a long, horrifying scream. And then he gazed into a long tunnel of utter darkness, and saw a single point of light. A spinning star, blue-white and cold as winter.

And then it, too, was gone, and he was spent utterly, gasping, on hands and knees. The world spinning around, hurtling through the cosmos, though no man seemed aware of it. No man.

An hour later Eldrich was still not himself. He sprawled in a chair by the fire, eating a bowl of soup. Practicing the arts always left him warm, except for augury, and that invariably left him shaking and devoid of body heat, as though he had fallen into a winter river. It sapped his strength for some time, leaving him tired and lethargic.

*It is the cold, dark void among the stars*, he told himself. *It enters into one, and is not easily driven out.*

"Lord Eldrich?" his servant said, concern in his voice. He had been saying something, and the mage had not answered.

"Yes, Walky, I'm listening. There is something stationed before the cave...."

"A great wolfhound, sir."

"Indeed...." This news actually focused his mind for a few seconds. "And is it natural, do you think?"

"I don't know, sir. It has only been reported to me. All I can answer for certain, sir, is that it is there."

"It can't be Erasmus'" he mused aloud. "Can it?" he asked the old man who stood so solicitously nearby.

Walky shook his head, clearly troubled. "I wouldn't think so, Lord Eldrich. I . . . I hope it isn't."

"Yes. I hope it isn't as well." Silence. He stirred his soup absent-mindedly, watching the vegetables surface, then drown in the broth.

"The problem is that it seems it will not allow anyone to enter the cave."

"Ah. I am . . . rather tired this evening. My mind. . . . Has anyone tried to kill it?"

Walky shook his head.

"So whoever reported it believed it unnatural?" Eldrich looked back down into his bowl. "Well, I will deal with it, then."

He stared down into his bowl again and suddenly thrust thumb and fore-finger in, bringing them out dripping, but holding a piece of meat. Setting the bowl aside he rose wearily and went to the window, pulling it open. He stood there, facing the night, and made an odd sound, somewhere between the call of an owl and a whistle, though low and long. And then he waited, seemingly with infinite patience.

Walky stayed where he was, not moving, which he believed was the wisest course. He was not exactly afraid of Eldrich's familiar, but the beast was un-predictable, as unpredictable as its master, and Walky was never sure that ei-ther of them would continue to treat him as a valued servant simply because they had done so for many decades. He simply wasn't sure.

Perhaps a quarter of the hour passed before Walky heard the sounds of the wolf as it came over the wall and into the garden. It was panting a little as though it had been on the hunt when the summons came. Unlike Walky, it never looked particularly concerned when it had kept its master waiting. There was a bond between mage and wolf that Walky could not fathom—something far more than man and . . . "pet" hardly seemed the right word.

Eldrich stroked the beast behind its ears somewhat roughly, and spoke low in the tongue of the mages. Walky could not quite hear the words. The wolf took the morsel in a gulp, hardly noticing, it seemed. A moment more of this show of affection, and then the wolf bounded away, leaving its master watch-ing, his hand still raised as though not finished with its stroking.

Eldrich lowered his hand to the windowsill, and supported himself, still fatigued from his efforts. It was certainly not his place to say, but Walky be-lieved the mage indulged in this practice too often. The servant was certain that there were more questions resulting from augury than answers. No, it was all right to See now and again, every few years or even once in a year, but very few weeks went by that the mage did not practice the art in some form. And what did it bring him? Too many possibilities, too many by half.

No, it was not worth the effort.

Walky looked at the mage, still standing before the open window leaning on the frame like an elderly man. It was a sign of desperation, Walky knew. This task Eldrich had been left. . . . Walky feared it was almost beyond him. All the centuries of augury had missed the most important truths, and now there was only one mage left to deal with the situation. The last mage of all, or so he hoped.

Eldrich cleared his throat and Walky put aside his musings, attentive to his master's needs.

"I am sorry about Erasmus, Walky."

The little man felt a wave of sadness settle over him, like leaves upon the earth. "I know you are, sir."

## ᧒ Thirty-Two

The countess shaded herself with a parasol and sat in the stern of the boat, smiling somewhat enigmatically. Kent was trying to smile as well, but the soft look of remembered pleasure on the countess' face made it difficult. He could hardly take his eyes from her all the same, and occasionally he would notice that a look of anxiety would transform her beautiful face, as completely as a cloud would turn the blue waters of the lake to gray. He wondered what matter pressed on her so, and despite his own pain at what he had seen through the window, he felt a desire to comfort her.

As he looked at her sitting so primly in the stern seat, dressed impeccably as always, he could not erase the memory of her in the act of love. It almost seemed to him that this had been some other woman, abandoning herself to pleasure. His jealousy toward Erasmus—and the fact that Erasmus had experienced this side of her nature—was driving him a little mad. He dipped his oars and drove the boat on a little more briskly.

Marianne sat in the bow puffing on a pipe, reading from time to time from her work in progress, and then disparaging what she had written. She was taking one of her periodic breaks to contemplate—though whether she was thinking about her book, meditating upon her own genius, or considering the beauty of the scene, Kent could not tell.

He dipped the oars and moved the boat again, hardly aware of the beauty of the hills behind the countess.

"Mr. Kent? Do you think my depiction of Frederick's response is realistic? I am asking you to speak as a man."

"How else could I speak, Miss Edden?"

She blew out a smoke-filled laugh. "As an artist, for certainly the artist has a way of seeing the world that transcends their own situation. Good artists, anyway."

Kent tried to remember what she had just read. The character, Frederick, was hopelessly in love with a woman who thought him her dearest friend in the world—though she had given her heart elsewhere, and very unwisely, too. It was not an original situation, but Marianne's description of the man's feelings was so exact, so unusual. Before he could answer, the novelist prompted him by reading from her manuscript.

"'While in her presence he felt as though he had been cast loose from his world. All the ties that bound him were severed, and he could no longer even imagine what his place had been. Suddenly he could not speak to children without feelings of terrible awkwardness and inadequacy, as though afraid all the while that he was making an absolute fool of himself. As though the judgment of children mattered. And this in a man who had lunched amicably with the King and had courtly flirtations with some of the most notable beauties in the capital. He floated in the sea of faces, adrift, adrift, adrift—and no one reached out a hand to him.'"

Kent nodded, unable to escape the thought that Marianne was not only describing him but trying to tell him something as well. Perhaps it was only his own reaction to his present predicament that made him feel so, but he blushed all the same.

The countess, mercifully, did not seem to notice, or at least pretended not to.

"I don't know, Marianne," the countess said. "I think Frederick far too strong a character to react this way. I simply can't believe it."

"But that is the point," the novelist protested. "The most successful, most assured people can suffer this same undoing. I have seen it. Certainly you have seen it. And perhaps those around Frederick who don't know him well do not notice—though he feels even children can see through him. Which is my point entirely. It is all internal and 'real,' if we can even use the term, only to him. Objective 'reality' hardly figures in our perception of the real at all. In this sense, the world of a novel is as real as this world we inhabit. If you believe it—it is real."

Kent looked off at the distant shore. He had long trained his mind in the habit of examining his surroundings, puzzling over how one would paint this or that. Today he was fascinated by the apparent haze of green surrounding certain trees, though this was only the forming leaves breaking free of their buds. Yet, from this distance it appeared that a rarefied green cloud hung in the branches.

Despite this attempt to fall back on old habits, Kent did feel cut loose from the stable grounds of his own life. *That is what comes of hopes and desires and absurd expectations*, he told himself. *Why in the round world did I ever imagine that this woman would be interested in me?*

But another part of him kept asking, *Erasmus?* She had taken up with Erasmus Flattery? Not some wealthy noble at all, but a man of substance. A man who could not even bother to dress in fashion. Even Kent qualified on at least one of these counts. Why not him? Was he not talented? Did he not have a certain charm and wit? Kent believed that he could be as handsome as Erasmus, even if he did not have the presence, for it was true that Erasmus commanded not just respect but attention, without seeming to make any effort.

"You are staring at the shore with an intensity that makes me think you are ready to quit the sea, Mr. Kent," the countess said.

"Oh, not at all, Lady Chilton. I apologize. It is a terrible habit of mine. I see something that catches my eye, the play of light, the shadow and light behind a hill, the color of the birch tree branches, and immediately I find myself trying to decide how I would capture that on canvas."

"Do you know what I think, Mr. Kent?" Marianne said, causing Kent to crane his neck around in her direction. "I think that if you ever applied your abundant talent to painting people so insightfully, you would be the foremost portraitist of our day. Wouldn't you think, Elaural?"

The countess' face revealed nothing, though Kent felt as though the boat had begun to sink around him and him alone. "I think that Mr. Kent would be successful at whatever he chose to do with his art, but what he does now is perfectly suited to him. But really, Marianne, can we not speak of anything but art? I, who have no talent whatsoever, am beginning to feel a bit inferior. Have you no gossip for a poor unaccomplished person such as myself?"

"Well, let me see. Erasmus Flattery and that astonishing Mr. Clarendon have gone down into this great cave everyone speaks of, which I'm told is not a little dangerous at this time of year because of the spring flooding raising the water inside. No one is quite sure why—unless you know, my dear?" she asked playfully.

"Mr. Flattery does not confide in me, I assure you," the countess said quickly.

"Someone has let the house of this man Baumgere, and no one seems to know who it is. There are even rumors that it is the crown prince, here to take the waters. Lord Skye was seen yesterday in the company of the Waldmans' very blond daughter. What was her name?"

"Miss Trollop, I think."

This made Marianne laugh. "And what else have I learned? These navy men who are about are said to be trying to catch an Entonne spy, though the one officer seems to be more interested in this same Miss . . . what was her name again?"

"My, she does get around, doesn't she?"

"I do love small towns. Imagine what they're saying about us," she said with some delight. "Think, Mr. Kent, in the minds of the people of Castlebough you might be involved in a love triangle with the Countess of Chilton and that strange novelist. What was her name again?"

"Busybody," the countess offered.

"There, you see—the perfect name for a woman trapped by her own desires."

"Who is in Baumgere's house, do you think?" Kent asked suddenly.

"Someone who might be interested in the works of Averil Kent, perhaps?" Marianne teased.

"No, seriously."

"Well, I don't know. I have seen the man they say is his servant, but he is no one to me."

"Well, if you know all the doings of Castlebough," Kent said, "why is Sir John Dalrymple here, and who is the man he is with? Bryce, I believe he calls himself."

"Ah, now that is a question. The town seems split on the matter. Sir John is either here to assist the navy men in capturing a spy, or he is here begging money from this man Bryce, to whom he defers, even when he means to give the impression that he does not. Who this man Bryce is, is another matter. A wealthy merchant, I have heard. A smuggler, which I think more likely. A dealer in fine jewels—also a possibility, but not nearly so interesting. Or a rogue who has made his fortune marrying wealthy women, and then pushing them off balconies. And I must say he is terribly attractive, don't you think, Elaural?"

"I don't know to whom you refer, my dear."

"Ah, too much time looking at stars," Marianne said wistfully. "But Mr. Kent; it was a surprise to find you in Castlebough, especially after you had visited the countess so recently."

"Mr. Kent often travels to paint, Marianne. Now please—stick to the gossip."

"What else have I heard?" she mused. "Another group have gone down into this cave everyone seems to be visiting—though this group had in its numbers a young woman. They apparently were prepared to be gone several days."

"A woman went into the same cave as Erasmus?" The countess leaned to one side so that she could see Marianne past Kent, and the jealousy in her voice stung him. The painter felt, suddenly, as though he were not even there.

Marianne blew out a long stream of smoke that curled around Kent, causing him to choke. "That is what I've heard. What's in this cave, do you think?"

"I . . ." The countess paused, looking terribly troubled. "Erasmus told me, and you absolutely mustn't repeat this, that he was going into the cave to look for two young friends who he feared did not understand the danger of what they did. He expected to be gone three or four days."

"Well, it is all very odd," Marianne said. "Why should we not repeat this? If Mr. Flattery has friends in trouble in the cave, should we not alert the town? Should not a rescue attempt be mounted?"

"I only know that he asked me to say nothing. He was not certain that these young men were in difficulty, but only went to be sure they were safe. It all seems a bit odd now, and it is quite a coincidence that these others have gone into the same cave. It is not safe at this time of year, you say?"

"That is what the locals claim. It is often visited during the summer, for it is a natural wonder, after all, but the local people stay out of it in winter and spring, for the water levels rise and fall without warning, and the lower entrances, which are on the shore of the lake are under water. I hope all and sundry are safe in there. Who were these foolish young men?"

The countess shrugged. "I don't know. Friends of Erasmus' . . . Kayes and Heller, I think he named them." She looked to Kent, who shook his head. He didn't know either.

"If he is not out in a day or two," Kent offered solicitously, "I will talk to the local people about mounting a search."

The countess tried to smile at him, but looked away, and Kent felt it was a rather pathetic offer he had made, but it was all he could think of. Hardly enough to have her throw herself into his arms with gratitude.

What was Erasmus up to, he wondered?

## ⌒ Thirty-Three

Hayes managed to pull himself together, considering what he'd found, and that he'd almost set himself afire in a space so tight he was still amazed he had managed to escape largely unscathed. He felt lucky to be alive.

Kehler bathed his hand in fresh water and bound it in a strip of linen torn from their cleanest shirt. Hayes drank some water and sat on his pack, still coughing from the smoke that had seared his lungs.

Kehler stayed close, saying little, perhaps feeling a little guilty at having exposed his friend to such horror.

Slowly Hayes began to recover from the fear and the shock, and the coughing subsided. Kehler made him a cup of their lukewarm tea, which in Hayes' state actually tasted good.

"I noticed something while you were gone," Kehler said. "Can you get up?" He lit a candle and led his friend down the passage.

"It was so quiet while you were inside, and I began to believe I was hearing something. I thought it might be my mind playing tricks, unable to bear the silence, perhaps, but I came down here, listening with all my attention. First I would think I heard it, then it would be gone again. A regular sound I can only describe as tinkling, almost metallic, but very even when I could hear it." He held up a hand. "Stop here and listen."

Hayes did as he was told, straining to hear sounds beyond their own breathing.

"Nothing?"

Hayes shook his head.

"Step along three paces. Now?"

Hayes listened again, trying to calm his ragged breathing.

"Something, perhaps. . . . Flames, it is so faint that I'm not sure."

"Exactly. Now come down here." He led them along another few feet and then bent down before a low opening. Inclining his head Kehler shut his eyes, his face tense with concentration. "Do you hear?" he whispered.

"Something, yes. Yes. There is a sound. Is it water, do you think?"

Kehler shrugged. "Likely. But watch." He brought the candle close to the opening, moving it slowly and then holding it still, his hand wavering just a little.

Ever so slightly the flame bent away from the opening, as though affected by air currents, and then it swayed the other way.

"What do you make of that?"

Hayes held out his hand, trying to feel the air movement. "I almost think I can feel something."

Kehler nodded.

"But does it mean anything? Is this passage more likely to contain what we seek, or is it less likely?"

Kehler shook his head. "I don't know, but it is the only one with any feature to distinguish it from the others. For that reason alone, I'm in favor of exploring it next. At worst, we'll simply have eliminated one more possibility."

Hayes agreed, as it was Kehler's turn to go next anyway. The two made a short meal, and Kehler cleaned and filled the lamp before he set out.

Hayes pulled their packs down before the opening Kehler intended to explore and wrapped himself in his coat and blankets. "You'll have to shout your loudest if you need me," he said. "I can't possibly stay awake."

He watched his friend crawl into the opening, dragging his feet in behind him, and when the light was gone he fell almost immediately to sleep.

Occasionally he would awake with a start, escaping a dream in which he was trapped in the stone, or in which the skeleton reached out for him. On one of these occasions he awoke calling for help, and then realized that he was not the one that was calling out.

"Blood and flames!" He thrust aside the blanket and got up stiffly, hunting around for a candle and the materials to light it. It took him a moment floundering around in the darkness with his one hand in pain and only half-useful, and then a flame was slowly born. All the while he heard the regular muffled shouts of his companion.

Careful not to blow out the flame, he went to the opening Kehler had entered.

"*Kehler!*" he shouted, but all he heard in return was an increase in the calling, not a word was clear.

"Martyr's balls," Hayes swore. "He must be lodged." With great trepidation he knelt down on the hard stone and started into the opening, still so fatigued that he could not imagine how he would make it more than a dozen feet, or what he would do when he reached his friend.

He was forced to rest every few feet, lying in the near darkness, his fingers cramping from holding the candle and unable to bring his other hand forward. When he rested, he would call out to let Kehler know he was coming, but if Kehler was as little reassured by this as Hayes was confident that he could help, the poor man must have been near to despair.

After he crawled beyond what he thought was the limit of his endurance, Kehler's voice was suddenly quite clear, almost near at hand.

"Hayes?"

"Kehler? Are you lodged, man?"

"Bloody martyr's blood! I thought you would never wake. I've been stuck for hours. Flames, man. . . ." But then he seemed to run out of words.

"I'm coming along as quickly as I can. Try to relax. If you could get in, you can get out. Don't worry." Hayes tried to sound confident, but he'd seen the skeleton and knew what it meant.

Finally, in the dull light of his candle, he saw the worn soles of Kehler's boots, a few feet away. As he drew up behind his friend, the lantern glow could be made out, though Kehler's body blocked it almost entirely, the passage was so small.

Hayes reached out and tapped the bottom of his friend's boot.

"Praise be," Kehler said, sounding genuinely relieved. "I am so desperate that I have had a religious conversion; may Farrelle be praised. I'm being punished for my theft of church property."

Hayes laughed. "Only you could find humor in this," he said.

"Hayes?" There was no humor in his friend's tone now. "I'm really in a jam, and I have worn myself to exhaustion trying to get free. I don't want to end up another skeleton in this particular hell."

"We'll get you out, Kehler, don't worry. Let's took at it logically. Where are you jammed?"

"My hips, if you can believe it. I got my shoulders through after some effort, but then I jammed my hips."

Hayes held out his candle trying to discover how his friend was stuck. "Don't move your feet, Kehler, you'll put out my candle." After wrenching his neck around for a moment so that he could look ahead, he had to lower his head to the stone to let the muscles rest. "Try to describe how you're jammed in there."

"Well, there are two ridges in the rock," Kehler began, focusing his attention on different parts of his anatomy. "They run across the ceiling in two bands about four inches apart. My left hip is jammed between them, and my right is stuck as well. If I could move one of them forward or back even two inches, I could go ahead."

"Go forward!?" Hayes said in disbelief. "You want to back out, Kehler, not get farther in. We want to get out of this place."

"But you don't understand. . . . The passage is opening up beyond this. I can see it. The largest section of passage we've found since our arrival. All we have to do is get through the squeeze, and we can go on. Flames, we can almost crawl on hands and knees in the next bit."

Hayes could hardly believe what he was hearing, but then the thought of having some space around him drew him in a way that he could not explain. Only feet away there was room to breathe freely.

"I can't really see why your right hip is stuck. It might be in a small pocket in the rock and you're just too exhausted to get it free. Let me see if I can pull it back, and you try to help me." Hayes poured some wax on the stone and stuck the butt of the candle in the soft wax, hoping it would stay upright. He gripped Kehler's ankle with his forward hand and, bracing himself, pulled as hard as he could. After about fifteen seconds of effort he had to relax.

Flailing for purchase with his free foot, Kehler managed to put the candle out, leaving Hayes in almost complete darkness and beginning to feel panicked himself.

"Kehler? I have another idea. I'm going to put my head against the sole of your left boot and pull on your right foot at the same time. Push on my head as best you can. Is that clear? We'll push your right hip forward and your left back at the same time. Are you ready?"

"No. Rest a moment more."

Hayes put his head down on the stone and tried to think of the world above. A world of sunshine, but he could not hold the image there in the darkness.

Kehler was silent so long that Hayes began to wonder if he had fallen asleep from exhaustion.

"Kehler?"

"Just a moment more."

"Are you all right?"

Silence, and then a very small voice came from the darkness. "What if this doesn't work?"

"Then I'll bring a rope in here and tie it to your foot, and then crawl back out where I can get some purchase. I'm sure all we need to do is get your lower hip to come back a few inches and you'll be out."

"All right. I'm ready."

Hayes grabbed his friend's foot and moved forward until he felt the boot sole contact his head. He expanded his shoulders against the stone and braced his feet as best he could.

He pulled with his hand and pushed his head against his friend's boot, feeling the pressure on his neck, not to mention the pain.

Nothing.

"Blood and flames!" he heard his friend curse and then suddenly the pressure went off his head.

"*Oh, flames . . .*" Kehler managed, "I'm bloody well through." His voice broke on the last word and for a moment the two of them lay gasping.

"Hayes?" Kehler said, his voice thick. "Well done." Kehler dragged himself slowly forward and light poured into the narrow passage. Suddenly Hayes realized Kehler's face was nearly filling the opening ahead. "Can you make it through? There's room to breathe here. Look, I've actually turned around."

Hayes crawled forward, running his hand over the rock where his friend had stuck. Seeing how his friend had lodged was of great help, and with Kehler pulling him, Hayes was through in a moment.

They could actually sit up, the passage was so tall—perhaps two feet and a half in diameter.

They slumped there like two survivors of battle, not a breath of energy left to carry them on, or even to speak. Kehler managed to raise his hand and clap his friend on the shoulder, but beyond that they didn't move for half of the next hour.

Finally Kehler made shift to go on. "I have to move to get some warmth, or I shall begin to shiver."

"Do you think we should?" Hayes asked. "Should we not go back and eat and get some sleep, gather our strength a little?"

"Let's just see how far this goes. If it narrows down again, I agree; we should go back for now. But if it simply ends in fifty feet . . . I don't want to come back in here just to find that."

"Neither do I."

Kehler started out on hands and knees, but around the next bend they were walking upright, though ducking now and then.

"This is more like it," Kehler said, unable to hide his excitement. They both knew this was likely to lead to nothing, but even so, it was the first time they'd found a passage that opened up and it lifted their spirits immeasurably.

Another bend and the passage began to angle up. Kehler stopped them at one point, holding up his hand for silence. "There. Do you hear it?"

"Yes. Without question. It is water running, isn't it?"

"I think so." They hurried on.

Around another bend and then they climbed natural stairs up a slope, the passage opening up to a dozen feet. They crested the top with Kehler a few steps ahead. When Hayes came up, watching his footing, Kehler put out a hand and stopped him, gesturing forward.

*"Martyr's blood,"* Hayes whispered, the words barely audible.

Ten paces before them, at the top of three man-made steps, stood the arch of a small doorway built of white stones. The two stared dumbly, Kehler lowering himself to a ridge of stone as though he could not bear to stand a second more.

Hayes took a step forward, but his friend reached out a hand to restrain him. "No. Stay back. Do you see the flowers inscribed on the keystone?"

"Teller. . . . Is that not what Clarendon said? Two vale roses and an unknown blossom."

"Yes. This is their chamber, but we might not be able to enter."

"What?! We have come all this way through such hardship, and we must stay outside?" Hayes felt his temper rise, and he was too exhausted to control it.

"I said we *might* not be able to enter. There could be charms protecting it."

"Charms? Spells, you mean?"

Kehler nodded.

"And do you have any idea how to deal with them?"

Kehler shook his head. "None at all."

Hayes laughed, he could not help himself. "Well, this has been the most futile endeavor I have ever been tricked into pursuing. Why did you not tell me this before? Is there anything else you are keeping back? You might as well tell me now."

Kehler made an odd face, almost a grimace, and shrugged foolishly.

"And there shall be no fame or fortune either, I'm sure." Hayes shook his head, half angry, half overcome with the absurdity. He could hardly believe that his good, solid friend Kehler tricked him so infamously.

"We should have brought Erasmus," Hayes said suddenly.

But Kehler shook his head. "No. I fear your friend would get word back to Eldrich, and then no one would ever learn of our discovery—whatever might lie beyond this door. No, Hayes, we must keep this from Erasmus."

"Well, I don't think we need fear Erasmus, who is the most decent of men." Hayes wondered if he sounded as guilty as he felt. Had Erasmus already begun searching for them?

"The most decent of men, yes, but he served Eldrich, and mages are not known for letting men go. Not only do I suspect Erasmus of knowing far more than he claims, but I'm distrustful of his loyalties. We absolutely must be sure that Eldrich learns nothing of this until such time as we reveal all. We will publish our findings and make it impossible for Eldrich to bury what we've found. Knowledge should not be kept in the hands of the few, who use it to suppress the many. If nothing else, I became convinced of that while I lived with the priests."

"So what do we do now?"

Kehler considered a moment. "It is my belief that one of us should attempt to pass through the door. I will do it as I'm the one who began all this. I am not certain what you should do, Hayes. I don't know if you will be safe, or if you should go back out to the main passage. I don't even know if you will be safe there."

Claustrophobia gripped Hayes at the thought of going back into that passage. No, they had come this far, going back did not seem an option. Not yet, anyway.

"I'll come with you."

Kehler considered this a moment. "You realize that might be foolish?"

Hayes laughed. "This entire endeavor has been foolish."

Kehler nodded, and Hayes gave him a hand up. Neither said a word, but only went forward, a bit tentatively, perhaps, but they went on.

They put their feet upon the first step and Hayes realized it was marble, not the stone of the cave at all. They paused briefly at the door, as though their nerve had failed, and then Kehler forced himself to go through, with Hayes close on his heels.

By the poor light of their lantern they could see a hall before them. And then a bright light flared, blinding them utterly, felling them like trees in a storm.

## ᕲ Thirty-Four

Since the incident at the lake, conversation had almost ceased. Deacon Rose was helpful and solicitous, never complaining about the arduous nature of their undertaking. Not that Erasmus or Clarendon were given to complaining, but they did not act as though the trials of the body were of no consequence, which was the impression given by Rose.

The priest would often make small talk at their meals and stops, displaying the kind of modest, self-effacing charm that he had exhibited when he first visited Erasmus. There was little doubt in Erasmus' mind that if the good deacon had not chosen the cloth, he would have made a very successful courtier.

Erasmus noticed that Clarendon did not respond to this display of charm, keeping his responses carefully neutral. Obviously he had reservations about taking the priest along, though Erasmus was not sure the savant would have chosen to let the priest drown as an alternative. Still, Clarendon was not happy, there was no question of that, and Rose could not have missed it.

They were wading along a waterway now, occasionally climbing down small waterfalls, so that they were wet and cold. According to Clarendon's survey, there was a falls not far ahead of them, which marked the farthest point Clarendon had penetrated into the cave in the past. The small man had claimed that it hadn't been worth the risk to go farther, which Erasmus found a bit ominous, for it was apparent that Clarendon was not a timid man.

They slipped and splashed their way down the slope, the water running cold and swift around their knees, boots ruined and their feet near to numb.

Erasmus was aware of a growing sound, though it was difficult to describe for it did not vary, nor did it have any particular defining characteristics. He was only certain that it came from ahead.

"How difficult is it to pass beyond the falls?" Erasmus asked Clarendon.

"I have never done it, nor have I seen it done, but it is said to be an intimidating traverse. Not really so hard if it were but two feet off the ground, but it is over a falls that plunges down into an abyss. It is more a test of nerve than skill, I think, but it is a great test of nerve, and not all have passed it. Several men have been lost there. Not two years ago a man fell and dragged his rope partner with him." Clarendon shook his head. "The danger is real, but I think we can pass it. I will go first and set a rope for safety."

"No, Randall," Erasmus said, "you have put yourself forward to explore all the tightest places. Let me lead the way across the falls. Don't forget, I can swim."

"Well, that is up to you, but when you see this falls, Mr. Flattery, you'll realize that even such skill in the water as you possess will be of no use."

They carried on for some time, and finally the roar of the falls drowned out all other sounds, and then they were at its lip, staring down into the darkness.

"There is no hope for swimming there," Clarendon said. "Do you still intend to go first?"

Erasmus nodded, gazing out at the rock face he would have to cross. "Where is the route, do you know?"

Clarendon pointed out the path that had been described to him, explaining as best he could how he thought it could be negotiated successfully.

"Deacon Rose," Clarendon said, "it is you who will have to hold the rope, for I am not large enough for this service. I will instruct you."

"I have traveled in the mountains, Mr. Clarendon, and have held the rope for many a man. Do not be concerned, Mr. Flattery. I shall not let you down, nor will the greater powers, I am sure, for I will pray as you go."

A rope was produced, and Erasmus prepared to start. Both Clarendon and Rose advised him to climb in stockinged feet, for boots would be too slippery on this rock, which was wet from constant spray.

When Rose gave him the signal, Erasmus stepped out over the roaring falls, glancing down once, and then focusing his attention on the route he would take across the stone. Rock dug painfully into his feet, soft from a lifetime of wearing boots, and his hands were already battered from the climbing and crawling that they had done. But he tried to put the pain out of his mind—the climb would require his entire focus. Clarendon called to him encouragingly over the sound of the falls, and gave instructions that Erasmus did his best to follow.

He knew that what Clarendon said was true; if he had been only a few feet off the ground, this would have been child's play, but with an almost certain, horrible death only a slip away, suddenly it was as difficult a climb as he could imagine. Rose held him steadfastly on the rope, but ropes often parted, and there was the story of the man falling and dragging his partner with him.

"You are past halfway, Mr. Flattery," Clarendon called. "Not much farther, now. Reach up with your left hand—is that a hold there? Do you see? Good. Now I would try to move so that your right hand is where your left hand is now. You're doing well."

Erasmus glanced ahead. It did not look so simple from here, at least not when one was out over a yawning gorge.

"Do you see what looks like a small platform ahead? You cannot stop to rest before this, for the holds and steps between are not large. Do you see?"

Erasmus was not sure that he did. All the holds that had seemed so large when he had stood looking from the top of the falls, appeared, upon closer inspection, to be very small indeed.

"Do not hesitate too long, Mr. Flattery. Better to do it before you begin to tire."

It was likely good advice, Erasmus thought, for already he was feeling his muscles knot—from being too tense, he was sure. He took a long breath and stepped out, moving as quickly as he dared. Then he was on the platform and forced himself on without stopping, as though the safety of the other side called to him. A moment later he was crouched in the mouth of the passage, catching his breath, which he was sure had been taken by fear and not exertion.

"It was not so bad," he called back. "Not with a strong man on the rope and another to give instructions. Who will be next?"

"Mr. Clarendon; and we will safety him from both sides," Rose said. "No, Mr. Clarendon, I insist. I will come last, for I have had the most experience in climbing, I think, and you can both take the rope from the far side. Can we send the packs and one lantern across first?"

This was done, and a few moments later Clarendon prepared to go. He would benefit from light from both behind and ahead now, as well as men holding his rope from either side. Rose tied the smaller man into the center of the rope and took up his position, sitting in the flow of the water, his feet braced against a rock.

Erasmus had done as Clarendon said, and found a spire of rock inside the new passage. He threw a loop over it and tied himself onto the tail so that he could sit just in the opening and take the rope around his waist.

Thus protected from either end of the rope, Clarendon set his stocking feet out on the path just navigated by Erasmus.

It was Erasmus' turn to call out encouragement and instruction. He concentrated on Clarendon and his efforts almost as much as Clarendon did himself, and because of this did not notice Rose moving across the falls.

"Erasmus?" Rose called out suddenly. "Hold fast!"

The priest had moved to the far wall, and with no more warning, he gave the rope a yank and pulled a flailing Clarendon off the rock. Erasmus was dragged forward almost a foot before the rope around his waist came taut. And there hung Clarendon, out over the terrible void, his feet dangling in the rushing water, the spray thick around him, and he cursed the priest without respite.

Erasmus tried to pull in on the rope and succeeded in raising Clarendon up a little, but Rose held the end tight and Erasmus was afraid the rope might break.

"Now who will be forced to tell the truth?" Rose called, more than a little triumphant.

"Rose!" Erasmus shouted. "You gave your word. You swore an oath."

"I swore I would not harm Kehler and his companion, but I said nothing of Clarendon. I think your friend is a follower of Teller, Mr. Flattery, and a danger to us both. Eldrich is his sworn enemy, and that means that you, too, are his rival. Is it not so, Mr. Clarendon?"

The man dangling over the falls, said nothing but began to twist about as though he could free himself.

"Well, I will have the truth, whether you will cooperate or no, Mr. Clarendon, for I have ways of dealing with your kind."

Erasmus thought the priest began to mumble, but the sound of the falls swept any words away. Clarendon had taken hold of Erasmus' side of the rope and begun to pull himself toward the rock. But the priest was too strong for the little man. Erasmus could see Clarendon's face was white with rage and fear.

Raising one hand, the priest closed his eyes, continuing to mumble as he made odd geometric gestures in the air. And as he did so, suddenly Clarendon produced a knife and cut the rope connecting him to the priest.

Clarendon swung hard into the rock below Erasmus, and as quickly as he could, Erasmus began to pull in on the rope.

"Randall? Randall, are you hurt?" Erasmus was surprised at how light the man felt.

"Mr. Flattery!" Rose shouted over the sound of water. "Do not go on with that man. He is your enemy. You cannot trust him."

Randall scrambled over the edge of the precipice, so enraged that he did not seem at all frightened. He was on his feet in an instant, shaking his fist at the priest.

"Cannot trust me!? Farrelle's blood, but I have never met a more deceitful man. And I have met all manner of men. Come near to me again, priest, and I will see that you never lie again."

Without warning Randall turned, lifted the priest's pack, and flung it into the abyss. The little man shouldered his own pack and snatched up the lantern.

"Come," he said to Erasmus, "I will not assist his crossing. Let him stay where he is, or plunge into the netherworld where he belongs."

Without waiting for Erasmus, Clarendon went stomping up the tunnel, carrying the light with him. Erasmus stayed for a moment, staring at the priest, who stood there meeting his gaze, holding up a lantern. Despite being soaked from head to foot, the priest still retained his pride. Certainly he did not look repentant. He stood at the top of the falls like a proud man falsely accused.

"You are in danger, Mr. Flattery," he said evenly, shaking his head a bit sadly.

"Mr. Flattery!" Clarendon called.

Digging quickly into his bag, Erasmus found a bundle of candles and some food. He tied these together and tossed them to the priest.

"Make your way to the surface," Erasmus called, and then turned and went after Clarendon. Every step he took into the tunnel he could feel the priest standing behind him—could feel the reproach in his silence.

## ∽ Thirty-Five

*I went to hear Asquith play, and I don't know by what magic this was accomplished, but I cried inconsolably for my lost childhood, and for the harsh and dread-filled place the world had become.*

*—The Countess of Chilton*

Kent could hardly believe what he was doing. He brushed at his frock coat, which was spotted with loose dirt and dead leaves. Lifting his glass, he pointed it toward the lit window and through the foliage could just make out figures moving—or so he thought.

He looked around quickly, listening for any sound. By starlight he had scrambled up a steep embankment and now stood in the farthest reaches of someone's garden. He did not have quite the view of the countess' house that he had hoped, but it was much safer than what he had done the night he saw her with Erasmus.

Flames—if he'd been caught! He would have been forced to move abroad and change his name. What a fool he was acting. And this—sneaking into someone's garden with his field glass—was almost as bad. Claiming to be looking at stars would hardly be believed—there were a hundred more accessible places in Castlebough that were not someone's private domain.

He focused back on the windows of the countess' house. Perhaps that was someone sitting by the fire—but whom? Kent looked around a little desperately. This would never do. He needed either a better vantage—difficult because the house of the countess backed onto a slope—or he would have to return to his place below the windows. And if he did that, it was only a matter of time until he was discovered.

But what was she doing? Had Erasmus returned? Was she visited by Lord Skye, and had that fool realized that the most beautiful woman in Farrland was mad for him? He shook his head. If he could only trade places with Skye for one evening.

Almost desperate, Kent decided to abandon all caution and return to the window.

*This is insanity*, he thought. *Utter insanity.*

Having made the decision, Kent decided not to go down the embankment again. Instead he went quickly toward the house and the street. There were lights in the windows, but the chances of anyone being in the garden at this hour were probably slim—it was not a warm summer evening, after all.

Emboldened by the passion that gripped him, Kent marched up through the garden, past the house and out the gate. In a moment he was at the corner of the countess' street, and here he stopped in the shadow of a tree that hung over a garden wall. Before the countess' house, a coach and four stood at the curb, and a small man was handing the countess up into the large carriage.

Instinctively, Kent stepped back around the corner as the carriage passed by, the night too dark for Kent to see into the coach.

The street, Kent knew, snaked back and forth up the hillside, and after a moment of watching to be sure what the coach would do, Kent went quickly across the street and up a narrow stair between the houses. The faint starlight barely penetrated here, and Kent stumbled more than once, striking his shins cruelly on stone.

At the stairhead he stopped, staying to the shadow, and waited for the coach to pass. When he was sure it would continue up and not stop at a house, he went on, taking the next stair. Here he fell again and lost his glass, wasting several moments searching in utter darkness. When he emerged on the street, the carriage had already passed and he sprang across the paving stones and onto the next stair.

If the stairs had only been uniform in height and depth, but there were landings that sloped up and every stair was a different size, forcing Kent to feel his way up like a blind man. Again the carriage had passed when he reached the street, and this time it was even farther ahead.

Kent was almost certain he would not catch it now, for he was struggling to breathe as it was. As quickly as he could, he plunged into the shadow of the next stair, and here was helped by lights in the windows. He sprinted up the steps, his breath coming in terrible gasps.

He met the carriage this time, and waited for it to pass before setting his feet to the next flight.

On he went, upward, the carriage gaining each time it passed, and then finally it did not appear on the street at all. Kent stood in the middle of the thoroughfare looking both ways, wondering what could have happened. He was certain he had not fallen so far behind. Had it stopped back around the corner where he could not see it?

Thinking there was no other explanation, Kent hurried down the street. But at the corner he found no coach, nor was there a gateway large enough to allow it to enter.

*Where am I?* he wondered, trying to recall the lay of the town, and how many flights he'd raced up. "There must be another road here," he said, thinking aloud. "A carriage cannot simply disappear."

He set off down the slope and in a moment discovered a small lane running out of the town, following the contour of the hillside. It was too dark to see if there were marks of the coach's passage in the soft earth, but he could not imagine where else the coach could have gone, and began to trot along the lane.

To his right, through the trees lining the lane, Kent caught glimpses of the lake shimmering far below. To his left lay a wood, broken occasionally by small glades. The town had not escaped its confines to take root here, despite the likely vistas, and tall grass grew down the center of the lane indicating how little use it saw.

After half of a long hour Kent was beginning to wonder if the carriage had actually come this way, and contemplated turning back, but then a familiar odor assailed his nostrils telling him that horses had passed this way, and recently too. The painter pressed on with renewed energy.

A few moments more and he passed through an open gate, and the lane suddenly sloped down toward a level bench. At the bottom of the hill he could see a large home illuminated by the stars. Near to the entrance a carriage stood, its lamps burning dully.

He slowed his pace and tried to keep to the grass to muffle the sound of his approach. Whose home this was Kent did not know. There hardly seemed to be an entertainment in progress—the house was all but unlit, and only one carriage waited.

Remembering what he had seen the last time he'd spied on the countess, Kent went forward torn between dread and excitement. Erasmus was supposed to be in the cave, so she could not be visiting him.

Kent was not sure how he would respond if he were to discover the countess had another lover—that she bestowed her favors so liberally and yet treated him no differently than she treated her friend Marianne.

Staying to the shadows as much as possible, Kent stayed high on the slope along the edge of the wood. Once he was convinced there was no movement in the lit windows, Kent decided to circle the house at a distance.

Certainly if the countess came here at such an hour, it must be for an assignation. What other explanation could there be? He felt a flash of anger toward her.

*This is why men she can't even remember meeting fight duels over her*, Kent thought. *Look at me. Look at what I do.* But still, he carried on, despite the fear that dueling with strangers would come next.

Kent slipped around the side of the house, keeping to the shadows wherever possible. The grounds had obviously not been tended in years. The hedges were overgrown, flowerbeds choked with weeds, lawns gone to seed, and fallen branches and leaves lay rotting everywhere.

As the far side of the house came into view, Kent saw the dull orange of a flame—an oil lamp burning inside a ground floor window, or perhaps a fire in a hearth. A little farther along he realized that the light came from inside a row of leaded-glass doors. Here there were people, he was almost certain, though there was much furniture and it was difficult to make out the shapes in such poor light.

Slipping partway down the hill, Kent stood in the shadow of a bush, peering down over an open section of lawn with his field glass. Something moved inside; a man, he was almost certain.

"Mr. Kent?"

The painter whirled around, raising his glass like a cudgel—but the man before him was familiar, even in the poor light.

"Sir John?"

"Yes," the man whispered. "Keep your voice down and come back from the house. I fear you will give us away if you stay here."

Kent hesitated, embarrassment was rapidly replacing fright. What in the round world was Sir John Dalyrimple doing here? Was he spying on the countess as well? Not knowing what else to do, Kent followed Sir John until they were some distance from the house and hidden by the corner of a garden wall.

Here, in the pale light, they crouched down, looking out only occasionally to see that they were alone.

"I would ask what you do here, Mr. Kent," Sir John whispered, "but fear you will say it is not my business, and rightly so. But perhaps the fact that we are here, watching this same house, might indicate common purpose, or so I hope."

Kent tried to read the man's face but the light was so poor. He could not even begin to guess why Sir John was here, other than for the same reason as Kent.

"I am here out of concern for a friend," Kent said.

Sir John nodded as though this made sense somehow. "Well, you are more noble than I, Mr. Kent, for I am here out of concern for myself. You followed the woman who arrived in the coach?"

Kent nodded.

"Who is she, pray?"

Does he really not know, Kent wondered? "The Countess of Chilton," Kent said, unable to think of a reason to lie—or perhaps to see Sir John's reaction.

"Of course," Sir John said, glancing down at the house.

"But whose home is this?" Kent asked.

"You don't know? It was the house built by Baumgere, the infamous priest. But who is staying here now, I cannot say." He paused, and Kent sensed that he was trying to decide what else to say, or how to say it. "I have a man who passes me information. . . . Invaluable information, I will tell you, but he is a complete mystery to me. I cannot say where he is from or name the source of his knowledge, and this troubles me, Kent." Sir John nodded his head toward the house. "I have reason to believe the man comes here, to this house, so I am here hoping to discover who it is that he meets. One wants to be sure one is not unwittingly embroiled in the plot of a foreign power."

"This is the man I met on the road to Castlebough—Bryce?"

Sir John nodded.

"And what has he to do with the countess?" Kent said quickly, afraid that jealousy was obvious in his voice. Had not Marianne Edden named the man handsome? Yet the countess had claimed not to know whom she meant.

"I . . ." Sir John stopped, shaking his head, the motion so small it was almost indiscernible. "Bryce is interested in Skye, for some reason, but I don't think Lord Skye is here."

"Who is, then? Did you follow Bryce here?"

"One does not follow Bryce, Mr. Kent. At least that is what I believe. No, it was luck only that had me see Bryce's carriage come down this lane. And so I am here, watching, not quite sure what I hope to see."

Sir John leaned out to look around the corner of the wall, and held his hand up quickly, stopping Kent from speaking.

Kent moved so that he could see past Sir John, and there, in the center of the ill-tended lawn, a man and a woman walked under starlight. Even at this distance he knew it was the countess, but the man was a mystery to him. Certainly not Skye. Nor was it Erasmus. Was this Bryce, then? And what had he to do with the countess?

"Is that your man?" Kent whispered, keeping his voice as low as possible. But even as he asked the question, he was sure that the answer would be no. The man on the lawn was tall, with a stiff posture and movement. *A king in pain*, Kent thought immediately, though he didn't know why—but that was what the man seemed to him.

Sir John shook his head.

Just as Kent started to raise his glass, a large dog appeared at the edge of the lawn. It hesitated a moment and then loped across the open space toward the people.

Kent was certain the woman froze with fear, but the man held out his hand and the beast, which he realized now was massive, circled them once. It didn't do this warily, Kent thought, but out of independence.

Sir John pulled back behind the wall again, drawing Kent back as well. Kent was not sure what had come over Sir John; he seemed to be suffering from some sudden ailment, and Kent feared it might be the man's heart. Sir John could not seem to catch his breath, and Kent was sure he could see sweat running in rivulets down the man's face.

"Is that beast a dog, Kent," Sir John managed, "or is it a wolf?"

It seemed an odd question, but Kent leaned out to look again. The animal had deserted the people and went back toward the trees, its head down, and neck stretched out. Definitely not a dog, and then he realized what Sir John meant and almost threw himself back behind the wall.

"*Eldrich*," he said, realizing the only reason that a wolf could cause such fear. "Is that what you think? It is Eldrich?"

Sir John could not speak but nodded his head, his breath coming in quick little gasps. "Farrelle . . . save us," he managed. "I had . . . no idea."

He grabbed the front of Kent's frock coat and levered himself to his feet, stumbling toward the wood. "*Flee*," he hissed, and Kent hesitated only a second, before following the terrified man into the utter darkness beneath the trees.

By the time they found their way back to the lane, they were bruised and their clothing torn and soiled, for the starlight penetrated into the wood only rarely.

Sir John had finally regained his breath, to Kent's relief, but the painter was now so concerned for the countess that he almost went back, despite his fear of the mage.

"Don't even think about it, Kent," Sir John said, sensing what was in the painter's mind as he looked back over his shoulder. "There is nothing you can do. Even if the countess needed rescue, you could not accomplish it. He is a mage. I can't quite believe we have escaped unharmed. Just be thankful for that, and do nothing foolish."

They went on, listening for the sound of horse and carriage, or the howl of a wolf.

At last they stopped so that Sir John could catch his breath. He seemed only slightly less terrified, even though they appeared to have escaped.

"Are you recovering, Sir John?"

"Recovering? My breathing, yes, but I shall never recover from the shock. I had no idea what I involved myself in, Kent. Eldrich!" He shook his head in disbelief. "Bryce is an agent of the mage. What shall I do? Whatever shall I do? I have been promoting the interests of a mage, unknowingly. And what does Eldrich want with Skye?" Sir John seemed to realize that he was ranting, and stared up at Kent, immense fear and regret apparent in his manner. The man looked so cowed, almost cringing where he sat.

He suddenly grabbed the painter by the arm. "Kent, you must promise me that none of this will go any further. I had no idea what I did, I swear. And at no time did I ever subvert the interests of my country. I swear to you, Kent." He looked down at the ground, almost ready to collapse, Kent thought. "How will I ever get free of this? *Eldrich!* He will never release me. What am I to do, Kent? Whatever am I to do?"

But Kent neither knew nor cared what Sir John should do. Why was the countess in the company of Eldrich? What was their involvement? That was all that concerned him. Was she in danger? Was she his agent? His mistress?

Kent sat on the step of a deep-set door, so that a shadow hid him from the street. It was the farthest point on the street from which he could still see the countess' home. Never in his life had he felt so utterly powerless, so unsure of what to do. Was the countess in danger? Or was it much simpler than that: she was the most beautiful woman in Farrland, and the histories were clear that mages were not immune to such things. He pressed his fingers to his eyes, which burned from lack of sleep.

But somehow he could not shake the feeling that the countess was in danger. No doubt his feelings for her held sway here—but even so he would wait and see.

The thought of waking Marianne Edden crossed his mind, but she was likely the countess' ally in all things, and would not be so sympathetic to Kent. He believed she thought he was a bit obsessed anyway.

What he wanted to do was ask the countess herself, so he waited, trying to imagine how he would approach her, what he would say.

It was too dark to read his timepiece, but Kent was sure that daylight couldn't be far off. He wondered what he had landed in the middle of, here in this odd little village in the Caledon Hills. Skye had a copy of a painting by Pelier which showed the structure Baumgere had uncovered above the town—though the painting, if it was a true copy, must have been done many years before Baumgere made his discovery. Erasmus Flattery, a man who had served Eldrich, had become an intimate of the Countess of Chilton, though Kent had thought she was in love with Skye. Eldrich was here! Not on his estate, which he was said never to leave.

And what was this about Erasmus going into the cave? And others had followed, apparently. And Sir John? What was this man involved in? He could not remember having seen a man so overcome by terror. Sir John was entangled in all of this somehow, and he was a senior member of the Farr government!

Kent had not the slightest idea of what went on.

The sound of horses and a carriage rattling over the cobbles echoed down the empty street. Kent pulled himself back into his shadow, trying to wrap it around him like a cloak.

The same carriage Kent had seen take the countess away, stopped before her door. A small, round man handed the countess down, and she slipped quickly inside. The carriage came Kent's way, and he regretted hiding on the street, now. He drew his knees up, pressing back against the door. Without thinking, he hid his face, not looking at the carriage as it passed. When its sound was barely audible, Kent forced himself to move. With absurd caution he stepped out onto the avenue, but the carnage was gone and the street deserted.

Kent crossed to the countess' door at a run, but when he raised his hand to knock, he hesitated. Despite all his thought, he still did not know what to say. If the countess was involved with Eldrich in some way, she would likely report him to the mage, and Kent certainly didn't want that.

For a moment he stood there before the door, unable to decide, and then he went immediately around the side of the house. He would see what he would see, and then decide what to do.

The faintest light came from the window he had crouched beneath before, and the thought of what he had seen then both propelled him on and made him want to turn away. As quietly as he could, he went to this window and peered in, showing as little of his face as he could.

The countess sat before a fire that had burned to embers. She sat rigidly straight in her chair, unmoving. There was something unsettling about her manner. Thinking that it was perhaps the greatest folly, Kent tapped on the window. There was no response. He tapped louder. Still the countess did not stir.

She must have heard, he thought. Pressing his face to the glass, he was sure that something was greatly amiss. He tried the door but found it locked, and it would not give way to pressure. He was becoming a little frantic, when he noticed a casement window slightly ajar. With a small blade he worked it open and went in as quietly as he could.

The room was dark, and it took Kent a moment to find the door that led into the hallway. When he entered the small sitting room, the countess still remained unmoving before the hearth.

"Lady Chilton?" he whispered, but she did not seem to hear.

Kent went nearer. "Lady Chilton?" Her eyes were opened, but it was as if she were deep in sleep.

Kent put a hand tentatively on her shoulder. He realized that she wore only a sleeping gown beneath her cloak.

What has been done to her? he wondered. She seemed to have been mesmerized. Was this the way a person acted when they had been bespelled?

He shook her ever so gently. "Lady Chilton? It is Averil Kent. Lady Chilton? Please . . ."

To his relief the countess took a quick breath, as though surprised, and then seemed to relax.

"Mr. Kent?" she said, startled.

"Yes. Do not be afraid. You're all right now."

She pulled away from him a little as her wits returned. "What has happened? What am I doing here? What are *you* doing here?"

"I will explain everything, though be at ease, Lady Chilton, I mean no harm." Kent pulled a chair nearer so that they could speak without waking the house.

"I was passing earlier this evening, returning to my rooms, when I saw you entering a large carriage. You were dressed as you are now, and seemed . . . I cannot describe it, but you were not yourself. Almost as though you walked in your sleep."

"Mr. Kent!" the countess exclaimed, obviously disturbed, "you are not serious?"

Kent nodded. "I'm afraid I am. This is what I saw. You entered the carriage and your manner was so . . . unworldly, that I confess I followed you. Out of concern for your well-being.

"I chased the carriage, running up the stairs through the village, and finally out along a lane to the manor house that this priest, Baumgere, built." He paused to gauge her reaction and was touched by her look of distress. "The house seemed deserted, but as I circled, keeping my distance, I saw you on the lawn. You were standing with a tall man I didn't know. And as I watched, what I thought at first was a large dog came out of the wood. But as it crossed the lawn, I realized that it was not a dog at all, but a wolf. A massive wolf."

The countess stared at him, uncomprehending.

"It is well known that a great wolf prowls the estate of Lord Eldrich. . . ."

The countess pulled away from him completely, as though what he said were so offensive that he could never be forgiven. Her beautiful face contorted in fear and rage. "What are you saying? That I was whisked away to see Eldrich in my sleep?" Then the fury gave way to sudden comprehension. "Farrelle save us,. Kent. . . . I woke here once before, having walked in my sleep, or so I assumed. Is it possible that I have been taken away before? Abducted from my house and have no memory of it." She pulled her cloak close around her, crossing her arms over her breasts. "What has been done to me as I walked in my sleep?" she said so quietly Kent could barely hear. "What does a mage want with me?"

Kent shook his head, not wanting to say what he thought.

"What should I do?" she asked suddenly, and though she did not really seem to be asking this of Kent, he felt he must answer.

"You must flee," he said immediately. "Leave Castlebough. Leave Farrland, even. To Entonne, perhaps, or Doom. Get as far from Eldrich as you can. He has hardly been away from his estate these thirty years past, I can't think that he will pursue you."

The countess rose from the chair and paced to the window, stopping to look warily out, as though she feared the mage was watching. "But what does he want of me, Kent?" she asked, turning away from the window. "Erasmus told me that Eldrich cares little for men and their concerns. That he will use them to his own ends without remorse." She stared at Kent, a sudden realization striking her. "Has Erasmus something to do with this? He served Eldrich. . . . And look at all that goes on here. Skye has his copies of the Peliers and pursues Erasmus to have the script translated. This man Baumgere found some great secret in Castlebough, or so everyone believes. It is all connected. It must be." She looked at Kent to confirm her fears.

"I think you are right, Lady Chilton." Kent was tempted to tell her about Sir John, to prove somehow that he cared for her well-being by revealing his secrets to her, but something stopped him. The fear Sir John had exhibited: it was one thing for Kent to risk himself, but to expose another, especially one so convinced of his peril, was unforgivable.

"But what goes on in this sleepy little town?" she asked.

Kent shook his head.

"I can't help but think Erasmus knows something more. . . . And then there is Skye. I will speak with him this very morning."

"Do you think that's wise?" Kent blurted out, jealousy overruling all reason.

"Why do you say that?"

"Only because I think you should not waste a moment. We should be off this morning. Within the hour. Who knows what plans Eldrich might have for you. You said yourself, the mages were always ruthless—Eldrich will be no different."

The countess looked at him oddly. "Tell me honestly, Mr. Kent. Were you watching my house?"

Averil felt fear at being discovered, but strangely he felt great indignation as well. As though the accusation was not entirely true. "Lady Chilton," he said, his voice shaking a little, "I assure you that witnessing your abduction was entirely coincidental."

She continued to fix him with that measuring gaze. "Then I apologize, Mr. Kent," the countess said, although she did not sound at all convinced. "I have had such odd things happen with men. You understand. . . ."

Kent nodded.

"It is almost light. I'm going to wake Marianne, and then send a note to Lord Skye. I hope you'll stay, Mr. Kent. I would like them to hear your story."

"Of course," the painter answered. Left alone, he banked the coals in the hearth and built a fire, conjuring the flames with a bellows. He was not happy with the countess' decision to call on Skye, or to bring Marianne Edden into this matter. What he wanted most was for her to flee, with Kent as her protector. If they were together for a month in Entonne, he was certain she would begin to feel differently toward him. She would begin to see things which perhaps weren't readily apparent in a quiet man like Kent.

Perhaps half of the hour later a servant delivered coffee and freshly baked pastries, and another fifteen minutes saw the countess return in the company of Marianne Edden.

The novelist greeted him rather perfunctorily, as though she suddenly did not approve of this poor painter. Kent found her entirely changed toward him. Servants brought more coffee and food to break their fast and for a while there was no conversation.

As the servants closed the door, Marianne fixed Kent with a look that could hardly be called warm. "You were out for a stroll, Mr. Kent, when you saw the countess taken away?"

"Yes, I could not sleep," Kent said, not liking where her questioning might be going.

"And do you recognize this?" Marianne asked. Reaching over to one of the trays the servants had brought, she snatched away a cloth, and there lay Kent's field glass. "A servant retrieved it from the rear garden."

Kent felt himself color. "Ah, that's where I left it. Yes, it is mine. Like many, I'm an amateur empiricist myself. I was looking at the heavens."

Marianne's scowl left little doubt that she didn't believe him. "And how did you come to be in the house when the doors were locked?"

"I confess, I came in a window left ajar."

"You stole into our house like a prowler and found the countess sleepwalking in little more than her sleeping gown? Mr. Kent, this is most irregular. What could have led you to take such liberties, I can't imagine."

"I know it seems very irregular, Marianne, but if you had seen Lady Chilton, you would understand. Her manner was so very odd—like a string puppet. I hesitated, not sure what to do, and quite unsettled by what I had seen. I almost knocked on the front door, but for some reason did not. Concern for Lady Chilton made me a bit reckless, I fear. I realize it is unconscionable, but I slipped around the back and peered in the windows. And there I found the countess, seated, unmoving, before the fire as though she had been shocked into immobility. I knocked on the window and she did not respond—even when I knocked quite loudly, she did not notice. Frightened, I tried the doors, which were bolted, and then in desperation I found the open window and let myself in. I woke the countess here, before the fire, and the rest I'm sure Lady Chilton has told you."

Marianne began to speak, but the countess interrupted. "Be that as it may, Marianne, the truth seems to be that I was outside the house this evening and completely unaware of it. I believe Mr. Kent is telling the truth there."

Kent did not much like the implication that he was not telling the truth elsewhere—even though this was the case.

"And you believe this story that it was a mage?" Marianne said, a little incredulous. The countess hesitated. "Marianne, I awoke here, wearing my cloak over my sleeping gown. But that is not the oddest thing. My feet were dirty and stained as though I had walked across wet grass. As Mr. Kent said, he saw me on an expanse of lawn."

"But you could have just as easily have walked out onto our own lawn."

"Marianne. What reason would Mr. Kent have for making up such a story?"

"To have you flee with him. With him! To Entonne, and who knows where. Men have been driven to even more foolish stories, and plans. I have been witness to it, and more than once, too." The novelist scowled at Kent.

"Mr. Kent," the countess said, a little warmth and vulnerability entering her voice. "Please tell me truthfully. . . . Did you see me taken away in a carriage? Truthfully, now."

"Lady Chilton, I swear that I did."

"And were you spying on the countess with your glass, Mr. Kent?" the novelist asked pointedly. "Now answer that truthfully as well."

Kent hesitated, feeling somehow that if he was not honest he would not be believed at all. "I did not actually spy on the countess with my glass," Kent said. "But I will tell you honestly, Miss Edden, that I did consider it."

"Kent!" the countess said, such disappointment in her tone that it made the painter utterly ashamed, "I thought you were my true friend."

"I am," he said quickly. "I just . . . I forgot myself. I . . . I have no excuse." He hung his head, unsure of what to say. An apology seemed terribly inadequate.

"Well, Mr. Kent," Marianne said. "I think you should leave us for the time being. It has been a disturbing morning, make no mistake, and we need some time to consider what has happened."

Kent went out into the newly risen morning, a bit dazed. He had been caught spying on the Countess of Chilton. He was ruined. There would be no redemption for such an act. But what had he seen! He stood on the street for a moment, unsure how to proceed.

*Eldrich.* The mage had taken the countess from her home, and she was not aware of it. Kent shook his head. She had not believed him. Or, more correctly, Marianne Edden had undermined her confidence in him. If only he hadn't left his cursed glass in the garden! What madness had led him to confess?

"What will I do now?" he asked aloud.

Somehow he had to convince the countess that what he said was true. Sir John was his only hope. Kent set off down the street with great urgency. But would the man help him? Kent could hardly remember seeing a man so frightened. But what other hope had he?

He almost ran through the sleepy streets. There was no other way to support his claims, for they did sound like the result of madness—a particular kind of madness that occurred around the countess with disturbing regularity.

"I will be ruined," Kent whispered, though the world did not seem overly concerned. "Utterly ruined."

He located Sir John's residence, and fortunately found the man awake.

"Kent, you look worried out of your mind, man." Sir John bade him sit, and a cup of coffee was put into his hand.

"I went to see the countess," Kent blurted out.

Sir John's eyes widened. "You didn't mention me, I hope?"

"No. Not a word. But I found her sitting in her parlor, completely dazed. Her eyes were open, but she seemed asleep. Unwilling to raise the entire household,

I slipped in the window and roused her. I related what I'd seen, not mentioning you, of course. But then Marianne Edden woke and she didn't believe my tale. She was certain that I had fabricated the story to convince the countess to run away with me." Kent shook his head, feeling himself color a little. "You know how men are with the countess. . . . I think she was inclined to believe me until Miss Edden arrived—and then the idea of what I had seen so unsettled her that she preferred to believe only that she had been sleepwalking, out into her garden." Kent spilled his coffee as he set it down. "I am ruined if I cannot convince them of the truth. Sir John. They thought I had been spying on the countess. Can you imagine? Spying. And then, of course, I slipped into her home unasked. Concocting this fantastic story to frighten her into running off with me. Flames, there will be no place where such infamy will not follow me." He tried to pick up his coffee, but his hand shook so that he spilled more into the saucer, and he set it back down quickly.

"And now you've come to ask me to support your story," Sir John said.

Kent looked up, his hopes rising.

"But don't you see, Kent, the countess is an object of interest to Eldrich? Think what that means. The mage might very quickly discover your interference. He must speak with the countess, after all. As noble as it was to try to warn her, it was more foolish, still. Eldrich will not tolerate interference in his affairs." Sir John let out a long breath. "I will tell you, Kent, you have greater things to worry about than your reputation."

"But what of the countess?" Kent said, realizing that he was pleading. "Who knows what Eldrich . . . intends with her? She has no knowledge of their meetings."

Sir John leaned forward in his chair. "Kent, listen to me. I realize you have feelings for the countess, and no doubt this situation she is in seems monstrous, but there is absolutely nothing you can do but draw the rage of Eldrich, and I will not have that fate visited upon me."

"You will not help me . . ." Kent said in disbelief.

Sir John drew himself up, his look defensive. "I will not. And I beg you to think what you do. You might as well dive into an ocean storm as try to stop Eldrich. Come to your senses, man. A mage is a force of nature."

## ☙ Thirty-Six

Hayes and Kehler scrambled up quickly as the light faded to a pale glow. It was not lamplight, but a cool white light, like the pure light of stars, that emanated from beyond the opening.

Kehler stood before Hayes, partially blocking his view. Neither of them moved for a moment, and then Hayes stepped up so he could see past his friend. A long corridor, perhaps a dozen feet in width, extended before them. Feeling no ill effects, Hayes pressed his friend forward, and they stepped through the door into the hall.

It seemed not to be a cave at all, but the entranceway to a great palace. The walls were straight and plumb, decorated with intricate carvings. Ten feet above the floor, a border carved like a twisting vine ran the length of the hall, and into this blossoms and unfamiliar characters had been worked.

The light emanated from above, and when Hayes looked up, he thought that he looked into a star-filled sky. A sky of infinite depth.

Kehler followed his gaze up and stood transfixed for a long moment.

"How many men living in this day can say they have witnessed the arts of the mages?" Kehler asked.

"But were they mages?" Hayes said.

They walked slowly down the wide hall, the sound of running water clear now. To either side, sections of the wall were covered in text of the same unfamiliar characters found in the border.

The hallway was long, a hundred feet or more to an arch at the far end. Hayes' initial impression of stepping into a palace, he realized now, was wrong. This felt like a temple, though none that he was familiar with; still, there was no doubt in his mind that this was a place of worship.

"Who built it?" Hayes asked.

"I don't know," his companion said, shaking his head.

"But you think it was Teller?"

"Perhaps. I can't say. In my reading I have come to the conclusion that there was a division in opinion among the mages—a period of internal strife. Not that they were ever particularly united except in their war against the church. But this schism was something greater than their normal individualism. Perhaps this chamber had significance to one of these groups, or perhaps it was a chamber known to all the mages."

To their right a tall doorway opened onto a stair. Hayes leaned in and found the stairway curved up and to the right in a long arc.

He leaned back and looked down the passage toward the end. "Up or on?" he asked.

"Let's explore as we go," Kehler said, and started up the stair.

Once on the stair they returned to the poor light of the lantern. As in the hallway below, the walls were decorated here and there with text and floral designs. Twice they stopped to rest. The stair was so long and they were utterly fatigued. Even the excitement of their discovery could not overcome that altogether. They were considering giving up this climb when they came abruptly to the stair's end. A large character of the type they had seen carved on the walls was the single decoration on the blank surface that ended the stairs.

"What does this mean?" Hayes asked.

"It means that however this chamber was built, the people who used it, or intended to use it, did not enter it as we did."

"You think this is a door?"

"Perhaps not a door, but an entrance all the same. Or perhaps it was merely meant to be an entrance one day. I would guess that the surface of the world lies not far beyond this wall."

Hayes stepped forward, pressing his hands against the stone, moving them across it as though its secret would be revealed to him by such an inspection.

"Remarkable. What does this character mean, I wonder?"

Kehler shook his head. "I don't know. . . ."

Hayes looked at him sharply. *So why had they risked their lives to find this chamber?* "Does anyone?"

"Eldrich, almost certainly. Perhaps Erasmus Flattery. Maybe Deacon Rose and a few others within the church."

"But what good will it do us?"

"Us? We have little to do with this matter, Hayes. It is about the hoarding of knowledge—worse by far than the hoarding of riches. Reformers talk incessantly about leveling society, doing away with the advantages of the wealthy and the aristocrats. But there is no leveler like knowledge. Who knows what is concealed here? It could be the great discovery of our age. For centuries the arts were in the hands of a select few—but what if that could be changed? What if you could suddenly heal the sick, as no physician ever can? Imagine what that would mean."

"But how do we know there is any such knowledge recorded here? Knowledge that can be used."

Kehler shook his head. "All we know is that Baumgere was willing to sacrifice a great deal to find this chamber, and that the church did everything in their power to hide it. The Farrellites have long been the greatest hoarders of knowledge. They would keep the population in utter ignorance if they could. Better if men could not even read. Whatever is hidden here has long been suspected by the church—suspected and kept secret. That is enough for me. It must be brought out. Out into the light."

They turned and descended the stair, the sound of water growing as they went—a sound that had not been heard by men in this place for many years.

When they came to the foot of the stairs and into the cool light, Kehler blew out the flame in their lantern and set it aside.

They continued down the long hallway, and found small niches on either side into which faces were carved in high relief. Both men and women were represented here. Around each niche, text in the same script was arranged. They stopped and looked carefully at each face, as though they might find there someone they knew. The faces were sensitively rendered, Hayes thought—noble and sad. More than one wore a circlet around its brow, often surmounted by a brilliant stone set into the sculpture. And then he realized that each face bore a stone. One in a woman's ear lobe. Another on a pendant around a man's neck. All different colors and brilliance, some so unusual that Hayes could not even guess what they were.

"Who are they, I wonder?" Kehler said softly.

Hayes stared at one face, unable to tear his gaze away. "See how sad they look. What could have made them so?"

Kehler shook his head, though he looked almost as troubled as the faces he contemplated.

They carried on past the sorrowful faces, most of them older, it seemed, but one or two quite young—the age of Kehler and Hayes.

"Either the artist who sculpted here was a genius," Kehler said quietly, "or these faces are touched with the mages' art, for I feel I almost know their stories. Do you feel it? The faces are so evocative. I look at them, and some knowledge seems to be just at the edge of my consciousness." He stopped before one—the long face of a man in his middle years. "Look at this one . . . noble and tragic. See how his brow is almost knit, as though he wrestles with a terrible burden. He is a man who has been much disappointed, and remained alone throughout his life—no wife or children, clearly. He dedicated himself to some cause, and paid a terrible price. Look at the depth of his thought. Those brooding eyes. Here is a tragic hero if ever there was one. A man who made choices that cost him dearly—yet he could make no others.

"And do you see this woman? How old is she? Thirty-five, do you think? What is that look? Is it pride? Not quite. Pride is too close to vanity. But even so, she has struggled against some terrible fate, and not surrendered. I cannot say that she triumphed, but she did not surrender." Kehler looked at his companion. "Do I sound like I'm raving?"

"Raving? No, I feel the same thing. These faces are touched by a great art, though I don't think it is an art of the mages, but merely the result of genius and inspiration." Hayes reached out tentatively and touched the face of the woman, brushing his fingers over her cheek—almost a gesture of affection. Lonely, was what Hayes thought when he looked at her. Hidden down here for how long? Centuries? Lost to the world—to all mankind. A portrait of loneliness.

They walked on, every few strides passing two more faces, none joyous, none even content.

And then a great hall opened before them. They stood in the archway and stared into the chamber—as long as the hallway they had just walked, but five times the width. Hayes didn't know where to look first. The ancient white walls were covered in neat, linear rows of script, the characters as high as his hand was long—thousands of them, for the walls were tall, thirty or forty feet, Hayes was certain.

Gingerly they stepped into the room, as though they were trespassers in fear of being caught, or in fear of spells left for intruders, but even the mysterious light did not alter.

In the center of the room, against one wall, stood a raised terrace of smooth stone, and it was from this that the sound of running water emanated, as it likely had for uncounted years.

Ten paces into the room they turned in a complete circle, overwhelmed by the wonder of their discovery.

"I feel like I am suddenly surrounded by mystery," Hayes said.

"You have always been surrounded by mystery," Kehler said, a hint of a smile appearing. "But perhaps we have reached to the heart of this one."

Hayes went to one wall and ran his hands over the letters, which were raised in relief, not inscribed. The script he thought exceedingly fair and yet curious, for it didn't seem to resemble the common or even the ancient scripts used around the Entide Sea. But it was almost definitely the same script that Kehler had included in his letter.

Hayes realized that he felt a little disoriented, finding himself in this vast chamber of light after the dark little tunnels he had navigated.

They crossed the room and mounted three steps to the raised terrace. Here the water flowed from the mouth of a wolf head set upon the shoulders of a man. A stream of water fell into a small font, and then apparently ran under the platform to appear again at its base, finally flowing in a narrow channel to the far side of the chamber where it disappeared into the floor.

Above the font, life-sized torsos of a man and woman grew out of the rock, the man wearing the mask of a fantastic crested bird, the woman a mask of a hawk or falcon, Hayes was not sure which. To either side of the figures text was inscribed inside a floral border.

"Look," Kehler said, staring down at the floor. "These lines lead to seven points, and at each point a circle is scribed and a different colored stone laid into the floor." He stood by one of these stones. "This one seems to have stars cut into it, though if these are constellations, they are unfamiliar to me. And that one has more written characters. This central stone has no markings at all."

The last was black and glistened.

"What material is that?" Hayes asked.

"It appears to be glass," Kehler said, bending down and touching it. He stood up, looking around. "Does this not feel like an altar to you? The center of the temple?"

Hayes nodded, though he could not begin to guess at the purpose of such an altar. His eye kept being drawn back to the man and woman above the font, their faces hidden by masks. When he had first looked, he thought they held hands, but now he realized their wrists joined into one and ended in the claw of a bird. Both their free hands were slightly extended as though in supplication, but the woman held a long-stemmed blossom in her hand.

"Everything I see here seems to have some meaning that is just beyond my grasp," Hayes said suddenly. "I have never felt so much that I walked in a dream. Do you know what I'm saying? Like you, I felt that the stories of those men and women whose faces we saw were just on the edge of my consciousness. And I feel much like that here. As though I can almost understand the significance of these figures, of this font. Of these stones set into the floor. Look at the way this man and woman hold out their hands. . . . I am touched by this, in some way that I cannot explain, as though my heart understands, but my head is not quite able to grasp it."

Kehler nodded. Hayes realized that his friend was close to tears. He had persisted in his efforts for so long, taken such risks, and now he was so overwhelmed by what they had found that he could no longer control his reaction.

He sat down on the step, hanging his head so that Hayes could not see, and if his shoulders shook a little, Hayes did not think it was unwarranted. Hayes was not far from tears himself, though largely because they had survived the ordeal of the cave. Tears for the child he had found and the horror of crawling through those dark tunnels. And he hadn't taken the risks in Wooton that Kehler had. Demon Rose did not pursue him.

Kehler rose suddenly, not looking at his companion, and went on, his attention apparently drawn to the script on the far wall. Hayes kept his distance, continuing to float through this peculiar dream, in which everything seemed to have ephemeral meaning, yet nothing was familiar.

Kehler walked along one wall, Hayes the other, running his fingers over the words as though he could absorb their meaning thus. He closed his eyes, hoping words would form in his mind, and felt yet again that the meaning was so close, but he could not quite grasp it—like a memory trying to surface.

The two met before the final archway, and gazed through, wondering what would be revealed to them here. But this room had no light of its own and what lay within was not clear. Hayes waited for Kehler to go first, for he found himself curiously reticent to enter. When his friend made no move, Hayes gathered his nerve and stepped through the arch.

His eyes quickly adjusted and he found himself in an oval room, its ceiling vaulted and carved to look like a beamed ceiling of intricate design.

In the center of the chamber stood a crypt of white stone, its cover sculpted to resemble a recumbent knight in full armor. His hands closed over the hilt of a sword, the point of which rested at his feet, and he held the stem of a small blossom entwined in his fingers.

Kehler had come in behind him and stood staring at the face of this knight. Like the faces carved in the hall, this man's countenance was marked with sorrow, his heavy brows and strong mouth speaking nothing else.

"And who is this they have laid here in such solitary state?" Kehler asked, quoting a well-known line.

Hayes turned away from the melancholy knight and realized there was yet another face sculpted into the wall behind him, but as he stepped closer, he realized that it had been left incomplete.

"Look at this," he said. "Everything we've seen was finished to the smallest detail, but this is hardly begun."

The face was unquestionably that of a woman, or would be when it was complete. The curve of her hair was clear, but the eye sockets remained unfinished and she stared blindly out at them. The nose would be relatively fine, and the lips full. The chin was small, but even so the face was strong. Hayes felt there was a personality trapped in the stone that struggled to emerge, to take form before them.

"It is like looking through frosted glass or fog. The features are not quite clear." Kehler squinted as though somehow that action would bring the face into focus. "Very odd. As you say, nothing else we have seen was left unfinished." He turned to examine the rest of the chamber. Text covered the back wall, and this, Hayes was almost certain, would tell the story of the man who lay in the crypt.

On the wall at the foot of the knight a second head was carved, this one a man and quite complete. Hayes moved closer, drawn to these mysterious individuals, as though they held the key to understanding the purpose of this chamber.

"*Farrelle's blood . . .!*" he said under his breath.

Kehler came up beside him, and stopped, putting a hand to the wall for balance. "It is Erasmus. . . . Isn't it?"

"So I thought, but now that I have stared at it a moment, I am not so sure. The likeness is not perfect, but it is so close that it can hardly be coincidence."

"Like the Pelier. . . ." Kehler said.

Hayes sat down, suddenly utterly exhausted. He put his back against the wall, drew up his knees, and buried his face on his arm. *What in this round world? Erasmus Flattery?*

A moment later he opened his eyes and found Kehler sitting opposite him, slumped against the crypt, his eyes fixed on the face that so resembled the man they knew.

"I came here," Kehler said, his voice trembling with fatigue and awe, "unsure what to expect, with little more than the maps and the painting of Pelier to feed my imagination, and what I have found is utterly unexpected. I thought I knew something before we arrived here. I thought I had delved into the secrets held by the church and knew things that others did not even suspect. And now I realize I am utterly ignorant. I know less of these matters than a child knows of the greater world. I . . ." He shook his head in bewilderment. "What have we stumbled upon, Hayes? Is it nothing more than an elaborate tomb? Is it the key to some secrets of the mages themselves? The recording hall of Teller's society? Or something else altogether? Something we cannot even imagine. Why is there a likeness of Erasmus Flattery here, in this chamber that must be . . . centuries old? What in the round world have we found?"

Hayes looked up at the face again. The likeness showed a younger Erasmus, or so it seemed to Hayes—a man in his early twenties. But was it Erasmus? The hair was curlier, and the features finer, but then clearly the artist had not been working from knowledge of the model.

"It must have been done from a vision," Hayes said, struck by sudden insight.

Kehler nodded. "Yes. That would explain it. But whatever does it mean?"

"I think that Erasmus is not so innocent of the ways of the mages as he claims. Perhaps the rumors are true, and he is a mage himself. Does he even know of this chamber, I wonder?"

Hayes shook his head. "I suspect he has never seen it, but considering our discoveries, I would not be overly surprised to find that he knew of its existence. We might even be performing the task of finding it for him."

Kehler had obviously never considered this, and looked sharply at his friend. "Do you think so?"

"Anything is possible. We are dealing with mages, with men who, it was said, could look into the future. Perhaps their vision was not perfect, or utterly clear, but they could see some things. Perhaps they even saw us."

Saying this, Hayes lowered himself to the hard stone and, using his arm as a pillow, surrendered to the sweet sleep that overwhelmed him.

## ᝄ Thirty-Seven

She stood before a small niche that time and water running over stone had etched into the rock. A crystal stalactite, thrice the thickness of a stem of grass, hung there, and on it a drop of water laboriously formed. *Like a swelling womb*, Anna thought. She could see a reflection of the lantern's flame flicker in the droplet, like a tiny, rapidly beating heart.

For a long moment the drop continued to swell, and then, with what appeared to be a final inhalation, it let go its hold and fell into the world. She watched the droplet distend as it plummeted toward the natural basin below.

Opening her mind at that instant, Anna stared into the water. The droplet created a hollow where it struck the surface, and in the depression she saw stars spinning.

And then she reeled away from the basin, clutching her head in pain. Hands took hold of her, lowering her gently to the floor of the cavern, which spun around her so that she spread her arms to keep her balance. She wept.

Gentle hands supported her, and after a moment the world resumed its normal ways; the spinning slowed and then stopped altogether. No one spoke for some time, and she kept her eyes tightly closed, trying to shut out the cold, the terrible feeling that she balanced on the edge of a precipice, and all around her was a dark, cold void.

"Anna?" It was Banks. She could hear the concern in his voice, though it was partly worry that she would lose the vision if she did not speak it soon. It happened sometimes. She would cling to the vision, but it would be driven out by the feelings of terror and anguish that augury engendered.

"I have it, still," she said, and no more, not quite ready to move. She knew that this attempt at augury would slow their progress by several hours, but it couldn't be helped. There were times when a vision announced itself, and she had learned to listen at such moments, listen very carefully.

"They are here, ahead of us. I saw them; a priest, a man, and a dwarf, climbing above a raging torrent. But there is more. Two men sleep, and an armed knight watches over them. And in a window I could see a man, Erasmus Flattery it seemed, and he looked in on this scene with great sadness. Behind him there was the shadow of another. Someone very large and powerful, I thought. On the wall I could see writing. . . ." She paused, pressing her eyes closed, focusing her mind. Trying to create a complete picture of the vision. "Landor," she said. "There are more words, but. . . . *Curre d' Emone*," she said suddenly, words coming clear to her.

Those around her waited as she tried to recall more, but finally she shook her head. "That . . . that is all."

"*Curre d' Emone*," Banks said. "Heart of the world."

"Landor's gate," Kells said, his voice echoing like falling water.

"It is only a story," Banks said, the disdain in his voice less than convincing.

"All stories have roots," Anna said, pulling her hand free of Banks'. "However remote and disconnected, they have roots."

She forced herself to her feet, swaying terribly, her head suddenly light. But she did not fall.

"We must make haste. We must drive ourselves until we are there. I fear

Halsey was right—the shadow behind Erasmus Flattery must have been El-drich. I can think of no other explanation."

"But if Erasmus is an agent of Eldrich, then we are already too late," Kells said, looking genuinely frightened.

Anna shook her head, trying to work the knots from her shoulders and back. "But I sensed that Erasmus was not knowingly the mage's agent. That feeling was very strong. We might influence him yet. I must try. But we must make all haste. With such a thing to be discovered, Eldrich cannot be far off."

## ᗡ Thirty-Eight

Clarendon kept staring at the survey, which he had spread in the lamplight on the cavern floor.

"'Beyond the Fairy Galleries.' This is the only passage that is shown, but clearly there must be another that hasn't been recorded." He nodded at the pool of water which ended the passage. "Perhaps we have passed some little bolt hole. Such things can be almost impossible to see, sometimes."

Clarendon made an effort to sound his usual self, but even Erasmus, who had not known him long, could tell that he was still affected by the incident with Rose. Erasmus was not sure if Clarendon was still enraged at the priest (very likely) or if he was a little chagrined by his own reaction. After all, he had placed Deacon Rose in more than a little danger when he threw the man's belongings into the void.

Despite his own hostility toward the priest, Erasmus was concerned about the deacon's well-being. If Rose were injured, or worse, on his journey to the surface, Erasmus would feel more than a little responsible. Perhaps he should have done more for the man, but then Clarendon had caught him utterly by surprise when he threw the priest's pack into the falls. Erasmus would never have allowed Randall to do that if he had realized what he intended.

Turning his mind from this, he began to search the immediate area, ex-amining the rock, looking for an odd shadow that hid a small opening. They had already noticed a few of these as they traveled through the cave. And then he spotted a tiny bit of flowing moonstone which was too gray-white to be real.

"Well, look at this." Erasmus dug a fingernail into the wax. "I don't think that this has been here too long. Certainly only days and not years." And then he realized that the letter H had been etched on the rock in wax.

Clarendon stared at the marking, his mustache twitching. "Our friends were here, that is certain. Perhaps they didn't know precisely where the passage was, but had to look for it themselves. At least it seems they arrived at this point unharmed. It gives me hope."

Starting at the pool, they began searching back up the passage, Clarendon holding the lantern and Erasmus investigating every niche and concavity in the rock. A short time later they arrived back at the Fairy Galleries.

"We have missed something," Clarendon said.

But Erasmus shook his head. "No. I don't think so. Not in that passage at least. Let's look at the survey again."

They made their way back to the pool, where they spread out the survey and stared at it as though it were a puzzle with a hidden solution, some trick that they couldn't quite see.

"I might be a fool," Clarendon said at last, "but I can't see anything here that answers. Perhaps there is an undiscovered passage back in the Fairy Galleries, but certainly there is nothing in this section. What did your young man's letter say?"

"'Beyond the Fairy Galleries. . . .' And that he would mark his route with the letter H."

They slumped down on the rock, both of them lost in thought.

"I can answer your question," a voice said softly.

For the briefest second Clarendon looked puzzled and then he was on his feet. "I warned you to go back!" he shouted down the passage.

Deacon Rose stepped forward, a dark form on the edge of the light. Erasmus found this apparition unsettling.

"That is true, Mr. Clarendon, but without me you will not go forward, that is certain."

"Will we never be free of you, priest?!" the small man shouted, and Erasmus rose up to calm him.

"Don't be so hasty, Randall," Erasmus said, putting a hand gently on his shoulder. "I'm willing to hear the Deacon out."

Clarendon shook off Erasmus' hand, glaring at him, clearly not intimidated by size. "Have you not heard enough lies? Enough promises? He put me in the gravest danger, swinging out over the falls because of his obsession. I don't believe there are followers of Teller still among us, and I have looked into these matters, Mr. Flattery. Studied the life of Baumgere, and much else besides. . . ."

The priest interrupted quickly. "Yet you are curiously reticent to allow me to perform a trial that would prove you, and these young men you pursue, innocent," Rose said, his voice as reasonable as ever.

"Because I do not trust you!" Clarendon said with feeling. "Because the church of Farrelle has always judged in haste and with little regard for the truth. I know your history, priest. I will not have you sit in judgment of me."

Rose came forward a step, and Erasmus could see that he bowed his head, almost like a penitent. "I cannot dispute what you say, Mr. Clarendon, for there is truth in it. Some truth at least, and despite what you think, some members of my church do care for truth. I count myself one of these. That is why I'm here. I believe that there might well be Tellerites still among us, but I will see no innocent men or women persecuted. However, if there are Tellerites, as I fear there are, their purpose will not be innocent.

"They desire the power of the mages, and you do not even begin to understand what that means. You claim to know history, Mr. Clarendon; look at the history of the mages. They did not even know the meaning of the word justice. If they did not bring ruin to men, it was not because they were just or fair, but because their energies were taken up with other matters. But the followers of Teller, who hope to replace the mages after Eldrich is gone—what are their intentions?

"I believe there is a reason the mages have dwindled to one. It is not an accident. They mean to leave no trace of their arts behind when the last of them is gone. But we will have new mages to take their place, and who can be sure that they will maintain the same indifference to the affairs of men? Are you willing to take a risk that these mages will leave men in peace? I am not."

"You have already persecuted the Tellerites without mercy," Clarendon said, his voice calmer now, but the tone of accusation hardly reduced. "What will be their intentions toward the church if they rise to power now? It is no wonder you are apprehensive. You have reason to be. It is not men who need fear, but priests."

"Can you be sure?" Rose asked. "Can you, Erasmus? You know something of mages, I think. You know how little they care for mankind. Shall we have new men of power rise up, when we know so little of their intentions, or their morality? I, for one, fear it."

"It doesn't matter what he says," Clarendon countered, appealing to Erasmus as the priest had just done, as though it were Erasmus who sat in judgment. "He is a priest and has already proven that he can't be trusted. I believe he is a danger, not just to me, but to Hayes and Kehler, and perhaps even to you, Mr. Flattery."

"But you have overlooked something, Mr. Clarendon. I know the way on. I saw what Kehler saw in Wooton, though at the time I did not quite realize what it meant. But I have located the way and could simply go on without you. I could confront your young friends, and there would be nothing you could do. But, you see, I am trying to make amends for what you believe was an act of bad faith. I will show you the way, and you can accompany me. We will find Kehler and his friend, and you can assure yourself that I will not harm them. I believe now that you are no follower of Teller, Mr. Clarendon, and I apologize, both for doubting you, and for my actions. I'm sure it was terrifying, though I will say I would never have done it if I had not had utter faith in the rope to hold your weight. Despite what you might think, I did not intend to endanger your life."

"Why?" Erasmus said suddenly. "Why do you suddenly wish to make amends for what you did to Randall?"

"Because it is a long and dangerous journey out of the cave alone," Clarendon growled.

"No more dangerous than traversing above the falls alone with no one to hold the rope," the priest answered. "Because I'm now convinced that you are not followers of Teller. Because if any discovery is made, I hope to be able to convince you of its danger, should it become known. If we find your young friends, there will be four of you and but one of me. If my powers of persuasion are not up to the task, you will override me and do what you will. I am only asking to be heard. That is little enough for showing you the way on, for I can guarantee that you will not find it without me."

"We should search on," Clarendon said. "I'm not ready to admit we cannot find the way."

"By all means," Rose agreed. "I will await your decision." He sat down, his limbs sprawling like a man entirely exhausted, and no longer caring about appearances.

"Have you food left?" Erasmus asked the priest as they passed him to return to the Fairy Galleries.

"Very kind of you to ask, Mr. Flattery. I have a little and am used to fasting anyway. What I need is sleep." The priest rolled onto his side on the cold rock and shut his eyes. Erasmus thought he would be asleep in seconds. He was almost that exhausted himself.

They left the priest, warmed only by the small flame of his candle, and went back up the passage carrying their lantern and the survey.

When they were sure they had passed beyond the priest's hearing, Clarendon turned to Erasmus. "I will never trust that man. I am suspicious of him even now. It is foolish even to leave him alone with our packs."

Erasmus nodded. "I agree with you, Randall. I'm not quite sure what Rose is up to, but he can't be trusted. Yet what has he gained by coming to us? Do you think he is after the contents of our packs? He intends to go on without us somehow? Perhaps one of us should wait here in the darkness to see what he will do."

Clarendon shook his head. "But he knows we don't trust him. He might even imagine that we would do such a thing. No, there is something else. Could the way on be in this passage and we have missed it?"

"We searched every crevice. . . ." Erasmus stopped in his tracks.

"Mr. Flattery?"

"What if it is through the pool?"

"What are you saying?"

"Imagine the pool extending beneath the wall, and then the passage opening up again beyond. Do you see what I mean? The pool could merely be a low spot in the passage where water accumulates."

Clarendon spun around and bolted down the passage. Because the tunnel was small, Erasmus was soon left behind, following the dull glow of the lantern, stumbling in the growing darkness. Once he hit his head so hard that he fell to his knees clutching his scalp in pain.

He heard Clarendon cursing beyond him, and tried to hurry on, but he was leary now of doing himself further injury. Light began to grow before him, and in a moment he found Clarendon crouched down in the pool reaching frantically under the wall. The priest was nowhere to be seen.

"I saw him, Mr. Flattery. The blackguard was disappearing under the wall as I came. I was not swift enough. May he drown for his lies and his false heart."

Erasmus waded in beside his friend and reached in under the wall as far as he could. The passage was narrow and completely water-filled as far as he could tell.

"I will chance it," Erasmus said quickly. "But we must think about how we will take our lantern through. How could he have light beyond?"

Clarendon pointed back at their gear, which was spread across the cave floor. "He had a lantern still and has taken a tin of our lamp oil."

Erasmus lumbered, dripping, from the pool, and to his dismay discovered that many things had been taken. From one of the packs a large section of canvas had been jaggedly cut.

"Here. He has wrapped everything in clothing and canvas and hopes that will be proof against water for as long as he is submerged. We will do the same." He found two candles and lit them, then blew out the flame in the lantern.

As soon as they felt the lantern had cooled sufficiently, they wrapped it as best they could and took up the bundles they would carry on with them. Erasmus tied one end of their rope about his wrist with a knot that he could easily release and went into the pool where he knelt in the cold water.

"As soon as I have found air, I will pull the rope through. Hold fast to the end. If all is clear, I will tug it sharply three times." He took three deep breaths and forced himself into the tunnel beneath the wall. The idea of being submerged was not particularly unsettling to Erasmus, but he was worried about how far he might have to go before he found air again. If Rose could make it, then Erasmus was certain he would manage—though he feared finding Rose drowned in the tunnel. The priest obviously didn't lack courage, but he'd already proven himself a poor swimmer.

Clarendon was more of a concern, but then Erasmus had seldom met a man with greater tenacity. If Rose and Erasmus could go through, then so would Randall Spencer Emanual Clarendon—have no doubt of it.

The dark waters seemed to cling to him as Erasmus clawed at the rock, pulling himself along as quickly as possible toward the air he hoped was near. Air . . . The urge to breathe began to take hold of him. If he went much farther and did not emerge, he might have gone too far to return.

Suddenly his survival seemed to depend on turning back immediately.

*Go on*, he told himself. *The priest did it, and he could not swim.*

And then as he reached forward to grab the rock, his hand broke the surface. A few seconds more and he sat upright in a pale, glowing pool, light coming from the candles on the other side. Rose was nowhere to be seen.

Erasmus scrambled out of the freezing water, shaking. The knots on the roll of canvas defied his cold fingers for a moment, but then he got them opened and pulled out his clothes and the lantern, only dampened from their brief submersion. He pulled on his shirt and breeches, drying his hand before striking the flint and lighting the lantern.

In a few moments he had hauled their remaining pack through the siphon, and then he stood knee-deep in the pool waiting for Clarendon, ready to offer assistance.

The water began to surge around him and in only a few seconds he had Clarendon by the hand and pulled him out into the air and light.

"Flames . . .!" the little man sputtered, trying to catch his breath. "I thought I should never come to the end of it. Farrelle preserve us, but that is my own version of the netherworld: dark and airless and unbearably close." He shivered uncontrollably.

Afraid of what the priest might be up to, they went quickly on, following wet footprints on the rock.

In less than half of an hour they came upon a section of cavern where innumerable openings gaped to one side. Here they found two packs, all but empty.

"I don't think we are far behind now," Clarendon said. "It is only a question of which tunnel they've entered."

Erasmus bent down and put his hand to the rock before the nearest opening, then reached inside. "I'm not sure if this is damp, but it is the most obvious choice." He bent down and peered into it, listening for sounds of a man crawling. "Flames, it is tight."

"And that is where I prove my worth, Mr. Flattery." Clarendon was still not dry from his encounter with the pool. His fringe of white hair was plastered to his scalp and his clothing still damp. But despite this his determination did not seem diminished.

"Let me go ahead," he insisted. "I fear for our young friends. I will take one end of the rope, and if this is the right passage I will signal you to follow. Just as we did at the siphon."

A moment later the man's small feet were disappearing into the opening, and Erasmus was left in candlelight, wondering what they had found. Worrying about Kehler and Hayes and Clarendon. And this treacherous priest.

Hayes was drawing carefully on the slightly mushy paper. Despite being meticulously protected in oilcloth, their writing supplies were damp, to say the least. Each line of ink spread out as it was laid down so that it looked like the efforts of a child, and any attempts at precision or elegance were futile.

In the hours since they had wakened, Hayes had come to realize that the inscriptions on the walls were much more complicated and diverse than he had originally thought. The walls were not simply covered in text, but also boasted diagrams, art, what might be a chart of the heavens, stylized figures, even a map. There were characters that Kehler was convinced were numbers arrayed in complex formulae. On the wall opposite the font, seven large intersecting circles were cut into the stone and surrounded by stars. Hayes was almost convinced that the lines scribed on the central circle depicted the Entide Sea, though Kehler was less convinced.

"Perhaps these represent our globe, but each view is a partial rotation beyond the last. Seven views of our world," Hayes had offered, but it was mere speculation, though in such a place one could not contain the desire to speculate, and they did so endlessly.

He stood by the font looking at the sculpture above. The avian masks of the man and woman looked less exotic and more macabre as time went on. The font and raised floor still felt like an altar to him, and he had a strange foreboding that the rituals that might be performed here would be dark and strange.

They had been so overwhelmed by exhaustion and by the magnitude of their discovery when they arrived that they had not noticed two urns that stood to either side of the font. These were made of white marble and sculpted to resemble blossoms—like the one the woman held, although the urns were much larger.

"What do you make of these?" he asked Kehler, who was sitting on the top step leading to the terrace.

He looked up from his work, a slightly dazed look on his face. His pen paused in midair. "What's that?"

"These urns. What do you make of them? Do you see, they were made to resemble the blossom held by this lady."

Kehler put the end of his pen to his front teeth. "You're right, I think." He rose stiffly and stood by his friend. "The top almost looks like it might have been made to lift off," he said, reaching forward. He jerked his hand back abruptly. "Flames! What was that?" Kehler looked over at his friend, his eyes wide. "Do as I did," he said.

"But what happened?"

"Nothing too serious, apparently; but try."

Hayes put his hand gingerly forward, and then he, too, jerked it back. "What in this round . . . ?"

Kehler shrugged. "I don't know. It wasn't quite pain, nor was it really heat. More like a tingling and numbness, but it was unbearable. I don't think I could possibly hold my hand there." He reached out again.

Hayes snatched his hand away. "I'm not sure that's wise. It is certainly not natural, whatever it is. I'm not certain we should toy with it." He looked up suddenly. "Did you hear a noise?"

They both stood perfectly still, straining to hear.

"I hear nothing," Kehler said. "What did it sound like?"

"Footsteps, I think—or scuffling, as though someone walked or crawled." He shook his head. "I'm sure it was just imagination."

The rope fed out slowly, water squeezing from the strands as it ran through Erasmus' hands. Occasionally it would stop altogether, worrying Erasmus, but he was afraid to shout into the tunnel for fear of alerting Rose, who might not realize his pursuers were so close.

Randall might have an indomitable spirit, but Erasmus feared that he would be no match for Rose physically. He hoped Rose was in such a rush to find Hayes and Kehler that he wouldn't wait to see if they followed, otherwise poor Randall could be in trouble. Erasmus had even begun to wonder if the priest would use violence. Clarendon had been right in the end; Rose was utterly deceitful.

"Hurry, Randall," he whispered. "Hurry."

*May we catch the priest before he can perform his knavery.*

The rope began to move again, like a languid snake. Erasmus realized that this rope would have to be carefully dried or rot would set in, for it still remained for them to make their way out and cross again above the falls.

Suddenly two feet of rope slipped quickly through his hands, and he dropped it lest he blister. But then it lay limp for a moment, Erasmus' concern growing. And then it began to run quickly as though it were being taken in, hand over hand. Three distinct tugs followed, and Erasmus sighed. In his mind he had an image of Rose waiting at the tunnel's end, and overpowering poor Randall, and then luring Erasmus to follow.

Erasmus had stiffened up considerably while he waited, and he got down on his belly to slither into the opening with some discomfort. His still-damp clothing seemed to stick to the rock and the effort it took to drag himself forward was enormous.

Randall had taken their lantern, so Erasmus carried a candle, which made this hand ineffective at pulling him forward. He soon had hot wax pouring on his fingers and after ten minutes dropped the candle and accidentally snuffed it out. He lay in complete darkness in the tightest passage he had yet encountered.

*Large enough for Randall*, he thought, *but what of me? Perhaps I cannot make my way through.*

He forced himself to go on, against growing panic, as though he were making a terrible mistake. The entire endeavor suddenly seemed a terrible mistake. But then a hint of light came down the tunnel ahead, or more accurately a hint of gray. The passage almost materialized.

"Mr. Flattery?" came Clarendon's voice.

"Randall? Am I almost through?"

"Very nearly, Mr. Flattery, though it is a bit tight right at the end. I assume if the others managed, you will as well. But hurry. I fear we might be too late."

Erasmus forced himself to push on, heartened by the thought of light and space, and a moment later he twisted himself through the constriction at the tunnel's end.

The passage was still small but seemed like a ballroom to Erasmus. He sat for a moment, taking long breaths, each one seeming to increase his sense of relief. Clarendon stood impatiently by, fidgeting.

"All right, Randall. Let's go on and see if our friends are here."

As quickly as they could, they set off along the passage, crawling on battered knees and blistered hands. To their relief the passage opened up, and Clarendon helped Erasmus to his feet.

"Do you hear a tinkling sound?" Clarendon asked.

"Running water, I'm almost certain."

A pale light seemed to illuminate the tunnel beyond the reach of their lantern's flame, though it was so faint they could not be sure. But as they went forward, the light grew. Not the light of lanterns or candles, but a pure white light—more like the light of the moon than the sun. Supporting each other, they increased their pace and a moment later came to a natural stair, its rounded steps ascending a low slope.

Erasmus looked up. "A doorway," he said, and the two of them stopped to stare in wonder.

"And there is Teller's symbol," Erasmus said, pointing to the three blossoms raised in relief on the keystone.

"I . . . I'm not so certain, Mr. Flattery. These blossoms are all the same, I think. There are no roses."

Erasmus went forward, up onto the man-made steps, and then he nodded his agreement.

They went up and through the door, dousing their lantern, and found themselves in a long, high ceilinged hallway bathed in what appeared to be starlight or moonlight. And then they heard laughter.

## ⌐ Thirty-Nine

Halsey sat working by the light of a poor lamp, bent close to the page so that he could see. His pen scratched across the paper rhythmically, and behind him a log moved in the fire, followed by a crescendo of sparks. There were no other sounds; both the house and the town were asleep.

Then, distinctly, someone cleared his throat. Halsey raised his head, registered what he'd heard, and then whirled around. A tall man stood by the hearth, hanging a poker back on its hook.

"Who are you?"

"I thought such an authority on the arcane would need not ask."

Halsey raised a hand to his face, so slowly it seemed almost to have moved without his knowledge. He felt a strange disconnection with his limbs, with the world. A nightmare unfolded before him. "*Eldrich* . . ." He whispered the name as though he named a fiend.

"Ah, you are an authority, I see," the man said mockingly. Eldrich shifted his position, though he made no movement that would imply fear or even concern for his situation.

"I warn you," Halsey said. "I am not without resources," but he could hardly catch his breath, and still felt as though gravity did not quite hold him.

A smile flickered on the mage's face. "I stand forewarned. You don't mind if I sit?" he asked, sitting.

Despite the strong sense of unreality, Halsey could not help himself—he stared at the man in utter fascination. *He was in the presence of a mage.* Certainly it meant the end of everything he had hoped to accomplish in his life—but even so he was utterly fascinated.

"How is it that you found me?" Halsey managed, his voice still quavering a little.

The mage shrugged.

But there could be only one answer. "*Skye* . . ."

Eldrich stared at the man, saying nothing.

"And Erasmus was meant to lure us as well?"

Eldrich continued to stare, his look of mild amusement not varying.

"You have trapped me, can you not at least answer my questions before . . . before you do whatever it is you intend?"

The two men regarded each other for a moment, and then Eldrich spoke. "Augury is a strange art—its subtleties almost impossible to teach. . . . Skye, you see, is my creature. I created him, in a way—created him to serve only one purpose. He was the grain of sand around which your vision formed."

Halsey was not even sure he understood. Eldrich had created Anna's vision? Was that possible?

The fire cracked, shooting sparks onto the floor, and the mage swept them, rather lazily, back into the coals with the toe of his boot. "After he appeared in your vision, I arranged to put Skye in danger. You, very gallantly, rescued him." He tilted his head as though to say: "It was not so difficult." "Though I will confess, I thought you might approach Erasmus first." He stared hard at Halsey. "This young woman—your mage in waiting—she has gone down into the cave with the others?"

Halsey said nothing, feeling like a belligerent child faced with an infinitely more powerful adult.

Eldrich glanced down into the fire, as though considering what he might do with this wayward child.

"I will confess to you," he said, his manner so offhand he could have been addressing a friend, "until two years ago I was beginning to think my augury was false—that you did not exist—but I had a feeling. Intuition perhaps, and a mage should always trust his intuition." He glanced up at Halsey. "And here you are." He tried to force some triumph into this declaration, but it rang hollow, and he looked suddenly tired and sad, almost melancholic.

Halsey said nothing, but sat and stared, aware that his threat had been hollow, knowing that Eldrich knew it, too. Anna . . . her impetuosity had been their undoing, though he knew she should not be blamed entirely. He had sanctioned many of her actions, however reluctantly. He shook his head. It was the oddest moment; his flash of fear had disappeared and now he felt only inevitability. He could not change what was to happen, but could only wait.

"But why am I here?" Eldrich said suddenly. He looked at Halsey expectantly, as though the question were not merely rhetorical. "Do you have any idea what is to be found in that cave?"

It was said one could not lie to a mage, and even Anna could usually discern truth from lie. "No, I haven't."

Eldrich raised his eyebrows, a distinctly human response. "They search for nothing?"

"They hope to find a chamber left by Teller's people."

Eldrich's face darkened at the mention of this name. He stared at Halsey for some time, his gaze unsettling. "I wish them luck," he said finally.

Halsey shook his head, suddenly finding his emotions. Angry at being toyed with. "I think I have little to add to this conversation. You trapped my brothers at the abbey. Trapped and murdered them."

"Me? I was not even born. Nor were you, I think. That is history, Mr. Halsey. And history is but memory—ever unreliable memory. . . ." The mage paused, staring at his captive, for that is what Halsey was, and he knew it.

"Do you know what Medwar said about history? It is fiction without dialogue." Eldrich smiled wanly.

"What will you do with me?" Halsey asked, unwilling to listen to jests from his likely executioner.

"To a large degree, that depends on you, Mr. Halsey."

"I will not betray my fellows. I have ways of averting that."

A smile pulled at the corners of Eldrich's mouth. "I have no doubt that you do, but let me ask only that you hear me out, Mr. Halsey, for there is a tale I would tell you, and at the end . . . Well, I think we will have more to discuss when I have finished."

"You cannot win me over. Even a mage is not that persuasive."

"I ask only that you hear me out, Mr. Halsey. The story, I think, is more persuasive than I could ever be." Eldrich rose from his seat and paced across the hearth, gazing down at the floor, seemingly unaware of the Tellerite.

*Flames, he does not fear me in the least*, Halsey thought. *Do we truly know so little of them?*

"It began with Lucklow in his middle years," Eldrich said, his musical voice even more melancholy. "He was skilled at augury, much more so than I. Much more so than you, Mr. Halsey. . . ."


## ∽ Forty

Walky rode up behind the cab of the carriage as though he were a footman. He had an unerring sense for the times when his master needed to be left alone, and this was one of them. He looked around at the night. Moonlight found its way through the trees in splashes highlighting a world drained of color. There were no coach lamps flickering fitfully, for the carriage of a mage did not require them. Driver and team traveled unerringly to their destination on even the blackest of nights.

Walky had served the mage for a very long time now, over seventy years, and he had never seen Lord Eldrich so troubled as he had been these last weeks. This constant reversion to augury was one sign, but to Walky there were others as well.

The mage revealed almost nothing of his thoughts, let alone his concerns, but Walky hadn't remained in his service for so long without reason. He was sensitive to his master's moods, and Eldrich's mood was dark and very troubled.

This entire affair was unsettling. Eldrich had returned from his encounter with the old man who followed Teller, and shut himself up alone for twelve hours. Walky had heard him pacing, back and forth across the room—forth and back like a caged wolf.

And now there was this young woman and her companions who had gone down into the cave, to perform all manner of mischief, no doubt.

The cave itself was a matter of the greatest concern, or, more precisely, what was hidden there. And then there was Erasmus. Even though Walky knew that he was still alive, he grieved for his former student all the same.

The knowledge that all of this was necessary hardly made it easier to bear, but it was all the comfort he had.

*We all die*, he thought. *Even the mage will pass through eventually.*

The carriage rocked to one side, and Walky took hold quickly. He saw a bird glide through a shaft of moonlight, making no more noise than a passing cloud—or a mage. An owl, Walky realized. Eldrich's great wolf howled somewhere out in the darkness—an unmistakable if not a common sound, for the beast was usually as silent as its master. Perhaps it howled the despair the master felt. Walky did not know. Nor would he likely ever know. He served the mage, and one did not ask questions of a mage.

The driver brought up his team, and as Walky peered into the darkness, he realized that the lane had ended. He climbed down from his perch, not nearly as quickly as he once had, and opened the door, lowering the carriage steps.

Lord Eldrich did not emerge, and Walky stood patiently by, never thinking to speak. The driver readied two saddle horses that had been tethered behind, and when he spoke softly to Walky to let him know the mounts were ready, the springs of the carriage rocked, and Eldrich stepped out. Without a word, he mounted a horse, and with the help of the driver his servant did the same.

Walky was almost sure they were on a path, though he could not see it. On occasion, when the need arose, the mage cast a spell over him that allowed him to see in the darkness. *Owl sight*, the mage called it, though Walky suspected that this was Eldrich's idea of humor. In any case, owl sight seemed to bathe the world in soft starlight. There was only the slightest shade of color to even the brightest objects, but even so one could see perfectly. Tonight, of course, Walky did not have to see. He could follow the mage, who could see perfectly, he was sure—and it would never occur to Eldrich to give his servant sight merely out of consideration. The mage did not think in such terms.

Walky, of course, didn't feel the slightest resentment over this. When he needed to see in the darkness, he was given sight. When he needed to know, he was informed. It was the life he had chosen, and he could not even imagine another.

Erasmus would never have been able to adapt to it, even if that had been the reason he'd come to live with Eldrich. No, Erasmus had questioned everything, and resented anyone who kept knowledge from him. From what the old man could tell, that had not changed.

Walky wondered if this was one of the reasons that Erasmus was where he was this night. But, no, even the mage couldn't be so petty. After all, Erasmus had been only a boy in those days. He could hardly be blamed for his actions, he had been so young.

Leaves brushed across his face, and he bent down quickly.

Ahead of him, Eldrich emerged into an area of moonlight so that Walky could see his slightly bent form almost clearly. The mage, with his head bowed, riding through a wood by night. There was an image to frighten children, and for good reason. Eldrich did not care much for men, at any age.

Although Walky had long ago accustomed himself to following blindly wherever his master led, whatever he did, this night the servant felt a vague uneasiness growing in him. What was it they did this night? Had it to do with some larger purpose? And if so, what?

They were somewhere above the great cave into which Erasmus had disappeared, Walky was sure. Erasmus and the others—the followers of Teller. He began to feel nausea creeping over him.

Walky knew that Eldrich would act without the slightest compassion toward those who opposed him, but Erasmus was in this same cave, had helped draw the followers of Teller there, in fact.

*Has that been his purpose all along?* Walky wondered. *Poor child. Poor sad child . . . Better to have burned.*

## ᔛ Forty-One

"Erasmus!" Hayes rubbed his eyes as though he might wipe away the image of his friend. Surely he could not be here.

Kehler turned quickly on Hayes, the accusation clear.

"I—I left a note for Erasmus in case we didn't return. I thought our friends might like to know where we'd perished."

"And it was a wise precaution," Clarendon said, almost crossly. Then he waved his hand about the chamber. "But what in this round world have you found?"

Kehler didn't look quite as furious as Hayes expected. In fact, he looked almost relieved to see the others.

"We aren't quite sure, Mr. Clarendon," Kehler said. "It is what Baumgere sought, or so I surmise, but beyond that I cannot say. The mark above the door seems to be Teller's, but that is about the only token we recognize."

"And even there you are mistaken," Clarendon said. "For the blossoms over the door were not vale roses. They were not roses at all." He stared at the sculptures above the font, his eyes darting here and there and then back again.

Hayes caught Erasmus' eye. "Do you have any idea what this place might be?"

Erasmus looked down, shaking his head. "I think only Eldrich might have that answer, Hayes." He looked up. "I assume you've seen no sign of Deacon Rose?"

"Deacon Rose!?" Kehler said.

Erasmus nodded. "Yes. I'm afraid he learned of our expedition into the cave and, suspecting our purpose, confronted us at the entrance. We thought it better to bring him, and keep him under our eye, than let him wander free, but he slipped away and got ahead of us at the pool. Now we don't know where he's gotten to."

Kehler slumped down on the stair of the terrace, suddenly limp with resignation. Twice he raised his hands and tried to speak but couldn't manage to find words. Finally he said; "But that is why I kept this so secret. Rose is a Farrellite 'inquisitor.' A priest trained to deal with matters that have to do with the arts of the mages. Men just like him burned the Tellerites who were discovered within the church—burned them for heresy. You cannot imagine how powerful he is. And his dedication is beyond all. The church will do anything to see that the arts do not live beyond the years of the last mage. They believe, once Eldrich is gone, that the church will rise again—and they will have no practitioners of the arts to deprive them of their rightful place. This man, Rose, he is more than just a fanatic. He would burn for eternity before he would fail in his duty. He would sacrifice any number of innocent people." Kehler looked up at Erasmus, his face drawn with exhaustion and fear. "I cannot think what he will do to me if ever he finds me," he said, losing his voice suddenly. "I can't think."

"He believes you are a follower of Teller," Clarendon said, watching the young man's reaction carefully.

Kehler's hands flew up as though they were on strings. "I am undone," he said.

"Can we not simply stand guard at the mouth of the passage?" Hayes asked. "No one could pass through there without us knowing."

"And then what will we do?" Kehler asked, his voice filled with accusation.

"I don't know, Kehler, for I cannot begin to imagine what this man can do to us. Can we simply keep him from exiting the tunnel? After all, a man in that passage is hardly at an advantage."

"You don't understand. Deacon Rose has been trained in the arts of the mages," Kehler said.

"No, he is trained in the lesser arts only," Erasmus said emphatically.

Everyone turned to him, a bit surprised. "The church has long had some knowledge of the lesser arts. They can detect certain things—people who practice the arts for instance, or have a talent for them. They have practiced augury with partial success. Perhaps they can even protect themselves from the charms of a person who has some small knowledge of the arts—but that is all. The mages would never have allowed the priests to retain more power than that. I'm sure this priest is every bit as fanatical as you say, Kehler, but he is not nearly so powerful as you think. Fear, I suspect, is his greatest weapon."

"How do you know?" Kehler asked, still utterly despondent.

"Because I did learn a few things in my time with Eldrich. We must be wary of the priest, certainly, but here are four of us and only one of him. He cannot overpower us." Erasmus looked around him, shaking his head in disbelief and wonder at what they'd found.

"What do you make of this, Erasmus?" Hayes asked, placing a hand on Kehler's shoulder. He felt a bit guilty about Erasmus' arrival, but he was also greatly relieved.

Erasmus did not answer, but turned in a slow circle. "It is a miracle that such a thing exists. And even more so that you found it." He shook his head again. "What lies through the doorway?"

"A crypt, or so it seems; and something you should see."

Erasmus and Clarendon mounted the steps onto the terrace, slowing to look at the font and the sculpture above before going on toward the chamber's end.

Inside the doorway they stopped, Kehler and Hayes hanging back, watching their friend's response. Clarendon reached out and touched the supine figure of the knight, resting his hand there as though it were the grave of a friend he had finally come to visit.

"Who was this?" Clarendon asked softly, his voice oddly filled with emotion.

But Erasmus shook his head. "Look at the arms on the breastplate. These are not Teller's signs."

"No, but who has been honored so?"

"Landor," Erasmus said, though the word came out reluctantly. His three companions stared at him, the question unspoken.

Erasmus pointed at the text on the wall behind the crypt. "I have seen that name before . . . in a book in the house of Eldrich."

"But who was Landor?"

"The first, perhaps the most powerful of the mages, or so say the myths. I don't know more than that." Erasmus turned to the sculpted face of the woman, gasping in wonder. Perhaps, like Hayes and Kehler, he felt that he should know her. Reluctantly he turned away and crossed behind the crypt to examine the text, his jaw tight, but his eyes glistening as though tears tried to form.

When he came to the end wall, Erasmus stopped so abruptly that Clarendon, who followed, was almost knocked off his feet.

"*Blood and flames*," Erasmus breathed, and said nothing more.

Clarendon stared at the face and then up at Erasmus. "But it is you, Erasmus," he said, stepping back quickly, as though he should not stand too close to this man. His eyes darted back and forth, from the face in stone to Erasmus.

"Is it me?" Erasmus asked, his tone a little desperate, as though asking to be reassured that it could not be. "Is it?"

They sat on the steps of the raised terrace in the perpetual starlight of the chamber, eating some of the food that Kehler and Hayes had brought through the tiny passage.

The conversation was quiet, punctuated by long pauses as they contemplated the meaning of what they'd found.

"Erasmus?" Hayes said. "It seems that you can read—some of this, at least. Will you not give us some idea of what is written here?"

Erasmus looked up at his young friend, and then turned his gaze to the writing on the wall. For a moment he said nothing, and Hayes was almost certain he would again deny having any knowledge.

"The language," Erasmus said, his voice quiet and solemn, as though he were in a place of worship, "is one of the root languages of Farr and Entonne. It is called Darian, in that tongue. Scholars today have small fragments of it, though these have never been translated. I cannot read it fluently, and most of what is written here is as much a mystery to me as it is to you. I could read the name 'Landor,' which was inscribed in the crypt." He glanced back toward the chamber where his likeness was carved. "The text begins in that corner and runs right to left for the first line, then left to right, and so on, back and forth, I don't know the first word, though it would appear to be the word or name of this chamber. The first line appears to say, '. . . was built to mark,' or perhaps it is, 'to solemnize the meeting of the two worlds, Tearalan and Darr.' Do you see the circles opposite us? Each is marked with a name. The one most central is Tearalan, the circle next to the right is Darr. The first word of the next sentence is Landor. Perhaps, 'Landor discovered this gateway in . . .' I think it is a date, but I cannot tell you what it might be. 'Honor and high praise to the great mage who opened the way. Let his name be remembered always. Let his . . .' perhaps 'praise.' 'Let his praises be sung by all who come after.'" For a moment he fell silent, his eyes scanning the script. "It appears to be a history. Seven mages passed through the gate, Landor and six who followed him. 'The land was fair, and they named it . . .' It is a form of Landor—perhaps 'Landoria' would be our equivalent. 'The tide followed them, sweeping through the land, and the arts grew in strength as the tide rose.' I know only two words of the next line. . . . I cannot make sense of it. Then, 'The King's Blood was spread upon the earth, and took root and blossomed. Thus ended the first years of the . . .' More words I do not know." For a few moments he said nothing at all. "I have forgotten so much. There are words I think I should know, but they escape me. It would seem that this chamber was built as a monument to Landor and to the others who were his followers or supporters. It marks the place where these first mages arrived."

"But from where?" Hayes asked, unable to contain his question.

Erasmus shrugged. "From Darr, apparently."

"Faery," Clarendon said. He gestured to the intersecting worlds on the opposite wall. "From a world beyond." He looked at Kehler. "Don't you think?"

Kehler shrugged. "There was so much to be learned in the archives of the Farrellites. Perhaps if I'd had more time . . . I came seeking Baumgere's secret, never knowing what it was."

Erasmus cleared his throat and began to recite:
*"And Tomas plunged into the mirror lake,*
*And emerged he knew not where*
*A land unnatural and unknown to man*
*And he wandered out by star and moon*
*To a land both fell and fair."*

"The Journey of Tomas," Hayes said.

Erasmus nodded. "I spoke with Deacon Rose before we came searching after you, and he reminded me of the tale. He said that whatever you were seeking, what you might find could be very different—as unexpected as Tomas' journey into a strange land."

"He seems to have known something, Mr. Flattery," Clarendon said. "Does it not seem so? Did we not plunge into a pool and emerge beyond? Does it not say here we are at the gate to another world?"

"Baumgere had several different versions of the lyric for the ballad," Kehler said. "That is how we found our way through the pool—he had written a note on one of the texts. Rose must have seen it as well."

Erasmus nodded. "He likely spoke of the ballad to see my reaction."

"We have not yet taken you up the stair," Hayes said. "You passed it as you entered. It spirals up and ends in a wall. And there a single large character has been carved. Perhaps it is the gate you spoke of—Landor's Gate."

"Perhaps," Erasmus said, though he did not seem at all inclined to go see this wonder. "Whatever the purpose of this chamber, Kehler, I doubt that we shall ever comprehend it. And I can tell you without a shade of doubt that we will never be able to use it as the mages did—even if we could read every word written here. It takes a man's lifetime to become a mage. Seven decades. Not three years, as some people seem to think."

"It does not matter if we understand," Clarendon said. His eyes still glowed with wonder. "We have found it. A miracle, as Mr. Flattery said. And we shall copy every word and reproduce every diagram, and this wonder will not be lost to man again."

"I don't think you understand the implications of this discovery, Mr. Clarendon," came a voice from the hall's end.

They all looked up to find Deacon Rose standing in the archway at the chamber's entrance. He raised his hands, palms out. "I carry no weapon, as you can see. And Mr. Flattery is right in what he says: I do not have the powers of a mage. You need not fear me. But I do hope you will listen to me, for I have some knowledge of things arcane, and more knowledge about our last mage, for he is of particular interest to my church."

Hayes looked over at his friend, who really did look as though he confronted a demon. To his right, Clarendon clenched his fists as though struggling within himself to not assault the man.

Rose didn't come forward, and though he was some distance away, his voice carried easily in the stone chamber. "I'm sure that if Eldrich does not know of the existence of this chamber, he certainly suspects that it exists. Even I have read a reference to it, though I believed at the time it was merely myth. Landor's Gate. *Poart Landorianné.*

"If you think you will publish what you have found here and not draw a reprisal from Lord Eldrich, you do not know much of the world. Nor do you understand the powers of the mage. I know your intentions are noble, Mr. Kehler. You wish to see knowledge spread to every quarter of society. I know you believe that my church hoards knowledge to keep its power, and I will freely admit that sometimes this has been true. But it is not as simple a matter as you make it out to be. Eldrich will make you pay a terrible price for what you have done here. This is a sacred place, if I can use such a term, for that is how the mages viewed it. Just being here is enough to earn you Eldrich's wrath. You had best pray to Farrelle that the mage never learns of our transgressions . . . as unlikely as that might be. I fear it is too late for all of us." He stepped out of the doorway, and for a moment he forgot what he was saying, and stared in awe at the chamber. But then he shook his head quickly and looked back to the others.

"I tried to stop you, Mr. Kehler, but you eluded me. And Mr. Flattery, Mr. Clarendon . . . once you had led me to the Fairy Galleries and I realized where Mr. Kehler must be, I tried to slip away, hoping you would not follow. I tell you honestly that I hoped to spare you this. . . ."

Clarendon stood suddenly, unable to contain himself any longer, but Erasmus took hold of his arm. "Be at peace, Randall. In this the Deacon does not lie. If Eldrich learns that we have defiled this place with our presence—and I can hardly imagine that he will not learn of it—he . . ." Erasmus stopped suddenly, his look very odd. "The price he exacts will be more than you will ever wish to pay, I assure you."

Hayes was truly alarmed. "Then what should we do?" he asked, a bit embarrassed at the apprehension in his tone.

"Leave this place," the priest said. "Destroy every scrap of paper you have written on. Leave this place and never speak of it to anyone—not even to each other. Let it be as though we found nothing. Never write a word of it in your most secret journals. Do not even think of it. And if we are fortunate and Eldrich does not already know of our discovery, we might escape his notice." He was agitated now, and began to pace across the chamber. "You cannot conceive of the powers of a mage. He might even now be aware of our trespass. Mr. Flattery is here, and though I believe that you are no minion of Eldrich, sir, still, you might be surprised at how much he knows of your endeavors. We should leave now—not tarry an instant more." He pointed up at the figure above the font, though Hayes thought he almost seemed to avert his eyes. There was a look near to horror on the priest's face. "We have seen too much. Things we were never meant to see."

Clarendon could be restrained no longer. "And when we leave this place with nothing to show for it, this priest will offer us up to Eldrich. When the mage is gone, the church will want to be sure that no word of this place escapes. Who knows what might be learned here? But the Farrellites will bury that knowledge. They will bury it, and we will be buried as well, frightened into silence, or betrayed to Eldrich. If we were not civilized men, we would leave your bones here, priest, for you are the danger to us. You and your desire to appease Eldrich." Clarendon stopped suddenly, his anger so great that it drove out his thoughts.

"Randall is right," Erasmus said, his tone so quiet and reasonable that it hardly seemed to belong to the same debate. "We always come back to this problem of trust, Deacon. If you go to Eldrich, the rest of us will suffer for our discovery."

Rose nodded, stopping his pacing. He looked up at Erasmus. "There is an answer to this, Mr. Flattery. You must go to Eldrich and tell him what has been found. Make him realize that no one understood what their discovery would mean. Plead our case. Eldrich would not likely accept our promise of silence, but the mages have ways of making people forget. It is our only chance, I think, unless you are willing to trust my silence—and I am sure you're not."

The others looked hopefully at Erasmus. Here, from this unlikely source, came an offered solution. But Erasmus did not look so hopeful.

He shook his head. "I am willing to try to take our case to Eldrich, though I will tell you honestly that there is no reason to believe the mage will even speak with me. He has forgotten me, I think, and was barely aware of me even as I lived in his house. I would not pin my hopes on this. Even if Eldrich heard me out, there is no guarantee of leniency or even justice, no matter how eloquently I plead our case."

No one spoke. Even Clarendon's anger seemed to give way to despondency. The little man sat down hard on the steps, glancing once at Erasmus and then quickly away.

"We have already desecrated this place," Erasmus said after a while. "It is too late to change that. We're all exhausted and our thinking no longer clear. Let's stay some hours and rest and then decide." He looked up at the priest. "Deacon Rose? I'm afraid we will have to ask you to make your bed in the chamber at the far end of this hall. We will sleep before the door. I mean you no harm, but we would like to decide our course together, if you don't mind."

The priest looked up at Erasmus, and then nodded once. He would not cross the terrace where the others sat so casually, but instead stepped over the small stream which flowed across the chamber.

The others followed the priest, staying a few steps away, as though he were a condemned man, and no one wanted to stand so close to anyone about to meet death.

Rose hesitated as he went into the poorly lit chamber. On the threshold he paused, leaning in to look, as though he feared foul play, but then Hayes thought the small room with its crypt had such a religious feel—though not of the priest's religion—that Rose hesitated entering.

When he did cross the threshold, he went slowly, still unsure, taking in everything without urgency. He passed behind the crypt, pausing to examine the unfinished face of the stone woman. He gazed for a moment at the text on the back wall, and Kehler caught Hayes' eye, his question obvious: *Can the priest read this?*

But Deacon Rose moved on, stopping abruptly when he came to the face that resembled Erasmus. He looked sharply back at Erasmus, but to Hayes' great surprise he asked no question. Backing away, he slumped down against the wall, his eyes still on the face that so resembled their companion.

*Yes*, Hayes thought, *how long ago was that face sculpted? And what does it mean?*

To Walky, Eldrich seemed to be listening, though he knew it was not the sense of hearing that was being used. But that was how he thought of it, for Walky had seen this before. Eldrich walked among the trees that grew in this small depression in the hillside, and then stopped, his head bowed as though completely given over to concentration—sensing things that other men were unaware of, things the mage could not explain, even if he were inclined to explanation.

An unseasonably warm wind, fresh from Entonne, hissed through the hills, sweeping away the clouds and leaving the sky unnaturally clear. Stars stood out, cruelly bright, and Walky could not remember seeing such a bright moon.

All around, tree branches waved in circles, and the new leaves fluttered softly. Gusts seemed to fall from above, pressing the underworld flat against the hill, and all the while Walky thought *the emotions of the world are in this wind*. A world disturbed by the presence of Eldrich and by his intentions. The emotions of the world; whirling up, ebbing, rising in sudden agitation, moaning and shaking the trees, then falling to despairing silence. He could feel the concern, the distress. The knowledge that the natural course of events was about to be interrupted.

And Walky had begun to feel much as the earth did, though he had some idea of what was to come.

*Poor child*, he thought. He so wanted to speak. To intercede.

Apparently unaffected by the concerns of the earth, Eldrich stopped near to the bole of a beech tree, its silver bark almost aglow in the moonlight. The wind blew his dark hair and tugged at his coat as though seeking his attention, but he was not to be distracted from his task.

"Sir?" Walky heard himself say, so quietly that the wind certainly drowned him out.

"Sir?"

Eldrich's eyes snapped open and he glared at his servant. "*Mr. Walky!*" he said, using the honorific and a tone Walky had heard only once before.

And the servant fell silent, realizing that his entreaties would have no effect. He swallowed hard, not because he had earned the displeasure of the mage, but because someone needed him and he had failed.

*But he is a mage, and I am merely a servant*, he thought. Even knowing this did not take the shame away.

Eldrich turned his back to his servant, a deliberate gesture. For a moment he did nothing but move his head very slightly as though listening. Walky knew the mage's eyes were closed. Then the man turned, his stiff movements a bit odd in the poor light.

Eldrich's eyes opened, and he moved a few paces to one side, stopping to look up at the stars. Walky saw the wolf glide across the edge of the clearing, as swift and silent as the shadow of a bird. A deep howl came from far off, like a beast in pain, but Eldrich paid no attention.

He crouched down before a flat rock that emerged like the back of a whale from the moss and ferns of the forest floor. Lifting his hand, palm down, the hand hovered above this stone for a moment, and then suddenly struck the rock with great force. Walky was sure he saw sparks fly from the impact, and he stepped back, startled. The wind muttered through the trees, disturbed.

The mage spoke in a low voice, addressing his words to the earth, it seemed, and he ran his hand over the stone in a pattern, over and over. Lines began to appear on the stone, lines of glowing silver, like moonlight or starlight.

Walky shut his eyes, knowing what was to come. He reached out and placed his hand against the bole of a tree. A tear escaped from one eye and, as it ran down his cheek, the breeze marked its path with a welcome coolness.

A troubled sleep was all Hayes could manage. He felt so guilty that his note to Erasmus had led the priest to them that he slept sitting in the doorway of the crypt to be sure the priest could not slip away. Every half of the hour, or so it seemed, he would wake, cock open one eye and find the priest had not moved. Around him the others slept, Kehler most fitfully. Twice he leaned over and shook his friend out of a nightmare, and both times Kehler awoke with a moan, putting his hands over his eyes briefly.

Later Hayes woke to muffled voices, far off, almost beyond the dream, and lay listening in the enchanted starlight. He closed his eyes after a moment, hearing only the sounds of his companions sleeping, and the constant voice of the water as it sang to itself. Sometime later he woke again, certain he heard a woman's voice; and then he fell into a sleep and saw a beautiful woman. She seemed to be making her way toward him through a tunnel in a thick mist, reaching out blindly as though she might find him by touch.

Later still, Hayes woke to find Erasmus standing on the terrace, staring up at the figures above the font. For a moment he watched, but when Erasmus made no move, Hayes fell back asleep without meaning to.

When he woke again, it was to a hand on his shoulder. Erasmus stood over him, and some of the others were already awake, trying to shake sleep from their minds.

"I've heard something. From back in the tunnel," Erasmus said. "Wake the priest."

"I'm awake," Rose said, emerging from behind the crypt.

Clarendon was on his feet, rubbing his eyes like a tired child.

Erasmus met the priest at the doorway. "Has someone followed us into the cave?" he asked.

"Not to my knowledge." Rose met Erasmus' gaze as he said this, and Hayes felt he was either the consummate actor or was telling the truth.

Erasmus shook his head. "I don't know who it is or what their intention might be, but we had best meet them at the entrance in case they do not wish us well."

"Is it Eldrich?" Hayes asked, unable to stop himself from voicing his fear.

"I don't think so, Hayes. The mage is not one for crawling through tunnels."

Erasmus set off across the chamber, and Hayes thought Erasmus looked both tired and very grim. Sensing his mood, everyone fell in behind, not even asking what he'd heard.

"Stay off the terrace," Erasmus said, stepping over the stream. "Something is very odd here. I can feel it."

Hayes looked at Kehler, who shrugged, his eyes a bit wide.

They passed quickly into the long hallway, the stone faces watching their progress with infinite sadness. At the arch leading back into the cave Erasmus stopped abruptly, and Hayes pressed forward so he could peer over Kehler's shoulder. There, at the bottom of the slope leading up to the three stairs, stood a woman dressed in the clothing of a man, and just then, behind her, a young man appeared.

They stood staring up at Erasmus and the others, like poachers caught in the act of trespass.

"I saw her . . . in a dream," Hayes said, certain this could be no other, though she was begrimed and exhausted.

She extended her hand, still looking a bit intimidated, and opened her mouth to speak, but suddenly she looked around her, frightened, and sank toward the floor.

Hayes felt something deep inside him, something disturbing that he did not recognize, like an internal vibration that gripped his heart. And then the walls before him blurred, and he lost his balance for no reason that he could discern. The woman and man down the slope both reeled as though they'd been struck.

"Come up!" Erasmus shouted, and then staggered down the steps, falling to his knees and crawling on. A terrible rumbling came through the rock, and Hayes felt himself fall atop someone. He lay there as the world lurched and vibrated around him.

*An earth tremor*, he finally realized, and then the world fell into chaos. A deafening roar and the sound of crashing stone seemed to strike him like a blow. And then a choking dust blinded him, filling his lungs and mouth. Light disappeared, and he lay in the pile of his companions, like a frightened animal whose only defense was to remain still and hope to avoid the notice of the terror.

And then it was still. Still and dark.

Hayes didn't move, but lay coughing and fighting for air, as did the others around him, he realized. Not knowing quite why, he began to crawl back into the hallway, or so he hoped.

*"Mr. Flattery?"* a small voice managed: Clarendon. *"Mr. Flattery?!"*

The fear in Clarendon's voice was obvious, but Hayes crawled on, his own terror greater. Suddenly his head exploded, and he fell limp and dazed.

*A wall*, he thought, *I struck a wall.*

He fought for air, trying to breathe through the fabric of his sleeve. And then a dull light began to grow. Dust. The air was filled with dust, which swirled and swept past him as though on a wind.

Sitting up, Hayes realized he had only crawled diagonally across the hallway, until he had struck his head. The others were spread about him, only Clarendon standing. He was bent over someone, thumping him hard on the back.

"Breathe, man," the dwarf was saying. "Breathe!"

And then the air was clear. Hayes continued to cough, pressing a hand to his scalp where the wound was slowly seeping blood.

The woman who had appeared at his door, rose to her knees suddenly, turning toward the archway.

"No . . ." he heard her say, her voice low and filled with anguish and disbelief. "The others . . ."

"Are we all here?" someone asked. "Are we all in one piece?" It was Deacon Rose, taking charge.

The priest stood, steadying himself on the wall. "Mr. Flattery? Thank Farrelle. Mr. Kehler? Are you well?" He nodded toward Clarendon, ticking him off mentally. "Mr. Hayes, you are injured."

"Not so badly, I think. Just a scratch."

A man Hayes had never seen sat up, coughing, and covering his mouth with both hands, but there was no dust left in the air. The light had returned to normal as well, if such a light could be called normal.

Hayes propped himself against the wall, and realized that he heard crying. The woman was sobbing into the shoulder of the young man who accompanied her. Hayes felt a strange surge of jealousy.

Clarendon helped Erasmus to his feet, though Erasmus bent over as though in pain, and clutched one hand to his back.

Scrambling up, Kehler pushed past the others and into the archway. He stared into the darkness for a moment, and then turned back to his companions, a look of utter hopelessness on his face.

"The tunnel . . ." he said through a dry mouth. "It collapsed. We're sealed in—utterly." He looked around a bit wildly. "Do you hear me? Do you hear . . . ?"

## ⌒ Forty-Two

Hayes put his hand to one of the smaller rocks and tried rather gingerly to move it.

"I shouldn't do that if I were you," Deacon Rose cautioned.

Hayes took his hand away. The passage beyond the entrance to the chamber was completely choked with rubble.

"But has the passage collapsed back ten feet or two hundred? That's the question," Kehler said.

Hayes nodded. It was the question. Was there any hope of them tunneling out?

Erasmus stood staring at the collapsed section of cave, though his eyes did not seem focused.

"Mr. Flattery?" Kehler asked.

Erasmus started slightly, as though he'd been wakened. "No amount of effort will allow you to make a tunnel through this. It was not a natural tremor that we felt and was certainly meant to collapse the main passage well beyond this. We weren't meant to escape."

The woman and man who had arrived as the passage collapsed stood near to each other, grief etched on their faces.

"It was Eldrich, wasn't it? He meant to murder us?" she said, a building rage kept in check by grief. "All of my people . . . we were lured down here for this." She put a hand to her face and tears appeared from closed eyes.

"I fear you're right," Erasmus said softly.

"But why us?" Hayes asked, surprised by the sorrow in his voice.

"We trespassed in a sacred place," Deacon Rose said. "As I warned you." He nodded to the woman. "And these people—followers of Teller—I would not be surprised to find Eldrich had been planning to trap them for years. Everyone had a part: you, Mr. Kehler, with your insatiable curiosity. Even Mr. Flattery. I have no doubt the Tellerites have been watching him for years. Wondering if they should approach him. Now they know."

The woman glared at Erasmus.

"I knew nothing of it," Erasmus said, "if it is even true. But you see, I am trapped as well. If I am an accomplice, I am an unwilling one."

The woman turned her back on the scene of ruin, standing for a moment looking down the long hallway. "It is not nearly so simple," she said. "You will note that not everyone perished. Some of us have been left alive, at least for the time being, in this place. Seven of us, to be precise. This was no accident." She began walking slowly down the hallway, staring at the sad stone faces as she passed, her companion in tow.

"What is she suggesting, Mr. Flattery?" Clarendon asked.

"I'm not sure," Erasmus said. "Seven was a number of great significance to the mages." He hesitated, not wanting to give voice to his thoughts. "I can't say more than that."

But Hayes was afraid that Erasmus could say a great deal more.

*       *       *

Hayes followed Erasmus into the chamber, where they found the woman and her companion staring in rapt wonder, their grief temporarily displaced by awe.

"Is this what you sought?" Erasmus asked quietly.

The woman glanced at him and then back to the wonders before her. She shook her head, as though the power of language had been temporarily lost.

The man at her side looked at Erasmus. "Until Anna had a vision, we didn't know what might lie here. Even then we did not believe it. You are Mr. Flattery, I collect?"

"Erasmus Flattery, yes."

"Josiah Banks. And this is Miss Fielding. Miss Anna Fielding."

Hayes saw that Rose had come up and stood staring at the two new arrivals, his manner less than welcoming. "So I finally see you with my own eyes," he said.

"And who might you be, sir?" Banks asked.

"This is Deacon Rose," Kehler said. "But don't let this modest title deceive you. He is the Farrellite Church's Grand Inquisitor."

Banks fell very silent, his look and manner changing. Hayes thought that this was the way a man would react when introduced to an infamous murderer. Shock, and then fear, and finally a perverse interest.

"You must be terribly disappointed, Deacon," the woman called Anna said. "It seems Eldrich has done your work for you." She did not seem at all concerned that this man spent his life seeking to find and eliminate people such as her. In fact, she looked away as though dismissing him from her thoughts.

"If we are trapped here together, with no hope of escape," Clarendon said, "then let us put aside our differences."

She looked at him sharply. "Differences? Here is a man sworn to discover people such as myself, and then do you know what he is to do, sir? Burn them for heresy. And this is not just some travesty of the past, it has been done in living memory. Perhaps our good Grand Inquisitor has done it himself." She turned and looked at the priest. "What say you, Deacon? How many have you burned for their alleged sins?"

Rose met her gaze, and then he slowly shook his head, looking down. "No, Miss Fielding, I have been spared such horrors. But Mr. Clarendon is right. We are trapped here. Why make our last hours a misery? I shall overlook your heresy if you will forgive me my loyalty to the word of Farrelle."

"I cannot forgive you your prejudice, sir, for we have no quarrel with your church, and yet you burned my brethren out of cowardice and jealousy. Afraid of the mages, and even more afraid that we might rise up one day and challenge the church, though this had never been our intention. I am surprised that you will so easily let me live even though we are trapped and doomed to die here. Is this not dereliction of duty, Deacon? And more important, how can you deprive yourself of such pleasure?"

"You do not know me, child," Rose said, his voice trembling just a little, "so you do not realize what injustice you do me. But my offer stands. We cannot live long in this place. Starvation awaits us all. There might be some comfort, yet, in the word of Farrelle. For any who wish it, I will offer what comfort this knowledge will bring."

Anna had drawn herself up, her manner hard and imperious. "I will die with a curse for Farrelle on my lips," she said. "Farrelle and his church. That will be comfort enough for me."

The priest looked at her and then turned away. He retreated back into the hallway, and a moment later they heard a musical chant begin. A rite for the dead, Hayes was certain. For some reason the singing touched him—its warmth and strange sadness oddly uplifting.

A look of horror crossed the face of the woman called Anna, but her companion drew her on into the chamber. "It will do no harm," he said to her soothingly, and she let herself be led away.

As they walked slowly along the length of the hall, all the others watched their reactions with great interest. Neither of the newcomers spoke, but occasionally they shook their heads, and both seemed overwhelmed by what had been discovered.

The terrace, with its font and sculpture, stopped them for several moments. They circled it at a distance, as though fearing to set foot there.

"The *nance*," she whispered.

"What?" Kehler asked.

"The *nance*," she said, but offered no more.

They stepped over the stream and continued down the hall.

"Do you know what this place was?" Clarendon asked after a moment. "Does it have a purpose?"

The newcomers gazed at the small man, a look like alarm on their faces, neither of them offering an answer.

"There is no point to secrecy now," Kehler said, his curiosity clearly driving him. "We will take anything you tell us to the grave, there is no doubt of that."

"You really don't know what you've discovered?" the young man asked.

"Mr. Flattery can make some sense of the writing, though not all of it. That is all we know."

The woman nodded. "I need some time to read and think," she said.

"But is it really Landor's Gate?" Kehler said, though Hayes was certain his friend asked the question just to see their reaction to the name.

Both the man and woman looked utterly unsettled to hear the name of Landor. "We . . . we need time," she said again.

They moved on, turning their backs to the others. Occasionally the two would share a look, as though they had both noticed something of significance, but they continued in their silence.

Finally they came to the crypt, and at the door they paused.

Anna stared up at the symbol inscribed above the archway and then put her hands to her face. She glanced once at her companion, who seemed as moved as she. And then Anna made an odd motion with her hand before her face and then over her heart. She mumbled something that Hayes could not catch, though he was certain that the words were from no language that he knew. She made a fluid bowing motion and then crossed the arch into the crypt. Banks did the same, and followed.

A soft light grew in the small chamber as she stepped inside, which had not happened on any occasion when the others had entered. Kehler began to follow her, but she looked at him so sharply that he drew back. Everyone stood in the opening, watching.

She made the same bowing motion before the crypt itself, mumbling again. She gazed at the face carved there for a long time, as though she memorized every feature. Once she reached out her hand to touch the stone of the crypt, but it looked to Hayes that she lost her nerve, and her hand fell limply to her side.

For a few moments she paused, apparently reading the text, and then began to move slowly to the left. The unfinished face of the woman drew her attention for some time, and she and Banks whispered together as they examined it.

They moved on, passing the text, and then stopped at the second face cut from stone. They both glanced back at Erasmus, and then spoke quietly to each other.

"Can you read what it says?" Kehler asked.

The woman turned to him and put a finger to her lips, and he fell silent.

They stayed in the crypt, reluctant to leave, for some time, and when they finally did emerge they came only a few paces into the main chamber, before Anna sat down on the stone, as though what she had seen had taken away her strength.

For some moments she leaned her forehead against Bank's shoulder, but finally she straightened up, composing herself purposefully.

"What is this place?" Kehler asked, voicing the question for all present. Everyone stood a few paces off, their body language odd, Hayes thought, for they were all turned slightly away, as though not to intrude on their privacy.

She glanced at Banks.

"It is a chamber in memorium," she said, clearing her throat. "A historical archive. A chamber of great power located at a nexus of the world's forces. It is a solemn place, almost a shrine. And it is a gate as well. A gate to places no man has traveled in . . . a very long time. It is a commemorative monument—to those who first opened the way, and ventured here as explorers. A monument to Landor—to the seven who made the gate and its key. And it is a place of arcane rites and sacrifice. And that is why we are here," she said, forcing her voice to be very even. "We are a sacrifice."

The newcomers to the dungeon, as Hayes thought of it, explored every corner of their subterranean cell, but even when they were done they offered no explanation. Hayes found he did not really care so much what the purpose of the chamber was unless this knowledge would help them escape.

Hayes also realized that he did not yet believe that they were trapped here. It was probably nothing more than a refusal of the mind to accept the horror of their situation, but he could not believe it. He was utterly sure that the stairway that led nowhere was significant. Why had it been built? Surely because it once opened to the world, or at least was intended to be opened. There could be no other explanation. Perhaps there were only a few feet of rock separating the head of the stairs from the light and air beyond. Perhaps there was only a foot. Hayes believed this was their best chance—use some of the fallen rock and try to batter their way through.

Hayes and Kehler sat on the stairs of the terrace, what Anna had called the *nance*, defying the superstition that the others were developing, which seemed foolish to them.

Anna and Banks emerged into the main chamber. They'd been up the stair for a second time. Hayes had been half afraid that they would perform some spell that would open a doorway and let them escape, so he was a little relieved to see them—and a bit embarrassed that he would worry about such a thing.

Noticing them on the stairs, Banks came forward. "Mr. Hayes, Mr. Kehler: you must not set foot on the *nance*. One must perform certain ablutions when venturing there."

Hayes rose immediately, stepping down to the floor, but Kehler remained on the stair.

"Then you must teach me," Kehler said, rising but showing no signs of moving away, "or I will go on defiling your sacred *nance*." He half-turned as though he would step up onto the terrace proper.

Banks held up his hand. "No . . ." But he stopped. It was clear that he was not about to teach Kehler the proper rites.

Banks almost turned away, but then reconsidered. "Mr. Kehler, you might be letting yourself in for some bad fortune by acting with such disrespect. This chamber is bespelled in a manner that we cannot even begin to comprehend.

That is hallowed ground you stand upon. It is neither prudent nor wise to treat it with disrespect."

Anna turned back to watch this confrontation, her gaze rather hard, as though she did not much care if Kehler brought disaster upon himself—if there could be a greater disaster than being trapped here.

Kehler continued to stare at Banks. "You want me to cooperate, Mr. Banks, yet we have no cooperation from you. Enlighten me. Tell me what you know about this chamber, and you will find that I am a most convivial companion. As was said earlier, we all lie in the same grave. There is no reason to keep secrets now."

"There are oaths that have been taken," Banks said.

Some of the others had drawn closer to hear this conversation. "I have taken oaths as well," Deacon Rose said, "but as it seems I will live out my last few days here, I would have my curiosity satisfied. I will answer your questions, Mr. Banks, if you will answer mine. In fact, I will go further. . . . I will tell you my story first if you will reciprocate by telling yours. Perhaps we all have a story to tell. Mr. Flattery certainly has a tale we would all like to hear. And Mr. Clarendon is a most interesting individual. I would even like to hear what Kehler found in the archives, though I suspect I know. What say you?" he asked, turning to the others.

No one spoke immediately, and Hayes thought their reluctance very curious.

"I will tell my story," Kehler said after a moment. "Why should I not? It takes some time to starve to death, I think, and we have little to do to pass the time. I will bare my soul if others will do the same. In fact, I will tell my tale even if others will not speak. Perhaps, when I am done, others will be more inclined to follow."

"You see," Rose said, turning back to Banks and Anna. "I will break my oath, for I'm sure it can do no harm here, and Farrelle will forgive me this, I think, considering the circumstances." He tried a weak smile on the two who were supposed to be his sworn enemies.

"Will you not come down, sir?" Banks said, his tone so very sincere that Kehler relented.

"You have been up the long stair twice now," Kehler asked, as though sensing this was the time to ask. "Was it meant to go to the surface? Can we break through, do you think?"

Again the Tellerites only stared back at him, saying nothing, but then perhaps Banks realized that Kehler would not cooperate if he received nothing in return. "It is not so simple, I fear. Much of what is written here suffers from ambiguity, to say the least. The mages were famous for it, as though they were always afraid that their writings would come into the possession of people who should not have them. Such as yourself, Mr. Kehler, or me for example.

But the stair . . . it could have had a number of purposes, I fear." He reached out and clasped Kehler's arm. "Thank you for coming down."

They gathered near the door to the vault—Landor's crypt—and sprawled on the hard stone. Clarendon had assessed their tiny food supply and realized that, even if rationed to the point of absurdity, it would not last three days. After that it was only a matter of time.

There had been a rather macabre discussion of how long people could live without food, and the longest anyone had heard of, that seemed believable, was nineteen days. Ten or twelve days seemed more likely given their exhausted state. Hayes had been hungry since they'd entered the cave. If he believed they were truly trapped, the prospect of starving to death would no doubt terrify him.

He stretched out full length on the stone, propping his head on his hand, and waited, not sure who would begin this confession. Certainly not him, for he had nothing to tell. He looked over at Anna, marveling at how different she looked dressed in the clothes of a boy—not like the elegant and somewhat threatening lady who had appeared in his dream. Her manner and her appearance were in contrast, for she looked tired, even pallid, but in her movements she was no more exhausted than the rest—perhaps less so.

She noticed him looking at her, and Hayes suddenly felt he must ask a question to justify his staring. "What did you mean when you said we were a sacrifice?"

She returned his gaze briefly and then looked away. "It would appear that Eldrich has been aware of us for many years. We were utterly wrong in many of our assumptions, and the mage long schemed to trap us." She glanced at Erasmus. "He used Mr. Flattery and another to draw us out into the open. . . ." She faltered, not quite answering Hayes' question.

"I think that Miss Fielding is right," Erasmus said. "Eldrich wanted to lure us down here, and not just any seven people. That means that you, too, were required, Deacon, though I cannot imagine why."

That left everyone thinking. And then Kehler looked around the circle. "Who will begin?"

"It started with me, or so I begin to perceive," Erasmus said, "so I will start." He sat with his back to the wall, his legs stretched out and crossed. Hayes had known Erasmus for many years and during all that time Erasmus had made few concessions to fashion, but even so he had always retained an inexplicable dignity—never looking even faintly ridiculous the way many scholars did. Even now, with his beard and hair unkempt, clothing dirty and torn to rags, Erasmus retained a certain disheveled distinction—like a prince in exile. He could not say the same for Kehler, or likely himself.

"It seems that everyone knows of my time with Eldrich," Erasmus began, looking up, his manner almost defensive, "though no one suspects the real truth of it, I'm sure. I will apologize in advance to Hayes if the story I am about to tell is a little different from the one he heard previously." He stopped, took a long breath, and looked over the heads of the others, his eyes focusing on another place and time. "I was sent to the home of Eldrich when I was aged ten years. It is true that I don't know the reason for this, though something my mother once said left me believing that it was at the request, perhaps even insistence, of the mage himself.

"I was given a room to share with another boy of about my own age: Percy. We were schooled together, and we were as close as brothers for those three years." Erasmus looked a bit distressed at the thought of this other boy, or so Hayes thought. "An elderly servant named Walky was our schoolmaster. He was a forgetful, kindly old man, and the closest thing to a friend we had in that strange house, so despite his eccentricities we loved him dearly. I will not bore you with all the details, but let us just say that Walky had obviously taught boys before, and he kept confusing our lessons with the things he had taught in the past. The subjects he had taught previously it seemed, were not always so mundane as our own lessons."

"Are you saying that Eldrich trained others, but it has been kept secret?" Anna asked, her surprise obvious.

"I have asked myself that very question many thousands of times, Miss Fielding. I have spent entire nights trying to puzzle it through, and I've never reached a conclusion."

"I have an answer," Rose said, "or so I think. The mages commonly had young men in their service, and almost all of them were taught some small part of the arts. Most, however, never rose beyond being servants and their knowledge was not great. This man Walky would be one of them. But many a failed apprentice to a mage was sent back to his family—and if he learned anything out of the ordinary in his time at the mage's house, he could not remember it. Some, it seems, remembered nothing at all."

"So Mr. Flattery has had his memories obliterated? Is that what you're saying?" Kehler asked, his curiosity so great that he actually spoke to Demon Rose.

"But I remember everything perfectly," Erasmus said. "Not every tiny detail, perhaps, for it was long ago, but there is no time unaccounted for in all my years there."

"Let Mr. Flattery finish his story," Clarendon said before anyone else could speak.

Erasmus looked a little unsettled by this discussion, as though his part were suddenly suspect. "As I said, Walky began to confuse our lessons. At the time I didn't think we were meant to be taught anything but the normal subjects for schoolboys. Now I am not so sure. . . . It seems Eldrich does nothing without purpose. We learned a script and some few words in another language, Darian it was called. Although we suspected Walky was not to teach us these things, we never questioned him. In truth, we were fascinated. We had never been told why we were there, and Percy developed the theory that we were meant to be trained as servants to the mage—not just servants, but to assist Eldrich with his pursuit of the arts. I think we both secretly wondered if we were to be mages ourselves, a thought that was rather terrifying, and attractive at the same time. We were only boys, after all, and had no real idea of what this might mean.

"And then, after we had been there almost a year, Walky left a book in the room we used for our studies. It was an intriguing looking book, its title, so worn it was barely legible, in the script we had learned, though the words meant nothing to us. *Alendrore Primia*."

"*The primer*," Anna whispered.

"You know it?" Erasmus said.

"No . . . I've never seen it," she said, apparently still reluctant to speak.

"A rough, incomplete copy exists," Banks said. "Made by Teller from memory. It is the first book in the training of a mage: the *Primer of Alendrore*."

Erasmus nodded. "For the first few days the book sat there, we were afraid to touch it, though it was seldom out of mind. When we realized beyond a doubt that the book had slipped from Walky's mind, we worked up the nerve to open it. You can't even begin to imagine the thrill this gave us—forbidden knowledge, after all. And it was a book full of wonders; diagrams of things arcane, written in an ornate, highly ambiguous language that filled us with awe—like a voice from the past, but the voice of a mage.

"It was not a slim volume, and the first section was devoted to language. After a fortnight we smuggled the book out of the room and hid it in the loft above the stables. Here we pored over it by the hour, though in the good weather we took it to the wood that surrounded much of the hill on which Eldrich's house stood.

"After the section on language, which we learned with a diligence that would have impressed Walky—but then the text was so impressive to us that we dared not approach it in our typical schoolboy manner—came a section of lyrics and poems. All extremely ambiguous, but fascinating all the same, for they seemed to speak of a distant and mysterious history, and like the sculptures in the hall, these poems seemed to evoke something more. That odd feeling that one knew more than was actually presented.

"The second year went on. It became clear to me that we were not mages in training, for most of our work was in the most mundane of subjects. But even so, we learned our lessons, including those that we were never meant to have learned—or so we thought.

"As we progressed into the primer, we mastered some very simple charms—tests I believe they were. Tests to determine our talent for the arts. Some of these might make good parlor tricks. There is one which employs a candle and a rose that is impressive, for instance."

Hayes noticed that the priest nodded his head when he heard this.

"Much of this first book had to do with the control of fire, which was very exciting to boys who, of course, love nothing better than to play with fire. I think that was the plan of it, for whoever wrote this book knew his readers well. Without Walky to guide us, though, our progress was slow, and we were constantly afraid that we'd be discovered. If we performed the simple enchantments we found in the book, would Eldrich sense it? We debated this endlessly, and then with the imprudence common to young boys, we went ahead. I cannot tell you how thrilling it was to bend the flame of a candle this way and that, to make the smoke behave in a manner completely unnatural. We could hardly have been happier, and for the first time stopped dreaming of returning home.

"During all of this time we never met the mage, and, in fact, were warned to keep our distance should we accidentally happen upon him. Once, while I was idling on a window seat, I did see a man I took to be Eldrich walking in the garden. He looked up at me suddenly—this is the story I told to Hayes—and I felt so utterly sure he knew about our book. That he could sense terrible guilt within me. I fled back to our room and put such a terror into poor Percy that he almost fainted from fright. But Eldrich did not appear, nor did Walky suddenly wonder where his book had gone.

"I wonder now if it was merely the overactive imagination of a boy, or if Eldrich put that fear in my heart, for I will tell you I have never known such overwhelming terror. Astonishing to think that a man of such power would take pleasure in terrifying a small boy, but I am not sure he didn't. Be that as it may, we went back to our book in a week or so. It was near the end of my third year there when we came to the method of lighting fire—a skill we thought useful beyond our ability to express. I was the dominant partner in this alliance, and in the manner of children, coerced Percy into first trying anything that seemed at all dubious to me. It is a tradition of sacrifice practiced by children the world over, I'm sure," Erasmus said, but the irony was tinged with sadness and regret. "In this case I could not imagine what this small act of cowardice would lead to. Percy performed the spell as it was described in the book, exacting in the preparation, or so we thought." He stopped and took a deep breath. "But the small fire that we thought to start did not materialize. I was standing several feet away, mindful of my own safety, as usual. We were in a small clearing in the wood, and Percy stood in the center of a geometric design we'd marked out on the ground.

"We had experienced failure before, and worked through the explanations in the book to find our error, and this is what I thought we would do again. I went to step forward, opening the book as I did so. And suddenly Percy screamed . . . and a column of flame erupted around him. I felt as though I was thrown back, and when I regained my feet, I saw Percy staggering toward me, engulfed in flame, such a wail of agony erupting from his throat that I can hear it still.

"As quickly as I could, I quelled the flame with my coat, and Percy lay on the ground, horribly burned, howling from the pain. Before I could even consider going for help, Eldrich arrived with Walky only a few paces behind him.

"The mage stopped, surveying the scene—the geometric markings on the ground, the book—and then he thrust me aside and whispered something over Percy, who seemed suddenly released from his agony. Wrapping the child in his coat, Eldrich bore him up, saying only, 'Bring the book, Walky.'

"I followed behind, terrified for my friend, overcome with guilt and shame. Walky sent me to our room, though not unkindly. I saw no one until the next day when Walky arrived to have me pack my belongings. 'But what word of Percy?' I asked. 'Don't you be worrying about Percy. You have other matters more pressing,' was all Walky would say. 'Where are you sending me?' I asked. 'Home, child,' he said. And that is what happened." Erasmus put a hand to his brow, hiding his eyes for a moment, and then, self consciously, moved the hand to his chin. In that moment Hayes thought that Erasmus looked utterly dejected and anguished, for clearly this was one of those great shames of childhood that some men bore. "That afternoon I was put in a carriage and taken home. To this day I cannot tell you what happened to Percy, though I fear the worst. Slowly I recovered from the horror, if not the guilt of what had happened, for I blamed myself. I was the leader of our small league, and I had let Percy do something so foolish. I realize now that I was only a child acting as children do, but only my head believes this—my heart knows differently.

"As I grew to be a young man, I found that the events of my childhood haunted me. If Deacon Rose is right and many who serve in the house of a mage can remember nothing afterward, then I can only think I was being punished by being left with my memory intact. But my curiosity had not been burned away by our terrible fire. I began to believe that for both myself and Percy, who I believe died of his burns, I would seek the knowledge of the mages. I would learn all the things that we were meant to learn as boys. Perhaps I would even find out if Eldrich could have healed my boyhood friend— something that would have given me great relief—for I could see that even the terrible mage was not unaffected by Percy's suffering." He opened his hands as though displaying something. "And this has led me here . . . and it seems now I will be truly punished at last."

There was no immediate response to Erasmus' story. No one asked the questions that had occurred as he spoke. Hayes wanted to comfort his friend, for it was certainly true that Erasmus had merely acted as children often do, but he could not deny Erasmus was being punished—for Eldrich was a mage and mages were vindictive. History bore this out over and over again. If Erasmus had not been meant to see the book, then he might well have earned the mage's anger. But if Eldrich had merely used Erasmus to lure the Tellerites out of hiding, as had been suggested, then why was Erasmus trapped here as well? Did Eldrich use people so callously?

"You should not censure yourself for what happened, Mr. Flattery," Rose said at last. "You were a child and could not understand the possible consequences of your actions. We do not allow children to play with knives or rapiers, for their inexperience makes mishaps likely. The book should never have fallen into your hands. If it was an accident, then the one to bear the blame would be this man, Walky, not you. Guilt is a consuming emotion, and it clings to us like no other. I sometimes think that we are more able to stop loving another more easily than we shed our guilt, though very often I have found men's guilt to be unwarranted. And that, I believe is the case here, Mr. Flattery. You were a child, and you have made penance enough over the years. And who knows, this young boy, Percy, might live a perfectly whole life, cured of his affliction, or less affected by it than you think. I would advise you to give up this atonement. Let your last days be free of this torment—this feeling that you deserve to be punished."

Anna looked at Erasmus. "I think you were merely playing a part in Eldrich's plan, Mr. Flattery," she said, her tone unusually warm. "You and your boyhood friend, used without remorse to trap me and my companions, and if you are innocent of any alliance with Eldrich, as you claim, then I am sorry for it. But the mages have always been so, even to the last, it seems."

Erasmus looked at them gratefully, a bit of relief on his haggard face, as though telling his tale had provided some small comfort. "What day is it, do you think?" he asked.

Banks and Hayes produced watches that did not agree, and Clarendon did the same, his timepiece committed to its own theory. It turned out that there was no concordance, and only an estimate could be made.

"Whatever day it is, and whatever hour, I think I must sleep," Clarendon said, and the others agreed. Only Anna did not seem so inclined.

She leaned closer to Banks, but Hayes could just hear. "I shall have all the sleep I want soon enough," she said, and rose, leaving the rest of them to find their own places to rest.

Hayes watched her walk toward the *nance*. She stood looking up at it for a moment, then began to whisper, making odd motions with one hand in the air. She bent down, almost reverently, and kissed the floor of the *nance*, and then, casting a quick glance back at the others, she went up the stair and immediately to the font. Here she went down on one knee, continuing to whisper, and then dipped a hand into the water, sipping a few drops carefully. She stood then and stared for a long moment at the urn to one side of the font. As she reached out toward it, Hayes realized that Rose had risen from his place.

"What are you doing?" he hissed, but it was an accusation, not a question.

She turned and glared at him as he came to the foot of the stair. And then with a quick motion and some half-whispered words, she spun and descended the far stair, crossed the chamber and disappeared through the arch at the far end.

Rose stood and watched her go, hands on his hips. For a moment Hayes was certain that the priest would follow, but instead he returned to his place and lay down on his side facing the *nance*.

Hayes was certain that Anna had gone up the stair again, making him wonder if there was not something more to this place than she claimed.

He noticed then that Erasmus, too, was watching the priest. Hayes lay back down, wondering what he had just seen. Wondering what would happen to them. There was not time to fight among themselves, he was sure.

*We are trapped with no hope of escape*, he told himself, but found he could not believe it.

Erasmus lay for a long time listening to the even breathing of the others. The questions he had asked all his life seemed no closer to being answered. Some part of him had always believed that one day he would find these answers. He had a fantasy that, once the mage had passed on, he would hear from Walky, still miraculously alive, and from the old man he would have all his questions satisfied. But not now. In a matter of days he would certainly be dead. It made all of his years of searching for knowledge seem terribly futile.

What had he to show for it? Had his efforts benefitted mankind? Had they even benefitted him?

The answer, undeniably, seemed to be that his efforts had profited no one at all—except perhaps Eldrich—which was, no doubt, what had been planned.

*I lured the Tellerites here*, he thought. *Despite what I believed, that has been my only purpose in this life.* He felt such a rage toward Eldrich that his muscles began to ache where they had knotted from anger.

Quietly, Erasmus slipped away from his sleeping companions and crossed to the chamber's far end.

Moments later he was ascending the winding stair, his anger driving him quickly on. He wondered what this rather cold and imperious young woman was doing up this mysterious stair. Thinking the end was farther, he rounded the corner to find Anna collapsed against the stair's end. Her knees were drawn up and her face was buried in her arms.

Hearing him she looked up, her face shining with tears. She let her arms fall limply by her sides and laid her head back against the stone, and still she cried as though she were alone, utterly alone.

Erasmus stopped, so taken aback that he had no idea what to do.

"*Bastard*," she said through her sobs, "he trapped us here. I was a fool. . . ." and then she began to sob so violently that she could not go on.

Unable to bear it any longer, Erasmus came and sat on the step near to her, reaching out and taking her hand tentatively. She leaned forward and buried her head in his shoulder and continued to sob. Erasmus laid a hand awkwardly on her shoulder.

He found himself making soothing sounds, saying the meaningless things that people say to comfort each other, though he did not believe them. They were trapped without hope—that was the truth. Buried alive.

It was a long time before Anna began to recover, and then she finally pulled away from him, rubbing at her eyes with the heels of her hands.

"I haven't even a clean square of linen to offer," Erasmus said.

"And you call yourself a gentleman?" she said, a weak jest. "I have been down here long enough that I would accept a soiled one, I think."

Erasmus produced his handkerchief. She held it up to examine it, and then laughed. "I guess I have not been down here quite as long as I thought." She returned it to him. "I must look a fright."

"You are the most beautiful woman in this entire system of caves," Erasmus said, his tone mockingly solemn.

She laughed. "Ah, when you are the only woman trapped with a roomful of men, you finally hear the things you wish to hear."

"Shall I leave you alone?" Erasmus asked.

"I gather I am not quite as beautiful as you suggested?"

"Not at all, it's just . . ."

"That you have no idea how to deal with crying women?"

Erasmus shrugged. "Something like that."

"I'm all right now. I will pass beyond it if you can."

Erasmus nodded. He was not quite sure what he would say, now that they were alone. Why had he come up here in the first place? To speak with her, certainly, but now he was not sure why.

"I had no part in this," Erasmus said suddenly. "I was manipulated and trapped, like everyone else."

She nodded. "I believe you. Eldrich is a mage, and loyalty is unknown to them." She looked up at him, her eyes still wet with tears. "But what do we do?"

Erasmus shook his head. "I don't know. I feel certain that there must be another way out, for surely the tiny hole we used to find our way in here is not the main entrance. I'm not sure I even understand its purpose." He reached up and flattened his hand on the rock. "This is the mystery to me. Clearly one did not climb all the way up here to admire a single character. Once, it must have gone somewhere, or been intended to go somewhere. Hayes believes the outside world might lie only a few feet away. Clarendon and I have studied the survey, but it is not clear how close to the surface we might be." He looked at her. "Banks said he did not understand the purpose of this stair. Is that so?"

Anna twisted her head around, looking up at the wall. "Do you know this character?" she asked.

"It is the Darian equivalent of our 'L.'"

"Exactly . . . or almost so. Spoken, it is not voiced as it is in Farr, or perhaps is only half-voiced, so that it is softer, almost a whisper, and hard for many to master. But it is Landor's initial and was used as his signature. Centuries later, Lucklow would pattern his own distinctive L on this one." She turned her head and looked down the stair, pondering. "I have been thinking much about this. In fact, I came up here to be alone and contemplate it more, not to collapse in tears as you saw." A tear streaked her cheek again, but she had mastered her emotions now and did not give way to them. "This entire chamber is bespelled, and with a sophistication that I can hardly begin to understand, let alone explain. The men—and women, for there were both in the seven who made this place—were skilled in the arts far beyond any who came after. Look at this chamber. It is true that it is hidden beneath the surface, but even so it is untouched by time. When the outer passage collapsed, the dust that at first blew into the hallway was then forced back out again. Did you not realize? One moment we were choking in dust and debris, and the next the air was clear. This chamber is protected, and Eldrich could only collapse the entrance." Anna paused, and Erasmus was sure tears would appear again as she remembered her colleagues who had died just beyond the safety of the chamber. "But we were allowed in, which indicates that it was meant to be discovered." She looked up at Erasmus again. "And in the vault which contains Landor's crypt, we find your likeness carved in stone."

"But could you read the text around it?" Erasmus asked quickly. "I couldn't make sense of it."

She nodded, still staring at his face. "It is a confusing phrase, for a direct translation is not possible. 'The last keeper of the gate,' is how I would render it."

These words chilled Erasmus utterly. He felt himself push back against the wall, as though drawing back from the meaning. "What does it mean?" he asked, afraid that he already knew.

For a moment she didn't answer, but continued to stare. "I am not completely sure. What I find odd is that the likeness is not more exact. Though perhaps there is a simple explanation for that. Halsey might know."

Erasmus didn't want to ask if Halsey was one of the people killed in the collapse—he assumed he was. "But what of the face of the woman? Why was it never finished?"

She looked at him oddly. "But these were not carved by human hand," she said, a bit incredulous. "Did you not know? The face is emerging, slowly. I don't know the role of the woman, but the face will form when it is clear who she will be."

"Clear to whom?"

She shook her head, puzzled by his response. "To no one. It is like augury, though it is a spell that was cast centuries ago. At some point the vision will be complete and the identity of the woman will . . . *emerge*. There is no human agent. The spell is the agent. Do you see?"

Erasmus had only the vaguest sense of what she meant. "Is it you?" he asked.

Her look suddenly changed and her eyes glistened again. "That is what Banks believes. . . ." She could not speak for a moment. "I don't know. If it was meant to be me, I think the face would have formed by now. I can't imagine why it would not." She shook her head. "I don't know enough to understand." She looked up and touched the wall, tracing the bottom of the character with delicate fingers. Erasmus realized then how young she was—barely into her twenties, he thought—and at the moment she looked even younger and quite vulnerable.

"But this gate, I began to say . . . It has a spell about it, if I can use that term. You understand, Mr. Flattery, you worked through some part of the primer. But I am not skilled enough in the arts to understand it. Unless there is some clue written in the main hall, I fear we shall never unlock this gate. And even if we could, there is no guarantee that it would lead to the surface."

"Are you saying it would lead to this other land? Is that where it goes?"

She shook her head. "No, it is not that sort of gate. It might open into another chamber, one that was not meant to be penetrated by anyone but a mage, and perhaps not just any mage. But I suspect we will never know, Mr. Flattery, for we haven't the skills even if we had time."

Erasmus reached down and worried the edge of the leather that flapped over a hole worn in his boot. "I am not the sort of man who will sit idly by and starve to death. I must try to find a way out. I can't believe there is nothing we can do." He banged his fist against the wall. "If we give up now, then we're certainly walking about in our own crypt, and I'm not ready for that. I'm not . . ."

She nodded agreement, rather unconvincingly. "Nor am I, Mr. Flattery. But I am not sure what we can do. Even if we could unravel the spells that surround the urns on the *nance*, I'm not certain we would be further ahead."

Erasmus looked at her quizzically. "I think you assume I know more than I do. What is this about urns?"

"I thought you'd read the primer," she said, surprised. "The urns contain the king's blood, or so I surmise. I can't imagine they would be so protected if they were empty. Can you?"

"I do remember references to king's blood. But I never understood what they meant."

She drew her head back, her look quizzical. "I am amazed, Mr. Flattery, but then I suppose the book was not meant to be read without guidance. King's blood is a plant—beyond rare. There are references to it in the chamber below."

"Yes! Of course, I saw one, but could make nothing of it."

"The seed is a powerful herb. It is said to be a physic able to cure the worst illnesses, and it is also believed that the seed was the source of the mages' long lives. But it does something more. It wakens the talent in individuals, if there is any talent there to begin with. But it is said that the seed exacts a price, for all who use it become habituated unless they have an iron will, or take certain precautions. But it was a key to the mages' powers, and they guarded it even more closely than their knowledge.

"The legend tells that Landor bore the king's blood with him from beyond, and it grew here only under uncommon circumstances. But if the urns contain seed . . . well, we must study the text on the walls with care and examine the chamber meticulously. Banks believes that it is even possible that there is a hidden door—an entrance from the surface. We must look. It could be anywhere. We must focus all of our energies on this task. All of us. Even this priest, Rose, will have to put his secret knowledge at our disposal."

Erasmus wanted to jump up and begin immediately, but Anna did not look ready to start just yet.

"How did you come to be down here?" Erasmus asked suddenly. "Were you following me?"

She pulled the stray hair that had escaped from its braid away from her face. "We knew that this young man Kehler was searching the archives at Wooton for Skye. His interest in certain events had caught our attention. We watched him as we could, for we are wary of the priests and thought they might be using him to tempt us. For some time we didn't realize that there was a connection between Kehler and yourself—Mr. Hayes. When we did discover this, we realized that . . ." She searched for words. "Events were converging. Happenstance is not something I believe in, not where certain individuals are concerned. Through Kehler, Skye was seeking the secrets of Baumgere, which we believed were likely hidden in Wooton, where we dared not go.

"When Skye set off for Castlebough, we felt almost certain that the time to approach you might be near. You see, the similarity of your life to Teller's is undeniable—or so we thought. You both apprenticed to a mage yet left his service. Both you and Teller spent your lives thereafter seeking out the secrets of the mages, or so it seemed to us.

"We practice augury—it is not so reliable that we base all our actions upon it, but we consider it in our decisions. We had a vision that you played a part in, Mr. Flattery. And here you were in Castlebough meeting up with this young man who had been in Wooton."

"What vision?" Erasmus asked, his tone flat, for he felt a little apprehension.

Anna did not answer, but he thought she colored a little. She simply could not answer.

"You are filling me with fear," Erasmus said quickly.

"No need," she said, her voice pitched very low, as though afraid they would be heard. "I have had two visions in which you played a part, or so I believe. In the first Skye opens an ornate bronze gate set into a stone wall. I pass through and inside I find a man who offers me a book and a white blossom—king's blood. . . . I could never see the man's face, though I long believed this might be you." She looked away. "The second . . . the second was not so . . . significant."

"Why do you say that? This first vision seems to have been wrong, entirely. Perhaps the second has more meaning?"

She took a breath, as though steeling herself. "We were on a hillside, you and I, beneath the stars, with trees all around. There was a bed of soft moss, and we . . ." She had looked down, but now she glanced up at him, not raising her head, and she colored, making her hair suddenly appear more red.

"I see," Erasmus said softly, feeling his own cheeks warm.

"It does not necessarily mean that we will. . . . It is a vision and must be interpreted."

Erasmus nodded quickly. For a moment he sat looking at her, and she did not meet his eye. He thought of the countess, comparing her to this young woman before him, in her boy's clothes, her hair a mess, her face streaked with dirt from her tears. And he realized that he felt immense pity for her, trapped here so young. She looked more vulnerable than he could imagine—unlike the countess who seemed so in control—in control of every situation.

He reached out a hand and touched her shoulder softly, meaning to offer her comfort in some way, but she moved forward immediately and came into his arms, pressing herself close to him. She did not raise her face, but kept it close beside his own so that he could not see her, but only hear her breathing close to his ear. Hear her catch her breath.

"Perhaps there is more truth in your vision than you know," Erasmus whispered. "Perhaps we will escape yet to see the stars."

## ⤳ Forty-Three

The message found Kent pacing the room, his confusion and chagrin not even slightly reduced. He had not slept that night and his exhaustion made his entire situation seem more dire. After hours of turmoil he'd sent a note off to the countess, hoping that she would see him so that he might try again to persuade her that he had been telling the truth. Even if she did not choose to travel with him, she must flee. It was imperative to her safety.

But his note had gone unanswered for several hours now, and he had begun to despair of it ever receiving a reply.

A knock caused Kent to start, and he rushed to the door, hoping that it was not merely a chambermaid come to change his bed. At the door he found a young local man, who presented him with an envelope.

"From Miss Edden, sir," the man said, waiting expectantly.

Kent handed the young man a coin, hardly aware of its denomination, and closed the door with barely a nod.

He began to tear open the envelope, but paused, knowing full well that a reply from Marianne Edden, not the countess, meant that his overture had been rebuffed.

He lowered himself rather gently into a chair and stared at the envelope, too dejected even to be angry at Marianne. Slowly he opened the letter, pulling the single page free and shaking out the folds.

*My Dear Mr. Kent:*
*Please, come at once! I clearly owe you an apology. Please,*
*please make all haste, I cannot tell you how worried I am.*

Fearing the worst, Kent snatched up his frock coat and bolted out the door.

When he arrived at the house of the countess, he was met by a maid who looked near to tears. Kent felt his heart sink utterly. The countess could not be dead . . . ? She could not.

"Oh, Mr. Kent, thank Farrelle you've come," she said. "Miss Edden is beside herself with worry."

Marianne appeared behind the servant, her usual quiet demeanor swept away entirely.

"Lady Chilton has gone," she said.

"Gone? But where?"

Marianne took his arm and drew him hurriedly into the house. "I was out visiting in the village and learned of her departure only when I returned. Gone without explanation." She looked expectantly at the maid, who stood twisting her apron in her hands.

"Yes, Mr. Kent," the maid said. "A small man came to the door asking for my mistress, and within moments Lady Chilton had me throw a few belongings into a trunk, and she went off with him. Went off without saying where, or even when she might return."

Kent closed his eyes for a second. "Did this man come in a large, old-fashioned carriage?"

The maid nodded. "A coach and four. Yes, sir. And a smaller carriage followed behind."

"She did not even leave me a note, Kent," Marianne said. "Not a single word. I've known the countess for years. She would never, never have done such a thing. I—I . . ." She completely lost what she had meant to say.

The maid interjected. "Has the countess eloped, do you think?"

Marianne looked at Kent; clearly she no longer doubted his story. She dismissed the maid and took Kent into the sitting room.

"I should have listened to you, Kent," she began, keeping her voice low, though it was filled with emotion all the same. "This is entirely my fault. It was just that . . . I have seen men concoct the oddest stories to gain the attention of the countess. . . ."

"It's too late to worry about that, Marianne . . ." But Kent did not finish his sentence, for at that moment the Earl of Skye arrived.

"Ah, Lord Skye," Marianne said. "I cannot thank you enough for coming so quickly." She glanced oddly at Kent, who was sure he looked at her like a betrayer. "I'm sure you've met Mr. Kent? Yes? I hardly know where to begin."

With Kent filling in his parts of the story, they related what had occurred.

"You believe it was Eldrich?" Skye said, when the story was completed. "You're sure?" He shook his head.

"I'm afraid there is no doubt of it. If only Mr. Flattery were here," Marianne lamented. "He might be able to tell us what to do."

This caught Skye's interest. "Perhaps we could speak with Mr. Flattery. I've heard he is traveling in company with a young gentleman of my acquaintance. Someone I would like to speak with in any event. Do you know where Flattery is staying?"

"Yes, but he remains down in the cave searching for those young men."

Skye looked up quickly. "You don't mean Hayes and Kehler?"

"Yes, that sounds right . . . but I don't remember exactly. Elaural mentioned their names only in passing."

"Farrelle's—" He let the curse go unfinished for Marianne's sake. "And is this the cave where Baumgere's confessor self-murdered?"

Marianne shrugged.

Skye rose and paced across the room, pausing before the windows.

"But what shall we do?" Marianne said.

"What?" Skye turned back to the others. "Well, you should have heeded Mr. Kent's warning," he said. "If the countess is in the hands of Eldrich, then the Farr army will not pry her loose." He turned back to the window again, obviously disturbed, but Kent was not sure it was by the plight of the countess.

"There is only one road from Castlebough back into Farrland," Kent said. "We can catch them yet—if we ride at once."

"And do what, exactly?" Skye said, whirling to stare down at Kent. "He is a mage, Kent." He paused, looking at the painter and Marianne, his features softening a little. "I'm sorry about what has happened to the countess, but there is nothing anyone can do. And to be completely logical about matters— you don't know that she didn't go of her own accord. It's true that the countess did not leave Miss Edden a note, and she rushed off in terrible haste, but—" He raised his hands. "You might catch them up, Kent, and if Eldrich is not in- clined to cripple you on the spot, then the countess could just as well lean out the window of her carriage and tell you to turn around and bother her no more. And whether she says this of her own choice or not, we will never prove. I'm sorry. But there is nothing to be done." He looked from one to the other. "How long has Mr. Flattery been in this cave?"

Marianne shook her head, hardly able to follow the change in conversa- tion. "I don't know!" she snapped. "Four days, perhaps."

"Well," Skye answered, "there is someone we can help. If Mr. Flattery hasn't appeared by tomorrow, I suggest we organize a search. At least *he* is not in the clutches of a mage."

Kent was beginning to feel the effects of lack of sleep, but he forced himself up the stairs to Sir John's rooms. The knight had obviously been sleeping, but when he saw Kent, he came completely awake.

"Eldrich has taken the countess away," Kent announced.

"*Flames,*" was all Sir John could manage. "Come in, man, come in."

"Is this man Bryce still in Castlebough?"

"No. No, he's gone. Why do you ask?"

"I don't know. He is a servant of Eldrich. Perhaps . . . perhaps he could assure me that the countess went of her own choosing. That she is in no dan- ger." Kent sat in a chair, hands on his knees, his head hanging down as though he had not the energy to raise it. "I must go after her," he said.

"Take hold of yourself, Kent, you're not making sense. You're not some hero off to rescue a maiden in distress. You're a painter, for Farrelle's sake. Come to your senses, man. There is nothing you can do. And do you even know if Lady Chilton was taken against her will?"

Kent looked up at Sir John, who asked the same question as Skye. "The countess had no memory of her meeting with Eldrich. The very thought of it caused her the greatest revulsion. How can I assume that anything but an abduction has taken place?" Kent sat back in the chair, letting his arms fall loosely to his sides. "Flames, I wish Erasmus were here."

"Flattery, you mean? Could he help?"

Kent shrugged. "He has a certain . . . affection for the countess, I believe. And who would know more about the mage than Erasmus? Assuming he had nothing to do with the countess' disappearance."

Sir John shook his head. "If Eldrich is out in the world again . . ." he muttered, letting the sentence die. "Can Mr. Flattery be reached?" the knight asked.

Kent shook his head. "I don't know. He has gone exploring one of the local caves for some unknown period of time. I cannot say if he is still there, or if he has, perhaps, emerged and even returned to Avonel."

"Well, let us endeavor to find out before you do anything rash."

Kent felt a bit embarrassed at his state. He knew that he had no claim on the countess and was acting a bit of a fool. "I don't think I can wait, Sir John. I need to know where he has taken her, at the very least. Perhaps you could take on the contacting of Erasmus Flattery? And I will send word back to you as to the whereabouts of the countess. I feel sure Erasmus will help."

Sir John did not look like a man who felt any degree of confidence in Kent's plan. "I think it more likely that he will try to dissuade you from interfering. Though I'm not sure, now, what my own situation is. I received a note from Mr. Bryce this morning saying that he was leaving Castlebough immediately and that I was free to return to Avonel. In other words, I have been dismissed— temporarily." Distress seemed to draw his face taut. "He has gone off after his master, I assume." Sir John lowered himself into a chair, staring at a spot on the floor just before him.

"I don't know, Kent. It is all very odd. Eldrich was in Castlebough for a reason. Bryce insisted I accompany him here, but now I'm not sure why. What- ever purpose he had came to nothing, it would seem. But even so, I have a feeling that something occurred here. And not something insignificant either." He pressed fingers into the corners of his eyes, clearly still tired. Then he looked up at Kent, his eyes red from exhaustion and worry. "Well, Kent, what will you do? I hold little hope that you'll listen to reason in this."

Kent knew the man was talking sense, but it did not matter. "I will heed your advice, in part. I will keep my distance from Eldrich and try to discover where he will take the countess. I'll then send word to you. If you will attempt to speak with Mr. Flattery. . . ." Kent paused for a moment, finding it difficult to keep his train of thought. "Skye is worried that Erasmus has been gone too long, that he has met with misadventure." Kent shook his head. "I can't believe it. Erasmus Flattery is an enormously competent man. I'm sure no evil has befallen him. If you will tell Erasmus what has happened when he emerges, I will set off immediately so that Eldrich does not outdistance me."

Kent shook his head, trying to make his mind function. Was there anything else he should say to Sir John? Unable to think of anything, he forced himself up. "Good luck to you, Sir John."

"And to you, Kent. Safe journey." He rose from his chair, reaching out to clasp Kent's hand warmly. "But, Kent, do keep your distance from Lord Eldrich. It is likely he has already learned of your interference. Take no chances, Kent, I implore you."

The painter nodded. Sir John pressed his hand firmly and then released it, and Kent went out thinking that Sir John treated him like a man going off to war. Like a man who would not be seen again.

The countess realized that she had been staring for a long time at the scene before her, but it had not registered until now. She shook her head and blinked, her eyes feeling like they had been scoured with sand.

Eldrich roused from his reverie and looked at her. "Ah, there you are," he said as though she had just appeared.

"Indeed . . ." She felt a peculiar confusion, as though just awakened from a deep sleep. "But where am I?"

"In a carriage traveling through the Caledon Hills. We have come from Castlebough."

She nodded. Yes, Castlebough. "My mind . . . it is not clear."

"It will become so in a few moments. Do not be alarmed," Eldrich said, his tone musical but not terribly soothing. She felt as though he mocked her; she was not sure why.

She pressed her eyelids closed for a moment, relieving the pain in her eyes, and tried to order her thoughts. She had been in Castlebough. With Marianne! Yes, now it was coming to her. They had gone there after Skye, though she could not recall the reason. . . . She took a long breath and searched her memories, which were terribly fragmented. A feeling deep in her center was familiar. Had she taken a lover there? Something told her she had; in fact she seemed to remember—everything but his face and name.

Erasmus! That was it; Erasmus, but she felt an odd sense of disappointment, though she was not sure why. Had it ended unhappily? Was he inadequate? Neither of these seemed to be true.

Putting this line of inquiry aside, she tried to remember the reason she had gone there in the first place. Skye. She was certain it had something to do with Skye. And his paintings! The Peliers. And this priest Baumgere. She took a long breath. It was coming back. But why was she here?

Certainly she knew Eldrich, but how? She was sure that she had not

encountered him before her journey to Castlebough, but she could not remember when they had first met. One did not forget meeting a mage. Curious.

She opened her burning eyes and focused on Eldrich, who looked at her
with disturbing disinterest.

"Why am I here?"

He did not answer but continued to stare, almost as if he had not heard.
She was about to ask again when he spoke.

"The explanation is lengthy, and I have provided some of it already. It will
come back to you. Give it time, something we have in abundance, for the next
few days, at least."

The countess straightened her skirt. "At least I have clothes," she said, not
sure why.

Eldrich smiled in amusement. "Are you disappointed?"

"No, I think not. What have you been doing to me?"

"Not what you suspect at the moment, though I will confess that I have
been tempted. But that would be tempting fate, quite literally, wouldn't it?"

"Would it?"

He did not answer.

The countess sat up straight, suddenly feeling very vulnerable. "Well, you
have all the advantage of me. I do not know where we are going or why."

He nodded agreement but did not offer an explanation.

One hand had gone to sleep, and she rubbed feeling back into it. "Nor do
I remember agreeing to such a journey."

"Were your relations with Erasmus intimate?" Eldrich asked suddenly.

"Sir! I am shocked that you would ask such a thing."

"In fact, you're not. And I'm glad to find that they were—intimate, that is."

She was about to protest, but he turned and looked out the window, as
though no longer interested in this matter. She thought his face changed a
little, the mockery replaced by sadness.

"Something has happened to Erasmus," she said suddenly.

He turned back to her, his look a bit surprised, or perhaps more impressed.
"Erasmus is perfectly hale, I can assure you."

"But where is he?"

"Do you really care?"

"Yes, of course I do."

He nodded, though she was not sure why. "It is often said that to practice
the arts one must give up one's heart." The look of sadness returned. "But I will
tell you that it is not so simple."

She did not quite know what to say, but suddenly her conviction that something had happened to Erasmus was not so solid. Did she care for Erasmus?
She remembered their night of love. Certainly it had given her great pleasure.

But had Erasmus engaged her heart that night? It almost seemed that if the question needed to be asked, the answer must be "no." And this made her a little sad.

"You did not answer my question," the countess said.

Eldrich looked at her sharply. "Have you not heard that it is unwise to anger a mage?"

She did not answer, feeling suddenly frightened, but frustrated and angry at the same time. Eldrich turned again to survey the passing countryside.

She felt a stirring inside and a blush spread across her skin. A memory of desire came back to her, but it did not seem to be connected to Erasmus. Eldrich . . . She had felt this desire for him—at his command, it seemed. And now the memory of it washed through her again.

*Is this his doing,* she asked herself, *or are these my feelings?*

Fear—she also felt fear. Fear and desire. The idea that these two emotions could live within her at one time she found loathsome, but her body did not care. And worse, she sensed a hunger in him that she had not felt before— hunger for her. It was hidden behind his mockery, by his stillness, but, even so, she felt it. She was desired by a mage. . . .

"I still do not remember consenting to this journey," she said, hoping that speaking would take her focus away from the confusion she felt.

Eldrich turned and looked at her, drawing himself up in his seat. "Do you know my age?" he asked, as though he had not heard her.

She shook her head.

"One hundred and thirty-three years. All other estimates you have heard are inaccurate. In fact it will be my birth day in just over a fortnight." He paused, watching her reaction to this information. "I am stronger than men a century my junior, my mind is still sound in all its parts. In every way I am a man in his middle years, except that, like all my kind, I cannot father children." He raised his eyebrows, cocking his head a little, as though a bit proud of these facts. "I will not stoop to asking how old I appear, for politeness begs a lie, even in my situation, but I do not look like an elderly man, of that I am aware." He paused again—his conversation was punctuated by pauses, all a little too long, and the effect was to discomfit those he spoke to, or at least it had that effect on the countess. "Do you know Lady Felton-Gray?"

She nodded, wondering if his mind was as sound as he claimed, for there was no apparent thread to this conversation.

"She is eighty-some years old, I believe. When she was your age, I thought her the most beautiful woman I had ever seen. At the risk of being terribly unkind, she is now a crone."

"It is rather more than unkind," the countess said before she thought. "Lady Felton-Gray is a woman of great distinction, I think."

He nodded. "But the men of Farrland, and even farther afield, sing the praises of the Countess of Chilton, not Lady Felton-Gray. You, Lady Chilton, are the great beauty of your generation. In ten years you might still look much as you do now. Oh, your hair will not be so thick and lustrous, and your skin will not have the glow that it does today, and lines will have begun to form at the corners of your eyes. But you will still be thought a great beauty. In twenty years you will be replaced by someone half your age. In thirty years you will be thought handsome and perhaps well-preserved. In forty years people will marvel that men whose names you did not know once fought duels over you. And when you are the age of Lady Felton-Gray . . ." He shrugged.

"And it gives you some pleasure to remind me that I am merely mortal and will suffer the same indignities that befall us all?"

"It might give me some small pleasure, I suppose, but that is not why I brought it up. I have been confronted recently with a dilemma, but I think I have found a solution. Would you not like to stay much as you are now far into your old age?"

"What are you saying? You can give me such a gift?"

He paused, and then nodded slowly, watching her face.

She looked at the man sitting before her and thought that he did not truly look like an evil man, yet she felt terribly threatened by him all the same. What he felt for her was not tender, she was sure of that. He did not care for her or anyone else. Eldrich was not a man as other men were. "I assume you will require something in return?"

He nodded again, but did not offer further explanation.

"And what might this be, pray tell?"

"Most would say that long life, youth, and vigor could not have too high a price," he said.

"I have read stories of people who made bargains with devils, Lord Eldrich. They never had happy endings."

He actually laughed, as though he found the comparison flattering. "Life never has a happy ending, Lady Chilton—old age, infirmity, death. One can only aspire to a rich life, and a fullness of years. But I am offering more: a chance to prolong your youth in all its parts. Your beauty and vigor and all your mental faculties. All of them. Youth, Lady Chilton—or at worst, middle age—until you have passed your centenary. Passed it by half a lifetime as men measure such things.

Some part of her brain believed she was being mocked or made to look the fool, but another part of her was not so certain. *Youth*—not eternal, but for many years. Oddly, tears welled up, and she struggled to keep them back as a flood of emotion swept through her.

She knew now that there was something more here—something more be-tween them. She remembered their first meeting and the things he had inti-mated. The idea of becoming part of his world was too frightening, too alien.

"I think I shall have . . ." She pushed her emotions down. ". . . Have to de-cline your generous offer."

Eldrich did not answer but only stared so that she looked away, casting her gaze out the window into the darkness. The carriage had slowed to negotiate one of the road's many tight turns, and suddenly it stopped. She heard voices—the driver apparently speaking to someone on the road.

Eldrich opened the door and stepped out, lowering the stairs and holding out a hand to her in a manner that was less than polite. For a second she de-murred, but then remembered that he had said he was not a gentleman, and she reached out and took the offered hand.

She climbed out, unaware of anything but the touch of his skin—infinitely soft, like the skin of a child. And warm, so unlike his manner.

*Warm hands, cold heart*, she remembered her mother saying.

"Why do we stop?" she asked, a bit short of breath.

"There seems to be someone on the road. Walky? What is it?"

"A woman, sir. She seems to be wandering, lost."

They rounded the team and, there, in the light of the coach lamp, found an elderly woman standing by the small man the countess had met before. Clearly the woman was confused, staring around her as though she could not under-stand how she had come to this place. Her motions were exaggerated and not perfectly controlled.

"My dear!" the countess said, going immediately to the woman who was clearly not a peasant. "Has there been an accident? What's happened to you?" The countess took the woman's hand, cold as snow. "Tell me, madame, what's happened? From where have you come?" There was no smell of drink on the poor woman's breath but she was not steady on her feet.

She stared at the countess curiously as though she recognized her. "I . . . I don't know. Where are we? What place?"

"The Caledon Hills, my dear. Near Castlebough. Is that where you've come from?"

"I don't know. . . ."

The woman sagged suddenly, clutching the countess' hands, and the count-ess tried to bear her up.

"Oh, Mr. Walky, can you lay down your coat?"

Walky quickly did so, and they lowered the woman to the ground where she lay, still confused, but conscious.

"Can you tell me your name, dear?" the countess asked.

"Name . . . ? Oh, yes. It's . . ." The poor woman squinted, trying to force the words up from her memory, but then she shook her head, and tears glistened in her eyes.

"Lord Eldrich," the countess said, "is there nothing you can do for her?"

"I don't think she wants my assistance," he said firmly.

The woman touched the countess' hair. "And who are you, child?" she whispered.

"The Countess of Chilton, my dear. If we help you, can you get into the carriage?"

"But you can't be," the woman said, her look even more confused. "I am the countess. There can't be two?" The old woman began to cry in earnest now. Pitiful tiny sobs. "You can't be me. . . ."

The countess felt herself draw away, staring down at the wrinkled old woman in some horror.

"You will be surprised how quickly youth is spent," Eldrich said. "How everything you take for granted crumbles and fades. And here you meet your future, Lady Chilton. Not eighty years, and not even your memories to bring you comfort. Stay with her for a while. Contemplate the choice you are making."

"I've seen enough," the countess said, starting to rise, but the old woman clutched at her clothing, holding her still. And the countess felt as though a vision of death had its cold hands upon her, dragging her down toward the earth. She pulled sharply away from the whimpering woman, feeling both guilt and revulsion—but revulsion was the stronger.

*It is an apparition only*, the countess told herself. *An apparition and nothing more.*

She turned to Eldrich, but the mage was gone, leaving her standing there in the coach light, confronted by her future. The common future.

For a long moment she could not tear her eyes away from the poor woman, who still held out her hands to her, begging her help. A wave of nausea passed over her, and she felt the world spinning, endlessly spinning. She turned quickly away, stumbling into the carriage.

Hanging her head, she closed her eyes and tried to control her breathing, her tears. The animal fear of death had come over her, and she knew that she was ready to fight to the last breath to stay alive.

*Look what he has done to me*, she thought. *He has stripped away my honor, my dignity. Reduced me to a beast, growling at threats in the darkness, prepared to do whatever is necessary to preserve my precious self.*

The vision of the ancient woman appeared in her mind.

*Farrelle's blood*, she thought, *preserve me from becoming that.*

*What a monster he is. What a terrible monster.*

The coach lurched into motion again and as it rolled the first few feet the countess stiffened, afraid she would hear the terrible whimpering. Blessedly, she heard nothing.

"Perhaps," Eldrich said softly, "we should begin this conversation anew. I require your cooperation, Lady Chilton, and in exchange I am able to offer something that no other living man might offer. What say you now?"

## ⤳ Forty-Four

Anna and Banks bent together over their translation of the wall text, hoping to uncover some hint that might indicate a way out of the crypt into which they'd been sealed. Occasionally they consulted with Erasmus, who seemed to be remembering more of his boyhood lessons by the hour. Only Deacon Rose continued to claim that he could offer nothing, though clearly the Tellerites did not believe him. If the priest could not help, he certainly kept his eye on all progress, and his actions were creating a palpable tension.

The others examined every inch of the chamber that could be reached, searching for a seam in the stone or any other sign of an exit. Hayes and Kehler worked together, starting in the long hallway. The walls seemed flawless to them, the rock carved and finished to a consistent texture, as though it had been meticulously shaped by hand, though from what Anna had said, there was some doubt that craftsmen had worked here at all.

"I am beginning to think this is futile," Hayes said, lowering himself to the floor to rest for a moment. His stomach growled, for the most recent "meal" had been so absurdly inadequate that Kehler had actually laughed when he first saw it, though the laugh had died rather abruptly and he'd been left with a dark look in his eyes.

Small amounts of food seemed to waken the appetite, and Hayes began to have some pain from his stomach and even a burning in his esophagus. A headache had come to reside in his temples, and he had to be careful to rise slowly or his head would swim.

"Perhaps it is futile," Kehler said, responding to Hayes, "but have we something better to do?" He pushed his back to the wall, bracing his legs out. "I put my hope more in the efforts of Anna and Banks. Perhaps there will be something written here that will help us." Kehler looked around the chamber. "I can't believe that our route in here was the only entrance."

"Nor can I," Hayes said, his tone a little defeated. "I think that our passage was left open so that the chamber could be discovered one day. So that the accomplishments of Landor and the others would be remembered. In some ways I think of this shrine as an act of colossal vanity. Can you imagine building a shrine to yourself?"

"Look at all the great houses and palaces in Farrland, Hayes. What are they but monuments to their owners, many of whom accomplished next to nothing?" Kehler fell to thinking. "And," he pushed himself up, "how many of these homes had passages built in them to allow escape in uncertain times?" He paused. "There must be a way out. I cannot believe otherwise. And we must find it before we're too weak to make use of it."

Two hours later they came to the end of the hallway and were in such despair that they could not look at one another. It was finally sinking in that they might die here, and their failure to find anything that might facilitate their escape only made that worse.

"Shall we go over it again?" Hayes asked, no great hope in his voice.

Kehler shrugged. "Do you think there's any chance we'll find something we've missed?"

Hayes looked out into the chamber where the others had gathered in the middle of the floor. "No. I'm afraid we'll find nothing more. Let's go see what the others have turned up."

The gathering in the chamber's center was a somber one. Hayes and Kehler sat down among their fellow inmates, and listened to the terrible silence for a few moments. No one seemed at all hopeful, and only the priest seemed at peace with their situation.

"Is there nothing useful in the text, then?" Kehler asked quietly.

Banks shook his head. "Nothing, though it is certainly a fascinating document, if one can call it that. Of course there are sections we cannot translate, but it seems a good part of it is a history. A history of the mages' arrival in Farrland from Darr."

"But do you believe this, Banks?" Kehler asked. "Do you believe the mages came from some other land that cannot be reached by mundane means?"

Banks glanced at Anna, a bit guiltily. When she did not react, he nodded. "I do, yes. But there is other evidence. You yourself were interested in the Stranger of Compton Heath, Kehler, and certainly that man was not from our own world—not even some unexplored part of it, I'm sure. And a mage took him away, for the mages have greater interest in these matters than anyone else."

"You know it was a mage?"

"Have no doubt of it," Anna said firmly. "It was a mage. Eldrich, I would say."

"And what became of the stranger?" Hayes asked.

Anna shrugged.

"More importantly," Erasmus took up the argument, "how did he get here, and why did he not simply return?"

Banks motioned with his hand as though about to speak, and then paused, perhaps finding his explanation inadequate. "There is no agreement on this matter, but I believe it is possible that there are times when the worlds touch and natural portals occur. I cannot explain how this happens, but it seems to me that at times individuals have come through these openings: the Stranger of Compton Heath; 'Mad Nell,' as she was known; a boy found nearly frozen to death in Doorn. There are any number of others. They were all confused, more surprised to find themselves here than we were to discover them."

"And do you agree, Miss Fielding?" Erasmus said.

Her mouth turned down. "Recently I have been forced to admit that this explanation is very likely true."

"You have met a stranger," Clarendon said quickly.

She pressed her lips together, barely shrugging, and looked down to her hand, which traced a circle on the stone floor.

"Well, if we are not to get out this day," Rose said, his manner composed, as always, showing no trace of despair, "then who will be next to tell their story?" He looked evenly at Anna and Banks.

"No," she said putting her hand on Bank's arm. "We will not reveal our secrets to you until we are sure there is no escape."

The priest nodded, casting his eyes down deferentially. "Who then?" he asked quietly.

"Why don't you tell everyone how you trapped my brothers and burned them for the crime of causing harm to no one?" Anna said.

"I was not alive when this occurred, Miss Fielding. I can, however, tell you another story—equally sad—but I think somehow you will want to hear it." Rose looked around at each person in turn. "I can tell you how the mages trapped the Followers of Teller and destroyed them."

"You know this story?" Anna said, looking up sharply. "The true story?"

Rose nodded once. He put his hands on the floor behind him and tilted his head to look up at the ceiling for a moment. And then he began. "After the terrible conflict that has come to be known as the Winter War," he said, his voice faltering. He stopped and worked some moisture into his mouth. "In the year 1415, a final great battle took place, though it was not between nations, and few ever heard of it. The field of this battle was somewhere near the ruin of Tremont Abbey—some say the abbey itself was the site." The priest looked around at the others. "The followers of Teller, who had hidden themselves for uncounted years, centuries in fact, made a grave error. They underestimated the patience of the mages."

Anna hung her head so that her face was hidden by her hair, and she became utterly still. Hayes wondered what went through her mind. Beside her

Banks looked like a man at a reading of his own funeral rites. Color drained from his face, which seemed drawn and rigid.

"No one knows how the mages learned of their rivals' plans, or even of their existence, for the followers of Teller hid themselves not only by normal means, but by means arcane as well. They believed that augury would not detect them." He leaned forward now, sitting cross-legged and putting his fingertips together. "But perhaps the story had its beginning an age earlier, in the tenth century. It is true, as is often speculated, that Teller's master died before Teller had completed his apprenticeship. The war between the Church of Farrelle and the mages was nearing its height then. Teller offended the mages somehow. One contemporary who actually met Teller claimed that he had delved into Lapin's books after he died. He even stole some of the texts to have for his own, hoping to make himself a mage without sanction from the other mages." He closed his eyes and drew a long breath. "For some reason Teller believed the mages would not allow him to complete his transformation to a mage. No one knows exactly why, but he fled them, and eventually came for a time to serve the church in the long struggle." He paused, thinking, the way he held his fingertips together reminding Hayes of making a church of his hands when he was a child. The priest stared into this structure as though it were an aid to meditation.

"Teller was only a reluctant ally, I think. Not caring for the word of Farrelle, but for a while he helped immeasurably. No one knew more of the mages and their ways than Teller. The mages did not expect to be countered by sophisticated arcane means, and though Teller was no mage himself, he was endlessly inventive. A genius, many thought. But when it became apparent that the church would not win, Teller vanished. The mages questioned the seniors of my church at length, but their renegade had slipped away.

"But miraculously the church was allowed to continue, much reduced in its power, but even that was something to be thankful for. In a rite that horrified the fathers of the church, they swore never again to employ the arts of the mages, and never to have commerce with a renegade servant of a mage. The penalty for ignoring this would be complete destruction of the church.

"Afterward, members of the church realized that much of what Teller had been doing during his time with the church was preparing his escape. Preparing his escape and hiding the texts and knowledge he had stolen from Lapin. Somehow Teller eluded the mages, which must indicate both great talent and skill in the arts. The Society of Teller was created. More clandestine than any secret society, for one whisper of their existence would see them destroyed. And there was something more, some other crime that Teller had committed: he had stolen a secret herb from Lapin. King's blood, as we have read here. And this, above all things, was a crime that could not be forgiven.

"There is no document that I know of that tells the story of those years, though perhaps Mr. Banks and Miss Fielding know more. Certainly Teller shared his knowledge with his followers, and increased his own, for he had escaped with a number of books. But it seems likely that those who came immediately after him had less of the talent needed to truly master the arts, for they couldn't recruit just anyone, no matter how talented. The society dwindled in power, if not numbers—each successive generation less skilled than the last. For centuries this dwindling of power went on, while the few who even knew of Teller thought his knowledge had been lost.

"But as will happen in any art, there was a renewal, a golden age, when men of successive generations were born with talent. The arts were greatly restored among the followers of Teller, and they grew in confidence. Finally, during the Winter War, the decision was made to perform a rite—I cannot tell you its exact nature—but it was believed that it would give them power. Perhaps it was the ritual performed to make a true mage—that is what some think. And they went to Tremont Abbey. There is an ancient lay. . . ."

"Mr. Flattery knows it," Clarendon said quickly.

Rose recited the words of the song that Erasmus had sung at Clarendon's home.

"*A delro, a delro. Ai kombi aré*," Banks repeated.

"Meaning what?" Kehler asked.

"'We are here, we are here. At the world gate,'" Anna answered, "or as we would render it: 'At the gate of the world.' It could also be translated: 'We are here at the beginning of the world,' but in this case I think it means 'gate.'"

"But what happened at the abbey?" Kehler asked, impatient for the story.

"To the few who know the story, it has long been said that only the five mages know for certain, but I will tell you now that this is not so. There was a young priest of Farrelle on a pilgrimage to pray in the holy places. He had stopped at the ruin of the abbey for the night when the followers of Teller came, singing their song of power, if we are to believe the ancient lay. They passed down into the cellars of the abbey, leaving him wondering what they did. But there was something forbidding about these men, so he stayed where he was, hidden in the ruin.

"The five came by moonlight, 'more ghostly than men,' but they did not ignore a pilgrim monk; in fact, they seemed to know he would be there. 'The witness of the Holy See,' they greeted him, and took him with them, down in the cellars. Brother Stephen was his name, and he is the only man who saw what befell the followers of Teller.

"'Before they descended into the cellars of the ruined abbey,' he later wrote, 'they drew a pattern upon the stone of the nave with the ashes of my fire, and then, with a candle, spread wax over this same pattern. A vial of starlight, or so they called it, was used to mark a second pattern within the first, and this glowed ghostly light on the floor. At a word, the outer pattern took fire and burned in thin, unbroken lines as fire should not. Many words were spoken in a foul tongue, and spells were woven and enchantments cast. Not till the mages were satisfied with their monstrous work did they descend the stair. Down we went, into the bowels of the old abbey. Down a passage unknown to men, and a secret stair that wound its way into the earth like a serpent hiding from the light. Down . . . until we came at last to an opening in the solid wall.

"'There the seven who had gone before performed a rite of terrible splendor. So involved were they in their wicked pursuit that they did not see the five who came; the five and the one who watched. Seven columns stood in a half circle around a font, above the base of which sculptures of a man and a woman had been cut from the rock. Lines glowed like starlight and moonlight on the floor, and the men cried out in inhuman voices in strange tongues.' Brother Stephen claims to have stopped up his ears, but it did not matter. He heard every dreadful word. 'From the font emerged a column of fire, and the man chief among them spoke to it in words of power and it obeyed him.

"'But then the mages began to chant, nearly silently, and around them dazzling patterns appeared in the air. Their voices grew until we could no longer hear the song of the seven. Suddenly the mages burst into the chamber, casting before them the white down of birds, which caught flame where it fell. With silver daggers they slew the seven to a man, slew them singing a horrible dirge. And the flame exploded around them, sweeping out across the floor, and the ceiling opened up to the vast dome of the sky, and we seemed to spin among the stars in the heavens.' Brother Stephen claims that he passed from consciousness then, believing that he was dying, and praying to Farrelle for his doomed soul.

"But he did not die. 'When I awoke, I lay in the sweet grass of a meadow beneath a warm sun. A spring bubbled a few feet away, and as I sat up in this fair setting, I realized I was not alone. One mage remained. "Drink from the spring," he said, "before you follow the path that will lead you back. And then travel to the seat of your Order and tell them what you have seen this night. Take them this warning." And he left then. Left me in this place which I think today is the fairest place I have ever seen. And so I drank from the spring, and by and by I followed the path beneath an arch of stone, out of the wood.'"

Rose looked around at the others. "Brother Stephen did as he was instructed, recounting the story as he understood it, and writing it down in the secret annals of the church. I confess to have read it many times, and apologize, for this has been a truncated, paraphrased version. But the center of the story is true to the original. Ah, there was one brief corollary: Brother Stephen returned to the abbey years later and could find neither secret passage nor stair. Nor could he find the beautiful meadow he described as the 'fairest place on earth.' Could not find it though he claimed it was but a short walk from the abbey. Some do not believe his story at all, but the song came from the others: 'the orphan, the maiden, the man,' and so I believe it, for it is too close to the story of Brother Stephen who was, by all accounts, of sensible disposition, and in all his later years blessed in every way; 'from drinking the water of the spring in that fair bower.'" Rose stretched his legs before him.

"That is the story as it is known to the church. Even the mages believed the followers of Teller destroyed. At least for many years they believed that. It seems they never suspected the hidden meaning of Teller's sign: three vale roses. One for each secret company he left behind, each unknown to the others. Or so I have come to believe." He looked at Anna, who still hung her head, and even Banks would not confirm or deny the man's speculation.

Suddenly Anna rose to her feet, and stepping deftly among the seated men, walked off across the chamber, her head up now, her manner stiff but filled with rage and dignity. Banks watched her with great distress, and then he rose and followed, without looking at the others.

"Perhaps, Deacon Rose, you did not choose the most appropriate tale to tell in these circumstances," Clarendon said, fixing the man with a hard look.

"In truth, Mr. Clarendon, I think that Miss Fielding wanted to hear that story. It is a piece of their history that has likely never been clear to them, for the other groups were never known to them until after their destruction."

"Perhaps, but she is like a child whose entire family has been destroyed, even those distant relatives she has never met. And now she, too, is trapped and doomed to die. I think it was cruel, Deacon Rose, cruel and unnecessary, but I'm sure it gave you great pleasure at least." Clarendon pushed himself quickly up, and walked off, disappearing into the crypt.

Erasmus thought that the priest did not look so concerned with the idea that he would die in this place as everyone else. "You are quite happy to die here as long as the followers of Teller die with you, aren't you, Deacon?" Erasmus said.

"You do me injustice, Mr. Flattery. I believe that I shall live beyond this life. That I shall be reborn in a better world. A world without poverty and sickness and strife, where only the virtuous live. Believing this, why would I be unhappy?"

Kehler got up and went to the corner of the large chamber, and began examining the wall with great deliberation. Hayes went to help him, and a moment later Erasmus rose and disappeared down the hallway. The priest was left alone, seemingly unaffected by his rejection by the entire group.

Erasmus set foot on the bottom stair, wondering if he did the right thing. Should he interrupt Banks and Anna? Clearly Banks had gone to comfort her, and Erasmus was sure that the young man held her in affection. Perhaps it was not his place to interfere.

Footsteps came down the stairs, and Erasmus stepped back into the hall, going to one of the stone faces and pretending to examine the text.

"Ah, Mr. Flattery." It was Banks coming from the stairwell. "Anna would like to speak with you, if you . . . would be so kind." He tried to smile as he spoke, keeping all signs of emotion from his voice, but Erasmus heard it all the same. The poor young man felt some pain at her asking for Erasmus. Pain that he tried not to show.

Erasmus nodded, not knowing what to say, and turned to ascend the stair, before realizing Banks had not quite finished.

"I think you have something more to say, Mr. Banks?" Erasmus said.

The young man struggled for a few seconds. "Do you think there is any chance we will get out of here?" he asked, though Erasmus knew this was not what Banks wanted to say at all.

Erasmus shook his head. "I don't know, Mr. Banks, but if we give up, we will certainly never escape. I don't want to die here, that is certain."

"But perhaps you won't, Mr. Flattery."

"What do you mean?"

"'The last guardian of the gate.' Perhaps you will live on to fulfill your purpose."

Erasmus felt something indescribable inside—as though his heart paused to listen to something utterly horrifying. "You cannot be serious."

"It is not impossible. We are dealing here with an art so deftly managed that we cannot even begin to guess what it could do. No, Mr. Flattery, I'm afraid it is entirely possible." He nodded toward the opening. "She is at the top of the stairs."

Erasmus ascended slowly, wondering if Banks had meant what he said, or if it were merely jealousy driving him to cruelty. He hoped it was the latter.

He found Anna at the stairhead, sitting with her legs drawn up and her chin on her knees. She stared off at nothing.

"You keep returning to this place," Erasmus said.

She shrugged, but offered no explanation. "Erasmus . . . may I call you Erasmus?"

"Certainly."

"I have been thinking and I'm convinced that Rose will not let us escape, even if we do find a way out. At least he will try to prevent Banks and me from getting away. I'm not sure about the rest of you."

Erasmus looked off at the same point in the distance that had so drawn her attention, and wondered if they saw the same things. "I'm not sure about the rest of us either, but it's possible he would prefer to see us all buried with what we've learned. If we discover anything at all that might help us escape, we must keep it from Rose. I'm not sure how we'd do it, but we would have to slip away without him." He pushed a hand into his hair. "Not an easy task, for I fear there are several among us who are not skilled at subterfuge."

"Poor liars, you say? Well, you cannot possibly mean Banks and me, for we have spent our lives hiding the truth. . . . Though look where that got us." She turned her head so that her check rested on her knees and she looked sideways at Erasmus. "It maddens me the way the priest seems so unaffected by our situation. I cannot believe that he has no fear of death—I do not care what his beliefs are. Men fear death. It is in their nature."

Erasmus nodded, still staring off at some point in the impossible distance, some point beyond the cave. He thought of the countess. Was she worried for him? Would she mourn when he was finally given up for dead?

And what of Rose? Why was he so . . . ? It was an odd epiphany, yet in this place it seemed completely natural. There was a very obvious reason for Rose's equanimity.

"Perhaps Rose is more devious than we realized. He didn't choose to tell that particular story just to cause you distress and to gloat about the triumph over the Tellerites. There was something more, I felt it even as he was talking. 'Why this story now?'" He turned and looked at Anna. "He believes he is to be the witness for the Holy See. That is why he shows no fear. Rose believes he plays the role of Brother Stephen."

Anna sat up straight against the rock, and closed her eyes. She was so still that Erasmus thought she forgot to breathe, but then she let out a long sigh and took in a quick breath. "I should have realized," she said, still not moving. "I don't know what's wrong with me. I seem to be missing everything. Eldrich lured us down here like fools. And then this priest follows us. 'Everyone has their part.' I believe that is true. Rose's part must be to witness for the church."

"But I don't understand why," Erasmus said, leaning back, trying to find a position that was comfortable.

Anna shook her head, her eyes still closed, as though she were afraid to open them, afraid of what she might see. "Why didn't the mages destroy the church? It is a question we have long asked. The usual answers are not even close to the truth, I suspect. There was something, some reason to let the church survive. It is almost as if the church had some hold over the mages, though I cannot imagine what that could be."

"Nor can I. But you're right. There is no explanation that I find adequate. It seems most likely to me that the mages found some use for the church. They would never have let it survive otherwise."

A silence settled around them, but it was not terribly awkward. The silence of people pursuing their own thoughts. The silence that existed between people who were not familiar enough with each other to know what the other was thinking.

"I saw you on the *nance*, examining the urns," Erasmus said. "Is there any hope that we could reach the seed? Would that help us?"

"It could, yes. The seed is necessary to the arts of the mages. If we could find some way to get at it, we could take it, you and I, and we might find that some secrets of the chamber would be revealed. The chamber is sensitive to our presence—Hayes and Kehler said there was no light when they first looked in. When I performed the proper rites, light appeared in the crypt." She waved a hand around them. "And now we have light here as well—ever since Banks and I ascended. I believe that someone who is on the path, someone with talent who had taken the seed, might gain control of some of the chamber's functions."

"But we haven't the knowledge, unless you are keeping much from me."

She shook her head. "You are likely right, though how will we ever know unless we try? But every time I go near the urns, the priest comes and stands by, watching me. He must guess what's hidden there, even if he will not set foot on the *nance*." She rubbed her hands over her face and pressed her fingers to her eyes, shaking her head. "I don't know why I am suggesting this, I don't know enough. It is very unlikely that I could break the spell. It is more than unlikely," Anna said, any small hope that she had expressed earlier abandoning her. And Erasmus felt it, too. He stifled an urge to beat on the walls as though he could demand to be set free.

They sat in silence for some time, pursuing their separate thoughts. Erasmus found himself wondering what this woman felt about him. She had pressed herself close to him before. They had kissed—only once—but it had been a kiss full of promise, Erasmus thought. Now he found himself wishing that she would touch him again. He wanted to reach out and put his arms around her, but something stopped him. The countess came to mind, and he felt a twinge of guilt.

*But I am likely going to die here*, he thought. *Should I deprive myself comfort? Is that not foolish?*

He realized suddenly that Anna was gazing at him, her eyes moving slowly over his face. "You have the eyes of a poet," she said, a small smile appearing, as though she were a bit self-conscious.

"Haunted, a bit mad, suicidal?" Erasmus asked.

"No. A bit sad and very thoughtful. And focused inward, not upon yourself, but not focused on the world around you."

"Distracted, you mean?"

She laughed. "You will not take a compliment, will you?"

"Ah, it was a compliment."

"Well, there is more implied in what I said, you see. I was telling you that you had beautiful eyes." She looked at him, the playfulness disappearing from her face.

Erasmus leaned forward slowly, and they met halfway, kissing tentatively. A smile lit Anna's face—a bit smug, Erasmus thought, and then she moved closer to him.

She whispered something to him in another language.

"What's that?"

"'My heart lifts like a water lily rising from the depths.' It is far more beautiful in Darian."

"There is love poetry in Darian?"

"Oh, yes. The mages had a book of lore and history and poems. It was called *Owl Songs*, though we have only fragments of it now. So much has been lost over the years of secrecy."

"Lost how?"

"Too much has always been trusted to the minds of my brothers and sisters—for the written word can give one away. But over centuries people die unexpectedly, and knowledge is lost before it is passed on. So our powers dwindle, and what we learn anew does not compensate."

"And the seed? Did Rose not say that Teller had seed? What became of it?"

She shook her head, close beside his own. "We had so little, and the secrets of cultivation were lost, or the seed, which is treacherous, betrayed us. It has been gone now for many years. We have failed in our endeavor. There was some hope that you might be our new Teller, Erasmus—that you might renew us—but you are here, trapped like the rest of us." She pushed herself closer to him, seeking contact.

"I was nothing but a lure set out to tempt you." He closed his eyes, seeing poor Percy staggering toward him, his terrified face enveloped in flame. It occurred to him that this was what the church did to heretics. "I had no other purpose."

*I have always felt cut adrift*, he thought. *As though my purpose was kept secret from me. All the years I sought to understand why Eldrich had taken me into his house, I never suspected the truth.*

"But you have a purpose now," she said, her fingers cool on his face, touching him as though she were without sight and wanted to know him. "Escape from Eldrich's trap. Escape, ultimately, from Eldrich. We have ways of hiding ourselves. We can slip away, as long as he believes, at least briefly, that we are dead." Her fingers traced his brow. Erasmus closed his eyes and felt her touch, cool and gentle on his skin.

Erasmus felt the unreality of the moment touch him. "I can never escape him," he said. "You don't know. Eldrich lets no one go. He would find me. Even if he had no further use for me, he would never let me escape."

She pulled him very close to her.

"But Eldrich does not plan to live in this world much longer. There is a reason he has sacrificed seven. He hopes to open the way one more time and slip through. That is his plan, I'm sure. If we can escape, we will strand him here. Eldrich will be trapped." Her voice seemed very hard suddenly. "I am not as kind a person as I seem, for the idea of revenge seems sweet to me now. To strand Eldrich in this world he would escape, and trap the priest here, alone, in this netherworld. These are the thoughts that bring me comfort, the weapon I use to drive away despair. Only let me live to have revenge. If I could appeal to a higher power, that would be my prayer."

## ∽ Forty-Five

Erasmus lay looking up at the dome of the chamber, so like a star-filled sky that he could almost imagine that he had escaped to the world above. He drifted in and out of sleep, rising to clouded consciousness, sinking down into the depths of dream. They were all becoming more and more lethargic—all except Deacon Rose and, oddly, Clarendon.

Erasmus tried to force himself to the surface, back to consciousness, but a current took hold of him, spinning him slowly, pulling him down. Erasmus could feel the great chasm below him, leagues of dark, silent ocean—the place he would drift for eternity, tugged this way and that, half in dream. The cold of the limitless sea seeping into him. A world of cold blue.

He tried to call out, but no sound came.

*Swim*, he thought. *I must swim.*

Up, if only I could. . . .

Suddenly he was swimming, following a trail of bubbles that escaped his lips. Up, straining toward air and light. Starlight.

When he broke the surface Erasmus found himself sitting up, gasping for air, covered in a cold sweat.

"Flames," he whispered. "Bloody blood and flames."

He looked around. The others lay here and there about the chamber, their posture strange as though they'd collapsed and were too weak to arrange their limbs for comfort. Anna and Banks lay near the crypt, Rose between them and the *nance*. Hayes and Kehler sprawled by the door to the hallway, and Clarendon stood silently, staring at the wall as though reading what had been written there.

Erasmus forced himself up, his head throbbing. Vertigo gripped him, and he braced himself, waiting for it to pass. A moment later he made his way slowly to the stream that emerged from beneath the *nance*. He knelt down and drank from cupped hands.

*If only I were a fish*, he thought. *I could dive into this stream and find my way out, out to the sunlight.*

He moved across the chamber, staring down into the opening that drained the water from the font. Clarendon appeared beside him.

"Are you well, Mr. Flattery?"

Erasmus continued to watch the water spin down into darkness.

"Mr. Flattery?"

"How wide do you think this opening is, Randall?"

Clarendon stopped, considering. "More than a foot. A foot and a third? Perhaps as much as a half?"

"That's what I would guess." Erasmus glanced across the chamber to where Hayes and Kehler slept. He pitched his voice low so that anyone who might still be awake would not hear. "Can you pass through such an opening?"

"One not filled with water, certainly. I think you could yourself, Mr. Flattery, though it would not be comfortable, but even so, I think you could."

Erasmus nodded. He crouched down, examining the small trench that carried the water across the floor. "How could we not have seen this? Look, Randall—what if we were to take rubble from the collapsed tunnel and dam the flow of water? We could build up a small dam down this side of the channel, across it diagonally to the wall. Do you see what I mean? Force the water out onto the floor and into the hallway. There must be gaps among the fallen blocks of stone—enough for water to find its way—and beyond the chamber the floor of the tunnel slopes down." He looked back at the opening in the floor. "It might be hard to stop all the water, but if we could reduce it substantially we could explore this pathway. We have a rope. We could lower you. . . ."

Clarendon stared down into the darkness where the water disappeared. "And if our dam gave way?"

Yes, Erasmus thought, that was not impossible. He thought of the boy in flame. "I will chance it. It could hardly be a death worse than the one we live now."

Clarendon nodded once, then glanced over his shoulder. "Come away from here for a moment." He led Erasmus to the chamber's far end as though he would show him something. "But what of Rose?" he whispered. "He will not allow these Tellerites to escape—not if he can in any way prevent it. I'm not convinced he will even let us escape. Did you not say that he believes he is to be a witness? That somehow Eldrich will free him?"

"It is possible, yes."

"Then all he must do is wait, and somehow this unholy bargain between the church and the mages will be honored. Perhaps our own deaths are even necessary." He put a hand to his brow, suffering the same throbbing ache as everyone. Erasmus almost reached out a hand to steady him, but thought better of it. Clarendon was a proud man.

"I'm not certain your idea will work, Mr. Flattery—we have such poor material to make a dam—but it is our best hope and I feel we must try it." He cast his gaze once more across the chamber. "Leave Rose to me."

"But, Randall, certainly we can't . . ." Erasmus had almost said "murder the man," he was so unsure of anyone's judgment. They were becoming desperate.

"I will not harm him if it can be avoided, but I don't know how we can take him with us either. We shall see. I will speak to the others. I think Rose is watching us this moment, afraid that we'll find some way out. Perhaps your plan has already occurred to him, but he has said nothing. Leave it to me, Mr. Flattery."

Clarendon went to Hayes and Kehler and roused them gently, leading them off, still half-dazed, down the *Hallway of the Seven*, as they had learned it was called.

Erasmus wanted to examine the opening in the floor again to be sure his judgment was not wildly mistaken, but he didn't want to arouse the priest's suspicions. The man hardly seemed to sleep, and was always watching.

A spasm of abdominal cramping bent Erasmus double, and he lowered himself to the floor, resting his back against the writing on the wall. A cold sweat broke out across his brow again, and in spite of himself he moaned quietly. If they didn't get out soon, they would certainly be too weak. They might not have the strength to follow Erasmus' scheme as it was.

Some time later Erasmus had gone to the end of the hallway and was examining the rubble that had fallen, blocking their exit. Although massive blocks predominated, there would certainly be a quantity of smaller material, more or less suitable for their purposes. Getting it out without causing further collapse would be the problem. They would likely need several cubic feet of material, which would make a hole in the rubble large enough to be dangerous—or so he thought. He was no quarryman, after all.

As he stood there considering the possible problems, a sudden cursing and shouting came from the main chamber, then the sounds of a scuffle. He ran as best he could and arrived in time to find Kehler, Hayes, Clarendon, and Banks wrestling Rose to the ground, Anna standing near, making quick motions in the air before her.

"You must gag him quickly. . . . Banks!" she said.

A moment later Rose was thoroughly bound, both hand and foot, and a filthy handkerchief had been used to gag him cruelly.

The others were near to collapse from the effort, and Rose was glaring at them with a viciousness that Erasmus would not have thought possible of a priest.

Clarendon saw him coming and raised his hands. "Now, I know you did not agree to this, Mr. Flattery, but we do not trust this priest to let us go. If our plan works, and once we are all safely away, you may release him and make your way out together. We are sure he will do nothing to harm you for fear of Eldrich."

Erasmus had not been warned about this speech, but it made immediate sense. Better Rose did not think he was being left behind.

"Why would he fear Eldrich on my account? The mage trapped me here as well."

"That might be so, Mr. Flattery, and I cannot deny that Eldrich has dealt with you in the worst manner, but we all know mages have their own ideas of justice and do not brook interference. I think this priest knows enough of Eldrich that he will not dare interfere with you."

Erasmus glanced at Deacon Rose, wondering if he believed this act, though Clarendon, at least, was quite convincing.

"I haven't the strength to argue," Erasmus said resignedly, having no difficulty finding the right tone, for he truly was exhausted. "We must be sure to let him drink, and to do him no harm. But let us get on with our task, while we have some strength left."

No one had imagined how arduous an endeavor they had taken on. Removing material from the collapsed passage proved both more difficult and more dangerous than expected, and the rocks and smaller fragments that they could get free made only an indifferent dam. Water poured through it as through a sieve, and though its flow was reduced, it was not reduced enough that anyone would dare the opening.

Exhaustion and hunger wore away at what little strength they had, and reduced them to taking longer and longer rests between trips to their quarry. Erasmus did not like the looks in the eyes of any of them, for he could see the doubt there—doubt that they could accomplish the task at all. And if they did, who would have the strength left to crawl down into this tiny passage that they all knew would steal their strength away in fifty feet?

Their labors drove them all to consume quantities of water, but no amount of water was a substitute for food, and they were all soon so exhausted that a few moments of effort were followed by many more of recovery—and occasionally one of them would fall into a sleep that could not be fended off.

*If we had only come in here with our reserves undiminished*, Erasmus thought, *but the journey through the cave taxed us all more than we expected.*

Anna emerged from the tunnel carrying a boulder the size of a skull—not such a burden really, but she struggled with it as though it were a hundred-weight.

"Is this any use?" she asked, nearly dropping the rock to the floor, and then sinking down beside it.

"I'm sure it is," Erasmus said, putting a hand on her shoulder. "Rest a moment," he said. "We must pace ourselves if we are to succeed."

She looked down at the stream of water that found its way through their makeshift obstruction, and Erasmus thought she might begin to cry.

"Clay is what we need," he said quietly. "Something to fill all the crevices." The problem of engineering their dam had fallen to him, and he did the best he could with it, while trying to keep up a brave face, which was the harder part.

Kehler and Hayes had proven themselves adept at extracting stone from the pile of rubble, and soon invented any number of dodges to shore up the pile while they pulled loose some stone. Every now and then they would stand back and heave rocks at the pillars they had made as braces and the pile would collapse again. Dangerous, Erasmus was certain, but no one had a better suggestion.

"How are they doing out there?"

Anna nodded. "Well enough. They have a bit of a stockpile waiting now. How much more do we need?"

Erasmus looked at their efforts. They had filled the channel for about three feet, but the dam was so porous that the water had not yet overflowed its banks. They had also built up a small dike along one side of the channel, but this would likely need more material if they ever succeeded in forcing the water to back up.

Anna pressed her hands to her eyes for a moment, and then forced herself up. She crossed the chamber stiffly and a moment later returned with a coat. "Try this," she said. "Perhaps it will stop up some of the holes."

Erasmus spread the coat over the inside of his dam. For a moment they waited, watching.

"It was a foolish idea, I suppose," Anna said.

"No, wait a moment yet. It is having some effect I think. And you've given me an idea. Kehler and Hayes dragged much of their gear in here. Did they not have oiled cotton bags?"

These were found, one split and laid in place, and they were rewarded by a noticeable backing of the waters.

They all stood watching the miracle, the water finally overflowing the banks of the channel. The low dams that were to direct the water away from the opening in the floor were only partly effective, but signs of success energized them all for a while. Two hours later a shallow pool of water covered the floor to one side of the channel and the *nance*, flowing slowly out into the hall and disappearing into the pile of rubble.

They all lay on the hard floor on the dry half of the chamber, unable to move, it seemed.

"We must not wait too long," Clarendon said, "for we cannot know how long the dam will hold."

Although several heads nodded, no one rose to begin their efforts. Hayes and Kehler were snoring.

They had consumed the last morsels of their food some hours earlier and Erasmus was now regularly seized by spasms of abdominal cramping that would last several minutes. He noticed that Banks suffered the same, though the others were less affected. He'd begun to wonder if he would make it out even if the passage proved viable.

Erasmus glanced over at the *nance*, with its macabre figures. What purpose did trapping them serve? Destroying the followers of Teller, clearly, but Eldrich could likely have done this less elaborately once they had revealed themselves. No, Erasmus was certain that Anna was right—they were a sacrifice. But was it that simple? Had they nothing more to do than die? It made so little sense. . . .

Rose squirmed around on the floor near the door to the crypt, and this prompted Clarendon to rise and check the man's bindings. They let him drink by soaking the handkerchief used as a gag, for Anna and Banks were afraid to let the man speak, which seemed to indicate that Rose might have more skill in the arts than Erasmus had believed. Not enough to loosen his ties, apparently.

As much as Erasmus knew Clarendon was right, he felt sleep drawing him down, into the infinite blue, at the mercy of currents and undertows and up-wellings.

Something brought him to the surface, though he could not say what. A strange warmth and tingling, almost luxurious, as though he had just had love. As though he had never gone into that hard, lightless place inside the earth, far beneath the roots of the great trees that bathed in sunlight.

His vision would not quite clear. Light, pale and cool. Starlight. He could hear a mumbling, almost singsong chant. And then—there—Anna standing beneath the masked figures. What was she doing? Erasmus tried to move his head for a better view, but he could not.

*I'm dreaming*, he told himself, for often, in his dreams he was frozen, immobile.

But then he heard Anna speak, her voice cracking and almost overcome with exhaustion. "Teller be praised," she whispered, "I've done it. . . ."

Erasmus tried to speak, but only a hoarse breath escaped him. Anna came down from the *nance*, Banks rushing to support her, comfort her.

Someone else was trying to speak. Erasmus could hear strange, gargling vowels, cursing.

And then the sea took hold of him again, rocking him on its gently lifting breast beneath a star-scattered sky.

"Mr. Flattery?"

Someone shook him from his sleep, from his drifting toward darkness. Clarendon.

"They've gone, sir."

"Wha . . . ? Who's gone?" He propped himself up on an elbow, somehow surprised to find himself still in the chamber.

"Anna and Banks, sir."

Erasmus came fully awake, though his mind could not quite escape the dream-fog. He looked across the chamber. Their dam still held, the mirror-calm pond spreading across the floor. Then he noticed the rope knotted around one of the urns on the *nance* and leading to the opening in the floor.

"When?"

"Just a moment ago, I think," Clarendon said, putting a hand to his head. "I watched but could not move. I—I'm not certain our sleep was quite natural." He shook his head, pressing his eyes closed in apparent pain.

Hayes stirred nearby, moaning. And Rose, Erasmus realized, was wide awake, his eyes wide with frustration and rage.

"Why did they go without us?"

Clarendon helped him to his feet. "One of the urns on the *nance* is opened, Mr. Flattery. It would seem clear that they managed to break the charm and fled with the contents. King's blood? Is that what you called it?"

Erasmus nodded.

Rose began to make a terrible choking noise, writhing on the floor. In an instant Erasmus and Clarendon had his gag off and were pounding him on the back.

For a moment Erasmus thought they would have to bear the responsibility of the man's death, but then he managed to catch a breath, and then another.

"They took the seed," Rose said, his voice only a hoarse whisper. "Water . . . Please . . . Water."

Erasmus untied the man's legs and they bore him up, supporting him for a moment on weak limbs, then led him to the dammed stream and lowered him to where he could drink his fill, slurping up the water like an animal.

"I'm not sure he will harm us now," Erasmus said. "It must be clear to him that Kehler and Hayes are not in league with the Tellerites." The priest's condition was causing him some guilt.

Clarendon hesitated, and then nodded once and addressed himself to the knots that held Rose's hands behind his back. Free, the priest staggered to his feet, and before either Erasmus or Clarendon could move, Rose threw himself at the dam, breaking it down with his weight and the force of his lunge.

Water flooded through the gap, taking parts of the dam with it, filling the channel, and swirling down the opening. Erasmus and Clarendon leapt to save the ruins of their effort, dragging the priest out of the mess, not without a few cuffs, shoving him rudely aside. Erasmus struggled into the rapidly dissolving dam, grabbing for the oiled bags that had held the water back. Without them they had no chance of rebuilding, though Erasmus wondered where they would find the reserves to perform such labor again.

Hayes and Kehler came up, wading into the rapidly receding lake, pulling out the stones they had collected at such cost, glaring at Rose, who knelt in the shallow pool, his eyes cast down, perhaps in prayer.

"I could not let them escape," he said, meeting no one's eye. "You do not realize what you would have set loose on the world. These Tellerites, they appeared to be the most gentle of people, but they are ruthless. Do not doubt it. They will stop at nothing to achieve their goal. And now two of them are free, and they have the cursed seed. You do not realize what that means, but it will give them power, a hundredfold. Our only hope now is that they have drowned, or that the passage does not take them to the surface. Only Eldrich can stop them otherwise. Once that trollop has begun to take the. . . ."

Clarendon hurled a rock at the man, and dodging it ended his tirade. No one wanted to hear the priest's rantings. All they could think of was that their only hope—the only possibility of escape—had been closed, and no one knew if they had the strength to open it again.

"There's nothing we can do until the water has all drained away," Erasmus said, looking at the currents that now flowed toward the opening in the floor. They would defeat any efforts they made. The water might only be three inches deep over the floor of the chamber, but that added up to substantial volume, and now it was all running toward the opening. They struggled to preserve what was left of their efforts.

Rose retreated toward the hallway, wading across the pond, and disappeared through the archway. This left Hayes and Kehler free to curse him, which they did with a passion.

An hour later the floor of the chamber was rapidly drying, only a few small puddles remaining. The group collected on the steps of the *nance*, staring at the destruction Rose had caused.

"It will not be so bad this time," Erasmus offered. "We have no need to collect or carry stone from the tunnel and this time I need make no experiments in dam construction. We know what needs to be done. It shouldn't take us three hours working together. And the result will be stronger, I'm sure."

"But what of Rose?" Kehler asked. "Will we leave the man behind? There is no trusting him, that is certain. I for one won't go easily down into that hole thinking that the priest will send a stream of water down to drown me."

The others nodded agreement. There was no sympathy for the priest at that moment, but nor were they certain they could subdue him again, now that they would have no element of surprise.

"I don't know what to do about Rose," Erasmus said. "Let us rebuild the dam and guard it carefully. That is all we can do. That, or give up and die, and I, for one, will not give up."

They began again, working more slowly this time, but as Erasmus had said, experience informed their efforts and the dam began to take shape, despite their exhaustion. Clarendon and Erasmus made the younger men pace themselves reasonably, and they all took frequent rests, at which they were too drained to speak, but sat with their heads hanging like beaten men.

But they were not defeated yet. Perhaps eight hours passed in this labor, and finally the water rose so that only a trickle found its way into the opening in the floor.

Clarendon argued with Erasmus about who would go down into the shaft first, and Hayes and Kehler lent their support to the small man, forcing Erasmus to concede, though he did not do so easily. Anna and Banks had managed it and though she was slim and likely more flexible than the men, Banks was of normal size—at least as big as Hayes and Kehler, though not so large as Erasmus.

The small man went down into the hole in the floor, holding tightly to the rope, scrabbling with his feet for purchase on the passage walls. Watching him go, Erasmus realized that he had come to view Clarendon differently after their few days together. His small size was no longer the characteristic that stood out—his indomitable will had superseded that. The man had courage out of proportion to his size. And here, where many passages were so small, his size was a great advantage. Clarendon led the way and the rest followed.

"How does it seem, Randall?" Hayes asked, trying not to show his own fear of the tiny passage.

"Big enough, I think," Clarendon said, trying to look down, his voice distorting strangely up the shaft. He worked down a little farther. Erasmus could see that he was struggling, weakened by his labors. A trickle of water still made its way through the dam and this was enough to keep the shaft wet and soak the rope, making both slippery. He only hoped that it was not far to the bottom, for a fall was a real danger, and injury would leave Randall unable to climb up again. Against Erasmus' urging, Clarendon had refused to let them tie a line around his waist and lower him down. The passage was small enough that he went with one arm down and the other stretched over his head, which could make it impossible to release a knot if it became necessary. Either way there was risk, and in their desperate state Clarendon had made the more courageous decision—though not the one with the least risk.

Clarendon's feet slipped suddenly, and his hand skidded on the rope before he checked his fall. Erasmus could hear his harsh breathing. They were all so frightfully weak. . . .

"How do you go, Randall?"

He saw the small man's head nod, though he spared no breath for speech. The size of the passage made it dreadfully difficult because it was all but impossible to look down and there was no way to carry a lantern. Clarendon had gone about ten feet now and already he was losing the light from the chamber. Soon he would be in utter blackness.

"You're all right, Randall?"

A grunt in response.

They should have sounded the shaft first, Erasmus realized. It would have been easy to do, but their wits were so clouded.

Fifteen feet now. The rope had originally been a hundred feet, but a section had been cut off to bind the priest.

Twenty feet.

If Clarendon slipped, how far would he fall? No one knew. It could be ten feet to the bottom, it could be a hundred. The small man was only just visible, but from the sounds Erasmus could tell that he was laboring cruelly.

*Don't fall*, Erasmus willed him. *Please don't fall.*

"Randall? Are you bearing up?"

"Well enough." The terse reply funneled up the shaft.

Forty feet.

They could hear Clarendon gasping for breath now. His strength was fading fast, and they all knew that in their exhausted state there were no reserves to call upon. One could not force one's strength to hold that moment longer. When it gave out, it did so immediately and without recourse.

*Hold tight.*

Forty-five feet.

"Flames!" Clarendon swore. "Thank Farrelle."

"Randall!" Are you all right?"

"Yes," came his tired voice though the relief was clear. "I found a little ledge for my feet and just in time. If this shaft tightens down to nothing at the bottom, I don't know how I'll get up again."

Erasmus did not like to think that Clarendon might come down upon the drowned corpses of Anna and Banks. "We'll draw you up, Randall, don't you worry. Is there any sign of the bottom?"

"I'm in the dark, here, Mr. Flattery. It could be ten feet or ten miles, there is no way to be sure. Let me rest a moment, and then I'll press on."

It was a long moment, which worried the others, for not only was Randall tiring quickly, but it did not bode well for them when their own turns came.

"Randall?" Erasmus said when his concern would let him wait no longer. "Can you go on?"

"Yes, Mr. Flattery. Best to rest while I can when the bottom is some unknown distance away."

Hayes glanced at Kehler, the meaning clear. They all worried that they would not be strong enough to make their way out.

Erasmus ran his eye over their dam, which so far appeared to be holding, but it was yet another cause for concern. They had been tending to it regularly, and how would the last man down manage that?

"Mr. Flattery? I'm going to go on," Clarendon called up, though he did not sound confident, as though he realized that no amount of rest would restore him to any greater degree.

"Take care, Randall."

Almost immediately they heard the small man's breathing grow harsh and quick, partly from fear, they were sure. They could not see him now, but marked his progress only by the sounds. The dull scrape of boots and the rasp of his clothing against the too smooth stone.

"How far is he?" Kehler whispered.

Erasmus shook his head. "Sixty feet? More? I cannot say. Light the lantern, Hayes, and we'll see if we can cast some light down to him. It might bring him comfort at least, even if it does him no real good.

"Randall? How goes it?"

"I cannot hold much longer," he said, his voice surprisingly calm, though very small.

Hayes jumped to light the lantern, fumbling with the flint, as though light would make a difference. They could hear Clarendon's breath coming in short, quick gasps now. And then suddenly, unmistakably, the sounds of him falling, and then, only a second later, silence.

"Randall?!" No response. "Randall?"

"I seem to be down," they heard the small man say.

"Are you injured?"

"No . . . not so much. I have wrenched my knee cruelly, but nothing seems to be broken. The passage turns here. Give me a minute."

They waited. Hayes lifted the lantern over the opening, and cast its dim light down into the darkness. They could make out something, perhaps Clarendon's fringe of white hair. Movement. Erasmus thought it might be a hand waving.

"Mr. Flattery? Can you send down the lantern?"

Quickly, Hayes hauled the rope up, and the lantern was sent down more slowly, care being taken not to shatter it against the stone. Finally Clarendon appeared in the descending illumination, though, still, he could not be clearly seen. He released the lamp from the rope, and then began to wriggle, painfully, disappearing from view.

The next minutes crept so slowly by that the others began to worry that something had gone wrong—Clarendon had passed out, or fallen again.

"Perhaps one of us should go down," Hayes said. "I will do it," he offered, showing his character, for surely none of them wanted to attempt this difficult descent less than he.

"A moment more," Erasmus said. He glanced around at a sound and there, by the door to the hallway, stood the priest, watching. For a moment Erasmus met the man's stare, but then turned slowly back to the opening in the floor.

Hayes and Kehler looked at Erasmus expectantly, clearly wanting him to make a decision. He took a deep breath. "As things stand," he said, "the three of us can likely draw Randall up again if the passage goes nowhere, but if one of us goes down after him, I don't think that the two who remain will have the strength to bring anyone up. We must wait, I fear, although Randall might be in danger, until we are all but sure he will not return."

They stared down into the darkness of the shaft, wondering if this pit offered any hope at all.

A splash behind him caused Erasmus to whirl, and there stood the priest, only a few feet away.

"Stay away from this dam!" Erasmus ordered, and Hayes put himself quickly between the dam and Rose.

"You need have no fear," the priest said. "The Tellerites alone were my concern. Even Kehler's betrayal of trust is of little matter, now. . . ."

"As though we would take you at your word, priest," Kehler spat out.

"But what I say is true, nonetheless," Rose said, his voice so utterly reasonable, that even after what he'd done, he made Erasmus feel as though they were persecuting him. "And besides, I can help you. As Mr. Flattery knows, I have spent some little time wandering in the hills and mountains. I know how we can all descend safely, and if need be I can help draw a man up. I will tell you honestly, that I no more wish to die in this foul place than do you."

"You want to pursue the Tellerites, if they survived your attempt to drown them," Hayes said.

"I wish to live, Mr. Hayes, just as you do."

Just then a dim light appeared at the shaft's bottom, and then the lantern appeared, followed by Clarendon's too white face.

"Mr. Flattery?" he called up in a thin voice. "It goes. . . ."

Erasmus felt Hayes clap him on the back, such relief on the young man's face that Erasmus thought tears might appear.

"What could you see, Randall?"

"Only a small passage with a stream running in it. Very wet, but hopeful. All the hope we have at least. It might come to nothing in a hundred feet. Perhaps only one more should come down so that we can explore. I'm a bit crooked, I think—this leg . . ."

"Who will go?" Kehler asked.

"Either you or Hayes," Erasmus said, knowing he must stay to watch Rose. "Whoever feels stronger."

The two candidates looked at each other, and then Hayes spoke up. "I feel quite recovered," he lied. "Let's get on with it. I fear Mr. Clarendon's injury could be more serious than he is saying."

Rose took a step forward, and everyone glared at him, which stopped him in his tracks. "I can make your descent much safer, Mr. Hayes, if you will allow me."

Erasmus looked at Hayes and nodded. He did not trust the priest at all, but he was quite sure the priest badly wanted to know if the Tellerites lived, and would pursue them if so, and that made it unlikely that he would try to destroy the dam again.

"If this is treachery, Deacon," Kehler said, "I swear, I will throttle you myself."

Rose did not respond, nor did he show anger, but only looked down at the floor—the posture of a man unjustly persecuted by his fellows. He stepped forward, his manner humble, his voice as reasonable as ever. "It is a simple thing, Mr. Hayes. Sit here, on the rim. Now take a turn of the rope around your boot and then hold it in your left hand. Yes, like that. There will be enough friction that you can control your speed easily—but you must keep your leg utterly straight and never let the pressure off, or the loop might come off your foot. If you feel it running off toward your toe, point your toe down a little. With your other hand, grasp the rope above your head. That's it. You should have no trouble, but have Mr. Clarendon move to safety, all the same."

"I am clear," came Clarendon's voice up the shaft, for clearly he heard every word.

Hayes let himself over the edge, letting the rope run jerkily through his hands.

"Good, good. That's it," Rose coached. "Try to let it run more smoothly, and then stop every few feet, for you will certainly burn your hand if you go too quickly and then you risk losing control of your descent entirely."

"Are you all right, Hayes?" Kehler asked.

"Yes. . . . This works well enough, though I fear I'm sawing my poor foot in two. Better than falling to the bottom, though."

They watched him make his slow descent, the rope hissing slightly at each drop, until he disappeared into the darkness. Every few moments they called down and he answered, and then, unexpectedly he was at the bottom.

"It is easier than a stair," he called up, a bit of laughter in his voice. They heard him speaking then but could not make out his words. "Erasmus? I will go on and have a look at this passage and see where it might go. If it appears to go some distance or branch, I will come back and you can follow. The dam is holding, I take it?"

"Yes, but go with care, Hayes," Kehler called down.

The men remaining retreated to the steps of the *nance*, for the entire floor had some water on it now, and here they collapsed, Kehler clearly fighting to stay awake, not wanting to leave the priest unwatched, Erasmus thought.

But try as they might, sleep would not be denied, and one by one they slipped into troubled dreams, dreams in which food figured largely.

Erasmus awoke when someone shook him, and found Kehler doubled over on the stair, his eyes dark, his face somehow seeming years older. "I heard a call," he said.

Erasmus started up, his wits still fogged. Rose awakened as well, looking around as though unsure of where he was. Immediately Erasmus went to the well.

"Hayes?" he called down.

"Ah, there you are. I thought you had all expired or escaped some other way. I cannot tell how far it goes, but some distance at least. There is a falls that will have to be negotiated, and once we've done that I doubt we'll get back up again, but I think we should chance it. Is there any way you can bring the rope with you? It would make the falls less treacherous, I'm certain."

"I don't know, Hayes. You've been down the shaft. Can one of us climb it without the rope?"

The hesitation was answer enough. "No. . . . I don't think you should try it. No, we'd be better to take our chances with the falls."

"How is Randall?"

"Injured. More than he is letting on, that is certain. He will need all the help we can provide. Fortunately much of it is crawling, which he seems more able to do. Are you coming now?"

"Yes. As soon as we've looked over our remaining gear to see if there is anything to bring. Stay where you are a moment and we will lower down our last tin of lamp oil and the few candles."

Light, Erasmus knew, would be their greatest problem. Once the lamp oil ran dry they would be forced to use candles—and even if they could keep them lit in the wet passage Hayes described, there were only a handful. Kehler had done an estimate and thought they might have eight hours of light—no more. It was fortunate that Anna and Banks had not taken all they had.

Once the few things had been sent down, Kehler took his place on the edge of the shaft, and following Rose's instruction, let himself down. Having the example of Hayes no doubt helped, for he went easily down without mishap, touching the bottom in no time.

Erasmus looked around for Rose and found the man carrying a large stone across the pool.

"I don't know if it will work, Mr. Flattery, but if we can jam a stone tightly in the channel and set it upon small rocks so there is a space beneath it, then we can wrap the rope around it. It will be doubled then, and may not reach the bottom, but, with Farrelle's help, we may be able to bring it down after us by hauling on one end. But first you go down as it is, and I will come after and try to bring the rope."

"But if this stone does not lodge properly, Deacon, you might bring it down on top of you."

Rose looked up sharply at Erasmus. "But will that not be the best of all possible worlds, Mr. Flattery? You'll be rid of me, and have the rope as well. Do not concern yourself with my welfare, but get yourself down unharmed and quickly. We have light for a few hours only, and once that is gone, the chances of us finding our way out are . . . Well, only Farrelle can help us in that event. On with you, sir. Just as I've shown the others."

Erasmus went down into the black well, lowering himself with the rope around his foot, water trickling down his neck as he went, running coldly down his back and chest. He hoped his ruined boot would stand up to the rope abrading it, for his chances of getting out of the cave barefoot would be slim. A broken foot or toe down here could mean disaster. Which made his concern for Clarendon all the greater.

For the first time in days Erasmus felt his hopes rise, even as he slipped down the shaft into the passage below. If only his strength would hold. Even using Rose's method for descending, he felt completely spent when he finally struck bottom, stopping with a jar that sent hot pain shooting up his back.

"Erasmus?" It was Hayes. There was some light around his feet, he realized. Erasmus stood in the tiny well, for he could do nothing else, leaning his head against the wet stone, the pain in his back so severe that he did not dare move.

"Erasmus?"

"Yes," he said through clenched teeth.

"You must come out feet first. It is a bit of a trick to get oneself into the passage and then turned over, but once done, it is no more than ten or twelve yards out into the larger passage. Light will do you no good, I'm afraid. Can you manage it? You're not too fatigued?"

"I'll manage," Erasmus said, not certain that he would. The thought of getting down into another cramped little passage had little appeal to him, but standing here waiting for the dam to burst and water to flood down was even worse. If the pain would just stop. He waited a moment more, the pain slowly ebbing, though not disappearing entirely.

"Mr. Flattery?" Rose called down, his voice echoing loudly in the well. "Are you clear? May I come down?"

"A moment."

Slowly Erasmus lowered himself, trying to slip his legs into the bending passage. For a moment he thought he was lodged and would have to try to pull himself up. Panic set in, and he cursed loudly. He was taller than Hayes and perhaps could not fit.

So frustrated and frightened was he that he felt tears sting his eyes, but then with a thrust he forced himself through, tearing the skin off his shins and knees. He slipped down into the passage that ran only slightly down, slopping about in the stream of water. He realized that if Rose released the dam now, in his weakened state he would certainly drown.

*He will do no such thing*, Erasmus told himself, but even the thought of it was almost unbearable. This was not the place he wanted to die.

Forcing himself to move, he began the painful crawl out, more difficult for it being feet first. He seemed to be inching along for hours, stopping to rest after every effort, each attempt carrying him a shorter distance, until he was resting every few inches. For some moments he actually fell asleep, one side of his face resting in the cold stream. Clarendon's voice called him back and the horror of what he wakened to drove him on again. Finally he felt hands take hold of his ankles and they drew him slowly out.

The passage he emerged into was small—not a yard high and perhaps half again as wide, but it seemed enormous after what he'd been through. He found his friends, sprawled in the water, too exhausted even to try to keep dry. Kehler and Clarendon were shivering, which did not bode well. They looked frightened and despairing, as though they had not really escaped at all, but had come from a place well-lit and dry, to this. A passage that they all knew would likely flood if there was a rain storm above. After the enchanted light of the chamber, the lamplight was pitiful, Erasmus thought, and it seemed to exaggerate the haunted looks on the faces of the others.

The passage sloped at an angle of some twenty-five degrees, water tumbling down it into a series of pools, one of which they all sat in now. Below them the passage extended the few yards the lantern illuminated, looking much the same.

"So this is our salvation," Erasmus said, but no one answered.

Erasmus leaned his head back into the dark tunnel and called up. "Deacon Rose? You must hurry. We are wet and cold and must go on quickly. Deacon Rose, can you hear?"

From far off a distorted, macabre voice echoed to him, the words incomprehensible. Erasmus thought he was hearing a voice from another world.

"How far to this falls, Hayes?" He did not really care but felt he had to bring some focus to this group, who looked more defeated than at any other time.

"Not far," Hayes said softly. "Fifteen minutes."

"Might I see your knee, Randall?"

Clarendon nodded, shifting slightly, which caused him to wince. The small man managed to prop himself up against the wall so that his knee came clear of the water. Hayes moved the lantern to give better light.

Clarendon's breeches had been slit, and the knee was blue and already badly swollen.

"Can you put weight on it at all?" Erasmus asked, his tone solicitous.

"I don't know, Mr. Flattery. Perhaps if I could get started on it and work past the pain. But don't you worry, I will go on one leg and two hands if I must. Or on my belly if need be, but I will not stay here."

"Well, a physician would recommend you bathe it in cold water and elevate it, but I think we can only manage one of those. But as for the rest of us, we should try to get up out of this water or it will sap away what little strength we have. Is there nowhere we might sit up on dry stone?"

"Down the passage," Hayes said, gesturing.

"Then let us go there, and I will come back with the lantern for the priest. Come along. Except for Randall's knee, we must try to get dry. We'll huddle together for warmth. Up with you." He took the lantern from Hayes, trying to hide the pain shooting up his back. Fortunately Hayes and Kehler helped Clarendon, for Erasmus was certain his back would not allow it, and they made their slow, painful way down the passage.

Erasmus had to rest for a moment before starting back, and when he got there Rose was calling, convinced he had been left behind in the dark. The truth was that Erasmus would have been tempted to do so, but with a little luck, the priest was bringing the rope, which they might well need. And the priest seemed to have retained more of his strength than the others, for he had spent none of it building the dam. He also possessed skills from his climbing outings that they might require. It was a sad irony that now they might need the man.

"Deacon Rose? Are you down?"

"Ah, there you are, Mr. Flattery. I thought you'd . . . all been swept away. Have I far to come?"

"Have you negotiated the corner? Then it is not too far. Did you manage to bring the rope?"

"I have it."

"Well done!" Erasmus thought they might have to forgive the man if he managed another miracle like that one, though he suspected the others would not agree.

A few moments later the priest emerged, clutching the end of the rope. He quickly drew it out, coiling it in shaky hands, and dropping the coil over his shoulder. With a nod to Erasmus they set out, half-crawling, half-slithering from one pool to the next.

In a moment they found the others, huddled in the dark. Erasmus could not remember seeing a more sorry company. Filthy and shivering, their eyes sunken and haunted. He thought then that if the surface was not very near they would never make it. They had used the last of their reserves to get to this place—a worse grave than the one they'd escaped.

"Can you go on?" he asked, afraid the answer might be "no," but they all nodded.

And so they went, slowly, taking turns to carry the lantern and bundle of candles, for they were so weak that any weight quickly became more than one could bear. Rose assisted Clarendon, whose condition was far worse than Erasmus had hoped, and Clarendon accepted the help, desperation having replaced pride. Every hundred feet they stopped to rest, Erasmus choosing a place where they could sprawl out of the water, though it hardly mattered, they were all so wet and cold that they shivered uncontrollably, barely able to master their limbs.

Erasmus did not speak his fear that this passage would continue down and down until it ended in a pool, and that would be their final resting place. As they went, he searched the walls for openings, hoping to find a passage that might lead them off in a more likely direction, but only one passage was found and it was filled with flowing water, which swelled the stream they waded through and made the going more difficult.

They came to the falls Kehler had mentioned and rigged the rope as a hand line. It was not really so steep, perhaps forty degrees, but more water seemed to be flowing here and they had so little strength.

They went down one at a time to save the rope, which Erasmus was beginning to distrust—it had been severely strained and wet now for days. Rot would have set in and weakened it.

Clarendon had to make his way down alone, clinging to the rope, sliding on his seat, buffeted by the current, gasping for breath. Twice his hands slipped on the slick line and he slid, crashing down on the rock, but both times he recovered before another could go to his aid. They all came down with only minor injuries, but were soaked again and had expended too much of their already reduced resources.

They rested, no one speaking, all hanging their heads, mouths agape, as though they had no strength to spare to keep them closed and no concern for appearances.

"On," Rose said over the sounds of the running water. "We must go on."

No one even nodded agreement, but Kehler pushed himself up, and staggered down into the next pool, Hayes following, and then the others. At least the passage had opened up so that they could walk upright, but Erasmus had examined the walls as they went and was sure, from the signs of scouring, that water ran at all heights here at different times of the year. Even a passage this size could be flooded. Spring rain, not an uncommon thing, could be their end.

The slope was less, now, allowing them easier passage, but even so, the stops were more frequent and longer. The lantern had been turned down to save fuel and the darkly orange flame cast the faintest light through the smoke-stained glass. Erasmus shook the lamp gently, and despaired to hear the tiny swish of oil within. It would not last the hour, he was certain.

Hayes looked up at him, and grimaced, as though telling Erasmus that he knew the truth. They would not find their way out—even if there was a passage they could hardly go another hundred yards. Both Kehler and Clarendon had begun to shiver with such violence that the others crowded around them and they held the lantern close to capture its almost inconsequential heat. They stayed like that for over an hour, turning occasionally to warm their exposed sides, no one speaking. The truth was there was little warmth in their frames to share, but eventually there was some small improvement. Food was what they needed, for they were traveling on nothing but willpower and desperation.

The lamp flickered suddenly, and Hayes produced a candle, lighting it from the shrinking flame. A moment they all watched, and then the thin little flame guttered inside the glass, brightened for an instant, wavered, and disappeared in a sigh of smoke.

More than one of them drew a quick breath, as though they had been holding their breath. There was silence, the small flame of the candle flickering, barely lighting the walls a few feet away.

The sounds of their rough breathing were like words—the language of despair and fear. The last flicker of their hope had gone, Erasmus realized. They would sit here until they died of exposure. Shivering out their last reserves in darkness.

"I think we will need to light a second candle," Clarendon said, his voice thin and a bit shaky yet. "If that one goes out, we will never use a flint in these conditions." The others nodded, though all knew this would mean they would have light for only half as long. Better light for a shorter time than none at all.

They still huddled around the lantern, drawing the last embers of heat from it, and then Erasmus took it and removed the glass chimney. With great care he cleaned this with his shirt, and then did the same to the bronze fitting where the wick emerged. Using a knife to bend the thin metal, he wedged a candle into this with difficulty, for his cleaning had not removed the residue of oil and wax did not stick so well. Lighting the candle, he replaced the glass and held this aloft, swinging it from side to side to see the effect. The flame wavered a little but held.

"Ah, Mr. Flattery," Clarendon said. "That will brighten our future, and extend our hours of light." He tried to make his voice steady, and push back the despondency in his tone.

They smothered the other candle and put it away, risking going on with one, knowing that if it went out, they would be consigned to darkness, which would much reduce their chances of escape. How easy it would be to be injured or to pass by openings in the dark.

With their candle lantern held aloft, they set out along the passage. Clarendon, bringing up the rear with Rose, spotted a small opening that the others had missed, which concerned Erasmus. How many others had they passed by? Kehler volunteered to explore it, and crawled in with the light, leaving the others to sit in the darkness, imagining an opening to the soft world above. Barely able to let themselves hope. A few moments later Kehler emerged, saying nothing, only shaking his head when he saw the others staring at him. Perhaps the hope on their faces stole his voice.

They let Kehler rest a moment and then went on, needing to pause within fifty feet. Then on again.

Suddenly Hayes, who was leading the way with the lantern stopped, bent over a pool. He reached out tentatively, and then drew his hand back.

"What . . . ?" But Erasmus saw what it was. "Banks?" he said, and Hayes nodded.

"Yes, though one would hardly know it. Look how battered he is."

They all stood staring, no one even glancing at Rose, for they could not bear to see the satisfaction that was, no doubt, written on the man's face. They body floated heavily in the pool, the skin white and swollen where it was not purple with wounds.

"He has been swept down here from much higher up," Erasmus said. "That is why he is so battered." He did look up at Rose then. "You should be proud, Deacon, no doubt your flood drowned him in the first tunnel. Likely we will find Miss Fielding not much farther on."

Erasmus had barely thought of her since they had begun rebuilding the dam, but now he felt an odd sensation. Was she dead, too, lying facedown in a pool, her faded gold-red hair streaming in the current?

Hayes handed the lantern to Erasmus and bent to rummage through the body, hoping to find candles, or anything they might use, but he found nothing.

"There is no seed?" Rose asked.

Hayes shrugged. "Search him yourself, Deacon," he said, and turned away, moving off a few steps.

The priest bent quickly over the man, searching him, and then he made a sign to Farrelle in the air, muttering some words that Erasmus was not sure were last rites.

They stumbled down the passage, a vision of death traveling with them. It was no mystery now. That is what they would become if they could not find a way out. It stunned them into silence, and both drove them forward and filled them with despair.

A second candle was wedged into the lantern as the first burnt down to a stub. Erasmus estimated that they had two hours and a little more from that candle—not very long—and they had only five more. A dozen hours of light, at most. And then they would be left wandering in the darkness—just as some myths of the netherworld described. But not wandering endlessly.

Down they went again, descending a small falls that left them all sprawled on the rock, gasping, their heads spinning from the effort. One more such obstacle and that would be the end of Clarendon, Erasmus was certain. The poor man had to expend so much more energy to move, and he was in constant agony now. It was written on his face. Even Hayes looked as though he would soon give up.

The passage had opened up considerably, until the ceiling was almost twenty feet over their heads and the walls almost as far apart. A torrent of water plunged down this in rapids, swirling into pools. Erasmus was not certain why the volume of water was so great. Either it rained in the world above and this had swollen the underground streams, or hidden passages added their water to the flow—he suspected it was the latter. Either way it made progress more difficult, and certainly more treacherous. But the increase in the passage size seemed a good sign to them and raised their spirits a little. At least they were not crawling through tiny holes more fit for rodents than men.

They struggled on, assisting each other more often—taking turns providing encouragement, convincing the others to go on. A third candle went into the lantern, and they stopped for a long rest, most of them falling into an odd sleep, rousing every few moments, but unable to stay awake. Erasmus did not sleep but watched the irreplaceable candle burn too quickly down—wasting their invaluable light—but it could not be helped. The others had passed beyond the limits of their endurance.

When he had seated the fourth candle into the lantern, Erasmus roused the others, forcing them up, making them all drink. They were cold again, and shivered terribly, but there was no time to warm themselves. They had, at most, five hours of light, and once that was gone, they were all sure that no hope would remain.

Clarendon argued that they should explore on without him, and come back if they found a way to the surface, but the others would not even discuss it, but simply bore him up, and he was too weak to argue. They took turns helping him now, two at a time, and changed this duty frequently.

They came down a steep section of tumbling water, and at the bottom found what Erasmus had most dreaded—a pool. Both Hayes and Kehler cast themselves down on a rock, hiding their faces for they knew there was no way out, now.

"We could have died in the light, at least," Clarendon said, as Rose and Erasmus lowered him to a rock.

"I cannot believe that I have come so far at such cost only to end here," Hayes said. "Flames, I will go with a curse for Eldrich on my lips!" And he put his head in his hands and silent sobs shook his shoulders.

"What will we do now?" Clarendon said, taking up the task of providing hope. Or at least an example of resolution.

Erasmus looked at their candle, which had burned down to its final half inch. Only one remained. "I will take the lantern and go back up the passage. Perhaps there is an opening we missed."

The priest shook his head. "Five pairs of eyes searched as we descended, Mr. Flattery. Looking again will be of little use."

"Have you a better plan, then?"

Rose thought for a moment. "How high are we, do you think?"

Erasmus was taken aback by this. "Why do you ask?"

"There are openings into the lake that are only accessible at the low waters found in summer. Could this pool connect to the lake? Clearly the water must go somewhere."

This caught the attention of everyone and they fell to musing.

"I think we are above the lake by some distance yet," Clarendon said, his voice drawn taut by pain. "The chamber was above the Fairy Galleries and they are quite high up the hillside as it is. We have come down only a little more than halfway, I think."

Silence followed his words, and they all sat apart, shivering, thinking about the end, and the two hours of light that the last candle would bring. Erasmus picked up the lantern and walked along the edge of the pool, holding the light high so that it would penetrate to the farthest reaches of the chamber. His efforts only proved that the dark patches were shadows, and not openings as he hoped. Disheartened, he sat down again. There was no exit from this room except the way they had come. It was the end.

He stared down into the black waters where a few bubbles floated, caused by the water falling into the pool. They bobbed across the pool in a fan, disappearing as they went, so that only a few touched the far shore.

Erasmus stood suddenly, holding the lantern high again. "Have a look here," he said. "Do some of these bubbles seem to disappear, there, in the far wall? Is that another shadow or a small opening?" He pointed. "Do you see where I mean? Just in the center."

The others gathered about and Erasmus handed the lantern to Hayes and put his foot into the water, testing to see if there was a bottom. Taking the lantern back, he waded out into the water, which was almost immediately chest deep.

"It is an opening!" he called back. "Right at the surface. Flames, it is small." The bottom dropped off so that he could no longer walk, and Hayes plunged in after him and took the lantern, holding it up as best he could while Erasmus swam the few strokes to the far side.

The current here was far swifter than he expected and almost swept him into the opening. He grabbed the rock and felt inside with his hand, and then a foot.

"It is deep. No. I can touch the bottom, but just."

The current grabbed him but he hauled himself back by gripping the stone.

"I don't know if it has air in it for any distance. There is less than a foot clear just inside."

"Sailors say that drowning is painless," Rose said, "though I don't understand how they would know."

"It likely doesn't have air for far," Erasmus said, "but give me the end of the rope and I will explore what I can. I would rather die trying than huddling in the dark."

Erasmus swam back to the others and Rose knotted the rope about his waist.

"Your voice will likely be indistinct, Mr. Flattery, so call like this. Call 'out' once for more rope, and 'in, in' for us to draw you back. Your words will likely to be distorted, but we will be able to distinguish between one word and two."

"Will you take the lantern?" Hayes asked.

Clarendon nodded. "You must, Mr. Flattery. We will light the last candle and guard it here, while you take the lantern."

Erasmus considered this. The idea of going into darkness was terrifying, but he was sure the candle would be doused in a moment, for he would need both hands to make his way in the current.

"Keep it here, but hold it low to the water and I will have some light for the first few feet. It likely goes no further than that."

Erasmus went back into the cold water, knowing that he would lose his strength within minutes, so there was no time to spare. He forced his muscles to obey, floating quickly into the opening, grabbing the sides as he could, but carried swiftly in. He would never be able to swim out but would have to trust to the others and the rope.

The feeble light from the lantern disappeared in a moment and he was in darkness, trying to feel ahead of him in case the ceiling came down and knocked him senseless. His strength faded, and soon he was swept along, struggling to keep his mouth above the surface. And then suddenly the rope went taut, cutting into his middle.

"*In, in!*" he hollered. "In, in!" he shouted again. "Flames, I will die here in a moment."

There was a tug on the rope, and then a harder one that pulled his head under, but he pushed himself up, bracing his feet against the sides.

Bit by bit he was drawn out, scrabbling against the sides of the passage, fighting to keep his head above water. Many mouthfuls of water later he caught a glimpse of fitful light, and a moment later he was out in the pool again, and splashing across to the others.

"Does it go?" Hayes asked, wading out into the water and helping Erasmus to the shore.

"I—I don't know. There was air as far as I went, but beyond that I can't say. Certainly I could not have come back without your help."

They all looked at each other, Hayes and Kehler shaking their heads.

"It is a great risk," Clarendon said.

"But certainly death will find us here," Erasmus said. "In two hours we will be in darkness, huddled together, starving, though we will die of lack of heat before." He looked back at the tiny opening, not sure that he was really ready to go in there again, in with no chance of returning.

Hayes rose to his feet. "Look, we can tie the rope around that horn near the opening. That will give us at least twenty feet more rope." He looked at Erasmus. "I will try it this time."

"No, Hayes. . . . It will be difficult if you can't swim."

"Yes, but if it goes anywhere, we all must go into it, and none but you can swim, Erasmus. Is it not narrow? Can I not pull myself up on the walls?"

Erasmus shook his head. "Not easily. You're so weakened. We are all so weakened. No, I will try it once more. Give the rope to me."

"Then I'll come with you," Hayes said. "In some of the deeper pools I felt myself float up, and by moving my arms and legs, I managed to propel myself forward. I'm willing to try. Better you not go alone."

Erasmus looked at the determination on the young man's face—far preferable to the despair that had been written there. Erasmus nodded and they plunged into the pool. Hayes tied a loop over a horn of rock, for Erasmus' fingers would not work, and then they took the rope in both their hands and went into the passage, their legs streaming out behind them.

Twenty feet in, Erasmus felt his fingers slipping. "Hayes! I can't hold on." Erasmus felt Hayes' hand take hold of his shirt, and they hung there for a moment, gasping for breath but unable to go back. Hayes was spitting out water, struggling to keep his head above the surface, and then suddenly Erasmus' fingers slipped, his shirt tore away and he was swept into the darkness.

"Go back!" he yelled and went with the current, no strength left to resist.

Hayes called his name, and then Erasmus was fighting to keep his head above water, the walls tearing at him as he swept by on the current. Once the ceiling dropped down, cracking him hard on the forehead, forcing him under, but he fought his way back up and found air again. Then he plunged down a smooth slide, coughing up water, scrabbling to rise, but the current had him, and he felt himself surrender. He could fight no longer. And the darkness took him.

Just as Erasmus felt he was lost, he found himself suddenly floating in calm water, coughing up great mouthfuls of the stuff. Rock came under his feet and he stood, stumbling back into the water, and then rising again.

"Flames . . ." he whispered. "I'm alive. Bloody . . ." He was racked by coughing, and fell again, but now the water was so shallow that he sat with it not even to his chest.

And then he heard splashing. Though he felt barely able to move, he plunged back into the water, thrashing around with his arms, searching the darkness. "Hayes . . . ? *Hayes!*"

He moved toward the sound of splashing and suddenly gripped a handful of hair and pulled the young man up, spluttering and coughing.

"Don't struggle! I have you. Damn it, man, don't struggle. Just here you can stand." He hauled the choking boy into the shallows and pounded him on the back. For a moment he thought Hayes would expire, and Erasmus began to beat him with all his remaining strength, and suddenly Hayes twisted away from him.

"You don't need to . . . murder me," Hayes gasped, and was gripped by another spasm of coughing.

Not knowing what to do, Erasmus kept dragging his companion into shallower water until they were on dry, smooth stone where they lay, shivering and coughing.

"Well, here we are," Hayes said at last, his voice coming out of total darkness, and though they were only a foot apart the sound seemed to have no source. "And the others will never know what has happened."

"And I'm not sure we're better off," Erasmus said, feeling an exhaustion in his limbs such as he had never known. "I haven't the strength to go another step."

"No. . . ." Hayes stopped. "Listen! Did you hear that?"

Erasmus tried to control his gasping for breath. "Are they calling?" He forced himself up, swaying on his knees. "Where is it coming from?"

In the darkness sounds echoed, seeming to expand to fill the chamber, their source mysterious. It was even difficult to tell where Hayes' voice was coming from. Erasmus waded back into the water, feeling the current and pushing against it. Hayes shouted behind him, the sound echoing around the chamber for an impossibly extended moment.

"This room must be enormous," Hayes called to him. "Where are you, Erasmus?"

"Here. Let me try to find the way we came in."

The flow of the water became stronger and pushed him away to one side, but finally he found the source. An opening much like the one they'd first entered, but discharging a strong flow of water. He pulled himself along the rock wall, leaning his head out so that he could call into the opening.

He shouted as loudly as he possibly could—no words, for none would carry—just a sound. Anything to let the others know he was alive. There was a long silence, and then a dull echo, garbled, unintelligible, as though the rock complained of its ancient pain. Erasmus shouted again. He waited and there was a response. Two distinct noises this time.

"Hayes? Is that an echo, do you think?"

"I . . . it is impossible to say. Call again."

Erasmus tried to copy what he'd heard, in both number and duration.

Three distinct calls returned. Erasmus called four, so they would not think it an echo.

"That is them," he said to Hayes. "It must be."

"What will they do, Erasmus?" Hayes asked. "Will they try to come through?"

"I don't know. All we can do is call and hope they realize we're still alive." Silence. Only the sound of water moving, and dripping down from overhead.

Erasmus did not know what to do. He shivered uncontrollably, now, his fingers slipping on the stone. He let the current take him, drifting him back.

"Hayes? Speak so I might find you."

"I'm here." They both floundered around in the water for a moment, and lumbered into each other, causing Hayes to fall, where he sat in the water, laughing.

"I don't know how in this round world you can laugh, Hayes, but I do admire it."

They helped each other onto the stone, sitting back to back for the little warmth of contact, wondering what they would do now.

"If you were the others, what would you do?" Hayes asked quietly.

Erasmus considered a moment. "I would likely try to come through, but then I can swim and haven't such a fear of the water."

"I would do the same. So we should be ready for them," Hayes said. "If one of them is rendered senseless as he comes through, he could float right past us and we would never know."

"Yes," Erasmus said, gently exploring the wound on his own forehead. "But if we go stand in the water, we will be even more cold than we are now, and I am near to freezing."

"I am as well. . . . Then we must listen."

They fell silent, imagining white swollen bodies floating by in the darkness.

"Do you think she got out?" Hayes asked suddenly.

"Anna? I don't know. She could not have been far ahead of Banks, so it is unlikely. I'm surprised we didn't find her, though. Can you imagine doing this on your own? No, even if she survived Rose's flood, she would likely not have made it through the tunnel that just vomited us out here."

"Yes, but what if she found some other way that we missed? It's not impossible."

"No, it's . . ." But he did not finish, for the sound of something floundering in the water stopped him.

Both Erasmus and Hayes leaped into the water, calling, and suddenly Hayes cried out.

"I have him!"

For a moment Erasmus could not find them, though he could clearly hear someone coughing and another pounding him on the back, but try as he might he could not get closer to the sound. Then his hand found Hayes in the darkness.

"Who is it?" Erasmus asked.

"Kehler, I think," Hayes said. "He makes a very distinctive sound when he's trying to drown. Kehler? Are you whole, man?"

Kehler continued to cough and it was some minutes before he could speak. "Rose and Clare . . ." He began to cough again.

"Clarendon, yes . . . What of them?"

"They're going to come through together. Bloody martyr's balls, that was the most terrifying experience of my life."

Erasmus found the young man in the dark and put a hand on his shoulder. Certainly it had been no less awful for them.

They fell silent, only their breathing and something that Erasmus identified after a moment as his own teeth chattering.

They listened, and suddenly heard the sounds of the others splashing. Hayes and Erasmus plunged back into the water, and in a moment had Rose and Clarendon out on the rock. For some reason they were not so badly off, and recovered more quickly.

The five of them huddled there in the dark, shaking violently, wondering what they would do now.

"Whose turn is it to t-tell their story?" Hayes whispered, and the others actually managed to laugh.

"Do we have the rope?" Erasmus asked.

"I tried to bring it, but it snagged and was lost," the priest said.

"Well, I thought we should tie ourselves together like blind men, but we will have to stay close. I have some strength left, enough to explore this chamber. There must be a way out. The water has to go somewhere."

"I will not go into another such passage," Kehler said. "Do not even ask me."

"I will stay here and die with Kehler," Hayes said. "But if there is a dry passage, I might manage a few more feet."

Erasmus pushed himself up.

"I will help you, Mr. Flattery," Rose said. "I will search one side of the chamber if you will tackle the other."

Erasmus went back into the water, not caring how frigid it was. He could not possibly be colder than he was. He swam a few strokes until his hand found rock, and then he lumbered awkwardly up onto a ledge. Here he began to search with his cold and battered hands until he found a wall, and this he explored as high as he could reach until the ledge ended in water. Making a mental note that the water's edge beyond this would need to be explored, he went back the other way, deciding to stay dry for now. He searched it all again for he could not tell where he had begun, but nothing felt familiar. His mind was not working as it should, that was certain.

"What are you finding?" Hayes called out.

"Rock," Erasmus answered.

"The same," Rose said quietly.

"I think we are in a giant stomach," Erasmus said. "We have been swallowed up by the world."

Erasmus tripped and fell hard to the stone, laying there for a moment, too exhausted to get up.

"Erasmus? Deacon Rose? Are you all right?"

"Yes. I stumbled," Erasmus said. "But I'm unhurt. Just need to rest a moment."

He lay there wondering if he would bother to struggle up again, his sudden energy gone, but then he imagined a passage just ahead. A flat, easy passage, dry, tall. And down it came the sweet scent of pine.

"I have something!" Rose called out.

"What? What is it?" Hayes called, his voice echoing from everywhere at once.

"An opening. Not large, though not so small." A pause. "I can fit into it easily, though I think I must rest before I attempt it."

Erasmus forced himself up, going carefully back into the water.

"Keep talking, Deacon, though quietly," Erasmus said, "and I will cross to you."

Out of the darkness came a sweet song, a hymn of sad beauty, and Erasmus stopped for a moment, so surprised was he to hear something so lovely in this harsh world. He followed the air, which echoed around the chamber so that it sounded like an entire choir, a choir singing in a great cathedral.

"Here you are," Erasmus said as he found the man, and the singing stopped, much to his disappointment. "Where is this opening?"

Rose led him to it, and Erasmus explored it with his hands, like a blind man would.

"It is not so small," he said. "Let me try it now. If I wait, I think I will grow weaker, not stronger."

Not waiting for Rose to agree, Erasmus pushed himself into the opening on hands and battered knees, ignoring the pain, and the humming in his ears. He stumbled down the passage, feeling before him as he went. It sloped up, not steeply but unquestionably up.

For a moment he stopped to rest, odd lights swimming before his closed eyes. *This is it*, he thought. *This is all the effort I can make. I'm too cold. Too exhausted. Flames, I am tired.*

He lay still, feeling sleep reach out for him. Warm sleep. He imagined a soft breeze caressing his face, the smell of fallen leaves. A smile touched his lips.

"Mr. Flattery," came a voice.

Erasmus shook his head. "Yes."

"What have you found?"

"Nothing yet," he called, forcing himself up on his elbows. He shook his head. "Ten feet," he whispered. "You can go ten feet."

He struggled on, not even rising to his knees, his head swimming now, a terrible ringing in his ears, like the body's own dirge for its passing. Even crawling, he lurched to one side, losing his balance in the dark. He collapsed again. And lay shivering, gasping for breath from his effort. His empty stomach heaved, and there was a hot burning in his throat. He heaved again and spat out bile, letting it dribble down his chin, uncaring.

"Flames," he muttered. "Flames. . . ." Then, "Ten feet, man. Any weakling can crawl ten feet. Percy would have managed it."

A murmuring seemed to fill the passage, and he stopped to listen, not sure what it was, then picking out the sound of voices. The others had gathered about the opening. Perhaps they came after him.

He forced himself to move his limbs, crawling through his own bile. He shook his head, trying to clear it, for he was dizzy and nauseated. Strange lights moved before his eyes now, even when they were open.

But he crawled a few feet. Rested a moment, his back spasming, and when that let up a little, he made himself go on. Five feet this time. Just five feet.

He saw a strange pinpoint of light that wavered and blurred, but at least it had the decency to disappear when he pressed his eyes shut. Five feet more.

There was some rubble of rocks on the floor of the passage now, and he crawled across this, the scream of pain from his poor battered knees and elbows seeming so distant.

"Mr. Flattery?"

*Go away*, he thought. *Can't you see I haven't the energy to spare to answer.*

He forced himself on, ignoring the calls of the others, though they seemed closer, now.

*I'm delirious*, he thought. *I'm half out of my wits. Is this what you feel before you die?*

He went another few feet, before being overcome by nausea again. When he opened his eyes, the point of light returned.

*What if it is the proverbial light at the end of the tunnel?* he thought. *But it is so small. . . . It would have to be a mile away.* He couldn't possible crawl a mile.

He squinted. Could it be sunlight infinitely far off? Or worse, could it be a tiny hole allowing light in but not large enough for any man to pass? Would he die with a view of the outside world?

He crawled a little farther, banging his head hard. He lay stunned for a moment, and then reached out with his hand, but it was not such hard stone. He put his cheek against it.

"*Flames*," he whispered. *Is this delirium?* He ran his hand over the surface, then rolled onto his back looking up.

The world seemed to spin and he shut his eyes. *But it was a tree!* And those were stars overhead, and that was the scent of pines. He had crawled out into the world. The world of light and air and trees and grass.

Erasmus tried to call out, but only a faint whisper emerged. A mumbling came to him, like someone chanting. A voice spoke his name a few feet away.

Hayes. The others were near, crawling out into the delirious warmth of a spring night.

He felt himself convulse oddly, and sob. And then he lay, curled up like a child, hot tears running down his cheek, collecting on a fallen leaf. A breeze moved the branches overhead, whispering in a soft, green voice, welcoming him back to the world, to the brief life of men.

# The Compass of the Soul

A man may move either westward through life, following the light, or eastward toward the gathering darkness. It is a kind of orientation of temperament that is set in our earliest years; an emotional compass. One either pursues one's dreams or one's memories, and it is an exceptional man who, once his compass has been set, can alter it even a point or two.

—Halden: *Essays*

# ⌒ One

She was reborn from the earth, emerging from a dark womb of stone into the ancient light of a new morning. A shaft of diffuse light lanced through the trees to caress her skin. Warmth . . .

*Let it sink into my very bones,* Anna thought, almost certain she would be cold to her center for the rest of her days.

A bird lighted on a branch not a yard away, regarding her with a darkly glittering eye. *"Chuff,"* it said, the single syllable floating up like a bubble of sound.

"Shoo," she responded. There was something about its bill—blood-red and decurving, like a scimitar.

*"Chuff,"* it said again, though less surely this time, and took two steps closer, shuffling its red legs along the branch.

"I am not food for you yet," she whispered, and managed to wave a hand, driving the bird from its perch. It settled a few yards away, staring back at her with its head cocked, an eerily intelligent look in its glittering eye. And then it fell to flight and sped off into the heart of the forest.

Anna closed her eyes. Sleep. She must sleep. Sleep for years, she was sure. And thinking that she drifted into a nightmare: swept helplessly along the course of an underground river, fighting for air . . . struggling to live.

Something bounced off her temple, and Anna opened her eyes to find the sun higher, providing a coverlet of delicious warmth. She had stopped shivering.

*"Chuff. . . ."*

The bird perched above her. "Whose pet are you?" she asked, then realized an acorn lay but an inch away. Had it dropped that for her?

She turned her gaze back to the bird, and then sat up, suddenly filled with wonder. "But you are no one's pet, are you?" she whispered. *"Flames!"* She patted a pocket in her waistcoat and removed a square of wet linen, then glanced back at the bird.

"Farrelle's ghost, but it must have begun already." Tentatively she reached out a hand to the dark-feathered bird—crowlike with a red bill and legs of the same hue. But the bird hopped away, only a foot; and there it stayed.

*"Chuff,"* it said again.

Anna laughed. "'Chuff' yourself." Gingerly, she unfolded the linen and spread it out on the ground in the sun. She separated each precious seed, blowing on them gently. The seed had been her salvation; without it she would never have found the resources to survive the trip out of the cavern, even though eating it raw produced only a fraction of its power.

The bird began to hop about excitedly, and she turned a warning gaze upon it. "This is not for you," she said.

Overwhelmed by sudden weariness, she leaned back against the bole of a tree, but kept her eyes open, afraid the bird might make free with her seed. Where were the others? Certainly they must be some hours ahead. She had waited as long as she possibly could before following them out.

Anna had arrived at the pool and collapsed, too exhausted to start back up the tunnel in search of another passage. There her candles had burned to darkness. Not knowing what to do when she heard the others approaching, she had crawled into a crevice and lay still, sure anyone could hear the pounding of her heart. By the poor candle light, Erasmus and the others had not seen her nor had they the energy or inclination to search. She had watched them go into the watery passage. Heard them shouting back and forth between the chambers. And when she thought she could wait no longer and still have strength, she had followed.

The thought of that water-filled passage caused her to pull her limbs close. She trembled.

"Do not think of it," she warned. "Do not."

She had survived! And here she was . . . on the surface of the world once more. Reborn to the light. Reborn—for certainly she had been in the nether-world these last days. Days! Could it have been only days?

"But what to do?" she whispered. Deacon Rose had been with the others, and she knew that he would soon be hunting her. Hunting her even now, perhaps. Did he think she had escaped ahead of them?

"What to do?" she whispered again, feeling her eyes ease closed. She forced them open. Up. She must press on. As soon as the seeds were dry, for she could not let mold touch them. They were more precious than diamonds. Almost more precious than life.

Had Halsey escaped, she wondered? Did Eldrich think they had all died in the cavern? Difficult to answer. She no longer presumed to have even the slight-est knowledge of the mage's mind. He had deceived them—trapped them with disturbing ease—and only she had escaped, and that only by a near-miracle.

The Entonne border was nearby, and Anna could almost feel it offering haven. If only her resources were not so depleted! Food and rest were utterly imperative, for she had endured beyond her limits. Food and rest and cloth-ing. And money. Anna had not a coin in her possession. But where? Where could she go that Eldrich would not suspect?

Perhaps Halsey had escaped unnoticed. He was wary and meticulous in his precautions. Eldrich might well have missed him. Flames, if she had only paid heed!

No use flogging herself with this. Survive. That was her task now. Her obligation.

Carefully she rolled the seed around on the linen, which lured the bird nearer, extending its neck to watch.

"What bird are you?" she asked. "Not a rook, I think, but some distant cousin. Cousin to the carrion crow. Dark-eyed and cunning. Cold-hearted, too, I'll wager. Perhaps you are the perfect familiar for me, then. For all those who were close to my heart are gone, and they will never be replaced. Not if I am to succeed in what I must do." Saying this she wrapped the seed up again and buttoned it carefully into her pocket before rising stiffly.

Her mind was made up. It might be dangerous, but she could not proceed without knowing what had befallen Halsey. If he had fled, he would leave signs. Things so subtle that even a mage might miss them. And if he had been discovered . . . Well, if he'd been able, he would have left signs of that, too.

A waning moon sailed west until cast up on a shoal of cloud: stuck fast in the heavens.

Anna crouched in the midst of a stand of shrubs, watching. The house that Halsey had leased was just visible through the branches. At intervals she could see the old man pass before the window, pacing, his stooped carriage unmistakable. It was his habit to pace when problems beset him. Maybe the pain clarified his mind somehow, or perhaps it was penance.

But still she watched, and had been doing so for several hours. He was alone, she was sure of that. Some time earlier, a local woman had arrived with his dinner, stayed to clean the rooms a little, and then departed, carrying away the tray of dishes she'd brought. No others had come or gone, or even strayed nearby. Still she waited. Impatience had been her undoing once. Their undoing.

When Halsey began to blow out the lamps, she moved from her place, still stiff and weakened by her ordeal. A woodsman had fed her the previous night; fed her and set her on the path to Castlebough. She had made a slow journey through the woods, accompanied by her chough, for that is what the woodsman called the bird—the obvious appellation.

She had hidden herself here earlier in the day, and had she the resources, would have watched another day yet, but her exhaustion was too complete. Knowing that warmth, food, and company in her sorrow lay so near weakened her resolve.

Before the last lamp was doused she tapped on the window. Silence from within. She tapped again.

*"Chuff,"* said her familiar, somewhere in the darkness.

Halsey appeared, standing well back from the glass, looking very unsure.

"Halsey . . .'Tis I. Anna. Can you not let me in?"

She saw him reach out to support himself, and then he hurried toward the door. A moment later she was inside where the old man took both her hands in his own and kissed them, as though she were a daughter returned from the dead.

"My dear girl. My dear Anna . . ." He looked at her, words clearly failing him. "What of the others?" he said, his voice almost disappearing.

She began to speak, but her own voice failed, and she merely shook her head and looked down, expecting tears to come—but they didn't. She was too exhausted to mourn. Farrelle's oath, but she felt empty.

He kissed her hands again. "Come inside, child. You look like you have survived the ordeal of Helspereth. Come in and I will bank the fire."

She left Halsey bending awkwardly before the hearth while she found clean clothing. Returning a few moments later, she wrapped herself in a thick blanket and curled into a chair before the flames.

"I am warming some soup," he said solicitously, "and there is bread and cheese. Not much, I'm afraid."

"Anything will be welcome. Only two days past I thought I should starve to death. . . . A crust would have seemed a cake then."

A blackened pot was suspended over the flames, and a board of cheese and bread produced. Again, Anna was surprised at how quickly her appetite was slaked. For a few moments they sat, saying nothing. Each time she looked up, Halsey was staring at her, the unspoken questions held in check only by compassion and concern for her.

She took a long draught of wine, and then resettled herself in the chair. "It was a long journey . . ." She swallowed the last word, and continued in a near-whisper, "down into the cavern." For a moment she closed her eyes, thinking of Banks drowned and the others buried alive. But she forced herself to go on. Forced some substance into her voice. "Long, arduous, and filled with wonders, though we had little time to stop and marvel. As we traveled, I sensed a vision, and despite our haste, we stopped so that I might search for it. None of us believed what I saw. Not even me. . . ."

The story took some long time to tell, and Halsey nodded in wonder again and again. When she spoke of the collapse of the cave and the murder of their companions, he rose from his chair and paced off across the room, shaking his head and raising his hand to stop her when she started to admit that he had been right. And then he came and settled painfully back into his chair and motioned for her to continue.

When the tale was finally told, they sat watching the flames inexorably consume the logs, turning them first to glowing coals and then to ash.

"He is a monster," Halsey said at last. "He . . ." But the old man did not finish.

"So he is," Anna whispered.

"Have you the seed still? Did you preserve it?"

She produced the small bundle, unwrapping it with extreme care, and held it out to him. In all the years that she had known Halsey, Anna had never seen him react so. His always stiff, unreadable countenance seemed to dissolve, and his eyes glistened suddenly. For a moment he sat unmoving, not even breathing, she thought, and then he reached out slowly. But just as his hand was about to close over the seed, he drew it back, and placed it tight to his heart.

"No. You keep it," he said. "You risked everything to possess it. And the others . . . they made the sacrifice so that you might have it. No, it is meant to be yours."

"But you have talent, as well. Talent and far more knowledge. Certainly we should cultivate it and both attempt the transformation."

He shook his head. "No. I am too old. Too old and no longer strong. It falls to you, Anna. That is clear to me now."

She sat quietly, trying to absorb what he was saying. Certainly this is why she had taken the risk of coming here. To find an ally, and to have his council.

"There is something more," she said. She went to the window and threw it open. Making the noise one might make to attract a pet, she leaned out, searching the shadows. "There! Do you see?"

Halsey came and stood beside her. "I can't make it out. What is it?"

"A chough, I was told. Much like a rook or a crow. It greeted me as I left the cave and has accompanied me ever since."

Halsey stared out into the darkness. "A *familiar*," he said. "Teller be praised. Such a thing has not happened since the days of Alan Dubry." He looked at her, his eyes shining. "Perhaps your vision was not wrong. Skye opened a door, and see what we have found?" He shook his head. "Who among us would not accept the greatest sacrifice to make a mage? A mage at this point in history."

She turned away from the window. "Don't say such a thing. Everyone, even Banks . . . No, I could not live with such a thought. That I had sacrificed them all to my vision. . . ."

He put a hand on her shoulder. "But you did no such thing, Anna. You could not have known. But even so, no one would have hesitated. A *mage*. A mage who will live beyond Eldrich. It is the dream we hardly dared to dream. You, Anna, will preserve the arts. You will rediscover what has been lost."

She moved away, perhaps unable to accept the responsibility.

"The cost was too great," she whispered.

"It was great, yes, but all the more reason to seize this opportunity. Let no one's sacrifice be in vain."

She nodded. There was wisdom in this, she was sure. Such a cost. Something must come of it. "Then what are we to do?" she said softly. "How must we proceed?"

He turned back to the fire, but his eye lit upon the seed and lingered. "We must vanish again. Perform the rites that will hide our escape from anyone using the arts to seek us. We must begin tonight."

*"But I am so tired—"* Anna began to protest, and Halsey turned on her.

"Tonight!" he said firmly. "Eldrich is near. Already he has almost destroyed us. I fear that it is this seed he seeks. Perhaps it has been this seed all along, for let me tell you something, Anna; this seed must be Landor's own. Do you understand? Not seed that was cultivated in this world, but which came from beyond. We have long known that the seed lost its power from one planting to the next—but this . . ." He gestured to the precious bundle. "Use it sparingly. And it must be cultivated—as soon as you can manage."

Saying nothing, Halsey disappeared, returning a moment later with a book. This he passed to her. "Here are some few things I've set down these past years. Knowledge that you do not have. It is in Darian, so there was little chance that it would have been understood if it had fallen into the hands of another."

"But why give me this now?"

"We cannot know what might happen. Now come quickly. We will perform the ritual and leave no trace of our flight for the mage or his servants. No one will be aware of us again until it is too late."

Quickly, they prepared the few things they would need to travel at speed. Horses were saddled, burdened with baggage, and led away from the house lest they sense the arts and bolt.

Halsey began to light candles. Seven tapers were arranged in a pattern on the floor, and then he took a scented oil and marked the walls with Darian characters. Using the same oil he began tracing a pattern on the floor, chanting as he did so.

"You will perform the enchantment," he said as he completed the pattern.

"But . . ." she began to protest, and then realized that he was right. She was the mage emerging: the spell would facilitate the process, and certainly now her powers outstripped Halsey's own.

She took up ashes from the fire and sprinkled the still warm powder evenly over the pattern. When she was finished, she made seven marks upon her face with the ash and then moved to the pattern's center.

*"Curre d' Efeu,"* she began. "Heart of flame. . . ." The enchantment was not long but it was rather intricate and required precise motion and control. Once Halsey prompted her, for her mind still suffered from fatigue, but she carried on, knowing the importance of what she did.

Fire erupted in the hearth again, and when she placed a hand near the floor and spoke, she drew a line of flame out from the logs. It spread around the pattern.

She was into the spell, to the point where it would be dangerous to stop, when a fierce tapping drew her attention. The chough was at the window, frantically beating its wings and beak against the glass.

Anna blocked out the sounds, the questions.

Halsey spoke unexpectedly, his deep, gravelly tones forming Darian with an authority that none of the others had ever mastered. But what was he doing?

The room seemed so far away, the world so remote, so dreamlike. Halsey sprinkled something over the pattern, holding an object in his hand—an object of dread.

And then the realization gripped her, dragging her back to the world, to the present.

"*Halsey!*" she called out, but he raised the hand that held the dagger and continued in his efforts—sprinkling blood from the wound at his wrist along the pattern.

"What are you doing?"

"Do not stop," he said, not looking up from his task. "Go on, child. You will ruin us both."

And so she continued, chanting a long string of words, drawing up the candle flames.

Halsey stopped, suddenly, just as she reached the spell's end. "Eldrich found me," he said, his face contorting in pain and guilt. "I was to wait here to be sure that none of our people emerged from the cave—a simple task, for Eldrich was all but sure no one had survived. For this small service I would be rewarded— something greater than I would have expected." He shook his head, a tear streaking his cheek. "But when I saw you . . . alive." He met her eye for a second, begging something. "Eldrich has put his mark upon me, Anna. I can never escape him." He began to speak Darian, a spell she did not know. The fire in the pattern rose up suddenly, and the characters on the walls burst into flame. He called out, and before Anna realized what he would do, the old man plunged the knife into his own breast.

He turned toward her as his knees buckled. "*You are free,*" he whispered, and toppled into the rising flames.

For a moment Anna stood transfixed. Unable to believe what she saw. Unwilling to believe the horror of it. All of them gone. Every one.

Alone. She was utterly alone.

And then a crashing against the window drew her, and she saw a tiny dark eye beyond the glass, and realized that the spell no longer offered protection. With one final look back at Halsey, enveloped in flame, she swept up her skirts and fled.

## ᗧ Two

Without a sign from anyone, the mage's procession of two carriages had rolled to a sudden stop, leaving the countess wondering what apparition they had encountered now.

Eldrich stepped down to the gravel and disappeared soundlessly into the wood.

The countess watched him go. *As silent as a shadow,* she thought, and shivered.

For the first time she saw all of her traveling companions: Walky, of course; a darkly handsome man of perhaps thirty; the drivers; and four other servants. The mage's entire entourage.

The drivers saw to their teams, and the others stood about in isolated silence, as though casual speech were forbidden to the followers of a mage.

*Silence,* the countess thought. *He lives in the silences.*

Under the pretense of finding the least obstructed view of the stars, she edged closer to Walky, finally catching his eye.

"What goes on, Mr. Walky?" she whispered.

The little man shrugged, put a finger to his lips, and slipped away before she might speak again. Thus chastened, she found an outcropping of stone at the roadside and made it her seat, vowing that she would never become as servile as these others.

*Why have I agreed to this?* she wondered again, though not yet sure what she had involved herself in. The ancient woman at the roadside—herself: the Countess of Chilton—the mere thought of this apparition quelled all of her doubts for a moment. She closed her eyes, trying to drive out the image—a woman pathetic in age and loss of mental faculties.

*Better any fate than that,* a voice inside her warned.

But there was more. A certain feeling of inevitability, a crumbling of resistance—the feeling of giving one's self up to a seduction, to another. And to desire.

*Desire.*

But was it real, or was she merely under some form of enchantment?

A shadow flowed out of the wood and onto the road: Eldrich's wolf.

She heard her breath catch and she froze in place, as though it were a wild beast and she its prey. For a moment it paused in the starlight, slowly turning its head as though searching, and then it darted into the wood again.

The countess let out a long breath. What did he want of her?

The moon sailed among the stars, illuminating the solitary clouds that passed before it. From deep within the wood a nightingale burbled its liquid song. The countess tried to silence her inner voice. To be aware of the night. Traveling with a mage would require that she learn patience and attentiveness. And silence.

She did not know how long she listened to the winds' whispered conversation, observed the heavens, before Eldrich reappeared—two hours, perhaps three.

The stooped silhouette crossed to Walky and the handsome man. She could hear them speaking; words like stones dropped into a brook and just as comprehensible. The three conferred briefly, and then Eldrich went directly into his coach.

Walky came to her.

"What is it?" she asked. "What has happened?"

"The unforeseen," Walky said hoarsely. "Come. I will ride with Lord Eldrich and the countess, if you will allow it."

She nodded, smiling at this odd gesture of consideration. As he took her arm and led her toward the carriage, the countess could see the others releasing the team from the second coach, which they began to turn around in the narrow road.

*They are going back,* she realized, as she stepped up into Eldrich's carriage.

They moved off as she settled herself.

At last, she could bear this dismissive silence no longer. Her anger boiled up, and she drew a long breath. "What has happened?" she asked, feeling her heart beating—like a child asking forbidden questions.

Dark silence was her answer, and she felt her anger boil over. Did he treat everyone with such disregard?

"There is a hunting lodge," the mage announced, his musical voice betraying no trace of emotion. "Not distant. We will stop there."

It was a concession, she knew, though hardly informative. Only where and what, not why.

The countess should not have been surprised to find that mages cared little for the niceties of property rights. Walky and the servants quickly had the building open and began setting it to rights, as though it were their own. Lamps were lit, fires built in the hearths, sleeping chambers aired and beds prepared.

*And where am I expected to sleep?* the countess wondered. She stood before one of the hearths, warming her back, her arms crossed stiffly before her. *I feel as uncertain as a young girl,* she thought. *But there is not a petal of romance in the air.*

*Will he want me?* That was the question. The desire was there; palpably so, but would Eldrich give in to it?

With other men she would know. Their intentions were easily divined, but the mage was not like other men.

Walky appeared from a dark hall. It seemed that Eldrich and his servants had no need of light—a strange thought. No need of light.

"A chamber has been readied for you, Lady Chilton," he said, taking up a candle.

She remained by the fire a moment more, suddenly reluctant to leave its warmth.

"Where is Lord Eldrich?" she asked, her voice oddly hollow in the massive room.

"Engaged," Walky replied.

Still the countess did not move.

"The mage is involved in matters of great import, m'lady," he said. "Matters that are little understood by others."

"So you do not know what goes on?" the countess asked.

Walky nodded. "I know very little, I'm afraid. Best Lord Eldrich answer your questions."

"He does not seem much inclined to answering questions."

"All in good time, m'lady," he said. "All in good time. One cannot rush a river, but wait and the stream will carry you where you wish."

"Rivers flow in only one direction, Mr. Walky," she said, not heartened by his choice of metaphor. "And I fear I have the patience of a mortal: I like my answers immediately."

"It is something you will adjust to, m'lady," he said softly and gestured for her to follow.

"Perhaps," she whispered to herself. Eldrich's words came back to her. *I am one hundred and thirty-three; all other estimates you have heard are wrong.*

The countess was but five and twenty.

She sat in a window seat before the open casement, her knees drawn up and clasped by woven fingers. A nightingale trilled its melodious song, and unknown insects added strange counterpoint.

The hour was unknown to her. Late, no doubt, but still she did not proceed to bed. She perched in the window listening to a nightingale offer enticements to a mate.

*At least he sings,* she thought. *A shred of gallantry.*

The bed, with its curtains and coverlets folded back, took up a much greater place in her consciousness than in the room itself. And it offended her somehow, like a statement of presumption.

"What does he want of me?" she asked the night, and leaned her head back against the cool wood. She closed her eyes and felt such sweet relief. The air seemed seasoned with such a complex fragrance. She drank it in deeply, as though hungry for it. Late. So late. And she was but five and twenty.

She awoke to a touch on her cheek. A kiss? Opening her eyes, she found Eldrich standing between herself and the bed. Oddly, this did not startle her at all. Indeed, she did not feel quite herself—as though she floated in time, somehow.

"Do I dream?"

"There are those who claim that life is nothing else," he answered, the music of his voice touching her, stripping away the last cords of gravity binding her to the world.

"The nightingale . . . he has stopped."

"Yes." His eye did not waver, but remained fixed on her—not unkindly, but not kind either.

"What will you do with me?"

A smile, like the shadow of a winging bird. "What would you have me do?"

*Yes, what?* "I cannot bear to be left wondering. I cannot. . . ."

His gaze did not waver. "No," he said quietly, a voice like a soft wind, "it is a terrible thing."

## ↜ Three

Kent walked his lame gelding along the black river of road, and contemplated his own recklessness. One did not canter by night along a road known for its potholes and washouts. Not with the moon hidden by overcast, stars visible only through tears in the cloud.

He patted his mount's nose, trying to calculate the distance to the next travelers' inn. Not far in miles, though several hours at this pace. Some knight off to save the fair lady he had turned out to be.

Kent crept along the road in the faint starlight, aware of the precipice to one side. The sound of flowing water floated up to him and increased the illusion that he walked along the dark surface of a river.

He stepped, mid-calf, into water, and brought his lame mount up short. Cursing, he peered into darkness, trying to gauge the width of the washout. To his right, the river of road seemed to have overflowed its bank and the substance of night whirled there in a slow eddy.

It was a spring, he realized. In that backwater of darkness would lie a drinking trough and a fount where humans might slake their thirst and take their rest upon stone benches.

"I think this will be our inn this night," he explained to his gelding, as he led it into the liquid shadow of the trees. Here both horse and man drank.

Kent tethered his mount where it could reach the grasses growing at the margins of the wood, and sank down onto a stone bench, pulling up his collar against the small wind. Daylight was some hours off, but Kent could not sleep. Thoughts of the countess haunted him. An image of a large carriage charging through the hills, drawing farther and farther away from him.

It even occurred to him that his horse's lameness might not be entirely natural. He snorted. No. Certainly that had been the result of his own imprudence, not the arts of the mage.

He shifted, seeking greater comfort, but the stone refused to yield.

*Is the countess Eldrich's lover?* he wondered again. Willingly his lover? He did not think so. Certainly she had been horrified when told she had been in the company of a mage. That had not been an act.

He stared up at the stars, picking out the constellations and trying to see new shapes in them, then giving them appropriate names. The Dragon became a woman weaving: the Weaver. The Twins, with some stretch of the imagination, became a carriage. And the Hunter could be nothing but a Mage.

*Does he know I pursue him?* Kent wondered. *Is it possible?*

Just then, the gelding whickered. He could feel its excitement in the dark. His first thought was wolves, yet then he realized the gelding's reaction was not fear but anticipation.

Someone approached.

Kent went out onto the shadowy road, gazing into the darkness and listening. Was that the sound of a horse? He stood, staring down, concentrating his senses and finally was sure he heard the sounds of horses—several of them, to the east.

He stared off into the night, relief washing through him. If luck was with him, he would be in Castlebough this night, and on the road again before midday.

Around the shoulder of the hillside a dark shadow appeared against the low stars, the sound suddenly clear: a large carriage drawn by a team, Kent was almost certain. And how quickly they came.

Then he realized that he had seen no coach lamps. He froze in place, confused, and then he rushed back into the shadow. Tearing the horse's reins free, he began dragging his mount up into the trees. It stumbled and tried to pull away, but Kent resisted, coaxing it along, blind in the dark. Up they went, diagonally now, on some kind of foot track—likely a path to a lookout point. He could not see the track but felt it underfoot, and the horse came along more easily.

When his breath failed him, Kent stopped and bent double—not enough wind left to even curse. The sound of horses pounding along the road came up, slightly muffled, through the trees.

And then it died.

Kent did curse then, in a whisper.

*Do they know I'm here, or do they stop only to water their team?*

He stroked his mount, jiggling its bit as a distraction. *Make no sound,* he willed it. *Make no sound.*

And then the horses moved again, the sound of hooves, slow, like tumbling rock. Kent realized they had delayed only to negotiate the washout.

"Flames," he swore. It must be Eldrich. Who else could see such a thing in the dark? But why was the mage returning to Castlebough? Racing back to the city he'd just left? There was no explaining the doings of a mage.

Was the countess with him? That was Kent's only question. Certainly she must be. There might be a chance that he could rescue her yet.

"What is it?" came a half-familiar voice, muffled by its journey through the trees.

"The road is washed away," came another voice.

"Shall I climb down?" The first voice drifted up to him again, teasing him with tones he thought he should know.

It couldn't be Eldrich, could it? The ramifications of this stopped him cold.

"It might be best, if you don't mind, sir."

Kent heard the click of a carriage door, and then the complaining of springs as the horses edged forward. A pause, then a surge as the carriage rolled up out of the trench.

"That will do, Mr. Bryce."

Again the door sound, and then the carriage set off, far too quickly on this dark night.

Bryce? The man who had accompanied Sir John? He felt a wave of relief. The man was clearly an agent of the mage. But why was he returning to the town his master had so recently abandoned? Kent could not imagine, but clearly Eldrich and the countess still traveled on.

Kent edged back down the trail, hoping his mount did not stumble and crush him. At the spring he let the gelding drink once more, and then set out, lame mount and all, along the dark river that bore the countess away.

## ∽ Four

The ruin was still smoldering when Bryce arrived, the stone hot to the touch. Out of the coals, cranial walls rose up, window openings gaping, glass melted into frozen pools, dripping from the sills. Bryce could sense the death here—the death of the house. Perhaps more.

The roof had collapsed, leaving only a few beams, blackened and burned to half-thickness, which angled down from the stone walls like the tines of a rusted rake. He turned over a roof tile with his foot and a gasp of caustic smoke escaped, stinging his eyes.

In what he guessed to be the center of the room, he probed into the ashes with a stick, dredging up a heavy object blackened by the fire but unmistakable. A dagger.

"He will not be pleased," Bryce said to himself. "Not in the least pleased."

There was other evidence of the arts as well, not all of it perceptible by the usual means. But beyond the house there was nothing.

"Flames, it was a powerful drawing," he said. He turned over more tiles with his branch, and was rewarded with more smoke, which seared his nostrils and lungs.

Crouching at arm's length, he plumbed the ashes and turned up something else. A charred object that stopped him. *"Blood and flames. . . ."* The bone slipped back into the ash, like a corpse into a pallid sea.

Bryce stood suddenly, looking around at the ruined house, horrified by what had been done. "The mage must know. Immediately he must know! He sacrificed himself—and there can be only one reason for that."

## ∽ Five

The five who escaped the cave had been transported to the sanitarium and put under the care of the physician and his staff. Not that they were badly injured—exhaustion and need of nourishment being the most dire of their physical hurts. Even Clarendon's damaged knee did not appear so serious in the light of day.

Erasmus stood before the mirror staring at the gaunt figure who looked back, apparently distressed by what he saw. The figure in the glass had somewhat sunken eyes and a slight hollow to the cheeks that even the freshly trimmed beard did not hide. But what struck him most was the cast of his face—a man who had learned a terrible truth.

*"There are truths men never recover from,"* Beaumont had once said.

*A mage tried to murder me,* Erasmus thought, and turned away, unable to bear the stranger's look.

Erasmus lay down on his bed, thinking that he might just let sleep take him once more—if only he could dream something sweet. Instead, each time he slept, he tumbled back into the nightmare of the cave: hopelessly lost; starving; cold to the soul; water rising relentlessly.

But the weariness was greater than his fear of nightmares, and his eyelids fluttered closed.

"Erasmus?"

Erasmus opened his eyes to the muted light of late evening. For a moment he wondered what chamber this was, and then realized he was not in the cave at all.

"Erasmus?"

A man sat on a chair in the center of the room.

Erasmus propped himself up on an elbow, squinting at this apparition in the shadows. "Who is that?"

His eyes adjusted to the light, revealing a precise, dark-eyed gentleman. A stranger, yet there was something vaguely familiar. . . .

"Do I know you, sir?" Erasmus asked, dropping his feet to the floor and perching on the bed's edge, his head swimming.

The man still said nothing, but stared at him for a moment.

"You don't remember?"

The voice: bitter . . . older. Erasmus found himself standing, as though drawn up by a will other than his own.

*"Percy?* Flames! Is it you? *Percy . . . ?"*

The man's gaze faltered, blinking.

"But I thought . . ." Erasmus stumbled to silence, his throat constricted. The room spun and he fell back to the bed.

*"You thought I had burned?"* the other said softly.

Erasmus could not bear the man's gaze, and looked down. "Yes," he whispered. "I thought you dead."

Erasmus stared at his unmoving shadow and heard every accusation contained in that silence.

He looked up suddenly. "All these years I thought you dead. I thought . . . I cannot tell you what joy it gives me to see you alive. Alive and whole."

Percy did not answer, but stared at Erasmus as though he had been paid the gravest insult.

Erasmus nodded. "Yes," he almost whispered. "I know what you must think. But I was only a child. How could I have known what would result?"

"So, unsure of the dangers, you pushed me forward to perform the ritual, not daring it yourself."

Erasmus looked back to his dark outline on the floor. "It was an act of cowardice. Yes. But the act of a child, all the same. I am sorry for your sufferings, Percy. No day goes by without my thinking of it—regretting it." He looked up. "But you are whole, thank all gods. Eldrich made you whole again."

Percy's face hardened, masklike, eyes narrowing. "Whole? No, I am not whole. And I am tied to the mage. Tied to him until the end, while you have walked free, inconvenienced only by your paltry guilt. But I am his servant, Erasmus. Healed, to all appearances, but his servant still. You cannot know what that means. You can't begin to know."

Erasmus stared at the man, and felt the rage and contempt hurled at him. All he could say in defense was that he had been a child, a mere boy—but that would not gain him pardon here. Not before the sufferings of this man, whose judgment had been passed long ago, and likely renewed every day for all these many years. No, Erasmus had been condemned in absentia, and there was nothing for it but to hear the sentence.

"It is long done, Percy, and my regrets cannot undo it. So what is it you will have of me now? My continued suffering, heightened by your lack of forgiveness? Or is there some act of contrition? Is that what you have come to ask?"

The man who had been his dearest friend and ally in childhood laughed bitterly. "Forgiveness? I have been tutored by a mage, Erasmus. It is a word without meaning to me, a human weakness which was burned away long ago. No, there is nothing you can do for me. The mage, however, is not done with you yet, Erasmus Flattery." For a second the mask became almost human as he said this, and the voice was tinged with a certain pleasure.

He lifted a foot and set the ankle on his knee. "Begin with the story of how you came to be here in Castlebough. Leave nothing out. You know how exacting the mage can be."

Erasmus shook his spinning head, hoping that he dreamed, but something told him he did not. This was Percy, returned after all these years. Returned with the accusations Erasmus had hurled at himself during this same span of time. Justice; very rare in the world of the mage.

Realizing that there was nothing else to be done, Erasmus told his tale, beginning with meeting Hayes in the brothel, and the bizarre story he'd told of Skye, the Stranger, and a mage.

During the entire explanation Percy's countenance did not alter. Even the failing light could not soften the bitterness and disdain.

*What has he suffered?* Erasmus wondered. *Did not the mage heal him?*

*Look! Is there the slightest scar or burn? No, he is a handsome man, of great bearing and presence. Yet he hates me still.*

The light in the room faded as the story was told—faded like hope—and when he came to the end, his inquisitor was nothing but an indistinguishable shadow in the room's center.

For a long moment Percy was quiet, and Erasmus could not see his face to judge the impact of his tale. "One would think, by your story, that you'd given up the ways of a coward," he said coldly. "What of this girl? You saw no sign of her after the drowned man?"

"None. But unless she could swim, it seems very likely she, too, was drowned and carried away by the stream."

Percy shook his head. "She did not drown. No, she is living yet. And Eldrich will not be pleased to hear of your part in this."

"Me? What have I to do with it?"

"Was it not you who managed the escape from the chamber? You were never meant to escape, Erasmus. You cannot begin to realize the harm you've done."

Erasmus could hardly credit what he'd heard. "Did Eldrich expect us to sit meekly in the cave and starve?" he said incredulously. "Even a mage must know more of human nature than that!"

Percy rose from his chair and went to the window where he looked out into the twilit valley. Erasmus could barely make him out—Percy's inhuman precision blurred to indistinct silhouette.

"What is it you want of me?" Erasmus asked again, guilt no longer bridling his impatience.

No answer. A silhouette as still as sculpture.

"Find this girl, and Eldrich will lift the sentence that has been passed against you."

"What? What sentence?"

"You trespassed in a sacred place, Erasmus. For that you were to have paid with your lives. And then you aided the girl's escape. All of you have earned Eldrich's displeasure."

Erasmus had turned on the bed so that he could watch his dark friend, and now he almost writhed where he sat. "What is it you're saying? Was I not to tempt the Tellerites out into the open? Was it not intended that I lead them down into the cave so that Eldrich could destroy them? Was this not my purpose all along? And yet, for doing Eldrich's unspoken bidding, my life is forfeit for violating the chamber? And then I am also charged with managing our escape?"

"When you stand before a mage, Erasmus, an appeal to logic is futile. They do not care much for the niceties of human regulation. You violated the chamber. There can be no 'mitigating circumstances.' You aided the escape of Eldrich's enemy. One should never interfere in the affairs of a mage, especially not one bent on revenge. If you and your companions can find the girl, you will escape Eldrich's judgment against you. Tell that to your friends."

"The priest as well?"

"The priest especially. The church . . . Eldrich will deal with the church." A protracted pause. "This girl took king's blood from the chamber. It must be surrendered to Lord Eldrich. Do not even touch it—especially you, Erasmus."

Percy turned toward Erasmus, but he was still only a dark mass before the window. "Find her," Percy said softly. He tossed a roll of paper on the bed. "And when you have her, this will allow you to alert the mage."

He swept out of the room, and Erasmus realized he no longer saw the erect, forceful man, but someone bent and broken. Someone scarred by fire and loathing.

For some time he sat, unmoving, then he went to the open window and looked out over the valley. The lake glittered in starlight.

So his nightmare had come true. Percy had returned from the grave to confront him, to accuse him. And what a terrible husk of a man he was. Burned hollow, no matter what Eldrich had done to heal him. Poor child. Erasmus could not help but remember the boy—innocent as rain, as trusting as a young bird.

What a monster Eldrich was. What a terrible monster. And all over this young woman—who, despite her duplicity, hardly seemed evil to Erasmus. No, she seemed far less malevolent than the mage. And now he must find her and offer her up to Lord Eldrich.

Remembering what Percy had said, Erasmus lit a lamp and unrolled the curling papers. Immediately he felt the room grow chill. The writing was Darian.

An enchantment.

He was halfway through before he realized it was familiar—*the spell innocent boys had used to summon fire.* The spell that had immolated Percy Bryce, burning away the germ of his humanity.

## ⌒ Six

The bruised joy of survivors was all but absent among those who had escaped the cave. They still wore the haunted look of men just awakened from nightmare. Erasmus thought they had been through quite enough.

Unfortunately, he could see no way to spare them. Their deliverance had been illusory. Erasmus regarded each of the silent faces in turn, and almost to a man their gazes slipped away. Only Rose was bearing up.

"I had a visitor this evening," Erasmus began, his voice uncertain. "Not a welcome one." He could see them all stiffen, as though about to receive a blow. "A servant of Eldrich."

All eyes snapped up briefly, alert now, like the eyes of animals surprised by the hunter.

"I'd hoped we had escaped. That our ordeal was over, but instead Eldrich has found us." His mouth was suddenly sticky-dry, the flesh like a sponge.

Only Deacon Rose did not appear frightened. Indeed, his eyes shone with interest. "I don't know where to begin. Eldrich claims that we have committed a great offense against . . . his kind." He was almost whispering now. "That is the crux of it. But all is not dark, for he has offered us clemency if we will but perform a single task for him."

"*Clemency!?*" Clarendon exclaimed, drawing himself up in resentment, one sign of life at least. "For what crime?"

"I'm afraid the Deacon was right, Randall. We trespassed in a place the mages hold . . . sacrosanct. For this alone our lives should be forfeit. We then added to this crime by aiding the escape of Eldrich's enemy, damning us doubly in his eyes."

Kehler began to protest, but Erasmus held up his hand.

"There is no court of appeals when dealing with a mage, Mr. Kehler. I know what you will say: 'Was it not Eldrich's design that we lead the Tellerites into the cave, to their ruin?' Yes, and yes again to any arguments of logic and justice, but the justice of men has no bearing in the affairs of the mages. Only their own mysterious code, and according to the strictures of that code our lives should be forfeit for what we have done. Unless we are able to accomplish this task."

The survivors looked at each other, all of them still, almost hunched, like the hunted. How battered they all looked, how haunted by their brush with death.

They were nearly buried alive, Erasmus thought.

Poor Kehler looked almost as aged as Clarendon, with his hair going gray too early, his posture stooped by fatigue. Even the bright curiosity of his eyes had disappeared.

Hayes looked only slightly better. His light hair and the blue of his eyes saved him from the dark look of his friend, but he no longer looked boyish, not even when he smiled.

Only Deacon Rose appeared unchanged by their ordeal. His vitality remained. Even his complexion still bore the mark of the sun, not the pale scar of their escape from the darkness. Deacon Rose retained his ability to appear at peace, his practiced charm. The eyes could still smile beneath the cap of gray hair.

Deacon Rose shifted in his chair. "We are to find the girl and her remaining colleagues," he said, not showing the least surprise.

Erasmus nodded. "Yes, but there are no others, only Anna."

"How do we know she is even alive?" Hayes asked.

"She is alive," Rose said, "or the mage would not seek her."

"But, Erasmus," Hayes protested, "certainly Eldrich can find her more easily than we. After all, we are not masters of the arts."

Rose interrupted, for he seemed suddenly rejuvenated. "But the Tellerites have ways of hiding themselves from practitioners of the arts. That is the reason for Eldrich's elaborate ruse to draw them out into the open—to force them to reveal themselves—and Anna will not make that mistake again. No, she must be hunted down by natural means, like any criminal."

Hayes sat up abruptly, his upper body swaying in a small circle as though he had been set off balance. "But what has Anna done to me? Nothing for which I would see her murdered, and that is certainly what Eldrich intends if she is found. Am I to participate in this crime to save my own precious skin?" He shook his head, pushing out his lower lip. "I will not be party to such a thing, no matter what the cost. It is not just Eldrich who has a code."

Both Kehler and Clarendon nodded, the little man muttering, "Hear, hear," under his breath. Then he looked up at Erasmus. "What of you, Erasmus? Will you carry out this errand of cruelty for Eldrich?"

Erasmus felt himself mired in some sort of mental ooze, as though still not quite awake—not quite back into this world from the murky world of cave and nightmare. Would he do this? What justification could there be other than self-preservation—and he knew what it was like to live with that.

He shook his head. "Let me tell you this, if any of us refuse Eldrich's mercy, it will not be a simple matter of paying with our lives. Mages are more vengeful than you know. Men have suffered a lifetime of unspeakable torture for angering a mage. You should think hard on that before you make any decisions."

Rose stood suddenly. "Listen to me. It is more than fear of torture that should be taken into account here. Eldrich has not set out to destroy the followers of Teller for petty vengeance—as notorious as his kind might be for such acts. I have read the confessions of the Tellerites, the heretics who hid within the church. The intentions of their conspiracy were not so innocent as one would expect from meeting young Anna and Banks."

Clarendon stood, red-faced, and Erasmus thought he would storm from the room, but Hayes put a hand gently on his arm. "It will cost us nothing to hear him out, Randall."

Rose paused to look at the small man, and then continued. "There has been much speculation about the disappearance of the mages. We don't know why only Eldrich remains, but from the confessions of the heretics I learned this: Augury was at the heart of the mages' decision." He began to pace stiffly across the floor between Erasmus and the others, looking at no one, as though he rehearsed a speech. "What, precisely, the vision revealed I cannot tell you, but it was frightening and apocalyptic—frightening even to the mages. It would seem that they were divided in their interpretation of the vision. How consensus was reached is unknown, but somehow it was eventually accepted that the catastrophe would result from the arts or their practice. How else could they have arrived at the decision to erase the arts from this world? To hide their last vestiges for the good of the earth, perhaps for the good of mankind?"

The priest stopped his pacing and met the eyes of his audience, all attentive now, even Clarendon captive.

"The Tellerites will keep the arts alive at all costs, that is their avowed purpose. They either do not believe in the augury of the mages, or do not care, I don't know which, but they are willing to take all risks to see their purpose accomplished. Do you see? Anna and Banks might have seemed innocent—and perhaps in some ways they were, but even so they are willing to risk the apocalypse to possess the arts. An apocalypse even the mages feared."

Rose stood in the center of the floor, looking around at the others, his fists clenched tightly at his sides.

"What do you say to this, Mr. Flattery?" Clarendon asked softly, like a man too tired to argue. "Is there any truth in the priest's ravings or is this another in his long string of deceptions?"

Erasmus shook his head. "I don't know, Randall. I don't know. Eldrich did not confide in me, nor did I learn much of the mages' history—a secret they guard assiduously. I wish I could say more, but . . . It is certain that Eldrich is determined to see the end of the arts in his lifetime, there can be little doubt of that. Is Eldrich driven by revenge to destroy the Tellerites? I think it would be naive to deny the truth of that, but given the circumstances it seems to be more than just revenge. The Tellerites clearly want to keep the arts alive—Deacon Rose is right in this—and it would seem that Eldrich is equally determined that this will not come to be."

"But the priest has lied repeatedly," Clarendon began, but Kehler interrupted.

"Be at peace, Randall, there is some greater evidence that the Deacon tells the truth, this time. I saw references to the Tellerites—the men the church calls Teller's bastards—in my researches at Wooton. Whether their confessions were true, I cannot say, but they were not just a convenient invention of Deacon Rose. According to the Tellerites, the mages did have a catastrophic vision. Teller's bastards were aware of some part of it, perhaps from their own augury, but they believed it did not apply to them, but only to the mages. I did not connect it to this—the disappearance of the mages. Only now have I heard that suggested."

Kehler bounced to his feet, animated, unable to remain still. He stole the floor from Rose with his outrage and frustration. "But what are we to do? If we were to choose the path of honor, we would refuse to involve ourselves in this conflict of the mages, this struggle in which we cannot even begin to gauge right from wrong. Yet Erasmus has put such a fear into us—into me at least—that it would appear our only course of action is to obey Eldrich or self-murder to avoid a lifetime of unimaginable horror." He threw up his arms and then let them fall limply at his sides. Suddenly he was very still. "Or do we accept that Eldrich has some reason other than revenge for his pursuit of the Tellerites, as the Deacon suggests? That there is some justification for what he does? Some justification that even we would accept?" He shook his head, touching a hand to his brow. "I cannot know the answer. It is not as though Eldrich will show leniency toward Anna if she is found—of that I'm certain. There will be no charity, no application of reason to turn her away from her purpose. No, if we deliver Anna to Eldrich we will be party to murder, in one form or another." He stood like a scarecrow, his arms rising as though waving ineffectually at crows.

"But, Mr. Kehler," Rose said, his voice calm and reasonable—the tone Erasmus had come to identify with his most egregious lies. "Many criminals do not comprehend the harm that they do, yet they go to the gallows for their crimes, all the same. We make no allowance for this other than madness. If we are to be utterly generous, we might say that it is not so different with Anna. She does not know what will come of her actions, nor, perhaps, does she want to know. But whether her intentions are good or evil, I am convinced that great harm will result all the same. An apocalypse, Mr. Kehler. An event so frightening that the mages would renounce the arts to avoid it. *Renounce the arts!*

"I think we can hardly imagine such a catastrophe, for surely it is more terrible by far than any war contrived by man. A war to wound the very earth itself. Who would not give his own life to prevent such a thing? I would, certainly. Better we live with the guilt of our actions than allow the apocalypse. Moral cowardice comes in many forms, Mr. Kehler, and all shades—not simply black and white. The life of one for the lives of many, and perhaps more besides." He turned in a slow circle, like a clockwork-toy, regarding each of them in turn.

Clarendon looked through him, addressing Erasmus. "What say you, Mr. Flattery? This priest could justify any atrocity, I think, if it would benefit mother church, but I distrust his ever-so-reasonable rationalizations. 'A tongue so sweet it should be cut out and fed to dogs,' were the words of Beaumont, and I feel they apply doubly here."

Erasmus rubbed his palms into his eyes, feeling the burn. "I fear we are too depleted by our ordeal to make wise decisions. One can always rationalize when one's life is threatened. This must be guarded against. Let us weigh all that has been said on the scales of our conscience, try to sleep, and decide in the morning."

The others nodded at this, perhaps happy to put off passing such a verdict.

"But I have already made my decision," Deacon Rose said, rising to his feet, almost lightly.

"Do not be hasty, Deacon Rose," Erasmus said. "Eldrich's servant intimated that his master would deal with you. It was ominously said. Best take this night and look into your soul. Sleep the sleep of the innocent, gentlemen." Erasmus turned and left the room.

Erasmus stood upon his balcony and stared up at the wandering star that had trailed across the heavens these past weeks. "A wondering star," he said aloud, for so he had misunderstood the term as a child. A star that wondered—as did he. What could such a star think about? The question of a wondering child, riding through the heavens on the back of this miraculous planet.

The ancients believed such natural phenomenon to be signs, portents—of evil, almost invariably, but sometimes of favorable events as well.

"And which do you presage?" he asked, the wondering child not quite absorbed into the knowing adult.

"Mr. Flattery?"

Erasmus started, unsure of the voice's source.

"Sir?"

One of the attendants stood, poised in the door.

"Excuse me, Mr. Flattery. I knocked but had no answer. I wouldn't normally intrude, sir, but you have a visitor. . . ." The man's eyebrows raised. "It is the Earl of Skye, Mr. Flattery."

"Skye?" Erasmus must not have looked pleased, for the attendant blanched.

"Is it too late, sir? I would have asked him to return tomorrow, but he seemed so anxious to see you, and . . . well, he is the Earl of Skye."

"No, that's quite all right. Can you show him up?"

A moment later the silver-maned Skye appeared, even his movements, strong and graceful, almost feline: the lion of empiricism.

"It is a great honor," Erasmus began, but Skye waved a hand to cut him short.

"Hardly. I must begin by apologizing for intruding like this and at such an hour. You're unharmed by your adventure, I take it?"

"Largely, yes."

The two men settled themselves in wicker chairs. Despite his obvious need to see Erasmus, Skye appeared curiously reluctant to speak. He kept shifting in his chair, looking as though he were about to begin—but then demurring.

Erasmus did not know what he could say that would allow the man to overcome his reticence.

"Mr. Flattery, I . . . Oh, where to begin?" the empiricist muttered.

"I know the Peliers Lady Chilton showed me belonged to you," Erasmus prompted.

Skye looked at him obliquely.

"Yes? Well, you also went down into the cave in the company of Kehler and Hayes. I don't know what they might have told you."

Erasmus nodded. He had assured Hayes he would keep his confidence.

"We were trapped in the cave for several days—a section of the roof fell in, you see. For most of that time we were convinced we would die there—taking anything said to the grave. I don't think they would have broken their word otherwise."

Skye nodded. "Indeed. Under the circumstances I cannot hold them responsible. I'm only glad they survived, for it was partly due to me that they came to be in that cave in the first place. Perhaps they told you this? Flames, but it is a long story."

"I have learned of a number of things: the story of Compton Heath and the Stranger; Baumgere's discovery of the crypt and his search of the caves; the Peliers, of course."

"And what did you find in the cavern?" He leaned forward, his gaze fixed on Erasmus in anticipation. "What was it Baumgere sought?"

Erasmus sat back in his chair. "We found nothing but a section of a cave never before explored. We almost found our deaths. As to Baumgere—I had hoped you might tell me. What was he looking for?"

Skye nodded, sucking air through his teeth. "Exactly. What?" He shifted in his chair again. "I believe he was searching for the way to the land of the Strangers. He wanted to know from where they had come, for the Stranger of Compton Heath was but one. There were almost certainly others.

"You saw the painting of the man crossing the bridge? Yes? It depicts the Compton Heath Stranger, I'm certain. He passes over a bridge from one world to another, and what awaits him? A dark carriage, just as the carriage came for the real Stranger." He looked steadily at Erasmus. "Was it Eldrich? Is that what you think?"

"I don't know for certain, but it seems very likely."

"Then mages were interested in these things. It is not surprising; but why, do you think?"

Erasmus shrugged. "The affairs of mages are a mystery to men, Lord Skye. If these Strangers came from somewhere else—Well, the mages were almost all possessed of an enlarged curiosity, something that I'm sure you understand."

"Of course, but from where did they come? That is the question." He rose out of his chair, agitated, and went to look out the window, hands on his hips, his frock coat thrown back. "Baumgere seemed to think that the entire myth of Faery resulted from the visits of Strangers. Do you realize what such a thing would mean to our concept of the cosmos?"

"May I ask you a question?" Erasmus ventured.

Skye faced him. "By all means."

"There is a group interested in such things. I have only met two of them. A man named Banks and a young woman who goes by the name Anna Fielding. She is unique looking, hair a faded red . . . I can't think how to describe her."

"Looks as though she has had part of her life drained away? Part of her very being?"

"Yes, that's her. She's in her early twenties, mid-twenties at the latest, though she does look drained. I have never seen anyone like her."

Skye returned to his chair. He appeared still, now, and lost in thought.

"Obviously, you've met her."

"Yes," Skye said softly, "or at least I assume it was she." He rubbed his hand over the chair's wicker arm. "It was an odd thing. I went to visit a friend at her home. . . ." He proceeded to tell Erasmus the story of meeting Anna, though it clearly unsettled him. When he finished, he sat brooding as though he had forgotten the purpose of his visit.

"It was an even stranger meeting than you realize," Erasmus said. "I think Eldrich arranged it."

"She was his agent?"

"No. She was the precise opposite. She is his enemy, or at least that is Eldrich's belief. Centuries ago a renegade apprentice of a mage—a near-mage—made off with some texts that had belonged to his master. It was during the war with the church so the attention of the mages was focused elsewhere. This man created a secret society, the purpose of which was to learn the arts of the mages. To eventually rival them. Anna was a member of that society."

"What? Are you saying that centuries later these people persist?"

"Not the same people, obviously, but others. Their descendants in purpose if not in blood. You were put into danger—from Moncrief—so that Anna and her colleagues would save you, thereby revealing themselves."

"That is preposterous!"

"So it would seem, but the mage uses people without them ever realizing. You see, the followers of Teller—that is how these renegades are known—practice augury. They had a vision of you, Lord Skye. In it you opened a gate for them, and beyond stood a man who held a book of lore . . . and other talismans of power. They had to keep you safe, you see. You were to open a gate to knowledge and power. That is how they revealed themselves to Eldrich, who sought them out to destroy them."

"You're seriously suggesting that I was a dupe in Eldrich's plot. That he would use me so? A man in my position! I can't accept that." The man placed both feet firmly on the floor and leaned forward, elbows on knees, hands about his face.

"Nevertheless, it is true. Eldrich cares nothing for rank, nor even genius. He would toss away a man's life for his own purpose without qualms. Indeed, he would deal with the King this same way, should it suit him. Mages are above the laws and morality of men, or so they believe. You were used, Lord Skye, as was I."

Skye stared at him now, his eyes wide, lip almost trembling with rage. "I appeared somehow in the augury of these people? Is that what you're saying?"

"Precisely. They catch glimpses of events that might come to be, but these are filtered, somehow, filtered through the recesses of the mind so that they emerge in symbols—visions. You have the Peliers. What did Pelier do but somehow catch glimpses through time?"

Skye said nothing for a moment, suddenly calm. But it was more than calm—he was shocked into silence.

"Lord Skye? Are you well, sir?"

Skye nodded, still saying nothing, then he rose slowly and went to stand before the window again, his shoulders drooping a little. He took several deep breaths of the cool air. "Have you seen the wandering star?" he asked, his voice both soft and weary.

"Yes."

Skye nodded. "Do you know my history, Mr. Flattery?"

"I'm sure everyone in Farrland knows something of your story."

"I find that surpassingly strange, but nonetheless let me acquaint you with it again. There are some few things of which most are unaware.

"I was an orphan, taken in by a kind family. At fourteen I fell from a horse and apparently lay near to death for several days, and though I recovered, the memory of my life before that time was lost. The physicians said that in time I might recover some of what was lost, though it was far from a sure thing." He rubbed his fingers over the palm of his other hand as though trying to erase the lines. "And memories do come to me at odd times. Occasionally in dreams, but often waking. I cannot explain these for they seem to be brought on by certain emotions, as though my feelings at a particular moment are so like those of a past time that some shard of memory catches in them. More often it is just the emotion—or a memory of emotion—and the incident from my past remains just out of grasp." He shook his head, lifting a hand to his brow. "However, odd fragments of memory come to me, and they are truly strange. They are of my younger years, but not of my adopted parents' home. Most often I have visions of a strange city that I cannot identify. Or I have what seem to be memories of ideas—as though they are not truly mine. The laws of motion came to me thus, and many other things as well. And in my dreams I sometimes fly through the air. . . ." He fell briefly silent, oddly distressed by this confession.

"I have had dreams of soaring like a bird," Erasmus said, feeling he must reassure the man somehow. "And certainly, when inspired, many have said it seemed knowledge they had always known."

"Yes, but these dreams and waking memories are so consistent, as though I spent my youth in another land. Much has been made of my manner of speech—it almost seems to be slightly accented. A result of my accident, everyone assumes. . . ." He looked at Erasmus over his shoulder, the starlight turning his mane of hair to silver, his face pale as snow. "Words come to me. Words no one has ever heard. They have no meaning, yet they are words nonetheless. I can feel that they roll of my tongue with great ease. And there is more. I remember characters—written characters—that I have never before seen."

"Like those in Pelier's painting?" Erasmus asked.

Skye looked back to the window, shaking his head. "No; unlike them. But neither are they like any script I know."

Erasmus struggled to make sense of Skye's words, to understand what disturbed the great man so. "Do you think you're having visions like Pelier? Is that it?"

Skye shook his head, pressing fingers to his eye's inner corner. "Perhaps. . . ." He paused, taking a long ragged breath. "But I fear it is madness," he whispered.

Erasmus was stunned by this sudden admission. "You have the most celebrated mind of our time, Lord Skye. Certainly your thoughts seem lucid, utterly logical. And if you are having visions . . . celebrated men and women have experienced the same. The mages practiced augury. Pelier was not entirely alone."

"Pelier went mad, you know—self-murdered." The great empiricist raised a hand, touching fingers to the glass. He pulled his hand away suddenly, animating his slumping frame. "Do pardon me. It was not my intention to burden you with . . . this."

Erasmus did not feel it a burden, though he didn't understand why Skye had chosen to confide in him. Did it explain the earl's interest in Pelier? Or was there something more?

"You cannot know what it is like to lose part of your life—your childhood. Years gone, and these fragments of memory—memories or dreams—floating up. They are like ghosts, but ghosts within. All so very strange.

"Do you know there are no records of my birth? I was a foundling, or so it is said. Though I have tried, I cannot find who my true parents were." He hesitated. "I am a mystery to myself. A stranger, in my own way." He fell silent again, moving his fingers over the glass, over the reflection of his face, Erasmus realized.

"Your parents have passed through?"

"Long ago."

"Had they no friends? Someone must remember your arrival at your parents' home. They had servants, a nanny?"

Skye continued to move his fingers, almost tenderly, across the cold pane.

"None I can find. The servants I remember had not been with the family long—my parents were not easy on their domestic staff." Erasmus could feel the man's burden of suffering in the silence. As distressing as Erasmus' own.

"I—I'm not sure why you have told me this."

"Nor am I."

Silence again. Skye dropped his hand, but continued to gaze at the glass, at his reflection and the darkness beyond. He turned toward Erasmus, not meeting his eye. "I've taken enough of your time, Mr. Flattery. Excuse my ramblings. You and the others are safe—that's the important thing. Pleasures of the evening to you."

Erasmus barely made the door to let the man out, and once Skye had gone, he found himself staring at the same window as though something would be revealed to him there, or he would see what Skye saw. "How very odd," he whispered. "What had he meant to tell me?"

Certainly Skye had been wrong about one thing. Erasmus knew precisely what it was like to lose his childhood. But what had Skye said? *I am a stranger—in my own way.*

Erasmus raised his hand to the glass to smear the slick of condensation and watched his reflection distort. And what was that he saw? A faint light? A wondering star?

## ⤳ Seven

The brook they camped beside chattered incessantly, the clatter of rocks rolling in the streambed. Aromatic pines scented the breeze and rippled in the gusts along the hillsides.

The beauty of the surroundings went unnoticed by Anna. She stared at the roughly drawn map again, considering. Could she make her way from here?

Her guide assured her that it was simple, the landmarks unmistakable, but still, she was born and bred to cities and tame countryside, not mountains and wilderness. She gazed over at her sleeping guide, the wind tugging at his hair, sun burnishing his young face.

"The sleep of grace," she whispered.

He had been the woodsman she'd met upon escaping the cave. After Halsey's sacrifice, she had returned to him, remembering his boast that he knew the hills better than most men knew their gardens. If he'd only realized where his immodesty would lead.

Anna folded the map with tenderness, as though it were the last letter of a beloved.

"Give me strength," she whispered to no deity in particular. "If I am to survive, this is who I must be."

In her years with Halsey and the others, she had been spared so much—so many burdens the others had shouldered.

"If I am to survive," she whispered.

She looked again at the young man, his face softened by sleep. So content and trusting.

They had lain together the three nights since she had found him again. Anna had not protested. It felt good to be held, to have a few moments of oblivion, escape from her sorrow. There had been some guilt in her surrender as well, knowing what the future might bring.

*I cannot tarry,* she told herself. *I am hunted.*

She drew a long breath and forced herself to cross to her companion, sinking down by his head. Gently she smoothed his brow. Gently.

"You will always have your hills," she whispered, but he did not stir.

Whispering phrases in Darian, she produced a small, silver blade. A tear fell onto the young man's cheek, running off as though it were his own. In a quick motion she cut the carotid artery, pulling her hand away from the blood, watching it spread out onto the ground.

The brook sang its hollow song. Rocks clattering over rocks.

She put a hand to her face for a moment, horrified by what she'd brought herself to do. The knowledge that she was left no choice did not comfort her. A flutter, and her chough landed on a saddle, watching the proceedings with keen interest.

Dipping her fingers in the warm lake of blood, she made marks upon the man's face, upon his chest. She spoke words in Darian and chanted mournfully, tears still falling onto his cheeks and mixing with the blood.

The rite lasted the morning. Time she did not have, but she was not yet as callow as a mage—as callow as she would have to become. Fire consumed the body, and smoke drifted up into the hills, releasing the woodsman to his mountains and the unfettered wind.

"Your spirit will always watch over this glen," she said to the flames, the twisting pillar of smoke.

The ash she gave to the brook, to the river it would become, the distant lake, and then, one day, the sea.

"You will return as rain," she said, as the brook turned the gray-white of spawn. "Or lie upon the hills as snow."

The chough bounced from rock to rock in the racing brook, intent on what she did, inquisitive, its intelligent eyes aglitter.

"Yes, I have become a monster, too," she said to her familiar. "As cold of heart as the carrion crow, swooping down upon the innocent to pluck out their eyes."

"*Chuff*," the bird said, releasing the single syllable with such conviction that one would think it an entire sentence, the articulation of avian thought.

"This man would have been my betrayer," she said to the bird, her voice a bit plaintive. "If I had let him go, the followers of Eldrich would certainly have found me." She paused, the chough's cold eye meeting hers. "But why do I tell you? You don't care what atrocities I commit—do you—cousin to the carrion crow?"

The bird tilted its head, staring at her one-eyed, as though struggling with the language of humans, then suddenly, dipped its blood-red bill into the murky water.

For a moment she stood appalled, then she thrust her hand into the milky waters and drank, tasting the salt of blood, the bitterness of ashes.

## ⤳ Eight

As the morning sun lifted, a line of shadow and light descended the hillside, illuminating each tree like a green flame.

Erasmus had wakened in darkness, too troubled to sleep, and at the first sign of gray, had stepped out into the sanitarium's sprawling garden.

"I have become a troubled man," he told himself.

He was troubled that morning by more than just the visit of Percy Bryce. His thoughts had turned to the countess, as though her company were a haven from the madness in which he found himself.

As soon as he had been able, he had sent a note to her, but no reply had come, and the silence was beginning to magnify his growing feelings of isolation. Certainly, she did not hurry to visit him or bring him comfort, and Erasmus was beginning to accept that it was but a night's indiscretion, soon forgotten—by the countess, at least.

"'The dove-gray wing of morning.'"

Erasmus, seated on a bench, turned to find Clarendon looking down from nearby steps, his wolfhound, Dusk, by his side.

"Ah, Randall! Is it Faldor? 'Awash in dew drop stars,' or some such thing. Is that the line?"

"Very nearly. You slept no better than I, I take it?" Clarendon put a hand on the great dog's shoulder as if to reassure him that Erasmus was a friend.

"I managed a few hours, but then woke and could not stop my fevered mind. And I fear I have little to show for so many hours of concentration."

Clarendon came down the stairs, favoring his injured knee a little. He lowered himself to one of the benches, Dusk sitting close by. The dog had found his master somehow, or perhaps having heard of Clarendon's escape from the cave, some kind soul had brought the dog up to the sanitarium—either way, the beast had barely left his master's side since the two had been reunited. "I have seldom experienced such indecision myself. We are being asked to take so much on faith. Could Eldrich not have provided even the slimmest of explanations? If the mage has perfectly good reasons for pursuing the followers of Teller, could he not at least have said so? Given us some justification? Farrelle's ghost, but I am not one to be bullied, I will tell you that. It is not my nature to make decisions out of fear—or ignorance. One would think a mage would be wiser in the ways of men."

Erasmus nodded. So one would think. "The mages have long used fear, or promise of reward, to motivate those who did their bidding. It would appear they think us little more sensate than beasts. They only seem to exhibit subtlety when manipulating those who are unaware. As though there is challenge enough, then. I'm afraid, Randall, that we'll get no more explanation than we have. Whether we accept the priest's reasoning, that the followers of Teller are a great danger to us all, is the question."

Clarendon nodded, reaching down to gently massage his knee. "Yes. If Kehler had not corroborated some of what the priest said, I would reject his explanation outright. The man is the greatest blackguard I have ever met—and he has his own reasons for wanting to destroy Anna. I think him as capable of vengeance as any mage!" He paused, obviously tired yet, searching for his train of thought. "Kehler, however, has forced me to have second thoughts. And there is this entire matter of the disappearance of the mages. The only explanation I have heard that makes sense is that they are erasing magic for fear of the harm it will do sometime hence. Even Kehler had read about their augury—a cataclysm." He met Erasmus' gaze. "Do we accept the truth of this and go seeking Anna's destruction, or are we merely grasping at any explanation that will allow us to survive? Are we motivated by cowardice?"

"I can't imagine that you have ever been motivated by cowardice, Randall.

Whatever your decision, it will reflect your integrity and courage. I confess, I trust your judgment in this more than my own."

Clarendon looked at Erasmus for a moment, lost in contemplation. "Mr. Flattery, I journeyed with you down into the cave and saw you prove your courage repeatedly. Beyond all doubt. Who among us swam the Mirror Lake? Led the traverse above the falls? And went into the water-filled passage in the end? No, your courage is not in question. One act in childhood, Mr. Flattery, does not make the pattern of a life. Every man among us, I'm sure, has some act that they regret—that they feel was not an act of bravery. The rest of us were fortunate that our small acts of timidity resulted in no serious injury to those we thrust forward. No, you will not choose out of cowardice. I worry more that you might choose unwisely for fear of being timorous. That is a real danger and you must guard against it, Mr. Flattery."

Erasmus was surprised at how grateful he was for this vote of confidence.

"Tell me, Mr. Flattery," Clarendon began, his voice dropping, "what do you think we found down there? Oh, I know, it was the burial chamber of Landor, but was it somehow a passage? The gate to Faery, that Baumgere sought?"

"I believe Anna suggested as much, though why we should accept anything she said as truth I don't know. But certainly it seems likely. It marked the place where the first mages emerged into our own world. Emerged like the Stranger of Compton Heath; if you believe in the Stranger. . . ."

Clarendon nodded. "What choice have I but to believe?" he said softly.

At that moment a tall woman appeared below them, walking along the edge of the man-made lake. She seemed to be seeking others, looking in at every bower, at each bench. Erasmus could almost sense a desperation in the way she moved.

Erasmus found himself rising from the bench to watch her. This movement caught her eye and she stopped, staring up at Erasmus and Clarendon. Quickly she began to toil up the small rise, and a moment later she appeared at the stairhead.

There she paused, as though suddenly shy or unsure of herself. Erasmus thought her a most interesting woman; tall and well formed, yet her hair was cut like a boy's, her dress plain. In fact, now that he could see her well, he thought her a mass of contradictions: boyish; womanly; wearing a badly fitting dress of cheap materials, but over that a knitted shawl of fine silk in subtle color and design. This could be no one but the countess' friend, Marianne Edden.

Erasmus felt the smile appear on his lips. The countess must be here as well, searching for him inside, perhaps.

"Mr. Flattery, I hope?" she said.

"Erasmus Flattery," he replied, making a leg. "And you are Miss Marianne Edden, I take it? This is my friend, Randall Spencer Emanual Clarendon."

She smiled at Randall, who made a low bow.

"It is an honor, Miss Edden," Clarendon said, "for surely I have read all your books, some of them twice, and I will tell you, they are all improved by a second reading."

Marianne nodded at this, hardly seeming to register the compliment.

"Is Lady Chilton here, as well?" Erasmus asked, both relieved and entirely flattered that the countess would come to visit him.

"No, Mr. Flattery. That's just it. The countess is gone. Run off. And I am worried beyond the ability of words to describe . . ." She hesitated, glancing at Erasmus' companion.

"Shall I leave you?" Clarendon asked softly.

"If you don't mind?" Erasmus asked, and with a gracious bow the small man brought his dog to heel and was off.

Erasmus felt the sudden need to sit, dreading what Marianne might say next.

Marianne came and sat on the adjoining bench. "It is strange beyond all measure," she began. "The countess went off in a carriage at a moment's notice and left not a word of explanation. This is utterly unlike her, I will tell you. And this just a day or two after Averil Kent came by late at night with the strangest story."

"Kent? What has he to do with this?"

"Well, it is not a short story, but I will try to explain. You see, Kent had apparently seen the countess entering a carriage outside our door late in the night. And she was dressed for the bed. He thought her manner so strange that he made shift to follow her." She went on to tell of Kent finding the countess returned to the house, but appearing to sleep sitting up, and then all that had happened since.

Erasmus only shook his head, feeling so utterly without resources, without hope in this matter. He had been barely a pawn of the mage—someone whose life could be tossed away without the slightest concern. What did this woman expect him to do?

Marianne had finished telling her story, and stared at him. "Has this been too much in your reduced state, Mr. Flattery?"

"No, it is nothing to do with that. Were I at the peak of my powers, I would feel just as I do now." But he did feel suddenly ill, and weak beyond measure. He felt his limbs tremble from just the effort of sitting upright. "I will tell you in all honesty, Miss Edden, that there is absolutely nothing that can be done—and no one regrets this more than I. Eldrich . . ." He groped for words. "The mage is a force of nature, Miss Edden. Completely remorseless, and without regard for our laws or principles. Eldrich cares no more for people than a lightning bolt cares for its victims.

"Whatever Eldrich wants from the countess, he will have. Flames, he can make a woman burn with desire for him if that is his whim. There is nothing to be done, Miss Edden, but pray. Pray—if you are able."

Marianne put her hands to her face, her eyes glistening. "Mr. Flattery . . ." she said. "Mr. Flattery . . ." but no more.

"I hope Kent does not catch up to them. I wish I had been here to stop the man." He hung his head at the thought of the painter encountering Eldrich. "But it is unlikely that Kent will overtake them. Mages can travel unnaturally fast when they so desire, and never change a team to do it." He shook his head. "No, Kent is likely safe."

Erasmus' head spun, and he broke a cold sweat. His thoughts seemed to scatter, like a flight of doves released—a mad flutter in all directions. At least Kent had shown courage—born of ignorance, unquestionably, but courage all the same.

And what of Erasmus? Erasmus who had experienced the countess' favors.

He shut his eyes for a moment, trying to stop the spinning. There was nothing to be done. One did not sneak into the house of a mage and steal away the fair damsel. Not in this world.

He thought of the countess lying close to him, the scent of her hair, her perfect lips tugged into an involuntary smile of pleasure and happiness. To think that Eldrich had simply stolen her away—against her will!

Marianne put a hand on his arm. "Can Eldrich simply abduct one of Far-rland's most noted citizens with impunity? There is nothing anyone can do? Martyr's blood, is it the tenth century? Do mages rule the land again?"

"They have never abandoned their rule," Erasmus said, "except to appearances. No, others have been spirited away by a mage and—But excuse me, I frighten you. Perhaps we are entirely wrong in our thinking. The mage is very likely treating the countess with all respect. It is not impossible that she went with him of her own accord. Mages can be very persuasive, even without employing the arts."

The clearing of a throat drew their attention.

Erasmus turned to find Hayes standing at the stairhead.

"Your pardon," he said. "We have convened in your room, Erasmus."

"A moment," Erasmus said, nodding.

He stood, too quickly, and the world wavered.

"You are in the same lodgings?" he said to Marianne. "I will come later if I can, or send word. Let me think on this, Miss Edden. I . . . Let me think."

They appeared almost to huddle close in the room, as though they were back in the cave clinging together for warmth and support. Only Rose sat apart.

"What choice have we been left?" Hayes asked, the bitterness not masked by the quietness of his voice.

"Very little," Clarendon said. "I, for one, would not be ready to accept the justifications of this priest—who would stop at nothing to see Anna dead—but for the word of Mr. Kehler." He looked over at Kehler, as though asking for further confirmation.

Kehler nodded. "I can only repeat my words of last night. There was some cataclysm feared by the mages, and, yes, I do believe that is why the mages have trained no apprentices. I think it is very likely that Anna represents a danger, and not just to the designs of Eldrich. But I am loath to turn her over to Eldrich's justice." He looked at Erasmus now. "What if we were to find her and then deal with Eldrich? Could we not ask leniency for Anna in exchange for giving her up to Eldrich?"

Erasmus felt his head shake. "It might be very unwise, Kehler. Angering the mage is likely to make things worse for all concerned."

"But if Eldrich had no choice but to negotiate?"

"And how would you hold him to his word?" Erasmus asked. "Let me assure you, Eldrich would not feel bound by any agreement we reached. He will do as he pleases."

"There are ways to hold even a mage to his word," Rose said.

The others looked at the priest in surprise.

"The church made pacts with the mages in which both sides were bound to fulfill their part. It can be done."

"If we could find her, it would be worth attempting," Hayes said quickly. "What say you, Erasmus?"

*If we find her,* Erasmus thought, *I shall alert Eldrich by immolating myself— a living beacon. Yet if I refuse to search for her, I will face the justice of Eldrich.*

"Even if we agree to try to treat with Eldrich," Clarendon said, "there is no way we can trust this priest to keep to his word. He has proven that repeatedly."

"I seek only to protect my church, Mr. Clarendon, and despite what you think, I would derive no satisfaction from Anna's suffering or death. I believe she does not understand the consequences of what she does. No, I do not wish her harm. Let us find her and then treat with Eldrich. I think Mr. Kehler is right. Even a mage must make bargains out of necessity."

## ᖇ Nine

A prism of sunlight angled beneath the eaves, delineated in dust motes and by a luminous rectangle on the polished floor. Particles moved within the geometry, their motion too languid to be real.

The awareness that this was no dream formed very slowly, and then crystallized suddenly. The countess pushed herself up on her elbows, realizing that she was in the offending bed and wore not a stitch of clothing.

"Farrelle preserve us. What has been done to me?"

For a second she shut her eyes, searching her memories. She had been sitting in the window, afraid to proceed to bed, and had fallen asleep. A nightingale had been singing. And then Eldrich had appeared. . . . But had he really? It seemed almost a dream now.

But how had she come to bed? Try as she might, she could not remember. The countess clutched the covers to her.

*Why did I agree to this?* The open window drew her eye. Could she slip away? Escape? Surely she had not made the decision to come here of her own free will. She must have been bespelled.

A memory surfaced of the woman at the roadside, and the countess collapsed back into the bed, covering her eyes.

"I am a vain, despicable creature," she sighed. But she knew it was not so simple—there was a fascination as well. She was in the company of a mage. *A mage.* A man whose powers and myth were beyond understanding. A legend. And the last of his kind as well.

"Some women are only besotted with rogues," she said. And though she had always thought them fools, she was suddenly a bit more sympathetic. "Is it the danger, then?"

She did not know. It was a mysterious attraction, like a spell perhaps, but often such things were. Or a kind of madness. All she knew was that she had not the mental discipline to turn her thoughts from Eldrich for long. And her thoughts of him were almost all encompassed by questions. Who was he behind his distant manner? What was it that drove him? How did he manage the feats that he performed?

"And what does he want of me?" she whispered. "Or has he had it already?"

A tap sounded at the door, and then it opened a crack.

"Lady Chilton?"

"Is that you, Mr. Walky?"

"Yes, Lady Chilton; Walky. We are to make a beginning this day. Will you break your fast in your room, or will you come down?"

"In my room, I think. We are to make a beginning . . . ? Of what?"

"Your part in the bargain, Lady Chilton. There is little time and much to do. I will return immediately after your meal, if you will allow it."

The false deference grated on her. She thought it highly unlikely that a refusal would be allowed.

"Until then, Mr. Walky." Now what was this? Somehow she had not thought her part of "the bargain" would be carried out with Walky.

Breakfast was simple but adequate. The countess found herself suffering a little disappointment. Couldn't mages eat exotic fruit out of season, famous and long-ago consumed wines with dinner? Could there not be some sign of these legendary powers? Or was the use of the arts for mere indulgence beneath Eldrich?

The countess held back her sleeve and refilled her glass cup with coffee. Lifting it, she remembered the sunlight pouring into the room when she woke. How like liquid within glass it had appeared, dust motes moving slowly, aimlessly through the liquid light. Touching each other only by chance.

*Like humans,* she imagined. *Floating through life with little thought or purpose, but see how the light illuminates them for an instant here and there.*

She glanced over at a mirror and, given the circumstances, thought she looked remarkably herself. Not tired or frightened. In fact her color was a bit heightened, as though she were in a blush of pleasure, like a woman newly in love. This caused her to color even more. Her dark tresses fell in lustrous curls, and her eyes, set too wide apart, appeared gray this morning, for they changed with her mood and the color of her surroundings. Men wrote poems praising her eyes—and her mouth, which was full and sensuous. She shook her head. What a terrible vice vanity was. A foolish weakness, and the countess knew that, in all the ways that mattered, she was no fool.

A familiar tap on the door drew her attention.

"Mr. Walky? Do come in."

The rotund little man appeared, and she found herself smiling. How like a caricature he was—or like a character in a children's book. A bit distracted, disheveled, but there was something more there. . . . Had Erasmus suggested the man's memory was not quite sound? The countess thought it unlikely. He would not still serve the mage if that were the case. Eldrich would not be one to put up with incompetence. No, Erasmus must have been wrong—but then he had been only a child.

Walky hovered by the door.

"I'm quite finished—well, except for my coffee. Would you care to join me, Mr. Walky? They have provided another cup."

"Kind of you," Walky mumbled as he took the second chair. The countess filled his cup, which seemed to fluster him a little. He was the servant, after all.

It was only then that she realized Walky had set a book on the table—a book with an ancient leather binding, its title faded to unintelligible hints of gold.

"So, Mr. Walky, what is it we shall do?" the countess asked as casually as she was able.

Walky tilted his head to one side and looked at her quizzically. "You do not know?"

She tried to hide her embarrassment by sipping her coffee. "Lord Eldrich has told me nothing."

"Nothing? Even yet? But you agreed. . . ."

She nodded, not sure what to say. *Yes, an intelligent woman can make a foolish bargain. Do not look so disappointed.*

Walky's eyebrows lifted, and then settled as his brow knit in concentration—as though he had little time to spare for contemplating the folly of others. He placed a callused hand on the book, gently. "We are to begin your studies, Lady Chilton, and here is our reader. The primer, or more properly, *Alendrore Primia*—the first book of Landor."

The countess had begun to lift her cup, but put it ungently down, staring at the book. "Erasmus told me that, while in the house of Eldrich as a boy, you left a book in the schoolroom. A book written in a strange language and filled with odd diagrams and drawings. He said that when it was discovered that he'd had the book, he was punished."

Walky did not look at her but nodded slowly, gazing at his hand on the book. "Punished? You need not worry, Lady Chilton. It is the mage's will that you begin your studies with me."

"To what end?"

"Best you ask that of Lord Eldrich, Lady Chilton."

She nodded at the book. "You are not really so forgetful, are you, Mr. Walky? And books of the arts are not left lying about for schoolboys to discover."

Walky did not answer, but continued to stare though his focus was inward now.

The countess reached out and placed a hand softly on Walky's arm. "Tell me honestly, Mr. Walky, will Eldrich use me so heedlessly? For surely Erasmus was supposed to discover the book—to suffer some terrible regret all these years, though what purpose this served I cannot imagine."

Walky had become utterly still. She could feel the muscles of his arm tensed beneath her fingers, yet he did not move his arm away.

*He has not known a tender touch in who knows how long,* the countess realized. *How old is this man and how long has he been living a monk's life in the service of Eldrich?*

She felt his muscles relax suddenly, and his eyes pressed closed. He sagged a little, as though something at his center collapsed.

"Please, Lady Chilton," he said, the constriction of his chest squeezing the words flat.

The countess gazed at the man, who seemed suddenly to be suffering, pressed his arm gently, then let it go.

Mr. Walky removed his hand from the book and sat back in his chair a moment, careful to keep his gaze cast down.

"The primer," he began softly, still not meeting her gaze, "is the first book in the study of the arts."

For a long moment the countess heard no more. *The study of the arts.*

## ∽ Ten

The baggage made a pyramid of battered leather in the corner of Sir John's room: a monument to his resolve, for he was in no hurry to return to Avonel. Having been abandoned here by Bryce, Sir John had been tempted to prolong his visit. Even a few days without worries of Bryce appearing at his door would be a great gift. Shirking duty was not, however, in Sir John's nature.

Bryce. . . . And to think he had asked Sennet to find out what he could about the man! Sir John was certain Sennet had not uncovered the truth, or anything like it. Bryce served the mage, and so, indirectly, did Sir John. A thought that invariably caused him such anxiety that his hands shook and blood drained from his face, leaving him sweating and slightly disoriented.

"Dinner," he said aloud, intentionally turning his mind to matters more appealing. It was unfortunate that Kent had run off on his fool's errand, it would be good to have company this evening. But Kent had his obsession with the countess driving him—driving him to ruin, Sir John was certain. Poor fool. These artistic types, they were so . . . *capricious.* Kent would come to regret it.

Sir John pulled on a frock coat of royal blue and regarded himself in the mirror. Still a passable-looking man, younger in appearance than most his age. A woman could do worse, he was sure.

A banging on the lower door interrupted his self-appraisal, and he watched his face sag as the confidence drained away.

"It is only the landlord, come to be sure I need no help."

Sir John took a lamp and descended the stairs, unbolting the door.

"I am hardly a ghost, Sir John," Bryce said. "You need not look so. Will you not invite me in?"

Sir John tried to regain his composure. "Certainly, certainly. I am surprised, as you see, as you had left so abruptly. . . ."

Bryce pressed past him, pounding up the stairs with his customary energy. Sir John struggled to keep pace, the light swaying around them in the narrow stairwell.

Bryce eyed the small mountain of baggage. "Just in time, I see. But what have you done? Purchased another wardrobe? You had less than half this when we came."

"It belongs to a friend, I'm carrying it back to Avonel with me."

"What friend is this?" Bryce asked.

Sir John hesitated, almost certain this inhumanly precise man would catch him in a lie. "Kent. Averil Kent. He's run off somewhere in his pursuit of beauty." Sir John shrugged. "Artists . . ."

"Ah." Bryce turned a chair slightly and took a seat, Sir John's deception apparently unnoticed. "Matters have changed, Sir John, and we have need of your services again." Bryce spread his hands and touched the tips of the fingers together. "There is a woman we must find. Find at all costs. She goes by the name of Anna Fielding, though she will not likely be using that name now. Fortunately she is uncommon looking: about twenty-three or -four, above average height for a woman. Her hair is straight and long—past the shoulder—and the oddest shade of red-blonde; as though it had been drained of color, or faded from too much time in the sun. 'Washed out,' is how one described it. But it does not stop there: her entire appearance is the same, as though she has had some of her life drained away, yet her manner belies this, for she is as vital as any her age."

"Is this not the young woman said to have gone down into the cavern after Erasmus Flattery and the others?" Sir John thought to cover his discomfiture with a question.

"The very one."

"But none of her party emerged. I have heard that Flattery and his friends all perished."

"She did not," Bryce said firmly.

Sir John shifted his weight to his other foot. "What am I to do?"

"You are to go to the Admiralty, to all of your most influential friends. This woman must be found and, above all, must not escape by sea. The ports have to be watched, watched as never before."

Sir John stared at Bryce. "And how am I to accomplish this? Am I to tell the Sea Lord that an unknown gentleman must have this girl for unknown reasons? Flames, Bryce, I cannot perform miracles!"

"Tell them whatever you must. That she is a criminal. That she has stolen something from one of Farrland's most influential citizens—which she has."

Bryce shook his head. He was tired of it. Utterly exhausted by the lie. "Why do I not simply tell them the truth?" he said, suddenly a bit breathless. "That Lord Eldrich wants this woman for his own reasons."

It was the only time Sir John had ever seen Bryce taken by surprise. No matter what happened now, he had that satisfaction, at least.

Bryce touched the corners of his mouth with finger tips, then he almost smiled—an act Sir John had thought unnatural for him. "Sir John, Sir John. Curiosity can be the greatest curse of man." Bryce rose from his chair, pacing across the room, the soft touch of his boots on carpet, then the brittle sound as they struck wood.

Bryce turned suddenly on Sir John. "You were better off not knowing, you realize?"

"So parents tell their children, but ignorance is a curse, I believe."

Bryce fixed him with his unreadable look. "Eldrich wants this woman found," he said firmly. "It would be very unwise of you to try to back out of our arrangement now."

"You need not threaten me, Mr. Bryce. I understand my position. But you ask a miracle of me. I am not the King's Man, after all."

Bryce gazed at him intently for a moment and then moved to the writing desk, uncorking the ink bottle and taking up a pen. After a moment he motioned for Sir John, and removing a small box and a thick sheaf of papers from his coat, placed them with the newly written letter into the knight's hands. "Take these," he said. "You will deliver them to a lodge on the road from Castlebough. You see, I have drawn a map." He went over the directions so that Sir John could not mistake them.

Sir John looked at this, and the folded letter in his hand, "I have sealing wax," he said.

This appeared to amuse Bryce. "Read it, if you like."

Sir John hesitated a moment, not sure why, then he unfolded the paper. But it was no script he knew. He heard his breath catch and he looked quickly up at Bryce.

"He will want to speak with you, Sir John. You may not think ignorance such a curse, then."


## ⤳ Eleven

When she watched his hands, she thought of a dancer. The movements were so fluid, the long, elegant fingers so sure. Even performing simple acts, like unstopping the bottle, they seemed to perform a dance. And everything he touched, he touched so lightly, as though the force commonly used by men was never required of a mage.

Eldrich tipped the bottle into the mortar and out tumbled small seeds, like peppercorns. He took up a pestle and began to crush them, releasing a pungent fragrance into the air.

"The seed was carried here by the first mages and has been cultivated by my kind ever since. It is the most precious commodity in the known world, for without it there are no arts, no 'magic.' One may study the arts for a lifetime and have talent in abundance, but without the seed to release that talent—" He continued to move the pestle, crushing the seed to powder, his beautiful hand moving in slow rhythm. "The elixir is simplicity itself to make, that is why we guard the seed above all else. It is death to touch this seed without the express permission of a mage. In my household only Walky may handle it. Teller stole seed, for which his life was to be forfeit, but he escaped us." He continued grinding the seed to a fine powder.

The countess began to feel distinctly uncomfortable, though she was not sure why. As though she were afraid her hand might slip, and she would touch the seed and pay the arbitrary price.

"When the seed is first taken, waking dreams often occur. Some of these are 'visions,' though that depends upon the nature of one's talent. One will often begin to dream vividly when asleep, as well. It is good to note such dreams down when waking, for one can never be sure of their significance and they are soon forgotten." He stopped and stared down into the mortar. Satisfied, he lifted the steaming kettle off its hook over the fire and poured water into cups. Taking up the mortar and a dagger, he apportioned the powder into the cups, stirring them with the blade. The countess watched it glint in the candlelight, a little mesmerized by the movement.

"A transformation is initiated by the seed, for the path from man to mage is not merely through learning. It is more profound than that—profound and irreversible." He lifted one of the cups and, leaning forward, set it before her. The second cup he raised, his dark gaze upon her.

"Me?!" she said, finally realizing that this was not to be a mere demonstration. "But I am no mage's apprentice!"

He continued to regard her. "No, but in this world you are the closest thing. Do not drink it all in one rush, but sip it slowly your first time. You might find the experience a bit overwhelming otherwise."

The countess drew her hands back off the table. Transformation? What in this round world was he talking about? "I did not agree to this."

"Indeed, you did. You simply did not ask what our bargain entailed." He held out his cup as though about to offer a toast. *"Raise it,"* he said, the music in his voice suddenly very cold.

She found this command so chilling, so utterly disturbing, that she moved her hands so they all but touched the cup.

"It is also the seed which lengthens one's years and preserves the vigor and appearance of youth—like the apples of immortality."

"But there was a cost to obtaining those apples," she said softly.

"There is always a cost. The seed is habituating. You will require it. There are other effects as well, but these can be mitigated. Think of it, Lady Chilton. You have but to drink, and you will avoid the fate you saw at the roadside. The fate of all those who do not die young. The ruin of age, the loss of physical powers, of one's mental acuity, of memory, of one's past. It is a loss of dignity, Lady Chilton, the likes of which most cannot imagine . . . until it is upon them. But not for you. Youth. Imagine it. I am a century and a third old. A century and a third. Fifty years ago I looked no more than thirty." He raised the cup to his lips, his eyes still on her, and then they closed—in pleasure, she thought.

She touched the cup, felt the warmth through its ancient glaze, for the cups themselves seemed very old. For a moment she stared down into the rising vapor, as though trying to see her future. The realization that this was a decisive moment, perhaps *the* decisive moment, of her life settled into her like glacial waters.

*There is no road back,* she told herself, numbness flooding through her being.

She raised the cup with two hands, for it had no handle, and inhaled the vapor. Her hands trembled as the rim touched her lip, and a drop spilled upon her dress. Closing her eyes, she tasted the liquid. It had no flavor she could name, though it was pungent and spicy.

She swallowed. And again. The liquid seemed to flow warmly throughout her body, as though it ran into the veins, driving out the numbness.

And then the dim room grew suddenly dark. She walked among the walls of a ruin, a castle or some great edifice. A moon rose above a toppled tower, and a hawk flitted from ledge to lintel overhead. Columns rose up or lay shattered on the ground. As the moon rose, it reflected on a pattern set in silver into the stone floor.

The beauty of the pattern struck her—intricate scrollwork winding among the precise lines of a geometric pattern. A silent wind rustled her dress. It was only then that she noticed the quiet of the place. Even her own footfall made not a sound.

Skirting the pattern she went on, deeper into the ruin. At a balustrade looking out over a moonlit valley she found a man, a small falcon perched upon his wrist.

For a moment she stood, afraid to approach. But then he turned slightly, and she saw that it was Kent, an aged and wrinkled Kent. For a moment he gazed directly at her, but registered nothing. Even so, she could see the sadness and loss in his eyes—as though she looked through them into the desolate valley beyond.

"Where am I, Kent?" she asked, but he turned back to the valley, the bird fluttering up from his outstretched arm.

A shadow moved among the columns, someone tall and stooped. "Lord Eldrich?" she tried to call, though her voice emerged thin and weak. The figure blended into the shadow of a column, leaving her unsure of what she had seen.

*I am alone. Alone but for a silent, aged Kent who cannot hear when I speak.*

For a moment she collapsed on a fallen column, overwhelmed by sadness.

Tears appeared, running down her cheeks, but when she went to rub them away, she found tiny, pear-shaped diamonds in her hand. They glittered in moonlight and shrank away, dissolving on her palm, leaving her skin cold where they had lain.

"*Flames,*" she heard herself whisper.

Surprisingly, she felt no fear, only a vague disquiet and uncertainty.

*This is a vision,* she told herself. *You have taken king's blood and walk within a waking dream. No harm can befall you.*

She entered a round courtyard, though perhaps it had once been a chamber, its roof worn away long ago. In the center stood a fountain, empty of water and filled with spiderwebs, the strands silvered by moonlight. A sculpture of pale stone rose out of the web—a woman bent back beneath her lover, her face half-formed but lost to passion. Her lover bent over her with both tenderness and passion, though she could not understand how both these states had been conveyed.

"It is not me," the countess said, her voice trembling. She pressed a hand to her heart and felt it beating wildly. "It is not Eldrich." But the man's face was obscured, and she could not say.

The bird that had perched upon Kent's wrist alighted on the edge of the fount and regarded her with its unsettling gaze.

She skirted the sculpture, averting her eyes, but it drew her, and she glanced that way again. It had moved, she was sure, as though animated by the slow passion of stone. She fled through the first opening that offered itself.

Here she came upon a second balcony, and looked out over the moonlit valley. A lake shimmered in the distance, but the valley was in shadow. Trees, she thought she saw, perhaps hedgerows, and here and there regular shapes that could be houses or the structures of men.

For the first time she heard sounds, a low dirge, like monks chanting. The sound seemed to float up to her from a great distance, and then she saw the singers—men bearing a litter up a blue-shadowed stair. They passed through a shaft of moonlight, and she could see it was a bier they carried, and the singing was indeed a dirge—a lament of great power and sorrow.

"What king is this?" she whispered, for somehow she was sure that such music could only befit a king.

A breeze moved her hair and seemed to whisper next to her ear. . . . *auralelauralelaural* . . . She looked up at the sky, filled with stars, their light diffused into soft haloes. The heavens seemed to be spinning slowly, and she turned to follow. Faster it went, and the world tilted beneath her. She fell.

"*. . . lauralelauralelauralelaura . . .*"

A hand rested lightly on the countess' shoulder; she could feel the warmth of it through the fabric of her dress.

*He is touching me,* she thought. Every finger was distinct, and her breath caught. The hand was so still. Only a mage could remain so motionless.

She opened her eyes and found she lay upon a divan in the great room, a single candle trembling on a table. Eldrich sat near her head, one hand resting on her shoulder. He was awake, she was certain by the sound of his breathing. But she was so tired. . . . Her eyes shut of their own accord.

"What do you want of me?" she whispered.

"What did you dream?" he asked, ignoring her question.

"I saw Kent standing on a balcony beneath a moon, looking out over a shadowed valley. A hawk rested upon his wrist. A pattern of moonlight was woven into the stone floor. . . ." She struggled to remember, to remain conscious. "And a dry fountain filled with spiderwebs held a sculpture of a woman . . . and a man."

"You knew them?"

"No," she said quickly, then remembered to whom she spoke. "The woman might have been me. The hawk lighted upon the fount as though it required something of me and I fled. Out onto a second balcony. Below me men chanted, a sad lament, and bore a body upon a bier. Only a king deserved such music, I thought. Only a king, yet there was no great train, no procession. Only a handful of men, as though this king died in exile. And then the stars began to spin, and I fell."

Eldrich said nothing, and she felt herself falling away.

"If it was a vision, does that mean I foresaw a death?" she managed.

"Perhaps," Eldrich said softly.

"But whose?"

"Sleep," Eldrich said. "Sleep in peace, and let dreams trouble you not."

## ⟿ Twelve

Kent walked through the night, through the moonlight that passed over the land like a searching owl. His increasingly lame mount slowed him, as did the shadows of hills, which flowed across the road in black pools.

And then the darkness began to pale, giving way to a still dawn, filled with the silence of calling birds—a world contained within a pearl.

The stableman looked askance at this city dweller who brought his horse in so injured, riding foolishly by night. Kent hardly cared what anyone thought, only let him sit and eat some food, then he would have energy to feel abashed.

He took a table in the near-empty common room, and leaned his head back against the wall, closing his burning eyes.

Food and coffee arrived after a moment. Guests came down to break their
fasts, the men stepping out to check on the readiness of carriages. The travelers
were bound for Castlebough or another scenic town, some few going to the border beyond and down into Entonne. They had that air of anticipation and release
that people on journeys so often displayed. A great contrast to his own state.

The painter leaned his head on his hand as he ate, slumping in his chair.

*I must look in a sorry state,* he thought, and though his appearance was
usually important to him, at that moment he did not care. How far ahead was
Eldrich? Too far to ever be caught by natural means? The entire endeavor
seemed even more foolish by the fresh light of morning than it had in the darkest hour of the previous night.

*Kent rides off to slay a mage and win the hand of fair lady.* Flames, but he was
likely making a perfect ass of himself. Luckily there was no one there to see.

"Kent?"

The painter looked up.

"Sir John!"

"Kent, this is as far as you've traveled?"

Kent nodded sheepishly as Sir John took a seat at his table. "Have you been
watching Eldrich?"

Kent shook his head. "No, they must be in the lowlands by now."

Sir John fell quiet, breaking eye contact abruptly. "Ah . . ."

"And what of you, Sir John? What's led you to be traveling by night?"

"I was called away suddenly," Sir John said.

Kent eyed him. "A servant of the mage passed me as I traveled—I heard
him speaking to his driver. It occurred to me later that this might be the man
with whom you had dealings. Is it business of the mage that you are on?"

"No, just . . . business." But the words had little strength in them.

"Well, at least I shall have a traveling companion until our ways part."

"But, Kent." Sir John stared down at his hands folded on the table, hanging
his head like a man suddenly ill. "Kent, I don't go to Avonel." He took a long,
uneven breath. "Do not ask me more."

Kent sat back against the wall, gazing at the suddenly wretched man. *What
does he do for the mage?*

"Will you want your carriage back?" Sir John asked, forcing his gaze up,
shaking off his mood.

"No. I should travel faster by horse. You managed through the night with
those wretched lamps?"

"Yes, well enough."

A servant came, and Sir John asked for a meal. The meal was interrupted
only by small talk, neither man speaking his real concerns. Finally, as Sir
John was about to rise, Kent put a hand on his arm. "Is there nothing

you can tell me? Do you know where the mage has gone? Where he has taken her?"

Sir John tugged his arm gently free. "Kent, there is nothing you can do. Nothing anyone can do." He leaned closer so that no one else might hear. "I have been forced to dissemble once to keep you from harm. I shall not get away with it twice. Kent . . . I implore you, give this up." Sir John swept from the room, the eyes of everyone on him, wondering what disagreement beset these two gentlemen.

The road wound its way along the bottom of a high valley awash in the translucent green of spring. The breeze fluttered leaves and the sunlight caught them like sparkles on the sea. Kent sat his horse at the valley's head, watching. His trap, which bore Sir John, appeared in a gap in the trees, then disappeared beneath a wave of phosphorescent green.

*"Have you been watching Eldrich?"* Sir John had asked.

The mage was nearby—it could mean nothing else. The countess was here, somewhere.

*Sir John must know I follow,* Kent thought. *But is he going to meet the mage?* Certainly Sir John had never encountered Eldrich before; his fear the night they had seen the mage proved that. There had always been an intermediary. . . . But at the recent meeting at the inn, Sir John had looked almost as frightened as he had the night above Baumgere's home, though this fear was overlain by resignation.

What, other than a mage, could inspire such terror?

Kent nudged his horse forward, out of the shadow of the trees. He felt like a knight riding into a hopeless battle. It was one thing to pursue a mage with little chance of ever catching him, and quite another to think that he might actually come face-to-face with this terror. Whenever these fears appeared, he would think of the gratitude of the countess, and this would drive him on, even if it did not drive the fear away.

The shadows of the hills sundialed across the valley, and the sky tones softened to near-pastels. Darkness was not far off, and yet Sir John hardly slackened his pace. Kent would catch glimpses of him between the green seas of hills.

The painter began to wonder if he had misread Sir John altogether. Perhaps he was not going to meet the mage. Kent wasn't sure if he felt dismay or relief at this, for his own courage ebbed and flowed by the hour.

Occasionally his mind would stray to what Eldrich might be doing with the countess, and the pictures that appeared in his mind caused him such anguish that the resultant anger would solidify into resolve. For an hour he would not care what Eldrich might do to him.

The limb of the sun bobbed on the crest of a western mountain and shadows stirred in the depths of the forest—restless for release.

Kent pushed his mount forward now, wanting to close the gap between himself and Sir John. Would the man travel in darkness? Kent still wondered how he had managed the previous night.

"The mage and his servants have no need of lanterns," he said aloud. A sign, surely, that Sir John's situation had changed.

Kent topped a rise which provided a long view of the road ahead, but there was no sign of Sir John.

"Martyr's blood!" Kent swore, and set his tired horse to race the gathering darkness.

Sir John brought his trap to a stop before the lane Bryce had marked on his map. Stepping down to the grass he paced quickly forward, looking into the deepening green of the wood. The lane wound into the trees, revealing no sign of men or habitation.

"Farrelle preserve me," he whispered. Sir John had never dueled, but he was certain approaching a duel would be no worse than this.

He thought seriously of climbing back into his carriage and hurrying on, down into the lowlands. On the coast he could take ship for some foreign port—escape. Escape Eldrich.

But some part of him knew this was impossible. One did not escape a mage.

He found his breath coming in short gasps, and his hands shook a little. His horse snorted, and Sir John jumped, whirling around.

"Take hold of yourself, man," he muttered, trying to calm his heart.

With utter resignation he climbed back into the trap and set off down the lane, into the heart of the wood.

It was only a short distance to the lodge, which stood in the midst of a lawn and a seemingly abandoned garden. The last light of the day found its way here, creating long shadows, like incursions into the world of light.

The lodge was stone and dark wood, and Sir John was certain that if it had been inhabited by anyone else, it would not have had such a threatening air.

Sir John could not imagine what would befall him here, but in his heart he knew that his life would never be the same after this night—as though he were about to make a pact with a devil. Flames, but he wished he had never met Bryce. Better ruin, both social and financial, than this. He was about to become the servant of a mage!

*But you have been one for some time,* he reminded himself, a thought that brought no comfort.

He stopped the trap before the main entrance. As he stepped down, the door creaked open and a mild looking, silver-haired servant appeared.

"Who are you, sir, and, pray, what is your business?" the man asked.

"Sir John Dalrymple. Mr. Bryce has sent me to deliver a letter."

The man nodded, and disappeared inside. The ordinariness of the servant's appearance and manner made the situation somehow more macabre.

Although it was only a moment before the servant returned, twilight rose from beneath the trees, shadows bleeding out across the lawn, enveloping everything in their path.

The servant held aloft a lamp. "Come in, Sir John," the man said as though it were not an invitation to give up one's soul.

The lodge was not well lit inside, and though it was a common structure for its service, it took on a more ominous appearance for its darkness.

The servant led him quickly on, saying nothing. They saw no one else, as though the place were empty but for the mage and this one aging manservant.

Sir John forced himself to go forward, his nerve very near to breaking, but he had passed a threshold and there would be no turning back now.

As they came to a hall below a heavily built stair, the servant bid him wait and disappeared down a hallway, leaving Sir John with only the light of the faintly flickering hearth.

He sat on a hard, wooden bench, and without warning, bile burned up his throat as though his rising fear had spilled over. *Farrelle's flames, man,* he chided himself. *Eldrich isn't going to murder you.*

The hollow echo of footsteps sounded somewhere above him, falling lightly, then descending.

*Could this be the mage?* Sir John wondered, and though he wanted to rise, to greet his fate standing, he shrank back into the shadow, fighting to catch his breath.

A faint glow tripped lightly down the stairs to his right, touching each step in turn before it spilled onto the polished floor. The footsteps followed, hardly more substantial—as light as a girl's, but even and purposeful.

The lamp appeared, and then its bearer—a woman darkly dressed, long tresses swept back from her beautiful face by silver combs.

She passed the cowering figure of Sir John without the slightest notice, and carried on down the hall, like an apparition.

*The Countess of Chilton,* Sir John realized, and he hadn't the wit to speak, to ask after her, as any gentleman should. Again he choked on his own bile.

*You are still of use,* he told himself. *Bryce came to you with instructions. They're not done with you yet, so you are safe from harm.*

The flames in the hearth flickered and pulsed, like a tiring heart. Sir John felt his slim hopes fade with the dying light.

A door opened, and a lamp appeared in the hallway the servant had taken. Footsteps reached him, loud in the silence—two sets this time. As the servant neared, Sir John could see that another followed behind, just on the edge of the light.

This time he forced himself to his feet, standing bent, his knees none too steady. The servant stopped before him, and the second man came into the light—a small round man of almost comical aspect.

Was *this* the great Eldrich?

"I am Walky," the little man said. "You have a letter from Mr. Bryce?"

Sir John nodded, speech having abandoned him, and reached into his coat for the missive, which he proffered in a trembling hand.

Walky took it, paused as though contemplating Sir John, said softly, "A moment," and then followed the servant up the stair. The lamplight retreated after them, flowing up the treads like a bride's train.

Sir John collapsed back onto his bench, staring at the embers glowing in the hearth, a lone flame that whisped up, wavered, and was inhaled into the glow. He waited in the dark, watching for the return of lamplight, listening for footsteps. For some moments he sat, his growling bowels the only sound.

"Have you never heard that a mage walks in perfect silence?" came a musical voice, and involuntarily Sir John threw himself hard against the wall. A shadow on the last stair might have been a man.

The hearth erupted into flame, but the shadow on the stair remained untouched by the light.

"Have you any idea what Bryce wrote?" the shadow asked.

Sir John could not speak but only shook his head.

Silence, as though a great beast contemplated him—wondering if he would be worth eating.

"He believes that you cannot gain the support I require from the powers in Avonel—at least not of your own influence. . . ."

Sir John was not sure if it was a question and remained frightened into silence. *Had his use ended? Was that why he was sent to Eldrich?*

"I'm waiting . . ." came the musical voice, perhaps touched by amusement.

"I would not gainsay," he gasped involuntarily, "Mr. Bryce."

"That is your answer?"

Sir John nodded.

The shadow stepped to the floor, and though it crossed before the fire Sir John saw nothing but a gathering darkness which passed silently down one of the unlit hallways. The flames in the fire died away, returning Sir John to the dark.

*He moves without sound,* Sir John thought. *Could be standing beside me at this moment.* He pressed himself back into the wall, half-raising his hands as if he would ward off a blow.

Footsteps sounded again, lamplight lilting down the stairs.

The servant and the small man appeared.

"We have prepared a room," the small man said, his voice not unkind.

Sir John nodded, but he found he could not rise.

"Sit a moment," the man called Walky said. "Many find their first meeting with the mage . . . strangely overwhelming."

The two men waited in utter silence, as though there were nothing odd at all in the situation.

Finally Sir John pushed himself up and, though not perfectly steady, thought he could go on.

He followed the others up the stair, terrified at the thought that he was expected to spend the night here—in the house of the mage. But to what purpose? Had he proven himself unworthy with his admission? What would be done with him?

He clutched the rail as they went, up to a landing and open hallway. A door stood ajar emitting a soft light. Here they stood aside and let Sir John enter. A lamp and fire burned within.

"The fire will take the dampness from the room," Walky said. "You will find everything you need here. Sir John," he said, making sure of the other's attention. *"Do not leave your room,* and I say this for your own safety. If you need anything at all, ring the bell. Do you wish food?"

Sir John shook his head.

"Then I bid you sleep well." He turned to go.

"But," Sir John hesitated, "what will be done with me?"

Walky shrugged. "Only the mage knows," he said, and the two men went out, closing the door firmly behind them.

The wandering star appeared, a tiny flame in a mother-of-pearl sky. Slowly the opaque dome dissolved to the infinite depths of night, and stars flickered into focus. Kent stood, immersed to the shoulder in the edge of the wood, his field glass trained on the lodge.

He'd found the lane, open gate, and the signs of Sir John's passing. Having hidden his mount he made his way through the twilit wood.

His trap stood before an outbuilding, proving him right—Sir John was inside. But was this where the mage dwelt and, more importantly, was the countess here? Kent hoped with all his heart to find her in an open window and whisk her away before even the mage realized what had been done. But most of the windows were dark, and those that displayed feeble light never framed a silhouette, let alone one so fair as the countess.

Kent stepped out onto the lawn, for moving through the wood made far too much noise, and slipped quietly along the edge of the trees. At the back of the house he scrutinized each window, with the same result. One would almost have thought the inhabitants asleep—perhaps like the old tale, asleep for a hundred years.

He passed behind the stable and paddock, arriving at the lodge's far side. The windows here provided no more information than the others. From far off a howl floated through the trees—not an uncommon sound in the hills at night, but with Eldrich at hand it sent a chill through Kent. For a long moment he froze in the shadow, listening like a frightened beast.

"A small bird," the countess said, "like a hawk, though more colorful. It hovered before my window."

"A kestrel," Eldrich said. "It is a small falcon. I saw one at the edge of the wood today—and did one not appear in your vision?" He nodded, as though giving his approval, though his gaze was far away.

"What will happen now?" the countess asked. "Will it . . . come to me?"

"A familiar is not a pet," Eldrich said, shaking himself from his reverie. "You might lose sight of it for days at a time—but if you are agitated, angry, frightened, it will appear. Not just then, of course, for it performs a duty. In times of danger you will see it, and you will know. The familiar has been called a reflection of the soul—but I think it is more like a shadow. Imagine if you stood with your back to the sun and looked down at the earth—and you saw the shadow of a hawk . . . or a wolf."

Eldrich began to eat again—something that he did with little sign of pleasure. Wine he appeared to enjoy—but food seemed a mere necessity. The silence returned, the silence in which he seemed barely aware of her. She watched his hands as he manipulated his utensils, the long fingers curling around the bowl of his wineglass, white against red.

The countess thought he had the most elegant hands she had ever seen, almost articulate in their movements. The fingers were long and fine, certainly the hands of an artist. A shiver coursed through her at the thought of his touch. She had begun to dream of his hands, hands reaching out of shadow and caressing her.

She glanced up at his face; his large eyes appeared to be focused on something unseen. His presence disturbed her, especially in the silences, and this often forced her to make conversation.

"I have noticed something else; my throat . . . It seems tight, somehow. I feel it when I speak—though not all the time."

Eldrich barely nodded. "Yes, it is the king's blood," he said, his voice reaching out and brushing her intimately. "It will give you a voice like . . . there is no description, for it is hardly human. But we will keep your voice as youthful and mellifluous as it is now. I will speak to Walky."

The countess nodded. She had barely seen Eldrich since their arrival here, and now she found him strangely subdued. Oh, he was as remote as ever—that had not changed—but the arrogance that so offended her was largely absent. He seemed like a man in mourning—as though he had lost someone close to him.

This impression was only offset by the two occasions during the meal when she had found him staring at her. The intensity of his gaze had unsettled her completely. She had known such looks too often to wonder what they meant.

*He desires me*, she thought. *Despite all of his feigned indifference, he desires me*. She felt a wave of warmth sweep through her core and her face and neck colored. If she had been standing she would have wavered.

*"What is it he wants of me,"* she had asked Walky, naively.

*"He will tell you in his own good time, Lady Chilton,"* Walky had said, but she had an answer, here. He wanted this, and something more. The something more was what frightened her.

He desires me, yet steels his will to resist. She felt her head shake, overwhelmed by confusion of thought and feeling.

Eldrich reached out and drew a sheaf of paper toward him, holding his hand upon it as though contemplating the content.

"From Mr. Bryce," he said suddenly, pushing the papers toward her.

He did not say if she was to read it or not—for all she knew it might have been an explanation for his state of distraction—but she took it up and began to read.

It was a long letter running to several pages, precise in the extreme, from the hand through the observations, which were few but stated with a vivid clarity. The letter retold the tale of Erasmus and the others who had gone down into the cave and dealt at length with a chamber they had discovered—Landor's chamber, they called it—and the escape of a woman named Anna with the seed of the king's blood.

A few days earlier the countess would not have understood, but now, as a somewhat-unwilling initiate in the seed, she realized this was a cause of the greatest concern.

Eldrich lifted his wineglass while she read, abandoning all pretense of eating. Walky came in and stood by silently, as though sensing his master's need.

"What does it mean?" the countess asked at last, mystified by what she had read. "Who was Landor, and why did he leave seed buried far beneath the surface?"

Eldrich looked like a man so overwhelmed that he was about to take refuge in wine. She could not imagine the mage acting in this manner. The mage!

"Landor . . ." Eldrich said, staring out into the descending darkness. "Landor was among the first—he *was* the first. First and most skilled of the mages who journeyed to Farrland from beyond. Why did he leave seed? For those who wished to make the journey back from whence they came. I can think of no other reason. But it is difficult to say what Landor might have planned, for he lived so long ago that he has become a myth. Yet it was Landor who found the way—the way by darkness. Landor who led the others, and laid the foundations for the arts in these lands." Eldrich paused, lost for a moment attempting to see into the past. "All of this is of little more than scholarly interest now. This woman, Anna, has the seed—Landor's seed. . . ." He rocked forward in his chair and stared down at the table, unsettling her with the strangeness of his manner. "It is a disaster beyond any I had contemplated," he whispered. "More than a disaster." He shook his head, beginning to raise his hands to his face as though in horror, but he caught himself and stopped.

"Have I been so unworthy, Walky, that I should be punished so?" he asked, not even glancing at his servant.

Walky shifted from one foot to the other, his wrinkled face etched with concern. "It is not a matter of worth, as you well know," Walky said. "It is the seed, sir, it is the arts themselves, struggling to live. They are like a man being suffocated; he will find his greatest strength just before the end." The little man shook his head. "The arts will not pass away without a struggle, sir. We have long known it."

Eldrich said nothing for a moment, then nodded agreement. "No, they will not." It was almost a whisper.

A sudden ferocious howling brought Eldrich half out of his chair—not startled, but alert.

A moment later a servant appeared. He said nothing at all, but Eldrich dropped his napkin on the table and he and Walky quickly followed the man out.

The countess found she could not continue with her meal and went to the double doors that looked out onto the lawn, hoping to see what all the commotion was about. Although she could hear voices, there was not a lantern or light to be seen.

"What has happened now?" she wondered aloud.

The voices faded away and she heard only footsteps crossing the lawn—the servants, not Eldrich, she knew.

*Will I walk so silently one day?*

Voices rumbled down the hall and into the room, no words discernable. She found herself gravitating toward the door, desperate for some clue as to what went on in this house. Some indication of what might be expected of her.

Quietly, she opened the door a little wider, leaning close, listening. She even dared to peek for a second but could see nothing at the hallway's end. Then, very distinctly, she heard her name, and from a familiar voice, too.

"My word," she whispered, but before she could pull open the door to go out, footsteps sounded, and grew louder. The countess retreated into the room, taking up her wineglass.

Whose voice had she heard? Not Skye's. Erasmus? That seemed most likely.

A moment later the door swung open and Eldrich came in—followed by Kent, of all people. Kent who had warned her to flee.

She knew immediately why the poor man was here: on her behalf. Now what would be done to him?

Eldrich paused, glancing back at the painter, who looked frightened near to collapsing. "Do you know this man?" he said, with more than a little accusation in his voice.

She nodded. "Yes. . . . But Kent, what are you doing here?"

"He is rescuing you, I take it," Eldrich answered. "Somehow he is under the impression that you are not here of your own choosing."

The countess felt near to tears, both from frustration with Kent and fear of what Eldrich might do. Some part of her was touched as well. What a noble fool the painter was, setting off to confront a mage.

Kent looked even more like a boy than usual—a truant, standing before his school master. His fair hair was in disarray, the skin around his eyes tight with fear, eyes bright with hope. Standing near to Eldrich he seemed small, almost fragile. She feared he did not understand the gravity of his situation at all.

"Kent," she said as softly as she could, "your journey has been in vain."

Kent did not respond, but only stared at her, deeply suspicious, blinking back tears, she was sure.

She turned immediately to Eldrich. "What will you do with him?"

Eldrich shrugged, taking up his seat at the table again.

She thought desperately for something to say, something that would save the poor man. "Averil Kent is an artist of surpassing abilities, Lord Eldrich. Can you not release him? He'll promise to interfere no more. Won't you, Kent?" she said looking at the painter, imploring him with her eyes to agree.

As she went to speak to Eldrich again, he looked away, and she stopped on the first syllable.

Finally Eldrich looked over at Kent. "Do you paint?" he asked, taking the countess completely off guard.

Kent nodded.

"Paint portraits of Lady Chilton and myself, and if I judge them worthy, I will release you." He nodded to Walky, who came forward to lead Kent away.

"But he is not a portraitist," she said, "and does he even have his painting box with him?" She looked back at Kent who shook his head.

"Everything he needs can be found here. Apparently much of the 'art' that graces these walls was painted by some talentless member of the family." He turned to his servant. "Walky," he said, needing to give no more instruction than that.

And Kent was led out, looking like a child-criminal leaving the court—and not to freedom.

The countess turned back to Eldrich, but he was no longer in his chair. She caught a glimpse of his shadow as it slipped silently out onto the dark lawn—the shadow of a wolf.

Despite the hour, Walky arrived soon after the countess' summons. He looked a bit concerned as he came through the door.

"Is something wrong, m'lady?" he asked, persisting in his use of the ancient form of address.

"No, nothing, but I wish to speak to Kent. Is that possible?"

"It would not be wise, m'lady," he said, shaking his head.

"I see. But would it be forbidden?"

"Only Lord Eldrich could say, m'lady."

The countess glowered at him for a second, but could not keep it up. The little man looked so genuinely sorry that he couldn't give her the answer she desired.

"Will he be all right?" she asked very quietly.

"All right, m'lady?"

"Yes, will Eldrich . . . harm him? Kent did not mean to interfere. It was only concern for my welfare that brought him here. Eldrich can hardly blame him for that."

Walky knit his brows together and looked at her, tilting his head a little. "But he is the painter, Lady Chilton. The first good sign we have had in days. I hardly think he will be harmed. No, my master will reward him—or so I should think."

The countess hardly knew what to say. "'He is the painter'? Whatever do you mean?"

Walky shrugged. "Lord Eldrich has been awaiting the painter—and he has finally appeared. Do not be afraid for Mr. Kent. No, there are other matters far more worthy of our concern." And with that he bowed and let himself out.

## Thirteen

It was absurd to even contemplate sleep, so Sir John sat at his window, open to the night, and stared out at the shadowed wood, and beyond it the hills silhouetted against the stars.

Insects and frogs filled the night with their peculiar love songs, and a nightingale held forth periodically, the sound like bells tumbling down a distant waterfall.

A family of deer came out onto the lawn to crop the soft grasses, and a pair of fawns gamboled awkwardly about the doe.

"What will he do with me?" Sir John wondered. He pushed the window wide, a breath of soft air cooling his face. When imagining the course of his life, the young John Dalrymple had never contemplated an occurrence such as this—held captive by a mage.

"Perhaps you are merely a guest," he suggested, as though he spoke to another—a guest who could not leave, however; not even his room.

Would he see the countess again? The thought of an ally in this place was very appealing. If he could speak with her, he could find out if Kent's fears were true, that she was here against her will—assuming she knew her own heart in this matter. But it would be good to know so that he might communicate this to Kent if he met the man again—which seemed very likely given recent history.

Suddenly the deer started on the lawn, held utterly still, then bounded off into the wood, passing quickly into silence. Sir John wondered what could have caused this action, but then he saw—a wolf padded quickly across the grass, head down, neck extended. Sir John felt his pulse quicken at the sight.

*What a ferocious beast,* he thought.

And then there was a sudden crashing in the underbrush, and the branches of a tree began to sway. The wolf released a terrible howl, and leaped at the trunk, twisting as it returned to the earth where it stared up into the branches, howling pitilessly.

Sir John almost reached to stop up his ears when a door banged open and men erupted onto the lawn. They kept their distance from the wolf, speaking in hushed tones, and then fell silent. Even the wolf ceased its howling, though it held its position, trembling with anticipation.

A shadow appeared among the servants, and Eldrich spoke to the beast, though Sir John did not know the words. The wolf suddenly slunk away growling and muttering, casting glances back over its shoulder at whatever had been treed.

Eldrich spoke again, this time in Farr, adding a string of foreign syllables. The branches of the tree began to shake and sway. A moment later a figure appeared in the poor light of the lawn, and even though it was barely more than a shadow, Sir John knew immediately who it must be—poor, foolish Kent.

Sir John did not know how much time had passed since Eldrich had discovered Kent, but certainly time enough for any kind of revenge, and Sir John had imagined several varieties, all of them unspeakable. Twice he had gone to the door, even placed his fingers upon the handle, but the futility of it coupled with Walky's warning kept him in his room. The thought of that wolf skulking the halls was enough to suppress any noble act Sir John might contemplate.

He returned to his view of the starlit garden, where he could discern very little but could imagine a great deal. What would the mage do to Kent? At least it gave him something else to consider while he waited, though the question had not changed but for the name.

*What would he do to Sir John?*

All the while his eyes played tricks on him. He thought he saw the wolf again, and then the deer, but could be sure of neither. Was that the countess crossing through the shadow of the trees? He listened, trying to parse the sounds of the night, searching for those that were human. A pale edge of light appeared, like the glitter of moonlight on a railing. This line extended and bent suddenly, tracing thirty degrees of arc, then bent in and crossed itself. This went on for some minutes until a figure of some complexity glowed on the lawn.

Moonlight on silver, or low flames of mercury. A shadow could be discerned now, moving slowly around the pattern. A shadow Sir John had encountered before. *Eldrich.*

Sir John had crouched down below his windows so that he could just see over the sill, wondering if Eldrich knew he watched. The arts were forbidden to men, after all.

*Perhaps he does not care what I see because my use is done,* Sir John thought.

A second shadow appeared, not so dark as the first. *Kent,* Sir John wondered, but then the person stepped into the pattern of silver light and shed her shadow like a robe. A raven-haired woman, as pale as the moon, for she wore not a stitch of clothing.

Sir John heard his breath indrawn. The Countess of Chilton; it could be no other. Despite his fear he felt a surge of sudden desire.

The musical voice of Eldrich began to chant, and silver characters appeared in the air briefly only to flare into nonexistence. The pattern grew in brightness, rising up until the countess appeared to stand in the center of an intricate silver cage. The musical chanting continued. It echoed in Sir John's mind, as disturbing as the event he witnessed, yet he could not tear his eyes away.

Suddenly the silver cage shattered, a sound like breaking crystal, and though not loud, painful to the ears. A shadow lay on the lawn, whimpering, Sir John was sure. The darker shadow of Eldrich bent down to bear the countess up, carrying her toward the house.

Sir John continued to stare at the dark lawn, the pattern burned into his brain. What had he seen, and why had it left him with such a feeling of horror—and why did this night linger so?

Servants arrived an hour after dawn, bearing hot water and the other articles for Sir John's toilet. He had barely finished dressing when a knock sounded on the door.

"Yes?"

The door opened a crack, and the small man of the previous night looked in.

"Ah, Walky, is it?"

"Yes, Walky. Lord Eldrich will see you now."

Sir John froze for a second, then nodded. He thought a condemned man might be allowed a final meal, but apparently such traditions meant little to a mage.

He followed Walky down the stairs, slightly bolstered by the morning light streaming in the windows, but only slightly. Fear was still tangible. He felt himself sweating, though it was not overly warm, and that sweat seemed to have an odd, sickly-sweet odor.

They came to a set of doors, which Walky opened just enough to allow a man to pass, and nodded Sir John through, his countenance maddeningly neutral.

Inside he found a large, bright room, but Sir John noticed nothing more, for his gaze fell immediately upon Lord Eldrich, who sat at a table bent over a sheaf of papers, sipping coffee.

Sir John stood utterly still, trying to catch his breath, wondering if he could hide any of his fear at all. Eldrich languidly turned a page, and continued as though Sir John were not there. The small box that Bryce had him deliver sat upon the table, closed, its contents still a secret. Despite the fact that it bore no lock, Sir John had not dared to open it.

"Few have set eyes upon a living mage," Eldrich said without looking up, the musicality of his voice strangely repellent now.

What was he to answer? That he was honored?

Eldrich continued reading. "And fewer still remember it after the fact."

The mage looked up suddenly and set his cup down, patting his mouth with a square of yellow linen. "I have need of the cooperation of the Farr government—meaning this man Moncrief, I assume."

Sir John nodded.

"Bryce explained what is to be done?" He raised an eyebrow, not without humor.

"Yes. This young woman who goes by the name of Anna Fielding must be found."

Eldrich nodded. "Though surely she will be using some other name now. To aid in this endeavor Bryce will send you an officer who actually met her, though he did not recall it immediately. No matter. She can be identified by him. I am most concerned that she not take ship for the island of Farrow. Is that clear . . . ? Good." He reached forward and picked up something from the table. "You will deliver this to Moncrief and await his response—which, unless the man is a complete fool, will be immediate and favorable. He is not a complete fool, is he?"

"By no means."

Eldrich sat back in his chair, clasped his hands, and eyed Sir John. "Bryce tells me you are a particularly valuable and astute servant, Sir John, and Bryce is sparing with his praise. It occasionally serves me to have gentlemen in places in society who are aware of whom they serve and might even have some small knowledge of my larger purpose. You are such a man, Sir John."

Sir John bowed his head, partly to hide his own shock. "I—I am honored."

"No, you are dismayed, but that is no matter. I trust you will serve me with utter commitment and unwavering loyalty. Do you know what that means, Sir John?"

"I think I do."

"I am not talking about the mere definition of the terms, you realize."

Sir John nodded, confused.

Eldrich stared at him a moment, letting the silence extend until it seemed it must fail. "Loyalty unto death, Sir John."

## ᕲ Fourteen

"I didn't like the sound of it. I said, 'Any man who wants to avoid the road returning to the lowlands is hardly to be trusted.' ''Tis not a man,' my brother said, 'but a woman, and a pretty one, too.'" The guide patted the neck of his sturdy mount, blinking rapidly.

"Did he tell you her name or describe her?" Erasmus asked.

"He said only that it was a woman and that she would pay him handsomely."

Erasmus glanced at Clarendon, who nodded.

"Do you know the way they traveled?" Erasmus asked.

The man nodded.

"Can you take us?"

"I was going to set out in three days anyway. I thought Garrick to be back yesterday. He hadn't intended to take her all the way, but only through the most difficult sections." He shrugged. "It is likely that he's taken her farther than he first agreed. The paths through the hills aren't so clear as a lowlander might wish."

"We need to find this woman—immediately. Can we engage you to take us?" Clarendon looked very intent. "But we need to leave today."

"That'd be hard, sir," the youth said. He could not have been more than sixteen.

"Hardship is to be expected," Clarendon said quickly, reaching into his pocket and finding three gold coins. "Would this hasten matters?"

The boy looked for an instant as though he'd been pricked by a pin. "Aye. But even so, it will be late in the afternoon."

"There will be five of us," Clarendon said. "I have my own horses and outfit."

"Five!" The lad was dismayed.

"Don't despair," Clarendon said, taking the boy by the arm. "We will all pitch in, as will my staff. Come along. We'll begin by seeing Mr. Tanner about horses. . . ."

They went single file through the highlands, along the narrow paths and hidden ways known only to huntsmen and the falconers who sought nests to rob in the high cliffs. Following the roll of the hills they passed through various bands of vegetation: On the ridges wind-sculpted pines, stunted and sparse, grew out of rock painted with orange-and-green lichen; in the valleys they found spring flowers and lush, deciduous trees. Along certain streams grew a golden-leafed willow found only in the hills—there could not have been a thousand of them in all the world.

Pryor, their guide, stopped to survey the path again, as he had been doing off and on all day. Erasmus was surprised to find that paths in the hills were not as rare as he'd imagined. They had even passed through two small settlements— large family holdings, he'd gathered, but still unexpected. No one had seen Anna or Pryor's brother, which was not surprising. Anna had a lifetime's experience hiding herself—if it was Anna they were following.

But who else could it be? A woman returning to the lowlands secretly. Rose had argued that only two should follow their guide into the hills, the others staying behind to search elsewhere. But it soon became clear that Rose was determined to take this route, which made the others suspicious. Clearly the priest was convinced this was Anna, though no one could guess why he was so certain.

Kehler worried that they were following a false trail—after all, the guide, Garrick, had conveniently told his brother where he was going. But then, the meeting with his brother had been accidental—if one believed in accidents.

Pryor searched among the bushes beside the trail, bending low to the ground, examining the branches. From among the foliage he lifted his hand, teasing out something invisible—then a glint of red-gold twined in his fingers and trailed in the breeze.

Erasmus dropped to the ground and took the strand of hair, holding it up to the light.

He showed it to the others who all nodded—not even Rose showing any elation.

"Well, we know we're not being misled," Kehler said. "Or, at least, it's very unlikely."

Pryor took the reins of his horse and led them on, eyes scanning the ground. When he was certain which path had been taken, he mounted again, and they traveled more swiftly along the valley floor, the new leaves fluttering nervously in the breeze.

Anna stared at the hand-drawn map again, looked up at the peaks around her, then back to the map. Nothing was where it should have been. She was lost. From her breeches she produced a pocket chronometer and used it, with the position of the sun, to determine south. Unquestionably this valley was running the wrong way. She had mistaken the pass, and now wasn't sure what to do. Retrace her steps and hope to find the right way, or carry on and see where this led? Her map didn't extend far enough to tell her what lay ahead. The chances of becoming even more disoriented were great.

"*Chuff?*" her familiar said, the syllable sounding distinctly interrogative.

"Back," she decided. "We must go back."

She checked her string of horses, mounted, and crossed over the small creek three times, muttering an enchantment as she went. On her first crossing she tossed the wing bone of a hawk into the stream; on the second, a coal black stone; on the third she let a feather fall. A feather from her familiar. It sailed off on the current, fluttering on the ripples, glinting in the sunlight.

At least she would lay down a false trail and confuse anyone who tried to follow, especially by unnatural means. Halsey had always said that apparent lost efforts must be put to use whenever possible.

Thoughts of the others caused her to bend over in her saddle, as though she were in actual pain. Grief had its grip on her, she knew. She caught Chuff looking at her oddly at times—that intelligent glittering eye. For a beast with a vocabulary of a single word it managed astonishing shadings in its speech, and one of those was concern. She was hearing this tone too often, now.

*One could hardly be cheerful after what I've been through,* she thought. But still, it was a danger. Grief led to brooding, and brooding took her focus away from the matter at hand: survival.

Eldrich would be looking for her, and for the first time a mage had a starting point; he knew where she had come from. She was in more danger now than she had ever been—even escaping the cave.

*He will learn that I have seed.*

Did the mage know what lay in the cavern? Somehow she suspected he did not. He would never have sealed the chamber off if he'd known what lay within. But once he learned, Eldrich would be desperate to find her. More than desperate.

"But where would he think I have gone?" she asked aloud, for that was the game. Each trying to outguess the other. Does he know that I am alone? Did Halsey tell him there were no others?

She traveled, lost in both thought and place, until she passed a small pool. Here she stopped for a moment, tethering her horses so they could not sully the pool. It was near to sunset. This would be her camp tonight.

She gathered a handful of tiny white blossoms, and then firewood. For a long time she sat by the edge of the pool, thinking, *I am stronger now, my talent deeper. There might be something to see.* Not merely darkness as there had been that night in the house where Halsey died.

The last light in the sky seemed to coalesce into stars on a black field. Anna took a long breath and began the ritual, careful in its preparation. The marks on the ground, the figure that burned in her mind. An eerie ringing—the songs of stars. She stared down into the pool, at the points of light which floated there, and then closed her mind, holding what she had seen.

*Pain!* Searing pain, as though white-hot iron had been thrust into her brain. She wavered but held her concentration. For an instant she opened her mind, reeling toward the void, then cast the flowers onto the water. She felt herself collapse at the water's edge, like a great bird too exhausted to land softly. She heard herself crying. Nearby Chuff spoke his single word of fear, over and over.

## ⌐ Fifteen

The brushes were inferior and the easel not to his liking, but under the circumstances such matters were trivial.

*You are painting to save your life,* Kent reminded himself.

He looked at the portrait he had begun of Eldrich, feeling more than a little satisfied. He had been allowed to make only one brief sketch of the mage, but the image was unusually distinct in his mind, even for Kent, whose visual recall was not particularly good. He suspected the arts at work in this were not entirely his own.

He had caught something of the mage's presence, Kent flattered himself to think, for Eldrich seemed to have a still center of power—the calm eye of the storm. The darkly brooding visage had not been so difficult—much could be done with shadow—but even so the eyes were not quite as they should be. How did one portray a gaze that penetrated even the walls of time? The thick black hair and dark brows could not have been more in character for a mage—as though an actor had chosen them.

"Yes," Kent said softly, "you may have imprisoned me, Lord Eldrich, but I have captured something of you as well."

He turned away from the portrait, back to the blank canvas sitting on the easel, and felt the jangle of nervous expectation. The countess was to sit for him, and should arrive at any moment. Of course it was utterly unnecessary that she model, but he did not tell Eldrich that. Kent could recall the countess as clearly as . . . well, there was nothing he could recall as clearly. Closing his eyes, her image came vividly to mind in a hundred poses and varying moods. No, Kent did not require that she sit for him at all. But to see her and speak with her again!

The door clicked and swung open, revealing the countess. She stopped as she closed the door, looking intently at Kent, her manner anything but happy.

"Oh, Kent. Why were you so foolish?"

Kent felt himself look down, his cheeks burning. "I thought . . . I thought the countess had been abducted."

She continued to stare at him unhappily, and then nodded twice. "But as you see, I am here of my own choosing, and you have endangered yourself for naught."

"I didn't know," he said softly and looked up. "But how can you be sure that you have chosen to be here? How do you know that Eldrich has not used his arts to influence you?"

"Because I know, Kent. Trust that this is so." She came across the floor to the chair that had been set out for her, then hesitated as she arranged her skirts to sit. "But should this not be a divan? Yellow with new-world foliage and warblers, wasn't it?"

Kent felt the blood rise into his face, but he nodded, looking down.

"It was a lovely portrait, Kent. Better than I deserved," she said, almost tenderly. "Thank you."

Kent picked up a brush and palette, words suddenly seeming utterly inadequate. He began to paint before looking at his subject.

Every time he did look that way, the countess' soft eyes were upon him. He could not believe what hope he felt each time their eyes met, but there was no joy or pleasure in the countess' look, only anxiety and sadness. Nothing to cause him hope at all.

"What did you think to accomplish, Kent?" the countess asked suddenly.

What indeed? Kent wondered. But he knew the answer—he was not that unaware of his inner workings. He hoped to prove the depth and truth of his feelings. He hoped to prove himself worthy. Even though Eldrich might strike him dead, she would know.

He shook his head. One could not admit something so adolescent. "I hoped to learn the truth of your disappearance—whether you had gone of your own volition or no. Beyond that . . ." He shrugged.

This partial lie was followed by total silence. She did not believe him, he knew.

"You followed Sir John?" she asked, giving up the censorious silence.

"He is unharmed, I hope?" The truth was that Kent had hardly thought of the man since the wolf had treed him.

"To the best of my knowledge, yes."

It was hardly reassurance. How much did the countess know of what went on in this strange household?

"This little man, Walky. Is he the man I saw handing you down from the carriage in Castlebough?"

"I assume so. He is the mage's servant; not a house servant, but servant in the arts."

Kent did not understand what this meant, but he continued to work. The light streaming in the windows illuminated the countess in a way he found particularly maddening. It was almost unfair that beauty should be concentrated to such a degree in one woman. Unfair and baffling. Even as he studied her for the portrait, the truth of her attraction eluded him. What was its source? Could he ever hope to capture it as it had captured him?

"Kent, do you know what has befallen Erasmus?"

"I . . ." The phrasing of the question was distinctly odd. "He had not returned from the cave when I left Castlebough."

She looked down at her hands twisting the corner of her shawl.

"Is there some reason for concern?" Kent asked casually, the memory of the countess and Erasmus coming back—causing anguish and taking his breath away at the same time, as it always did.

"Something the mage said. Perhaps it meant nothing." She realized she had started referring to Eldrich as Walky did—the mage. *One can't help but acknowledge his difference,* she thought.

"What will happen . . . when I finish the portraits?" Kent had begun to ask what would become of her, but felt he had no right to pose such a question.

"I don't know, Kent. I hope Lord Eldrich," she made herself use the title, "will keep his word and release you."

"You say that as if there were some doubt?"

She stared at him intently. "I don't mean to frighten you, Kent, but he is a mage."

Kent nodded. And as such not bound by the mores of men. Unless certain rituals were performed, or so the old tales said. A mage could be bound to his word by the arts, though, if it were true, likely no one alive today would know how it was accomplished.

Rays of sun created a slanting backdrop of pure light to the countess' black curls, and Kent began to paint the sunlight using brighter colors than he would have expected—yellows and near-white. As though he were trying to heighten the contrast between the mood of the countess and the brightness of the spring day—almost a contrast of seasons. It was one of those unforeseen occurrences that invariably filled Kent with delight—a decision made on some other level, surprising for its rightness.

He glanced up and found the countess hanging her head, as though absorbed in some private pain.

"Lady Chilton? Should we pursue this at some other time?"

She straightened up immediately. "No. The mage wants our portraits done with all speed." She tried to smile. "Have I changed my position altogether?"

Kent considered, shook his head, continued to gaze at her a moment more, and then returned to his canvas. It might be true that the countess was here of her own choosing, but he had seen it—profound doubt at this decision. Profound doubt and near-despair.

## ꙮ Sixteen

"The ulna," the mage said softly. "One of the bones of the forearm." Eldrich turned the charred fragment over gently. He had contemplated it for a day, consulting certain texts frequently. "Halsey was more resourceful than I realized," he said to Walky. "Men are so easily underestimated. It is a lesson mages have never learned. And if I do not learn it . . . ?"

The house creaked around them, in the grip of the storm. A wind dropped down the chimney, setting the fire in the hearth fluttering. Eldrich continued to stare at the bone Bryce had sent. It lay in a dusting of black ash upon a square of linen, so fragile that, left to the elements, it would be worn away in hours. Halsey's last remains would vanish on the wind, as Teller's followers had always done.

"Resourceful," Eldrich said, picking up the train of his thought, though not really speaking to the ever-attentive Walky, "but in the end he didn't quite know what he was doing. His knowledge was not complete—fortunately." The mage sat back in his chair, looking up at Walky. "Bring me seed."

The mage ground the seed to powder, breathing in the aroma released when the husks cracked. From a hook above the fire he took a kettle and poured, steaming water hissing into the ancient cup. Eldrich felt his nostrils flare—even after all these years—his eyes closing with pleasure, anticipation.

He watched the slow swirl of liquid as he stirred, the steam coiling up in the firelight. Into the cup he spilled black cinder scraped from the bone, watched it float, spinning on the surface, then slowly soak through, turn slick, and founder. He stirred again, muttering a line of Darian, and raised the cup to his lips.

"I will know you now."

Dipping a finger into the cup he bent to the floor and outlined his shadow, whispering the lines of an enchantment, and felt himself begin to float. He drained the cup and stood, the storm breaking around him in foam and spray. Yet for all its fury the wind barely rustled his coat. Eldrich walked across the rolling seas as though upon a dark, writhing landscape. Pale crests rose up, then toppled, tumbling to ruin. Far off, bright wires of light shot from cloud to cloud or flashed deep within the storm. Eldrich turned slowly, surveying the world, feeling the turmoil—his turmoil. From long experience he knew one must accept the reality—not argue with it.

All around him was the rumble and hiss of seas as they raced and plunged to chaos and rose again. A whale's back glided by, glistening, spume blown off on the wind. A storm petrel skittered across the surface, a prisoner of the wind.

*"Where are you?"* Eldrich whispered.

Beneath his feet a knot of kelp slowly rolled to reveal a face; bone-white blossoms for eyes.

No one he knew, Eldrich thought at first, but then . . . "Halsey? Have I found you despite all?"

A wave crest tumbled to foam, tearing away strands of the kelp, bits of the lips and jaw.

The mouth moved. "I have found you," it said.

Eldrich felt himself lift on a crest, foam breaking around his knees.

"He's come for you, Lord Eldrich. Even now he is near. Nearer than you know." The face grimaced, the blossoms that were its eyes fluttering in the gusts.

"Who?"

But another wave fell upon the decaying face, tearing it apart and leaving nothing but a carpet of pulp and detritus spread upon the sea.

"Who has come?" Eldrich said again.

He went on, not really walking but somehow floating above the seas that crumbled and lifted beneath him. The taste of salt and king's blood, the bitter ash of Halsey's death, fresh in his mouth—like blood and iron.

Something dark before him. An enormous leviathan, he thought at first, but a flash of lightning revealed a ship, thrown on its beam ends, foundering in the crashing seas, its crew washed away.

Eldrich stood upon the seas, and watched the great vessel heave up one final time, then in a rush of water and escaping air, it rolled and slipped beneath the surface, into the lightless world below.

For a moment Eldrich remained, his emotions as confused as the sea—horror, and wonder, and fear. There was nothing but visions of death.

Then he realized the top of a mast bobbed in the water, almost vertical, a pennant or scrap of sail fluttering from its tip. He went closer, drawn to see the flag, but a few feet away it became a coat worn by a sailor clinging to the last fragment of ship. A dark, little creature, shadow-eyed and light-limbed, not quite human. It eyed the mage warily, curling back its lips and hissing as Eldrich approached.

The mage hesitated.

A wave swept over the small man, burying him in pale foam—liquid starlight.

The mast top swayed and bobbed as the wave passed, the creature still clinging desperately, its coat torn away. In the eerie light its feet and legs appeared to have fused in shadow.

He bared his teeth at Eldrich again, though no noise was heard. Then, to the mage's amazement, the creature uttered a curse of demons in Darian—the mage tongue.

"What are you?" Eldrich asked.

It only cursed him again, making a quick sign with a hand that was swiftly returned to the moving mast. A third wave broke over the creature, and for a moment Eldrich thought this one would do for it. But again it was there, the mast spinning slowly, gyrating like a top about to topple. And there it clung, its clothing torn away to reveal a dark, glistening skin, like a whale back—an odd shape to its hips and legs, more fish than man.

Suddenly the water erupted all around, wingless birds rolling into the air, only to slip back into the chaotic seas. *Dolphins,* Eldrich realized.

They curled out of the sea at every side, describing their perfect arcs, as numerous as raindrops. The creature on the mast was suddenly alert, chattering in Darian.

Yet another crest broke nearby and swept toward them, dolphins capering in the foam. And in the bright sea foam Eldrich thought he saw a shape—a woman borne by the wave.

The creature cried out as the wave overwhelmed him. Casting free his grip, he leaped into the sea, in among the dolphins and the sprite, if that's what it was.

Once its head broke the surface, searching out Eldrich, and it bared its teeth again, in triumph now. It called out once more in Darian and was lost in the storm—a last slap of its tail upon the broken surface.

*She comes not for you,* it had called.

A glow, bone-white, broke through the cloud and spread over the shattered sea, chasing wave crests like streaming veils. Eldrich turned to see a bubble moon float up, casting his shadow on the water like a stain upon the spinning world.

## ᔔ Seventeen

An unsettling wind, disturbed in its patterns, invaded the Caledon Hills. It swept down slopes, moving the branches of trees like an army of advancing giants.

Horses became skittish, dancing away from the madly swaying branches and forcing their riders to struggle for control. Erasmus felt his own nerves begin to fray, and was surprised to hear Clarendon upbraid Kehler when the younger man's horse shied in front of him.

"There is no profit in this," Clarendon said suddenly, embarrassed by his outburst. "Let us find some shelter from this cursed wind and make a camp."

There were no dissenters to this plan.

As they searched along the valley bottom, lightning splayed toward the eastern horizon—a jagged tear in the dark cloud. A moment later they felt the drumbeat of distant thunder. The initial flash seemed to be a sign, and the sky was shattered over and over.

Their guide, Pryor, in better control of his mount, had ranged ahead and appeared now and then among the trees, searching for a suitable site to make camp. Finally they caught up with him, off his horse, staring at something on the ground.

Erasmus and Clarendon came up next, and saw the dark stain of ashes, the charred remains of logs sticking out like blackened bones.

"Quite a cooking fire," Erasmus said immediately, noting the size.

Pryor nodded, his eyes still fixed on the ashes.

Clarendon dismounted. "This is as likely a spot as any. There is water and we might find some shelter from the wind in that stand of trees. We shall have rain soon enough, and I fear we will have to manage as the beasts do and simply endure it."

The others began dismounting, relieved to be off their nervous mounts. Hayes and Kehler took charge of the horses, glancing over at their guide, who had not moved from the fire pit.

"Pryor . . . ?" Kehler prompted.

The lad stirred, looked up, clearly not sure why he had been disturbed, then realized he shirked his duties and roused himself to help.

Erasmus began to collect firewood, which was in short supply in the immediate vicinity. Returning with a small armload a short time later, Erasmus found Rose crouched down and stirring the caked ashes with a stick, watching a stream of gray carried away on the wind.

A scorched fragment surfaced, like something dredged from the seabed. The priest remained immobile for a second, realization sinking in.

*Bone . . .*

"Why?" Erasmus whispered.

"To leave no one to tell where she had gone."

"But can a mage not take away a man's memories?"

"Yes, but she is not a mage. Who knows what she can do and cannot do?" Erasmus' coat billowed around him, fluttering like a sail.

Rose shook his head, dropping his stick and sitting back on his haunches. "It is said an enchantment can be strengthened by blood."

"Not human blood," Erasmus said quickly.

"Yes, human blood, too, though even the mages had strictures against such evil." He nodded at the fire. "If she believed he had to die—"

Erasmus let his armful of wood fall in a clatter about his feet—sticks bleached and bone dry.

Hayes and Kehler finished dragging their tack in under the low sweeping branches of a fir, and left the horses to Pryor. The boy was a willing worker and took seriously his responsibilities as guide, making his earlier lapse seem oddly out of character.

Kehler was about to make his way back to the fire pit, but Hayes motioned for his friend to walk with him. They set off up the draw, the wind suddenly pushing against them with such energy that they leaned their entire weight into it—like soaring birds.

Finding a flat stone in the lee of an outcropping they sat themselves down, and there, beneath the wind, what seemed like quiet descended. Now that he had his friend alone, Hayes didn't know how to begin. Kehler waited, appearing to listen to the wind, to gauge the growing darkness. In the distance the lightning continued unabated, branching like veins of pure, instantaneous light—then gone.

"You don't need to say it, Hayes," Kehler said softly, his words all but buried beneath a roll of thunder. "If I thought for a moment that all our endeavours would lead to—" His voice caught and in the gathering dark Hayes could see him shake his head sadly. "I only thought we would make a great discovery. That we would write a book that everyone would want to read and that we should make a tremendous success of it all." He turned to Hayes, his voice very low. "And I thought you would escape your poverty, Hayes. That is what I hoped. Never for a moment did I think it would come to this, and that in the end we would have nothing to show for it." He hung his head. "If only our notes had not been ruined. . . ."

Hayes was a little taken aback. He had not for a moment intended to accuse his friend of . . . of anything. "No sense regretting that," Hayes said as warmly as he could. "Eldrich would never allow us to publish our story anyway. It was a great adventure, Kehler, but no one beyond our small band will likely ever know of it. Mages have ways of insuring silence. Poor Doctor Ripke proved that."

"Not quite. In the end he spoke to me. Remember? But I know what you're saying." A peal of thunder silenced them a moment. "I fear that, rather than improving your circumstances, I have made them appreciably worse, Hayes."

"Worse?" Hayes regarded his dejected friend. Poor Kehler was not doing well. "They could hardly have been worse. But no, Kehler, rather than making matters worse, all that we have seen and done has made them better. You see, I feel . . . I don't quite know how to explain . . . I feel more whole, somehow. I don't know what it is. . . . Perhaps seeing the wonders we have seen has altered my perspective on the world. The concerns of the educated classes seem suddenly terribly foolish and petty, and as a result my fall in society seems rather insignificant." He smiled, though not with joy. "In some way, I am the better for what has happened. Do you see? My circumstances are not improved, but I am. If we survive, I shall thank you for it, Kehler. I shall thank you, despite all."

Kehler gazed at his friend through the murk, as though wondering if he jested or perhaps had lost his reason altogether.

Hayes thought poor Kehler did not look bettered by their adventure. The young scholar seemed reduced somehow. It was not just that he had lost weight and his bones and joints had grown more prominent—but he seemed smaller, shrunken. Shrunken, the way old men appeared shrunken. The skin on Kehler's face had lost its youthful luster, and the area around his eyes darkened as though he'd been bruised. If Hayes had not known better, he would have guessed his friend to be seriously ill. Fortunately Kehler's energies had not failed, and he remained almost as wiry and nimble as ever.

"You did not bring me out here to blame me for our ruin?" Kehler said, somewhat surprised. "To excoriate me for leading you into this. . . ."

"No, anything but. In fact, riding through these hills in silence has brought a kind of clarity to my mind. I've been mulling over everything that's happened these past months—the recent weeks most prominently. When you look at all the events clearly, you realize how truly odd some of the coincidences were. The fact that the family of Erasmus Flattery, the man who served Eldrich, were my neighbors, and that I should have found him at the brothel—where I was taken by sheer chance, or so one would assume."

Hayes could barely make out his friend in the growing darkness, except when lightning flashed and illuminated his face in a shockingly unnatural blue-white.

"Yes, it is very odd," Kehler said, sounding both relieved and tired, "but we have said as much before. Even Erasmus has mentioned it. Clarendon has said several times that he does not believe in coincidence, and I am coming to agree with him."

Hayes nodded. "Yes, Clarendon." He took a long breath and plunged on. "I have been mulling over the events that led us to this pass and have begun to realize that I know why *we* are here; Skye set us off on this quest which eventually led down into the cave where we hoped to make our names, to say nothing of monetary considerations. Erasmus is here because he has always been involved—as the child who lived in the house of Eldrich and the man the mage hoped might draw out the Tellerites. Rose is here because of his church and their determination that no one gain the arts now that the time of mages wanes. And that leaves Clarendon. Curiosity is his avowed reason. He led Erasmus down into the cave hoping to learn what Baumgere sought."

"Yes, but he is here now because Eldrich has commanded it," Kehler said, involving himself readily in the dialogue, which seemed a confirmation of their friendship, somehow—the cause in which they both believed.

Hayes nodded his agreement. "So it would appear, but he displays a determination that no one but Rose seems able to conjure up. I have begun to think that Clarendon's purpose is something else, certainly something more than he claims. We both know how difficult it was to journey down into the cave, how frightening it was at times, how dangerous. Curiosity, even strong curiosity, would hardly be enough to make a man take such risks."

"Well, I don't know about that, Hayes. We were largely driven by curiosity."

"And the desire to make our names and perhaps a tidy profit." Hayes smiled. "We also have, according to Erasmus, 'the impetuosity of youth,' which Randall cannot claim. But look at how Clarendon proceeds now. He is a man with purpose. I don't quite know what the purpose is, but he does not seem to have the ambivalence toward this task that we feel. He may have begun by protesting and proclaiming his principles and opposition to Eldrich, yet I see little evidence of this now."

Kehler tilted his head to one side, thinking. "It seems to me to be rather a thin argument, Hayes. What is it you think he seeks?"

*Yes, what?*

"I confess, I don't know. But consider our first evening at Clarendon's house. Do you remember? He told us his personal history almost immediately, as though he could not wait. Is that not odd for a gentleman? We were only acquaintances of a few hours, after all. It was as though he had to tell the story quickly, as if by doing so he might forestall any questions. As though he did not want us to start wondering. Clarendon is so genuine and has led such a difficult life, or so he tells it, that who would question him?"

"I was rather touched by the trust he exhibited, telling his history to strangers," Kehler protested.

"As was I, but think of it. We have hardly thought to question his motives since. However, Teller left more than one band of followers behind, each unaware of the other."

"Now, Hayes," his friend protested, "this is not mental clarity but overactive imagination!"

Hayes felt blood rise in his face, partly from embarrassment. Was he grasping at straws? "Really? The man has a beast that will hardly leave his side—a wolfhound, yet. And what is the familiar of our last living mage but a wolf? It is an odd coincidence, and Clarendon does not believe in coincidence, I might remind you."

Kehler shook his head, almost smiling, but a flash revealed that the smile would not hold and dissolved into troubled shadows. "Do you really think he is a follower of Teller?" he asked, lowering his voice.

"Well, I don't know. It isn't very likely, I suppose. I only meant to point out that I don't believe we know why Clarendon is here. There is more to his story than he has told, or so I believe. He is a mystery masquerading as a tale of hardship and betrayal—an excellent ploy to gain our sympathy and trust—but there is a mystery there, all the same."

Kehler looked up at his friend, the doubt almost visible through the darkness. "If what you say is true, is he a danger to us, do you think?"

"Randall? No, I cannot believe that. Certainly, he seems to bear us no malice. I . . . It is only a question of his purpose, Kehler. Why did he attach himself to us, and why does he pursue Anna with such determination?"

Kehler leaned back against the rock. "Perhaps we should speak to Erasmus about this," Kehler said after a moment, which was what Hayes had hoped to hear.

"If you think we should . . ." Hayes said.

They sat in silence, watching the lightning-shattered sky, and then Kehler turned to his friend.

"I know you have tried to make me feel less responsible, Hayes, but I have not forgotten that it was my impetuosity that got us into this situation. I swayed you with hopes of wealth, even though your common sense told you not to become involved. No, what I am saying is true. You would never be here but for me promising you a way out of poverty, though in truth I had not the slightest reason to believe we would find anything of value in the cavern." He paused, faltering. "It was treacherous of me to promise you profit. It was worse than treacherous. I was lying, Hayes. Lying. And now we are involved with Eldrich. I don't know how you can bear the sight of me. Certainly no one has ever done you a worse turn. Flames, Hayes, but you should hate me. Hate me utterly."

There was the merest second of silence wherein Kehler looked down at the ground, and then he jumped up and hurried off, shaking his head. Hayes watched him go, dumbfounded by this outburst. Perhaps he *should* despise Kehler. Perhaps he should blame him for all that had happened. But Hayes could not. He really felt that what he had said was true. Samual Hayes had found himself through adversity—though it appeared the same claim could not be made for Fenwick Kehler.

They had found an overhanging rock that provided some shelter, though the wind whipped about to all points of the compass and even occasionally seemed to blow directly down so there was no escaping the elements entirely.

The storm was still dry, the dark clouds passing overhead ominously, holding back their rain as though harboring it for a final onslaught. Once they had cooked, they let the fire burn down so that they would not be subject to its smoke, which in these conditions could not be escaped for more than a moment by shifting upwind. The darkness was near total, except for the flicker of distant lightning, which lit their faces in quick, ghostly flashes.

"You are quiet this evening, Pryor," Clarendon said. "Have you nothing to tell us of this area of the hills?"

Pryor looked up, his face flickering into being. Etched with sadness, Hayes thought. "It is this place," the boy said. "I find it . . . I haven't the words."

In the next flicker of light Hayes thought he saw Rose and Erasmus look at each other solemnly.

Pryor roused himself and with some difficulty lit a lamp, heading off into the darkness to see to the horses, though Hayes thought he had really gone to be alone.

"What ails him, do you think?" Kehler asked.

A gust of wind beat down upon the trees, which creaked and complained. When the gust was done, it seemed to have carried off any answer to the question, for no one spoke.

Hayes had rolled himself in a blanket and sat with his back to the rock. If not for the wind and the branches of lightning he could have believed himself back in the cave, huddled against hard stone in the overwhelming darkness.

Suddenly Clarendon pulled aside his own sleeping rug and stood up, his movements oddly jerky in the intermittent lightning. "Someone should see to Pryor," the small man said, concern in his tone.

Kehler rose as well. "I'll come with you, Randall. It is too miserable a night to go off alone."

The two of them picked their way down the few feet of rock and disappeared among the swaying trees.

They sat for some time, and then Hayes leaned closer to Erasmus so that he might be heard above the wind. "Tell me, Erasmus, why do you think Randall involved himself in this endeavor in the first place?"

Erasmus turned toward him, drawing his head back as though wondering what had led Hayes to this question, but then he nodded. "I have wondered the same thing more than once. Something more than we have been told, I think—as do you, I collect?"

Hayes nodded. "Yes. Not that I fear his intentions . . . I think there is a story he has not told, but then we have not all taken our turn to relate our tale." He glanced at Deacon Rose, remembering how the priest had avoided telling his own story while they lay trapped in the chamber—telling of the destruction of the Tellerites by the mages instead.

Rose looked back at him. "I am gratified that others have come to have doubts about our friend Clarendon," the priest said.

"I do not doubt Randall Clarendon," Hayes heard himself say, "but only wonder if we have heard all of his story." As soon as Deacon Rose voiced suspicions of Clarendon, Hayes found himself defending the man. After all, had not Clarendon been proven right about the priest at every turn? Deacon Rose was not to be trusted.

In the next flicker of light Hayes saw the priest smiling. "If I criticized a demon, you would rush to his defense," Rose said.

"Randall's done no one harm that I'm aware of," Hayes said firmly.

"Let us not argue again amongst ourselves," Erasmus interrupted, his voice almost as deep as the drumming thunder. Hayes could see his face in the flickering light—like his neighbors in Paradise Street—flickering into being, then gone. "A man's past is not always so easily revealed to strangers, and despite any liberties with the facts, I think you will find that there was truth in Randall's story—the pain was certainly no exaggeration. Men often have good reason to keep their pasts from others. Let us judge Randall by his actions. By that standard he has earned the respect of us all. Let him paint his past in any shades he might wish, and I, for one, will bless him for it."

The lightning flashed again, and all of them started, for a figure stood at the edge of the firelight—a grimly sad Clarendon staring at them, his pain obvious.

"It is the curse of my difference," Clarendon said as the thunder rolled to silence. "I shall never be free of it."

Suddenly they heard a call above the sounds of the passing storm. Each of them became still, straining to hear, for it was not the first time that they thought they had heard a voice in the wind. Then Kehler appeared in a series of flashes, moving jerkily toward them.

"The horses! They're gone," he called out, and everyone was up, stumbling through the bowing trees.

A parted rope was all they could find of their mounts, scattered by the storm like so many leaves. Nor could they immediately find Pryor.

"He must be searching for the horses," Erasmus yelled above the thunder.

"Madness!" Hayes said. "We won't find them now until daylight."

"He will not likely come to harm this night," Erasmus said, "but someone will surely get lost if we go searching for him. Best we keep to our shelter until there is light."

"We cannot be lost between here and the cliff," Kehler said. "Let us separate just enough to comb back through the trees. The horses might not have gone far."

They split up and made their way back toward the shelter, finding their way by the flashes of lightning that drove back the darkness every few seconds.

Erasmus walked through the center of their line, and after a few moments emerged into the small clearing where the stream flowed. Here the lightning revealed two crouching figures. Erasmus hurried forward, sure that someone had fallen and been injured—easy enough to do in this alternating light and darkness.

As he came a little closer, Erasmus realized it was Deacon Rose bending down with his hand upon someone's shoulder—Hayes, he thought, but then realized it was their guide, Pryor.

Erasmus was brought up sharp. A flash revealed the face of the young man, contorted in pain, streaked with rain—yet it was not raining.

*He knows,* Erasmus thought. The poor boy. That is his brother's pyre.

And then the rain came, driving down upon them in thimble-sized drops. The little, burbling stream rose instantly to a torrent, swelling beyond its banks until it flooded across the fire pit, carrying the ashes and scattering them like memories.

## Eighteen

Moncrief received the letter from his secretary, a grimly serious man who had suffered Moncrief's employ for some twenty years. The King's Man looked disdainfully at the envelope, which was clearly not part of the day's post.

"From Sir John Dalrymple, sir. He . . . Sir John is waiting upon your reply."

"He came with a letter demanding instant reply? I should make him wait the entire day."

"He did say it was urgent, sir."

Moncrief rolled his eyes. "I'm sure he did. Send Sir John home, and accept no argument. Thank you, Horton."

Moncrief took the envelope, glancing at his name on the front written in an unfamiliar hand. It bore no title or honorific, merely Sutton Abelard, as though he were a commoner, a man of no consequence. He felt his anger well up. Sir John was proving to be more than an annoyance.

He slit the envelope quickly, and opened the letter.

*Sir:*

*You will place all the resources in your power at the disposal of Sir John Dalrymple beginning immediately and until such time as Sir John releases them. If I suspect for even a moment that you have not complied in every way with this order, you shall wish you had not been born into this life.*

There was no signature.

Moncrief felt such heat rise into his face that he could hardly speak. "What kind of joke is this?" he spluttered. "Has Dalrymple gone mad?"

He read the letter again, as though unable to believe that anyone could send such a missive to him. As he read, his hand began to shake with anger, and then, without warning, the paper burst into a ball of flame, burning his hands, the light paining his eyes.

He dropped the letter, stumbling away, blinded for the moment.

"*Horton!*" he called, thinking that the papers on his desk would catch and the whole building go.

The secretary burst into the room at the tone of his master's summons.

"Lord Moncrief? Are you unwell?"

Moncrief waved his burned hand at the desk. "Put it out!"

"Sir?"

The bewilderment in the man's voice brought Moncrief up short. He opened his eyes, the white flame still burned into his vision. But there was no fire. He stood mystified for a moment and then crossed to his desk. The letter was gone, and the envelope as well. He examined his hands.

"They are not burned?" he asked, showing them to Horton.

"No, sir."

"Did I fall asleep? Was it a dream?"

"What, sir?" His secretary looked very concerned, as though his employer were babbling.

"Did you bring me a letter from Sir John just a moment ago?"

"You know I did, sir."

Moncrief looked at the desk, and then at the floor beneath it.

"Have you lost it?"

The truth came to him, and he put out a hand to steady himself. The arts of the mages—of the mage. *Eldrich.* He actually felt the blood drain from his face. Quickly he sat down.

"Sir?"

"I must have fallen asleep." He took a long breath. "Very odd dream." He tried to smile reassuringly but failed utterly. "That will be all, Horton."

"If you're sure, sir," Horton said, clearly not ready to go.

"I'm sure."

Horton nodded and backed up a pace, examining Moncrief as though he might just call a physician anyway. Then he turned to go.

"Horton?" Moncrief said as the man reached the door. "Is Sir John still waiting?"

The servant shook his head.

"Have my carriage ready, I shall be going out for a while."

"Immediately, sir."

Sir John sat at his desk, unable to concentrate to even the slightest degree. There were a dozen reports staring at him, unread all the days he had been in Castlebough. He turned and looked out the window into the common across the street. How did one carry on the normal routine after the experience he'd just had? And now Moncrief was being most difficult. What if he did not bother to read the letter at all? Eldrich would not be pleased.

"Flames," he said quietly.

A knock startled him, and his secretary's face appeared in the open door. "Lord Moncrief, Sir John."

"Here? Now?"

"This minute, sir. He says it is most urgent."

Sir John had an urge to make the man wait but had no time for such pettiness. The door was left ajar; a moment later it swung gently back, and Moncrief stepped around it rather gingerly. He still wore his cape, hat and cane clutched in his hands.

Sir John had never seen the man look so pale, as though he were very ill. The King's Man stood there for a moment saying nothing, gazing at Sir John, his look neither malevolent nor defiant. The predatory Moncrief, with his beaked nose and eyes set too close together—the pinched look of disapproval—he appeared cowed! Sir John could hardly believe what he saw. Moncrief looked cowed! Moncrief! What was in that letter?

"I did not realize," the King's Man said at last, his voice very small. "I had no way of knowing. You need not be concerned . . . I . . . Pray, let there be peace between us, Sir John. Think of me as your friend, your ally in all things. Ask whatever you will of me. I am your servant in this matter."

Sir John nodded, not so far gone that he could not enjoy this moment. He smiled rather malevolently at the King's Man.

"We . . ." Sir John began, but then changed his mind. "*I* am looking for a young woman. A dangerous young woman. She has recently been using the name Anna Fielding. A captain of His Majesty's navy will arrive posthaste. He can identify her." Sir John held out a piece of paper upon which the woman's description had been written. He waited until Moncrief realized that he must cross the room to take it. "It is imperative that she not take ship, especially for the island of Farrow. Is that clear?"

Moncrief nodded, perhaps a little surprised by the request. He stood there like a minion, unsure if he was to be invited to sit or if he'd been released.

"I shall put the agents of the Admiralty to work this night. The pleasures of the day to you, Sir John," Moncrief said, bobbing his head and raising his cane slightly in salute. He backed out the door, closing it quietly behind him.

Sir John went to the window and watched Moncrief scurry into his carriage. Word of this unprecedented visit to Sir John would get about immediately. It was almost worth a life's servitude to the mage just to have had that experience. Moncrief currying favor—as he likely did with no one but the King. He heard himself laugh.

What had Eldrich written? Whatever it was it had frightened Moncrief like nothing else. And why did Moncrief believe it? Certainly anyone could have written the letter and signed Eldrich's name, though only a complete fool would do so, for if Eldrich learned of it the man would suffer. Sir John was not quite sure what, but one did not anger the mage. Or fail him.

## ᑫ Nineteen

A vapor wraith streamed up from the cup, fixed in the eye by a flash of lightning. Anna sipped the elixir made from king's blood, her hand trembling perceptibly.

Wind gusted down the slope and flattened her fire, spreading the tongues of flame so that they wavered but could not speak. A dry gale off the sea, and on the distant edge of the world a lightning storm the likes of which she had never seen.

The smell of king's blood was familiar to her now, and the taste. Her body reacted to it with a kind of hunger, even as her mind felt growing revulsion. There were precautions she would have to take soon, for the seed had other effects—none of them desirable—and one readily became habituated.

She closed her eyes and sipped again, the lightning still thrown against her retinae. The liquid ran warm into her center, entered the blood, and flowed outward, invading the rest of her body—or so she imagined. Blessedly, the elixir blunted the sharp edge of pain that cut into her brain—the hangover from augury. She pulled her cloak close around her, sinking back into the cedar boughs she'd cut for comfort.

*What did the vision mean?*

Men pursued her, a group of them: Erasmus and the others from the cave, she was sure. But there had been one among them who was only a shadow. Was it Eldrich? Eldrich seeking her in the hills? Mages commonly used minions for such tasks. Or was this a measure of how desperate Eldrich was? Of how badly he wanted Landor's seed and the words written in the chamber?

The meaning was clear. Somehow they had discovered that she had not died in the cave even though Halsey had sacrificed himself and she had taken a life so that this knowledge would never surface. A life for nothing.

"They come after us," she said to her familiar which hunkered down on a branch nearby.

No response. He did not like this storm and appeared to be sulking, pulling his head back into his shoulders, fluffing his feathers. He rode his wildly swinging branch through the gusts with almost comic determination.

Her eyelids fluttered like wings and closed. Anna began to feel herself drift as though she were floating away from her body. Of course, the vision had not been so simple—such was the nature of augury. She had also seen herself in a circle of columns and at each column stood a man: Erasmus was one; Hayes and Kehler; a priest; another she could not quite see; and again the shadow figure. They performed a ritual—a rite that would make her a mage.

*They will destroy me or help me,* she thought. *But which? Should I run or seek them out?*

Visions never offered answers—only possibilities.

Although she kept her eyes tightly closed, shadows formed at the periphery of her vision, hissing voices whispering unintelligibly, only the loathing articulated.

Anna emptied the bitter dregs of the cup, and lay her head back, the folds of her cape fluttering about her face like the wings of bats. Lightning branched toward the world's edge, rending the fabric of night.

She felt herself rise and opened her eyes to find herself crossing to the horses, the landscape oddly illuminated, almost dully luminescent.

She slipped the hobble on her gray mare and with neither saddle nor bridle swung up onto its back and set off across the meadow, voices hissing from the shadows.

Among the trees they found a path that led up into a cleft between hills. She did not question where they went; she was in the grip of king's blood and obeyed its dictates. The shadow figures seemed to follow her, silent now, but increasing in number.

The mare stopped suddenly as though the way were blocked, and Anna heard a hiss like brittle leaves in the wind. There, rising out of the ground, was the face of Banks. He bobbed as though floating up from the sea, hair plastered to his forehead, white shells for eyes. He rolled slowly, turned by an unseen current, and his shell-eyes looked up at her, ghostly blank.

"*Farrelle's oath . . . Banks?*" she exclaimed, her voice barely rising above the wind. "Banks? Is that you?"

He opened his mouth, but only insects emerged, scurrying off into the night. Again he tried, but the wind carried the words away.

Anna had slumped over her horse's neck, the horror held at bay by the king's blood. "What? I cannot hear. Banks!"

"*There will be a price,*" he hissed, and he slipped beneath the surface, one white shell left upon the ground like a tiny moon.

She slipped off her mare and plucked up the shell, turning the delicate object on her palm. *Armor,* she thought. The armor of some fragile creature.

"*Banks,*" she whispered. "A price for what?"

She went on, leading the gray horse by its halter. Tears slipped down her cheek but were flicked away by the wind. "Banks," she said again, "so many have died."

The path twisted upward among the swaying trees, over a landscape of gnarled root and shattered stone.

"*An-na,*" someone whispered.

She looked around, searching the ground. "Banks?"

"An . . . na . . ."

The voice did not come from the ground, and she looked up to see a form hanging from a tree. Reluctantly she moved forward.

"Kells? Farrelle's blood!" she cried. "What has been done to you? Kells?" She could see him now, his neck caught in the crook of a branch, his body hanging limp.

For a moment he struggled to breathe, trying to swallow, breath gargling in this throat like a death rattle.

"I will get you down, Kells," she said.

"You cannot . . ." he managed, ". . . help me."

"Kells—" her voice choked off in a sob. "Is this what becomes of us?"

"Not . . . you . . ." She could see him blinking, and then he began to choke again, his breath cut off. Anna closed her eyes, unable to bear it. But then the choking subsided and she could hear him drawing shallow breaths.

"He watches," Kells whispered hoarsely. ". . . listens . . ." His breath caught. And for a moment there was utter silence, as he fought to draw a breath, his throat seemingly blocked. No sound, only the lifeless body and the gaping mouth, bulging eyes.

She could not bear it anymore and, almost running, pulled her mare forward.

*"Farrelle's blood,"* she heard herself say again and again. Was this a vision of death? Was this what awaited her?

*"Not you,"* Kells had said, but what had that meant? Her fate was different? Worse?

She stumbled along the path, half-blinded by tears, unsure if the shadows to right and left were trees animated by the storm or creatures of nightmare.

She burst through branches into a small clearing and there a fire burned. Was she back at her own camp?

But no, it was not the same. And someone sat on a fallen tree near the fire.

She edged closer, fearing what she might find. The branches of the fallen tree reached up, tipped in white blossoms. The woman was rocking, humming to herself. Anna could see her now. A large woman of indeterminate age, wisps of gray hair threaded among the dark.

The woman looked up, her face kind. She cradled a baby at her breast, bundled in white, and sang softly.

*"My heart will keep the storm at bay*
*The wraiths, the rain, the whispering night.*
*The eye will see what's foul and fey,*
*The way by darkness*
*Into light."*

For the briefest instant Anna's familiar settled on her shoulder, but then took flight again, agitated, muttering its single syllable like a curse. The chough was battered by the wind, which then dropped to complete calm, though the shadow trees still writhed and swayed. Only here, in this small vale was it tranquil. Beyond, the world had succumbed to madness.

"Ah, child," the woman said, smiling at Anna. "You look chill. Will you not warm yourself by the fire? I've nothing more to offer, I'm afraid. Just fire."

Anna came and sat on a rock across from the dancing flames. She could see the woman more clearly, now, and was less sure of her age. Fifty? More? She shifted, great doughy rolls moving beneath her arms, visible through her blouse. The woman was thrice Anna's weight, she was sure. And she had borne a child—at this late age?

"You look sad, child," the woman said, her voice grandmotherly and filled with concern. "Sad and frightened."

Anna did not answer, although she found herself wanting to tell her troubles to this woman, as though a complete stranger could put her massive arms around Anna and bring comfort, protect her.

"My friends," Anna said, then stopped.

*"He watches,"* Kells had said, and the thought stopped her from speaking.

The woman nodded, her smile wavering. "They are among the whisperers," she said softly, nodding. She looked down at the babe at her breast, making soothing noises. "There my sweet child. There, there. It's only a wee slip of a girl. She can't harm the likes of you."

The woman looked up and gave Anna a tight smile. "It is a terrible, gathering storm. But what can we do? A gale can't be outrun. Even the birds, carried on its winds, fall exhausted at last. Sea birds swept a hundred miles inland, fall on ploughed fields, and are turned into the earth. Their sea memories weeping into the soil." She shook her head. "It is the way of the world. The way, the way.

"But why am I telling you, daughter? You journeyed through the earth's darkness. Only the darkness of the soul is more complete. There, most are lost. The one who seeks you—that is his failing . . ."

"Eldrich? Is that who you mean?"

But the woman looked down tenderly to the child again, and apparently did not hear.

"I suckled him," the woman said, not looking up. "Nourished him. Saw the light grow in his eyes. The light of the world." She shook her head. "Breaks a poor woman's heart."

"What does?" Anna said, confused. Was the woman making sense but the king's blood was muddling her brain, or was the woman raving?

Anna shook her head, pressing her eyes closed.

"What is it, child?"

Anna half-expected the woman to be asking this of the baby, but when she opened her eyes, she found the woman's kind gaze upon her—filled with concern.

"I don't know where to go."

"But you must. You must. He cannot live without me," she looked down at the baby again, clucking her tongue, and smiling. "Nor you," she said. "Women are the way to life. No other. Aye, by moon and tide, we are the way."

The warm light of the fire danced across the old woman, across the folds of the skirt that covered her massive legs, like the trunks of trees.

The woman took the child from her breast, which appeared like a great pendulous moon, and Anna could see crimson scars, a drop of blood forming on the nipple. Calmly the woman pulled her clothing into place, and then her smile brightened.

"See what a beauty he is," she said. "See the look in his eyes. Was there ever more promise than that?" The woman leaned forward, tugging back the swaddling folds.

But there, wrapped in white, lay a bundle of dried thistles and thorns. No child at all.

"Ah, look at how he smiles at you. You see what a pretty girl she is? Yes. Means you no harm at all."

Anna stared in frozen horror, and then the chough's wing brushed her face as it dove, screaming between them, fluttering above the flames. Anna was up, staggering away. She stumbled into the swaying wood, the grasping branches.

She fell, but as she stretched out her hands toward the ground, she seemed to tumble through and was suddenly spinning among the stars, their brittle voices echoing coolly in her ears.

The hanged man. The drowned man. The earth mother. Anna knew all the symbols, as did anyone familiar with even the lesser arts. Water, the stuff of life. There were poems that used the same imagery. Essex had made much of death by water. Death by life.

But what it all meant in her case was unclear.

Banks had drowned in the cave, so it was no surprise that he had appeared to float up out of the earth. *There is a price,* he had said. She shivered at the memory. A price for what? For her escape? A price to be paid for all the lives lost that she might go free? He might have even meant there was a price for entering Landor's chamber. Or stealing the seed. Who knew what charms the great mages had left on their chamber? They might be working their wickedness even now.

She flipped open Halsey's book again, holding it closer to the fire, trying to make out the fine hand. There had been no records set for travel that day, the day after augury and her dream vision. Anna did not think she had been more exhausted upon her escape from the cave.

Still, if she was correct in her assumptions, she was back on the trail that would lead her down into the lowlands—or at least into the right valley.

She read the carefully inscribed Darian, many of the passages followed by Halsey's explanation. The section on dream visions was not particularly enlightening. The only thing she learned was that her particular emotions during the vision could be significant, but as her emotions had seemed deadened and terribly confused, she was not sure what to make of them. Certainly, after the fact, she had been left with a feeling of dread, which might mean nothing. Or so she hoped.

Kells strangling in the tree was another enigma. Kells, who had always been the most articulate of them. The hanged man was usually the innocent, falsely accused, though not always. He could be paying for his crime—relating to Banks' foreboding "there will be a price."

*He watches,* Kells had said. *He listens.* Eldrich, undoubtedly. She didn't doubt that it was true. The mage had somehow known their visions. He knew they watched Skye, and Erasmus, though that was easier to understand—the man who so resembled Teller.

Could he be watching yet? She had not known it had even been possible, so best to assume Eldrich still knew more than he should. But did he know she would escape the cave? Was that part of his plan? She would carry the seed out to him? But Halsey had betrayed him?

Anna shook her head. Her mind was too overcome by fatigue to muddle through these questions. If Eldrich knew something of her visions, then how would she set her course? What depth of understanding in the arts this indicated! More than she had ever thought possible.

Death by water . . .

She could not shake the dream vision out of her mind. The earth mother who spoke as though she had brought the mage into the world. Or perhaps the mages. An image only. Not reality. But still what had that part of the vision indicated? The half-mad woman suckling a bundle of thistles and thorns. The lacerations and, most significantly, the drop of blood forming on the nipple. She suckled her infant with blood.

Anna put her head in her hands, and closed her eyes. The world still seemed to be spinning. She could bear no more. Erasmus and the others were after her, Deacon Rose among them, she was sure. Now was the time for speed. If she could only stay to the path . . .

She felt sleep overcoming her, bewildering her senses. Thoughts connected oddly to emotions. She sank down on the ground in the dull glow of her fire.

A sharp pain in her chest roused her. Looking down she found a thorn embedded in her breast, a crimson tear forming at its base.

## ∽ Twenty

The storm blew itself out by night and left only ravaged clouds scudding on the trailing wind. The travelers had found their horses and pressed on, but by mid-afternoon stopped to rest their mounts and let them graze in a small meadow. Each of the travelers had slipped off on their own, apparently requiring time to themselves.

Both Kehler and Hayes fell asleep in a sheltered place warmed by sunlight. In the cold stream Deacon Rose bathed and performed his ablutions and meditations, while a much subdued Pryor saw to the horses. Erasmus went looking for Clarendon.

The little man had said almost nothing since overhearing their conversation the night before, but he would meet no one's eye and rode behind, snubbing Hayes' and Kehler's attempts to engage him in conversation.

Erasmus had chosen to leave the man alone, feeling that Clarendon would need to nurture his hurt for a while before his more rational side began to assert itself. After twenty minutes of looking, he found the dwarf settled with his back against a fallen tree, writing in the sunlight.

Clarendon looked up warily when he heard footsteps, but his face brightened when he saw it was Erasmus.

"Well, at least you, Mr. Flattery, defended me against the disparagement of that cursed priest," Clarendon said. "He will work to undermine us, to divide us, for he knows we are strong when we stand against him and his scheming."

Erasmus crouched down, feeling the ground which was still wet from rain. "Actually, Randall, I don't think it was Rose who began the conversation. I don't know how much you heard."

"Only you coming to my defense, Mr. Flattery, though it seemed you had your own doubts of me as well." He squinted at Erasmus as though expecting an explanation or perhaps an apology.

Erasmus opened his mouth but could find nothing to say. It was true; he had expressed doubts about Clarendon.

The small man nodded, staring off toward the edge of the meadow. For a moment he said nothing, the bitter look on his face slowly softening.

"The truth is, Mr. Flattery, you were not so far off the mark. I have not told you my story—not all of it anyway. Not for dishonorable reasons, I assure you, but only because . . . I have not lived the common life of a man of my time." He shook his head as though confused by his own decision. "I have experienced things that others would likely not even believe." The little man fell silent, his shoulders drooping suddenly, his face stretched as though in pain.

"Randall, it is your story. You need not share it with me if you'd rather not. Trust that I do not doubt your intentions for a moment, nor do I doubt your friendship. We survived the cave together, and that told me more of Randall Spencer Emanual Clarendon than a complete and detailed history could ever tell."

Clarendon's face softened a little. "You are a friend, Mr. Flattery. A gentleman as the term was once used." Clarendon looked down, his gaze coming to rest on the paper in his lap.

Erasmus' eyes followed this glance, and he realized that the script was Darian.

"The text on the walls in Landor's tomb," Clarendon said, shrugging. "I cannot read it, but even so my powers of recall allow me to recreate it—perfectly." He tilted the page toward Erasmus. "I thought it should be preserved. I don't know why. Perhaps one day you will make sense of it, Mr. Flattery."

Erasmus reached out and put his hand on Clarendon's shoulder. "Even if I understood the words, it is unlikely that we would ever truly grasp the meaning. That is one of the odd things about men—we so often miss the meaning. The story you told us that night at your home, Randall . . . the meaning was clear, the emotional truth there for anyone to hear. The facts," he shrugged, "facts should not be mistaken for truth."

# ᨑTwenty-One

Three vertebrae, a dozen small willow wands, a tiny wolf head formed of gold, shells, a desiccated wasp, feathers, a butterfly wing, raven's beak, fire opal, garnet, a thimble of tin. A bit of colored string terminating in a noose, four flat stones, a crystal, the tooth of a carp. A ring of hair bound in ribbon of red, a braid of leather, a signet ring, the tail of a rat.

All these were spread at random across the table, and leaning over it, the mage, lost to the world.

The countess took a chair, keeping her silence, not expecting to be acknowledged. She looked at all the objects on the table, and except for the golden wolf, thought they looked like nothing so much as the treasures of a small boy. A child's hoard of precious nothings.

Yet this man, who had not a trace of childhood left in him, pored over them as though nothing in the world mattered as much.

After perhaps half an hour of being ignored the countess cleared her throat and said, "Augury?"

No reaction, and then slowly the head nodded, the dark curls barely shaking.

She was about to leave, though had made no motion toward rising from the chair, when Eldrich finally spoke.

"Not really augury in the truest sense. I don't know what one would properly call it. I'm sure no one in the world practices it but me. It is a useful complement to augury. It is properly called, well, *the Paths* might be a Farr equivalent." He waved a hand at the collection of odds and ends spread across the table. "Imagine that each object represents an event, a point in time or a person—perhaps even a place. All but the wands and the string—well, the string is more complex than that. The wands represent paths, though sometimes arrangements of objects indicate paths as well. These paths can be geographical, though more often they are paths through time.

"See how the wands are all different lengths and thicknesses? That is not accidental. Now imagine that time moves in one direction—different each time you cast the Paths, but discerning the direction time moves is one of the easier tricks to learn.

"All the objects on this side represent events that are already past. These in the center are due at any moment, some today perhaps. And this side of the table is the future—or the futures. More than one is indicated, unfortunately." He put his hand to his chin and resumed his contemplation.

Some moments passed and the countess began to think that was all the explanation she would receive, but then Eldrich spoke again, still not raising his head.

"Nothing is fixed except the past, and that is open to interpretation. Each time the Paths are cast, it is different. Each time an event is overtaken, decisions made, it changes." He held his finger above a jumble of objects—a smooth stone, the butterfly wing, and a wand. "Here is a locus, a way-point. This is the critical juncture. From here events can unfold in different ways. This wand that touches the stone comes from the past—the path taken to get here. But look at the array of wands fanning out from here. The string is near, and this trail of objects looks like stepping stones. Five possible directions at least." He shook his head. "This juncture . . . this is the point at which the ones I sought entered the cave. When cast before, all these paths terminated here."

"But Erasmus was in that cave."

"He was."

"But you told me he was alive and unharmed."

"And that was true. But he was never meant to have escaped. Yet he did. They all did." He went on as though this lie meant nothing. "Augury is a bit like gambling, you see. The odds of rolling a die to the same number five times consecutively are very slim. Yet it can happen. Men can escape a cave believed inescapable. Now the pattern has altered radically. It continues beyond the cave; but goes where . . . ? This course," he indicated a wand leading to a white stone curled within the tail of the rat, "it leads to disaster—utter and complete. It must be avoided at all costs."

"But what is this disaster, do you know?"

"The escape of my enemy, aided by my servant, or so I believe."

"Who?"

"Erasmus, I think, though it could be Bryce."

"But your servants are so loyal. Walky."

"Ah, yes, but Bryce and Erasmus are not Walky. They despise me." Before she could form her next question he answered, "It was necessary.

"Along this path, to the white stone, she escapes with my servant—the white stone is from a river, and water is life. Along this, to the wolf, she comes to me. See this . . . it terminates at the wasp. On this path I believe she dies with another, for the wasp is a twin. But look how the white stone and the wasp are almost connected by the string. As though the path where she dies and the one where she lives are connected. . . ."

"What does it mean?"

Eldrich shook his head. "Even I do not know." He almost brushed one of the objects with a finger, though it was clear he was careful not to disturb them. "But if this path is followed, it will mean Erasmus has betrayed me."

"So he will escape. . . ."

"Escape? He can never escape." Suddenly he was still. "No. That is not true. He escaped the earth when I believed it impossible. I have watched Erasmus Flattery all of his life. I would have told you that I knew, almost without doubt, the course he would take through the years. But now . . ." The black curls shook, his focus riveted to the table and its peculiar array of deadly whatnots.

The countess could hardly credit what she was hearing. Was this not Eldrich? Was it not the mage who moved all around him while he remained still? Yet he sounded like a man filled with doubts, a bit desperate, even melancholic. A man. Not this superior being that she had come to believe in.

"And where am I on these paths?" she asked, surprised to hear her voice emerge as a whisper. "Or am I too insignificant to appear?"

Eldrich lifted an elegant hand, indicating a willow wand with a long finger. "This is your path," he said.

She bent forward to see what was indicated, and saw the wand—perhaps the longest on the table. It led directly and unmistakably to the golden wolf. The countess felt her eyes shut for a second—as though the inevitability were unbearable. As though her freedom to decide had been stolen from her long ago and she had realized it only in this instant.

"Do not look so," Eldrich said, regarding her for the first time. "It is not that you have no choice—it only indicates what your choice will likely be. Do you see? Erasmus and the others escaped the cave. A man named Halsey self-murdered to thwart me. Self-murdered, which I had not thought him capable of doing. Nothing is carved in stone. But this . . . it is what you will likely choose."

She felt herself nod, though she still stared at the wand which led to the wolf—actually touched it. "There is a second wand leading off, into the future. Your path?"

He shook his head, still regarding her with those dark, unsettling eyes. "It is yours."

"Mine," she repeated dully. "But it is not so distant from these recent events."

"No, it is not. You will complete the task I have been given."

She heard herself gasp. "But I—I am merely a . . ." She could not find a word. She was an aristocrat. A person of leisure and no particular abilities.

"You are the woman who was created to tempt me." His musical voice tinged with sadness. "But I will turn you against those who believed I could be so ensnared. You were born with a talent for the arts. Do not look so surprised— you have an intuition far beyond those around you. I'm sure you have long known this. And fortune smiles upon you. Small signs, but they have always been there. There are other things as well. But I have tested you further." He looked down at the table again. "The task I leave you to complete—nothing might be required of you at all. Everything depends on this." He gestured again at the tabletop. "On the decisions made. Things learned. Encounters between individuals. And on the choices made by Erasmus. You see, I created him in a certain mold so that the . . . so that those who came after Teller would be drawn to him. Now this might work against me." He shook his head again. "So many possibilities." He fell silent, his shoulders actually sagging. Then he sat back in his chair and looked into the fire. The storm shook the house again, and she heard a wolf howl in the forest. Already she had learned that this would always be Eldrich's familiar. No natural wolf could bear to be in its hunting grounds.

"There is a strategy at the chess board. . . . Do you play? It has been used by several great masters of the game, but it requires a depth of understanding— an ability to look into the future that is almost beyond human. It depends on you understanding the opponent's design better than he understands it him- self. Then you allow him to pursue it, apparently unhindered, your own moves appearing defensive or harmlessly offensive. The game proceeds thus until, with a single move, you take the initiative—at that point your opponent can but react to your attack; there is no opportunity for him to pursue his own offense—and for good reason. . . . If you allow him a single move, the initiative will be his. You must pursue your own attack relentlessly." He closed his eyes for a second, as though exhaustion had suddenly gripped him. "I have allowed my opponent a move."

The countess paced across her room, glancing up now and then as a barb of lightning shattered the sky. Thunder seemed to tumble and roll up the valley. She always felt thus after a meeting with the mage—disturbed, confused. The heat of desire building. And tonight, something else. He had touched her in some new way. He had seemed so sad, so disheartened. Before this meeting she had never imagined that he could be anything but arrogant—maddeningly so. But tonight that arrogance was gone.

The countess slumped down on a footstool. What went on in her poor con- fused heart? What of Skye? And Erasmus? What were her feelings for them? Suddenly she did not know. She worried about Erasmus, but partly that was sympathy for someone caught up in something he did not even begin to understand—caught up in it since childhood. And Skye? He had not been banished from her heart altogether. It was just that Eldrich's presence was so overwhelming that it left little room for others in either heart or mind.

And then there was Kent. Poor, noble, foolish Kent. The man had put himself in danger where no one else had, and entirely out of concern for her well-being. She had even begun to suspect that some of his affection for her was genuine, not just infatuation. Not just reaction to her unnatural appeal. And this touched her. Of the men in her life only Kent seemed to care enough what became of her.

Eldrich. Well, she did not know what Eldrich felt. He was a mage, after all. But certainly he was using her to his own end. Skye did not appear to return even a hundredth part of the affection she felt for him. Erasmus was too entangled in the web of the mage to ever have a life of his own—if he survived at all.

And that left Kent. Kent who was willing to do battle with a mage for her. It was utterly foolish of him, especially considering that she had never indicated any depth of feeling for the painter, but still he had done it. And now he, too, had become useful to the mage—had become ensnared. If she managed nothing else, she would have him set free unharmed. As soon as he finished his portraits.

She draw a long breath and thought of the strange scene with Eldrich and his array of oddities. Had she only known what path she would find herself on—perhaps she would have run off with Kent when she had the chance. At least she would have a companion who genuinely cared for her. But what did she feel for him?

## ∽ Twenty-Two

Her eyes sprang open at the sound of a man clearing his throat. Anna lay still for a heartbeat, then turned to meet her captor. A few feet away crouched a priest, looking at her solemnly. He bowed his head in what seemed a deferential greeting.

"I hope you will pardon me for waking you," he said, his voice rumbling like lazy thunder.

Who in the world? Some minion of Deacon Rose, certainly.

"Have you long been lost?" he asked, his voice seeming to echo in a massive chest, though in truth he was a slight man.

Anna propped herself up on one elbow, quickly inventorying her possessions. "Am I not on the path to Wicken Vale?"

He nodded. "Not quite on it." He raised a hand and pointed roughly south. "You are one valley to the north."

A pain in her breast reminded her of the dream vision—and the thorn that was no dream. She wanted to touch the wound, which was still painful, but with the priest there—

Was he really as innocent as he sounded? Not a minion of Rose at all?

"You're traveling alone?" he said.

She nodded. "My guide was thrown from his horse and broke his neck." She stopped, as though struggling with her loss. "I have been wandering since."

She sat up, wrapping her blanket around her. "Can you put me on the right path?"

He nodded. "But would you not care for food and a roof over your head?"

"People will be worried," she said. "I must press on. There is the family of my guide to think of, as well."

He considered this for a moment, surprised, perhaps, that someone lost would refuse hospitality.

"I have been told that curiosity will be my undoing, but I can't help wondering . . ."

"What I am doing here, traveling by such out-of-the-way paths when there is a perfectly serviceable road?"

He nodded.

"Roads lead many places, Brother, but seldom to adventure." She smiled at him. "I'm writing a book—a traveler's tale of the Caledon Hills. But what would be interesting about a journey so many have made? So here I am searching for sights others have not seen or even heard tell of, though it seems I shall have to title it 'Lost in the Caledon Hills' rather than 'A Journey Through the Hidden Hills' as I intended."

"Your guide . . . from where did he hale?"

"Somewhere near Castlebough. Garrick was his name. Garrick Lake."

"There are Lakes enough in Castlebough, and in Wicken Vale, as well. Poor man. What did you do with him?"

"I performed the rites as best I could and set him on a pyre. May Farrelle preserve him." Again she paused, then glanced up. "But I am no priest and fear what will become of his immortal soul."

"I think if your intent was good, as it surely was, then you need have no worry." He tried to smile, to reassure her. "But then I am a hermit and have come to believe many strange things, I'm afraid. I have only a poor man's hospitality to offer, but come at least and break your fast, and perhaps there will be some foodstuffs I can provide to see you down to Wicken Vale."

He stood, pointing off into the trees. "There is a path, and perhaps something for your book. Come along when you're ready."

When she was alone, Anna rolled out of her blanket and dressed quickly. Certainly she should be sleeping in her clothing now, in case her hunters surprised her. She broke camp and loaded her horses, having no intention of visiting. He had not told her his name—surely an indication of how long he had been outside society.

Anna stopped as she tightened her saddle girth, realizing that she must visit with the priest at least long enough to have him put her on the right path. There was nothing to fear from him, she was certain of that. She would have sensed it, especially now, with her king's blood-heightened senses.

Trailing her horses behind her, Anna made her way up the path the priest had followed, and in a few moments, to her great surprise, found herself before a sizable monastery. Abruptly, she pulled her train up. Had he not referred to himself as a hermit? This was not a hermit's hut.

But then she realized the buildings were in various states of ruin: roof tiles dislodged, their careful columns in disarray; climbing plants swarming over the walls. It was an ancient monastery, and had not seen use for many years.

Anna tethered her horses in the meadow and left them to the new spring grass. The gate to the monastery was left ajar in invitation. She found herself in a good-sized courtyard, shaded by trees, with water burbling in a fount. Half the area was given over to a garden, which here, in the protection of the walls, was farther along than she would have expected. It was also artfully laid out, and immaculately tended.

The buildings which surrounded the courtyard were of a locally quarried stone, weathered to the color of dark leather, but mixed with stones of natural, deep reds and occasional intrusions of quartz.

The tile roofs sprouted small meadows of grass and even shrubs, and the birds made free with window ledges and niches for the building of nests. Nature had begun to make this place of man its home.

Anna walked beneath the trees to an open door, and as she entered, heard the sound of singing, *basso profundo,* as she would have expected.

It was cooler within the massive walls, and smelled of stone and emptiness. As though the monks, in their austerity, had passed through leaving not even the scents common to the living places of humankind.

A swallow fluttered past Anna and perched on a rail of the stair high overhead, chirping at her insolently.

*Let not my familiar find you speaking to me thus,* she thought, and wondered where Chuff had disappeared to. He came and went on his own mysterious errands. "Familiar" seemed an odd choice of name to her, for the bird was anything but.

The singing drew her on.

*To be wrecked upon the shoals?* she wondered. In a great hall, once the gathering place for meals, she found the priest bent over a table which appeared to be covered in clumps of vegetation.

But this was not what drew her attention. Some climbing vine had gained entry by high windows and spread itself across the ceiling and down the walls. White flowers, like morning glories, bobbed in the small breeze that found its way in the glassless windows. It was as though she were in a vast chamber made entirely of these heart-shaped leaves and gently fluttering white blossoms.

The priest looked up and smiled, the song retreating into its own echo, and disappearing in some small corner of the room.

"Do you like my great hall?" he asked. "The Hall of the Morning Bells, I call it. Though not everyone can hear *matines* being rung with such delicacy." He smiled again, a surprisingly pleasant smile given the yellow of his teeth.

Anna realized that the clumps of sticks and grass and reeds spread over the table were the nests of birds. Some were hardly larger than thimbles, and made of soft grasses and down, while others were hat-sized.

"My collection," the priest said. "I am Brother Norbert, by the way. Do excuse my manners—I get so few visitors." He did not wait to hear her name, so Anna did not offer it.

"It is my ambition to collect a specimen of nest from every bird that breeds in this corner of the Caledon Hills," he said. "Though I have some distance yet to go."

"But they have eggs in them as well," Anna said, wondering how these had been preserved.

"So it would appear," he said, lifting an egg from its nest and dropping it in her hand. It was far heavier than she expected.

He smiled at her surprise. "I seek out stones of the correct size and form, or near enough that I can polish them into shape, and then I paint them as realistically as I can. I can't bring myself to steal the eggs the poor mothers go to such trouble to lay, although it is a common practice among naturalists, I'm told." He gestured toward a door. "I have a kettle on and can offer soup and bread as well as tea. . . ."

Anna nodded, the thought of fresh bread actually causing her to salivate. Clearly she had been too long in caves and wood.

The song of birds caught her attention, and she looked up to see more swallows in the air overhead, picking their meals off the branches of the air.

"It is really the swallows' monastery now," Brother Norbert said. "I am merely tolerated by them."

She followed him from the hall into a smaller room where a fire burned in a hearth, and the smell of bread was on the air—the scents of man reclaiming this one small room, at least briefly.

They took their meal beneath a grape arbor, Anna too hungry, she found, to speak, so Brother Norbert, contrary to the practice of monks, made conversation while he ate.

"You might wonder what I am doing here alone," he said. "As I was curious about your own journey. You might also find the history of this monastery interesting—perhaps it could even find a place in your book. There is an artesian spring here, which is the origin of the fount in the courtyard. Thus the name of the monastery; Blessed Springs, though I think originally this place was merely called the Pure Springs.

"The monastery was built, in stages, during the sixth century. A Farrellite Order, the Order of the Sacred Fire, dwelt here originally. And, no, they were not burners of heretics, but burners of books and other art they felt too 'worldly.' They even went so far as to burn some of the art commissioned and possessed by the mother church, for which they were banished to the Caledon Hills and ordered to do penance. They faded into obscurity in a few short years, and all that can be said of them after they were sent away from the larger world, is that they became master builders, for this place would hardly still be standing if not for their diligence.

"The monastery was generally inhabited after the eclipse of the Brothers of the Sacred Fire, but by different Orders with different purposes. It is so far out of the way that many of the more unconventional sects within the church found their home here. Mystics inhabited the buildings for centuries—until the Tautistian Heresy. You know to what I refer?"

"I don't remember the details but know of it generally."

"The details, as you call them; the matters of belief of doctrine are so esoteric as to make one wonder how a veritable war resulted, but suffice it to say that a struggle for power within the church itself played its part, whether Farrellites like to admit it or not. It is a blot upon the church to this day, many of us think."

The priest looked off toward the wall of the courtyard, his face drawn and a little pale. "There was a battle fought here, between the Farrellite forces and the Knights of Glamore, but the Farrellites were greater in number, and the monastery fell." He stopped to swallow. "In the meadow before the gates . . . all of the monks, and the knights who did not escape, were burned as heretics. To this day no tree will grow on that ground."

Anna noticed Brother Norbert's hand shook as he lifted his tea. "The monastery was abandoned then, and for all the intervening years—until I came. My thinking had begun to wander down paths that made my superiors decidedly uncomfortable, so it seemed the life of a hermit monk might suit me best. With the 'blessing' of my bishop, I came here." He looked over at her and raised his eyebrows, trying to smile. "The monastery has an evil reputation in the Caledon Hills, and people don't like to talk of it—likely explaining why you'd never heard tell of it. It's believed the place is haunted, and no one who visits will ever stay beyond dark." He did not smile when he said this. "So I have a strange ministry here, one which my church would never approve of, if I were fool enough to tell them. I am putting to rest the spirits of the dead monks and knights."

He watched Anna's face carefully as he said this, and for a second she thought he jested, or perhaps said this only to shock her. "It is a noble cause," she said evenly. "How goes it?"

"You . . . you do not seemed surprised?" he said.

"Spirits wander the world. I hope the spirit of my guide will stay in the glen where I made his pyre and watch over it and bear no one ill. But these monks— How terrible their end must have been!"

He nodded. "Yes. You see, I am learning their tales." His voice dropped to a rasping whisper. "The winds blowing through the windows at night carry voices, whisperings. And as I learn each tale, I speak with the tortured spirit, and I seek forgiveness for what the church has done. I try to bring them peace and let them pass through."

Anna thought it was no wonder his superiors were happy to see him off to an uninhabited corner of Farrland. She wondered if he were a bit barmy, as some spirit knockers tended to be, or if he was a man sensitive to worlds beyond their own.

"And what has this meant to you, all alone here with the spirits of tormented men?"

He raised a hand and then let it sink gently back to the table. "It has been my nightly hell, and my salvation. . . . It has given me purpose, but I wonder how my spirit will rest after I have heard of all the horror."

"And you do this for your church?"

"For the men who were wronged and foully murdered. To bring contentment to this little corner of the world, for it was once a place of peace and beauty." He paused. "And for the men who committed the atrocities against their will—believing they did the work of Farrelle, and only later realized what this meant to their immortal souls. They are more tormented than any. I sometimes think they will never find peace."

Anna felt a tear well up, quiver on the lashes, and then streak quickly down her cheek. "Yes," she whispered.

"But look what I do," he exclaimed, seeing her tears. "I try to tell you something that might be of interest for your book—a bit of Caledon Hills history— and end by sending you into melancholia." He touched her sleeve, not the flesh beneath, but where it lay on the table. "Let me tell you the good things that I have seen here. I believe that each time a bird builds a nest within the walls of the monastery it is a token—and each nestling that fledges and takes to the sky is the sign of another soul who has shaken off his burdens and gone free. And see how many they are . . . !" He waved a hand at the swallows that darted in and around the walls of the decaying buildings, lost to the joy of flight, the ecstasy of their brief life in this world.

Anna swung up into the saddle, feeling strangely renewed. She looked down at Brother Norbert, his slightly unkempt beard, his stained smile.

"You feel confident of my directions?" he said for the third time. "You don't think I should ride with you until you find the path again?"

"They could not be clearer, thank you Brother." She marveled to hear herself saying thank you to a priest of Farrelle and meaning it, too. She bent in an odd, equestrian curtsy and then turned her mount. But not thirty feet on she stopped.

"Brother Norbert? If my spirit appeared to you one day, would you forgive me and help me find peace?"

"I would, yes."

"No matter what I had done in life?"

"No matter what you had done," he said, a vertical crease appearing between his eyebrows.

The two considered each other for a moment longer, then Anna nodded and turned back to the trail. He had never asked her name.

## ⌒ Twenty-Three

Hills hidden in a sheen of fog and rain. A windless day, sounds seeming to originate from no discernable point but simply out of the air. Anna had stopped her horse to listen yet again. The sounds of the forest were heightened, though strangely hollow. Somewhere a raven croaked.

"Only my own horses," she told herself. Not some others following. Not yet.

Chuff appeared out of the pale air, and landed on her packhorse, muttering his signature word—a complaint, she was sure. Even the birds found such weather unsettling.

She clucked her tongue at her horse and led it on. The path was too easily lost in this fog, so she had chosen to walk, much of the time bent close to the ground. There was undoubtedly an enchantment to keep one from losing one's way, but she didn't know it, nor did it appear in Halsey's book.

She touched a hand to her breast, over her heart, feeling the tender flesh where the thorn had penetrated. No coincidence. She feared that it might even be the work of Eldrich—the child of thistle and thorn. As though he had marked her.

She forced her attention back to her path, which disappeared often, for it was only used occasionally by hunters, and perhaps a bit more regularly by game. If this was not the path Brother Norbert had drawn on his map, it was at least very close, probably even parallel. There should be a river soon.

Anna made her way through the dripping woods, rain running off the tip of her nose, seeping through her protective clothing. Her skin felt numb and softened, as though it might easily tear and she would not know.

She stumbled over rock the color of fog, finding her footing on dark, caked mud. The raven croaked again, making her feel very alone. It rattled its bill, an eerie sound in this enfolding mist.

A sound like onrushing rain came to her and she ducked her head down, prepared to be even wetter. There was no point in seeking shelter now, unless she began to shiver uncontrollably, then it would be time to make a fire—something she could do now without flint or tinder. She might even risk it—a brief use of the arts.

The sound grew in intensity, like a downpour on flat water and broad leaves, but she could not tell from what direction it might originate. A breeze, at least, should precede it, something to carry the squall to her.

Chuff landed on a branch, warning her bitterly of the coming rain.

She held up an arm to brush soaking fir branches aside, but they sprang back, slapping her face with wet, green hands. She spit out fir needles, and then the ground opened before her.

Anna slipped as she stopped, her horse stumbling into her, and the one behind driving it on. She was thrust toward the cliff and only saved herself by grasping a branch that mercifully did not break away. How her horse didn't go over the edge she did not know. The bank gave way under one hoof that came too close to the edge, and the horse seemed poised to pitch into the void, the others jostling behind. She hauled on the reins, and the horse desperately thrashed for footing, somehow saving the moment.

She stood looking down into the gorge, the jade-and- white river rumbling below—the sound of an approaching torrent—and she felt as skittish as her horses.

"Blood and flames," she said several times. "Blood and bloody flames." Her chough landed momentarily on her shoulder; she felt its small, blood-red feet grip her coat.

"Yes, I know. I did not listen to you, Chuff. I was tired and distracted and thought it was coming rain. But it was a gorge. Flames! Being able to swim might not have helped me here."

She stepped away from her horses as her familiar took to the air, flying out over the terrible space. Kneeling, she leaned over the edge, staring down into the green waters. A fairly calm pool lay beneath her, fed by several falls. Below this the water turned to white, flowing between rocks as it dropped from one green pool to the next—water the color of arsenic, she thought.

Two hundred feet farther along, a bend hid the river from view. Anna lifted a stone and tossed it into the pool, watching it make a star of white and then sink into the deepening green.

She looked around, rose, and stepped back from the precipice. She had almost fallen—like the night of her vision. Fallen and landed among the stars.

## ↩ Twenty-Four

They would descend into pools of mist that hung in the valleys as though they were walking down into mountain lakes. Erasmus felt each time like a forest sprite or some other creature of myth and magic. But once into the pool their pace slowed to some fraction of normal. If Anna was far enough ahead not to be caught in this same situation, she would be rapidly escaping.

Pryor assured them that they would be down in the lowlands in two days, that is if they were not in fog for most of that time.

Erasmus wondered how the lad was doing. He caught only occasional glimpses of the boy through the fog—bent inertly over his shaggy horse. Pryor was so lost to his grief that Erasmus feared he might lose the trail from lack of concentration. The poor boy was so despondent that he was not even contemplating revenge. If not for his charges chasing this woman—this woman who had murdered his brother—he would likely have lain down in the rain and never moved again. Nothing mattered to the boy—as though his future had been erased and there was no longer any reason to strive.

Grief, Erasmus thought. He was not a stranger to it himself. For several years after being sent home from the house of Eldrich he had experienced bouts of it over Percy's death.

"Mr. Flattery!" It was Clarendon calling through the mist, still insisting on using formal address for some unknown reason.

Erasmus was afraid to pull his horse up, for Pryor would likely go on, and they would lose him.

Clarendon managed to catch up with him though the path would not allow them to quite ride side by side.

"Mr. Flattery, there are signs of horses joining the trail just behind us."

"Pryor!" Erasmus shouted, shaking the boy out of his reverie. "Did you hear? Randall has seen signs of horses."

Pryor slipped off his mount, dropping the reins to the ground, effectively anchoring his horse to that place. Erasmus and Clarendon fell in behind the boy as he passed, his face so lifeless that Erasmus actually felt alarm.

They passed the others, and in a moment Pryor was crouching down, touching the marks of horses that were rapidly washing away in the rain.

"Is it Anna?" Hayes said, coming up. Pryor had an uncanny ability to tell the hoof prints of one horse from those of another, and they had seen Anna's often enough now.

Pryor moved a few feet, never looking up. Then he shook his head. "Ours," he said.

It took a moment to sink in.

"That's enough for today, I think," Erasmus said. "No point riding in circles. It's only three hours until sunset—not that one can tell on such a day, but let us rest and hope the fog lifts by morning."

Camp was struck and a rough lean-to made from cedar boughs. Fire proved even beyond the skill of their guide, so they ate a cold meal and settled down as best they could, pressed too close.

Erasmus, who had great need for privacy, was feeling the proximity of others. Couple that with the frustrating day, and he found he had to exercise great self-control to remain civil. The others were irritable as well. Erasmus could feel the strained politeness. Deacon Rose was particularly quiet, sensing the mood and knowing that it was most likely toward him that any ugliness would be aimed. Indeed, Erasmus thought Kehler and Hayes were just waiting for the priest to give them an opening.

Clarendon had not quite recovered his usual gracious manner, but he seemed to have overcome his recent bitterness and was making some effort to rebuild his bonds with the others, though awkwardly—he was a man too used to being mocked and rebuffed.

Since Clarendon had admitted to Erasmus that he had not told his whole story, he'd seemed different. Somehow he had formed an attachment strong enough with this group, and perhaps Erasmus in particular, that he could no longer live with the lie.

*He feels shame,* Erasmus thought.

Erasmus felt that the very air was thick with confusion and misunderstanding, emotions close to the surface, as though the worst of human frailties had been exposed by their encounter with Eldrich. Not the first the mage had done this to, Erasmus knew.

*Why does he bring out the worst in men?*

Hayes was being very solicitous of his friend Kehler, making a concerted effort to cheer him, though to little effect.

This is what came of meeting a force that could be neither reasoned with nor defied.

Suddenly unable to bear the company of others, as the melancholic often could not, Kehler rose, muttered some excuse, and slipped away into the falling dusk.

An unsettling silence followed Kehler's retreat.

Clarendon took a long breath and said softly;
*"Dark, dark the night*
*And my heart is no lighter.*
*Bleak will tomorrow rise*
*And each day thence no brighter."*

They all turned to stare at Clarendon, barely visible in the gloom. Pryor rose suddenly and stepped out into the fog without explanation. Erasmus almost thought he heard the boy muffle a sob.

"If that was an attempt to cheer us, Mr. Clarendon, then I must tell you it failed utterly," Hayes said.

"I—I did not mean . . ." But he didn't finish.

"You might have some consideration for the boy," Rose said. "He has suffered great loss at the hands of that . . . woman." He fell quickly silent, realizing he had meant to keep his peace that evening.

Clarendon eyed the priest with obvious disdain. "We all saw you break down our dam and drown poor Banks," he said coldly. "Do not grow suddenly solicitous of others. It is as much a lie as all the other lies you have concocted."

Erasmus could not make out the priest's face but could see his silhouette stiffen.

"And who is it who speaks of truth and lies? A man who has been so completely forthcoming with his friends that they have all come to doubt him. Lies? You have lied to us from the beginning, Mr. Clarendon, and we all know it."

Clarendon began to bluster, but this fizzled out into a protracted silence in which Erasmus could almost feel the little man's pain.

"You have all sided with the priest, is that it?" the small man managed after a moment, his tone bruised and quiet.

No one answered for a moment, and then Erasmus cleared his throat. "Perhaps, Randall, it is time that you completed your tale . . . as you suggested when we spoke."

A long silence followed. Erasmus could see Clarendon hang his head, though in the dark he could not tell if this was shame or merely contemplation.

"You do not know," Clarendon said after a moment. "You cannot." He raised his head as though contemplating the others through the dark. "You were all blessed at birth. Born neither infirm nor deformed. You can never understand what it is like for those like me. Yes, I did not tell my story in its truest form, and all I can offer in defense is that much of it is difficult to tell, or to contemplate." He paused. "I have long thought that no one would believe it, for it is hard to credit—and at times I have had trouble believing it myself. You should also remember that even Mr. Flattery did not begin by telling his true story."

Erasmus could feel the others look at him. Even if they did not, he knew why he had felt sympathy for Clarendon in his obfuscation. Not everyone's past was a tale of joy.

In the fog-bound silence Erasmus could hear the others breathing, sense them waiting for what would be said next.

"Most of what I said was true, or true in essence, if not fact. Yes, I was a performer in the traveling show I spoke of. And my father did indeed drink himself to death. His so-called wife, Lizzy, did gain custody of me. All of that is true. But beyond that . . . there begin some deviations from the strict . . . facts.

"You see, we did not leave the traveling show as soon as Lizzy gained custody. We . . . I remained for some months. During this time she did fall victim to a cad—the aforementioned Colonel Winslow Petry. But events were not quite what I claimed." Clarendon shifted where he sat, his voice now quiet and laden with sadness.

"I know that life with Lizzy was less than perfect, for she had her own peculiarities, and it became even less than ideal when Petry appeared. The man was a brute. . . ." Clarendon drew a long breath to calm himself.

"And Lizzy, who was liberal with her affections, too often gave him excuse to misuse her.

"One of Lizzy's eccentricities was a belief in spiritualism and the ability of some to contact the spirits. She was a victim of every table knocker in Farrland and beyond, I sometimes think. Odd in a woman who was so shrewd in other ways.

"A new conjurer joined the traveling show not long after my father's demise and, among his many other gifts, he claimed to be able to contact the spirits. I was still quite young at the time, and though not living in surroundings that encouraged innocence, I remained, in many ways, somewhat trusting and naive." Clarendon's voice changed as he spoke, charged with sadness and loss, but with some undercurrent of pleasure as well, as though memories of Lizzy warmed him.

"This conjurer was a man of some interest, and not just because I was a child and fascinated by such things. I must have been aged about eleven at the time. He did tricks that no one in the show had seen before—and they had seen any number of such performances in the past, most of them variations on a few themes and well-worn ruses.

"Magnus was a man of some presence—tall and dark with a vast mustache that he waxed up into impressive points. He had a smile that all the ladies in the show remarked upon, and their finer qualities did not go unnoticed by him either, I suspect.

"But I digress. On a particular night Magnus offered to make contact with the spirits and perform some other feats as well. Most of the people who were paying to be part of this sham were locals, but a few were members of the traveling show—my cherished Lizzy among them.

"'*The calling*,' as it was named, took place in a tent used for one of the side-shows. As Lizzy would be inside and Petry's attentions were taken up with a bottle and one of the other women in the show, I contrived to conceal myself near a flap where I could watch what occurred without being seen.

"The obligatory tapers were burning and the participants clasping hands in a circle about a table when I slipped into my place. I had actually hesitated a while before I came, afraid that Magnus, who seemed to have abilities that no one understood, would discover me. But curiosity won out in the end, and with a thumping heart, I watched.

"Magnus was as good a showman as conjurer and held us all in thrall while he worked his 'magic.' He began having the table lift—a common enough trick for table knockers. He then performed a ritual of sorts, calling out in what I now guess was a faux language. There were several parts to the ritual, and I will not burden you with needless detail, but at the end the candles all blew out and a strange milky light appeared to hover high above the table. To this he spoke, and, in turn, it answered." Clarendon paused for a moment. Erasmus could feel the pain, as though he watched a man open a septic wound.

"A distant-sounding voice came from the milky light, though it did not speak Farr or any other language I had heard; and, as you know, my memory for such things is unsurpassed. Magnus interpreted what was said, and soon those present were allowed to ask questions which were then interpreted to the being in the light, or so it seemed. No one was allowed to speak directly to the spirits they sought, but everything went first through Magnus, and then through his counterpart in the spirit world. Despite this device being problematic in every way, the responses appeared to affect the people, causing them often to gasp and occasionally turn rather ashen.

"The evening proceeded in this way, people breaking down in tears as they heard from their lost loved ones, Magnus consoling them, especially the prettier women. I hardly noticed a carriage come to a stop near the tent, and when I did, assumed it was a lady arriving late. Contrary to my assumption, a gentleman stepped down from the coach, though I could not see him for shadow. A moment later he appeared behind me. As I made to cry out in surprise, he put a finger to his lips, and I was struck dumb. Nor could I animate my limbs to flee. I will tell you I have never been so frightened, though this man made not the slightest threatening gesture." Clarendon might have shrugged in the dark.

"He merely watched the proceedings, vaguely amused, or so I thought. I remained in my stricken state, too frightened to even notice what took place. And then the seance broke up, several people leaving, though two—Magnus' confederates—stayed behind to dismantle the apparatus.

"Magnus led Lizzy out into the night," Clarendon paused and drew a ragged breath, "which was warm and bathed in the light of a full moon. The dark gentleman set out in their wake, gesturing for me to follow, which I did only because I was too terrified to disobey. I could hear Lizzy's laughter and was struck by a fear that this terrible man might want something of her—for men always seemed to want something of fair Lizzy. Even then I realized he must be a mage, though I did not know his name.

"Lizzy and her conjurer went out into the meadow, and the laughter gave way to murmuring, sighs, things I had heard many times before. A round little man had appeared, following a few paces behind—the stranger's servant, I surmised. For some while we watched from shadow. I could see the conjurer unbutton the front of Lizzy's dress, two silhouettes in the moonglow. And then something unexpected—something unheard of. The heavens seemed to lose focus and shift, as though a pane of imperfect glass had passed across the sky, blurring the stars. But the world seemed to move as well. I felt it tremble beneath me and fell to my hands and knees. The meadow appeared to change, trees in different places, the faint lights of a house appearing, a copper moon over all. A rushing wind whipped about me, and then all was still, everything as it had been—except that Lizzy and Magnus were nowhere to be seen." Clarendon paused then, lifting hands to his face in horror, as though he saw it all again. But then he went on in a whisper.

"'What did you see, Walky?' the mage asked. I did not grasp what had occurred. Certainly Lizzy and Magnus were still there, somewhere. People did not disappear into the air. 'I saw the worlds . . . *overlap*,' the servant said, 'blend one into the other. And then with a wrench they separated again, tearing the woman and man away.'

"I could not believe what I had heard. Lizzy could not be gone. One did not walk out into a meadow and disappear! One did not! And what was this talk of overlapping worlds? 'What you saw was history being made, Walky. Never before have we been able to predict when such a phenomenon would occur. We are the witnesses to a historic event. What did you see, boy?' the mage asked, turning to me.

"At first I could not produce words, but then I realized that my safety depended on speaking and speaking true. I delved into my memory. 'The stars changed. They blurred, sir, and there were more of them, some moving, and then the meadow changed as well, trees appearing as though in fog, and the lights of a house. And then they all grew smaller, sir, as though disappearing

into the distance. And Lizzy was . . . gone. All I have, sir. She is all I have. . . .'
I began to weep. 'Can't you bring her back, sir? Please,' I begged. I fell to
my knees. 'No one can bring her back, boy,' the mage said. 'Not even I can
do that.'

"'But where has she gone? Where can I find her?' The terrible stranger
seemed to take pity on me, speaking softly. 'She cannot be found, child, for she
has gone the way of Tomas and you cannot follow. But I shall make you forget
this night, forget the pain you feel.' He crouched down before me, staring at me
with dark, unsettling eyes. He spoke words I had never heard, but then he
suddenly stopped. *He has the curse of memory,*' he said to his servant. 'Poor
child, I should put him from his misery.' '*Sir,*' his servant said, as though in
caution. The mage stood, staring down at me still. 'Give him some coins,
Walky. There is little more we can do for such a child.'

"And they left me there, my hands filled with silver, crying like an animal
wounded—wounded in spirit."

Clarendon fell silent then, still covering his face. In the darkness he
could have been the child again, weeping for his loss, for the pain he could
never forget.

## ↩ Twenty-Five

The world dripped with rain. The forest, the vines covering the walls of the
lodge, the eaves; even the windows ran with tears.

*A world overwhelmed with sadness,* the countess thought, and noted her
own mood was in sympathy. She realized that Kent was staring at her, and it
was not with his customary curiosity (the look he donned when he was painting) or adoration (the gaze he turned toward her the rest of the time).

"Am I fidgeting? I am sorry, Kent, it's just . . ." She was not sure what she
meant, and finally gestured toward the windows.

Kent turned his softly penetrating gaze there a moment, and then nodded.
It was like him to understand immediately what she meant.

He returned his attention to the canvas, though he did not raise a brush.
How unlike Eldrich's was his gaze, the countess thought. "Softly penetrating,"
she described it. Kent approached all of his subjects with a certain respect,
even humility. He insinuated himself into the heart of them, whether it be
nature—or human nature. She felt it herself. He made a place for himself in
her, like a sparrow building a nest.

Eldrich's gaze, on the other hand, tore through all impediments until he
held the heart. His approach was essentially destructive. Kent's desire was to

slip in unnoticed, take an impression, and slip away—disturbing as little as possible.

*Kent will pay a terrible price,* she thought suddenly. *He opens himself to the world, bears his breast to the knives. The very thing that makes him great will devour him.*

He looked vulnerable, contemplating his canvas, brush in hand.

She could destroy him herself. Destroy him without meaning to.

"The light is not cooperating, is it?" she asked.

Kent did not answer for a moment, but continued to stare at the canvas. "It is worse than that," he said, turning to her and blinking oddly. "I believe I'm finished."

The countess did not move, realizing what this announcement meant, then she rose fluidly and went and stood beside the painter.

She felt it a bit unseemly, too narcissistic, to stare at her own portrait, yet she could hardly help herself. It was not like gazing into a looking glass, though that was her first thought. This was the Countess of Chilton filtered through the sight and mind of one Averil Kent. This was how another saw her.

*He is in love with me,* she reminded herself. *But even so . . .* Certainly he had made her seem beautiful, though it was not this that stood out for the countess.

"Do you really think me so unhappy?" she asked softly.

Kent glanced at her, eyes widening a little, and then back to the canvas. "I had not thought of it. I simply try to capture what I see, what I feel. . . ."

"Is this sadness yours, then?"

Kent did not answer for a moment as he considered, and then she saw his shoulders fall a little. "It is ours, Lady Chilton," he said barely loud enough to be heard.

Yes, she thought, his sadness was there as well, mingled with her own. Sadness that she would never be his. Sadness that he would be forced to leave this terrible house.

She gestured toward the portrait. "I do not mean to criticize, Kent, but I'm sure my hands are not so long and elegant. In fact, I think those are your hands, Kent!" She teased him now, trying to lighten the mood, spoil the intimacy toward which he strived. "It is overly generous of you to give me your hands, but it is hardly painting what you see. Let me sit again, and I will try not to fidget—though perhaps we might wait until tomorrow? The light might be better."

Kent's shoulders did not rise as she'd hoped, but he nodded slowly. Outside the world continued to weep.

"It can't be changed, Kent," she said, placing a hand on his arm.

Kent took her hand, turning toward her. "But if you are here by choice, as you say, then can you not choose to leave?"

She could not bear the compassion in his eyes, and looked away, though she did not attempt to remove her hand from his. "No. I cannot explain, but it is too late to change course. I . . . it is too late, Kent. I'm sorry." She took her hand back then, glancing up once at the terrible sadness and loss in the painter's face, and then she went out, trying not to look as though she fled.

Back in her room, the countess threw herself down in the window seat, staring out at the weeping world through rain running down the panes. She drew up her knees and buried her face in her arms, but no tears came. The world might weep, but the countess could not afford to.

Sitting up she noticed a spot of deep red upon the soft place between her thumb and index finger: paint, from Kent taking her hand.

"So you've left your mark upon me, after all, Averil Kent."

Kent stood looking at his painting for a long while, trying to separate his sadness from that of the countess. No, certainly that underlying sadness was there in her. He had not simply painted his own heart. She was deeply unhappy—or perhaps unhappy at her center, though years of social schooling allowed her to hide it. But not from Kent, who was trained to observe.

*"Too late,"* she had said, and Kent felt all that he desired, all that he hoped for, slipping away. Like the words themselves, which for a moment vibrated on the air, and then dissolved to nothing. Leaving him with what?

*"Memories are but the ghosts of past events."* So Beaumont had said—a man who knew something about being haunted, apparently.

"Tell me, Mr. Kent, if you will—what are you thinking as you stare at your work?" It was the musical voice of Eldrich. The mage had entered the room unheard.

Kent did not turn, though he felt a strange wariness—as one feels when perceiving a threat from behind.

"'Memories are but the ghosts of past events,'" Kent said.

"Lapin," the mage said, his voice closer now.

"I thought it was Beaumont."

"And so it was, though Lapin said it first. Men often quote the mages and take the credit for themselves." Eldrich was standing directly behind Kent now, and the painter could feel the hair on his neck standing on end, as though it were the wolf and not the man who stood so close.

"The countess' praise was not undeserved, I see. Even I am affected. What is it, Kent, that goes beyond mere technical ability to make such a work? What is it that reaches out to others? 'Art,' I suppose you will say."

Kent shook his head. "Love," he said, speaking the truth, speaking it because it did not matter. The world of human emotions meant nothing to Eldrich.

"Ah . . ." the mage said, though Kent did not hear the mockery he expected. "And thus the talk of ghosts and memories." Eldrich was standing at Kent's shoulder, where the countess had been a moment before.

*Let him do with me what he will,* Kent thought. *It cannot matter.*

"The exquisite pain," the mage said.

"Sir?"

"It is what Halden called the memory of love."

Kent nodded. Perhaps the world of human emotions was not entirely foreign to him.

"Your work is finished here, Kent."

"The countess is not happy with the hands."

Eldrich laughed softly. "More than adequate for our purposes, I assure you. Tomorrow, Kent. I will speak with you before you go."

Kent remained staring at the portrait, not sure if the mage still stood at his shoulder. If so, did he see the sadness? And would it matter to him?

He began to clean the brushes mechanically, replacing each in the vessel from which they protruded like rigid tails. But then he noticed one brush he had employed only the previous day bore a tint that he had not used—a deep purple, like winter plums. He lifted the brush and held it to his nose. Certainly it was fresh paint.

"But it was not me," Kent said, and wondered how many painters Eldrich had hidden away in this strange house.

The countess looked up at Walky and then back to the text.

"I fear the countess' mind is not on her work," the small man said.

She had become "the countess" through the same process by which Eldrich had become "the mage"—or so she assumed. "Lady Chilton" was, after all, the proper form or, given that Walky was a servant, "Your Grace."

She sat back in her chair, looking at the gray old man—not quite what she imagined from the descriptions of Erasmus. Walky's mind appeared to be perfectly intact, for instance. "I confess I am worried about Kent," she said. "I know you assured me that he is in no danger, but . . . well, I find Lord Eldrich less than predictable."

Walky sat back from the table, a signal that this evening's lesson was complete. "It is not the mage who is unpredictable, it is others. Kent is in no danger, I think. Why would he be? Oh, he acted foolishly, and intruded on the mage's privacy, but even so . . . it is hardly a capital offense. No, Kent need only keep his bargain and not make a fuss. The mage will not bear interference or argument. If Kent will say nothing to anger him, he will leave no worse for the experience. My master is not vengeful in the common sense of the word—no more than the courts are vengeful to criminals. Do you see?"

"Yes, though all but the most benighted criminals know when they have transgressed upon the law. How would one know if one had violated the mage's code? It is rather different, you see."

Walky shook his head, sticking out his lower lip as he did when disagreeing. (Did he do this with Eldrich? she wondered.) "M'lady, there are a thousand tales written that describe in detail what one should and should not do to earn the disfavor of a mage. It is hardly secret. Never provoke a mage. Never. Not in the smallest thing."

"I fear I have already broken that law," she said softly.

Walky smiled. "Well, you have a special place in the mage's house."

"And what is that place?" she asked quickly.

Walky drew back into stillness as he did when questioned about certain subjects. "There are certain questions the countess must ask the mage."

She was the countess again. Not "m'lady" as she became when he was feeling less formal—less formal and more affectionate, if one could accuse Walky of affection.

"I think we must be done for the evening," he said, forcing an awkward smile. He did not like to be questioned about Eldrich. Clearly this was one of the mage's laws. The countess was aware that Walky held her in a certain affection—as though he were an old family retainer who had watched her grow from childhood to prominence with subsequent pride. Not the usual reaction she had from men—even very old ones. This meant it hurt him to not answer her questions, but he was the servant of the mage, after all.

He bade her the pleasures of the evening and made his way to the door. Halfway out the old man stopped, and stood in awkward silence for a moment. "Kent will be gone tomorrow," he said. "If you are concerned about his welfare, tell him to do nothing to provoke the mage."

It took a moment for the countess to absorb what had been said—*Kent was leaving in the morning!*—but then she nodded, and Walky slipped out.

Her reaction to the news was not what she expected. Kent was leaving. . . . She would be left here all alone, with no ally. No one who truly cared for her—cared enough to risk the mage's anger. This thought left such a hollowness at her center that she thought tears might well up. *Kent was leaving.*

She went to the window, finding only her face reflected in the night's dark mirror. What sadness had found its way into her countenance. And yet the turmoil she felt inside was revealed in no other way. No, this self-possessed woman did not appear as though she would fly apart at any moment, burst from too many contradictory emotions.

The school of Avonel society had taught her well. Only the sadness bled through, like Kent said paint sometimes would, no matter how many layers were brushed over. Only the sadness.

Even Kent had not seen the turmoil. Poor, loyal Kent. Kent who had risked everything just to prove his love. And how had she returned this loyalty? At the very least, she could carry Walky's warning to him. At the very least.

She tossed a shawl over her shoulders, swept up a candle, and went quickly out.

She knew approximately where Kent's rooms were situated, or thought she did. There were only a handful of people in the lodge, so it seemed that finding light under a door in the guest wing would answer—unless there were others there she knew nothing of. She feared that in the house of Eldrich this was not impossible.

She crossed above the great stair and waited a moment to be sure no one was below. Eldrich, of course, could walk the halls in darkness and utter silence, but there was nothing she could do about that. He would either see her and ask where she was going or not. As Walky had intimated, she was allowed to break some rules—to provoke the mage. Whatever it was he wanted of her, it gave her special status—a diplomatic impunity. Or perhaps the right to be undiplomatic.

She turned a corner into the next hall and froze in place, back against the wall. Eldrich's wolf was sniffing outside a door, and then along the baseboard. It seemed unaware of her at the moment—although that was clearly impossible. She bore a candle, after all, and had gathered in such a gasp as to be heard by the house entire.

*"Farrelle preserve me,"* she whispered. "Farrelle preserve . . ."

The great beast, far larger than she expected, had progressed to the place where she was standing, and sniffed around her feet. She looked down at the massive back and realized that a beast so muscled would tear her to shreds before any rescue could arrive.

*A mage's familiar,* she thought. As she herself possessed, since taking the king's blood. A completely unnatural creature, tied to its master in ways she did not understand. Did it know her? Know her scent? Was Eldrich's mark upon her so that it would leave her in peace?

It nosed at the hem of her dress, lifting it a little so that she felt its breath as it sniffed her ankles.

She pressed herself back against the wall, and found she drew her face back and away, as though to protect it should the beast lunge.

A rough tongue rasped across her ankle.

*Farrelle's blood, what if I am to its taste?*

Slowly she withdrew her foot, just a few inches—and the wolf growled, hair standing up along its shoulders.

"Flames . . ." she whispered, actually feeling the teeth bare. At any second it would lunge and bury those fangs in her too soft flesh, and she did not know what to do to avoid it.

Suddenly it did lunge, but to one side, ignoring her altogether. She almost dropped the candle in her fright, starting back, hardly able to catch her breath.

The great beast had something with its paws and mouth, and then came up with it—a squirming mouse, its tiny feet running madly in the air—and then it was gone into those terrible jaws. The countess slipped away, keeping her back to the wall, a hand to her heart.

The wolf went off, sniffing along the wall again, but blessedly away from her—hunting mice, of all things! She almost laughed aloud.

The countess sank into a chair and let her racing heart come back to its normal rhythm. She shook her head. Never come between a mage's familiar and his dinner. It was not a rule that Walky had taught her. Perhaps it was in one of those old tales of which he spoke. She laughed, though largely from release. She had come face-to-face with a creature from myth, only to find this terror hunting mice! If only she could tell Marianne this story one day.

Thoughts of Marianne brought Kent to mind, for some reason, and she resumed her search.

Not three doors on she found what she sought—a glow from under a door. She stood close to it for a moment, but hearing nothing she pressed her ear to the cool wood.

Something inside. A man singing softly, and footsteps. But was it Kent?

What if this were Eldrich's room, and she knocked on his door instead. Even the thought of this quickened her pulse.

*He is an uncaring creature, hardly more human than his wolf,* she told herself. Briefly, she pressed her cheek against the door, trying to drive out thoughts of Eldrich and the feelings these thoughts called up.

And then she knocked, her heart in her mouth.

The singing stopped. A hand on the doorknob—she saw it tremble—and then the door opened a crack, a single eye appearing in the gap.

"Lady Chilton!" the painter said, and paused before drawing the door open. He stood there quite embarrassed, for he was in his stocking feet and wore no coat or waistcoat.

"Oh, Kent, do not worry about your dress," she said. "Only let me in. I've just encountered Eldrich's wolf and fear it might return."

Quickly he stepped aside, and she came in, shutting the door firmly behind her.

Kent was clearly taken aback to find her in his room so late, and she could see that he was torn between his hopes and not wanting to appear foolish.

"Will you invite me to sit down, at least?" she said, though not unkindly.

"Yes. Yes, of course." He took the candle from her and placed it on the mantlepiece, gesturing to a chair.

The room was dimly lit by a single lamp, and Kent had clearly been sitting close to it reading, for a book lay open on the table. There was also a bottle of wine and a half-empty glass. Clearly, Kent was on better terms with the servants than she was.

"You will be sent off tomorrow," she said, coming straight to the point. "I talked to Walky."

Kent nodded, his eyes searching hers. "I know," he said after a moment. "Eldrich came to view the portrait after you left." He stood by the mantlepiece and looked down at her, hoping for some sign, some indication of why she was here.

"Kent, I don't know if we shall ever meet again," she blurted out.

His gaze dropped to the floor for a moment, then back to her again. "And if we do, will I even remember? Is it not the practice of the mage to destroy the memories of those who have dwelt in his house? Will I remember that I painted your portrait and had the pleasure of your company for those too few days? Oh, that I had never learned to paint so swiftly! Will he tear these memories away from me?"

She could not predict what Eldrich would do, but she was afraid that Kent was right. He would remember nothing of his stay in the house of Eldrich. Remember nothing of his fool's attempt to rescue her. His noble attempt. "I don't know what Eldrich will do. I really don't. I only know that Walky gave me a warning to pass on to you."

Kent looked at her differently now, the distress pushed back a little. He listened intently. His blue eyes were soft in the low light, pupils large. His loose shirt, unbuttoned at the top, showed a glimpse of pale skin. For a moment she closed her eyes.

"Do nothing to antagonize the mage," she said. "Offer no arguments. Provoke him in no way. Do you understand, Kent?"

He looked away from her, shaking his head. "What do I care what the mage does to me?" he said.

"Kent!" She rose quickly, taking up his hands, aware of the extreme warmth of them.

He looked into her face then, so close.

"Do not speak so. Please, Kent. Do nothing foolish. I will never forgive myself if you come to harm. Promise me. . . ."

Kent resisted for a moment. "But he will take everything from me," he whispered. "Send me away from you and rob me of my memories. All that I have."

She touched a hand to his cheek. Poor Kent. He was sick with love. Desolate at the thought that he would not even remember their time together. Was it really so precious to him?

"Do you see? I will lose you in every way. Every way."

She nodded. There was no denying this. He would forget her. Forget his infatuation. Forget this night, this very moment. "But I will remember, Kent. Remember that it was you who came searching for me—unconcerned for your own safety. I will never forget."

She kissed him. Not a peck on the cheek but full on the mouth. For a second they stayed close, his wine-sweet breath warm upon her. And then he kissed her in return, and took her in his arms.

*He will remember nothing,* she told herself. *Not a thing.*


## ❧ Twenty-Six

Marianne Edden was more distressed than she could remember. Her carriage—actually the countess'—rolled through the Caledon Hills on a beautiful morning, birds brightening the air with both flight and song, and she hardly noticed.

She glanced over at the anonymous portrait of the countess, her only traveling companion—the countess' lady's maid had insisted on giving Marianne her privacy and was riding up with the driver, a rather transparent explanation, for there was clearly sympathy between the two. The countess stared out from her frame, beautiful and somewhat troubled.

"Too beautiful," Marianne whispered. Such unnatural radiance was bound to bring trouble, if not tragedy. Any trait in overabundance was worrisome. Too much money, significant talent, a title, great beauty, charm and wit—they were like lightning rods. The countess stood too tall among the crowd—as did Marianne herself, in her own way.

It was the reason she had always avoided the court and certain circles in Avonel, and why she was attracted to simple things and uncomplicated lives. The countess had been a rare exception, but then who could resist the attentions of the Countess of Chilton? Even women were flattered beyond imagining just to be noticed by her. Marianne often thought that she was the countess' only true friend—or at least the closest thing the countess had to a friend. After all, Marianne was unlikely to ever suffer fits of jealousy or envy—the novelist was admired in her own right, and for entirely different reasons. They were simply never rivals.

*I am doing precious little to help for the person who professes to be her only friend,* Marianne thought. She could think of no other plan than to use her contacts in Avonel to gain an audience with the King, or at least with the King's Man: that despicable Moncrief. What else could be done? The King was the most powerful man in Farrland. If the King could not intercede with El-drich, then no one could.

Certainly Erasmus Flattery had proved a disappointment. It might be true that he knew of what he spoke, but still . . . to simply accept that there was nothing to be done! It did not speak highly of him. Even poor Kent had rushed off to try to save the countess though she feared he had not come to a good end over this.

Poor Kent, foolish with love. It was not so much bravery, she knew, as hopeless desire. That point of madness where one will die to prove one's love and thereby gain the affections of the beloved. A bit pathetic, really. Better to live in disappointment than commit what amounted to self-murder to gain a love that one would not be able to enjoy from beyond the grave. After all, most lived with disappointment. It was the nature of things.

Marianne let out a long sigh. She wanted to leap from the carriage and thrash the bushes with a walking stick. She felt such frustration, such helpless-ness. It was an emotion she was familiar with, but only at a remove—she wrote about it but almost never experienced it. Marianne Edden was a person with too many resources to feel frustrated often.

The carriage rocked, suddenly slowing, and finally lurched to a halt.

"Ma'am?" It was the driver.

"What is it?" She pushed the window open.

"A carriage with a broken axle, I think. Shall I stop and offer assistance?"

"By all means."

Someone hailed them. She could see the carriage now, a large, old-fashioned affair. Marianne pulled her head back in and took a deep breath. Was this not the carriage Kent described coming for the countess? But certainly the mage would not suffer a broken axle, like normal men?

Steeling her nerve, she pushed the door open and climbed down before the driver could lower the step.

By the listing carriage stood two gentlemen and a driver, all with their sleeves rolled up.

"Ah, fortune has found us," a dark-haired man said.

"Miss Edden?"

"Lord Skye! What an unlooked-for pleasure. You're returning to Avonel, too, I collect?"

The empiricist nodded his silver mane quickly. "May I introduce Mr. Percy Bryce. Miss Marianne Edden."

Pleasantries were lost on Marianne. Hadn't this man been rumored to be in the employ of whoever let Baumgere's old mansion? The mansion where Kent claimed Eldrich had taken the countess?

"You do seem to have had some bad luck, Lord Skye. Can I carry you on? There must be an inn within a few hours. They can certainly send someone to repair your carriage."

A few bags were quickly shifted, and Bryce and Skye took their place in the carriage with Marianne and the portrait of the countess. An odd situation, all in all, and a bit of luck that Marianne did not intend to let slip away.

Just who was this man Bryce and what was his place in Eldrich's house? Certainly he was no servant in the common sense of the word, but one could serve in many capacities. And what was Skye doing in this man's company?

"We are a bit of a traveling art exposition," Skye said, clearly trying to make polite conversation. "I have the Peliers the countess had authenticated."

Marianne nodded. The Peliers—she had almost forgotten them. The man crossing the bridge toward the dark coach. Skye had claimed this to depict the Stranger of Compton Heath. And the other, which showed the crypt Baumgere excavated above Castlebough. Prophetic paintings.

"Have you seen Lord Skye's Peliers, Mr. Bryce? What do you make of them?"

Bryce had been staring out the window, apparently lost in thought. Now he shrugged. "I must admit, Miss Edden, that I know little about Pelier. People say he had a gift, and far be it from me to deny it." He smiled apologetically, and as soon as it seemed even remotely polite, he returned his attention to the passing scene.

"Eldrich has an interest in Pelier. Did you know?" She wasn't quite sure what she was doing, other than falling back entirely on her novelist's intuition.

This brought Bryce back from the window, a suitably neutral look fixed on his face. Too neutral, Marianne was certain.

"Eldrich? Really?"

"Yes, Mr. Flattery told us much about the mage. I had heard that he would not speak of it, but then when he realized the countess' interest—I don't think men keep many secrets from the countess. Wouldn't you agree, Lord Skye?"

Skye barely nodded, clearly trying to warn her off with his eyes. All of a sudden he looked quite unsettled.

"Mr. Flattery could read the writing on the crypt depicted in the painting. He even made me several examples of this script. Remarkable, really. I plan to incorporate it into a book. Imagine how people will react when they discover I have the actual language of the mages in a novel! That should increase my readership, don't you think? My publisher will be pleased." She smiled at them expansively. What *was* she doing? Making this servant of Eldrich believe she knew more than she did, and that she was about to publish it in every city around the Entide Sea.

"We are actually stopping to visit friends along the way, Miss Edden," Bryce said. "I'm sure they would be delighted to meet you, and it would break up your journey."

She nodded. "Why how very kind of you. Nothing would please me more."

Marianne felt herself sag back in her seat. *Pray that I have not miscalculated and that this "friend" is Eldrich. Certainly Bryce would not do something unpleasant to me without consulting his master. Not to Marianne Edden.*

*Why, then, did Skye look as he did? One would think I had entered the den of a hungry lion.*

Marianne walked beneath the trees of the terrace of the inn. The buildings perched on the edge of a gorge high above a picturesque river. The terrace, walled and shaded, lay among the buildings, so that it was almost a courtyard. Emerging from under the spreading trees, she came beneath the canopy of stars. The cold clarity and sheer numbers of them stopped her momentarily, and she stared up into the depths of the heavens, as enraptured as the ancients who had organized their lives by the movements of the stars.

"Do you see the wandering star?"

Marianne started and then realized it was Skye, standing in the shadows beneath the lime trees. How long had he been there, watching?

She looked back up to the stars. "There are so many." "Yes, but this one is unlike all the others. Look toward the Ship. Do you see there, as if hung in the rigging, like sea fire."

"That milky blur? That is a wandering star?"

"Yes. What do you think you are doing?" Skye asked suddenly. He emerged from the shadow, his mane of hair silvered by starlight. "You have guessed who my traveling companion is?"

"A servant of Eldrich, I think."

He nodded in agreement. "You think you are being clever, having him take you to the countess, but what will you have accomplished? You will have angered the mage who does not like to have his time wasted by others, no matter how talented or celebrated they are."

"You speak as though you know him," Marianne said.

"Like the countess, I have visited him in the past, though my memories of these visits were clouded. You did not tell Bryce the truth at all, did you? Flattery told you nothing, I will wager."

She did not answer, realizing he could ruin her plans, if he had not done so already.

"I will explain this to Bryce, and perhaps he will let you go on your way."

"No!"

He came a step closer so that she could make out his face, ghostly in the starlight with only shadows for eyes. "Miss Edden, you do not understand what you involve yourself in. Do you think your gift for invention will help you rescue the countess? The mage detects lies more easily than even a novelist can manufacture them. I am surprised Bryce did not see through your story. You are only letting yourself in for a trial. Mages are not patient."

"Someone must do something," she said. "At least let me speak to the countess and reassure myself that she is not there against her will. If I can do that, I will be satisfied. Why is it no one but Kent and myself are willing to take a risk for our friend?"

Skye did not answer immediately, and when he did, his voice was very tight. "Because there is nothing one can do . . . unless proving you are loyal to the point of foolishness is important to you—as it apparently is to Kent."

"And you, Lord Skye. Why do you wish to see Eldrich if his tolerance for humankind is so slight?"

He did not answer, but walked a few steps to the wall and stared down into the gorge where the dark river ran like an artery of the world. "Because he has the power to unlock memories. Unlock the past. . . ."

Marianne shook her head, moving to the wall near him. "People are in thrall to their past. Many spend all the years that remain to them trying to forget, for their pasts were terrible. Perhaps you will be one of these. You have always been a visionary of empiricism, looking to the future. Why do you take this chance?"

Skye continued to stare down into the gorge, as though listening to voices in the darkly flowing river. "Because until I know, I will always be a stranger to myself. A kind of changeling. People are in thrall to their pasts, you say. One can be equally in thrall to a mystery. Imagine if several days of your life could not be recalled—not a thing about them. Would you not wonder? Would you not imagine all manner of incidents that might have befallen you, or things that you might have done? Imagine that you had committed some terrible crime, something so revolting that your mind could not bear to look upon it? Such things happen to men who fight wars. They see such atrocities that they can no longer recall entire battles—yet they dream of little else and waste away because they cannot bear to sleep.

"Who was I before my accident? I was adopted, but from where? Do you see? I am a changeling, a man who sees things others do not: my laws of motion; the naval gun; and much else besides. I am different, marked. Appearing from nowhere as though created whole in my teen years. And you counsel me to abandon my search?" He was gripping the stone of the wall with both hands, but now he loosened his hold, his shoulders sagging. "No, if Eldrich can unlock my past, then I will live with the consequences. They cannot be worse than what I experience now."

There was nothing to be said to this, Marianne knew. No argument would convince Skye to change his course.

"But what of me?" Marianne said softly. "You may choose your course, not even knowing if Eldrich will grant your request, yet you advise me to turn away. Who are you to decide for me, as though I were a child? I will tell you in all modesty, Lord Syke, that there are few people in all the land more calculating than I. Everything I have ever done or been has been weighed upon a scale that balances with a precision most cannot imagine. You talk of being created whole as a youth, but I am my own creation, and made myself whole even later in life. Marianne Edden, the eccentric genius that everyone knows something of, is my greatest character, created with perfect attention to detail. I have a colder heart than anyone knows, and yet I am willing to risk everything to be reassured my friend is unharmed. I have only one friend, you see—a thousand admirers and passing acquaintances, but one friend only. And as you say, I am willing to take great risks, not just to prove my loyalty, but because I will be forced to live with the knowledge if I shirk. I have lived with my calculation, my flawed heroine, long enough, I do not want anything more to haunt me."

The whisper and weave of the river flowing. A breeze making small banners of locks of her hair.

"Be up before sunrise," Skye said. "Bryce likes to be on the road at first light."

He walked away without saying good night, though she felt no insult. They were alike, she and he, hidden in among the population, appearing as others did, yet as different as crows raised in a nest of doves.

## Twenty-Seven

Kent was let into the room by Walky, who stood guard over his master's privacy with a dedication that no royal guard could equal. The painter stopped inside the door and waited for the mage to take notice of his presence.

Eldrich bent over a book at the table, a breakfast roll in one hand that he nibbled periodically without seeming aware of this action—as though his body had learned to seek sustenance of its own accord.

The two portraits—one on the easel, the other on a chair—were turned toward Eldrich, as though he had been viewing them, and Kent found that he suddenly craved the man's approbation. Had he no opinion? Did mages have no concern for such trivial matters as art? Any art but their own, that is.

"You are ready to travel?" the mage said. As was apparently his habit, he did not look up at Kent as he spoke.

"I am."

Eldrich seemed to nod, though perhaps it was only a random movement. Kent was not used to being treated as though he were not there—not in recent years, at least—and he did not much like it.

"Then I shall pay you your price, Kent," Eldrich said. He rose where he stood, eyes still fixed on the book. Only reluctantly did they give this up, and the mage turned his disturbing gaze upon the painter.

"You realize that you cannot go from this place knowing what you know?"

Kent felt his eyes shut for a moment. He called up a vision of the countess, her touch. Her lips. The sounds of her pleasure, her passion.

*Elaural. . . .*

"Kent?"

The painter nodded. "Will I remember nothing?" he asked in a small voice.

*Promise me you will not provoke him,* the countess had asked. And he had promised. But now. . . .

He looked up at the mage, half a head taller than Kent, even though Eldrich seemed to stoop a little.

"Nothing," the mage said.

The pain was so great that Kent shut his eyes again. "Then the price is too great. You receive your portraits, but I lose everything."

"Hardly everything," Eldrich said, his musical voice hardening. "I have let you have your life in exchange. Have you forgotten?"

"I do not value it as highly as I believed."

"Have you never heard that it is unwise to try the patience of a mage? Especially over things of little consequence."

"Matters of the heart mean more to men," Kent answered, not caring what happened. Who was this man to steal away his precious memories?

Eldrich looked at him and shook his head. A smile might have flickered across his face.

"For your insolence I should send you forth from this place." He stopped, took a long, calming breath, and let it out in a sigh. "Flames, Kent, you are young. I will leave you this," he said. "You shall not forget your rather over-valued feelings." He held up a hand. "Say a word, and I will withdraw my offer. Show some wisdom, Kent."

The painter looked into the eyes of the mage and thought that perhaps there was a trace of humanity there—not much more—but a trace.

The mage wove a pattern in the air with his hand, and began to speak words that Kent did not know. He felt himself falling . . . into a star-filled sky.

*       *       *

The lodge was clearly not used just for the hunt. There was every sign that the people who owned it spent significant time here as a family. Without nosing around too much, one could chart the progress of the children—and not just by portraits. The countess was sure there were two girls and a boy. She found their cast-off toys and games, as well as signs of other pursuits—the kind that parents insisted on because they were "improving." In rather mysterious ways in some cases, or so the countess thought.

One large room was set aside for a children's playroom. She had found it soon after they arrived, but had not visited it again. There was something about its atmosphere of abandonment that affected her. Childhood, not so much lost as repudiated. She remembered it, that impatience to become adult. And look where it led. . . . No, children had the best of the bargain, she was sure.

Why Eldrich had asked to meet her here, she did not know—an odd request. But then very little about the mage's household could be called ordinary, at least by the standards she was familiar with.

The countess pressed open the door to the playroom, and stood looking in for a moment. As always, she carried a candelabra, for the halls were unlit, Eldrich and his servants apparently having little need, and even less affection for light. But this room was lit, by candles and a lamp or two. Still she hesitated at the door, the feeling of loneliness growing, though she could not say why.

*Kent was gone.* And she was alone in this strange world, as Erasmus had been as a small boy.

Looking into the room, with its playhouse and dolls, its toy carriage drawn by a team of rocking horses, caused a terrible sadness to settle over her. A woman without child, she thought, by way of explanation, but knew it was not the truth, or only a very small part of it.

A music box began to tinkle, slightly out of tune, and too slow. She went in, and found Eldrich looking down from his great height at the music box on a miniature table. A girl in a long skirt and a dashing soldier spun on the top, dancing in the candlelight.

As was his habit, Eldrich did not look up as she entered, but continued to regard the tiny dancers—his mind elsewhere, the countess was certain. Focused on this great task that he wrestled. The task left to him by the other mages. She thought he looked more forlorn than usual, and that was saying a great deal.

While she waited to have her presence acknowledged, the countess let her eyes wander the room. On her previous visit she had not noticed the border painted high around the walls. It depicted a well-known children's tale, with its magic doors, wise wizard, and heroic children caught up in the strange events. She thought the section depicting them riding a raft down a torrential river was the best.

Shelves of poppets stared out at her from an open cabinet, their too-large eyes seeming to regard her with a certain malicious glee. Toy swords and shields stood at attention in a corner, beneath falling banners, their colors faded. Shadows, sharply defined, slanted among the blades and for some reason these seemed more solid than the objects that cast them.

The rocking-horse team, drawing a coach large enough for small children, made the countess wish she were small enough to play in it herself. It was so perfectly wrought; painted a vivid blue with wheels of yellow. Two large dolls sat inside, traveling endlessly across this children's landscape.

*Popidon, Popidon where do you go?*
*Down to the sea to see the men row.*
*Popidon, Popidon why do you weep?*
*The boats are ashore, the rowers asleep.*

"It is an odd little museum, is it not? Such effort focused on preserving childhood. Did your parents keep such a shrine to your younger years?"

The countess shook her head, looking over to find Eldrich gazing at her.

"Nor did mine. But then I had so little childhood to feel nostalgic about for I was sent off to the house of the mage when only seven."

The music box wound down so that the last few notes sounded like afterthoughts, the dancers barely twitching to this dying fall.

Eldrich had been taken away as a child, like Erasmus. It had never occurred to the countess before that this would be the case. Indeed, it was almost impossible for her to imagine the mage other than he was now.

"I have always said that having no childhood was a blessing, for it saved me from this current fashion for constantly complaining about one's younger years. No, everyone should have been sent off to serve a mage and saved us this endless prattle, that's what I think."

He fell silent, and began a slow circuit of the room, stopping here and there to contemplate one object or another.

The countess saw the room differently this time. It was not the children's abandonment that struck her, but the parents' efforts at preservation.

Eldrich paused before a wizard's cap and staff, and to the countess' surprise he actually picked up the staff. He studied it a moment, then thumped it once on the floor, speaking words of Darian as he did so. The head of the staff glowed with a soft green light, like sea-fire, and with this he etched the letter E in the air, where it hung for a moment before fading, as did the glow on the staff. Eldrich put it carefully back in its place and looked up at her. "It still works," he said, and then continued on his rounds.

The countess was too surprised to laugh. What was this? Charm from the mage? She did not think he even knew what it was. Irony, tending to sarcasm, seemed to be the closest he ever stood to humor.

Eldrich continued on his rounds. "Why have they preserved this room thus, do you think?" he asked.

The countess looked around her. "Museum" was a good description. But it was more than that. It was homage to a time, an age of life, as well as to children who had obviously been very precious to their parents.

"Despite the current vogue for complaint, there is a nostalgia in our culture for childhood. We forget all its trials and frustrations and remember only the days when the mundane world and the world of make-believe had very thin walls between them. That is what I think; we remember the magic, the stories, the hours of play—if we were lucky enough to spend our hours in play."

Eldrich nodded, seeming to consider this.

"Do you long for such a world?"

The countess had never thought of it in such terms. Did she? "We all long for simpler times," she said, wondering where this conversation was going, and why Eldrich had summoned her here. "There is very little magic in people's adult lives," she said. "Very little to surprise."

Again the mage nodded. He stepped behind a marionette theater, and one of the marionettes hanging there suddenly raised its drooping head. It looked around.

An arm lifted, as though relearning animation. It almost seemed to shrug its shoulders, as though working out the stiffness from so many years of inactivity. It took a few uncertain steps, then suddenly found its confidence. It did a little jig and threw up its hands, leaping for joy.

Eldrich looked up from his puppeteering, his eyes running sadly over the room and its contents. "I wonder if the children feel the same way about childhood as their parents? It is a critical lesson of life, knowing when to move on, when one's time is done."

The marionette slowed in its motion, like a music-box figure running down. Its head fell slowly to one side, limbs collapsing, and again the near-human figure hung lifeless.

With some care Eldrich hung the marionette back in its place, and without another word went out, leaving the countess alone.

She sat down on a tiny chair and felt her shoulders begin to shake. Why had she agreed to help this man? Was it really this promise of prolonged youth? She looked around the room at the preserved treasures of coddled childhood.

*It is a critical lesson of life, knowing when one's time is done.*

But youth had less to do with her decision than she realized at the time. Curiosity had taken its part, but even more than that was a sense that there would be purpose. Her life would have purpose.

For what had she been doing with her given days? What would she ever do?

She looked around the room again, seeking the feeling of childhood, the state of it that was somehow lost within her—yet it eluded her.

And here she was, in the house of a mage, with magic all around her, and she did not feel as she did as a child. Had she moved on? How could she know that it would all be so deadly, so grave? And yet she was not entirely clear what Eldrich would do. He would erase all of the mages' arts from the world, for reasons that were not perfectly clear. And she might play some part in this. She . . . And so she stayed, while others fell away. Erasmus. Kent. Marianne. Even Skye. And she stayed with this man—this near-human, feeling his contained desire for her. Wondering what purpose long-dead mages had created her for, and if Eldrich made a mistake believing he could turn her to his own uses.

Odd to go through life so convinced that one knew who one was and for what purpose one was intended, and then suddenly to discover that this was not true at all. Like an artist discovering that their art was larger than they; perhaps even overwhelming.

She stayed to find out who she was and prayed she would not be overwhelmed.

## ∽ Twenty-Eight

Anna looked back down the long valley, thinking the situation was a great deal less than perfect. It was all a matter of distances, of timing. She would see them first—assuming they came down this path, and she had left as many signs of her passing as possible to draw them on. If there was no fog, the smoke from her fire would almost certainly alert them.

When they crested the rise, she would play at being surprised—and herein lay the problem. The distance from her camp to the river had to be gauged with precision. If they caught her before they reached the gorge . . . Well, she did not like to think about what that might mean. No, they had to pursue her, be almost upon her when they broke through the last trees at the edge of the chasm . . . and then it would be too late. She knew the cliff was there, and trusted they did not.

Anna had studied that final stretch of trail with great care. There was no margin for error.

She threw another piece of wood on the fire and walked back up the rise to resume her vigil. A swallow cut an arc through the air and disappeared into the wood, reminding her of Brother Norbert and his promise—which brought her some small comfort.

*        *        *

Pryor bent low to the ground, touching the marks with a finger. He moved on, still crouched, glancing up to see where the trail led.

"They're recent," he said, standing straight for the first time since he had found his brother's pyre. "Yesterday, late, 'twould be my guess."

"But is it she?" Hayes asked, hoping, perhaps, that it was not. That he would not be forced to decide.

The guide nodded, taking up his reins and swinging quickly up onto his mount.

Erasmus looked around at the others, not all of whom were as ambivalent as he. Deacon Rose spurred his horse on and took up a position immediately behind Pryor. It was clear what these two would do; but what of the others?

Deacon Rose stood in the center of the narrow trail, holding up his hand, a finger to his lips.

"Smoke," he said, his voice low, if not an actual whisper.

Erasmus dropped down from his saddle. "Are you saying we've found her?"

The priest nodded. "Unless it is some other." Rose and Pryor had ranged ahead of the others, widening a gulf that Erasmus knew now would never be bridged. If they captured her, he would have to perform the ceremony Percy had left him.

Erasmus glanced back at Hayes and Kehler, both of whom looked a little ill.

The priest motioned them close in order that he could speak low. "The smoke appears at the head of this small hill, so it is not far. Even so, she will hear our approach if we go on horseback. Yet if we slip forward quietly on foot and she perceives us, she will mount her horse and flee, and we'll be left foolishly on foot.

"What we have decided is to go forward at the gallop, and though she will likely take to her horse, we will ride her down. There are five of us, after all."

Rose looked at Hayes and Kehler, who did not respond with even a nod. "Let Pryor and me do your work for you," Rose said to them. "We will dirty our hands, for after what was done to his brother, Pryor has no doubt of her character." He turned back to Erasmus. "I have taken the necessary precautions, for she has some skill in the arts, and perhaps more, now. But when we run her to ground, let me approach her first. Let her not practice upon you with the skill of her tongue, for she will say anything to save herself, and she will happily slit any throat that she might go free." He looked up at the two younger men. "Will you ride with us, or will you let us sully our hands to save your necks, brave lads that you are?"

"No," Kehler said, glaring at Rose. "I will not let another commit the crime that saves my life. And as nothing short of your murder will stop you, I am bound to be part of the crime."

Rose met the eyes of the two young men who sat their horses, staring down at him with obvious dislike. "It is often that men do evil, believing that they do good," the priest said, "but it is less common that men do good believing it to be evil. Even so, this is such a case, it seems, for the woman is a threat to all that you know. In years to come, you will understand that this is so."

He looked back to Erasmus who, feeling no more confident than Kehler and Hayes, nodded his head. Bryce would have his revenge at last. A revenge of fire.

They fell in behind the priest, and in a moment found Pryor, hidden in a thick stand of pines. They each took a moment to tighten saddle girths, and then, at a nod from Deacon Rose, they set off at a gallop up the narrow path between the hills.

As they crested the rise, Erasmus heard the priest shout, spurring his horse on. Determined that Pryor and Rose would not do Anna harm before she was delivered to Eldrich, Erasmus forced his tired horse forward, clods of the forest floor flying all around him.

In a moment they swept past the fire, glimpses of a rough camp, horses dancing on tethers. And then they were into a thicker wood, jumping a fallen trunk, branches snatching at their faces and tearing clothing. Hooves pummeled the fragile earth. The scene passed more quickly than perception.

A terrible scream—*Anna*. Horses in panic; Rose bellowing to stop.

Erasmus pulled his horse up sharp, and for the first time heard the sounds of water. Then he felt the dampness. He was off his horse before Hayes and Kehler appeared, racing along the path.

Even on foot he almost went off the edge. There he could see a horse slashing the surface with its hooves, in the grip of the current, dark against the poisonous green.

Rose stood a few feet away, his face ashen. He clutched one hand to his heart and with the other he steadied himself by a ridiculously inadequate branch.

Erasmus shouted back to the others as he heard their horses coming, then slowing suddenly.

"Pryor?"

"He went over, as did my own horse after him. I still don't know how Farrelle preserved me. I don't know."

Erasmus saw a flash of dark movement in the roiling waters and without hesitation dove toward the deepest green.

It seemed like an infinite time that he was in the air. Below him he saw a horse swept, thrashing, into the torrent, engulfed in white. A kingfisher plunged into the pool, the sun catching its jeweled feathers.

And then he hit the cold water, the impact driving the breath from his lungs. For a moment he hung there, suspended in thickened green light, gliding slowly down. And then he forced himself to swim. His head broke the surface, and flicking the water from his face, Erasmus bobbed up, searching around. Someone shouted from above, but his words tumbled into the torrent and were swept away.

On the cliff above, figures pointed, but it was impossible to see where. He swam farther out and then realized that the current was sweeping him toward the pool's edge. He struck out strongly at a diagonal, aiming for an eddy which curled behind an egg of rock. But the flow was stronger than he realized, and in a moment he was at the lip, then falling again, plunged down into the depths, a weight of water on top of him. A moment later he was mysteriously on the surface, gasping for air.

Erasmus realized that he would find Pryor only by a miracle. Best not to fight the current, for it no doubt swept Pryor away, and would spin him to the surface again. And Anna. Where was she? Had they accomplished Eldrich's aim, hardly intending to? Was the last follower of Teller gone from this earth?

The current carried him forward quickly now, into foaming and confused waters. He fought to keep the surface, but was dragged under, and battered against rock. Twisting and tumbling, he struggled for air. Just a mouthful here, and then another. Just enough to live. Again he struck stone, and felt the cold river close over him, a muted roaring driving out all else. And then silence.

Hayes ran along the cliff top, trying to keep Erasmus in view, but in a hundred feet the cliff had been cut back in a deep V and by the time he had found his way past this obstacle, Erasmus was gone. There was no sign of horse or man. Pryor, gone. Anna not to be seen. And Erasmus last seen struggling to keep his head up in the world of light and air.

"Can you see them?" Kehler called, coming along behind.

"No one," Hayes hollered above the river sound.

A moment later Kehler appeared at his side, panting, and the two stood, looking down into the chasm, searching for people they knew were gone. Down the river. Alive still, perhaps, but swept away and quickly tiring.

"If Erasmus can find a rock to climb onto . . ." Kehler said at last.

"Yes," Hayes whispered, "we can hope. Could Pryor swim, do you think?"

Kehler considered for a moment, as though trying to remember if this had been mentioned. "I doubt it. So few can: only Erasmus out of all the souls I know."

Hayes nodded. "But what of Anna? She survived the cave. Perhaps she can stay afloat."

"Perhaps, but then, we survived the cave, and neither of us can swim a stroke. Or at least I can't claim to. No, it is likely that we have seen the end of the Tellerites. Deacon Rose and Eldrich will be pleased. I am sorry for poor Pryor. Both brothers gone over this woman."

"Yes, and we're alive." Hayes sat down suddenly on the bank. "Alive and done with the mage, or so I hope. All I want is life to return to normal. I would welcome a creditor or two, now. They no longer seem much of a threat."

Rose came up then, his customary vigor having returned, though he was surprisingly subdued. "Is there no sign of Mr. Flattery?"

Neither answered nor looked at the man, then Hayes relented and shook his head.

Clarendon hailed them. The small man was limping along the cliff top, and as they came up they could see that he was bleeding from a cut on his skull, and looked shaken.

"Randall, what's happened?"

"I was thrown from my horse, but never mind. Where is Mr. Flattery? Where is Pryor?"

"Pryor and his horse followed Anna into the gorge. Erasmus dove in thinking to save the boy. And all of them have been swept away out of sight. Only Erasmus was still on the surface when last we saw."

Clarendon slumped down onto the ground, looking dazed.

"Randall, you're injured."

The small man did not respond. "It is what Eldrich does. Steals away people's lives. I curse him. I curse the day he was born into this world, for surely it must have been foreseen that he would feed upon men like a wolf among lambs."

A slow, rhythmic slap of water. The sea speaking along the shore. Erasmus opened his eyes to see a rippling pattern of light sprayed over a dark surface. He felt a chill in his back.

"Erasmus?"

A face came into view, hovering over him, long tendrils of hair tumbling down to touch his cheek.

"Erasmus?"

"Anna . . . I'm cold."

She nodded. "Can you try to sit?"

He was not sure. Lying still felt so good—but for the chill.

"You're lying in an inch of river water. Come sit up. I will help."

She tugged at his arms, and with surprisingly little effort he came upright.

"It is warming a little as the sun finds its way into the gorge." She stared at him a moment, her look very pensive. "I fished you out," she said. "Plucked you from the waters though it will mean the end of my scheme. Two horses passed but no riders, until you came."

"Pryor," Erasmus said. "He plunged in behind you. Rose lost his horse but managed to save himself."

"And you dove in nobly after this man Pryor," she said. "It is so like you, Erasmus."

"Pryor's brother was your guide," Erasmus said. His wits were coming back a little.

Anna looked intently into his eyes then nodded, looking quickly away. "Yes," she whispered. "I thought I could be as terrible and pitiless as Eldrich. But I have a conscience, after all." She looked down, her hands still supporting him unnecessarily. "I hoped that no one would be hurt. That only I would go into the gorge, and all others would be spared."

"And we would think you dead?"

She nodded. "Yes, and perhaps you would not have been wrong. It is only a miracle that I survived, let alone found you."

"A desperate measure, Anna."

"Yes. But what choice had I? Eldrich would pursue me to my death, or leave others to do so. It was one thing to hide from him when he did not know where to begin searching. But to elude him now . . . now that he knows who I am—It is near to impossible. He is stronger than we realized. Stronger and more cunning."

Erasmus looked around. They were on a flat ledge of rock beneath an overhang of stone, hidden to anyone on the cliff top. "How long have we been down here?"

"A few hours now. Three, perhaps four. I have not heard your friends for some time."

The slapping of water against stone, here where the river ran quiet.

Erasmus stretched, assuring himself that he was whole, and though he was much battered, no serious damage seemed to have been accomplished. "I will tell you true, Anna, though I owe you my life, I cannot lie to Eldrich. He will know."

She nodded, pulling her knees up into the circle of her arms, and laying the side of her head down upon her arm. Erasmus thought she did not look so drained now—as though life were being restored to her.

*The king's blood,* he realized.

She raised her head again, looking at him intently. "You can escape Eldrich," she said. "Escape him finally. They will soon give us up for dead, if they haven't already. I can hide us. Hide us from the arts of Eldrich." She reached out and grasped Erasmus' arm. "Even now he does not know if I live or die. But if he believes me dead—us dead—then he will pass through and leave no heir to his knowledge. We will be free of him. You will be free of him."

"I can never be free," Erasmus said.

"But you can. The others will report you dead, and I will hide you from his arts. We will slip out of Farrland and live quietly until he has passed through. It can be done, Erasmus."

Erasmus looked at her, at the hope in her eyes. "And what will we do then? It is the belief of the mages that their arts must pass away. That some cataclysm will result if this is not done."

"Even the mages did not agree on this, Erasmus, but the dissenters were overruled by the others, who were stronger if not more numerous." The light went out of her eyes suddenly, and she looked very sad. "But I will tell you true, Erasmus, I am no longer so certain that the arts should be kept alive. The cost has been so great. I only know that I am not willing to die so that Eldrich can assure this. Let us survive Eldrich, and then we will see. I have some skill at augury. If the mages' vision was true, then I, too, will find it in time."

"That is not the sworn purpose of your society," Erasmus said.

She rested her cheek back upon her arm. "There is no society. Only me." She laughed bitterly. "Is it not ironic that the moment Teller's dream is finally within reach—for I have Landor's seed and ample talent as well—his only remaining follower is no longer sure of his dream." She laughed again. "Certainly he did not foresee that. Nor did Eldrich. I have but one ambition now. Escape Eldrich and die of old age—and not a moment before." Anna fixed her sad gaze on Erasmus.

"The arts are passing, Erasmus, whether Eldrich succeeds or not. No, that is inaccurate. It is the power that is waning. Do you remember the seven touching worlds depicted in the cave? The ancients believed that the power, the power the arts draw upon, moved through the worlds like a tide, ebbing and flowing over the ages. The power is ebbing now. That is the truth of it. That is why the mages seemed less skilled from one generation to the next, whereas in truth they were likely more skilled, but the power they drew upon grew weaker."

"If this is so, then why would Eldrich care about erasing the knowledge of the mages? Why would it matter?"

She shrugged. "Their vision—of the cataclysm. Perhaps it is closer than we realize. Perhaps it is predicted before the tides have ebbed altogether. Farrelle predicted an apocalypse as well, and Pelier painted at least one canvas that is said to depict this final battle. Who knows, other than Eldrich—and the mage might not even know, for he is following a course set by others."

Erasmus stared up at the patterns of reflected light on the ceiling of stone. A breeze flooded down the gorge, causing him to shiver. "We will be cold here tonight," he said, not sure that he'd really made a decision. He needed more time to think.

*To be free of Eldrich!*

"We will have to stay close," Anna said, "but you are right. We daren't go out by darkness. Nor can we risk the others seeing us. How will they proceed, do you think?"

Erasmus considered a moment. Rose would want to be thorough—as certain that Anna was dead as he could be.

"They will look for us, either alive or dead. They will search along the cliff top—for not less than a day, I think, even though a few hours will really tell the tale. Certainly it will not occur to them that we are hiding here. Did you know of this place?"

"No. It was luck only, if one believes in luck. I had counted on being swept down the river. I have a map that shows the end of the gorge not far off. I hoped to crawl out there, if still alive, and hide myself until you were satisfied that I had not survived." She reached down and made a pattern on the surface of the water with one finger. "There is a ritual that we must perform this night. A rite that will hide us from Eldrich's prying eyes, for he seeks us with augury and much else besides."

"And where will we go?"

"Have you yet a house on Farrow?"

"Yes, but the island is so small. We would not be there two days before everyone would know. No, it will not answer. Into Entonne and down into Doom. We might find a boat and live among the string of islands beyond where only the fishermen and sparmen go."

Anna nodded. A black bird fluttered down from above, landing in the inch of water, into which it dipped a blood-red bill.

"Chuff!" Anna said, brightening a little.

Erasmus looked at the bird a moment before realizing. He turned to stare at Anna. She almost looked guilty in the face of this.

"When did this happen?" he said.

Anna nodded. "He awaited me outside the cave and has followed me since."

"Then you have taken the seed?"

She nodded. "I would not have survived the cave without it. After Banks was drowned." She looked up at him oddly.

Erasmus felt his eyes close as a memory returned. "Rose got free and broke down the dam. Was Banks caught in that terrible shaft?"

"In the small tunnel at the bottom. Such a flood of water came down. Banks all but filled the passage, blocking the flow. I could not get him out until after the water had drained away. He was so close. Only a few feet more and he would have . . . lived."

Erasmus touched her arm. "Rose caught us by surprise. We would never have let him destroy the dam. No one but the priest wished you ill."

She did not shake his arm off, but looked at him somewhat coldly. "But you have hunted me from Castlebough."

Erasmus removed his hand, letting it drop into the cold water. "Yes. Though with little will. Eldrich sent a messenger. . . . We sought you under threat and with the assurance that you would cause immeasurable evil even if that was not your intent."

"Ah," she said, staring off into the gorge, where the last light of evening lit green ferns growing from the blank wall. They moved moodily in the breeze.

"Is it true, I wonder?" Anna asked. "Or is it merely another lie from the mage—who has no particular allegiance to the truth."

Erasmus could not answer. Was she really suffering such doubt, or was Rose right when he warned them not to listen to her—that she would say anything? But she had saved his life. Pulled him from the river and certain death.

"Why did you save me?" Erasmus asked in a whisper.

Anna did not answer for a moment.

"Because too many have died. I cannot live at such cost. Better to die than to become like Eldrich. Better to die."

## ᕫ Twenty-Nine

Eldrich paced before the many-paned glass doors, dark against the morning brightness. After several slow passes, he turned to look at his servants, Walky and Bryce, who waited with studied patience.

"I am disappointed in you, Bryce."

His servant swallowed and nodded.

Eldrich glared at Bryce. "What would lead you to do such a thing?"

"She claimed Erasmus told her many things. Showed her writing in Darian."

"Erasmus would do no such thing! Really, Bryce, Erasmus is a man of some character and intelligence, not the youth you remember. You cannot think the worst of a child because he acts as a child any more than you can judge a horse for having no sense." The mage looked at Walky. "What does she want, do you think?"

Walky tilted his head to one side, considering not so much the question as the woman he had met. "I think it is safe to say that she wants only to be reassured the countess is unharmed and here of her own choosing. I do not think she is so foolish as Kent. Miss Edden has not come here with thoughts of rescue."

"Is she attractive, this writer?" Eldrich asked suddenly.

"Well, she turns herself out very plain, sir," Walky answered, showing no surprise at the question, "but she has a great deal of charm, a dry wit, and a lucid intelligence. Attractive? In the larger sense, sir, I would say, yes."

Eldrich actually smiled. "The countess will become jealous, Walky. Careful how you go." He paced again. "Allow her to see the countess. I will speak with her this evening after I have seen Skye." He paused to look at Bryce again—as though reappraising the man in light of his recent actions. "If Erasmus and the others went into the hills after this woman, as you say, then they should emerge soon. I want you there when they appear. Bring them to me, especially this man Clarendon." He continued to look at Bryce for a few seconds and then turned away. "I trust there will be no more surprises this day."

The mage did not say more, but went back to his pacing, servants dismissed from his mind, his thoughts entirely taken up with other matters; dilemmas he pondered in his silence and essential solitude.

The countess released Marianne from their third embrace, held her back at arm's length, and shook her head. "I still can't believe it. How in this round world . . . ?"

"Well, you *will* hardly believe it," Marianne said, disentangling herself from the countess, a bit embarrassed by such a display of emotion, "but I found Skye at the side of the road. His carriage had broken down, and he was traveling in the company of this man Bryce. You remember, he was said to be the servant of whomever was staying in Baumgere's house. Well, I knew from Kent that this is where Eldrich was secluded, so clearly Bryce was a servant of the mage."

"But you did not believe Kent!"

"I did once you had been whisked away." Then her eyes narrowed, almost closing at the memory. "Yes, I know this is all my fault. If only I had listened to Kent, you would have slipped away into Entonne and all this would have been avoided."

"Yes," the countess said, "but we doubted him, and I did not want to believe that I had visited the mage and kept no memory of it."

"Then Kent was right; you are here against your will?"

The countess shook her head. "No, I am here of my own folly. Caught by curiosity and—Well, suffice it to say that I entered into a bargain with Lord Eldrich—a devil's bargain, certainly. But one does not break one's word to a mage." She looked up at Marianne and tried to smile.

"Then you would leave if you could."

The countess shook her head. "No. I . . . I would not leave. It is complicated, Marianne, and much of it the mage would not want me to repeat. Trust that I am here of my own choosing, and that I am not the victim of any enchantment. It is the truth, if overly simplified."

"But, Elaural . . ." Marianne looked suddenly deeply hurt and unhappy. "What will become of you? Will you ever return to us? To your friends?"

"I have only a very few friends, and I hope I will return to you in time. I . . . I cannot say. The mage is secretive, and to be honest, I think even Eldrich is not sure of events." She slumped down suddenly on the window seat, and Marianne took the place opposite her.

"I am confused by much that goes on here, Marianne. Augury is not at all what I thought." She opened her hands and let them drop into her lap. "Imagine that you were navigating a ship through fog in changing winds and currents. Every now and then the fog opened up enough that you might see you steered toward rocks, so you change course, but the fog settles in again, and because of the changing winds and current, you can't be sure of your course. All the same, you do what you think you must to avoid the rocks.

"Outside forces, currents and winds, are operating ceaselessly. The fog might open again and show the rocks all but beneath your keel, or you might have passed them safely by, only to see some new danger. I know this hardly makes sense, but this is how augury appears to me. Nothing is fixed. A long time ago the mages had a vision of some terrible cataclysm. Clearly, this is the reason they have disappeared and taken their arts with them. The cataclysm would result from their arts. Do you see? So they have allowed themselves to become extinct, as it were, to avoid this event. But nothing is carved in stone. Events might arrange themselves so that the arts survive, despite all that they do, and the cataclysm takes place all the same. Do you see? It is not that things are fated, prescribed. Our actions have effects, though we might never understand what they will be.

"I suppose it is rather like life. We take actions that we think will be to our benefit and sometimes, despite all, they lead to tragedy. And Eldrich is caught up in this . . . trying to see deeper into the future than others. Watching the changes, trying to understand the forces at play. And I am part of it, somehow. Almost a hedge against possible events. It is not yet clear if I will have a part, or what it will be.

"It is difficult to describe, for Eldrich is convinced that others arranged events so that I would be here to tempt him in some way. Oh, I don't really understand. It is all so strange and sounds perfectly preposterous when spoken aloud like this." The countess looked up at her friend, seeing the worry written on her face.

"But, Marianne . . . what will Eldrich do with you? Why has he allowed you to see me at all?"

"I don't know. I convinced Bryce that Erasmus had told us all manner of secrets about his time in the house of Eldrich. So he brought me here, as I hoped. I wanted to see you, to reassure myself that you were unharmed."

The countess tried not to let her concern show. "You should never have done this. The mage is not patient." She looked out the window at the line of trees that marked the boundary of her world.

"It is so very odd. I came with Eldrich thinking I would be isolated from my friends, and you have all come to me. Kent was here—and oddly they were almost expecting him. Oh, not him precisely but a painter.

"And now you. And Skye is here, too, you say? Skye . . . I had thought I'd never see the man again. I had almost put him from my mind." She shook her head in wonder. "I've come to believe that I do not understand life at all, Marianne. Eldrich spends all of his time trying to part the veils of time, but it does him little good, for matters seem to change continuously. He does not seem to believe in coincidence. In his world nothing happens by chance—as though there is a pattern, however fluid. When Kent arrived, noble foolish Kent, Walky named it a good sign, saying they had been 'awaiting the painter.'" She looked up at Marianne, a smile spreading across her face. "And then Eldrich had him paint two portraits, one of him and one of me, and sent him off. And just when I had begun to despair that I would be left alone in this strange house, you arrive and bring Lord Skye in tow. I cannot begin to imagine what will occur next. I cannot."

Marianne laughed, raising her eyebrows. "It's only recently that you've come to believe that you don't understand life? I've never understood. People praise me for my 'vision,' but I will tell you, I have none. Not as they mean it, at least. I write about people caught up in matters that mystify them, making intelligent decisions that go wrong, or drawing foolish conclusions that come out right.

"Why, I know some utterly ridiculous people—not a sensible thought in their heads—who cannot seem to do anything that does not turn out brilliantly. If they were to buy shares in a company that was bankrupt, they would discover the next day that their offices sat upon a field of gold. And they think themselves geniuses! Yet they are nothing more than lucky, for lack of a better word—repeatedly lucky! And I'm sure we both know people who are the opposite. And that is to say nothing of who is deserving and what happens to them. How can anyone make sense of it?" A silence fell between them as though neither of them could keep up this false exuberance.

Marianne fixed a very serious look upon the countess. "What are you to Eldrich, Elaural? And what is he to you? Is there . . . *sympathy* between you?"

"Sympathy . . . ?" The countess was surprised at how guarded her tone had become. "No, I would not say that. There is . . . magnetism would perhaps describe it. And there is something more. I was meant for him, Marianne. To tempt him in some way. To lead him into some fatal error that would allow the arts to be renewed. That is what I have come to believe from the few hints the mage has given and the odd thing I have managed to pry from Walky." The countess looked up at her friend, wondering if she looked as forlorn as she felt at the moment. "Do you see? All along I have had some other purpose. This mad attraction that men feel toward me . . . it is not real, not me at all, but a result of the arts. And Eldrich was never meant to realize it. But they underestimated his skill, it seems, for he did realize. So I am here, partly to find out what my place is in this larger story. Can you understand, Marianne? I am like a character in one of your novels who realizes she is in a book but continues on just to see how it all comes out, what her part is."

"That made no sense at all," Marianne said, "and it frightens me a little that I understood what you meant. But if you are intended to tempt Eldrich into some terrible mistake, why does he keep you here? Why does he not send you away, or worse? Would that not be the safest thing? To not let you endanger his purpose?"

The countess shook her head. "I am not sure, exactly. Perhaps those who bespelled me knew he would not send me away—that he could not, even if he divined my purpose. It is impossible to say, Marianne. He is complicated and secretive. You have never met a man so secretive. And his pride is great. I sometimes think that he hopes to turn me to his own purpose, as though to prove his skill greater than those who sent me—as if he could prove something to the dead."

"Now that sounds more like a man. The 'great men' I have met, at least. Their pride is beyond all." Marianne raised her eyebrows. "Now, I should not pry—"

"You should not," the countess agreed quickly and firmly.

Marianne nodded resignedly.

A long silence overcame them, extending to several minutes. "Have I angered the mage, do you think?" Marianne finally asked, her voice softly harsh. "Will he exact some . . . retribution for what I've done?"

"I don't know, Marianne," the countess said, relieved that the subject had changed. "Kent was sent off unharmed, I'm sure. I think the mage will do the same with you—he does not seem to be quite so fearsome as the legends indicate. But you must realize one thing—you will not go from this place with the memory of your visit intact. Eldrich does not allow that."

Marianne's gaze flicked up, her mouth opening a little in surprise. "What are you saying? That he will do to me what was done to you? I will awake as though from a daze, and not even know if you are well or no?" She rose from the window seat, half-turning away. "Elaural . . . I transmute my memories into gold. Do you understand? They are more precious to me than fame or fortune or reputation. They are the raw materials from which I build. He cannot touch them. . . . He cannot!" She turned back to the countess, her face ashen. "You must speak with him. He must not tamper with my mind as though it were some hack's manuscript—cutting out what does not please him. You must tell him, Elaural. You must. . . ."

Skye did not remember. Bryce had said that he'd met Eldrich before, but he had not even the slightest recollection, not the vaguest image of what the mage might look like. More memories that had been stolen from him, but in this case the cause was known—as was the cure. Eldrich could restore what he had taken, of that Skye was certain. The mage might even be able to do more.

Skye had been abandoned by Bryce and put into the care of a round little man of distracted disposition who now took him to see the mage. It was odd that a man of Eldrich's forbidding reputation should have as a servant an innocuous little man easily mistaken for a retired schoolmaster. This had set Skye's overwound nerves at ease, a little.

Even so, he was not relaxed. Not so much because he was intimidated, though he would admit that he was, but because this was almost certainly his only chance. If he could not find a way to have Eldrich restore his memories now, then he would almost certainly live without them the rest of his days. It was an opportunity not to be thrown away.

And yet he knew almost nothing of the mage. Like all of his kind, he was said to be arrogant and insensible to the concerns of others. It went without saying, then, that he had no patience for men, whom he considered to be vastly his inferiors. How did one appeal to such a man?

The irony of the situation was that Skye, in his dealings with others, was usually in the position of Eldrich. Men, even accomplished men, were intimidated by him, by his vast reputation, and he had little patience for them, considering them a bother. They interrupted his important work with foolish questions and harebrained schemes. And the truth was, he was often less than polite to them.

And now how did one proceed? How did men catch the attention of the notoriously impatient Skye? Most often, they didn't, and the truth of it was that it depended on his mood and what they had interrupted. When he did take time to listen, it was usually to men who spoke politely, but directly, and who did not presume too much. Men who obviously had common sense, and did not ask much of him. After all, Skye had been the patron of more than one promising young empiricist, the champion of a few causes. He was not as selfish and impossible as he was made out to be. Was he?

The man named Walky stopped before a door, tapped softly and then opened it a crack. "Lord Skye," he said into the room beyond, and pushed the door open, nodding Skye through.

A singular tingling seemed to run through Skye's body just below the skin. It was not a sensation he'd had before, and it left him feeling cut off from himself, like his personality had been set adrift from his body. Somehow he managed to move forward.

Was this some spell? Some enchantment that emanated from the mage? Skye felt he might lose his balance at any time.

A dark-haired man sat in a chair before the window reading what appeared to be a very ancient book. On the table, a single candle flickered, emitting a furtive light that left most of the room, which Skye sensed was large, in shadow.

Six paces distant Skye waited, and after the threshold between impolite and outrageously rude had been breached he considered clearing his throat—but didn't. Somehow he thought this would not have the desired effect.

The thought of turning around and leaving crossed his mind, but stories of mages rooting people to the spot were numerous, and though Skye was a little doubtful of these, still—

Eldrich finally looked up, the book remaining open, held by one elegantly formed hand. Eldrich regarded him for a moment, with an unsettling disinterest, and then nodded. "When you met that woman at the house of Mary Finesworth—you remember, there were some few agents of the Admiralty there in various states of stupor."

Skye nodded.

"There might have been things you observed but later did not recall. I want you to turn your mind back to that night again. Close your eyes. Imagine every tiny thing you did or thought. Tell me: You arrived by carriage. . . ."

"Yes." Skye closed his eyes as he had been bidden, forming a picture of that night. Had it rained?

"A woman answered the door?" Eldrich prompted.

"The faded woman . . ." Skye felt himself falling into a dreamlike trance. He almost believed he was there. He could smell the evening, feel the night on his skin. It had rained, though barely. The door opened, and a woman appeared.

A hand on his arm guided him through the dusk—no, he was inside in poor light.

"You're perfectly hale, Lord Skye. Just through the door now." It was the small man, returned, and he was leading Skye out of the room.

*Eldrich.*

Skye tried to shake his arm loose but found himself too weak. "No. . . . I—I must speak with Lord Eldrich." Unable to free himself, he planted his feet and twisted his neck to look back. A tall man stood before the window, a single candle, twinned in the dark glass, touched him there and here—as though he were composed, for the most part, of shadow.

"Let him speak, Walky," came the oddly musical voice. Why did this sound chill him?

"Sir," Skye began, trying to remember what it was that was so important. "Sir . . . I suffered the loss of my memories as a child. I don't know if I have been of any service to you, or if I can be, but I would gladly exchange anything I might have, any service, to have these memories returned to me."

Eldrich did not turn around but spoke to the glass, his words seeming to take on the night chill as they reflected back. "Exchange? But people serve me, willingly or no. What have you to exchange that I cannot have at no cost? No, Lord Skye, it would be a bad bargain—for both of us, I fear. Would you be so intent on this if I told you that you'd be a happier man not knowing?"

Skye was taken aback by this. He had been only a boy; what could a boy have done that he would be happier not knowing? Or was it what was done to him? "I would have my memories, all the same."

"Would you, indeed? I will see the woman now, Mr. Walky."

The small man tugged at his arm. "Say nothing more, sir," he whispered. "It will not profit you."

And Skye let himself be led out into the hallway, his past remaining in the darkened room with the man made of shadow.

Marianne settled herself in the chair by the single candle, drawn to the light in this strange place.

*He will not harm you,* she assured herself. *Whatever else he does, he will not harm you. Even Eldrich would not be so arrogant.* She counted the King among her ardent readers, for Farrelle's sake. The King! Who could say—it was possible that even the mage might read her books!

After all, there was a book sitting on the table, the light of the candle falling upon its leather binding. But how old and worn it was, the leather as thin as decaying leaves in some places, any title erased long ago. It was her habit to note the titles of the books people read, only partly to see if it might be one of her own, so it was natural for her to wonder what book this might be. She almost reached out to open it, but then the realization struck. This was no common book.

This was a book of the arcane, forbidden to any but a mage.

"Flames," she heard herself say. Suddenly this was an object of fascination. She could not tear her eyes from it, as though staring would reveal something. *A forbidden book:* to a woman who loved books and sought knowledge, there hardly could be anything more alluring.

"Why don't you open it?"

She looked up to find a tall, stooped man standing in the garden doorway.

Marianne found that she could not open her mouth, not a word would come.

"You are fascinated, clearly. Open it."

She only stared, caught by his musical voice, the way the shadows played about him. He was more forbidding than Elaural had described. Stranger.

She reached out her hand, feeling somehow that she must not back down from this challenge. Just as her fingers were about to touch it, she stopped. "Will I be harmed?"

A smile lit his face for an instant; mocking, as she'd been warned. "Why? Do you feel knowledge is dangerous?"

"Unquestionably, when possessed by the wrong people, but I was thinking of more arcane things. A protective charm or some such."

He shook his dark hair. "No, in that way it is completely harmless."

Gingerly, she touched it, curling two fingers under the cover, but she hesitated to open it. Eldrich watched her intently, she could feel it. She took her hand away, and looked up at him, feeling a thin smile tighten her face, then dissolve.

The two gazed at each other a moment, and then Eldrich shifted on the threshold. "Wisdom as well as talent," he said, no mockery detectable in his tone. "That is not so common." He came into the room, sliding a second chair toward her.

"Eldrich," he said, bobbing his head in her direction.

"Marianne Edden."

"Let us put aside this ruse that brought you here. Erasmus told you nothing about his years in my house."

She nodded.

The mage looked a little saddened for a moment. "Bryce is always ready to believe the worst of Erasmus." He looked away from her, appearing to stare at the candle's reflection in the glass. "I trust you have been reassured that I did not abduct Lady Chilton or that I am keeping her here against her wishes?"

Marianne nodded, feeling the breath in her lungs disappear for a second. Was he angry that she thought this of him?

Eldrich sat back in his chair, almost sprawling, and interwove his long fingers before him. "How old are you?" he said, gazing at her in a manner that she thought less than polite—as though he were unaware of the etiquette of educated society.

"Twenty and nine," she said.

He pressed his lips out, as though in thought. "What would you say if I could tell you the year of your death?"

"I thought augury was less than exact," she said, hearing the wariness in her voice. Was this some jest at her expense? She did not like the sound of a mage speaking to her of death—her death!

"Oh, this is not augury. Not in the usual sense, at least."

Marianne could not remember feeling fear in a good many years—not real fear. Anxiety that she would be embarrassed or that she would not be a success, yes, but not fear for her life. "I think that I would rather not know. After all, what good would knowing do?"

"Very little, in the larger sense. You would not be able to change it. Still . . . it might allow you to complete the things that are important to you. Do the things you have always dreamed of doing. That journey to Farrow, or that book you have long planned."

"There is that, I suppose," she said. "Is this your purpose? To tempt me with some forbidden knowledge?"

Eldrich laughed. "It is a terrible vice, but you see, I am interested in knowing how long you will live for my own reasons, and I thought as I will have this information it might be of interest to you. It is freely offered."

"In all the stories I have read, I cannot once remember a mage offering something freely." As Marianne spoke, she feared that she had overstepped her bounds.

"I see that you are a friend of Lady Chilton's," he said, with a touch of humor in the irony. "But those are merely stories, almost none of them real. Fiction. And not the type that is more true than truth." He rose from his chair, suddenly, and went and stood by the door. Far off, she heard a high wail, and then realized that it must be the wolf. The famous familiar of Eldrich.

"Let me tell you a story, if I may presume to tell a tale to the teller of tales." He was about to speak when Marianne interrupted.

"Why do you bother, when I am assured I'll remember nothing that happens while I am here?"

Eldrich looked down at her, his face suddenly tight. "Do you fear you will forget your precious feelings for the countess, like Kent?"

"You misunderstand me," Marianne said, struggling to keep her tone mild. "My memories are the stone from which I build. Without them I am no different from any other unmarried woman my age. It does not matter if you have no respect for me, but if you respect my art at all, you will reconsider."

"Ah, this is about art." The mocking smile did appear, then quickly disappear. "I must tell you, Miss Edden, yours is a comparatively minor art, however elevated by your class, compared with the ancient art I practice. Excuse me if I appear vain in this, but you evoke things only in the minds of your readers. I evoke them here, in the world in which we presently dwell." He turned and gestured into the room. "There are spirits in this house. Did you know? Two children who died of influenza while still very young. The countess can almost feel them. Can you?" He began to move his hands in the air, tracing lines of glowing silver, a tracery of symbols and marks. Chanting in a language she did not know, he gestured to the candle near her elbow and its flame split into seven tongues and wavered up, so that she recoiled in fear.

A moment more, and there, in the center of the room, two children appeared, a boy and girl, staring at Eldrich, their eyes unnaturally wide and dark.

They whispered to each other, their gaze hardly leaving the mage. Once, the girl looked at Marianne, their eyes meeting, but Marianne was of little interest.

"Do you see?" Eldrich said softly. "The ghosts of the past. Can you feel the sadness? The loss? Aged three and seven, and wandering here still. Have you ever evoked a character so thoroughly? I think not." At a gesture the children disappeared, and Marianne felt an odd warmth, though in her heart she was cold.

"Now let me begin again," Eldrich said, the musical voice soft and sad, as though he could speak in a minor key—*pianissimo.* "I was taken to the house of the mage, Lucklow, when I was but seven years. Seven years. I hardly recall the time before . . . my true childhood. It is lost. Lost in a dream that slips away as you wake.

"And I awoke to find myself in the house of a mage, a ruin of a castle which was haunted by more than memories. I was a child alone in that terrible place. I would stare for hours out over the surrounding forest, dreaming of the world beyond, the world from which my parents had sacrificed me." He paused and drew a breath. "I feared Lucklow utterly. He was short-tempered and prone to cruelty. His familiar was an adder. . . ."

## ᕦ Thirty

Deacon Rose took the warm ashes from the edge of the glowing coals and filled the cupped hands of each of the mourners—Kehler and Hayes and Clarendon. Hayes found the warmth of the ashes disturbing.

Rose strode the few paces to the water, chanting words of Old Farr in his strong voice. He released a ribbon of ashes, which streamed out on the wind, and marked the sign of Farrelle on the flowing waters.

Each of them in turn did the same, and then together they released the remaining ashes into the river, into this artery of the world.

They had searched the whole day and all the afternoon before, becoming more desperate and more despondent as the hours passed. Much of the time Clarendon and his great dog had ranged ahead, wading in the margins of the current, clambering over rocks as though his years meant nothing. Often they saw him standing on some higher rock, surveying the opposite shore. Hayes had almost felt the concentration the man called forth, felt him willing

Erasmus to appear on the distant bank—appear alive with their young guide in tow.

Hayes watched Rose as he knelt by the river and prayed, the Old Farr sounding regal and solemn in this place. Any triumph the priest felt at Anna's destruction was tempered by the loss of Erasmus and Pryor.

When the prayer came to an end, Clarendon spread a handful of wild roses on the water, their scent swirling in the breeze that coiled out of the gorge.

Hayes watched the roses go bobbing over the waters, lost to them in a few seconds, and then he turned away, feeling the salt of tears. He went quickly up the bank, back into the trees to be alone with his grief.

Would all this have happened if he had not involved Erasmus in the first place?

Clarendon kept assuring him that coincidence played only the smallest part in any of these events, but even so—If they had not met at the brothel, would any of this have occurred?

He found an open place three dozen feet above the river and sat himself down there, staring out over the sunlit waters. The constant flow comforted him, somehow—the steady, uncomplaining procession toward the sea. They would all go that way, or back into the earth to become part of some great tree or the ferns that grew in the underwood. So Erasmus had gone, escaping Eldrich at last, escaping the hidden scars that he bore within.

Dusk appeared out of the trees, greeting him perfunctorily, excited to be here in the wilds with his master. A moment later Clarendon came out of the wood, his small boots making barely a sound.

"Ah, here you are, Mr. Hayes. Do I interrupt you?"

Hayes shook his head. "No. No, I am ready for some company. I am just sitting here watching the river flow, and it has comforted me."

Clarendon lowered himself to the grass, a little stiffly Hayes thought. "Yes, I always find water comforting as well. I can see the lake from my home in Castlebough. And when I travel in the winter, I usually stay by the sea or some other body of water. It is not really intentional, but it just seems to come out that way. Do you know the old song? Anonymous, I think.

*"We are borne within the clouds*
*Sailing landward on the winds*
*Falling sweetly to the grasses*
*Sipped by mothers, born again."*

The small man smiled wanly. "So we all shall go. 'Down to the ship-proud sea.' Whole continents will go that way, if these natural philosophers are to be believed. Mr. Flattery has gone earlier than he should. Earlier than his friends would have had it, that is certain. But we will all follow. Likely, I will not be far behind, and I do not say that in self-pity, but it is merely the truth, for people born with my particular condition seldom are blessed with a natural span of years." He gazed out over the flowing river, suddenly a little sadder.

Hayes did not speak or try to offer comfort, and the two of them remained silent for some time, perhaps still hoping for a miracle. Hoping Erasmus would appear, swimming among the folds and creases of the river.

"One would think that of the lot of us, Erasmus would be the least likely to drown," Hayes said. "Yet, in the end, it was his ability to swim that brought about his ruin. None of us would have dreamed of leaping into the gorge. And so his skill betrayed him."

Clarendon nodded. "I think it is often the way. Our abilities are what lead us into danger—not our shortcomings, which we learn not to test."

Hayes nodded. "What will happen now?" he asked. "Rose said something about a ritual that Erasmus was to perform if we found Anna. . . ."

"You did not speak to Mr. Flattery about this?"

Hayes shook his head.

"Well, it was not so much to alert the mage as it was a revenge upon Mr. Flattery. You see, he was to perform the ritual that had caused Percy's terrible immolation."

Hayes turned to look at Clarendon. "Do you think Eldrich was aware of this?"

The small man shrugged. "I don't know. Who can say with a mage. But certainly none of us are prepared to do it. Only the priest likely has the knowledge or talent, and certainly he is not going to risk his precious hide now that he has accomplished his purpose. No, I think we will have to find some way to contact Eldrich. Deacon Rose will likely take on this responsibility, and despite what I feel about the man, I will accompany him. I have a bargain to offer Lord Eldrich." His vivid blue eyes, which had seemed near to tears all along, glistened.

Hayes touched Clarendon's shoulder. "Randall, you will gain nothing from meeting Eldrich. Did the mage not say that Lizzy had gone where none could follow? Certainly everything we have learned would indicate this to be true."

Randall seemed almost to square his shoulders. "Eldrich knew what would happen to Lizzy. He came only to witness it—to be proven right. And there was Baumgere, who spent half a lifetime searching for a gateway to the world of the Strangers, to Faery, where Tomas had gone. A gate which I think we found, though we could not open it. And beyond must lie the world of the mages—the world Anna called Darr—and if that is where Lizzy has gone . . ." He fell silent, embarrassed, as though he had not meant to speak so openly.

"I will tell you, Randall," Hayes said softly. "I don't think Eldrich will care in the slightest that you seek a lost love. Such things mean nothing to mages."

The little man nodded, looking down and running his hand over the earth.

"Perhaps," he said softly, and then picked up a small stone from the ground and hefted it, but did not seem to have the energy to toss it into the river, as Hayes expected him to do.

How many years had it been? Hayes wondered. Forty-some? Fifty? Eldrich had poisoned all of their lives—a poison that never seemed to leave the system. Would he be so in fifty years? Unable to forget what had happened? Unable to go forward in life for want of gazing always back?

"I will not feel comfortable, seeing you ride off with Rose to look for Eldrich."

Clarendon shrugged. "I am aware of the depths of his deception, to what lengths he would go to preserve his church. I do not think he can surprise me now, unless he were to display compassion or behavior one might conceive of as noble. Do not be concerned."

A dark bird soared past on the breeze billowing out of the gorge; for a moment it hung in the air before them, its blood-red bill gleaming in the sun, and then it angled away, like a ship sailing across the wind.

"Do you know," Clarendon began, "I had great respect for Mr. Flattery, even before we met—his accomplishments demand it—but this became even greater as I grew to know him. And he treated me . . . I can hardly describe it. As though my abilities and shortcomings were no different than any others. Do you understand? My small stature was no greater handicap or advantage than extreme height would have been. There were things I could do that others could not—and things I could not do. Just as a large man would never have been able to negotiate the small passages we traveled—yet he might be stronger or have a greater reach. But to Mr. Flattery, I would have been that man's equal. And as to my mental faculties . . . I think he understood the advantages and terrible failings of those, and again they were not judged, but accepted. Do you see? He did not judge me by my size alone, disregarding all else. Nor did he see only my unusual mental abilities, and not realize that I had shortcomings, as well."

"I have not noticed these shortcomings in your mental abilities, Randall."

"Ah, but they are there. I am too emotional and let my passions overcome my reason. A terrible failing in certain circumstances, I can assure you. And I have not an artistic notion in my head. Oh, yes, I learned to play the pianum, but I am no more a musician than are these devices that will hit the keys in the correct order and 'play' a tune. My mind is a calculating device, with near perfect recall, but I have little capacity for the imaginative. I could never have invented calculus, as Lord Skye did, yet even that great man has not the ability to do calculations in the mind that I have. So there you have it. Mr. Flattery saw me for what I was, and I will tell you, few have managed that." He paused. "And though I knew him only a short time, I shall miss him terribly. It is yet another tragedy we can lay at Eldrich's door." He threw the rock suddenly, far out over the moving river. Its splash attracted several wheeling gulls, crying miserably above the voice of the water.

They would not likely survive another night on this ledge awash in ice water. And even if they did, Erasmus was certain they would have no strength left to swim out, if they had the strength now.

At dusk they slipped into the water, having carefully surveyed all the river that could be seen. They planned to let the current carry them a hundred feet, then they would try to swim into the eddy behind a jumble of rocks. Erasmus was certain that it looked far easier than it was, and it did not appear easy.

Anna squeezed his hand once before lowering herself into the waters.

"When you emerge from the gorge," Erasmus reminded her, "don't become disoriented. Land on the opposite bank. We will hide another day before crossing."

The chill of the water was like a slap to a sleeping man. Erasmus could barely move for a second and then the current reached out and grasped him and be began to paddle furiously to keep his head in the air. If he had realized how weak he would be, he would have chanced the ledge for another day. Flames, but it would be a miracle if he survived this.

The rocks that were his goal swept past, and two strokes told him that making the calm of the eddy was impossible, nor could he see Anna there. They were at the mercy of the river and would survive only if their strength held and if they were not bashed to pieces upon the rocks.

The river carried him forward, the cold, green stream like a sinewy muscle stretched between the bones of the rocks. Erasmus spun about in the current, scraping along water-smoothed stones, dropping into jade pools that were emerald at their center. He surrendered himself to it, to the undeniable force of the river, and was drenched in the blood of the earth. Let it take him now, if it would. Let it grant him escape.

Let him float to the surface in some calm arm of the vast river, turning slowly beneath the sun. Wash ashore on warm stone to be picked clean by carrion crows and roving bands of insects, carrying bits of him back to feed their young. Let him return to the earth and start anew.

And then there were fist-sized boulders beneath his boots, and he danced along in the current, three yards to a step. Darkness had settled into the gorge, trees along the banks indistinguishable in their species. He found himself crawling up on a gravel bank, so exhausted that he collapsed for a moment upon the sun-warmed stones, and lay listening to the night.

Anna . . . What had happened to her?

A nightingale began to sing, its fluid notes counterpoint to the river sound.

Erasmus forced himself up, climbing the few feet of embankment into the shelter of the trees. He crouched there, shivering, trying to find a place where he would be out of the cooling breeze.

He looked out over the river and saw the light of a fire reflecting off the upper ramparts of trees. His traveling companions. How he wanted to cross the river and reveal himself to them, appearing like a ghost in the warm light. He could sit by the fire and bask in the glow of friendship.

What had happened to Anna? He hadn't seen any sign of her since they slipped into the river. It was not out of the question that she had perished this time. After all, Erasmus would have drowned if not for her—after all the years he had chanced the waters.

He lay down in the shelter of a fallen log where he could see the dance of the firelight across the river, see the shadows of his companions as they moved about. He realized he could not go back to them. They would start the search for Anna again, and perhaps find her. Erasmus would have to perform Percy's ritual. The fire ritual. And if he survived, he would be in thrall to Eldrich yet again. No, better to be dead, to be a ghost, wandering in the wood. Better to have no name than to be a servant of Eldrich. To be twisted by hatred as Percy had become.

"Solve your own 'dilemma arcane,'" Erasmus whispered. To be free of Eldrich, of searching for answers in old histories, in long-forgotten letters, that was what he wanted. To think of Eldrich no more than any man who traveled the streets of Avonel. To find out who Erasmus Flattery was beyond the reach of Eldrich, beyond the obsession.

*There will be no Erasmus Flattery,* he reminded himself. He rolled on his back and stared up at the irregular plot of stars visible through the branches. He could not see the wandering star—his "wondering star." Perhaps it had found its place, its place among the stars, and would stay anchored there in peace.

## ∽ Thirty-One

Hayes was the first to appear, rising before the sun. He made his way down the bank, stopping to survey the river before bending to drink. In the muted light, the pewter morning, he appeared small, childlike, as he crouched down by the running water, the sky above him rose and gray. Dusk appeared, and Erasmus froze in place knowing the wolfhound might sense him where the others did not.

But the dog bent down beside the young man and lapped up the water with a long tongue, raising his head to survey the world warily, as wild animals did when they came to drink.

In turn, each of his companions came down to the river. As they departed, Erasmus said a silent good-bye to each; Deacon Rose next, then the determined Kehler, and Clarendon last. Oddly, this was the hardest parting. Randall Spencer Emanual Clarendon; the small man with enormous heart. There was something about his gentleness and fits of passion, his unwavering loyalty, that Erasmus found difficult to leave. Kehler and Hayes were young and bright, they would do well; it was hardly in question. Rose, well, he was another matter. Fanatics, true fanatics, were never wrong, and this sustained them through being both persecuted and persecutor. Rose would go to his death believing that Anna's murder was Farrelle's will—and Erasmus' death in quest of this, merely unfortunate.

Clarendon made his way back up the bank as the edge of the sun seared the horizon. Dusk gamboled beside him, but when his master did not respond, the dog became quiet, even pensive, if a dog could be pensive.

Two hours later Erasmus watched them ride off, leading several riderless horses. Despite being weak with hunger, and suffering the blackest of headaches, Erasmus remained hidden for some time.

What would he do if Anna did not appear? If she were dead or had abandoned him?

The sight of his companions riding away had left him feeling . . . as he had felt when delivered to the house of Eldrich, those many years ago. But now he felt ghostly as well. While his companions were camped a stone's throw away, he could still give this up—step out onto the riverbank and shout. And there would be food and warm clothing—a horse to ride. Friends.

Instead he was alone in the hills without food or the tools of survival: an ax; a knife; a bow.

Several hours passed, giving Erasmus ample time to contemplate starvation. His reserves had been so depleted by the time in the cavern that he began to wonder seriously if he could even walk out of the hills now. Certainly a grown man could not starve to death in the Caledon Hills? No, he decided, even if he wasn't born in the hills, he knew enough about the natural world to survive. There would be crayfish in the river, and fish, if he could fashion a spear. A dozen plants could be eaten. Birds' eggs would be a last resort. He would survive.

Sure that his companions were gone, Erasmus emerged onto the gravel bar, looking up and down the river. Here it flowed so tranquilly that he could hardly believe a torrent lay just upstream. Downstream the waters were shaded by overhanging trees, the shadows broken in places, sunlight turning the water iridescent green—the color of a hummingbird's throat.

As he looked, something took shape in the shadow, then stepped out into sunlight. Anna, her long legs golden in the sunlight. Erasmus moved toward her, and as he did, realized she wore only a long shirt. They met at the edge of the water, both silent and grave.

Then she smiled. "You stayed," she said.

Erasmus nodded.

Her smile broadened. "I am drying my wretched clothes. Come, swim with me, and I will show you where I've hidden the food."

She began stripping off his clothes, laughing, her smile bright and mischievous. And then, suddenly, she went bounding into the water shouting, "We're dead, we're dead! They all think we're dead." Peeling off her shirt and tossing it onto the shore, she pitched herself into the water and then emerged, throwing great arcs of water with her arms. She laughed with such abandon that she lost her balance and fell into the water, emerging in a fit of laughter and coughing.

Erasmus plunged in, feeling the shock of the cold after the warmth of the sun. He surfaced before her and she reached out and took his face between her hands.

"You realize we're dead?" she said, trying to sound serious though neither her face nor voice would comply. "Eldrich thinks we're dead. . . . Or soon will. You understand what that means?"

Erasmus said nothing, not quite caught up in the moment.

"We are free of him, Erasmus. *You* are free of him. Free of him! We may go where we please. Do what we wish. Become whom we will. Do you see?" She began to chant. "Freefreefreefree." And then she jumped up and ducked him, pushing down on his shoulders until he went under, and then she relented, slipping down, her body softly pressed to his. Their lips met as Erasmus surfaced, a long, luxurious kiss.

He could feel each of her ribs. That was his first thought as they kissed. She had come so close to starving. They both had. Flames, he was all bones himself.

When they parted, she released him, taking his hand. "Come," she said, "there is food, and then I think we can find a bed of moss. We'll have to do without starlight. I can't wait that long."

They lay close, by the light of a small fire, and gazed at a map they had spread on the ground. Anna lay half over Erasmus, propped up on an elbow, and the soft warmth of her was like a second fire, glowing against his skin. She aimed a long finger lazily at the map. "We cannot go into this village. That would be an error. No, we must go past, overland. It will be all meadows and fields and small woods. Not so hard as traveling in the hills."

"But we need to buy horses, food. Find rooms to sleep."

She nuzzled his ear. "Clearly you have not been hiding from Eldrich all your life. You can afford no mistakes. You must remember that no one can lie to him, or keep their secrets. Leave a single witness to your passing and Eldrich will hear of it." She kissed him softly. "We will travel by night, stay clear of houses and their occupants. If we must, we'll take a bit of food, and leave a coin or two—for I know you're too noble to rob the less fortunate." He could hear the grin in her tone, and she kissed his neck, wrestled the blanket around to her liking and put her finger to the map. "Here. What town is this?"

"Cobblers' Hill. Or 'Cobblers' Hell' as it is known locally."

"Why is that? Should we stay clear of it?"

"No, it is just a peculiarity of the local pronunciation, where 'hill' is 'hell,' and a 'mill' a 'mell.'"

"No one knows you there, I hope?"

"No. I've just heard the name. It is a prosperous town, by all accounts. Large enough so you can't know everyone's name or business. We'll buy horses there, I take it?"

"And a small carriage, if we can find one. Nothing that would stand out, but a lady traveling by horseback will likely be noticed."

"A dog cart," Erasmus ventured.

"Exactly. You know, when I was child, I thought such a cart would be drawn by dogs! Not carry them."

Erasmus laughed.

"I imagined all kinds of such carts. A cat cart. A goat cart . . ."

"Now there is such a thing as a goat cart."

"There is not!"

"Oh, but there is. We might even see one as we go. Usually used to draw milk to town, for some odd reason."

"You liar!"

Anna tried to tickle him, to no avail for he had not been susceptible even as a boy. After a moment she gave up. "I didn't realize you were a man of so little sensitivity."

Erasmus didn't respond, but remained still, staring at the map. "Where are we going?"

Anna sensed his mood, and grew more serious herself. This was characteristic of her, Erasmus knew—this sensitivity to others. Perhaps it was even a manifestation of her talent. It told her when to apply her abundant charm, to which Erasmus was susceptible.

She lay her head on his shoulder. "We must go to ground for a while, Erasmus. Let Eldrich become confident that we are dead. There is a place—Eldrich will not know of it—it is isolated, the house not easily found. We could live there thirty years and no one would bother us."

"And does this place have a name?"

She looked at him for a moment, as though wondering if she could trust him with such information—if she trusted him at all. "Do you know Beacon

Head? There is a small island in its lee: Midsummer Isle. Very few people live there. Fisher folk, a few farmers. There was a town, but it was long ago abandoned. It is mainly known for Halden once having stayed there a year. It is said he wrote *About Ashleen* during that time. A few eccentrics have taken to living there—people who, for various reasons, no longer desire the society of men. I have a house there. High on a cliff overlooking the sea. It is dark and rainy all winter, but the summers are often fine, if not overly warm. We won't be bothered, I can assure you."

"But what will we do?" Erasmus asked.

"Well, I was hoping you might be interested in more of what we've been doing this night. . . . No, I understand what you say. We will await the death of Eldrich. That will be our primary task: to outlive the mage."

"It sounds rather a . . . slim purpose to have in life."

"Survival? It is the one common purpose of the living, though mankind often forgets that. Survive and procreate. Our lives needn't be reduced to an animal level entirely, though." She smiled. "There are other things."

Erasmus shifted around so that he could see her more easily. "Anna, why did you rescue me from the gorge? I was hunting you. I might have given you away. Tell me truthfully."

She sat up, wrapping the blanket around her, the colors of fire playing in her disheveled tresses. "Is it difficult for you to believe that I could not let you drown? Yes, yes, I know—there was Garrick. But I had a vision that he would betray me. Survival, Erasmus. The animal desire to live." She hung her head as though ashamed. "We are alike, you and I. Eldrich used you terribly and trapped you in the cavern to die. If there is anyone who should want to escape the mage, it is you, Erasmus. If you continued to serve him, what would he do next? He cares for you not at all, Erasmus, for you or anyone else." She reached out and put her hand gently on his heart. "And I wanted an ally, a companion, for all of my fellows are dead . . . murdered. We might find something like happiness together, or at the very least, peace."

"Peace," Erasmus echoed.

They fell silent, listening to the dark sounds of the night and the river.

Anna snuggled down close to him as the fire burned to coals and in a moment she was breathing regularly, deeply asleep.

Why did she save me, Erasmus wondered. Certainly everything she said might be true, but these explanations were not the reason she had kept him alive. She was more cunning. He remembered her escape from the chamber with the seed. No, Anna had her own plans. Just how they involved Erasmus Flattery was the question.

He closed his eyes, but they sprang open again as it occurred to him that she might have murdered her guide thus—as he slept.

## ❧ Thirty-Two

Marianne woke from a restful sleep and found herself in the countess' carriage descending a long slope among the hills. And then she remembered; she was coming from Castlebough where she had left the countess to continue her foolish pursuit of Skye. Poor woman.

She shook her head and stretched in a manner that would not be deemed ladylike, but then she was alone in the carriage, and what cared she for such strictures anyway?

"Odd," she said aloud. She did not usually sleep so well in carriages; in fact, she never had before. It was something of a miracle that she had not been thrown to the floor.

She thrust open the window, feeling overly warm, as though the sun beat down on her carriage, which it did not, for the sky was nothing but cloud.

She sank back into her seat, watching a crow's erratic flight into the wind, *blown like newsprint,* she thought, and then rummaged for her notebook to jot that down.

Opening it she turned through the pages she had filled, searching for clean paper. But there, on the last written page, she found a hand not her own.

*I am perfectly hale, as you will not remember—for Eldrich has blotted your memories. Such are the bargains made with a mage. Absolutely do not worry or try to contact me! I will find you when first I can.*

*Elaural*

Marianne stared at the note for a long time, wondering if this was some strange jest. Eldrich? Marianne sifted back through her memories, verifying them against her journal entries. Yes, they had traveled to Castlebough with Skye's paintings, meeting Averil Kent there. And Erasmus . . . And then nothing was quite clear. There were shards of things she could dredge up. The anonymous portrait. A meeting with Skye. Erasmus had disappeared. It was so hard to concentrate, as though every time she tried to remember, her focus wavered and fixed on something else—as though purposely distracted. Most unsettling.

And her journal. Had she really made no entries for so many days? When was the last time that had happened? The last time she had been so infatuated, she had temporarily abandoned the practice of her craft, that was when. But there had been no one in Castlebough. The countess had enjoyed a dalliance, though, had she not? Was it Flattery? Kent? Again her mind seemed to slide off and onto some other track that caused her less distress. Certainly this note was a jest. Certainly . . .

Marianne opened the small window to the driver and had him stop. For an hour she questioned him mercilessly, until the poor man complained of a wretched headache, which she also had herself. But this questioning did not put her mind at ease. He suffered the same problem as she in that he could barely bring his mind to focus.

She closed her eyes and put her head in her hands. Had she met Eldrich? Was this true? And he had stolen her memories? Stolen her precious memories! No, she could not accept it, and the more she tried to consider it, the worse her pain became. Pain and strange distress.

"This is not right," she said aloud. "This is not natural. I have been . . . plundered. Raped. There is no word. A part of me has been stolen. And what did it contain? What secrets might I have learned? And what has become of Elaural?" She had half a mind to have the driver turn back, and might have if she had any idea where they should go. Back to Castlebough, apparently, but she was not even sure of that. It was like waking from a dream and discovering the dream was true, not the world from which one departed into sleep.

She felt tears sting her eyes. How could anyone have done this to her? And why? Did this bastard mage not realize who she was? That her mind was sacrosanct, her memories precious? Had he no regard for anyone at all?

*Such are the bargains made with a mage.*

The line came back to her, as though she had read it the first time but had not been able to accept it. Had she made a bargain with Eldrich? She felt her heart sinking, and a terrible stillness came over her. What had he offered her?

And what had she promised in return?

It was not an original image, but the countess had come to think of Eldrich as a spider in the center of a web. On each strand it seemed some victim struggled, many not even aware that they were caught. Whenever it suited him, he drew another in, filling them with venom or feeding off them if he hungered. And then he let them go again, out into the world where they did his bidding. Some few might have escaped—Kent and Marianne, she hoped—but then Eldrich could have use for them again one day. As he did for her.

Despite Walky's protestations that she enjoyed special status in the house of the mage, she was well aware that she was no different from anyone else. He filled her with venom whenever it suited him—in this case the king's blood.

If Eldrich treated her with a certain respect, it was because he had to, though she was not sure why. He needed her willing cooperation, it seemed, and to get it he had refrained from his usual methods—though not entirely, for he had made a bargain with her, holding out something he believed she desired in return for what he wanted. It seemed only Walky served the mage without coercion or promise of something—and that "something" usually appealed to people's baser nature.

"He is not human," she said to the rain. "He has no compassion, no heart." Her kestrel flittered across the edge of the wood, landing on a branch. Occasionally it came closer, once landing on the ledge when the window had been ajar, but she did not encourage it, for it was connected to Eldrich's schemes, and as such unsettling to her.

It was surpassingly strange to feel such physical draw to a man and be repulsed by him at the same time. Oh, yes, she knew his story now. He had rather transparently sent Marianne to repeat it to her. Poor Marianne who was led to believe her memory would return to her in some years, and she would write this tale of the last mage. Unlikely, the countess thought. Eldrich did not care if people knew of him, or understood the reasons for the things he did.

No, Marianne had been meant to tell the story in this room, and nowhere else. And it was a terrible story, and likely true. The countess found it difficult to imagine that Lucklow had been born of woman! So it seemed that Eldrich had suffered in the house of the mage far more terribly than Erasmus.

But that did not forgive Eldrich's heartlessness, his inhumanity. Not by the countess' measure of things. Eldrich was a man of vast intelligence and could make his own choices. After all, he had collected over a century of experiences to draw from.

She wondered what Marianne would make of her hastily scribbled note. It had been difficult enough to manage, for Eldrich had guessed correctly that Marianne would write a detailed description of everything that had happened since leaving for Castlebough—and this he had expunged. The countess had had only a second to jot a few words . . . and she was not even sure why she had done it.

Rebellion, she guessed. Rebellion, and because she could not bear to stand by passively while Eldrich committed this terrible crime against Marianne— or so Marianne would have seen it—if not a crime against art. But then, Marianne had agreed to this bargain, had she not?

A knock on her door roused her, and she crossed the room to open it.

The small form of Walky stood in the dark hall. Often he carried no lamp or candle, but made his way through the unlit house as easily as a mage.

*Owl sight,* he called it, and said she would learn it herself, by and by.

"Ah, Walky," she said, standing aside that he might enter. She could hardly think of another man in the world she would let into her bedchamber without hesitation—but Walky, though not immune to her charms, was so much a gentleman, and so loyal a servant of the mage, that he was to be trusted utterly.

"I have brought you a book," he said, proffering a small, untitled volume.

This one did not seem so old as the other books she had encountered in the house of Eldrich, though it was hardly new, even so.

"Come in, sit," she said, realizing how much she missed the company of others. "And what is this? Enchantments? Hidden histories? A book of terrible secrets?"

"It is enchanting, I think, but it is poetry. Poetry and songs," he said, taking a seat. "Although it has no title on the cover the book has become known as *Owl Songs*. Very odd, for to the best of my knowledge, owls hardly sing. It is a book of lore, in its own way, but little is plainly stated. We will use it in our study of the language. Here, let me give you an example." He took the book back and found a page. He read a short poem in Darian, and then looked up at her.

"I think I gleaned about seven words."

"Allow me to offer a rough translation," Walky said.

*"Worlds spun upon the web of time*
*The ebb and flow and ebb again*
*Of shoreless seas and waning light*
*Unknown to worlds of sleeping men.*
*Across the seas the seven came,*
*With book and blossom in their flight,*
*To land upon the island world*
*By star and moon and fairest night."*

Walky looked up from the book, his face oddly unreadable.

"What does it mean?" the countess asked.

"Mean? Well, it is poetry, m'lady, and, by its nature, means many things. It is likely only a fragment, as well, of some larger work. Upon its surface it is merely a description of the first mages' arrival in this world. 'Across the seas the seven came.'"

"They came from somewhere else? Some other land?"

"Yes, of course. The arts were not made whole in the lands around the Entide Sea. They are far older than that. Older than the Entide Sea itself, I would wager. But let us write it out in Farr, and you may study it. Nothing so ruins poetry as having it explained by another. You must find its meaning, for it is different for everyone."

She was always somewhat amused to see Walky write, for he did it with such deliberation and so slowly that she invariably thought of a child learning his letters. He finished and slid the page across to her.

They sat quietly a moment, and just as Walky was about to take his leave, she spoke.

"Why do you serve him, Walky?"

The softly benign look that he always wore altered into one of confusion— as though the question made no sense.

"He is the last great mage, m'lady. Could one need reason more than that? I have always served him. It is my purpose on this earth."

"But, Walky, certainly even you must see that he is cold and cruel. Of all those who serve him, only you do so willingly. All others, even those who might wish to serve him, are coerced, offered tawdry bargains, their weaknesses preyed upon. He has no compassion, no humanity. And yet you serve him with utter devotion. How can you?"

"But he is a mage," Walky said, wrinkling up his brow. "One does not judge a mage by the laws of men, any more than one would judge a falcon by the ways of a sparrow. A falcon is without remorse. It has no pity, no compassion, no humanity—but then it is not human. It is a lord of the skies. And so, too, is the mage, m'lady.

"He is not as you and I, if you will forgive me for saying it. He has duties and trusts that we can barely comprehend. He is the master of an ancient tradition, a discipline that few may follow. A bearer of perilous knowledge and all of its attendant responsibilities. You must understand this one truth of mages, m'lady. He cannot afford the luxury of humanity. His duties are too grave for that. One does not pity him for this, for he would not understand it, and it would anger him, but one must at least show patience and tolerance. It is a calling that one pursues at great price. One surrenders one's heart to become a mage."

They were silent for a moment, the countess taking in what had been said, surprised that Walky was suddenly so effusive, for usually he would avoid speaking of his master.

"I thought a mage had no duties to any but himself," she said, "and perhaps 'his own kind,' as Lord Eldrich likes to phrase it."

"That is the common perception, m'lady, but the truth is more complex, as the truth always tends to be." He tapped the book. "As is poetry. We will study this and perhaps you will begin to see. *Owl Songs,* the book is called, and owls see through the darkness."

## ᗌ Thirty-Three

The trail became a path, the path a track, and finally a lane. A tumbledown old house appeared on its bank, smoke streaming from the chimney, but with no inhabitants in view. The way went down quite steeply now, and they encountered a few houses that had been pushed out of the too-full town. And then they were in Wicken Vale, packs of children and dogs running along beside their horses, for it was not often that gentlemen appeared out of the hills— gentlemen and a priest.

They quickly found the only inn the village possessed and handed their horses over to the livery boy. The proprietor looked them over as they came in, and jerked a thumb toward the ceiling. "There is a gentleman here asking after others who might have made their way through the hills. That would be you, I take it?"

"And who might he be?" Clarendon asked, a bit warily.

"A Mr. Bryce."

"Ah," Rose stepped to the fore, "the very man we seek. Will you please inform him of our arrival, and then we would like rooms and baths for a party of four."

Rose appeared at the door to their room as Hayes was rubbing his hair dry.

"Deacon. Dinner has not been served without us, I hope."

The priest shook his head, his gaze shifting away from Hayes' then back again. "We are to set out at first light to meet Eldrich."

Hayes dropped his arms to his side. "All of us?"

The priest nodded.

"You spoke with this man without us?"

Again the priest nodded.

"Was even Clarendon present?"

"No one but me."

Hayes felt anger boil up through his incredulity. "What would lead you to believe you had the right to speak for us?"

"There was little discussion—merely a command to attend the mage."

"He questioned you, surely. . . ."

The priest nodded, rather reluctantly.

"And what did you tell him?"

"Only that we believed Anna had perished and, sadly, Erasmus Flattery with her. He asked to see Mr. Flattery's belongings, but I knew what he was after and had brought it to him—the text of the ritual Erasmus was to perform."

Hayes tried to understand. What wasn't the priest telling him? Why had the man snuck off to speak with Bryce without them? It was more than suspicious. "Does Clarendon know you've done this?"

A shake of the head.

"Farrelle preserve you when you tell him." And without another word, Hayes closed the door.

Deacon Rose rode in the carriage with the servant of Eldrich, whom none of the others had yet spoken with. Clarendon was in a dark rage and kept entirely to himself, riding behind the others. Even the day was somber, as dark banners of cloud fluttered over in a harsh wind from the sea.

Hayes and Kehler hunched down over their saddles, as though to make themselves smaller targets for the wind. They said very little, though it was perfectly obvious what was on their minds: Eldrich and what he would do with them.

Both young men had hoped they were quit of this matter, and Hayes was even looking forward to returning to his debt-ridden life in Avonel. Not that he had a place to live or any prospects. His hopes to enter the foreign service had been abandoned, as the positions for winch he had gone up were, no doubt, filled—and he had not even been in Avonel to answer a summons should one have come.

But before all of that there was Eldrich, and the anxiety of this meeting made all else seem very paltry and remote. Survive the meeting with Eldrich and anything else in life would seem child's play. Obscurity and pauperism would be almost pleasure.

"We are not traveling in the direction of Eldrich's estates," Kehler said, trying to keep his voice low.

He looked even more dispirited since their summons. Hayes was almost more worried about his friend than about their coming audience with the mage.

"What? No, we're traveling south. Apparently the mage is not in residence. Rose speculated that he was in Castlebough while we were below ground. He didn't think it likely that Eldrich could have collapsed the cave from any distance."

"Are we returning to Castlebough, do you think?"

Hayes shrugged. He felt a shiver run through him at the thought of the town, and it was not from the cold. The skeleton of a child reaching out . . . the stone constricting around him as he crawled through the dark. All to what end? He could hardly remember what had led them there to begin with.

He looked over at his friend, who slumped in his saddle, barely raising his head, trusting his horse to follow the others, lost in his own thoughts—all of them dark and filled with foreboding. Hayes knew what he felt, having lived in poverty. He knew how impossible it became to believe that anything would ever turn out right. That there would ever be light again.

He looked back over his shoulder to be sure that Clarendon was still with them, and saw the little man some way off, almost a smaller version of Kehler at that distance.

*What a ragtag company we have become,* he thought. *It will be a miracle if our meeting with Eldrich does not destroy us.*

Hayes longed to say something to Clarendon, something to soothe him, but he knew there was nothing that would ease the man's anger. As Clarendon had said himself, he was a victim of his passions. Even Dusk was tentative around him when he returned from his expeditions over the fields and through the woods. No, Clarendon would have to stew in the bitter juices of his anger and resentment, emotions that were too ready to rise up in the small man.

Hayes only hoped that he would not become like Clarendon in time.

Clarendon appeared so small and forlorn upon his full-sized horse—an elf prince out of song. A gray drapery of rain wafted out of the hills, then, and Clarendon was almost obscured from view in the downpour. Hayes looked back to the carriage where Deacon Rose sat in comfort, protected from the weather. Life was often thus, for certainly Clarendon had suffered and overcome enough in this life that he deserved respite. He deserved to be the one protected from the world's vagaries and injustice.

Hayes had given up guessing where events would take him next. A hunting lodge in the Caledon Hills would not have been one of his guesses anyway. They arrived in the midst of another spring storm, tired and somewhat miserable, and were left to wait in an unlit hallway beneath a stair. From a window somewhere above, occasional flashes of lightning cast angular shadows of railings and balustrades, making Hayes think, for some reason, of a jail. Thunder followed the flashes almost immediately, the lightning striking nearby. The protracted rumbling was so deeply felt and so powerful that Hayes thought it sounded like the earth splitting, breaking apart around them.

"You look rather calm and unruffled, Deacon," Kehler said. "The journey was not too arduous, I hope?"

The priest shrugged, as though to imply that sarcasm deserved no reply. Or perhaps even Deacon Rose was frightened and could think of no response.

Clarendon stood apart, still wrapped in the rage that had surrounded him since Wicken Vale. What treachery was this priest involved in? That was the question on the little man's mind. And there was more. There was this bargain that Clarendon had spoken of—something he would offer to the mage—though Hayes feared that even Eldrich could not offer what Clarendon wanted in return.

An explosion of thunder was followed by the sound of footfalls—like very distant echoes—and a wavering candle appeared, dimly illuminating a round-faced little man. He stopped some yards from them. "Follow me," he said, and started back the way he had come. There was a moment of hesitation, and then the priest set off after the man, the others rousing themselves to follow.

Hayes could hardly make out Kehler's face in the dim light, but his friend looked terribly grim. Men went to the scaffold looking thus, Hayes was sure. And he felt it himself. A strange weakness in all his limbs—a hopelessness. Here is where their curiosity had led—to a meeting with this dreaded mage. Anger at Kehler welled up in him. Had he the strength, he might have struck his companion, such was the ferocity of it.

Clarendon caught up with the candle bearer. "Are you Mr. Walky? Mr. Flattery spoke kindly of you."

"But it is not Walky who will judge you," the small man said as he put a finger to his lips.

Too soon they came to the hall's end. The small man opened a door and motioned them through. Hayes stumbled into darkness, the room lit only by a fire that had burned to glowing coals in the hearth. A hand gently pushed him forward as he stopped. And then he realized that something moved beside the fire—a shadow darker than the rest.

With a sound of wings fluttering, flames erupted in the hearth. Hayes could make out the figure now, a large man sprawled in a chair, patting a massive beast that sat at his side.

*The wolf of legend,* Hayes realized.

The four of them lined up a few paces away, coming no closer than they must. Walky had disappeared somewhere behind them. The mage continued to stroke the wolf, kneading behind its ears. Suddenly he pushed it forward, making a hissing sound through his teeth, and the beast came straight for them. Hayes drew himself up, becoming utterly still.

It snuffled about his feet and knees, then passed to Kehler, leaving him almost as quickly. But Rose interested it somehow. Excited it, in some way. The hackles rose on its neck, and teeth were bared; a low growl emerged. Hayes was sure that it would have attacked the man, but a word from the mage sent it on to Clarendon. Here again, something seemed to incite it, but again the mage spoke, and it went bounding away into the dark.

A long silence followed. Hayes almost wondered if they had been forgotten, or if the mage learned all he wanted without even having them speak. Perhaps they were speaking, and he did not know.

"You . . . we've met before," the mage said, his voice surprisingly melodious. "What is your name?"

"Clarendon," the small man answered, his voice barely audible. "We met—"

"I remember," the mage said, his voice harsh despite its music. "As do you. Did I not say it was your curse?"

"Where is Lizzy? Is she yet alive?" the little man whispered, barely forcing the words out.

"Who? Oh, the woman? She is gone, gone this half-century. Not a short time, even to me. Is she alive?" The mage shrugged, unconcerned for the fate of some unknown woman.

Clarendon was trembling now, as though he struggled just to keep his feet.

"I have knowledge. Only I have it. I will offer it to you freely. . . ."

"Indeed you will," Eldrich said. "And I will pay you nothing for it. She is gone, little man. Gone where you cannot follow, unless you have the knowledge and skill of Landor."

"Not the skill, but the knowledge, I think. . . ."

Eldrich did not respond for a moment. One long hand passed over a candle which flickered to light and held, yet this light did not touch him. "She exploited you," he said coolly. "Used you terribly, though you were perhaps too young to realize. I could have let you go with her." He ran his fingers over the candle flame again. "I seldom do men favors, but you . . . your existence was hard enough. Men do not care for those born . . . unlike them."

Silence but for Clarendon's ragged breathing. In the poor light Hayes could see the little man, bent as though he would collapse from the pain.

"Step forward, priest," the mage said, turning his attention from Clarendon and his precious bargain. The music gone from his voice. "Say nothing!" he cautioned, as the priest opened his mouth. "'A tongue so sweet it should be cut out and fed to dogs.' I should have given you to the wolf, and I might yet. If you make any attempt to use that silver tongue here, I shall teach you the lesson that life has neglected. Do you understand? I have much to settle with you and your church for all that you think you have hidden from my kind these many years. Your precious Farrelle spoke of atonement . . . and so shall we."

The priest nodded quickly. *Afraid to speak,* Hayes thought, and he would have felt some satisfaction if he were not so frightened himself. If he were not sure his turn was coming.

"You found no bodies? Neither Erasmus nor this woman? Not even the boy?"

No one answered.

"You, Clarendon. Speak up."

"No bodies," Clarendon breathed.

Lightning lanced into the earth nearby, revealing a large room, a shadow before the fire. Windows rattled with the deep throbbing thunder, its echo impossibly long.

Eldrich rose from his chair by the fire and went and stood before one of the tall windows, staring out at the night, his silhouette flickering into being with each streak of lightning.

"Perhaps they are dead, swept away by the river. Perhaps. But I am not convinced. Not yet. Your task might not be done. There is still a ship rolling in a strange sea. But first I will have each of your stories, and I caution you to leave nothing out, and to tell only the strictest truth. You cannot lie to me, and I have no patience for those who waste my time. I have particular interest in what you saw within Landor's chamber. That which was inscribed upon the walls. Which of you is Kehler? You met with Skye: begin there."

*      *      *

The mage bent over Clarendon's carefully copied text, the writings from Landor's chamber. He glanced up briefly at Walky, and then turned his gaze quickly back to the page as though overcome by fascination and horror. Then he shook his head and sat back in his chair, closing his eyes. He muttered something under his breath.

"Sir?"

"Tell me I sleep, Walky, and that this is nothing more than a nightmare. The nightmare of all my kind."

"What is it, Lord Eldrich?"

"It is the cataclysm, Walky, the apocalypse. The ruin of all that I have planned."

Walky had never heard his master speak thus and found himself staring at the text with great alarm.

"We must pray that this woman is not alive, and if she is, that she has not the knowledge to understand what is written here." He took a long breath. "And she has the seed. . . ."

"If she survived, sir."

"Yes, but the Paths have not indicated her death—not yet. And they found no body. Neither she nor Erasmus."

"Nor the boy," Walky added. "It is likely they were all swept . . . away." Walky choked a little on the last word, causing the mage to look up.

"Are you all right, Walky?" Eldrich asked quietly.

The servant nodded.

"Do not be so sure that Erasmus is dead, simply because these men believe it. I told you of my vision? It wasn't until later that it occurred to me that the creature clinging to the mast could be Erasmus. His obvious hostility to me, his half-fish, half-man appearance—one caught between two worlds, two desires. And then he leaped into the waters to join a nymph and the dolphins. Sailors believe that the spirits of men lost at sea inhabit dolphins and won't harm these mammals for any reason. How neatly it all fits. Erasmus plunged into this raging river and died with this woman. But water is life, Walky. We swim in it until birth. No, I am not convinced they are dead, so do not despair."

"But if he has joined forces with this woman, sir, that is worse," Walky said.

Eldrich looked at the small man briefly, then cast his gaze down, nodding his head. "Yes, there are worse things than a clean death." The mage reached out and brushed the pages spread before him. "I am worried about the emerging faces in Landor's crypt. Almost everyone thought one to be Erasmus—though none were absolutely sure. But the other—It has barely begun to form. Could it be this girl, Anna? Or is it our countess? Do you see what I'm saying? The art that made that chamber was great. Far greater than my own, or even

Lucklow's. The faces forming there are more critical than the people caught in the chamber realized. Absolutely critical, for the art that forms them is subtle and beyond our understanding. Will it be Erasmus?" He shook his head. "That seems unlikely now. And the woman? What if it is Anna? Is that possible?"

Eldrich looked down at the table, flipping over a page. "Imagine not being able to forget a thing," he mused. "A remarkable little man." Eldrich gazed at the writing for a moment.

"Everything is so unclear," the mage said, "so muddled. How I wish they had found bodies." Eldrich realized that Walky almost flinched when he heard this, and turned to examine his servant. "If he perished trying to save this young man, Walky, then it was a noble death; better than he might have found. Most die for no reason at all—and live for little more. But I'm not yet convinced of his death. Not yet." He turned back to the text, staring at it with a look Walky had never seen in his master's face before—fear.

A blind child, raggedly dressed, made his way along the wall, running his hand over the stone. Twice he stumbled and fell but stiffly raised himself and carried on with the stoicism of those who did not know they suffered injustice.

Eldrich watched, his mind too focused to even wonder who the child was or what this scene might mean. It was better to ask no questions now. Better just to watch, to let the vision unfold.

A moon floated up from behind a stone wall, casting its cool light down upon the child, who stopped, confused—as though he could sense the light somehow, almost see it. He turned about and his face was suddenly illumined.

*Clarendon. . . .*

The dwarf turned away from the light and continued along the ruined street, stumbling again at the foot of a long stair. Eldrich followed, keeping his distance. The small man went slowly up the stairs, using his hands on the broken treads.

The mage followed, not feeling the stairs beneath his feet, but up he went all the same, following the child-man who went, crablike, ahead. On each stair Eldrich saw a thin smear of blood from Clarendon's hands.

*Where are you leading me,* he wondered, but then turned his mind away from speculation.

A massive beast appeared at the stairhead—a wolfhound—and Clarendon took hold of its shoulder and followed.

By the time Eldrich crested the stair, man and beast were gone. Slowly he turned about, surveying the place: the ruin of an ancient city or fortress made mysterious by moonlight.

"Where have you gone?" the mage wondered aloud. "Where?"

The moon slipped behind a cloud, and Eldrich woke in a chair before a tall window, lightning forking down in the world beyond, his familiar scratching frantically at the glass before him.

## ᔕ Thirty-Four

The dog cart rattled along the rutted track between hedges, and turned abruptly into a field. Erasmus climbed down briefly to open a gate and latch it again as the cart passed. Sheep had browsed the grasses short, leaving only the odd sentinel thistle, purple tufts weaving in the wind. Anna had abandoned her practice of traveling only by night, and had offered Erasmus no explanation.

"Why exactly are we stopping here?" Erasmus looked around. "If you have in mind what I have in mind, this is hardly the place."

Anna dropped down beside him. "It was not what I had in mind—at least not until you mentioned it—but there was something I wished to see." She walked out into the field, her skirts wafting in the breeze. Erasmus thought that she looked amazingly restored, though he was also aware that it was not just rest or passion that had accomplished this: it was the seed that she took in tiny quantities. Even her hair did not look so faded, and her face glowed with youth and vigor. She had grown remarkably more attractive, he thought.

Twenty paces out into the field she spun on her toes and pointed to the north. "Do you know that town?"

Erasmus followed her gesture and found a few rooftops showing through the trees. Looking back to Anna, he shook his head and walked toward her.

"Can you not make a guess?" She smiled, teasing. "I will give one hint. It was made famous by an incident that was immortalized in oils."

Erasmus wondered what she was on about. He looked toward the town again as he caught up with her. "Is it Compton Heath?"

"The very place. I am guessing that this is approximately the point the Pelier depicted. Do you see? There is even a brook, though it seems only to flow in one direction, unlike the one you described to me."

They continued down the slight incline to the water, looking around.

"There is no bridge," Anna said, "but then we must consider artistic license in this matter." She shaded her eyes and gazed off toward the town. "What say you, Erasmus, is it at all like the Pelier?"

Erasmus nodded, considering. "It is, and it is not. The trees are not quite right, that small wood there was larger in the painting, and this pasture seemed a natural meadow, without hedges or gates. Of course the church stee-ple is gone—and has been for some years. But all in all, considering that Pelier was likely never here, it is quite remarkable." He looked at Anna. "Why do I not think this visit is idle curiosity?"

"I think you are coming to know me rather better than I would like," she said, turning full circle. "I wish to employ the arts here, briefly, though I fear that we might be seen."

"It is a risk," Erasmus said. "And what would this use of the arts be in aid of?"

"Knowledge," she said, "or, at the very least, curiosity. You see, if this is really the place where the Stranger appeared, as the painting suggests, then it would mean the worlds lie closer here—or at least did briefly. Even so there might be some trace of it. Indulge me for half the hour, Erasmus, for it is a question I would have answered. Wouldn't you?"

Erasmus nodded. "How obvious would it be to anyone watching that we . . . you were practicing the arts?"

"That depends on the proximity of the watchers, and their perceptiveness. Perhaps more obvious than we would like."

"Let me take a walk along the edge of the field and see if anyone is about. Was it not you that said we should take no chances? I am becoming rather fond of being dead."

"As am I. Have a look, then, and I will begin my preparations," she said.

Erasmus struck out across the field, crossing the brook on stepping stones. From the top of a stile he looked into the next field, then walked along beside the hedgerow and the edge of the wood. It appeared they were alone, though it would not have been hard for any curious onlooker to step back out of sight while he passed.

When he returned to Anna, he saw that she had made peculiar marks in the sod with a knife and built small cairns of river stones in three places.

"You might want to go stand by the horse, Erasmus. Animals often react badly when they sense the arts in use. Lead him out of sight—onto the road, perhaps."

Erasmus did as he was told, though he wanted to see what was done. As he was trying to decide if he would leave the cart and walk back, the horse suddenly shied, and it was all he could do to stop the animal from bolting. A quarter of the hour later Anna appeared, looking exhausted and flushed.

She slumped into the cart as though stricken with the vapors. Erasmus waited patiently until she finally pushed herself upright.

"I'm recovering," she said. "Press on, but I don't think we should pass through the town. Can we get up onto that high point, do you think? I would like to look at the surrounding terrain and have my empiricist explain its formation to me."

They wound their way up the odd hill that Anna had indicated. When they got to a suitable outlook, they turned the cart off the lane under the shadow of some regal oaks. Then they climbed down and walked a few feet in order to have the best vista.

"Well? Tell me about the geology."

Erasmus looked out over the countryside and tried to dredge up what he knew from Layel. "This long flat plain was once the floor of a large lake or arm of the sea. There are places not far from here where you can see perfect beaches, twenty miles from the sea. All of Farrland was scraped by massive glaciers, or so many believe, and the few hills hereabout, such as the one upon which we stand, were formed by the glaciers, though we don't really know how."

"But what of that?" Anna asked, pointing off toward a rather broken-down hill, like the ruin of some vast fortification.

"Ah, now that is different. That is a very ancient volcano, called Kilty's Keep, like the ancient song, though which came first scholars still debate. It is a geological feature of some interest. I visited it once, and found it surpassingly strange, for it does appear to be the ruin of fortifications, but on a vast, inhuman scale. One can imagine it was built by some race of men far more powerful than our own, which is what people believed in ancient times. If we could see back to the west there is another like it, though not nearly so large. They form a line, a fault of some kind where the molten core of the earth would well up and spew forth. The fault extends back into the Caledon Hills, though farther north, as though the line curved."

"And where exactly is Tremont Abbey? Do you know?"

Erasmus turned around and looked back toward the trees which hid the view to the north and west. He swept a small arc with his hand. "In that general direction."

"But near to this flaw in the earth?"

"Yes, very near, I should say."

She nodded and, finding an area of grass to her liking, spread one of their blankets. They sat down, close to one another, kissing briefly.

"And what has all of this proven?" Erasmus asked.

"Well, clearly you see what I am getting at."

"Tremont Abbey and Compton Heath both lay along the fault that runs through Kilty's Keep. Volcanic activity took place here in very ancient times. There is some connection between this and these other worlds of which you have spoken."

"I could not have put it more clearly. Though I cannot tell you more. Perhaps this volcanic activity is caused by the proximity of the other world."

"I think Layel and his followers would find this a little difficult to accept."

She shrugged. "Many things the mages believe empiricists would find difficult to accept. These men of reason even doubt the arts existed at all. I have heard that some say it was all trickery—conjuring on a grand scale—but you and I know better." She held his eye for a moment, and then smiled. "Finally, before we give up this subject all together, does this line of vulcanism— Is that correct? Vulcanism?"

"Correct in every way."

"Does this line extend toward Beacon Head?"

Erasmus felt himself sit up, suddenly not so comfortable.

"This island upon which you have a house, is it volcanic? Is that where this is going?"

"No, that's where we are going." She smiled at her poor jest and put her hand on his cheek. "Do not look so suspicious, Erasmus. We have long thought this island to be a place of power, which is how the mages thought of such sites—Tremont Abbey, for instance. Farrow as well. But it is nothing to be concerned about. I have no nefarious plans. No Tellerite conspiracy to bring to fruition. We seldom used this house at all, keeping it as a refuge in case all our plans went awry. I hope it is still standing." She leaned forward and kissed him tenderly at the corner of his eye. "Do you think people come up here often or might we be left undisturbed for an hour?"

Erasmus covered Anna carefully with a blanket, stood for a moment watching her sleep, and then walked out under the shading trees. He sat upon a rock and looked out over the valley toward Kilty's Keep. The town of Compton Heath lay below, twisting along a road that curved into a hollow of the hillside. This was where Baumgere had first encountered a Stranger and started on his quest—a quest that led to a child dying in isolation and terror far beneath the fair surface of the world.

*The surface of the world . . .*

Anna seemed to believe that this was but one of several "worlds infinitely far away yet close at hand."

It did not begin here, he reminded himself, any more than it began when I found Hayes hiding in an Avonel brothel, or when I was ordered to the house of Eldrich as a child. No, it began when the seven journeyed here from Darr— if it is not merely a myth.

"You saw the chamber," Erasmus reminded himself. And the face forming in stone; a face that must have been him—the last Guardian of the Gate.

But he had escaped the chamber and its gate, escaped Eldrich's attempt on his life.

"But can I escape him again?" he whispered, for certainly that was why he had taken up with Anna—that and he owed her his life. She would have been far safer to let him drown, but then perhaps she knew him well enough to realize that he could not betray her now. Eldrich had attempted his murder, and Anna had saved him from certain death. . . .

But it was a desperate thing they did, attempting to elude Eldrich. Erasmus could feel the desperation in both of them. It woke them from nightmares and was present even in their lovemaking. If they were found—well, he did not like to contemplate that.

Better to think about what life would be like if they escaped Eldrich. Perhaps he would finally lay to rest his shattered childhood and live life anew. It was worth killing Erasmus Flattery to be free of Eldrich. He only hoped that isolation and secrecy would not drive him to madness.

Erasmus rose and walked a few steps, looking off toward the sea. Great, billowing, white clouds—the escaped sails of an entire fleet—lifted up above the horizon. A hawk circled effortlessly over the fields, turning its head slowly, searching for movement.

Searching.

The sea was not quite visible from this height, though he could imagine it, lying silvered beneath the great reef of cloud.

Did he trust Anna? Lovely, seductive Anna?

No, she had some purpose of her own, some reason to have rescued him. But what could it be? He thought, though, that he had a much better chance of resisting Anna than he did of resisting Eldrich. Better to throw in his lot with someone who could not so easily overpower him.

"Be thankful you are dead," he said aloud. "Even Eldrich cannot murder the dead."

It occurred to him suddenly that the countess was with Eldrich now. Had he abducted her? Unlikely that she would go willingly, but then, mages could be very persuasive. Odd that Eldrich would have an interest in this woman, at this point. Certainly in their younger years, before they passed their centenaries, many of the mages were known to have a weakness for the fairer sex. To the best of his knowledge, Eldrich had not been one of these—not that he had likely lived as a monk, but women were not his passion as they had been with some. But Eldrich had passed his hundredth year some time ago, no one knew exactly when, and here he was abducting the fairest woman in all of Farrland. There must be some other reason.

For a moment Erasmus entertained the idea that Eldrich had done it to spite him, but no, the truth was that Erasmus was probably not so important to Eldrich that he would be driven to such revenge or even to wreak a little more havoc on Erasmus' already battered life.

"Is he lost in thought and melancholia?" Anna's voice came from behind. "Or is he merely contemplating the beauty of the world which stretches out before him?"

"It is the clouds," he said not looking back. "When I was a child, I imagined that there were worlds within the clouds and that magic ships existed that could visit them, sailing across the blue of the heavens, landing on islands of clouds which were all inhabited by strange races, usually with beautiful women."

She sat down and wrapped an arm about his neck, putting her head on his shoulder. "What do you mean, 'when you were a child'? Are you saying this isn't true? That we will not be able to find a good sky-ship and make our escape to the clouds?"

"Well, it is not a fancy I give up easily. But then there were some who believed that the way to Faery lay through the cave—yet we did not find it."

"No we did not, though that doesn't mean it was not there. . . ."

"You're beginning to sound like Clarendon."

"How so?"

"He . . . he was fascinated by Strangers and the idea that Faery might not be merely myth."

Anna nodded. "Myth it is, I think, but there certainly are lands beyond— Darr, from where Landor journeyed, and other worlds besides; one of them Faery, perhaps. Who can say?" She ran fingers through his hair, and shut her eyes, still in need of sleep.

"Will we escape Eldrich, do you think? Have you tried augury to see?"

"No, I have not attempted augury. Eldrich knew of our visions in the past. I . . . I am a bit afraid to use it now. Will we escape . . . ?" She shrugged.

"But you have the seed now. A familiar follows you. Do you fear him still?"

"More than I can say. There is no one who should not." She hesitated. "That is not true. Another mage need not fear him. They had strictures—No, it was more than that. There is a curse. One mage cannot murder another without bringing down this curse upon all mages."

"But there is only one remaining in all the world."

"So there is," she said. "So there is."

## ᴄᴈ Thirty-Five

The soft, almost hesitant knock was becoming familiar to the countess. In fact, she had begun to look forward to Walky's visits, often remembering what Erasmus had said about the man being a good friend to him in a difficult situation.

"Mr. Walky," she said, curtsying primly.

This took him somewhat aback, it seemed.

"Do I interrupt you, m'lady?"

"No, Mr. Walky, not at all. I was simply so happy to see you that I forgot myself for a moment." She laughed and took hold of his arm, drawing him into the room and closing the door.

"I have tea," she said. "Or wine if you prefer."

"Tea would be very welcome, m'lady."

She sat him down and poured tea. "It is not entirely fresh," she said, "as I expected you earlier." She raised a hand to prevent his next response. "No, you are not coming too late. I am only sorry about the quality of your tea."

She set his steaming cup before him. "Now, tell me. What will it be tonight? More *Owl Songs*, for I will tell you I have been trying to read them, but I have not enough of the language yet to make much headway. It is tough sledging, as an instructor of mine liked to say."

Walky, she noticed, looked rather subdued this evening. It might have been her imagination, but his eyes looked a bit red and puffy.

"Is something wrong, Walky?"

He made as if to speak, and his mouth quivered slightly as though it struggled to open. "I have received some news that, though not unexpected, was still very sad, m'lady."

"Oh, Walky, I am distressed to hear. Can you tell me what this is, or is it business of the mage and therefore not for mortal ears?"

"It has to do with a . . . friend, m'lady. I do not mean to pry, but I collect you had more than a passing acquaintance with my former charge, Erasmus Flattery?"

She nodded, closing her eyes involuntarily. She felt a peculiar numbness.

"The mage is not utterly convinced this is true, but we have received news that Erasmus had an unfortunate accident." He struggled with the next word, his mouth quivering again, ". . . *drowned,*" he managed.

"Oh, Walky." She felt tears appear upon her eyelashes, and she reached out and took the old man's hand. "Farrelle preserve us—preserve him. How did this happen? Could not Erasmus swim? Did he not tell me you had taught him?"

The old man nodded. "Yes," he whispered, "but not well enough, it seems." A tear streaked down from the corner of one eye. "The poor child," he said. "The poor, sad child. It was written in the stars. . . . What hope had he with all that was arrayed against him? What hope . . . ?" And the old man broke down and wept bitterly, the countess crying with him, for the loss of Erasmus Flattery, and the fate for which he had been born.

"It is nothing to be ashamed of," Hayes heard the priest say. "We were all afraid."

Hayes propped himself up on one elbow and looked around.

"Ah, he returns to the land of the living," Deacon Rose said.

"Hello, Hayes," Kehler said so softly he could barely be heard. "Do you feel as beastly as I?" Kehler sprawled in a chair looking like a man near death, his face positively gray.

"I have a headache for which there is no descriptor, but it is a long catalogue of ailments and probably no different from your own." Hayes closed his eyes.

"You resisted," Rose said, "which was a mistake."

Hayes noticed Clarendon collapsed against the wall, drawn into himself like a child who'd been beaten.

"Randall? Are you . . . ?"

Clarendon looked up, tried to smile, and then let his head drop again.

"Flames," Hayes said, "what did that monster do to him?"

"A favor, apparently," Rose said, looking thoughtfully at the small man. Then he shook his head. "This is about his lost love and nothing more. He was not misused any more than the rest of us—not last night, at least."

"Let him be now," Kehler said mildly, not opening his eyes.

Hayes sat up painfully. "What . . . what exactly happened? I have only the vaguest memory."

"I was just telling Mr. Kehler that Eldrich used the arts to be sure Anna had not left any form of enchantment upon us. He was also very interested in our memories of the chamber. But for the terror of it, I think we are unharmed."

Hayes nodded, closing his eyes. Yes, the fear was not easily forgotten.

"And why is it that you have so clear a memory of what happened, Deacon?"

"Because I offered no resistance, Mr. Hayes, and had I known what would be done to us, I would have cautioned you to do the same. You cannot resist a mage. But you did not do it by choice, I'm sure, but out of fear, and that is only natural. The arts are frightening and the mages even more so."

Hayes pressed his hands to the sides of his head, trying to stop the throbbing. "Blood and flames, I have never felt so battered. What will become of us now?"

Rose shook his head. "I cannot say. The mage was not pleased by our efforts. The fact that we found no bodies bothered him immeasurably. Though it would likely have bothered him more had we found the others and not Anna. It is probable that the current swept them away or down into some pool with an undertow, or lodged them under overhanging rocks. But still . . ."

"Still?"

"The mage did not seem convinced. He still suspects that Anna is alive; Anna, and perhaps Erasmus as well. Only poor Pryor has been forgotten entirely." Rose made a sign to Farrelle.

Truncated paragraphs of memory were coming back to Hayes—flashes of scenes, suddenly illuminated as though by lightning. "I will say, Lord Eldrich did not seem overwhelmed with regret at the death of Erasmus," he said.

Rose nodded at this.

"An insignificant loss to be rid of his enemy, wouldn't you say, Deacon?" It was Kehler, still with them, though he appeared to be nearer the state of Clarendon.

Rose glanced over at Kehler, his look pained. "Like all of you, Mr. Kehler, I came to esteem Mr. Flattery greatly. He was a man of substance and incisive intellect. I had begun to think of him, almost, as a man from another age. A better time when men were honorable and principled in ways that many today are not. It might be true that Eldrich does not mourn the loss of his former protegé, but that is not true of me. I mourn him, far more than you will believe, I'm sure."

Hayes rose from the bed and made his way to the window, where the pale light of morning illuminated the world. He looked down into the empty garden, which dripped still from the storm. "I guess an escape is not to be contemplated?"

"Only if you can outrun a wolf—and an unnatural one at that."

Hayes cringed at the thought. Kehler had come and stood beside him, and they both stared out into the dreary morning. Kehler looked like a man who had lost all desire to continue, as though his encounter with the mage had overwhelmed him entirely.

Hayes searched desperately for something to say. "What . . . what can we do for Randall?" he whispered after a moment, "for there is no one other than us to tend him." It was a clumsy attempt, he realized, but Kehler no longer cared for his own well-being so Hayes hoped to interest him in another.

Kehler turned to look at Clarendon, and this seemed to effect him somehow. He drew himself up a little. "I don't know. For the moment I think we should let him mourn, for it is a natural thing for men to do. But if this state of catatonia persists—Well, the man must eat and drink. We can't let him lay down and die. He must go on, as we did in the cave. We bore each other up then, and we will do it again."

"Yes," Hayes said, "as long as we never give in all at the same time."

Walky knew all the signs; the pale sheen on the face, the sunken eyes, the lassitude. Eldrich had gone searching in the vision world again, searching for Anna, searching to know if she lived and, if so, how she could be found.

The mage sprawled in a chair, his eyes half closed, the dawn light making him look even more ghostly and ill. "We must let Clarendon go with the others, Walky," the mage said.

Walky felt his heart sink a little.

"Is there no other course, sir?" He did not need to say that Clarendon carried the knowledge of the chamber—the ritual to open the gates.

"If she runs, Walky, we will never find her. She must try to make herself a mage, perhaps even open the gate."

"If she lives, sir, or did you see her in your dream?"

"No, but she could be hidden from me." He raised a hand, then let it fall back weakly. "Let us imagine that she is still alive. Put yourself in her place. What would you do, Walky?"

"I would find a place to live quietly, most likely in Doom, and wait. . . ."

"Until I am dead—you can say it, Walky. It's not as if I am unaware."

"That is what I would do, sir."

Eldrich closed his eyes, and for a moment Walky thought he slept. "But you have the wisdom of your years, Walky. Anna is young and impetuous, and though, no doubt, she believes she has learned patience, she does not yet know the meaning of the word. No, I think she will not be as wise as you. But it would help if she could be panicked. Frightened into believing she had no other course. Do you think she understands what was written in the chamber?"

"Perhaps in time she will, sir. It is not easily understood."

"Yes, that is likely so." Eldrich shifted his position, his eyes still closed, as though the faint light pained them. "Let us hope she has no record of what Landor wrote. None of the notes the others took survived their near-drowning. Only Clarendon appears to have the knowledge."

Walky stood quietly waiting for his master to speak again. The mage shifted in his chair again, as though in discomfort. "I will send out this priest and the others once more. And Bryce must make contact with his minion in the government. I will not give up this search, Walky. Perhaps it is madness searching for someone who is dead, but we cannot afford to make a mistake. Teller's people hid themselves so long—they have ways of doing this that even I don't understand. Foolish of me to not have questioned Halsey more thoroughly. The search must continue. Unless there is a sign. Bring the priest and the others to me in three hours."

Walky remained where he stood, waiting to be released. Unlike the countess, his patience was nearly infinite: he would quite literally wait all day and feel no resentment.

*He is the last of his kind,* Walky thought, *the final chapter of a story that is to be lost forever.* Even now, while one still lived, men were less and less inclined to believe the stories of the mages and their powers—but Walky knew the truth.

"Is she to be trusted, Walky?" Eldrich asked softly.

"This woman, sir?"

"The countess, Walky. She is from a decadent class. Has had no purpose in life but to please herself. Everything has been given to her. Everything. What will she do when I am gone?"

"It is not my place to say, but, for my money, she is a person of substance. A woman who would have the courage to take the difficult way if it were necessary, sir."

"Yes, I believe she would make her way through difficulty. But there will be some hard decisions, Walky. Decisions where some must make sacrifices. I fear she could not bear that burden."

Walky nodded. "That is not impossible, sir. She has a . . . a good heart."

"And I do not?"

Walky knew this game. Would he tell the truth or resort to a small lie, knowing the mage could detect lies. "Yours has a hardened shell, sir."

The mage nodded, the trace of a smile appearing. "That will be all, Walky," the mage said quietly, his breathing suddenly deep and regular.

The servant waited a moment, watching over his master, observing the troubled sleep. He heard him mutter in the secret tongue, yet there was nothing he could do to bring him peace.

Walky slipped out of the room. Almost as silent as a mage.

## ⤳ Thirty-Six

*Dusk upon the harvest field*
*Gilded stooks afire,*
*Aflame the shivering sky.*
*Clouds bubble up, burning,*
*And night,*
*The terrible night,*
*Is upon us.*

*—Ansel Bead, "Harvest"*

The countess gazed at the portrait, wondering what it was that so unsettled her. At a glance it was a flattering likeness, for Eldrich had a presence like no other, and all of that was there. The mystery, the brooding silence, the irony which verged on cruelty, the complete disinterest. But there was something else as well.

Sadness, certainly, though this did not begin to describe it—the right word eluded her. But even this was not what she found unsettling. She leaned a bit closer, narrowing her eyes.

*Eyes.*

Yes, whatever it was resided in the eyes. Dark, almost black, beneath heavy brows. A bit too sunken to be really attractive, though Eldrich's eyes had a way of unsettling her. It was likely the disinterest. The coldness. As well as the feeling that he looked through her. She might as well have been naked before that gaze, for it stripped her bare every time.

The countess shivered.

*Fear.*

No, it couldn't be that. He was Eldrich, the last mage; certainly the most powerful man in the known world. What could such a man fear?

She turned the question over in her mind, and came up with the not too very remarkable answer that his fear was no different from anyone else's.

"Flames," she whispered. *Is he near to death? Could that be possible? Has it come stalking even the long-lived Eldrich?*

The words from the Book of Farrelle came to her.

*And the river into darkness shall carry you, away from this desperate world and the memories of men.*

And there had been the Paths, the golden wolf, and from there only her path continued. In his attempts to part the mist and look into the future he had discovered his own end, and it was not distant.

"Farrelle preserve him," she whispered.

Kent had seen. Even if he had not known, he had seen it all the same.

Hayes was disobeying his very clear instructions. They had been billeted, two to a room: Hayes with Clarendon, oddly, and poor Kehler with Deacon Rose. As though the youngsters needed an older stabilizing influence.

But Hayes was worried about Clarendon, who had lain down on a bed and not moved in several hours. Neither would he answer to Hayes' entreaties, nor respond to shaking, even fairly violently done.

He was also concerned about Kehler left alone with the priest. Holding up his candle, he stared into the gloom of the hallway, searching for wolf-sized shadows. But no shadows moved. He hoped Kehler was in the next room along, and was relieved to see the faintest glow beneath the door.

Afraid of discovery, he did not knock, but only pressed the door open, looking in. "What in . . . ?"

He stared into the dim room, lit by a single candle, thinking that he looked into a land of wonder. A tiny carriage pulled by miniature horses, a castle barely taller than he . . .

"I hope, for your sake, you are not a robber," came a lovely female voice.

Hayes searched for the source, but could only tell that it came from a shadowed area by the window.

"No. No, I am a guest."

"Then you will not mind telling me the name of your host," she said quickly, though if she thought him a robber she did not seem the least frightened.

"Lord Eldrich."

"Come in then, and close the door; the beast is afoot."

Hayes did as he was told, and quickly.

"It is proper to tell a lady your name. . . ."

"Samual Hayes, ma'am."

"A pleasure, Mr. Hayes. I am the Countess of Chilton."

Hayes was sure she heard his indrawn breath. Could it really be? "The pleasure is mine, Lady Chilton."

"And what brings you to be a guest in the house of Eldrich, if I am not prying?"

His eyes were adjusting a little, and he could see her shape dimly now, sitting in the window, touched by starlight.

"Bad luck and even worse judgment, I'm afraid."

He could see her head nod. "The common reasons, I see." She turned to look out into the night as a small bird flitted before the window, nearly hovering there. She reached out her hand, and the bird darted away. "I will tell you, wandering around this house at night does not suggest that your judgment's improving."

Hayes felt a little chagrin at this slight mockery from such a woman. "I—I was looking for a friend. I thought this was his room. You see, I am worried about Clarendon."

"Randall Clarendon? A very small man?"

"The very one."

She rose, her movements full of grace. "Take me to him."

"Ma'am?"

"Take me to him." Then she paused. "He knows a friend of mine of whom I seek news, but then maybe you do yourself. Erasmus Flattery?"

Erasmus knew the Countess of Chilton? "I knew him, Lady Chilton."

He saw her reach out a hand to the window frame, and a long silence ensued, Hayes unsure what to say.

"What has befallen Mr. Clarendon?" the countess asked in a near whisper.

"Despair, I fear. It is a long story, and one which he might not wish repeated—not that his part was anything less than honorable. . . ."

"Of course. Let me see him, Mr. Hayes. Perhaps I can make myself useful in this small way at least, and then you can tell me what befell Erasmus."

Hayes opened the door, gazing out again, the countess close behind. He could feel her presence, like a source of heat. They slipped quietly out into the hallway, and through the door to Clarendon.

The little man still lay upon his bed, as though he had not moved at all.

The countess stopped and stared down at him with great solemnity. It was the first time Hayes could really see her, and he thought no description he'd heard did the woman justice. Thick, dark hair and perfect brow, her manner pensive and unbearably sad. There was nothing he would not do to comfort her, to take away the sadness—and they had barely met. The power of the attraction shocked him.

"It is not natural, Mr. Hayes," she said.

"What Eldrich has done to him?"

"No, what are you feeling. I was bespelled, or my grandmother was, I don't know which, but it works upon the men around me. What you are feeling is caused by the arts, and is an illusion. I am not really so appealing. It is good to remember." She went to the bedside. "Mr. Clarendon?" she said, but he did not stir. "Sir . . . ?"

Still there was no response. She sat down beside him and gently took his hand, and leaning forward, kissed his brow tenderly.

He stirred then. "Lizzy?"

"No, Mr. Clarendon, I am sorry to disappoint you. I am Lady Chilton, I believe we met briefly. Erasmus spoke most highly of you."

Clarendon did not open his eyes but was like a man half-roused from the deepest sleep. "Erasmus. . . . Gone, you know."

"So I have been told. May he find peace beyond this life."

Clarendon nodded, stretching a little, then settling back as though he would sleep again.

"Mr. Clarendon? That is a dream you return to. A pleasant dream, I have no doubt. A dream in which the dead live again, perhaps, but a dream nonetheless and everything that happens there is illusory. Illusion, Mr. Clarendon, no different from that which Eldrich perpetuates when it suits him." She lifted up his hand and touched it with her lips. "There are those in this world who rely upon you, who care for you. Come back, Mr. Clarendon, you will find the long sleep soon enough."

Randall opened his eyes and sighed. "Why does everyone wish to see me suffer, even you, lady?"

"No one wants to see you suffer. Certainly I have no such wish. Many, I think, would sacrifice much to see you free of pain. Mr. Hayes was willing to brave Eldrich's wolf out of concern for you, and few would risk that, I will assure you. No, your suffering brings pain to all who care for you. You have lost someone, it seems, other than Mr. Flattery?"

Clarendon nodded, looking up at this vision with wonder. "Lizzy," he breathed.

"Will you tell me about her, or would you rather not?"

"She was my guardian," he said, "my guardian angel . . . before Eldrich found us."

Hayes saw the countess shut her eyes tightly at the mention of the mage, but then she glanced up at him, and toward the door. Hayes took up his candle and went out into the fearful hallway, hoping he would find Kehler's door before the wolf found him.

Hayes returned later to find Clarendon tucked into bed and sleeping peacefully, not lying insensible, as he had been. For a moment he stood there, struggling with himself, and then went out, and into the peculiar room where he had first found the countess.

"Is that Mr. Hayes?"

"It is, Lady Chilton."

"I have been expecting you."

"Ma'am?"

"It is the enchantment, Mr. Hayes—I fear it makes men rather predictable. Most men, at least."

"Shall I leave you in peace?"

He heard her sigh. She was perched in the window where he had first seen her, the single candle burned down to a stub.

"No, come in," she said, her voice tired. "You promised to tell me a story, if it is not too . . . distressing for you."

"It is not a story to lift one's heart, that's certain," he said. "But it deserves to be known, all the same."

Hayes found a seat in the window, setting his candles atop the tiny carriage where they cast their light upon the countess. He was a little flattered that she awaited him, here, even if just to learn what had befallen Erasmus.

"I looked in on Clarendon just now," Hayes said. "I think you performed something of a miracle. He was sleeping peacefully."

"Let us hope that he wakes feeling so, though I think it will be some time before your friend finds peace." She pulled up her knees, encircling them with her arms as though she were still a young girl, not yet trained in proper ladylike deportment. "Mr. Clarendon says you found no bodies?"

Hayes shook his head.

She fixed her lovely eyes on him. "Do you think Erasmus is dead, Mr. Hayes?"

"I . . . I fear that he is, Lady Chilton." Hayes could not bear the sadness in her gaze and looked down. "Anna would, no doubt, have hidden herself had she survived, but there was no reason for Erasmus to do so, or our guide, for that matter. No, I fear they all perished and were swept away. If you had seen the waters there, you would likely think the same. I'm sure it is challenge enough to stay afloat in calm waters, let alone fast-running rivers with whirlpools and rapids and falls. I don't think anyone could have survived. Though it was the measure of Erasmus that he dove in after young Pryor without hesitation, for Pryor was no one dear to him."

The countess nodded. "I did not know Erasmus at all well, but I feel the loss all the same. I am gratified to learn that he did not falter when it came to saving another, even at great risk. I—I had wondered. . . ." She looked up at him again. "Had you known Erasmus long?"

"All my life," Hayes answered, "or nearly so."

"How was that?"

And Hayes began to tell the story of his association with Erasmus, the fall of his family's fortunes, and his "chance" meeting with Erasmus in the brothel. It took some time to tell, for Hayes held back nothing, not even his own fears and humiliations, and if he enlarged the parts played by Erasmus and Clarendon—well, it seemed to be what the countess needed to hear, and one did not wish to disappoint the Countess of Chilton.

She listened raptly, and the complete focus of her attention flattered him immeasurably.

When he finally finished his tale, the countess shook her head. "He is completely without heart, isn't he?" she said bitterly.

"Eldrich, ma'am?" Hayes lowered his voice. "I think that is being too generous."

"But it is a wondrous tale, isn't it?" she said, as though trying to pass beyond her anger toward Eldrich.

"Yes, I certainly never expected to see such things in my lifetime. It is like an old tale, from the distant past, all of it larger than life. I suppose no one will believe it in years to come."

"I don't suppose, though it is not likely anyone will ever know of it or the parts played by Erasmus and yourself, Mr. Hayes."

"My part has been small and largely accidental, I think."

"And I think you are being too modest, though it hardly matters. No one will know; Eldrich will see to that. He is secretive—strangely so, in fact." She turned and opened the window slightly, staring out at the rain and struggling storm. "Do you know, for the first time in my life I have begun to see the use of diaries. I had always thought them the most foolish vanity—the desire by the eminently unremarkable to be remembered. But now I am less sure. What else illuminates our passing through this world? We spend all our lives collecting memories, accumulating experience and some sliver of wisdom—and to what end? So that it all might be surrendered in our dotage, when memories are lost. One by one, the treasured experiences of our lives, gone. Is it not tragic, Mr. Hayes, that we lose everything in the end? I have seen great men reduced to the state of animals, unable to speak, to feed themselves. And the people who cared for them treated them with such disregard! It was shameful. As though they had not left their mark upon society—upon the world, in some cases.

"The vast majority of people born are too quickly forgotten, Mr. Hayes. And so we keep journals, hoping at least to remain in people's memories a little longer. A vain and foolish endeavor, perhaps, but completely understandable, I think. Don't you?"

Hayes nodded. "I had never thought much about it. I only know that I have never kept a diary beyond three entries, myself."

"Yes, but you suffer the illusion of youth, Mr. Hayes, if you will excuse me for saying so. You believe life is long, when it is absurdly brief—brief and shadowed by anonymity."

Hayes thought he caught a glimpse of a slim form in an upper window, but could not be sure. He smiled at his own reaction. Had not the countess said it was an enchantment that caused this response among men? She had said it so seriously that he had been half inclined to believe her. Whatever the cause, he now knew why men made complete fools of themselves over her.

An evening of conversation, and he was ready to do battle for her himself.

*Steady on, now,* he thought. *She certainly gave you no indication that there would even be a continued acquaintance.*

Despite that, the world did not seem such a bad place that morning. Not in the least bad. Even his continued servitude to Eldrich did not seem such a terrible burden.

Hayes glanced over at Clarendon, and this deflated him a little. Randall had not met anyone's gaze all morning, but busied himself about his horse, lifting each of its feet and cleaning the hooves with a hook.

Hayes should have looked as melancholy as poor Clarendon, for they were being sent to do the mage's bidding still. After all his hope of having escaped Eldrich . . . Apparently the mage did not believe Anna dead, for they were to seek her again, along the coast this time. It seemed Eldrich's greatest fear was that she would find a boat to take her to the island of Farrow.

Hayes glanced over at Kehler, whose mood was so downcast and black that the others were reticent to speak with him. In such a temper Kehler looked as though he had aged substantially in recent weeks: the lines on his face cut deeper, his hair appeared more silvered in the morning sun.

*Yes,* Hayes thought, *this is what comes of meddling in matters that were none of our business. We knew Eldrich might have an interest in what the church kept hidden in their archive.*

Knowing one had acted the fool did not help. Hayes was also vaguely worried about money, of which he had none, and now that Erasmus was gone he did not know where it was to come from. Certainly this expedition would cost a pretty penny. He let go a long sigh—nothing could aggravate him for long that day, and surely he had more important things to worry about. Someone would pay, even if Kehler could not: Deacon Rose or Clarendon both had ample resources.

He put a foot in the stirrup and swung up onto his horse, the poor beast hardly more recovered from their flight through the hills than Hayes was himself. He had never fully recuperated from their ordeal in the cave and felt constant fatigue, as though he had aged and would never recover—and despite the cause, missing much of a night's sleep had not helped.

Bryce stood in the door of the house watching their preparations—a darkly precise and intimidating man, and not just because he was the mage's servant. Hayes could not wait to be out of the man's sight, and away from this dreadful place.

Rose was on his horse, waiting. There would be no carriage for the priest this day. Hayes felt some satisfaction at this. Eldrich had shown so little regard for the priest and his church that even Hayes had been taken aback. The Farrellite church was a force around the Entide Sea, though one would not have thought so the way Eldrich had dealt with its emissary.

They all were mounted now, Kehler and Hayes taking the leads for their baggage horses. No one seemed ready to lead, so Hayes spurred his horse forward, glancing back once at the window.

"Kehler!" he hissed. "Look back. At the upper window." But when he turned again, the figure was gone.

"What was it?"

"I could have sworn it was Skye. I . . ." Hayes shook his head. Perhaps it had been a trick of light, silvering the head of one of the servants. What would Skye be doing here? What in the world had the Countess of Chilton been doing? He had neglected to ask, so delighted had he been to find himself in such company.

Riding out the lane to the road, Hayes wondered if his memories would disappear as he crossed some invisible line back into the natural world, for certainly he had been in a dream world since he arrived—nightmare and dream.

But they emerged onto the road and began, once again, the descent from the Caledon Hills, and Kehler found he could remember every word of his conversation with the countess. After the terror of Eldrich, her company had seemed like an elixir.

"Perhaps I am dreaming," he muttered.

"You look rather chipper this morning, Hayes," Kehler said, his mood lightening perceptibly. "Has the escape from the house of Eldrich caused such relief?"

"That and a night of fair dreams. Do you not feel some sense of relief that we have escaped that terrible place no more harmed than we are?"

Kehler inclined his head to one side. He was making an effort to sound his usual self. "Perhaps a little, though I would feel better if we were not still doing the will of the mage. And I, for one, have had nothing but nightmares since our meeting with Eldrich."

Hayes saw his friend shiver.

"I know; it was terrifying. For hours afterward I felt . . . as though . . . I cannot describe it. Do you know what I mean? It gave me the crawls to think that we had magic performed upon us. Eah! I can barely think of it."

Kehler nodded. "Yes, better we had never met Lord Skye and started on this whole terrible business."

"I will tell you, Kehler. It is odd, but I have begun to pine for my grotty rooms in Paradise Street, wax nostalgic for my days of poverty."

This brought a genuine smile to Kehler's anxious face. "Ah, yes. If only we could be impoverished again. . . . Wouldn't that be grand? Flames, I miss the cramps from lack of nourishment."

"And dodging creditors. Remember what fun we had!"

"Ah, yes, those splendid creditors, capital fellows. If only we could be poor again, how happy we'd be!" Kehler slapped a pocket. "Speaking of poverty, I haven't a sou, have you?"

"Not a coin of any denomination."

"Well then, our wish has been granted. HOORAY, WE'RE PAUPERS!" he shouted, causing Rose and Clarendon to look back at them, mystified.

The two friends laughed.

"I think we are a bit barmy from having escaped Eldrich," Kehler said, "though I shan't soon forget the fright of it."

"You might be wrong, there. I was told that Eldrich seldom lets those who serve him go with their memories intact."

"Who told you that?"

The countess had told him, but she had also asked him not to mention their meeting to anyone else. He did not know why but he was not prepared to break his word to the Countess of Chilton. "Well . . . Erasmus, I think."

Kehler looked at him quizzically.

"Is this another fool's errand?" Hayes asked quickly. "Is there any possibility that Anna is alive?"

Kehler looked out over the vista that had just opened up, the lowlands adrift in mist. "I would have said no, but if Eldrich has doubts—who can argue with a mage? All we can do is search, and hope this will be the last time El-drich calls upon us." He continued to stare at the distant lands. "Hayes? I'm dreadfully sorry for dragging you into all of this."

Hayes felt a smile light his face; he couldn't help it. "Oh, don't start again. I hold no grudges." He laughed.

Kehler stared at him intently. "You are odd today. Is there something you know that I don't?"

"Only that we are away from the house of Eldrich, and, who knows, per-haps it is all a dream. Perhaps we will wake and find we never left Avonel at all."

"You mean you'll still be poor? What a pleasant thought, Hayes."

## ᗡ Thirty-Seven

An ancient fishing boat acted as the ferry, its owner more ancient still. A life at the sea had weathered his features until they were not unlike the distant cliffs Erasmus could see looking out over the currently passive channel.

Anna leaned against the rail beside him, gazing off toward the island, her mood thoughtful and silent.

Across the twilit deck a few islanders gathered, speaking quietly among themselves, casting the odd questioning glance at the "come-from-aways." Their interest unsettled Erasmus, but Anna seemed unconcerned—though at the moment nothing in her immediate vicinity seemed to draw her atten-tion. Clearly, her thoughts were elsewhere.

Catspaws rippled over the slick surface of the sea, and the captain played these with skill and concentration, determined to get his passengers into har-bor that night.

Anna touched Erasmus' arm softly, and nodded toward the island. "There, do you see?" she said, keeping her voice low. "Among the trees?"

"With the slate roof?" Erasmus asked.

"Yes. Our honeymoon cottage, Mr. Townsend."

They were playing at being newlyweds, thinking this would explain to the neighbors why they sought privacy—and perhaps even allow them a little of it—though Anna said the islanders kept much to themselves. She had also taken some care to turn them out in modest fashion; they might be gentlefolk but not of the wealthy variety.

Fishing wherries rounded the tip of the island, sails barely bellied in the soft airs, their motion slow as though tired from their day's labor. The sky behind was awash in the deep hues of twilight, and a crescent moon hooked itself to the heavens. The stillness was absolute, broken only by the whispers of the passengers, who, respectfully, did not speak aloud.

It was entirely dark when they finally made their landing on the island. Erasmus borrowed a fisherman's handcart and wheeled their few belongings up the starlit lane to Anna's house, where they were half an hour lighting lamps and opening shutters to let the soft air of evening in and the mustiness out.

Anna gave him a tour of the house, which upon inspection was not so small. It had, Erasmus thought, a certain rustic appeal, and he felt comfortable there immediately.

"I spent a year of my girlhood here, though I was hardly allowed the luxury of a childhood. Our situation was too serious for that. But even so, this is the house I think of as my childhood home. Odd, really when there were so many, and some quite a bit more civilized, but the magic of this place—and I am speaking here of the commonplace variety—was something I never forgot."

"But where did you come from? How did they find you?"

"Halsey had his ways, I suppose, but he was a secretive man and would not say. I was an orphan, you know. I fancy my mother was a doxy, likely barely more than a girl herself. It is the common thing. But I exhibited some manifestations of talent early, and Halsey found me and brought me here. There was an old nurse who lived in the house then, a kindly woman who, though not fully a member of Halsey's little band, was an adherent in some way." Anna led him into a small room with a view out over the water toward the mainland. "She mothered me, as much as I was mothered. This was my sleeping chamber," she said, turning in a circle.

It was not particularly girlish in its adornments, Erasmus noted, just as one might expect of a girl whose guardian was an old man.

"Wait until you see the view in the morning. I loved it even as a child, for it is . . . everything a view of the sea should be, and perhaps a little more." She turned to Erasmus, putting her arms around his neck and gazing at him with very liquid eyes.

"I am only beginning to know you, Erasmus Flattery, and many of your looks are still a mystery to me. Are you anxious, Erasmus, or is it something else? Do you regret running off with me?"

"Regret, no, not in the least. But I find it difficult to believe it can be this simple to hide from Eldrich. To me, it seems we should be father away: Entonne, at least, and even more distant would be better. It isn't four days' journey from this place to Eldrich's estates. Too close. Too close by many leagues."

"Precisely. Would people not expect us to run, to get as far away as possible? Do you know there was a criminal haven in Avonel for years all but directly opposite the night watch's station? The best place to hide is where you are least expected—beneath the night watch's nose, or in the village nearest

Eldrich's home. Do you realize how long followers of Teller hid within the church? Over three centuries!"

"Yes," Erasmus said, "but they were caught and burned, let us not forget."

"But Eldrich will not last the decade, Erasmus." Her arms had fallen to her sides, and she looked vulnerable standing in the center of this austere room. "Surely we can stay hidden that long. I will tell you a secret of this way of living, Erasmus: one might as well surrender to Eldrich as spend every moment in fear of apprehension. You develop the habits that keep you safe and then put it from your mind, otherwise it will drive you to madness. Believe me, our people learned much of this. You divide your life in two, very distinctly in two, and live your public life like everyone else. Otherwise you will arouse suspicion. You must acquire the proper habits and then learn to live as though nothing in your life were out of the ordinary.

"Almost no one visits this island, so to the locals you must be cordial, otherwise they will begin to talk. They will understand our desire to keep to ourselves, for we are gentlefolk and they are not, but if you begin to act though you fear discovery, in a twinkle the speculation will begin. We are criminals, we are adulterers run off from our families. It will go on and on.

"I will spread the rumor that you have been ill and have come here to recover, and work on a book of . . . natural philosophy? No, that is too much like the real you. Poetry, perhaps. You needn't worry, no one will ask to read it." She smiled at him, cajoling. "Trust me, Erasmus, and I will be your teacher in this, for I have been hiding from Eldrich all my days."

Erasmus did not want to point out that Eldrich had trapped and almost murdered her once.

"Tomorrow I will go out to purchase what we need and you can stay here— to rest and recover from your illness. I will put forth our story—or let them draw it from me, bit by bit. By tomorrow evening everyone on the island will think they know our business, and we will be quickly forgotten.

"Do not forget; Erasmus Flattery and Anna Fielding died tragically of misadventure. There is no reason for anyone to be seeking us. The notable Erasmus Flattery is dead. His family will hold services for him within a fortnight, and your many accomplishments will grow in everyone's mind until you are a genius of the rank of Skye. Already I wish I'd known you."

She gave him a gentle shake. "It was a jest. You should laugh politely."

Erasmus could not laugh. "I never believed I'd be free of him, not even if he died, for who could know what task I might be left? I still cannot quite believe it. Free of Eldrich? It is as likely as having an amputated limb grow back. You cannot know how I have been haunted by him—since I was ten years old. Haunted by my time in his house, wondering what my purpose was, why I had been taken there. Eldrich has hovered at the back of my mind all this time, like a terrible shadow. I am not quite sure how to make that shadow go away, how to banish it."

Anna pressed him down into a chair, perching on the arm.

"It will take time. Do not expect it to go away overnight. The mages haunted the followers of Teller for centuries. We learned to practice vigilance without living in constant fear. Fear of discovery will gnaw away at you, Erasmus, if you let it. Be on your guard." She went to the window and cast it open, looking out over the dark, still waters that bled into the shadowed land, the shoreline indistinguishable. "The mages hoarded their power with great care over the ages. They never numbered more than eleven at one time, and commonly there were fewer—nine, often; as few as six, occasionally—and now there is only one. One mage to hold the power, to complete the final tasks."

"And what are the final tasks?"

She glanced at him over her shoulder, then turned back to the open window. "To leave no person or text that could seed a rebirth of the arts . . . and perhaps other things as well."

"But what of me?" Erasmus said. "I have some knowledge of the arts—" But he stopped, the answer to his question obvious.

"Yes," Anna said softly. "He trapped you in the cave with the rest of us. Deacon Rose, who is the church's authority on the arts—the man who is tainted that the others may remain pure—young Hayes and Kehler. Even Clarendon, I suspect, is not without some knowledge. Banks, myself . . ." she drew a breath, "and all my brothers." She reached out and put a hand on either side of the frame. "Imagine the skill it took to manipulate events so that we should all converge in that one place. One must stand in awe. But you, Erasmus, you thwarted him and discovered the way out. Pray that he thinks we are dead. That he completes his task, leaving us behind—and that he trains no other to stand vigil."

This thought had occurred to Erasmus as well. "Would it not make sense for him to do that?"

"He will do it only out of utter necessity. It is a danger, leaving someone with knowledge of the arts. That person might be the one who maintains them so that the arts might one day be known to others. Others who have no allegiance to the original mages."

"Then I will pray that he thinks we are dead, though to what gods I would appeal I don't know, for I am a child of reason."

He could just see her jaw move—a smile. "You are a child of magic, Erasmus." She shook her head. "How can one be a man of reason when raised in the house of a mage? Our kind are capable of such contradictions. Are there not empiricists who remain within the church, though the church condemns many of the beliefs of these same men of reason?"

"Yes, though I have never thought of myself as being like them." He shrugged.

She turned to him, leaning back against the window ledge, half-sitting. "Have you ever wondered if you're dead?" she asked earnestly. "I mean really dead, not merely conveniently dead, as we are. Perhaps when we die, we slip into a dream and our life continues on with us blissfully unaware. And that is what has happened. We died in the cave or in the gorge, or a hundred other points in our lives where we might have perished. And this is a dream."

"Mine or yours?" Erasmus asked.

"Mine, of course," she smiled. "But do you know what I mean? Has this only occurred to me?"

"No, in fact I have thought similar things myself. After all, we don't know what happens after we pass through—and this is as sensible as many of the explanations that have been offered. Perhaps this is death, and life is what comes after."

"You mock me, Erasmus Flattery," she said, wagging a finger at him.

"Not really. It is not impossible that we are truly dead, and not just conveniently so, as you have said." He gestured to the room. "Then this is the house of the dead, and that makes me, madam, a necrophile."

This made her laugh, and she took two steps, landing softly in his lap. He could feel her smile as they kissed.

"And that, sir," she laughed, "was the kiss of death."

## ᕲ Thirty-Eight

She found Skye in the garden in the early morning. He lounged on a bench set for privacy behind a screen of lilac trees. As she appeared, he started, then quickly rose to his feet.

"Lord Skye," she said, noting that he did not smile or look pleased to see her in any way. Why was this one man so immune to her charms? "I have wondered why we have not met."

"I have been cautioned to avoid you," he said. No greeting, nor did he make a leg.

This brought her up abruptly, but as she blocked the only exit from this small arbor, they stood there awkwardly. Certainly Skye would have fled if he could.

"The mage said this?" she asked, looking for anything to fill the silence.

"No, it was Mr. Walky."

"Oh, well, Walky. Take no notice of him. Please, sit. I'm sure a few words cannot do any harm." She tried to smile as though nothing were in the least amiss or even out of the ordinary, but all she could think about was why he had been cautioned to avoid her.

"You accompanied my friend, Marianne Edden, I collect?" she said when it became obvious that Skye would not speak. He perched on the edge of the seat and kept glancing up at the entry to the arbor as though expecting the mage to appear there out of thin air—which Eldrich actually seemed to do at times. She stole a quick glance, too, and then chastised herself for it.

"Was it the Peliers?" she asked quietly. "Is that what drew the attention of the mage?"

Skye shrugged, a little helplessly. "As astonishing as it is to me, Lady Chilton, I seem to have been an object of interest to Lord Eldrich for some time. I am not sure how long. He seems to know even of my distant past—the time lost to me. I—I cannot explain it. I have long been part of a design. . . ." Again he raised his shoulders in a gesture of complete mystification.

The countess reached out and gently touched the arm he had slung across the back of the bench. "Yes. It is shocking to discover such things. I found it a little hard to accept that I had met the mage on more than one occasion and had no memory of it. It was most disconcerting. But here we are. I had thought I might never see you again."

Skye nodded, forcing a tight smile.

"Has Eldrich told you of your past, then? It must be a relief to finally uncover—"

"He will say nothing," Skye broke in quickly. "Not a word. It would seem to take so little effort for him to relieve me of this suffering, yet he will not." He shook his head, anger and terrible disappointment appearing on his face. "What are we but the result of the lives we've lived, and if some part of a life is lost—then we are not whole. Part of us has been severed. That is what I think. But Eldrich would tell me not a thing."

The countess was not much surprised to hear this. "It is not his way to make such gestures to others, to show compassion for no reason. He is more likely to keep such information in the event that it will prove useful. Perhaps there is yet some task he wishes performed and nothing will insure your utter devotion to its success more than dangling the possibility of your memories before you. He is not compassionate as we understand the word," she said sympathetically.

She wondered how it was that his prematurely gray hair seemed to make him look younger than his actual years. Was it the contrast between the gray mane and the almost unlined face?

Skye looked down at the bench. "No, he is not compassionate, but then neither was I when in a position where it would have taken little effort on my behalf. Perhaps I am reaping the rewards of my own callousness. Perhaps the mage is teaching me this lesson."

"Oh, do not think that! No, Lord Skye, trust that Eldrich cares almost nothing for how you have conducted your own affairs. No, the concerns of men are of little consequence to him, for he considers himself above 'petty morality.'"

Skye nodded. "Yes, I suppose you're right. It just seems so odd. I was brought here by this man Bryce, spoke once with Eldrich, and then have been largely ignored. I am going a little mad with no one to speak with. One begins to have the strangest thoughts when there are no others about and one is thrown back entirely on one's own company." He looked up, apologetically. "I must sound a bit pathetic. Do excuse me, it's just . . ."

"Do not apologize. This is the most irregular household in the world, I'm sure. Left here entirely on one's own, kept in the dark as to what transpires and what the mage's intentions are: it wears on one's nerves. I have found it myself. Fortunately, I have had others to speak with, and Walky has become something of a friend."

"Yes, he seems the only spark of humanity in the entire place, present company excepted, of course. Why are you here, Lady Chilton, if I may ask?"

She glanced over at the entry, then at the lilac trees. "Well, it is difficult to explain. The truth is, I am not entirely sure myself."

"Then you are here against your will?"

"No. No, I am here . . . well, let us just say that the mage has a task for me, and that he was able to offer me something to insure my cooperation."

"Ah."

For an instant she thought he would ask what, but then he remembered his manners, even under the circumstances, which the countess thought so strange as to almost call for a rewriting of the rules of conduct.

They fell silent, the countess wondering what she should say next, acutely aware that Skye wanted nothing so much as to escape.

"The mage said absolutely nothing that would indicate what purpose he had for you?" she said when he seemed about to rise.

He shook his silver mane. "No. Well, I have mulled over the little he did say so often that the few words have taken on every possible meaning—and therefore have become meaningless. I don't know. He wanted to know about a woman I met once briefly. Beyond that, he warned me that I might not be so happy to have my memories restored, as though there were something in my past that . . ." He shrugged. "I have even wondered if this was said merely to torment me. Mages are not above tormenting cruelly, or so I understand. Is that possible, do you think?"

"Possible, though not likely. Not unless you did something to raise his ire. He does have a cruel streak that can come out at such times. I have begun to think that he is like a man who, at intervals, suffers some terrible agony, and when one of these bouts is upon him, he loses all patience and can become vicious. Knowing when he is suffering, that is the key. So far I have not been able to tell."

"But surely Eldrich cannot suffer from illness or injury. He is a mage."

"No, I said only that he was *like* a man suffering pain. Though I think the truth is even more strange. I believe he suffers fits of despair. Despair that he will fail in the task he has been left. I cannot even tell you why I think this. I have been told my intuition is good." She glanced at Skye. "Though occasionally it fails me spectacularly."

Again the awkward silence, Skye looking at the entry, perched on the edge of his seat. The countess could see that he was vastly relieved to have someone to speak with but was also terrified of discovery.

Skye suddenly sat back on the bench, slumping against the back, his face collapsing in a like manner. The look he fixed on her was one of desperate appeal. "Have you any idea why I am being kept here? Any idea at all?"

She shook her head, somewhat devastated that she could not give him an answer, still hoping to please him, she realized, to win him over, despite all. "No, I haven't, I'm sorry to say." Then she brightened. "But perhaps I could find out. I could certainly ask Walky: I am likely to get nothing from the mage, but Walky is sometimes surprisingly forthcoming. I could try."

Why was she making such an offer? Did she retain some feeling for this man that presently she could not find?

"I would appreciate it more than you could know," he said with feeling, his despair lifting a little with this small ray of hope.

"Lady Chilton," he said with great seriousness, "I really should not tarry. I do not want to do anything that would endanger my chances with Eldrich. Who knows. Perhaps he will answer my question yet."

She nodded, tilting her head toward the opening in the trees—releasing him. This time he did make a leg, even forcing a smile.

*Yes,* she thought, *as long as he wants something of me . . .*

Although it was really Eldrich from whom Skye wanted something this time. And as far as she could tell, the mage never granted anyone what they wanted.

## ᔐ Thirty-Nine

The ships in the harbor foundered in fog, the stars slipping into this same thin sea. As the carriage bumped over some rut in the cobbles, Captain James was thrown forward, and he reached a hand automatically for the windowsill.

One would almost think he dwelt in carriages these days, ever since he had been assigned this duty—the search for the faded woman. The one he had met . . . his mind would not provide the name of the village and the effort to dredge it up caused a peculiar uneasiness. And here he was again, rattling along the coast, pursuing another possibility.

For a sailor, Captain James was not a superstitious man, or so he held, but this duty was changing that. There was something very odd going on in the Admiralty. Everyone who was involved in the matter spoke of it in whispers. All very dark and peculiar. They sought a mistress of the King, some said, or an illegitimate daughter. But these theories were not near the mark—not for James' money. No, it was all more macabre than that. Like his inability to remember certain things. The way his mind would shy away from them, almost slide off onto some other tack, and there he would be, thinking of something else.

His hand lifted in an unconscious warding sign.

He wished to Farrelle he were not mixed up in this matter. Better a battle at sea, a battle with the chance of a clean death. He shivered at the thought of his spirit left wandering, endlessly wandering, but he feared such could be his fate if things went awry on this duty. Though not an overly religious man, he made a sign to Farrelle.

And there had been disturbing dreams, as well. Nightmares in which he spoke to a shadow—a darkly malevolent shadow. Many of the strange events that had transpired in past weeks surfaced in dreams. The men leaping from the high window in Paradise Street, but rather than floating down as they were witnessed to do, they turned into nightjars and flew off, mewling in high, thin voices. Enough to make one's skin crawl. The woman who self-murdered in Avonel Harbor floated through the sea of his dreams, as well, muttering dark imprecations. Words that he could not remember properly when he woke.

A bell echoed through the fog-bound town, which meant sunrise drew nigh, though in the world beyond the carriage there was only darkness and mist.

The carriage slowed, almost stopped, and then rolled on another twenty yards, as though the driver searched for a house number. Suddenly the rig drew to a halt, and James felt the springs flex as the driver climbed down to open the door and pull down the small steps. The man saluted smartly despite the hour.

"I believe this is your destination, Captain."

James stepped out into the damp night, brushed out his coat, and then reached back in for hat and cane. A guard, fully armed, appeared to a knock on the door and insisted James produce his warrant, which was carefully examined. They were being cautious, which he was happy to see—though a little speed at this hour would have been appreciated.

An officer appeared in the hallway, pulling his clothing into order and trying to shake himself into wakefulness. "Captain James? Lieutenant Beal. We have her upstairs." He gestured down the hall.

"You found her where?" James said as they mounted the creaking stair.

"She had procured passage from Helford on an old coaster."

James nodded, his interest increasing. Coasters didn't commonly bear passengers. There were far more comfortable methods of travel. Ideal for someone hoping not to be noticed.

"What brought her to your attention?"

"Well, she certainly fits the description, sir, though she is not quite so refined—but that could be an act. Claims her name is Ann Fairfield, which is close enough. And she cursed a sailor who was too bold with her, and he fell from the maintop and pulled his arm from its socket catching a buntline. A wonder he survived at all."

"Well, there's proof for you," James said.

"Aye," his companion agreed, missing the irony. "What has this young wench done that we're turning half the kingdom end-over searching for her?"

"It's a complicated story, Beal."

The man looked at him expectantly.

"And I'm not at liberty to tell it."

Two more guards stood outside a door, and here Beal shook out a massive ring of keys—a man who measured his importance in keys, as some did. He turned the lock, gathered a candelabra from a shelf, and gently opened the door.

James heard his breath catch, the moment was so unreal. He had been sent here to identify the woman, and the truth was that he didn't know what she looked like, precisely. *But he had been told that when he saw her, he would know.* Who had told him that? This was always the part that was difficult to remember. A dark-haired man, exceedingly well groomed. Bryce, or Price. Something like that.

"We managed her arrest strictly as ordered," Beal said quickly as he lifted the candles to afford James a view.

A young woman lay on a cot, bound hand and foot and roughly gagged. One eye was purple and swollen closed, and the rest of her face was covered by a curtain of hair—faded red hair.

James glanced at the other officer.

"We were told to descend upon her before she was aware of our intent, and not let her utter a word, sir. It went badly for her, but that's orders, sir. Is she a spy, Captain?"

James did not answer but took the candles from the man and bent down.

"Some are saying that she is some kind of witch, sir." James ignored the man, reaching out to tuck the woman's hair behind her ear—his hand trembling a little. She drew back from him as much as her bindings would allow.

No light of recognition lit in his mind. She was a stranger to him, of that he was sure.

"Poor child," James said. "Here take this." He thrust the candles at the man, and proceeded to remove the woman's gag.

"Sir! We were expressly warned not to do that. Captain James!"

"It is the wrong girl, Beal. There you go; Miss Fairfield, is it?"

She took a long gasp of breath.

"Here, let me get your hands."

"I didn't curse no sailor, sir. I—I swear it. You look a kind gentleman, sir. I'm no witch or whatever it is they t'ink." Tears began to run down the young girl's face. "I swear, sir. I'll swear it 'fore a priest. . . . I will."

"I know you're not a witch, Miss Fairfield, and His Majesty's government will compensate you for your inconvenience and injury. You can be sure of that. In fact this officer, Lieutenant Beal, is going to find you a room at the best inn this town can offer and send you on your way in comfort. Can you sit up, do you think? There's a girl."

A clamor sounded in the hallway and unfamiliar faces appeared in the door: two young men, a priest, and a brightly dressed dwarf.

"Who in this round world . . . ?" Beal took a step toward these strangers, his manner threatening.

"It's all right, Beal. I know them—or at least know of them." He turned to the door. "Is one of you Clarendon?"

"I am." The small man stepped forward, performing a graceful leg. "Randall Spencer Emanual Clarendon, at your service."

"This is not the Anna Fielding that I . . . know," James said. "I trust you concur?"

"Completely. But who has mistreated this woman so?" The dwarf glared at Beal as though the man weren't twice his size.

James stood up. "Send her on to the Admiralty in Avonel, Lieutenant, and they will see she's properly compensated. In a navy ship, mind you, not a coaster or a carriage. We don't want anything befalling her again."

Introductions were made, and without further farewell James followed the others out, leaving a mystified Beal bobbing in their wake.

There was some light in the fog as they emerged from the building.

"Well, gentlemen, it is my intent to find an inn and break my fast. As we seem to be assigned to the same duty, perhaps you would care to join me?"

The four glanced at each other, and then one of the young men—the cheerful-looking one—spoke. "I, for one, could use food, so it would be a pleasure, Captain James."

Forgoing carriages—it seemed they had all been cramped up in them for too long—they began to walk along the quay, certain to find an inn by the harbor. Within a hundred yards they were given the choice of three. They quickly settled on the most prosperous looking, and found a table commanding a view over the small harbor.

"Well, I think that makes an even dozen red-haired young women," Hayes said, "but not one our late, lamented Anna."

This gave James pause. *Late, lamented?* Certainly this must be a private jest. All James knew about these gentlemen was that they were searching for this same young woman and were to be given every assistance—up to and including the use of the navy's ships, personnel, and property.

"You know her?" James asked.

"Of course. Don't you? Isn't that why the Admiralty sent you down here?"

"Indeed it is," James agreed. "It's just that . . ." He waved his hand in a gesture of dismissal. "It is not worth discussing. Do forgive me. I have seen, I think, eight potential Annas, including this one whom we are both adding to our tally. I make that nineteen. How many women are there in Farrland with faded red hair and a slightly sallow cast?"

"I fear quite a number more," Hayes said, "though I hope they will not all be as misused as that poor girl."

"Yes, this entire matter is being pressed rather . . . vigorously."

"Well, you know the mage, Captain," Hayes said. "He cares little for the suffering of others. That poor girl might have been murdered, and he would not even take notice."

James wondered if his face had paled. *Eldrich*. . . . Obviously it could be no one else. Why had he never thought of that before? Whenever he considered this subject, his thoughts became so muddled that his head would soon begin to throb. *Eldrich!* This girl was being sought by the mage.

"And how is it you became involved in this matter, Captain?" the priest asked quietly. The man's question had no challenge in it, only polite curiosity, but he regarded James with a probing, intelligent eye.

"It is a difficult question to answer, Father, for I am not exactly sure. I seem to have trouble remembering. It was a man named Bryce or perhaps Price . . . ?" He pressed a hand to his forehead, which pained him suddenly.

The others nodded, and Samual Hayes touched his arm.

"Don't tax yourself attempting to recall, Captain James, it will only bring you suffering. The man's name, for your comfort, was Bryce. Percival Bryce."

"*Mr. Hayes,*" cautioned Clarendon.

"Mr. Hayes has offered you good advice, Captain," Deacon Rose said. "Trying to remember will gain you nothing. Better to know as little as possible. That's my counsel. And do be careful whom you take into your confidence on this matter."

"I am an officer of His Majesty's navy," James shot back, "not a gape-mouthed fool." He had not meant to speak so forthrightly, but the pain in his head made his temper flare.

The priest gave him the thinnest smile and a nod. "Of course," he said.

"It seems a bit odd to have us all gathered in one place," Kehler opined. "Would it not be more efficient to have us spread along the coast? Why on earth does it take the four of us and Captain James as well to identify the woman? Certainly one person would do."

"I think it was merely a mistake," Captain James offered, speaking softly now, the pain subsiding. "This young woman seemed very promising—she went by the name of Ann Fairfield, did you know?—and we were all summoned with the idea that someone would get here quickly, no matter what delays the others suffered."

A midshipman came quickly into the room, glanced around once, and crossed directly to their table.

"Captain James? And your companions, sir: Clarendon, Deacon Rose, Hayes, and Kehler?"

The captain nodded. What now? Another woman he must rush off to see?

"I'm to deliver this gentleman to you so that you might hear his story." The young man turned and looked back to the door where a rather unkempt Farrelite priest stood, looking somewhat abashed. At a nod from the midshipman he approached the table, though not quickly. James was oddly struck by the softness of the man's eyes, the modesty of his demeanor, as though he were not concerned about his place in the world. A glance back at the priest named Rose revealed a great contrast. There was no question in James' mind who was the true follower of Farrelle.

"And who are you, Brother?" Deacon Rose asked.

"Brother Norbert—of the Blessed Springs Monastery," he said. "In the Caledon Hills."

James exiled the midshipman to a distant corner of the room, and a chair was provided for the monk.

"Well, Brother Norbert," Rose said, "don't keep us in suspense."

"Men came searching into the hills these few days past, and dragged me from my home and my pursuits," he said, though if this were an accusation, it was stated very mildly. "They were searching for news of a young woman—Anna Fielding by name. I told them of a visitor whom I had found wandering lost, and apparently she fit the description." He looked up. "She was a woman of singular appearance—red-haired, vivacious. One might almost describe her as vivid."

James noticed the others glance at each other, a bit surprised.

"Not pale or faded?" Hayes asked.

"Not at all, sir. She had been riding beneath the sun for some days and had the color of it, but no, she was vital, even . . . vibrant. A most unusual woman."

"And what was she doing in the Caledon Hills, and what name did she offer?"

"She did not offer her name, and I did not ask. . . ."

"You didn't ask her name!?"

The priest shrugged. "No. It's only a word and seems very unimportant to me. Too much stress is placed on names, I think, which is why we brothers of the church give up our given and family names. I did not ask; she did not offer."

"She claimed to be writing a book of her journey through the hills. That is why she was visiting the out-of-the-way places. As she explained, readers would hardly be interested in localities that had been visited by half the people in the kingdom."

"And she traveled alone?"

"She did, though she had set out with a guide. A young man named Garrick Lake. He had taken a tumble off his horse and broken his neck. She was most distressed at this loss—most genuinely distressed."

"And when did you meet her, precisely? The date."

The priest considered a moment. "The morning of the twelfth."

Clarendon, who for the most part seemed unhappily quiet, interjected, "That was before the gorge, so it means little."

The others nodded.

"Did she say anything else, Brother? Did she tell you where she was going?"

"To Wicken Vale." Brother Norbert considered a moment. "In truth she said very little, especially about herself." He thought a moment more. "Though she did pose an odd question as she left. She asked, if her spirit appeared to me one day, if I would forgive her sins and help her find peace. I said that I would, and she asked, 'No matter what I had done in life?' and I said, 'Yes, no matter what you had done.'"

"Very generous of you, Brother, but you did not know what atrocities she had committed already in this life." Deacon Rose seemed to dismiss the priest from his thoughts then, looking at the others.

"But she seemed a kind, good-hearted young woman to me," Brother Norbert said mildly. "She shed tears for her guide and wondered if the rites she performed would bring him the peace of Farrelle."

"Which of course they wouldn't as she was no priest. And likely the rites that she performed would damn him for all time. You do not know whom you are dealing with, Brother. Have you anything more to tell us?"

Brother Norbert opened his mouth to speak, reconsidered, and then shook his head.

There was a tense silence following Rose's berating of the kindly priest, and then Clarendon spoke.

"Has her spirit appeared to you, Brother?" he asked, his voice quiet and serious.

Brother Norbert looked at the small man in some surprise. "It has not."

Clarendon nodded at this news. Saying nothing more, he turned to his food.

## ∽ Forty

Erasmus walked among the overrun gardens, occasionally looking out across the sound to the mainland beyond. Fishing wherries and coasters heeled to the breeze, stained sails among a smattering of small, white crests.

He had left Anna poring over Halsey's writings, stepping out to get some air. There was only so much time a man could spend reading—or making love, for that matter. He was going a little stir crazy. Escape from Eldrich did not seem such a bargain at that moment. In exchange, his life had been reduced in size until it seemed bounded by the walls of the garden—an area he could encompass in a quarter hour. Too small.

"I have exchanged all the world for this," he said aloud.

He looked out to the boats under sail, sturdy, seagoing little ships, and all he could think was that perhaps one of these could carry him away—over the horizon and into the great unexplored world.

"I am being locked up in this fair prison," he said aloud.

At least he was not alone, and though Anna spent many hours in study and contemplation, she was, the rest of the time, quite attentive to him. He had even begun to wonder if her affections for him were real. Whether real or feigned, they took great, if somewhat desperate, pleasure from each other, and that was making his captivity bearable.

Anna's chough landed on the top of the stone wall that topped the cliff. It eyed him, jealously, Erasmus thought.

"*Chuff,*" it muttered in disapproval.

"There you are," Anna's voice came to him, and he turned to find her brushing aside the branches of a laburnum. Although she carried Halsey's book and looked the part of a dutiful scholar, she favored him with a kiss that was anything but dutiful.

She held him at arm's length, gazing at him closely. "You are prowling about like an animal in a cage, Erasmus. I have begun to feel as though I have locked you up here, and against your will, too."

"It is . . . an adjustment. The world seems to have shrunk to this two acres, and I have not yet become used to it."

"You need to find some endeavor to occupy your mind. I know I have said this before, but can you not pursue your interests here? There is an old glass house that we could put into repair. Certainly horticulture can be studied as easily here as in Locfal?"

Erasmus disentangled himself from her and they both perched on the low, stone wall. "For some reason these things don't seem to draw my interest at the moment. Perhaps in time . . ."

"Well, you could assist me. I will try to propagate the king's blood. I will have need of it in the future."

This elicited an uncomfortable silence from Erasmus.

"It can't be helped, Erasmus, I am becoming habituated even now. You cannot imagine the agonies of giving it up. It is even said that it has never been done." She gazed at him intently, worried by his response.

Suddenly Anna offered him her hand. "Come with me," she said simply, and led him off through the garden and out a wooden gate set into the wall.

"Where are you leading me?" Erasmus asked.

"Astray, my dear Erasmus. You will see."

They followed a path that wound up the wooded hill behind the enclosed gardens.

"Whose lands are these?"

"Mine. Ours, now. Perhaps forty acres, or thereabouts."

They continued to climb, stopping to rest once, for it was not really so long since their ordeal in the cave and flight through the Caledon Hills, and neither of them had yet fully recovered.

Finally they came up onto a narrow, natural bench cut into the hillside. This sloped up gradually into a dense thicket of holly and gorse. They made their way slowly, leaving bits of hair and skin and clothing behind on the many thorns.

"I hope this is a vista worth the blood," Erasmus complained.

Anna laughed but said nothing, leaving Erasmus to wonder. Finally they burst through the thicket and found a stand of mature trees, evenly spaced, on a kind of natural terrace. A small spring spilled from the rocky bluff behind, and with the sun filtering through the leaves, it was a place of great charm indeed.

Erasmus turned to look out toward the mainland, but the view was almost entirely hidden by the branches of trees. He began to go forward, thinking to quench his thirst, but Anna restrained him with a hand. She seemed very solemn, suddenly.

"Before you go forward, you must first perform this short rite." And she made a motion with her hand, chanting a string of Darian.

"A *nance*," Erasmus said, realizing what he saw. It was akin to the ruin on Farrow, though made up of natural elements. Instead of columns, seven trees; two chestnuts, a pair of hawthorns, two silverleaf oaks, and a single black walnut. The trees were arranged in a half-circle radiating out from the rock wall, each tree opposite its mate, the black walnut opposite the wall.

Erasmus copied Anna's ablutions, and moved into the center of the trees, their boles standing straight, the many branches reaching up, supporting a green roof.

"You did not tell me of this," Erasmus said.

Anna shook her head. "No." She whispered as though they were in a place of worship.

"Is this a gate as well? Like Landor's Gate and the Ruin on Farrow?"

"No, it is a memorial. The gates are ancient sites, used in ages past. This is no older than the trees you see. In truth, it is more like the field outside Compton Heath. A Stranger appeared here once. My people traced it most carefully. She came into our world on this very spot, some two hundred years past." Anna put her arm out straight. "And along this line lie Compton Heath, Kilty's Keep, and the ruin of Tremont Abbey." She gestured in the opposite direction. "And far out to sea, Farrow sits, though it might not lie on this same fault—this line of power. You are standing at a place where the worlds meet, Erasmus Flattery. Or at least met in the past. On that day the earth trembled, and a great storm appeared to sweep down out of the sky. The worlds intersected here, and a Stranger appeared: an elderly woman. She did not live long—a year or two—but long enough to prove something that had been in doubt for a thousand years. The other worlds, the worlds of ancient stories, existed, and they could still be reached."

Conversation ceased, and they both remained very still, listening to the mumbling spring, and the breeze sighing through the trees.

Erasmus thought of Clarendon and his story—of seeing a man and woman disappear under moving stars—worlds intersecting. He was coming to believe it himself.

"You have never told me what you learned in the field outside Compton Heath," Erasmus said.

She crouched down with her back against a tree. "I could feel the world turning," she said. "And then I saw the heavens."

"In broad daylight?"

She nodded. "Yes. But there were no constellations I recognized."

Erasmus turned to her, surprised. "What does it mean?"

"That Eldrich has long planned to escape this world. It is why he is so desperate to complete his task. The worlds are drawing closer, aligning in some way, and there will be a chance to open the gate between—perhaps the last chance for centuries, perhaps forever."

Erasmus crouched in the center of the *nance* so that he could look directly into her eyes.

"What do you hope to do, Anna? What do you truly hope?"

She considered this a moment, biting her lip gently. "To live, Erasmus. That is the only purpose for both our lives now. To live, for surely Eldrich will destroy us if he can."

Erasmus asked the question that had weighed upon him ever since he had woken in the gorge and found Anna was his savior. "But what of this vision of the mages? This cataclysm? If we escape Eldrich, will we bring this catastrophe upon man?"

She shook her head. "I don't know the answer to this. I do know that the mages were not of one mind regarding it, as perhaps I have said. The more powerful mages overruled their fellows. Certainly Halsey was never able to see this alleged vision of the apocalypse. But in all honesty, Erasmus, I cannot say what will happen. Perhaps even Eldrich is not sure."

"But he does not seek our death for his own amusement. . . ."

"No, he does not, but that does not mean his reasons are right. What have we done to deserve such an end?" She looked suddenly as if tears would come, but she turned and looked away, her jaw tight. "He could offer a truce. I would listen to reason. I am the only follower of Teller left in this world, and I renounce his aims. Let Eldrich convince me, and I will renounce the arts. Do you think the mage could be convinced to do that?"

Erasmus did not need to consider this. He shook his head quickly. "No. He will seek your death—and mine. Eldrich treats with no one."

Anna met his eye. "No one but another mage—"

The question must have been clear on Erasmus' face.

"There was this stricture among the mages. They could not take the life of another mage. It was more than a law, it was a curse, and a mage's curse is a deadly thing. There was one moment in the ritual which created the mage when the emerging mage could be killed, but beyond that they were immune to any threats from their fellows."

Anna met his eyes with a gaze of great intensity. "He cannot harm you, Erasmus, if you undergo the transformation—if you become a mage."

## ⌒ Forty-One

"If I didn't know it was impossible, I would swear that he'd played a joke on us." Eldrich shook his head and continued to stare at the canvas. Walky stood a pace back, tilting his head to one side.

"Do I intrude?" the countess asked, for neither had acknowledged her, not that the mage made a practice of doing so. She wondered if the edge of ice was noticeable in her voice.

Eldrich glanced up at her and then at Walky. He looked annoyed, and the countess was not quite certain if it was with her unexpected arrival.

"No," Eldrich said. "Indeed; perhaps you can make something of this painting for us." His attention slid back to the canvas.

She came around the easel, taut with anger which appeared to go completely unnoticed by the mage. The story that Hayes had told her—Erasmus' story would not leave her in peace.

*He used children! One of whom was set aflame to fulfill his ends. Set aflame!*

Walky made a hasty bow, not nearly so insensitive as his master.

"By your leave," the little man whispered. The door closed behind his retreating form just as the countess' gaze came to rest on the painting.

She felt her balance give way oddly beneath her, and her anger toward Eldrich evaporated. "Is—is it a Pelier?"

The mage shook his head, apparently unaware of her reaction. "No. It is an Averil Kent, though painted under an enchantment that I hoped would allow him to imitate Pelier in more than just style. But what in this round world does it mean? That is the question."

Mean, indeed. The countess braced herself mentally, the same disturbing feelings that the Pelier had engendered coming over her. The painting was of a storm, or so it seemed; leaves and broken branches and detritus from the forest floor all airborne and awhirl. Rain, in streaks and torrents, spun on this same dervish wind. She could almost taste it, feel the breath taken from her, the leaves and dirt forced into her mouth and lungs. It was unbearable.

For a moment she shut her eyes, but the painting did not disappear, and in her mind's eye she could see figures in the maelstrom.

Her eyes flicked open. Yes, there they were—a woman and a man. And was that a white blossom in her hand, or merely something carried by in the torrent? The man braced himself against the wind, reaching out a hand to his companion. The countess could not tell if the woman had hold of the man's hand or not, but both of them looked as though they would be swept away at any moment.

The motion in the painting was astonishing, manic. The clothes of the figures billowed and swirled, almost seeming to move as you looked, which she could only bear to do for a few seconds at a time.

"Kent did this? A prophetic painting?"

The mage nodded, his attention on the canvas.

The countess gestured at the figures. "Who . . . ? Who are they?" she asked, her words seeming to spin away on a wind.

Eldrich shook his head. "That is what we were discussing. The woman would seem to be you." He reached out his hand, pointing a long finger. "Do you see this? The dark area? Your curls, I think. Though, if you tilt your head, they seem to be nothing but burned leaves and shadow afloat on the wind." He tilted his head experimentally. "The man is another question. Walky believes it is Kent, though I am not so sure. I think I see something of Erasmus in the stance, the silhouette, but who can be sure? See this, however." He gestured again. "That is the top of a column and a broken lintel. Like the Ruin of Farrow, though Walky believes that is mere wishful thinking. Do you see?"

"Yes. That is a column, I am sure. And it is carved with some . . . I don't know. Shapes that I cannot identify. Yet see this corner of sky! Kent told me that Pelier was unsurpassed in his treatment of cloud and sky, but look at this! I think Pelier has a rival, after all."

The mage cast an odd glance at her.

"Look closely at this woman. You have gazed into a looking glass—is it the Countess of Chilton?"

She tried to focus on the figure, but the more she tried to concentrate, the more the figure seemed to disintegrate. To see it at all she had to look away slightly and place the figure at the edge of her vision, as though it were not real but made up of the windborne leaves and detritus. "I don't know. The truth is that others always see you most clearly. What does Walky think?"

"He is not sure," the mage said, an edge of despair in his voice. "Perhaps it is you."

"But what do the other elements mean? Is that not a king's blood blossom in the woman's hand? And the column—These things must have meaning."

"Must they?" Eldrich stared at the painting, his usual unreadable countenance observably sad. He turned and walked away a few paces, then returned his attention for a moment. He sighed and threw himself down in a chair.

"I think Kent's price was too high, for he gave me nothing in return."

"Then the portraits meant nothing?"

The mage glanced up at her, raising an eyebrow. "No, they might yet have their use. We shall see."

His peevishness seemed to drain away from him as he sprawled in the chair, and suddenly he seemed fragile and tired, his dark, unsettling eyes sunken. For a moment he laid his head back and closed his eyes.

The countess felt her anger return as she looked at him, sprawled rudely in a chair, concerned only with the world of Eldrich. "Not everyone you use performs as you would like, do they? Perhaps, after all, coercion is less effective than willing participation."

His mouth turned down, as though he grimaced in pain.

"I have neither the time nor temperament to win people over," he said. "My task is more crucial than that."

"Nor do you have the respect for others that it would require."

He opened his eyes and regarded her almost coolly. She felt herself step back, but checked herself there.

"And what, pray tell, is all this? Have I offended your delicate sensibilities in some way?" He raised his eyebrows, the mockery appearing.

She felt her own anger boil up. "You would have offended the 'sensibilities' of every civilized person, if they only knew what you did."

He tilted his head slightly, the eyebrows arching up again.

She could not bear the mockery a moment more. The smugness drove her to fury. "You used children—*children!*—on this sacred quest of yours! How could you set an innocent child afire, and leave another to bear the guilt of it all his years? It is . . . *unspeakable.* It is the act of a monster. A despicable, heartless monster! And you look to me for comfort? You who feel no remorse. How could you prey upon children? How could you?" She drew a ragged breath, fingernails tearing the flesh of her palms because her fists were so tight.

Eldrich continued to stare at her, apparently unaffected by the outburst—as though he were mildly interested in the behavior of some animal.

"How could I?" he said, the mockery strong in his tone. "It was not difficult. I am a monster, after all. A man who surrendered his heart to become a mage." His gaze was suddenly not so disinterested. "How could I expect understanding from you—a spoiled child of a decadent class. You have never made a hard decision in your life. After all, what color gown you choose to wear is hardly earthshaking. Do not go on to me about what a monster I am. I would sacrifice a thousand children to accomplish my task. I would sacrifice you and every member of your inbred class, and they would be no more able to understand it than you. Now leave me in peace."

She stood appalled by his declaration, sure that it was not exaggeration. He would do it, and more. For a second she stood her ground, but then saw the futility of it and left with as much dignity as she could manage, as though she had hardly been wounded at all.

She perched on the miniature throne in the playroom surrounded by the landscape of a pampered childhood—a room outside of time. Twilight cast soft shadows across the floor and walls, imbuing the room with melancholy, though she could not say why.

It was here that Hayes had told her Erasmus' story—his time with the mage and what had happened. How Percy had been engulfed in flame—the screams Erasmus heard in his dreams even as an adult. If she closed her eyes, she could see the child burning. . . .

"I cannot be what he asks," she whispered.

Since her argument with Eldrich, she had felt a peculiar lassitude. What would she do now? Go back to her old life, all memories of this strange chapter of her days gone? Go back to worrying what color gown to wear to a ball? His words had cut her more deeply than she liked to admit.

"I have led a frivolous life," she said. Yet somehow it had brought her here.

*Perhaps I cannot leave,* she thought. *I am bound to fulfill my part of the bargain, though what that will entail is still far from clear.*

She looked around the room, the carriage and its rocking-horse team journeying endlessly toward make-believe. Reminders of the childhood that was stolen from Erasmus and his companion, Percy.

It was true that Eldrich had his childhood stolen as well, and had been subjected to the random cruelties of Lucklow. . . .

She shook her head. It did not matter. Generals did not send children of ten to fight their battles.

*"One does not judge a mage by the laws of men, anymore than one would judge a falcon by the ways of a sparrow."* Walky's words came back to her. *"He has duties and trusts that we can barely comprehend."* But did he? What, beyond this obsession to erase all knowledge of the arts, all real memory of their practice? *"You must understand this one truth of mages, m'lady. He cannot afford the luxury of humanity. His duties are too grave for that. It is a calling that one pursues at great price. One surrenders one's heart to become a mage."*

In this, at least, Eldrich had been more than successful.

Across the room a movement caught her eye.

*Who has found their way in here?* she wondered.

A shadow moved, and the countess froze. The wolf?

But, no, it was something else; a small phantom of starlight and darkness—a child . . . and then a second.

The countess heard her own indrawn breath.

They stood near the tiny coach, a boy and girl, difficult to discern, but certainly there. And they looked about as though lost, clinging to each other's hand, their moonlight-eyes wide and filled with sorrow.

"The children for whom this shrine was made," a musical voice said softly.

The countess started. Eldrich stood a few feet away.

"But what are they?" she asked, overwhelmed with an inexplicable desire to have peace between them, and unsettled by these spirits appearing before her.

"Ghosts, you would call them. Spirits of the dead children."

She looked around the room and realized this was what had disturbed her all along. The room was a shrine, not a museum. The children were dead.

"How old?" she whispered.

"Three and seven," he said softly.

"Why do they appear now?"

"They often appear when I am near. They are drawn to my talent for the arts. It is surprising you have not seen them yourself before now."

The countess watched the two children wander among the treasures of their childhood, forever unable to touch them. "They look so . . . *lost*."

"They seek a way back to life," Eldrich said, "but there is no path that can take them there."

"So they will wander here always?"

"Always? No, but for many lifetimes."

The countess could not take her eyes from these apparitions. She felt a tear tremble on her lashes. "How unbearably sad."

"Yes, but I can release them," he said softly. "Would you have me do so?"

She glanced over at him, but the mage did not look her way.

"What would become of them?"

She saw his stooped figure shrug. "What becomes of anyone?"

A silence.

"They suffer," Eldrich whispered. "Can you feel it?"

She nodded. Yes, they suffered, but it was not oblivion they sought.

"I will release them from that suffering if you will say but a word."

"Why is this choice mine?"

"Because you believe such decisions are easily made. What will you have me do?"

Nearer the children came, and though they were drawn to Eldrich, to his power, their eyes could not find him.

"I will leave you to consider," he said and was gone into shadow. She heard the door latch tick.

And before her the children were distraught. They felt him go, all their futile hopes disappearing with him. And then they sensed her, as though she were a lesser light that they had not noticed. They came toward her, mothlike, hands outstretched and groping. She backed away in horror, and still they sought her. A moment more and she fled the room, scattering a shelf of poppets as she went.

## ⌒ Forty-Two

The ringing of bells sounded from all points of the compass. Samual Hayes and Fenwick Kehler stared out into the darkness where occasional sails would slip by, ghostlike in the fog.

"It is the Lochwinnie fishing fleet, or so I heard someone say."

Hayes nodded. A slight breeze moved their ship over a calm sea, and though a fog surrounded them, overhead the stars shone clear among the sails.

Kehler nodded his head toward a solitary figure who stood farther along the rail: Brother Norbert.

"Why in the world did Rose force the man to accompany us? I'm sure this will be nothing but another 'false Anna.'"

"Well, clearly, to see if Anna's spirit does appear to him."

They both laughed, and tried to cover it up.

"Do you know, Hayes, I believe the stains on his robes are from birds!"

Hayes laughed softly. "I'm quite sure they are. He told me that his monastery houses mostly swallows now, and he is merely tolerated by them. 'I am the one making my home in their eaves,' is how he put it. For all his eccentricities he is a good-hearted soul. If all of Farrelle's priests were like Brother Norbert, I think I might respect the church more."

An odd, vaguely human sound bubbled up from the water, surprising both Kehler and Hayes. Something bobbed in the fog.

"*Martyr's balls . . .*" Kehler whispered.

The object, barely visible, was long and thin with an uplifted round end. The sound of soft laughter emanated from it.

Then Hayes chuckled. "It is a gull on a log. A laughing gull, so called, or so I would guess."

They watched the apparition, so like a drowned man, float past, and then Kehler nudged his friend. "Look at our mystic."

Brother Norbert was leaning well out over the rail, his eyes wide, straining to see through the mist.

"Perhaps that was really Anna, but our unschooled senses could not perceive it," Hayes offered.

Brother Norbert turned to them then, his eyes no longer wide, face collapsed into grief. Both Kehler and Hayes went quickly down the deck to him.

"Did you see?" he rasped, barely able to find a voice.

"A log ridden by a gull," Hayes said.

The priest shook his head, half-collapsed against the rail. Kehler took the man by the arm to bear him up.

"No, 'twas a man." Brother Norbert was sobbing softly. "A drowned man, young and fair. Crying for his brother lost, swept down to the sea, to the breathing, shoreless sea."

"Pryor?" Hayes said, incredulous. It was no apparition, just a gull on a log. He had seen it clearly himself, as had Kehler.

"What a tragic end for one so young," Norbert said, "what a terrible thing—caught up in matters beyond him, with people whose concerns were far greater than his own. The concerns of the world." He fell down upon his knees, bent over like a man in agony. "May he find peace," he said, and made a sign to Farrelle. He began to pray, mumbling in Old Farr.

Hayes backed away, a bit disturbed by what went on, and realized that Kehler did the same. A few paces back he came abreast of Clarendon, who stood looking on solemnly, Dusk at his side.

"Has Anna found him?" he asked softly, his voice heavy with melancholy.

"No, he has had a vision, or so I gather. It would seem to have been Pryor." Hayes gestured out toward the sea. "Yet Kehler and I saw the same thing—a laughing gull perched upon a log, half-hidden in the mist. Hardly unnatural. It seems the man's visions spring from a fertile imagination."

"But that is the nature of visions, and visionaries. What you see will be perfectly mundane, but what they see—Do not discount the vision because you did not see it, for you are not given to visions, Mr. Hayes. Nor you, Mr. Kehler. This must be why Rose insisted the man stay with us, for there was time yet for the visions to appear. If he has not seen Anna in a few days . . ."

"Then you believe this, Randall?" Kehler said.

The small man nodded, his wolfhound nuzzling at him for more attention. "Oh, I believe many strange things—have seen many strange things. After all, when I was but a boy, I saw a mage appear and take my world away. I have crawled into the very bowels of the earth in search of impetuous friends, and found the tomb of a mythical mage, perhaps even the gate to Faery, and many other things besides." He shook his head, the fringe of hair pale in the starlight. "Perhaps Anna will appear to him yet. Perhaps even Mr. Flattery."

"But what if she doesn't? What if neither of them appear?"

Clarendon shrugged. "Then I will allow myself to hope that Mr. Flattery is yet alive, for it is terrible to lose all of one's friends at once." He looked at Hayes and Kehler, meeting their eyes for the first time since his encounter with Eldrich. "You two go carefully. I could not bear to lose everyone dear to me." Saying nothing more, he turned away and disappeared into the shadow of the sails and the mist that drifted over the rail.

It was much later, the night waning, when Hayes woke and could not entice sleep's return. Finally he rose and climbed up on deck. He heard the sound of sharp tapping on the planks, and Dusk appeared, gamboling, licked his hand, then bounded back into the shadow of a sail. It was here that Hayes found Clarendon, leaning on the rail, which rose to chest height on the small man.

"Have you been awake all this night, Randall?"

Clarendon nodded.

Hayes put a hand on his shoulder. "I should not speak, Randall, for I have no experience in such matters, but even so, I cannot bear to see you waste away. It has been a very long time. Can you not give her up now?"

His words were met by silence. Hayes took his hand away, fearing that he'd caused offense.

"It is easier for you," Clarendon said softly, "you can forget. Everyone forgets—in time—even the loss of a cherished wife, a child. Memories lose their vividness, and healing begins, for part of healing is the forgetting, the softening of memories. But I forget nothing. I can see Lizzy as clearly as if she just spoke. I hear her voice—as real as yours, Mr. Hayes.

"Time wears everything away—mountains, men, and certainly the recollections of men—but my memories are the one rock that will not wear away. Time will not touch them, Mr. Hayes, I don't know why. To me, Lizzy left this morning, Mr. Flattery but ten minutes past. To heal from loss, you must forget a little, and I cannot. It is the curse Eldrich named it, and I wish it on no man.

"But do not concern yourself overly on my account, Mr. Hayes. I will not heal, but nor will I founder. No, I am made of good timber—old, gnarly oak. I shall keep myself afloat, even if Mr. Flattery could not. We owe it to him."

Dusk came up and set his chin on the rail at his master's elbow, docile, sensing the sadness. Clarendon stroked him slowly.

"Is there nothing that anyone might do, Randall?"

"Take away my memories. . . . But even Eldrich could not manage that. It is always good to have solid friends in difficult times. That is quite enough. Quite enough, Mr. Hayes. Now get some rest, if you can. I fear our road will grow more difficult before it's done."

## ᕲ Forty-Three

He lay upon cushions spread over a bench seat upon the terrace, his great wolf by him. The stars still circled westward across the sky, their nightly migration nearing an end. The pearl of dawn would soon overtake them, and then the infinite blue.

Walky stood in the door looking out into the soft night, watching his master rest from his labors. He needed to rest more now, and this small sign of mortality Walky found oddly disturbing. As though the mage were human, after all.

Lately, there were other indications as well. A softening of his master's demeanor, signs of regret over past actions. Small acts of compassion. It was the influence of the countess, Walky was certain. Even the mage wished to please her, though he would never admit it. But no, it was more than that. Her own compassion and heart forced even Eldrich to see himself anew.

Walky shook his head. She was a wonder.

The two, mage and countess, had been circling each other as warily as duelists for some days now, both seemingly unaware of it. She would not give herself to a man without a heart—he conscious of the folly of it all. A peculiar dance to watch.

"You should sleep, Walky," the musical voice said softly.

The mage's eyes were still closed, and he lay breathing evenly, like one asleep.

"Is there nothing I might do for you, m'lord?"

"Discover if this girl still lives. Tell me if my task is complete. Decide what I should do with this beguiling countess. Oh, and make me some coffee, as well."

"Will you not rest now, sir? It has been a long night."

"And it will be a longer day, yet. Coffee, Walky. I will break my fast later."

The mage pushed himself up, his wolf rising with him, joyful, as though his master had been absent. Eldrich put a hand on the beast's head, scratching absentmindedly.

"Time is running short, Walky." The mage rose to his feet, his slightly stooped carriage seeming even more pronounced. "There is much to do. This moon and the next, that is what the stars tell us. Landor's Gate has been rediscovered and Strangers walk among us. It is a propitious age, Walky, a time of wonder. But we cannot falter in our task. Not now, so near the end. But one cannot save the world without that unparalleled elixir."

"I shall fetch you seed, sir."

"I was speaking of coffee, Walky."

The servant did not smile. This did not seem the time for jests. But perhaps Eldrich had seen a vision in his sleep, a sign that all would come out right in the end. He could hope.

Walky was about to turn to go when his master spoke again.

"She thinks she can hide him from me," he said, perhaps to himself.

"Who, sir?" Walky asked, not sure if he was meant to be part of this conversation.

"Erasmus. She believes her art is deep enough, her skill great enough, but I am not so sure. I have had my sting in Erasmus Flattery all his life. Not long, perhaps, but long enough. We will see if her confidence is warranted. I will wager that Erasmus dreams of his days in the house of Eldrich. If he lives, he dreams of me yet."

The mage had spent all the long hours of light in his preparations, allowing no interruptions. Walky had seen this many times before, the mage lost in his labors, his meticulous arrangements for an enchantment. At such times he would forget to eat, sometimes for days. And his servants would creep about the house, never speaking above a whisper, and that only if absolutely necessary. These were always unsettling times, and Walky was not quite sure why.

Men were never comfortable with the arts. Even men who lived in the house of a mage. They acted upon a man at some level that could never be quite articulated, touched him like the cold caress of death—something one feared so completely that the rational mind held no hope of controlling the reaction to it. The arts were disturbing, and that was at best.

Walky set a plate of food on the edge of the worktable, reaching out to take the one left earlier, which remained untouched. The mage did not raise his head or acknowledge the old man in any way, but continued to bend over his work, completely absorbed.

Walky paused for a moment to see if there were any orders or requests. He seldom pried into his master's efforts, and the truth was that despite his years of service, he did not truly understand them. But tonight he could not help but notice a child's frock coat lying on the edge of the table, and this struck him as very odd. Certainly the objects Eldrich used in his toils could be very strange, even rare, but he had never before seen anything that belonged to a child.

And then it struck him. This sky-blue coat had belonged to Erasmus Flattery. If he closed his eyes, he could almost see it on the child as he raced across the lawn, going nowhere in particular in the headlong manner of boys.

*The coat of Erasmus Flattery.*

*May Farrelle preserve him*, the old man thought, and he slipped out the door.

## ᔕ Forty-Four

Walky woke her in the night, setting candles on a bureau near her bed. The countess thought the little man looked more distressed than she could ever imagine.

"What is it, Walky?"

"A catastrophe, m'lady. An absolute catastrophe. Erasmus is alive. Without doubt, alive!"

"What are you saying?" She sat up, sweeping her hair out of her eyes. Was she dreaming? Certainly Walky could not be distressed by that news. "Erasmus is alive! How can that be anything but good?" She felt her own heart rise at the news.

Walky shook his head, his look of distress becoming more extreme. "But he is with her, he must be. With this woman who will destroy everything my master has accomplished, and worse. You must rise with all haste. We travel within the hour. Up m'lady, please. Do not delay him this night. Do not."

And Walky was gone, almost running from the room. The countess forced herself up, the brevity of her rest causing a hollowness at her core.

"What in this round world . . . ?" She stood beside her bed in a daze. What was she to do? What would she pack? Did Eldrich still need her at all? They had not spoken since the night the mage had given her the terrible choice. Only a day, but it seemed so much longer. And she had not been able to choose. How could she?

She shook her head. Madness. There was so much that needed to be said. So much that required clarification. But what was she to do? Demand Eldrich stop and speak with her now—in the middle of crisis?

She began to pull on clothing, astonished by how often she did not seem to make clear choices but was merely swept along by currents more powerful than she. As though she were aswim in a dark river, the banks beyond sight, what lay ahead utterly unknown.

## ᴄᵌ  Forty-Five

A lamp and several candles were spread around the perimeter of the table. The haphazard nature of their arrangement told Erasmus that they were not part of some enchantment that Anna practiced but served the more mundane purpose of providing light. She bent over a large sheet of paper, unaware that he stood in the door.

Her familiar, Chuff, hopped back and forth across the surface of the table, resentful when she shooed him off the paper. Once he took the quill she used to write with in his mouth, and she was so engrossed in her work that it took a moment for her to understand why her pen no longer obeyed her will.

"Off with you," she said, chasing the bird from the table. He landed on the window ledge and vented his resentment in a single, indignant "chuff."

She turned back to her task, then realized she had seen Erasmus standing in the door and looked up, smiling wanly, her eyes rimmed in red and glistening from her efforts.

"What has you so involved you forget to eat?"

"So that is what causes this discomfort in my stomach. Did I really forget to eat?"

Erasmus nodded. It was almost midnight, and he had not seen Anna since noon.

She put down her quill carefully and covered her eyes for a moment. "Farrelle's ghost," she exclaimed.

Erasmus came and stood behind her, softly rubbing her neck and shoulders.

"Mmm. . . . Farther to the right."

Erasmus stared down at the paper covered in strange symbols and writing, all connected with the most intricate geometry.

"What is this?" he said.

"Your horoscope," she laughed. "You shall meet a tall red-headed stranger. . . ." She uncovered her eyes, staring down at her efforts. "It is a somewhat incompetent attempt to find some pattern among the appearances of Strangers. In the past three hundred years there were about a dozen fairly certain appearances, and about an equal number of disappearances. Have we spoken of these? Cases where people have vanished in odd circumstances? Halsey was certain they became the 'Strangers' of another world. So I have charted them, trying to see if there is a pattern. Halsey did much of this work, I am really only reproducing it, and rather incompetently, I fear."

"Have you added in the disappearance Clarendon witnessed?"

This caused her to pause. Erasmus could almost feel her thoughts scattering at his interruption.

"No. When was it, do you think?"

"When he was aged ten—about fifty years past, I think—but what time of year I cannot say."

"Unfortunate, but even the year will help. More importantly, though, was Eldrich's prediction of the exact hour and place where Clarendon's Lizzy disappeared. Do you see? This exercise may not be entirely in vain. Eldrich managed it, though likely he had been engaged in this endeavor for a long time." She returned her gaze to the sheet of paper. "All I have been able to conclude with any certainty is that there seems to be an increase in frequency of the appearance of Strangers, but if there is a pattern that can be discerned . . . well, I have nothing but admiration for Eldrich if he managed to find it."

"What would be the point of the exercise, Anna? Other than the great satisfaction of solving a puzzle?"

"It would tell us if the worlds converge and if Eldrich thinks he can leave this world for another, leave it by knowing where to be at what time, as Clarendon witnessed."

Erasmus stared at the paper a moment, trying to make sense of it. Could it really be Eldrich's desire to leave this world? And if so, why? Yet, if Clarendon was to be believed, the mage was interested enough to witness Lizzy's disappearance—and there was the mage who came for the Stranger of Compton Heath, who was very likely Eldrich. Erasmus was certain the mage did little out of idle curiosity.

"I would like to question one of these Strangers," Erasmus said suddenly. "Hear firsthand of these other worlds. . . ."

Anna stared at him a moment, her look penetrating though softly pensive. "Fill a lantern," she said, rising to her feet and leaving the room.

Fifteen minutes later they were on the path that ran along the cliff top back toward the small collection of houses that passed for a town on Midsummer Isle. They made their way up the main road, unseen by the islanders, for most were asleep, and it was only the odd window from which light escaped.

It was a relatively steep road, and they were soon harboring their breath, neither speaking. In half an hour they met an empty lane that ran off between rows of chestnut trees. They set out beneath the overhanging branches, and Chuff appeared suddenly to land on Anna's outstretched wrist, his manner animated, as though there were about to be some excitement of the kind that choughs approved. After a moment he winged off down the lane, disappearing into the shadows of the trees—a chough that apparently did not fear the fabric of night or the owls that dwelt within its folds.

Anna kept their pace deliberately quick to avoid conversation, avoid telling him where they went. Erasmus was well aware that there might be no actual reason for this, other than her naturally secretive nature, and the delight she took in surprising him.

Finally they came upon the ruin of an old cottage, overrun by vines, the waving branches of an ancient willow hanging down through an opening in the roof. Anna held aloft the lantern to spread the light.

"There," she pronounced, "you have never seen such a house before."

"A tumbledown cottage?"

"No, the dwelling of a Stranger, for it was here that the old woman lived for the short time she survived. Mother Green was what the local people called her, though the reason for it has been forgotten. She appeared in the place I showed you, and the local fisherfolk took her in, unable to understand a word she said. Like the Stranger of Compton Heath, they thought she had survived a ship-wreck. So provincial were they that they believed her to be from some out-of-the-way part of Doorn or even Entonne. And she came to live here, in this broken-down cottage, and had it not been for some of her writings, which were preserved, and the local legend, she would have been forgotten. One of the great wonders of the world, and she passed almost unnoticed." She shook her head.

"It was a simpler time," she said softly. "And who would have thought she could be anything more fantastic than a foreigner. Why, I'm sure that was exotic enough for the people of this island, who were never more than inshore fishermen, forgoing the deeper sea."

From a bag she carried over her shoulder, Anna removed a clay jar and pulled the stopper so that a feather of steam appeared.

"You want to see a Stranger, Erasmus," she said. "Well, here is your opportunity."

The aroma from the bottle reached him. He knew it from Anna's use, infrequent as it was. "King's blood," he said in a hushed voice though he did not know why. "Did you not warn that it was habituating?"

"I did, and for good reason, but this is diluted many times and indulging yourself once will not bring you to ruin, I think."

Erasmus hesitated, feeling the draw of it, his own curiosity. Chuff flitted out of the darkness, flapping about Anna, speaking excitedly.

"Why would I do this?"

"To see a Stranger, or the ghost of one, for she dwells here still, our good Mother Green. And who knows—the seed will produce visions for those with talent. You might see more."

Erasmus looked at the steam, which coiled out of the jar like a snake, and his nostrils flared at the stark, pungent odor. He could feel the vapor curl into him, twisting down through his lungs, spreading outward . . . touching his heart.

He turned to the fallen-down house, to the shadows within.

*Did the mage take you to his house only that you might lure this woman down into a cave and die?* The question spoke within his mind in a voice which hardly seemed his own. *But I have defied him and lived. . . . Defied Eldrich.*

Gingerly Anna held the jar out toward him, and he took it, touching it to his lips before he could reconsider. The liquid ran warm into his mouth, the aroma filling his nostrils, almost overpowering. He swallowed it down and felt the truth of it—not the vapor which barely caressed him, but the torrent which streamed hot down his throat. Almost before he lowered the jar, the world lurched, shadows taking on dimension, pressing out of the broken doors and windows as though they had gained substance. But there was movement within them now, darker shapes within the darkness.

Anna took his hand and led him forward.

They stepped into the shadow of the door that seemed to swell outward like a bubble. He felt this darkness cool upon his face. Things moved and scuttled in the corners, just beyond vision, and he heard whispers and hissing, the sounds of branches stirred by the wind.

A stair rail came to hand and Erasmus felt himself step up. A cool light glowed faintly above—moonlight or starlight. He no longer felt Anna's hand within his own, but drifted free, as though gravity had all but released him.

Up the speaking stairs, up into the loft where the branches of trees grew from the walls and roof. And there, in the corner, made of moonlight and lamentation, an old woman hunched over her needlework, rocking back and forth and singing softly to herself.

After a moment she glanced up and blinked, a look of confusion on her face.

"Who's that?" she said in an odd whisper. This was no accent of Doorn or Entonne.

"A friend," Erasmus heard himself say, and saw her cock her head as though struggling to hear.

"Wind and mice," she said, "forest and owls." She bent back to her work, rocking again, singing a different air this time.

Erasmus moved closer. He could see her unbound hair, dull silver in the moonlight. It fell like water to her waist. Whatever it was she toiled at could not be distinguished, as though she stitched something out of the threads of night.

"Who are you, child?" she whispered, not looking up. "And why have you come to haunt me? Can you not see I am poor and of no use to any?"

"I am here to learn from where you came."

She continued to stitch, unable to hear him, apparently, and then she returned to song.

*"Upon a hill, upon a cloud,*
*Upon a haystack golden.*
*Within a wood, within a lake,*
*Dwelt the lady Sollen."*

As she sang, she rose from her stool and went to the window, moving with fluid grace, almost floating, as silent in her movements as a mage. And in the light from the moon Erasmus could see that she was young, a girl of twenty, dancing before the window.

*"Above the wood, above the world,*
*Above the hidden bower.*
*Along a path upon an isle*
*She danced away the hours."*

It struck Erasmus suddenly that she was singing Darian, not Farr at all! Darian—the mage tongue.

She spun into a shadow, and her voice changed, suddenly heavy with age, creaking like old timbers bent with the weight of years. And the song ended sadly, Mother Green humming the last lines distractedly as though the words had slipped her mind. A hand appeared out of shadow, delicate and smooth, the hand of a girl touched by moonlight. The fingers seemed to extend toward him, and after an instant of hesitation, he reached out and found the hand soft and cool.

He would not allow himself to be taken into the shadow but instead drew the hand steadily, an arm appearing, then Anna, laughing.

"But was it you all along?" Erasmus said, confused.

"Not at all, it was a spirit. The ghost of Mother Green. But let us see what more might be found, for the night is filled with whispers. Do you hear?" She unstopped the jar again, and offered it to Erasmus, who took it this time without hesitation, excited by what he'd seen, by what might be revealed to him yet. Again the liquid filled him with its warmth, and he felt that sense of lifting. Rising like a cloud.

Around him walls of stone rose up toward the stars. A ruin, Erasmus was sure. A ruin of such massive scale it seemed impossible that it had been built by men. Yet time had laid waste to it so that almost nothing was recognizable—and even so it seemed familiar. As though he had been here before.

*Kilty's Keep*, he thought, though it could not be, for this *was* a ruined castle. Yet Kilty's Keep it was.

A shattered stair came underfoot, and ahead he could see ghostly moonlight. Up again, and around a corner, and there, illuminated by the moon, a single tree, the only living thing in this dead city—and it bore white blossoms, gently waving in the breeze.

Erasmus stepped forward but stumbled and fell endlessly, landing upon a surface soft and level.

Lifting his head, Erasmus found himself lying atop a cliff, the moonlit land stretching out before him, windless and still—a stark geometry of fields and hedgerows, rivers and roads. And then movement. A dark line, like a flight of crows low over a road. But then they emerged from shadow into moonlight, and Erasmus could see two carriages racing as though pursued. *And they bore no lanterns.* Nor were there drivers. They raced on by moonlight, and there, upon the high after-seat, perched a small boy, staring fixedly ahead. Erasmus as a child, wearing his favorite blue frock coat.

He scrambled up and fled into darkness.

"Erasmus?"

It was Anna. He knew her voice even if the shadow he could see did not resemble her at all.

"I saw—"

"Do not try to rise yet. Lie back and rest, Erasmus."

"*But we have no time to rest. He has seen me! He travels toward us even now.*"

"Eldrich?" Erasmus felt her stiffen. "How do you know? Did you see the mage?"

"I saw the carriage and another in flight across the countryside at night. No drivers guided them, nor were there coach lamps. Only a small boy—myself—sitting high up at the rear. But it was my—the manner of this small boy; so utterly fixated on the way ahead, so deadened of emotion. Like one given into madness and near catatonia, or a person in a trance."

He felt Anna sit back, suddenly very still. "It might mean only that he seeks us, which is hardly news. I . . . I must consider it. Was there anything more?"

"Yes. I was wandering in a massive ruined city. Ancient, I thought it was, and built to a scale that men could hardly imagine—massive. I saw the glow of moonlight and went toward it, and there, in what might have been a court-yard, grew a single small tree, white blossoms waving in the ghostly light. And I heard singing, though no music I knew. A dirge, it seemed, a requiem. What does it mean?"

"The city, I don't know. The singing? A death, certainly. The white blossoms were king's blood. The sign of the arts. Eldrich is near his time. That is what I think."

"But could it not be us? We have Landor's seed, after all."

She nodded, and rocked him gently, singing softly.

*"Above the clouds, among the stars,*
*Beyond the sacred mountain.*
*Beneath the sun, beneath the world*
*A gate lay ever open."*

## ﹏ Forty-Six

The mage traveled at a pace the countess would have thought impossible, but when drawn by horses sustained by the arts, the countryside swept past league by league. They had come down out of the hills in darkness, and followed the high road as it wound among field and wood toward the sea.

The countess slept as best she could in the swaying carriage, nearly jarred from her seat more than once, and each time she opened her eyes found Walky poised to arrest her fall, as though he never needed sleep, or could not rest while another might need his attention. The perfect servant, always.

After nearly being thrown from her seat for perhaps the tenth time, the countess tried to force herself into wakefulness. She squinted at the passing scene, sunlight and shade in rhythm as they passed down a row of evenly spaced trees.

"Have you not slept at all, Walky?"

He shook his head. "I've felt no need, m'lady," he said, though the countess thought the old man's eyes were a bit red.

*He is far older than you*, she chided herself, *and yet he sits awake seeing that you come to no harm.*

"Well, I've returned to the land of the living now, so you might rest if you've a mind to."

He smiled. "Perhaps, by and by."

She shrugged off the traveling blanket and rubbed knuckles into her eyes in a gesture that she thought terribly unladylike. She longed to stretch, but knew that would be going a bit too far.

"Where are we?"

"Just crossed the east branch of the Brandydrop River."

"My, but we are flying across Farrland! I don't think my kestrel could manage it more quickly."

Walky nodded. "When the mage has need . . ."

"Are Mr. Bryce and Lord Skye traveling with Lord Eldrich?" Since their meeting in the children's room, two nights past, she had not heard from nor spoken to Eldrich, and she wondered now what he did and what the state of his mind might be. He had very pointedly not requested her company in his carriage.

"Bryce and Skye have gone ahead to prepare Lord Skye's ship. He keeps a small vessel for his own pleasure. Did you know?"

She nodded. Skye's foibles were much discussed in Farr society, and none more than his ship. There was a saying in Farrland that a man who would go to sea for pleasure would fight a war for a holiday. Travel by sea was looked upon as particularly evil necessity.

"Mr. Walky?" the countess said, pitching her voice low, as though she might be heard above the rattle of the carriage. "Where is it we go? Is it Farrow? Is that why Skye prepares his ship?"

A bit of pain crossed Walky's face, as though it were terribly unfair of her to ask such questions of him. "We go in search of Erasmus. I know nothing more than that, m'lady."

She nodded, sitting back in her seat. She was having trouble believing that Erasmus was yet alive. The story she had heard from Clarendon and Hayes was so convincing. If he had survived the gorge, why had he not revealed himself to his companions? Had he been injured?

"Do you believe Erasmus is still alive, Walky?"

"The mage believes it, m'lady."

"But if it is true, why has he not revealed himself?"

Walky shrugged.

"Only the mage knows?" she asked, not really meaning to mock him.

But Walky looked very serious, as though he did not realize she was quoting his own much-used phrase. "Even the mage does not know everything," he said.

The countess smiled. "You should rest, Walky. Who knows when you shall have the opportunity again."

It was late night when the entourage of the mage entered Portsdown, a small port at the mouth of the Inglbrook, which was no brook at all but a broad river here where it met the sea.

They disembarked almost immediately for a ship, all of them in a longboat. The countess could see Eldrich wrapped in an old-fashioned cloak, his collar up against the dampness. Even sitting, he seemed stooped to her, bent under the weight of the impossible tasks he had been left.

She realized that she did feel a little sympathy for him. Perhaps a result of the choice he had given her—and that she had been unable to make.

How crucial were the responsibilities he had been left? Important enough that one would destroy the life of a child? It was not impossible, she thought.

A memory of being sought by the ghost children surfaced and she shivered. Their terrible, unhappy eyes, as they groped toward her, toward life. Would that she had been allowed to choose life for them. . . .

But perhaps Eldrich's choice had been no less difficult. She would likely never know, for he would not tell.

They came alongside a small ship and proceeded quickly up the boarding stair. And then, after all their hours of urgency, they were told they must await the turn of the tide, for there was not enough wind in the harbor to allow them to fight the flow.

The countess watched from a few paces away as Eldrich listened to Skye and his captain, a man who looked distinctly frightened by this apparition that had boarded his ship. Sailors, the countess knew, were superstitious by nature.

"There will be wind enough, Captain," Eldrich said, his musical voice distinctly odd here, upon the silent bay. "Indeed, there shall be all the wind you require—and more."

"But where do we travel, my lord? What course shall we set?"

Eldrich strode to the binnacle, glanced down at the compass rose, and began to chant almost beneath his breath. He drew his hand across the bronze binnacle, and the green sea fire appeared at the deck, like a glowing wreath. It spread upward slowly, until the entire binnacle was wrapped in viridescent fire.

"There," Eldrich said. "That is your course."

The captain stood back from the sea fire, frightened into silence. Eldrich spun around and went quickly below, leaving the sailors muttering among themselves, faces ashen in the fading green light.

Walky stepped forward, staring down at the glowing compass. "Due east," he said calmly, as though this were an everyday occurrence. "Captain," he said, nodding, and then followed his master below.

In the ensuing silence a small zephyr fluttered the pennant at the masthead, and then hissed across the deck like the whispering of a ghost. It began to build into a breeze. Still muttering, the sailors scrambled up the rigging, crablike against the stars, stiff with fear of who had come aboard and the ill fortune that accompanied him.

*       *       *

Her cabin was too small to pace, even if it had not been slanting at ten degrees and pitching slowly up and down. She hardly noticed how lovely the appointments of the cabin were, how unlike any ship she had heard tell of. Instead the closeness of the cabin reminded her of her situation, how trapped she truly was. Somehow the lodge in the hills had masked the truth, for she had the run of it and the grounds. But here, there was barely two square yards of cabin, and the little room felt claustrophobic.

She could almost feel Eldrich's presence, as though the heat of his body emanated through the thin bulkheads. She was sick of it. Sick of not knowing where they went, or why. Sick of rising in the night to be carried off to some unknown destination for some secret purpose. Sick of asking questions that no one would answer.

It was as though she had wakened from a sleep, or thrown off an enchantment, and the reality of her situation had struck her.

"Have I been bespelled the whole time?"

Never in her life had she so felt like hammering upon the walls, as it was said prisoners did—beating upon the walls until their fists were bloody, the bones of their hands shattered—but tonight she could have.

"This can't go on," she said firmly, taking herself in hand.

Sweeping up her cloak, she threw open her door and went looking for the companionway up to the main deck.

She emerged into a beautiful night, a near-full moon traveling into the west, the ship underway to a sailor's wind and only the most innocent of clouds abroad. The wind had the warmth of the south in it and ran its fingers through her dark curls in a most gentle manner.

She felt all of her pent-up frustration was suddenly illusory. The vast horizon spoke of a world without boundaries—world without end—and the magic of the night promised nothing but possibilities. She traveled with a mage, after all, the last of his kind, and magic enveloped them like the breeze. Anything might happen. Anything at all.

*I am going mad*, she thought. *One moment I'm ready to strike out and swim for shore—anything to escape—and then I feel I am truly blessed to be here. The most fortunate woman in Farrland.*

"Lady Chilton . . ."

"Lord Skye. I thought there would be no one awake."

Skye nodded. "I have suffered the insomnia ever since I can remember. I think it is my dreams, they are so disturbing. . . ."

In the weak light of the ship's lanterns he appeared pale, his face drawn—as a man might who had wakened from nightmare into a situation hardly less strange.

"These are dreams of your lost past?"

He nodded. "But like so many dreams, when I awake, they are just beyond my grasp. But even so they are more numerous since I have come to the house of Eldrich, more numerous and even more unsettling. As though they were more vivid and even closer to the surface, yet still I cannot reach them. I do not mean to press you, Lady Chilton, but you mentioned that you might speak to Lord Eldrich about my request."

Yes, he always wanted something of her—and almost invariably she offered it, though it was never what other men wanted. "And I must confess I have not, Lord Skye, for which I apologize. It is not that I have forgotten or been remiss in any way. The opportunity has not presented itself, and if truth be known, I think I am hardly in the mage's favor at the moment."

Skye nodded stiffly, the sadness that her words caused hardly masked.

"Well, there is little hope that the mage would grant my wish, for as he made abundantly clear, I have nothing to offer in return. One cannot make a deal with a devil unless one has a soul to offer. I, apparently, do not." He nodded off in the direction the ship traveled. "Where do we go now, do you know?"

The countess shook her head. "Farrow, I assume."

"But those are the lights of a village in the distance," Skye said. "We are sailing up the coast, not out to sea."

The countess was mildly surprised, but then why would she believe she could predict the actions of the mage?

"Then I cannot say where we go."

"Or why, I take it?"

She shook her head.

"What is it, Lady Chilton, that you do with Walky in all these hours you spend together?"

The question, and the way it was phrased, was so discourteous that she felt her face begin to flush with anger. But no sooner did the emotion rise then it seemed to have been carried away on the breeze. Like so many other things, the common politeness of Farr society was of no consequence in the house of a mage—who had little concern for such niceties himself.

"I study the arts of the mages, Lord Skye," she said, watching his face. But he was neither as surprised as she expected nor as she'd hoped.

"Then perhaps I will not need the cooperation of Eldrich."

"I can assure you," she said quickly, "that I have so little skill in these matters that I would not even know how to begin to recover what you have lost. I'm sorry, but do not look to me, Lord Skye. I have barely begun to learn even the language of the mages." She met his eye. "And I have not the slightest understanding of what use the mage will put my paltry learning to."

Skye nodded, his hope, however slight, fading.

They fell silent a moment, the breeze whispering around them, laden with the vowels of the sea and the silent language of human misunderstanding.

"Skye?"

It was the voice of Eldrich, and it startled the earl.

Skye backed away reflexively, and without even a nod to the countess, hurried below. She heard his boots scurrying down the companionway stairs.

Eldrich wore his old-fashioned cloak wrapped about him like a shadow. Unlike Skye, his boots made no sound as he came and stood beside the countess at the rail.

He said nothing for a moment, and the countess began to wonder if he had no more purpose than frightening Skye away.

"Why do you torture Lord Skye?" she said impulsively. "He will do anything to have his memories returned."

"Skye? He has brought evil enough into this world without his memories. Do not waste your compassion on Skye, Lady Chilton. He is the scourge, the outrider of destruction. I would never have let him walk abroad if I'd not needed him to find my enemies. It is a strange irony, and a tragic one. No, Skye shall not have his memories. If I were as heartless as people think, I would murder him this night." Eldrich's voice actually sounded overwhelmed by fatigue, something she had not thought possible. Where was the music now?

"He does not seem evil," she said.

He glanced at her, skeptically she thought. "No. Men seldom do. These larger-than-life, madly evil characters are generally the stuff of novels, I'm afraid."

The two remained a few moments in strained silence, mage and countess. She was about to curtsy and excuse herself, for it seemed that Eldrich had nothing to say to her, or if he had, would not say it. But then he broke the silence, his voice nearly a whisper.

"We have bargained once, Lady Chilton," Eldrich said, his voice flat and strained, "but it seems we must do so again. What will it take to have you fulfill your part?"

The countess reached out a hand to the rail, steadying herself. Eldrich was making an offer of peace. It was unheard of. Her thoughts were suddenly awhirl, and she tried to force order upon them, not wanting this moment of advantage to go to waste. "If Erasmus is alive, what will you do with him?"

Eldrich considered for a moment. "He aids my enemy," he said.

"I would have you spare him," the countess said quickly, thinking of the poor child Eldrich had so cruelly used. "Release both Erasmus and Bryce."

"Bryce can never be free," Eldrich said quickly.

"But he was harmed even more than Erasmus. Will you not spare both the children you have injured?"

"Do not concern yourself with Bryce," Eldrich said firmly. "He is another matter entirely."

"But he was a child, and the victim of terrible burning."

"Yes, but there will be no recovery for Percy Bryce. Even I cannot grant him that. The fire reached inside and burned him hollow; the fire of bitterness and recrimination. There is nothing left now but a shell. You see how fastidious he is? He is protecting the only thing he has—a husk. No, do not meddle in the world of Percy Bryce. It will not profit you, nor will it him. Erasmus is another matter. He betrayed me in my time of need."

"Betrayed you!" she interrupted, unable to contain herself. "You sent him down into that cavern to die! All he has done is survive—and try to escape you. You who would have murdered him! He cannot be faulted for that."

Eldrich rocked from foot to foot. She could feel him about to explode with frustration. He was not used to negotiating to get what he wanted, perhaps had never done it in his long life. "What do I care for the justice of men," he spat out, but caught himself, taking a long, slow breath. "I will consider what you ask. I can promise no more than that."

"And what will you have of me in return?" the countess asked, her voice a near-whisper.

Eldrich nodded. "Your part of the bargain."

"But you have never stated clearly what my part would be."

"Because I cannot know what will be asked of you." He turned to look at her. She could just make out the shape of his face, the dark shadows of his eyes.

"Walky will tutor you, guide you. Perhaps there will be no reason for you to do anything at all. But if the arts survive me—"

"But I know nothing of such matters! How can you give such a task to me?" She almost stamped her foot with frustration.

"Because there have been signs, portents. You will be the last Guardian of the Gate."

The words had almost no meaning to her, yet she found them chilling all the same. She wanted to beat upon his chest with her fists, demand that he speak in terms she could understand.

"What does this mean? Guardian? I have no idea to what gate you refer."

"The gate at Tremont Abbey, I believe, though perhaps it is Farrow."

She wanted to fall down upon the deck and weep. It was like falling into a madness, her time with Eldrich. Nothing was ever clear, or predictable. No day was like any other. Cause and effect seemed to have broken their alliance.

Eldrich reached out and touched her arm, disorienting her even more. He never touched her.

"Did Samual Hayes tell you about the sculpture in the cavern? The one with the emerging face?"

"Yes," she answered, barely able to find her breath.

He stared at her for a long, chilling moment. "It is you."

"But how can you know?" She heard herself almost pleading.

"Because I am a mage. You will stand vigil when I am gone, until all but the last vestiges of the arts have faded from the world. There will be no ember left that any can rekindle."

So there it was. Not unexpected, really, for he had all but said it before.

"But can you keep your part of the bargain?" he asked, stepping closer, and pitching his voice low. "Can you make the sacrifices? Sacrifices of others, if need be?"

"How can I answer when I do not understand what will be asked of me or even why this is being done?"

"But if I preserve Erasmus?"

"And what will I do in return? Murder a thousand? Send children into the conflagration? No! I need something more. If I am to pledge myself to your holy crusade, then I must know the reason. . . ."

Eldrich nodded once and turned to the rail, looking down into the sea. From within his cloak he produced a handful of shells which he tossed onto the sea, chanting words in Darian. There was a flash of silver, as porpoises broke the surface, and there, where they sounded, the water was suddenly still and gray and of infinite depth. And here something appeared, as though through mist.

The countess could see a city of ordered streets, alive beneath a warm sun. And then from a strange, high-flying bird, a seed fell, so distant it was little more than punctuation, the full stop at the end of a line.

A shattering of light staggered her. Light like the opening of the heavens, white, mysterious, infinitely powerful. And then a roiling cloud reached up, a thunderhead of dark beauty, blossoming at its height like an opening flower.

In its wake the city was gone, only a few shattered ribs of buildings sticking up as though from a mass grave.

She reeled away from the rail, from the vision in the water, the death of the city. An entire city gone in a heartbeat! Every soul in it turned to light, carried away on that terrible cloud.

"If the gates are not shut," she heard Eldrich say. "And even then such an end might find us. Even then."

## ⟿ Forty-Seven

The ship lay through the evening calm in the sound between Midsummer Isle and the Farr coast. Up on the maintop, Samual Hayes sat watching the sky fade through its paling palette toward darkness.

"First star," Kehler said, heaving himself up onto the maintop. "Make a wish."

"'Tis a planet, and therefore will not answer."

"Ah, perhaps that's why my wishes are never granted." Kehler settled himself beside his friend. He seemed slightly recovered, slightly more than Hayes remembered, as though every mile they put between themselves and Eldrich expressed itself in healing.

Hayes waved a hand toward the mainland. "I take it this little fishing village is our destination?"

"So I understand. I heard the master saying they would anchor in the 'roadstead' if they ever got wind to carry them there. Anchoring in the roadstead sounds rather like running aground to me. One should leave roads to carriages and horses, I say."

"It is a term describing an open anchorage near to the shore, and quite free of coaches and all horses but the seahorse."

Kehler laughed. "And here we have another false Anna to meet. Another innocent woman who has been set upon and gagged and is wondering if the world has gone mad?"

"Which it has. I learned something speaking with Captain James. This 'Anna,' who is not using that name, was accompanied by a gentleman, and it would appear that his description could fit Erasmus."

This silenced Kehler for a moment. "But imagine how many men would fit Erasmus' description. 'Tall, dark-haired man with rather forbidding deportment and acerbic wit.' A third of Avonel, I should think."

"Yes. That's what I thought. We'll see." He pointed. "There's a star."

They both made a silent wish, not even needing to ask what the other hoped for.

"Kehler? Could Erasmus and Anna have survived? Is it madness even to hope?"

Kehler considered for a moment. "Brother Norbert had a vision of Pryor, though unaware of the boy's existence." He paused as if to weigh what he had said, wondering if it sounded utterly foolish. "We have both seen enough strange things in the last month to make me wonder if there isn't some truth in Brother Norbert's claims. And he has yet to see a vision of Anna, or Erasmus, for that matter."

Hayes nodded. They were accepting such things as evidence now. But Kehler was right. They had both seen many peculiar things this past month. Flames, they had even met a mage!

"What if we do find Erasmus and Anna alive?"

Kehler kept his gaze fixed on the returning fishing fleet. "Anna killed Pryor's brother, at least that seems fairly sure. I would no longer be so concerned with what befell her. Let her meet Eldrich—as I have done. But Erasmus—We have received no instructions regarding Erasmus."

"I hardly think that will matter to the mage. If Erasmus betrayed him and allied himself with Anna, Eldrich will not forgive it. What do we say to the mage? 'Oh, we let Erasmus go. We were given no instructions pertaining to him.' I hardly think so. This isn't school after all. No, if we let Erasmus go, Eldrich will make us pay."

Kehler considered a moment. "Even so, I am not willing to take Erasmus back to Eldrich, and I am as much in fear of the mage as anyone." He looked at his friend, his manner very calm and sure. Since the escape from the cave, and even more so since the encounter with Eldrich, Kehler appeared to have aged. More gray hair could be seen among the dark, the wrinkles around his eyes grew more pronounced, and his skin seemed to have lost its glow of youth. He had begun to look like a spry old man, rather than the youth he was.

But then, how did one measure age? Hayes was sure that he had aged several years in these last weeks alone, and in the year before that he had thought his maturation vastly accelerated.

*At this rate I shall be ancient at thirty*, he thought.

"Why would Erasmus take up with Anna?" Kehler asked suddenly.

"Don't get ahead of yourself. I'm sure this Anna will be no more real than the others, and this Erasmus, too, for that matter." He paused to contemplate the question. What if this were Anna and Erasmus? Why *would* their friend take up with Eldrich's enemy? "Hatred of Eldrich," Hayes offered. "Or perhaps a chance to escape him. There was also the ritual Percy had left Erasmus. Self-immolation would drive me into Anna's arms, I'm quite sure."

"I dare say," Kehler said. "Remember how they kept disappearing up the stair together when we were trapped in the chamber? Banks was getting quite jealous."

"What do you imagine was taking place up there?"

Kehler smiled. "I suppose one last romance before starving to death is not out of the question, but somehow I doubt that was it. That was certainly not what was on my mind. But it seemed even then that Anna was trying to win him over, earn his trust. She was capable of augury, remember, and may have had some vision in which Erasmus played a part."

"I had not thought of that."

The ship's bell rang the hour, and as if it were a signal, a small breeze came in from the sea and bellied the sails.

"Well, it is a breeze," Kehler said, "though just. It will still be some time before we are at anchor."

"It doesn't matter. There's likely nothing we can do until morning

anyway." Hayes looked out at the rapidly appearing stars. "If we actually find Erasmus, what will Deacon Rose do?"

"I have wondered the same thing. And there is Captain James to consider. It would be better if we found Erasmus before they did." He looked out at the shore, not three miles distant. "A pity we can't swim."

The anchor was down within the hour, and the Admiralty agents were soon aboard. Hayes managed to squeeze himself into the captain's cabin to hear what they would report.

"They went over on the ferry some days past. Any number of people saw them. A vibrant-looking young woman with red hair and the bearing of a lady, and a somewhat older gentleman," the navy man reported. He stood abashedly before Captain James, smelling of spirits, for clearly he had been caught unawares by the ship's arrival. "Both were well spoken. They took up residence in a house which overlooks the sound on the cliff east of the landing. With a glass, one can just make it out from this shore."

"That's it?" Captain James said. "We have been rushed down here for that? The woman we seek is known to be faded, tired looking. Is that not so, Deacon Rose?"

"The woman Brother Norbert met was vibrant . . . 'vivid,' I believe he said."

"Yes, but was she the woman we seek?" He looked back at the Admiralty agent, who fumbled for something to say.

"Sh-she was the right age, sir, and keeping somewhat to herself. . . . It didn't seem impossible that she had recovered from whatever had ailed her, and was looking more hale."

Captain James shook his head in disgust, his mood quite black. Hayes could see how much he detested this duty, and could sympathize. The state of this agent of the Admiralty was also an offense to the captain, who was clearly consumed by duty.

"Was there anything else at all?" Deacon Rose asked mildly. "Did anyone overhear this couple's conversation? Was there something that marked them as uncommon in any way?"

The man shook his head ruefully. "Not really, Father. Oh, someone said the woman had a pet bird. Not a caged bird, sir, but one that flies free. A chough or corn crow."

Rose looked over at Captain James, and then back to the Admiralty agent. "If this turns out to be the truth, Captain James might even overlook your present state of drunkenness."

Hayes quickly found Kehler and told him what he'd learned.

"Deacon Rose thought this pet of great significance, or so I gathered."

Kehler nodded. "Yes, I can see why. It is probably nothing more than a woman who has rescued a young bird at some point, but one can never be sure."

"A familiar? Is that what you think?"

"I will wager that it's what the priest thinks. What is the plan now?"

"They will go at first light with a party of sailors. We'll not be invited, by the way. Rose convinced Captain James that it would be unfair to ask the friends of Erasmus to arrest him, if it turns out this is Erasmus."

Neither spoke for a moment.

"Kehler? The priest seemed to become very . . . *still* when he heard about this bird. As though he were hiding his excitement. Do you think it could be Erasmus and Anna?"

"I don't know but I will say again; I'm damned if I'll let Erasmus fall victim to Deacon Rose and the ire of Eldrich."

Clarendon came upon them just then.

"Your manner hardly looks suspicious," he said. "Don't huddle so, and stop whispering. That's better. Now tell me what this is all about?"

Dusk greeted them, prancing a little so that his nails clicked on the deck.

"This woman the Admiralty have found, she has a pet bird. Not a caged bird but a chough or a crow that flies free. And she is in company with a man who fits the description of Erasmus. Deacon Rose was quite taken with the thought that this woman might have a familiar."

"No doubt!" Randall said, lowering his own voice. "Is it possible that Mr. Flattery is yet alive? That he did not perish?"

Hayes and Kehler shrugged.

"We don't know, Randall, but if there is any chance that he survived the gorge, we want to warn him before he falls into the hands of Eldrich, though how we shall manage this I don't know."

Clarendon gestured toward the lanterns that appeared to drift slowly about the calm sea—boys out fishing.

"Rose and Captain James will not be pleased," Kehler said.

"When did we begin answering to them?" Clarendon asked as he leaned out over the rail. "*You, lad.* How's the fishing?"

"Not as bad as all that, sir. I've nearly hooked three."

"Nearly hooked? That will hardly provide breakfast. Would you like to make a sovereign for your night's work?"

"Indeed I would, sir!"

"Then keep your voice down and come over here, lad. And put that lantern out."

The boys, for there were two of them, were quickly alongside. Taking a look around the deck and finding the watch rather uninterested, Hayes and Kehler sent Mr. Clarendon down and then passed down Dusk, lest the beast bark and give them away. Hayes was about to slip over the side when Claren-don pushed the small boat free of the ship.

"Randall, what are you doing?"

"They will miss three of us more than one," he hissed, and had the boys back the oars. "If Erasmus is alive, Mr. Hayes, rest assured, I shall warn him." And with that, the boys bent to their oars, the boat carrying the small man away across the starlit waters.

## ∽ Forty-Eight

They were preparing to take flight again. Anna's plans to remain hidden on the island until the mage passed through were to be abandoned. Erasmus could not believe he had let himself hope that he would escape Eldrich. He found he had stopped packing their few belongings and was staring at the wall, seeing again the carriage racing across the night landscape, the entranced child upon the roof.

It might mean only that Eldrich sought them—that the mage believed Eras-mus remained alive. But it might also mean that he journeyed toward them, led somehow by his connection with Erasmus as a child.

Erasmus buckled up the case and took it down the stairs into the entry hall, where he found Anna staring hopelessly at several cases. They had thought it wise to procure the clothing and accoutrements expected of educated people—so they would not stand out—and now they were burdened with them.

"We are all packed up, but where shall we go?" Erasmus asked, putting his case with the others.

Anna raised her hands and let them drop helplessly. "I don't know. Farrow seems a danger if Eldrich does think you're alive." She shook her head, staring down rather sadly at the baggage. "Entonne, and then on to Doorn." Suddenly she looked up at him, her eyes bright. "Unless you have thought more about what I said. Eldrich cannot harm another mage. . . ."

Erasmus sat down on the second stair. "But I had hoped to end my involve-ment with the arts forever. To escape not only Eldrich, but all vestiges of El-drich, all memories."

"It is a lovely dream, Erasmus, but only a dream. Sometimes we can avoid the battle, but other times we must gather our resolve and wade in and fight it. There can be no other choice if we are to survive."

The truth of this, Erasmus knew, was becoming more and more difficult to deny.

"But you said yourself that Eldrich would have people watching Tremont

Abbey, perhaps even Farrow by now. Do we not need a place of power to perform the ritual?"

"Yes, and I believe we have one." Anna came and crouched down before him and took his hands. "You remember your vision: the seven-branched tree with white blossoms waving in the moonlight? The ritual which makes one a mage is performed at the full moon, and the tree was certainly king's blood growing. And it was seven-branched, the mages' number of power. But even more importantly, you knew the place. Kilty's Keep, you said."

"But it was and was not. It . . ." Erasmus lost his train of thought. "I don't know. It seemed to be a ruin, but somehow I knew it was not. I can't explain."

"There is no need to explain, Erasmus. It was a vision induced by king's blood. Accept the truth of it. Kilty's Keep lies on the same fault as Tremont Abbey. The same line of power. Trust what you saw and what you felt was true."

Erasmus closed his eyes and tried to recall the vision, recall the feelings he had experienced. Somehow it was Kilty's Keep even though its appearance was not quite as it should have been.

"Erasmus?" But Anna did not finish, for there was a knock at the door.

They both stiffened for a moment, and then Anna said quietly, "I rather doubt the mage would knock, and even so, once he is at our door, there is nothing left to do."

She rose quickly and went to the door, impulsively swinging it wide. And there, in the opening, stood a brightly dressed man not four feet tall.

"Randall!"

Clarendon nodded, looking a little shaken and pale.

"Are you well?" Erasmus asked as he rose from the stair.

"It's just seeing you alive, Mr. Flattery." He glanced at Anna.

Erasmus crossed the hall and embraced the little man, the two pounding each other on the back.

"Randall, how in this round world . . . ?"

"The mage is seeking you yet, Mr. Flattery. Rose and some navy men wait upon a ship across the sound. They will be here at first light, sooner if they realize I am gone."

"Blood and flames!" Erasmus glanced over at Anna, who looked no less distressed than he.

"He is telling the truth," Anna said quickly. She tore open a bag. "Take only a change of clothes. The barest of necessities."

Clarendon held up his hands. "But there is more, Mr. Flattery. Give me a moment to tell my tale."

Anna did not stop what she was doing but shifted part of her attention to the small man, nodding for him to go on.

With the door still open so that he was framed by the night, Clarendon began. "We were met by this man Bryce as we came out of the hills, and he led us to a hunting lodge on the road to Castlebough. I will not burden you with every detail, but we were taken to the mage." The small man paused here, wiping a hand across his eyes. "Taken to see the mage, and questioned closely, me most of all. I had spent some time writing out the text from the chamber—everything that had been written upon the walls, and this interested Eldrich more than anything. The mage pored over it, speaking with his servant, Walky.

"'It is beyond imagining, Walky,' he said. 'Beyond dreams. Look at this! The art of Landor, lost more than a thousand years!' He was beside himself with pleasure. He read parts of it aloud, shaking his head in wonder, as though it were the greatest work of literature ever created. He questioned me about Anna and Banks, having me repeat every word you had said about the text and the chamber—and as you know, I misremember nothing.

"'She must not have understood. Is that possible?' the mage asked. 'But she will realize in time; she must,' the servant said. And then there was some debate of whether you would have the text at all, for all the notes the others had written were destroyed by water in our escape from the cave." Clarendon looked from one to the other. "'But what will it profit her to open the way?' the servant asked. 'It will only profit her in that she can escape me,' his master said. 'But that would be to our benefit,' Walky said, but the mage only shook his head. 'If she can pass out of this world, Walky, she can return. Return after I am gone. No, the gates must be closed. Closed for all time." He pointed at the text I had so carefully preserved. 'This must die with me, Walky, as we both know." Clarendon closed his eyes for an moment. "And as it seems even the mage cannot take away my memories, I knew what that meant for me."

Erasmus looked to Anna. "Can this be true? The text was an enchantment to open the gates?"

Anna nodded. "It could be so. Banks thought it possible. It was so arcane, so complex, written in an older form of Darian, and obscure even by the standards of the mages. But if Eldrich says it is so—"

"But can it be used?" Clarendon broke in. "Used to open the way to this other world? Can you do it, Anna?"

She shrugged. "One would have to be a mage, not a near mage as I am. Could I do it, then? It would not be without risk. . . ."

"But could we not escape Eldrich thus?" Clarendon asked. He came and stood before Anna, suddenly animated.

"Randall," Erasmus said, "you have let your hopes blind you. Lizzy has been gone these fifty years. If she is alive at all, she would be very old."

"You do not understand. Eldrich will see me dead with what I know. My need to escape is as great as yours. But even if I do hold onto hope of finding Lizzy, it is not utterly foolish. Time does not run at the same pace in these other worlds—that is clear in the Tale of Tomas, and Eldrich referred to the old story himself. She might still be young, as was Tomas."

Erasmus shook his head. "It was a tale, Randall. An ancient lay."

"But based on some truth." He appealed to Anna. "Was it not?"

Anna shrugged. "We haven't time for this debate. We must fly. Find a boat and get ashore before Deacon Rose arrives."

"But fly where?" Clarendon asked. "Eldrich will catch you without doubt. Without question. And then what will we do? Throw ourselves upon his mercy?" Clarendon reached into his coat and drew out a sheaf of neatly folded papers. "But with this we might escape him. Escape him for all time."

## ∽ Forty-Nine

Deacon Rose walked around the razed house, glowering alternately at the ruin and than at Hayes and Kehler.

"You let him go, knowing full well that he would warn them?"

Neither Kehler nor Hayes answered. They had been seen the night before lowering Clarendon into the fishing boat—though the sailors on watch had no orders to interfere with civilians, and gentlemen at that.

Rose stepped gingerly into the ruin, testing the remains of the collapsed roof.

"Have a care, Deacon," James said.

Rose seemed not to hear, but went slowly on, perhaps relying on Farrelle to protect him.

In the center of the destruction he stopped and turned a slow circle, his lively eyes fixed and unwavering. He ran a hand over his cropped hair and made a sign to Farrelle.

"Were they . . . inside when it happened?" Hayes asked quietly.

Deacon Rose shook his head, his concentration not wavering.

"No," he muttered. "Better if they had been. Better for all concerned. But no, this house was burned deliberately. Burned so that they could not be followed by means of the arts. Clearly Clarendon warned them, may Farrelle damn him for it. But they are not far ahead now, and we shall catch them."

The Deacon looked up, his jaw set tight and his eye very clear. He picked his way carefully out onto the lawn, coming straight to Hayes and Kehler.

"What did you think you were doing, getting Clarendon off the ship?"

"Warning Erasmus," Kehler said, unintimidated. "If he were alive."

"Oh, he is alive, or likely so," Deacon Rose said. "Certainly Anna still lives, and who else would the gentleman be who fit the description of Erasmus? Eldrich will deal with the two of you."

Brother Norbert stood three paces behind his fellow priest, saying nothing, his face completely neutral.

"Captain James," Rose ordered, "you must put these two in confinement. They cannot be trusted." He shook his head, turning back to the ruin. "Well, we begin yet again. Anna and Erasmus Flattery have fled . . . somewhere. We must find their track. Find it and run them down." He turned back to the others.

"We must determine if they have fled by land or sea. That is our first task. Captain James, let us best detail your men to accomplish this." With a curt nod he set off across the lawn, taking Captain James and Brother Norbert in tow. Half a dozen sailors came forward to escort Hayes and Kehler, who glanced at each other. Rather than looking frightened, Kehler was red with suppressed rage. Hayes thought he might suddenly throw himself at their escort, then murder Deacon Rose with his bare hands. Hayes knew precisely what his friend felt. One grew sick of it. *He wanted his life back.*

They had been confined in a storeroom below decks, with only a small scuttle to allow in air, but no light.

"Who would have guessed the bowels of a ship are as dark as the bowels of the earth," Kehler said.

It had been some hours, neither knew how many, since they had heard Deacon Rose and his party depart, and they sat there miserably, imagining what Eldrich would do to them when their reckoning finally came. It was not a pleasant way to pass the hours.

"I still cannot fathom how Erasmus and Anna escaped us in the gorge. They could not have planned the entire thing."

"Leave it be, Kehler," Hayes said. "If Erasmus is still alive, then I think he will have had good reason to do what he did. Who knows what Eldrich had planned for him? Remember the ritual that Percy Bryce gave him? Self-immolation is hardly a reward for a job well done."

They fell silent, hearing only the slapping of water along the hull and their own quiet breathing.

"We seem always to be left in the dark."

*"Kehler,"* Hayes cautioned.

Hayes could hear his friend shift in the darkness.

"It is true, Hayes. We have not understood for a moment what we're involved in. And I'm sure we don't even yet. But what is really choking me now is the thought of Rose out there tracking down Clarendon and Erasmus. He has hated Clarendon from the moment they met, I'm sure, because Randall saw what a hypocrite Rose really was. And now he will have the pleasure of handing him over to Eldrich." His anger brought him to silence.

Small waves slapped along the hull in even rhythm, followed by a jingle of metal.

Hayes sat up.

"Ah, they have not forgotten us," Kehler said, stirring to rise. "Our evening turn on the deck. I am ready for it."

"Shh, keep your peace," Hayes cautioned.

And then the lock turned, a bolt was drawn back, and lantern light spread about the tiny storeroom.

"Brother Norbert?"

"Please, Mr. Kehler, keep your voice low." The hermit held a finger to his lips. "It took three bottles to lay the bosun's mate low so that I might lighten him of his keys. Do not let my efforts go to waste." He crouched down in the door. "There is a ship's boat lying alongside to starboard. Only two men stand watch, and they have sequestered themselves with another bottle on the foredeck. It is a full two hours until the change of watch." He motioned behind him. "Let me go ahead to be sure the way is clear, and then we will be over the side and gone before anyone is the wiser."

"'*We*,' Brother Norbert. Will you not suffer greatly for a betrayal of the church?"

"Perhaps, but I will suffer longer for my betrayal of the word of Farrelle. I have long known this was my choice, but hiding alone in the Caledon Hills allowed me to avoid it. Now it is no longer possible. Deacon Rose is what the church of Farrelle has become; a man who practices the very arts he has vowed to destroy, as the church is beset by all the evils they publicly condemn. Follow me to the ladder, but then wait until I give the word."

Brother Norbert slipped away, the lantern swaying as he walked. They waited at the ladder's foot, listening for the sounds of sailors. Norbert appeared, a disheveled apparition in the opening above, and motioned them on.

A moment later they were out into the night, the swimming moon caught overhead in the net of rigging. The boat was precisely where Norbert had said, and they were quickly away, silently dipping oars into the reflected sky, stars sent whirling.

Shore was their only goal—to land and slip away before the sailors missed them. Once they were ashore, the navy men likely wouldn't know what to do, and by the time the Admiralty had been contacted for orders, they would have escaped, pulled along in the wake of Deacon Rose.

"But what will we do now?" Hayes asked as the boat ran up on the beach.

"Find Erasmus and Clarendon. Take them bodily away from Anna, if we must. But Anna—she is on her own." Hayes turned to the monk. "Erasmus was convinced she murdered her guide, Brother. I am not sure why—something about the ritual performed. But this was not just some fabrication of the Deacon's to demonize her even more."

Norbert nodded. "Yes, and for this she should pay a price. But to a court of law. As to her soul: Farrelle taught that all sins could be forgiven. Whatever the case, it is not for me to judge."

They struck out into the town, wondering how far ahead Clarendon and Erasmus were, and how close behind Deacon Rose and Captain James followed.

"There must be an ostler in town somewhere. We need horses," Kehler said, suddenly energized, almost bouncing.

"Yes," Hayes said, "so that we might ride off into our uncertain future."

"Not so uncertain as all that," Kehler said, but he did not smile.

## ⌁ Fifty

The moon, two days from the full, lit the roads and allowed them to ride by night. And ride they did, changing horses often, pressing the poor beasts on without regard for their well-being, or for the black looks of ostlers. Erasmus had never known the countryside to pass beneath him so quickly. Poor Clarendon looked like a man who had fought a war, and Dusk was being run to skin and bones.

*Eldrich can rival the speed of a bird if he has need*, Anna had said, and pressed on. They hardly spoke, for when they stopped, they fell upon their food and drink like the starving, and during their brief rests they descended into a sleep that was near to stupor.

Anna dressed in the clothing of a man, not that she was trying to pass herself off as one, but only for its convenience. And much to the scandal of ostlers and innkeeper's wives, she did not ride sidesaddle.

"Time," she said, "has become our enemy. More even than the mage."

And so they rode, stiff and sore and blistered, into the interior of the kingdom, until Anna's horse stumbled and fell, nearly landing atop her.

"I'm unhurt," she said when Erasmus and Clarendon reached her, but she appeared pale and shaken. They made her sit a moment at the roadside, and she became so nauseous that she was almost ill.

"It will pass in a moment," she said. "It will pass." Then she gestured at her mount. "Has it a broken leg?" she asked.

Erasmus regarded the beast as it tried for the third time to rise, obviously in agony, one limb hanging limp. "I'm afraid it does."

"You must put it from its misery, Erasmus. Look at the poor beast. . . . Have you a dagger?"

Clarendon cut the beast's throat as quickly and cleanly as he could, and with some effort they retrieved Anna's tack.

Using the other horses, they dragged the dead beast into a thicket, and then went on, Anna riding with Clarendon, though more slowly as a result.

In two hours they came to an inn and fell down upon benches to eat while new horses were readied. The patrons tried not to stare, for certainly they had never seen people of the educated classes who looked so . . . well, who looked as though they fled the law.

Clarendon took food outside to see to Dusk, leaving Erasmus and Anna alone.

Erasmus tried to smile at the innkeeper, to put him at ease, but he had not the energy to concoct a story to explain their strange flight. If they had not obviously been of good families, certainly the innkeeper would have reported them to the local authorities—and might still do so when they left.

"Tomorrow by midday," Anna said, tearing off a chunk of bread, "barring further accidents."

Erasmus nodded. "Good. I don't think I can go further. Will we have time to make our preparations?"

She shrugged. "If the mage is not upon us."

Eldrich walked around the edge of the razed building, a stooped shadow in the moonlight. Twice he stopped and performed a brief rite, drawing lines on the ground in silver fire. The countess stood well back, watching. Bryce had made his way into the middle of the ruin, his passage releasing the pungent odor of smoke and ash. Eldrich asked him a question, then sent his servant searching among the still-standing walls.

They spent an hour in that place, the countess wondering if this was the work of Eldrich, and if the enemy he sought had died here, Erasmus with her. Or if fire had been carried here by the fanatical priest of whom Walky spoke. Erasmus seemed to go from one death to the next—first in the cave, then the gorge, and now, just when Eldrich was sure that he still lived, this. *The final death*, she thought.

Walky came from his own searching, near enough that she caught his attention.

"Has . . . anyone survived?" she asked.

"Everyone, m'lady," Walky said, surprised at the question. "At least no one died here."

"What of Erasmus, then? Was he here?"

Walky shrugged. "Only the mage knows," he said, and passed on.

The mage emerged into an opening in the wall, pausing in his circuit. Where he stood, moonlight fell between the smoke-blackened stone, but seemed to pass him by.

*Even moonlight shies from him*, the countess thought. *If it cannot penetrate the shadow and silence, how can I?*

She watched him disappear again, behind blackened stone, his servants keeping their distance. She, too, stood back from him.

*I have become like all the others who serve him*, she thought, *governed by his moods.* She shook her head.

From around a corner the mage appeared, crossing the lawn, tilting his head to Walky, who immediately waited upon his master. The music of Eldrich's voice reached her, but not the words. It was a sad music now, minor in key. Walky nodded and hurried ahead, leaving her to follow in her usual ignorance of what went on, of what was planned.

They followed the path along the cliff top, in a single line, no one talking, each seemingly unaware of the other. Thus it was in the house of the mage, the countess knew. Each person isolated from the others, as though Eldrich's silence and remoteness had infected them all. Everyone went before, walking through the night without lanterns, moonlight marking the cliff edge, the too-narrow path one must tread.

A nightjar roamed the sky, its buzzing call trilling through the air. She stopped and watched its flight against the stars, touched by moonlight, as it hunted. She felt as much kinship for this lone flyer as she did for those who served Eldrich. Even Walky seemed especially distant that night.

"Why do I follow?" she whispered. But she went on, along the moonlit path, the others lost from view. The vision in the water came back to her, and she shuddered.

In a few moments she came to the small wood where the path disappeared into darkness. When she had passed this way before, she had followed the others, but now—

"M'lady?"

It was Walky, standing in shadow beside the path.

"I have a gift for you," the little man said, holding out his hands like a child with a lightning bug.

When he opened them, saying a few words of Darian, she felt a strange light cast upon her eyes, and the world had changed.

"What in this . . . ?"

"It is owl sight, m'lady. From the mage."

All around her the world seemed to glow with a faint, unnatural luminescence. She held up her hand, which also seemed to gleam faintly.

"Please, m'lady, we should not tarry. It will not last long."

"I'm sure it won't," she said. Gifts from the mage seldom did.

The countess did not bother to ask how they had found carriages—from some country estate nearby, no doubt. And she again found herself in flight across the countryside, desperately in need of rest, a bath, and some civil company. This time she found herself riding with Skye.

"Did you see? They have paintings, or so I assume from the bundles. Immediately I wondered if they were Peliers."

"Kent's, I think," the countess said.

"Averil Kent?"

She nodded. "Yes. He was a guest of Lord Eldrich as well."

The great empiricist shook his head in amazement and dismay. "What goes on? Why am I here? What does he want of me?"

"It is the question many of us ask, Lord Skye," the countess said.

"I think, sometimes, that he only keeps me about to torture me."

She had seldom met a man more self-absorbed. "It seems unlikely to me. Whatever small pleasure the mage might derive from that would seem insignificant in the present situation."

"Yes, but what is going on? Do you know? We are racing about the country like . . . Well, I don't know what we are like, but certainly I have never heard of such a thing. Is it all about this girl I met? The faded one?"

Despite her need for company, the countess had quickly tired of Skye. "Only the mage knows," she said.

How had she once thought she was in love with this man? Hopelessly in love?

She feared that her time with Eldrich would make everyone appear thus— rather petty and absorbed by the most trivial matters.

But there had been something else with Skye, something besides the enormous regard in which he was held throughout all the lands of the Entide Sea—he did not respond to her. She shook her head at the thought. She had not been able to bear it. He was the only one. The only man she had met who reacted to her not at all. It shamed her to admit it, but there it was.

*What a child I was. A spoiled child, as Eldrich once said.*

She looked out at the countryside racing by and wondered what they would do now. Where they went.

*Let there be an end to this soon*, she thought. *Let there be some clarity, some understanding. I will go mad otherwise.*

## ⤷ Fifty-One

They stopped only to kill and skin a snake and gather a vial of starlit water, then continued on their mad way, careening across the Farr countryside like the most hunted of highwaymen.

The final hill defeated Anna's exhausted horse, so they led their mounts slowly up through the fading light. The moon, in its silver splendor, had not yet risen, and in the warm light of the fading sun, the ruin of the ancient volcano was strangely imposing. Erasmus thought it would be easy to imagine that this was the ruin of an ancient citadel, though a citadel of giants.

None of them spoke—they had not the breath to—and Erasmus could almost sense Anna's whirling thoughts. She kept her eyes fixed on the uneven path, but when she glanced up, it was with such a haunted look that Erasmus was taken aback. He couldn't begin to guess what it meant.

The path, almost a road, wound up between steep walls of dark, coarse rock—as a road might wind up through a hilltop fortress. Here and there the rock was columnated, nature having forced the hot stone up in elongated pillars, and these were worn and broken and tumbledown.

"It is difficult to believe this is not an ancient city," Clarendon said, his voice hushed, as though afraid of disturbing ghosts.

"Yes, especially in this light," Erasmus answered, "but it is natural all the same." He looked over at Anna, who was pale even in this golden light. "Are you well?" he asked.

She shook her head, not meeting his eye. "The last time my brethren tried to make a mage they were trapped—all of them murdered. . . ."

Suddenly Erasmus felt his fatigue even more. The little energy he had left him like the dying light of day. He looked over at Clarendon, and a sudden realization penetrated the overwhelming fatigue.

Erasmus drew his horse up abruptly, but the others went several paces before they noticed he had stopped and turned to look back at him.

"What is it, Erasmus?" Anna asked, her voice terribly weary.

"Why did Eldrich let Randall leave his house with all that Randall knows?"

Neither Anna nor Clarendon answered.

"Think about it. He uses others without them knowing. Consider how he manipulated events to send us all into the Mirror Lake Cave at the same time. Randall knows things that no one but Eldrich knows: the way to open these precious gates. Yet he sends Randall looking for us, knowing full well that Randall feels no loyalty to him, that he would do anything to find the woman he lost so long ago." Erasmus looked around him, as though he might find Eldrich hiding in a shadow.

"There is no spell upon Clarendon that might be used to find us," Anna said, then dropped the reins of her horse and began to sprinkle the starlit water in a pattern on the ground.

"Come quickly, Erasmus. Pass by me up the path."

The two men took the horses, which were too exhausted to bolt even though they shied and swung their heads when they sensed the arts in use.

They forced themselves up the shadowed path, laboring for breath. A moment later Anna came up behind them.

"Eldrich is not here, nor is he nearby." She took hold of a saddle to steady herself. "We will be warned now if any come up this path. I can do no more than that." Anna nodded and they set out again, forcing themselves to make each step.

Finally they came to the path's end. Anna stopped and slowly raised her eyes. She made an odd sign with her hand and muttered beneath her breath.

Before them lay a slope of shattered stone angling up between steep walls. Overhead, stars began to appear upon a sky in transition from darkest blue to deepest black.

"It was on a night such as this that my brethren were trapped by the mages," Anna said. "Trapped and murdered."

Erasmus found himself nodding. Trapped without the slightest warning, led on by their deepest desires.

Anna dropped the reins of her horse, pulled the bag from the saddle, and began to pick her way up the slope. Every few steps she would stop and raise her head, as though she looked upon some inescapable horror.

"They had come to make a mage," she said softly. "*A mage*. That miracle of all the ages. And they were murdered—murdered at their moment of joy—for it *was* a moment of joy, not triumph." She slumped down upon a rock for a moment, fighting to catch her breath.

Erasmus leaned against the rock wall. Dusk came down the path from above, where he had ranged ahead.

"But why did he let you go, Randall?"

The little man shrugged. "I had not thought of it, Mr. Flattery. He sent all of us who had been seeking Anna. I had carried this knowledge with me before, after all."

Erasmus thought this answer inadequate, but felt none of them could bring their minds to focus on the issue. Exhaustion had robbed them of their mental powers at the time when they might need them the most.

Anna turned suddenly to Erasmus. "Does this remind you of your vision? Is it the same?"

Erasmus cast his gaze around. "It resembles the place in my dream hardly at all. But it feels the same. . . ."

Anna nodded, pushed herself up, and began to climb again by sheer force of will. The others stirred themselves to follow, all the unanswered questions traveling with them.

They struggled over a massive shoulder of stone and found themselves upon a level bench. It could almost have been a terrace, with broken-down walls on three sides and open to the southeast. Against the central wall a spring bubbled up, forming a small pool.

Anna looked around and smiled for the first time in days. "Here, you see? Your vision did not fail you." She waved a hand at the spring. "Can you feel it? There is a power here. If my brethren had only known, they could have avoided Tremont Abbey and their meeting with the mages." She turned around in a graceful circle, as though the power she spoke of had invigorated her.

The moon was lighting the horizon, rising like a great, blind eye above the eastern hills. Anna greeted it in Darian, raising her hands as though she held the globe aloft. And then she collapsed upon a stone, her vitality evaporating, and stared off at the beauty of the rising moon.

"What must we do?" Clarendon asked.

"There is nothing we can do until the moon has risen higher." Anna moved down onto the ground and leaned against the rock. She closed her eyes. "I must rest an hour, and then we will begin."

"And what if Eldrich comes upon us before we are done?"

"Then, Mr. Clarendon, we will no longer suffer this misery."

Sleep eluded Erasmus, but he sat with Anna's head in his lap, his back pressed against a stone wall, and watched the moon float free of the eastern horizon. Chuff prowled the upper reaches of the rock walls, appearing in a flutter every now and then, cocking a single, dark eye toward Anna, and then springing back up into darkness.

No familiar had appeared to Erasmus, despite his use of the seed, but he kept alert watching for this miracle. The waking dreams were not so strong now, more like mild bemusement—though Anna said they could likely be induced again by a stronger elixir. Often he saw the dark carriage racing across the landscape, a small boy perched atop, alone.

"Mr. Flattery?"

He had thought Clarendon asleep, his breathing had been so even.

"I am awake, Randall."

"Will you become a mage, sir? Will you go through with it?"

The very question he was avoiding. He smoothed Anna's hair, assuring himself that she still slept. "I don't know, Randall. Anna is convinced there is nothing else that will protect me from Eldrich, but I am not so sure. He has spent all his later years dedicated to eradicating the arts from this world, I cannot see him allowing another mage to live, whether there is a curse or no."

"Exactly my thinking, Mr. Flattery, which is why I think we should try to open this gate, sir. It might be our only chance."

Erasmus felt his shoulders lift. "I don't know, Randall. She said herself it could not be done without risk. . . . But perhaps you are right. There will be no other escape for her in this world."

"I did not hear you include yourself, Mr. Flattery."

Erasmus looked up at the pure ball of the moon. "Did I not . . . ?"

There was a sudden pealing of a bell, a sound not entirely incongruous in this place that so resembled a city.

"What in Farrelle's name—"

Confused, Anna roused and sat up, rubbing her eyes. "Someone comes," she said, rising stiffly. She called out in Darian, and her chough appeared. She sent it winging off down the path. A moment later it was back, fluttering before them and speaking its single word excitedly.

"It is not Eldrich," she said and sat back on the rock to wait.

"I hear horses, I think," Clarendon said.

Then Erasmus heard it, too, the hollow sound of hooves coming slowly up. And then it stopped.

Finally the sound of voices, and boots on stone, then, in the near darkness, a man appeared. He stepped out of shadow into moonlight and stopped as though confused by the pale light.

"Mr. Hayes? Is that you?"

"Randall? Erasmus?" He turned and called out. "I've found them!"

Hayes swayed on his feet, tried very hard to smile, then collapsed on the ground. He held up a hand as Erasmus and Clarendon crossed to him. "I will be all right in a moment." He looked up at his two friends and shook his head as though unable to believe he had found them.

"Deacon Rose and the agents of the Admiralty can't be far behind. We managed to outdistance them by riding unnumbered horses into the ground. Your trail has not been so hard to follow, I will tell you."

"But what of Eldrich?" Anna asked. "Where is the mage?"

Hayes fixed her with an odd look, as though assuring himself that she was not a ghost, and then he shrugged.

Fenwick Kehler appeared upon the terrace, and then, most oddly, a Farrellite priest.

Anna shook her head. "Brother Norbert? What in this round world has brought you here?"

"Ill fortune, I fear," the priest said. "Men came looking for you in the hills. When they heard my tale, I was taken away from my home and my work and embroiled in this . . . madness."

"Brother Norbert helped us escape," Hayes said. "We would not have been able to reach you otherwise. But there is little time for stories, Erasmus. Although we managed to pass Deacon Rose, for his party was larger and consisted of too many sailors, we cannot have left them more than a few hours behind. Perhaps not even that."

Fenwick Kehler hobbled painfully into the patch of moonlight. "Yes, Erasmus, you must flee," he said. "Deacon Rose is near, and I worry that Eldrich is not far behind."

"No," Anna said softly. "We cannot escape them—not now. Not in this world."

They collapsed at the foot of a wall, protected from a rising wind which moved among them almost silently.

Hayes and Kehler kept looking to Clarendon, and then at each other, both so exhausted that they could hardly bring their minds to bear.

"There is no choice, nor time for soul searching," Anna said suddenly, then covered her eyes for a moment as though her vision swam. "I will attempt the ritual of Landor, and if we open the gate, you may pass through or not. It is your decision, but the ritual will be easier the more people who are involved."

"I will come with you," Clarendon said quickly, rising to his feet. He swallowed once, hard, and looked at the others for support, though his stance evidenced a desperate resolve.

"As will I," Kehler said, shaking his head as though he could not believe what he was saying or perhaps what a pass his life had come to. "I saw what was done to Doctor Ripke. Better to become a Stranger than suffer that." He turned to his friend. "Hayes . . . ?"

Hayes got slowly to his feet. "I—I will but no more help," Hayes said, fighting a sudden panic. *To pass beyond the world.* It was too frightening, too inconceivable.

"There will be no mercy from Eldrich, Mr. Hayes," Clarendon said, "and you will never escape him. You have no choice, whether you realize it or not."

"But I do not want to pass into the land of the Strangers," Hayes said plaintively, "even were it possible. Despite all my ill fortune, this is my world, here; Farrland and the Entide Sea."

"But, Mr. Hayes," Anna said, her fatigue filling her voice with emotion, "Eldrich is likely on his way to this place as we speak. He will make you pay the price for your betrayal."

Hayes nodded. He felt near tears from exhaustion and from the decision being pressed on him. "Yes, well, it will be my price."

Anna rose almost noiselessly. "There is no more time. If you will not help us, then I suggest you go now. Better not to be here when Eldrich arrives. Even Deacon Rose and his followers are to be feared."

"The time for discussion has passed," Clarendon said. "Come, those who will, let us begin. And any who will not—I wish you all speed." The little man turned away, though not before Hayes saw a tear in the small man's eye.

The despair in Clarendon's voice could not be missed.

*Let him go with Anna*, Hayes thought. *Let him pass from this world that has so injured him.*

Hayes looked at the forlorn figure of Randall Spencer Emanual Clarendon, his fine clothes torn and dirty. There was no thought of the future with the small man now, but only of escape. Memories had overtaken him like a storm at sea; it would be a wonder if he did not founder.

"I will help if I may," Brother Norbert said, his deep voice very solemn. He had risen with the others but stood apart. "Despite the teachings of the church, Farrelle never spoke against the practice of the arts. I will help in whatever way I can. Let Eldrich do with me as he will, I follow my own conscience now."

"I think you have little reason to fear Eldrich," Erasmus said. "It was not chance that brought you here. Just as it was not chance that took a priest to Tremont Abbey the night the mages trapped the followers of Teller. You will be the witness for the Holy See. And you may pray for us as well."

They all turned silently to the spring and the open area before it.

At Anna's instruction they placed seven rocks in a semicircle around the spring. Taking out a dagger, she began to etch lines onto the stone that recreated the intricate geometry Erasmus remembered from the *nance* in Landor's chamber. The same pattern that was etched on the floor of the Ruin of Farrow.

"We must perform the ceremony without mistake," Anna cautioned. "Let no one set foot on the *nance* without the proper ablutions, for it will endanger us all."

Hayes found his heart had begun to palpitate oddly, and he had not a drop of moisture in his mouth.

Each in turn did as Anna instructed: speaking words of Darian in dry mouths; gesturing as she demonstrated; then going to the spring to drink a cupped-palm of water. And then she began to teach them their parts, fear focusing their minds completely.

## ⤚ Fifty-Two

Even horses driven by a mage must stop for water, and the countess found herself on a riverbank at the bottom of a deep, narrow valley, waiting while the horses were tended. The trees on the hillsides bent to a rising breeze, and the river seemed to clatter past, as though it tumbled stones through the shallows. Dusk was gathering in the east, even as storm clouds climbed the southern sky.

The countess had taken the opportunity to escape from the confines of the carriage. They were following Eldrich's familiar, which was apparently tracking a wolfhound that belonged to Clarendon. The odd thing was that this did not seem the slightest bit strange to her. So they were careening across the countryside led by a wolf that anyone would describe as magical; what of it? Such absurdity now made up the fabric of her life. After all, who was she but a woman under an enchantment that made men foolish with infatuation?

She shook her head.

Sweeping aside a branch she found Skye and Eldrich standing on the riverbank, and though the conversation had lulled, their bearing spoke clearly in the silence. Eldrich was half turned away, his shoulders hunched, looking down at the empiricist with undisguised disdain. Skye stood back, his arms slightly open, palms out as though in appeal.

"From where?" Skye said, sounding as though he had been punched in the chest.

"A world where your great discoveries are common knowledge, *Lord Skye*. Where children know the laws of motion. So all of this puffed-up vanity over your great genius is nothing but so much empty posturing. That is what I have kept from you. Are you not overcome with joy and gratitude that I have revealed the truth at last? Now pester me no more." Eldrich swept off along the embankment, leaving Skye stricken, wavering on his feet. The empiricist took two steps and then seemed almost to collapse, sitting down in a heap on the grass.

The countess came and stood by him, tempted to reach out a hand to console him, but somehow she could not. "It isn't true," she said, not sounding terribly convincing. "It was said only in a fit of anger and cruelty. They were always thus, the mages."

But Skye shook his head, staring down at the ground. "No, it is true. I am a Stranger. I have always known it. Have always known my discoveries were but memories—nothing more." He put a hand to his brow, shaking his head almost desperately.

"What can I do for you, Lord Skye?" the countess said, almost a whisper.

"Lord Skye . . . ? That is not me. I am . . ." He shook his head again and, rolling awkwardly to his feet, pushed aside the branches and disappeared.

For a moment the countess stared after him, but then she turned to look for Eldrich. She knew he was caught in a fit of anger, and at such times would say whatever would hurt most—truth or lie. In this case she hoped it was a lie, and that she would be able to tell Skye so. Poor man. He might be a genius, but provoking Eldrich would hardly prove it. Of course what was she about to do?

This brought her headlong flight to a sudden stop. Perhaps this was not the moment to confront the mage over this matter. There was so much afoot, so many things she did not understand. Eldrich's mood was dark. Dark and fearful, she was sure. He had been left such terrible responsibilities. She remembered the vision he had shown her—the vision in the water.

Beneath a willow leaning out over the river, she found Eldrich plucking leaves from the branches, muttering to himself. Darian, she realized, and kept silent.

She remained a few paces off, afraid to intrude, wondering suddenly what he had decided. Would he release Erasmus unharmed? He had never clearly answered yea or nay.

For an instant he glanced her way, but went immediately back to his task, stopping only when he had a handful of the new leaves.

"It is not in my nature to gamble," he said, his voice and manner mild, and she sensed that he regretted the scene with Skye. The mage stared off over the river. "I allowed Skye out into this world against my better judgment only because I could trap the renegades of Teller no other way. I knew it was likely that some of his knowledge would surface in time. And now I have been forced to do the same with Clarendon—and he bears knowledge of even greater danger." He shook his head. "Is it not ironic?"

He shook his head, then crouched down by the river, his oddly bowed posture making him look like a penitent—something the countess suspected he had never been.

He began to chant, moving his free hand in intricate patterns. Across the bank before him, he drew his fingers, and a pattern glowed upon the grasses. Dusk seemed to flow up the valley, like flood waters, overtaking them. The mage continued his chant.

The countess was familiar enough with Darian now to glean a few words, and knowledgeable enough to guess that this was augury that Eldrich performed—something Walky said his master resorted to too often.

Caught by the wind, the willow branches writhed around him, like tendrils, she thought, as though animated by the arts.

With a final powerful syllable, Eldrich threw the leaves upon the water, staring fixedly where they fell, and then he toppled forward almost into the river, struggling to balance himself as though the riverbank tried to throw him off.

The countess fought through the grasping branches and took hold of his shoulder, pulling him back from the water. He flailed awkwardly with his arms, as though blind or stupefied.

He still mumbled, half in Darian and half in Farr. *"The* nance . . ." he kept saying. *"They are upon the* nance . . . !"

At that moment Walky appeared.

"I will tend to Lord Eldrich," he said, making it very clear that her presence was neither required nor wanted.

"Walky?" the mage said, staring blankly as though his sight had left him. *"They are upon the* nance. . . . *Do you hear? Upon the* nance!*"*

A moment later the countess found herself bundled into Eldrich's carriage, the mage slumped against the side, wrapped in his enormous old cloak; shivering, she thought, though in the failing light it was difficult to be sure.

He looked suddenly frail—frail and old—and this she found quite disturbing. So much so that she turned her attention to the dark window, the passing scene barely distinguishable now. Far off she thought she perceived something— something on the edge of hearing, on the edge of the world. *Thunder.*

Eldrich was staring at her. She realized it before she turned her head to look. His eyes seemed as dark and cold as ever—no sign of age or frailty there. In fact, he looked to be quickly recovering.

"What is the *nance*?" she asked.

Eldrich continued to regard her, and then finally spoke, the music still there, but brittle. "It is a place of ritual and power, and it is a gate. In the past, a gate that led to other lands . . . infinitely far away yet near at hand."

"And this woman is there? This woman you seek?"

"And Erasmus, yes."

"What will you do with him?" she asked quickly.

"It will depend upon the degree of his betrayal."

"What does that mean?"

He stared at her, eyes darker than the dark corner he inhabited.

*Yes, he does not like to be questioned*, she thought. She steeled herself for what she would say next. "We spoke of a bargain," she said, forcing out the words. "How else will you assure yourself of my cooperation?"

"You saw the vision of the mages," he said evenly.

Yes, she had seen it. The end of the world, or so it appeared. What would she not do to avert that? Her bargaining position was not strong, and he knew it. Her chance of saving Erasmus was slipping away.

"Is it true, then, that one can trust a devil more than a mage?"

"I have never met a devil," he said, the old mockery returning to his voice.

"If Erasmus is harmed, I cannot guarantee that I will be able to keep my part of the bargain."

"You would allow a cataclysm to spite me?"

She forced herself to meet his gaze. "Can you be sure I won't?"

He continued to stare. "Do you really care so much for him?" he asked after a moment.

The question caught her off guard. Did she, indeed? Why was she making such a fuss over Erasmus Flattery? Certainly the mage treated any number of people callously—Lord Skye, for instance—and she was doing nothing on their behalf. A memory of her evening with Erasmus—the way she had used him to gather information for Skye, and how he had reacted.

Perhaps that was it; the feeling that Erasmus, despite all that had befallen him, was a man of essential goodness, and considering how few such men there were, he had been terribly misused.

"Yes," she said, knowing it was said partly to wound. "Yes, I do."

*But he is a mage*, the countess reminded herself, *and can sense a lie. Can sense a lie and its purpose.*

Eldrich turned away, staring out at the passing night.

"Do you remember the Paths?" he asked, his voice mild and matter-of-fact.

"Yes."

"I have cast them recently, and something has changed. There are two paths now: one on which I live and another on which I die, or perhaps merely leave this world."

"Which will you take?"

"I am not certain I shall have the choice."

"Why are you telling me this?" *Sympathy*, she thought. *He wants my pity.*

"Why? So that you might prepare yourself. . . ." And he would say no more.

## ⤺ Fifty-Three

There was a mage at large in Farrland for the first time in perhaps five decades, and Captain James wondered what in this round world could have roused Eldrich from his slumber.

*A faded woman whom Captain James would know only when he saw her.*

James glanced over at Deacon Rose riding beside him. The truth was he did not like the priest. He much preferred Hayes and Kehler and their diminutive friend, but Clarendon had slipped away to warn those the mage sought, and the others had aided him. Captain James had been left no choice but to throw in his lot with Deacon Rose. He had been ordered to offer all assistance to these people, never guessing that they were not all of one mind.

By default the captain ended up supporting Deacon Rose, a priest of the church of Farrelle who was far too much of an authority on the mages and their secret knowledge. The arts were proscribed, after all, and certainly it was a mortal sin to pursue them. Yet here was this priest, only a deacon in rank, who knew more than any priest should about matters arcane and had an air of authority that belied his modest station. And he sought the faded woman, apparently knowing a great deal about her—more than James could say.

*When you meet her, you will know.*

Moonlight lay upon the road, shimmering the gravel and casting ruts and potholes into shadow. The river chortled along its course, and wind raced them down the valley floor. From all his years at sea, James knew this to be a storm wind, yet there was not a cloud to be seen. Instead, the sky remained unnaturally clear, the stars bright and large for such a moonlit night.

The man who led them, a local huntsman, halted his horse suddenly, pointing at a path winding into the trees.

"They were seen going this way; a redheaded woman and a dark gentleman, and not long ago three horses were found wandering on the roadside, all of them spooked and lathered."

"Then that will be all we require of you," Deacon Rose said. "May Farrelle smile upon you and your endeavors." He turned away, dismissing the man. "I will go first, Captain James."

As they went into the shadow of the trees, whispering broke out among the Jacks, like flames among grass. Their uneasiness with this priest and his involvement with things arcane had festered to the point where open mutiny was no longer just a remote possibility. For his part, the priest didn't seem to care what the Jacks thought, perhaps believing that the navy was like the church, where those lower in the hierarchy did as they were bid, and kept their peace. Captain James, however, knew better. He hadn't enough armed officers here to ensure the Jacks would follow orders, especially if these orders required they face the arts. It was a volatile situation, and the priest's utter insensitivity to it made it much worse.

What appeared to be a ruined city endured upon the rise, alchemic moonlight turning stone to muted silver. Out of shadow, two horses appeared, like limping ghost mares.

"They are here before us," Rose said, and spurred his exhausted mount on.

After half an hour's climb they came to a place where the horses could not pass, and Deacon Rose jumped quickly down, pulling a bag from his saddle.

*Fanaticism makes a man strong*, James thought.

The priest dropped the bag upon the uneven ground and pulled open its fastenings. Not paying any attention to James or the gathering Jacks, he began to spread out articles in the moonlight. Softly he began to chant, and a small brand caught fire.

The Jacks reacted by backing away, making warding signs, and uttering oaths. The Deacon began to sprinkle gray dust, like fine ash, upon the ground, drawing careful lines and curves. Touching these with the flaming brand, the design caught fire, revealing a finely drawn geometry. The Jacks fled in dismay, Captain James making no effort to stop them, but only watching the priest in terrible fascination.

Deacon Rose continued to chant, and flames, the green of sea fire, rose to envelop him.

And then, at a word, they died away, leaving only a flickering pattern traced upon the ground.

Deacon Rose looked at James, and then his eyes widened. "Where is your crew?"

"Gone. Threats of death would not have held them, for they fear death less than this." He waved a hand at the dying flames.

Deacon Rose picked up the still-burning brand and turned in a circle. "Then there is only thee and me," he said, "but if we are in time, that will be enough. Draw your sword, Captain. We might have need of it." He took up his bag and began to climb, holding his flaming brand aloft.

Up they went, among fallen boulders, then along a narrow ledge that looked down over the valley below from a great height. Twice the priest stopped to perform rites, flame from the brand forming strange patterns in the air.

"They try to thwart us, Captain," Rose said. "Do you see? But they shall not, for I am more skilled than they know. With this flame I can protect us from arcane assault, but you must not hesitate to use your blade—against man, woman, or child, no matter wealth or station. You must be utterly ruthless, Captain, for everything depends upon it. Everything."

They continued up until Rose stopped. From above voices echoed. The priest beckoned him, and not for the first time Captain James found himself reluctant to continue. Place him in an action at sea and he would face death unwaveringly—nothing less was expected—but this . . . ! It was more than the unknown. It was the darkness, the secret arts.

Despite his fears he crouched down beside Rose, feeling the cool rock press against him, reassuringly substantial. From above, a strange light wavered and a single voice spoke: a woman's voice.

"Thank Farrelle; we are in time," the priest said, his voice almost breaking. "You must stay close and be prepared to defend me at all costs, from that woman most of all. She is the true danger."

They toiled up the last thirty feet, and there, in the center of a level area, a woman was bent over in concentration, red tresses falling about her in a torrent. *And he knew her!* Without realizing why or from where, James knew her! Like a dream long forgotten, suddenly surfacing. He felt some strange triumph in this.

Rose began to draw in the air with his flaming brand, speaking low in another tongue. Without stopping, he nodded to James and went nimbly forward.

They were in moonlight, and high up among ruined walls, as though in a tower taller than any known. He hardly had time to notice more than that. Somewhere before them water fell: he could hear it slapping stone.

The woman had moved to the edge of the clear area now, and bent to her labors again, so focused that she did not see them, but someone called out in warning and she rose, tossing back her hair.

"Ah, Deacon," she said, "we have awaited you. Do not step on the floor, Captain James, or you will be consumed by fire. Only those within the ritual may set foot upon the *nance*."

"But you are too late," the priest said. He cast his eye around the others, measuring the situation. "I cannot imagine Eldrich's rage when you meet him next—and he approaches even now."

"Do not listen to his ravings," Anna said, her voice mocking, more than a little triumphant. "We will be gone before Eldrich comes, and Deacon Rose can be our witness, for all who follow me will escape."

"So that is what she has told you," Rose called out, his voice strong and reasonable, "that you will escape to this other world? But I am here to tell you that you will not. No mage in a thousand years has opened a gate to elsewhere, though many of the greatest spent a lifetime in this pursuit. No, she will make herself a mage. That is what she intends—just as Teller always planned. A mage to stand against the last master of the arts.

"You know something of these matters, Mr. Flattery. Think on it. . . . Only a mage can open a gate. Even if she were planning this escape, still, she must first become a mage. And as such she will bring calamity upon the world. An emerging mage at this point in time—it is a curse that even the mages feared." He waved his brand in the air as though to emphasize his words. "Mr. Kehler. You have read of the fears of the mages. Here they are, manifest in this woman. It does not matter that her intentions are not evil, evil will result—the worst evil ever brought upon mankind. Here is the moment the mages feared above all others. *Do not do this*, I implore you."

"We have heard your speeches before," Clarendon called out, unable to contain himself. The little man stood in his appointed place upon the makeshift *nance*, and shook his fist at the priest. "Even Eldrich warned that your tongue was charmed. We shall not fall victim to your 'reason' again. No, priest, you are the last person we shall believe, for you have uttered nothing but lies since the ill-fated day we met. Stand and watch if you will—your church dearly loves to have witnesses—but we will not heed you again."

Anna had gone back to her preparations, ignoring the conversation around her and the threat of the intruders.

Captain James noted a shadow move beside the spring.

"Is that Brother Norbert?" he asked.

Rose took a step forward, holding his flame aloft.

"Brother Norbert! What madness is this? You will be damned for all time for what you do."

"And you, Deacon. How is it you practice the forbidden arts and escape this same fate?"

"Perhaps I will not, Brother Norbert, but I do it for my church. I will die the true death so that all of you might live. Come away from this now; I order it. In the name of the mother church and all that we hold sacred. Come away while we might still save your mortal soul."

"No, Brother, I no longer believe such threats. I have seen the evil that priests have done in the name of mother church. I will no longer condone it, nor will I be allied with it. I will make my own decisions about what will endanger my soul, for certainly a murderous church cannot."

"Leave him be," Erasmus called out. "Nothing you say will change our course now. Eldrich created our fear and hatred, let him pay the price. In an hour we will have done what no man . . . no mage has done in a thousand years. You saw it, Rose, written upon the walls in Landor's crypt: the enchantment to open the way. And we have Landor's seed. It is enough. May the devils take you and your world of lies."

Anna had gone to the spring and, whispering a few words, cupped her hands and drunk. To each of those upon the *nance* she carried water, whispering as she let a few drops fall upon their tongues.

Taking up a jar of palely luminescent liquid, she unstopped it and began to sprinkle it over the pattern upon the floor, where it glowed like the substance of the moon. Rose's brand went out as though snuffed by a sudden wind. In the pale light James could see the priest put his hands over his eyes, then quickly reach to his tunic, patting his side. And then in the silence, Rose began to pray.

When her pattern was complete, Anna poured seed from a bag into a mortar, crushing it with a small pestle. From a second bottle she poured an inky liquid, mixing it with the seed. A pungent odor reached Captain James, igniting a strange hunger. Anna lifted the mortar with great care, raising it in both hands, and stepped to the center of her pattern. After speaking a few words she drank the mortar dry and cast it into the small pool of water at the wall's foot. She stood and hung her head, wavering as though she would fall.

But then she drew herself up, staring at the wall before her as though steeling her nerve. She opened the cuff of her right sleeve, and reaching down, wrapped something about her exposed wrist—the skin of a snake, James realized. Her other hand she raised aloft, and a crow—a crow with a blood-red bill—lit upon her wrist. Rearing back, the bird struck, tearing open her skin so that drops of crimson appeared, some few falling to the floor. She stamped her foot hard on the stone.

"*Curre d' Efeu!*" she called out, the words echoing in the chamber. "*Curre d' Emone!*"

Erasmus felt the words resonate inside him.

"*Heart of flame! Heart of the world.*"

And behind it all, Brother Norbert chanting; . . . *naisannaisanna* . . .

He struggled to keep his wits about him, to keep his focus, for it was either history being made, or his last moments of life. Either way he wanted to be conscious and aware.

Erasmus had no illusions. Anna was very likely not capable of opening the gate and having them pass safely through. Lucklow had not managed it, nor any who came before him, and they had spent their lifetimes studying the arts. But what other course was there? Only the retribution of Eldrich, and that would be a hell as terrible as any he might find. No, better to risk this than face Eldrich again. Better death than that.

"*Your servant calls out in darkness.*"

Out of the corner of his eye, Erasmus saw Deacon Rose fall to his knees in prayer.

Anna was making herself a mage. . . . Rose was right in this. Only a mage could open a gate. But once a mage, what would she do?

"*Vau d' Efeu. Ivanté!*" Anna called, her voice gaining strength and resonance.

*Voice of flame. Come forth!*

Again she called out in Darian.

*Speak from the mouth of your child.*

Erasmus found that he trembled, his knees weak, heart pounding like a stone upon the wall of his chest. He fought to breathe, and then called out in Darian, words he did not know.

A sound like water and wind funneling down a narrow gorge, and then flame erupted from the pool and Brother Norbert disappeared in a blossom of fire.

Captain James staggered back as the flame erupted, raising his hands to ward off the heat and light—but only a warm breath touched him, though the fire boiled and curled barely yards away.

Beside him, Deacon Rose continued his prayer, hands clasped before him, eyes tightly closed, as though even a glimpse of such blasphemy would endanger his soul.

The navy man found himself sinking down beside the priest, for there, where Anna had stood, a great serpent struggled with a massive bird, locked in a deadly battle. He shook his head to clear it, but still the vision persisted, though not quite clear or focused. The bird and serpent seemed to have climbed into the towering clouds, thrown hard against the dome of stars.

And then they fell, writhing, to the earth where they burst into flame as they struck, lying still, locked together in death.

But when he thought there would be peace and an end, they rose again, like martyrs from the pyre, and battle was renewed.

Seven times he saw the serpent arise and seven times the bird struck, and each time they fell in flame, flame that consumed them both.

Captain James felt as though he floated within a dream, where things made some terrible sense that could not readily be explained, as though another logic held sway here.

Finally, a woman lay broken upon the floor in a pattern of cold fire, her face hidden in a blaze of red hair.

Anna lay like one who had fallen from a great height—still, as only the dead could be still. A breeze wafted a few strands of hair. Erasmus wanted to go to her, to cradle her, push back the hair from her face, say some final words, for surely she had failed.

But then a hand moved, searching, as though it had a will of its own. Then a quivering arm. Her chest heaved as though life had slipped back into empty clothing, and with a moan she rolled and began to force herself up on trembling limbs. But she could not rise past her knees. There she stayed, head bent, shoulders shaking with silent sobs. And then she straightened, pushing back the mane of hair.

"*Tandre vere viteur . . .*" she whispered.

*Hear me*, Erasmus translated.

"*C'is m'curre.*"

*Here is my heart.*

From somewhere she produced a sprig of green—*king's blood*—and tossed it toward the flame. From above, her chough swooped down, taking the offering in the air, winging straight into the fire where it vanished with barely a swirl of flame, the sound of a wave dying on the shore.

And then darkness. Erasmus felt his knees strike stone, and struggled to keep his balance.

They were in a high place, or so it seemed, among the stars. A cool breeze tugged at his clothing, and a high keening, almost beyond hearing, blended in strange harmony.

Anna rose from the floor beside him, bent like one in prayer.

"*Where are you?*" Hayes whispered in a voice not his own.

"Alone," Anna said, her voice small and flat, "among the alone. Among the stars."

*"What do you hear?"* Clarendon asked in that same terrible voice.

"The songs of stars."

*"Tell me your true name."*

"Annais."

*"Then you may scribe it here, among the stars."*

And they were returned to the keep, a high note still ringing in Erasmus' ears.

Anna knelt in the center of the *nance*, weaving intricate patterns with her hands, speaking words of power. Erasmus felt the cool wind blow through him, stripping him bare, as though he were exposed to the world in some way he had never known before.

Captain James still knelt upon hard stone, his sword lying before him, forgotten. What had he seen? A mage being born? Born among the stars? Had anyone alive witnessed such a thing?

Movement caught his eye, and he realized Deacon Rose had risen from his place, and was moving deliberately forward toward the *nance*. The priest chanted, tossing something before him—white down, James realized—and in his hand he grasped a blade. But then a shadow coalesced to rise in the priest's path, moonlight turning it into a great dog. It stood before Deacon Rose, fangs bared, barring his way—the wolfhound of Clarendon.

The priest stopped. Then, as he went to step forward, the dog lunged, faster than moonlight could trace, and Deacon Rose stood, pressing a hand to his wrist, the dagger lying on the stone.

"Do not move, Deacon, or he will savage you again," the seaman said.

"Take up your sword, Captain, and slay this beast for me."

"I will not, Deacon, for it is not a natural beast and is not to be trifled with."

Deacon Rose began to protest, but as he turned toward James in anger, the dog growled, and the priest froze in his place.

Around Anna the pattern came to life again, and Anna rose, speaking the words of Landor's enchantment—the ritual for opening the gates.

It was long and complex, and even if Erasmus' Darian had been up to it, he likely would not have understood what went on. He felt the power of it, though, felt it grow within him, felt the majesty of it, like some glorious music rising inside him, reaching toward a crescendo.

And then, when he was sure the time had come and some glorious opening would appear, the flame rose up again, trembled against the heavens, and then fell upon them like a great wave.

## ↶ Fifty-Four

The countess came over the shoulder of rock behind Eldrich and Walky to find a priest and an officer of His Majesty's navy kneeling upon the rock like stricken men. And there, before them, a great, towering flame trembled, split in two, and in its center a cavern seemed to have been opened into the solid rock.

"They have opened the first gate," Eldrich said. "Flames, but we have no time to waste. Bryce!" he called.

Bryce appeared, assisting Skye, who was clearly not used to such exertions.

"Come, all of you. We must go in, but once inside, we will be separated, lost in a colorless land. I have no time to explain. You will see things that are not possible, but you must not falter. You must always go forward. If you falter, you will be lost. Make your way up, always up. We seek a long stair to the highest point, and if you find each other, stay together. Make all haste. All haste. You, priest, come with me. We must stop them by whatever means we can. Bring this sailor—even he might have a part."

Not waiting for any discussion, Eldrich plunged into the opening in the flame, speaking words of Darian as he went. The countess hurried after, fearing to be lost in this colorless land.

Erasmus stood upon a rock awash in a sea of fog—a gray ocean whirling slowly in the complete and unsettling silence. Across the colorless expanse, reefs of barren stone broke the surface, solitary and oddly substantial in the vaporous landscape.

The mist lapped about Erasmus' knees, a languid wave, and then drew back, revealing more of the island upon which he had been cast away.

It was the top of a wall, Erasmus realized. A ruined wall. And there, far off, a shattered tower thrust up out of the fog, mist breaking around it.

*A ruined castle*, Erasmus thought, *or an ancient city*, and somehow that did not surprise him, though he did not know why. He began to feel his way along the narrow isthmus of stone, his boots making no sound.

A moon shone down through a high, thin overcast which diffused the light of the few visible stars. Featureless, pearl-gray clouds hung almost motionless in the heavens, like daubs of plaster on the dome of the sky.

*"Where am I?"* Erasmus said aloud, the words seeming to come from far away, as though they were echoes.

The mists parted some distance off, and for a moment a figure was revealed—the silhouette of a man. Erasmus waved, but the figure looked elsewhere, and then the mists closed again, seeming to sweep the figure off its perch.

For a long moment Erasmus remained in place, turning slowly, surveying the strangely illuminated world. There, three stone arches surfaced, and he thought he saw movement. But after a long moment no one appeared. He considered shouting but found the place so unsettling that he feared drawing attention to himself.

*It is a king's blood dream.* But how had it begun? When had he taken the seed?

A silent wave of mist combed over the wall, submerging it in gray. Erasmus dropped to a crouch and felt his way forward. Abruptly the wall turned to the left, and it was only by luck that he did not pitch off . . . into what?

*It is a dream*, he told himself, not sure if he could suffer injury in such a place.

Suddenly he was on a stair, and as he descended, the mist settled with him so that he seemed to be wading in fog to his waist. Level stone came underfoot, and in a moment the mist had streamed away like an ebbing tide. Movement caused him to whirl, but he caught only a glimpse of something disappearing into shadow among the ruin. *An animal*, Erasmus thought.

He went on, through the ancient city of dark stone. Down another stair, past a pool of mist, across a bridge arcing over a finger of the gray sea.

Up again, and then, over a parapet, he saw movement below.

"Randall . . . ? Is that you?"

"Who is that?" came the small voice, distorted by mist and stone.

"Erasmus."

"Do I know you, sir?"

"It's me, Randall. Erasmus Flattery."

He could see the small man shake his head. "But who is Randall?" he said, and was swept by a sea of fog.

*"Randall . . . ?"* But there was no answer.

Erasmus went forward, wandering aimlessly, now driven up by inflowing mist, or turning this way or that to stay in the clear air. Twice he was submerged in fog so thick that he crept forward, groping like a sightless man.

And then he heard a sound, a high, thin keening like some small animal in pain or terror. It echoed among the stone, seeming to originate from nowhere. Erasmus searched for what seemed a very long time before he found the source—a small child curled up in the high window of broken wall.

"What is it, child?" he asked. "Have you lost your way?"

The boy raised a darkly twisted hand, and pointed with a finger blackened and charred.

"Percy . . . ?"

But a snuffling caused him to whirl about, and there was Eldrich's wolf, regarding him coldly. Erasmus felt himself back away and ordered himself to stand his ground—show it no fear.

The wolf had its ears pressed back, fangs partly bared, hackles raised like scales. For some reason Erasmus noted that its shadow, cast by the moon, was not canine at all but long and stooped.

"Take me, then, and leave this child in peace," Erasmus whispered. "He has suffered enough. We have all suffered enough."

The wolf bared its fangs and growled, raising one paw as though about to spring. Erasmus bent and swept up a heavy fragment of stone, but as he did so, the wolf leaped past him, snatched the child from its perch, and disappeared into a tongue of mist. Erasmus threw himself into the fog, but in a few steps he was lost and could find no trace of the wolf.

He tripped and sprawled on the ground, and felt tears form, like ice upon his cheeks.

It was a city like the one in her vision, where she had seen Kent and heard the lament for a lost king. She walked on, mist appearing now and then to blind her, and in this unnatural mist she thought she saw the scenes of her life drift by. Lovers, her late husband, the half-formed spirit of a miscarried child. All of these things wafted into view, dreamlike, then faded into the mist, the crying child-that-was-not most disturbing of all.

The countess didn't know where she was or how she had come to be here. Even the idea that it might all be a dream did not occur to her. She was merely here, in this colorless world, this ancient, abandoned city—here without reason or meaning.

And she wandered among the ghosts of her past, which seemed to haunt her but never came close enough to touch or even to be clearly seen. Kent appeared, his lips forming soundless words—but this was an aged Kent, wrinkled and bent, yet with the light still in his eye: vivid blue in this world bled of all color.

Marianne chasing leaves carried up on a breeze—leaves like escaped words. Erasmus standing on a stair, alone. He would not look at her, nor did he seem to hear when she spoke, but looked always away—abashed. Ashamed.

*"Why did you not come after me?"*

But he ascended the stair and dissolved in moonlight without answering.

Through an arch she found a fountain filled with mist, as though a cloud had settled into this small bowl. Reaching down, she swirled the mist and her own reflection appeared, the stars behind.

But it was not quite her, for she seemed as gray as the world around her, as though drained of . . . what?

*"Glamour,"* she whispered. "The countess without her enchantment." She stared for a long moment, then closed her eyes. "How plain I am," she whispered.

She looked again and reached out tentatively, but her hands found only ash, cold and fine between her fingers.

She fled that place, wandering aimlessly, and came upon a balcony which looked out over the ruined city swept by a sea of moonlit mist.

*What a cold, inhuman landscape,* she thought. *But who had built this place? Had men not dwelt here once?*

It seemed to her they had not. That the race that built this place was not quite a race of men.

And then she heard the song, a swelling of voices in a strange tongue. A dirge, it seemed. A song of great power and sadness. A lament for some fallen hero or king, and oddly familiar to her. Where had she heard this?

"Death stalks someone here," she said, and turned away, the music fading as she went.

She came into a sculpture garden, the statues broken and eroded upon their pedestals, and there she saw movement—two small children hiding among the statuary.

"You still have not chosen." It was the musical voice of Eldrich, oddly insubstantial here. She could not see him, for the voice emerged from shadow.

"What choice was I given? To let them die. But I would choose life for them, for that is what they desire."

"Look around you. Regard this endless, lifeless night. This world without warmth, or compassion. Would you choose this for them? This for many lifetimes of men?"

"You must give the choice to them," the countess said, and fled.

They pursued him, the cacophony of voices, the thousands and tens of thousands, and he ran; stumbling among the fallen walls, plunging into the pools of mist, scrambling up stairs and over balustrades. Closer they would come, and the noise of their voices would almost overwhelm him. Stopping up his ears was little help, but running, keeping ahead of them, that was his only hope.

"*Randall . . . ?*" someone called, someone who was not of the hordes that pursued him, but he did not know the voice and ran on.

Cold stone at her back: a pillar around which her arms were bound. About her feet a green flame flickering out of a rubble of stone—the tongues of a malevolent earth, but cold beyond enduring. Through the flame, her accusers silently watched, their shadowed faces ghostly grim.

Garrick. Pryor. Banks. Kells.

"*I am not a witch*," she said, but her words came out as silence.

"You, Banks, Kells. I did what you asked of me. I became a mage. A mage...."

But they remained as still and uncaring as the ruined walls. The flame flickered around her knees, catching at the hem of her robe.

Someone appeared among her tormenters, someone touched by moonlight which shimmered in his gray robe.

"Brother Norbert!" she called out, her hope suddenly rising. "You gave your word that you would bring me peace."

"Yes," he said, and led her tormenters silently away, leaving her to the flames.


"Kehler? Thank Farrelle! Kehler, it's me; Hayes. Samual Hayes."

Kehler lay in a huddled heap at the foot of a stone wall, his back near a small opening.

"I cannot go through with it, Hayes. I cannot. I don't care if I die, but I will not go back in there."

Hayes put his hand gently on his friend's shoulder, dismayed by his state. "You don't have to go into the passage, Kehler. It's all right. We will stay out in the open. In the moonlight. Come on—up with you now. Out of this, lad. We must go on."

"But there is never an end," Kehler sobbed. "There is only this dark world forever. Cold stone. Passages choked with water."

Hayes began to gently lift his friend, bringing him to his feet. Flames, but he felt light! He had not realized how badly their ordeal had depleted them.

"He is in there, Hayes," Kehler said, pointing to the opening, and backing away. "Inside, waiting. Reaching out. Don't go near!"

"Come away from this place," Hayes said, turning his friend away.

"But he spoke to me—the buried child. Asked why we meddled in the affairs of the dead." Kehler shook his head, leaning heavily on Hayes. "Asked why we would come to join him when we could be buried in the living earth. Oh, Hayes, Hayes. We are dead, and wandering. Wandering where memory and dream can never be pried apart."


Erasmus climbed the tower stairs and then up the stone to perch upon the wall. The gray and endless sea spread beneath him, made substantial by moonlight. High
up like this, he almost felt more than heard a cold and brittle music. It drifted down to him as though falling from the heavens—falling like snow.

*The choral stars*, he thought, not sure from where that knowledge had come.

On a section of shattered wall, like a jagged peak, a robed figure appeared, and a flight of swallows swept down from the sky to weave an intricate pattern about him, like a spell. All the while he turned slowly within it, hands half-raised, as though in awe.

"*Brother Norbert*," Erasmus whispered. "*Look what honor they give him. The very birds of the air.*"

And then the mist washed over the scene, and it was lost.

He found Anna huddled in a corner, shivering, muttering to herself.

"Leave me," she whispered, though it was almost a hiss. "Have you not haunted me enough? Will I not pay all the rest of my days, and beyond?"

"Anna? It is Erasmus."

She raised her head slightly but not enough that he could see her face. "Erasmus . . . help me," she whispered desperately. "I am a ghost. A shadow. I will dwell here always for what I have done, for the crimes I have committed."

He crouched down and put a hand on her shoulder. She flinched away. Through the flimsy robe he could feel her flesh was cold—ghostly cold.

"Anna, come with me."

"Where could we go that would be different? You don't understand, Erasmus. We are ghosts. Spirits. We will wander here for a thousand years."

He shook his head. "No. I remember. We are lost in the ritual. Like a king's blood dream. You were attempting to open the gate, perhaps did open it."

"Then we failed, and we are lost in the limbo between the worlds."

"No, it is something you once spoke of: the way by darkness. It is an ordeal of sorts, and we must go on."

Erasmus wrapped his frock coat around her, then took her in his arms, trying to give her warmth. She leaned against him, shivering so badly that her teeth actually clicked.

"Why are you so kind to me?"

"Because you have been haunted by Eldrich all of your days, as have I. We have common cause in our fear and hatred."

He felt her head nod. She began to sob bitterly. "But it led here, to this toneless world, this world without desire or sustenance or human warmth."

"Can you not feel warmth from me?"

She hesitated. "Yes. . . . Yes, I can."

"Then perhaps we are not quite ghosts yet. The others are here. I have seen some of them. Perhaps even Eldrich, for I saw his familiar. Rest a moment, and when you are ready, we will seek them. Perhaps there is a way out of this limbo."

Anna shook her head. "No, I shall never escape what I have done. Three times they have burned me this night, and I fear they shall burn me a thousand times more before the end. Whether I escape or no."

*      *      *

The moon crept endlessly across the sky as though the celestial clock had run down. The night lingered beyond enduring, and Erasmus wondered if a sun ever rose here.

*Are we between the worlds as Anna said?*

The mist had begun to rise again, as though the tide flowed instead of ebbed, and this drove them up through the bones of the city. Up to the crest of a hill.

Once, they heard a piercing howl of despair. It froze them, and then they forced themselves to go on warily.

At last they came to a great stair down which a cloud seemed to pour like liquid, lapping over each tread, spreading eerily about their feet, then dissipating as it flowed from the open square. They went up without discussion, as though both knew there was no choice. Up the cloud-stair, toward the moon and stars.

At the top they found an officer of the King's navy, huddled on the stair, mist breaking about him.

"What brought you here?" Erasmus asked.

"Eldrich," the man said, not stirring.

"Eldrich. . . . Is he here?" Erasmus asked. "Does the mage know the way out?"

The man looked up, eyes wide with fear. "Better seek a sea devil or the eye of a storm than seek the mage. This is what comes of meddling in the arts. You lose your soul and wander here. Wander until the world ends."

"You're not a ghost yet, Captain. Come along with us. We seek a way out of this limbo, for surely there is a way. A way to the world beyond."

The officer followed in their wake as the cloud swirled around them, leaving a curling furrow behind. They went down a columned avenue, and finally arrived at the foot of a flight of seven stairs.

"Here is the way out, if such exists," Erasmus said.

"But where are we?" the navy man asked.

"At the *nance*, Captain," Anna said, suddenly straightening. "The nexus of this world. The gate to the worlds beyond."

At the stair's head they found seven palely tinted columns; two of rose, a pair in white, two of green, and one of shining black.

Anna no longer seemed lost and overcome with despair. She drew herself up and looked around with a clear eye.

"We might manage it yet, Erasmus. Do you remember? We opened the first gate, but there is a second. Where are the others? Where is my charm? I hope nothing has befallen Brother Norbert."

"I saw him," Erasmus said. "The swallows paid homage to him. It was surpassingly strange. Men have been made saints for less significant occurrences."

"Not in this world," Anna said.

## Fifty-Five

Kehler and Hayes appeared first, helping each other up the final stairs. Anna bade them perform the proper rites before they set foot on the *nance*, and then they collapsed with their backs to a pillar.

"There, we have found our way out, Kehler," Hayes said. "We are not ghosts after all."

"I am recovered now, Hayes," Kehler said, the edge of desperation gone from his voice, which now sounded only profoundly fatigued. "I . . . I was lost in my own fears, the horror of the crawl into the chamber and our escape. You see, I remember it all now."

Anna stood looking down on them. "You saw no others?"

"None that I knew," Kehler said. "Only Hayes, who rescued me from my demons, it seems." He looked over at Erasmus. "I hope your own journey here was less harrowing than mine."

Erasmus shrugged. He remembered it with something less than clarity. He had seen Clarendon and Brother Norbert. And the countess . . . or had that been a dream?

The naval officer whom they had found—the man who had accompanied Deacon Rose—stood looking up at the figures carved above the fount. He seemed like a man lost—far more so than sailors normally did on land. The captain was out of his depth and knew it. His only hope now was to return to the world he knew; other than that, he no longer seemed to care what this struggle was all about.

Erasmus closed his eyes and felt himself begin to drift. He snapped his eyes open, but found himself still upon the *nance*—the others there as well.

He shut them again and drifted into a dream of a fair green place, where sunlight played upon the forest floor and a sweet breeze spoke among the trees. He could almost understand what it said. Almost.

A hand rocked him gently, then again, and Erasmus opened his eyes.

"Ah, Mr. Flattery," Clarendon said, for the small man was there, as was Brother Norbert. "We must all awake from our dreams now. Dreams or nightmares. Anna says it is time." The small man smiled at him in open affection, looking more than a little adrift.

Erasmus scrambled up, shaking his head to clear it.

"What must we do now?" he asked.

"The second gate must be opened," Anna answered. "Take your places as before. We must not tarry. Erasmus saw the wolf among the ruins, and I do not think it was illusory. Captain James? You must remove yourself from the *nance*. It will be dangerous for you otherwise."

The man stepped quickly down onto the top step, not needing to be asked twice, but then turned and addressed Anna. "Is there any hope that I will see my own land again?"

Anna gazed at him a moment. "There is hope, yes. You must return to the gate from which you came, Captain, and not tarry, for it will close soon after this gate is opened."

"But I don't remember how I arrived here. I only recollect being engulfed in a wave of fire and then found myself wandering, bewitched and lost."

"You must go down, Captain." Anna pointed. "Down to the edge of the sea of mist. The gate is there. I can tell you no more."

The sailor's gaze dropped to the ground, and he shook his head, more than sorry he had ever become involved in the affairs of mages.

Anna bent to begin her preparations when Clarendon called out.

Deacon Rose approached the stairs to the *nance*, his manner as determined and malevolent as ever. Without thought, Erasmus pulled Captain James' sword from its scabbard and pushed the surprised seaman so that he stumbled down the stair.

"Ah, Deacon," Anna said in mock solicitation, "you have arrived too late once again. In a moment we shall take our leave of you—unless you have it in mind to pursue me into the other world. . . . Don't look so disappointed, at least you are rid of me—though not in the manner you would have preferred no doubt."

"Eldrich is here," Rose said, barely containing his fury. "I have seen his familiar."

"But even he has not arrived in time, Deacon."

"Do not let him up the stair," Anna said, and turned back to her preparations, leaving Rose fuming below. A fair voice was suddenly lifted, chilling everyone who knew it.

"But it seems you are wrong, Anna. I have arrived in time."

Erasmus looked up to find the stooped figure of Eldrich approaching at the head of a small band, all masked in shadow.

Anna quickly drew a line of green fire across the stair head, and stood beside Erasmus, who held up his sword, certain that it would seem little threat to Eldrich. The others gathered around Anna, as though determined to make a stand, however futile. Deacon Rose backed away deferentially, quickly retreating from the field between Anna and the mage.

"Come no further," Anna said, her voice trembling. "I am more skilled than you know. Stronger than you guess."

"Are you, indeed?" Eldrich seemed amused, but stopped all the same. "One hundred thirty-three years I have lived, one hundred twenty-six of them steeped in the arts. Give me some credit, child. You are but four and twenty, after all. It takes seventy years to make a mage—a true mage—which you are not."

"I have undergone the transformation," Anna said, her voice no more steady, though more defiant, "and won my struggle with the snake."

"Won? You never win. It is but an uneasy peace, though perhaps you will manage that. More than I would have expected for one so poorly prepared. I was sixty-five when I stood upon the *nance*, and that only because Lucklow was near his death, and there was a task to be completed. And even so, *I* was not ready."

Erasmus could see the countess, now, lurking behind the mage in the dim light, and this sight somehow made his plight seem even more hopeless. Walky and sad Percy Bryce were there as well—all the lives that Eldrich had ruined. He looked again at the countess, who was coldly beautiful in the moonlight. Did she hold a memory of their evening together that was near as sweet as his? Did she keep a memory of it at all?

And then another appeared, silver-maned—Skye, of all people. Erasmus had no time to wonder what Skye's part was in this. Eldrich was here, and all their hope of escape was gone. They had been so close! So close to being free of him.

"You cannot touch me," Anna said, her voice very quiet and unsure. She seemed exceedingly young, suddenly, not even four and twenty, but a mere girl confronting an angry parent. "I have knowledge of the curse. . . ."

"But not enough, it seems . . ." Eldrich said.

A spray of white down fell over Anna and Erasmus, catching fire where it touched the *nance*, and then suddenly Anna was tumbling down the stairs, in the embrace of some other—a whirl of red hair and priestly robes. At the bottom the priest rose over her prostrate figure, speaking words of Darian, crimson hands clutching a dagger.

At his feet Anna shuddered once, tried to rise, but fell back trembling, her mouth agape as though searching for air. And then she was still, a coil of hair moving in the breeze, blood pooling around her ghostly pale face.

What Erasmus noticed was the horror of the countess, and then Clarendon snatched the sword from his hand and leaped down the stairs before any could move. With all the force of his charge, the dwarf plunged the blade into the chest of Deacon Rose, and then in a fury, pulled it free and struck again. The priest was driven to his knees, the dagger clattering to the stone. Again Clarendon struck him, cursing him with each blow, and even when the priest toppled forward over the fallen Anna, Clarendon still cut him.

Then the little man dropped the blade and fell to his knees, sobbing.

Erasmus descended the stair and put his arm around the small shoulders, edging Clarendon back from the bodies. Poor Anna, lying there, her fugitive life at an end. Erasmus felt such cold in his heart at that moment—such utter cold.

"*I have done murder,*" Clarendon wept. "*Farrelle help me, Mr. Flattery. . . . Murder.*"

Eldrich stepped forward, chanting solemnly over the bodies, his hand moving quickly in the air. Then he looked up at those standing before him. "That is enough killing," he said, all the mockery gone. "Life is short enough." He looked down again at Anna and the priest. "The last follower of Teller has fallen. My task is done."

"You let him do it," Erasmus said, eyeing the mage, feeling his own anger rise. "You saw the priest with his blade and let him murder her."

Eldrich stared at Erasmus until he realized his former charge would not look away. "She could not live, Erasmus. She had the knowledge and the power to open the gates, and that could not be allowed. She is dead, and so is her murderer. Let it end there. Let it all end."

"And what of me?" Clarendon asked, suddenly very still. "I have the knowledge as well. . . ."

Eldrich stared down at the dwarf, and Erasmus could hardly credit what he saw. Compassion softened the mage's face.

"You shall not outlive me, little man. But you will have to come along. There is no other choice."

"Where?" Clarendon asked, Erasmus hearing the hope in the small man's voice.

"We shall make the journey of Tomas. But there is no time for talk. Even this tardy moon sails toward the west." He turned to Bryce. "Bind up her wound and carry her up onto the *nance.*"

"But she is dead, sir."

"Yes," Eldrich answered, "but she is a mage, for all that she has done, and I cannot leave her to wander here. Bear her up." He strode past Erasmus and Clarendon up the stairs, speaking Darian as he went.

Quickly everyone was arranged; Bryce next to Erasmus, then Skye. Anna was laid before the central pillar, then Hayes, the countess, and Clarendon, still shaken and white. Brother Norbert stood by the small stair that led to the perch above the fount.

Eldrich approached the hermit, the only one there who did not draw back when the mage came near. For a moment Eldrich stared into his eye, and then nodded. "A priest who is pure of heart. . . . Live long enough and even one's most cherished prejudices are shattered," the mage said. He beckoned Kehler, who came near reticently. For a moment the mage spoke quietly to Norbert and Kehler, who nodded frequently, then bowed as the mage finished.

Walky then delivered a long roll to his master and the two stood whispering softly. Erasmus heard nothing but the murmur of Eldrich's musical voice, the sound of water on stone. Walky did not look at his master, but kept his gaze cast down, nodding often. For a moment nothing was said and then Eldrich reached out and placed a hand on the small man's shoulder. Walky looked up as Eldrich turned away, and even in the poor light Erasmus could see the servant's eyes rimmed in red.

And then Walky hurried off the *nance*.

Finally Eldrich spoke to the countess, the mage glancing once at Erasmus, the two nodding, and then he saw them take each other's hands before Eldrich returned to the center of the *nance*.

The rite began with Eldrich bringing the pattern to life, so that it glowed as though made of the substance of the moon. Brother Norbert chanted a word Erasmus did not know—the mage's true name: *Adorian*. In the mage tongue it meant *last*.

And then Eldrich called fire from the fount. From there it was all a blur to Erasmus' mind. The clarity of the scene dissolved, and Erasmus felt himself slipping into dream—like a king's blood-induced vision.

Erasmus as a child, balanced atop the driverless carriage, gazing fixedly ahead. And then an uncurling rose; Percy blossoming into flame, crawling toward Erasmus, screaming. His howl of pain cut into Erasmus' consciousness so that it rang always in the ear.

Eldrich walking in the garden below, a child perched in the window overcome by a fear that he felt in his heart, in the center of his being.

And then an old woman before a fire, suckling a baby and singing softly to herself.

*"Upon a hill, upon a cloud,*
*Upon a haystack golden.*
*Within a wood, within a lake,*
*Dwelt the lady Sollen."*

A warm wind crossing a bay, far off the sound of surf and strange birds. Night. A procession winding up a mountainside through lush vegetation, bearing an old man wearing the mask of a bird and a cloak of feathers. Overwhelming sadness and loss.

A woman before him, dancing among tongues of flame, many armed, blonde hair streaming, and Erasmus felt himself chanting in Darian, felt a presence within.

He did not know if minutes or hours passed, but finally the flame trembled open—a gate into the world beyond. A place lit by the soft light of stars and moon. Erasmus inhaled the scent of flowers, of spring and woods and meadows.

The roll Walky had carried had been spread upon the *nance* and now fire burned about it like a frame, the portrait of Eldrich appearing to float, wavering upon some invisible surface.

Eldrich spoke and sent the flaming likeness floating through the gate, and then he turned to Clarendon and then Skye. "Follow close behind me," he said.

The mage bore Anna up as though she were no burden at all, her hair falling in an arc like the skirt of a gown. He laid her in the center of the pattern, brushing the hair from her face and laying her hands upon her breast. Quickly he bent and kissed her on the brow.

He stepped back from her, then, and intoned words of Darian. Green flame began to burn around her, and then it spread across the still form, hiding her from sight. For a moment it persisted, and then flickered and died. Anna was gone. Gone utterly.

Eldrich bowed to the dying flames, speaking Anna's name three times, and then he straightened and looked around.

"Mr. Bryce," he said quietly, and then straightened his stooped form and walked slowly through the gate, growing immediately distant, as though he'd crossed a field in three strides.

A dark shape shot through the opening—Eldrich's familiar.

Clarendon hurried behind, barely hesitated at the flaming gate, then quickly stepped through, glancing back once. Skye went forward, faltered, gathered his resolve, then walked on, his shoulders squared—a Stranger in search of his past.

"*Erasmus . . . ?*" It was Percy Bryce, his voice low and harsh. He moved toward Erasmus, trembling, a sheen on his brow.

"*I cannot,*" he whispered. "*The fire . . .*"

"He calls you, Percy," Erasmus said. "You must go."

"Not into the fire. Not . . . fire."

"*Bryce . . . !*" It was the voice of Eldrich, strangely distorted, stripped of its music.

Erasmus reached out and took hold of Bryce's shoulder. "Close your eyes, Percy. I will guide you."

Erasmus steered him toward the gate, which seemed to have grown smaller and pulsated strangely.

"Hurry, Percy," Erasmus said. "I see the mage coming back for you."

Bryce dug his fingers into Erasmus' arm, moving forward stiffly, each step so small.

"*Erasmus. . . .*"

"A few steps more, Percy. You're almost through."

The portal was weakening now, Erasmus was sure. It wavered before him as though about to collapse. He pressed Percy on, hardly able to continue himself. Eldrich seemed to be running now, waving an arm, but Erasmus could hear nothing over the sound of the blazing gate.

And then Percy spun toward him, striking Erasmus hard on the temple with an elbow. Erasmus stumbled, and felt Percy shove him, fear making the man strong.

Erasmus sprawled on the floor and Percy fell upon him.

*"Now you shall know my pain,"* he whispered, dragging Erasmus up.

The world spun beneath Erasmus. He tried to take hold of Percy, but his fingers would not grip.

He felt himself thrust forward, falling.

And then he collided with something solid. The world went red, then dark, spinning madly. And then pain, like fire running along the strings of his nerves.

Fire.

## ᔐ  Fifty-Six

Stars wavered overhead, spinning slowly. Erasmus closed his eyes again. He lay upon a surface that seemed to be moving, like the deck of a boat. More than that he could not say. Searching with a hand he found his throbbing brow.

"Mr. Flattery?"

He knew that voice. . . .

"Walky?"

"Yes. Are you well, sir? Are you . . . whole?"

It seemed a strange question and even more strangely phrased.

"My head is throbbing terribly."

"Yes. Mr. Bryce struck you savagely, sir. And we have all been . . . sleeping."

"I must get up, Walky. We must make our way back."

"We are back, sir. Back to this odd ruin of a mountain, and it is night, sir, though whether the same night I cannot say."

Erasmus opened his eyes again. The world spun, then caught and seemed to hold, like a boat suddenly aground.

Walky crouched over him, his face drawn and profoundly sad.

"How can we be back?"

"I don't know, sir." The little man shrugged. "The arts are mysterious, or perhaps it was the work of the mage. I cannot say, for no one has opened a gate in more than a thousand years." He paused. "Only the mage knows."

Erasmus struggled to prop himself up on his elbows. "But I have a memory of pain, of going into the flame. Was that not true?"

Walky nodded. "The mage managed to save you, sir. Do you remember? Mr. Bryce forced you into the fire, but you are untouched by it."

Yes, he remembered. Percy had duped him into venturing near the flame. And he had felt it. The memory was strong. It had touched him, burning along the paths of his nerves. He felt himself cringe involuntarily.

"Are you hurt, Mr. Flattery? There is no sign of it."

"No. No, I will recover." Erasmus took a long breath. "What happened to Bryce?"

"I do not know, sir. He went into the gate as it closed. Whether he is in the other world or not, I cannot say." A strange hesitation. "Nor can I say what happened to the mage."

Erasmus heard Walky's breath catch, and the little man sat back a little.

"Walky?"

"Perhaps he is safely on the other side, sir. That is my hope."

Erasmus shut his eyes, trying to remember. The entire night was a blur. Nothing but vague images that he could not connect into any logical sequence, as though the narrative had been lost.

Could the mage have actually died? Died saving Erasmus? He could not conceive of Eldrich dead. It seemed impossible.

But even if it were true, Erasmus could feel no remorse. No guilt. He was more than surprised that Eldrich would make the slightest gesture to save him—the mage, after all, had tried to kill him once. But somehow Erasmus felt the mage owed him as much. After what he had done to Erasmus, Eldrich owed him a life.

"Who else?"

"Do you remember, sir; Rose murdered Anna."

"Yes, and Clarendon avenged her." He searched inside himself for some reaction to Anna's death—they had been lovers, after all—but there was nothing but a terrible numbness. As though the flame had burned away all feeling.

"Clarendon passed through, as did Lord Skye," Walky said. "Though Skye will not find what he sought. He did not come from Darr, but from the worlds to the east. The worlds of reason, not magic. All others are unharmed."

"And Anna—He set her upon a pyre. Is that right?"

"She was a mage, Mr. Flattery. He would not leave her to wander in the dark."

"But what of Rose, then?"

"The priest was a different matter," Walky said darkly.

Erasmus felt a small shiver pass through him. He was ordering his memories of the gray world. Was Rose condemned to that place? Erasmus was not even sure he would wish such a thing on the treacherous priest.

"And what of you, Walky? Are you whole?"

"Untouched, sir. Which is lucky, for I have much to do."

Erasmus looked closely at his old teacher. Walky drew in a long breath, and his face fell a little.

"It was his time, Mr. Flattery. The mage knew. And he passed into the other world—the fabled world, sir. And though few will ever hear of it, he took his place among the great mages of history. And at the very last he saved you, sir. An act of compassion. I am not a religious man, Mr. Flattery, but it seems an act of redemption to me. Somehow, an act of redemption. May he find peace now. Certainly he did not find it in this life."

Erasmus nodded. But poor Percy had been bitter and treacherous and murderous in the end. If he was lost between the worlds, what a horrifying ghost he would be. Erasmus shuddered at the thought.

"The countess is well?"

"Yes. Perfectly, sir. And the others are unharmed, in body, at least." The little man hung his head, his gestures small, voice suddenly very old and frail.

*He grieves*, Erasmus thought. *In mourning for his master.*

"Mr. Flattery?" It was another voice. Deep and solid.

"Brother Norbert?"

"Are you well, sir?"

"I appear to be unharmed—at least to the eye."

The hermit came into Erasmus' view. He looked very solemn. Very still.

"We are ready to make our way down. Will you need help yourself? Or can you manage?"

"I will manage, I think."

Brother Norbert nodded. "Will you take up your sea fire, Mr. Walky, and light our way?"

The little man rose stiffly, and he and Brother Norbert helped Erasmus to his feet. For a moment he wavered, but then he seemed to gain strength. Walky's doing, he suspected. The old man knew more of the arts than he ever let on.

The others were there. Kehler and Hayes. The countess, strangely distant. The captain sitting alone, staring off at the horizon. Kehler and Hayes came over to greet him, though they were hardly exuberant. They looked like men who had not yet assessed the cost of their adventure, but feared the result. Still, Hayes patted his shoulder, and spoke warmly.

They began the climb down from the Keep, single file, their way lit by the moon and Walky's flaming brand.

Brother Norbert began to sing, his strong voice echoing like water running over stone, swelling in a song of sadness and great beauty.

They struggled down, all of them exhausted and near to collapse. It seemed they'd crossed a kingdom when they finally found the road where carriages were drawn up, and horses were being tended by the drivers.

Brother Norbert turned back toward the looming mountain and made a sign to Farrelle and spoke a prayer. No one objected, perhaps feeling, as Erasmus did, that there should be some ritual or rite to mark such a solemn occasion. The last mages had passed from this world.

*The last mages.*

## ⤳ Fifty-Seven

They sat in a circle around a small fire, watching the eastern sky turn pale, the moon still riding into the west. Dusk had found them, going anxiously from one to the other, as though seeking news of his master.

They all seemed reluctant to leave. Kehler and Hayes sat upon the ground, their backs to a stone. The others perched upon stones or logs that had been set about the fire pit.

All of them seemed lost in their own thoughts, emerging occasionally to make a statement that almost invariably did not lead to conversation.

Erasmus could not describe what he felt—hollow, empty. None of these words did justice to the void he felt inside. He could hear his own thoughts echo.

*It was fire*, he thought, *the unnatural fire. It burned me away inside, and like Percy, there is no sign of it on my skin.*

But perhaps it was merely exhaustion and the trauma of what they had been through these last weeks, beginning with their exploration of the cave, and if so, it would pass. Certainly it would.

"I wonder if poor Clarendon will find his lost Lizzy?" Hayes ventured.

"He had no choice but to go," the countess said softly. "His memories were ravaging him. He could not escape them. Going through the gate was desperation. Perhaps he hoped Eldrich would help him, would take away some of the pain of it. He was a singular little man, bearing a terrible burden of memory, wrongs he could never forget, betrayals, all manner of cruelty because of his difference. And yet he had created a persona for the world that belied the truth. He did not seem haunted when one first met him. Indeed, he seemed to be a man at peace." She shook her head.

"He was an individual of great complexity, Randall Spencer Emanual Clarendon," Erasmus said. "We knew him only briefly, and though we saw him under the most revealing circumstances, even so . . . I think it would have taken many a year to know him well. He had been so injured by the world of men that he seldom ventured forth into the light. I felt honored that he trusted us enough to reveal what he did. But the countess is right; he hid his scars well."

*Unlike Percy*, Erasmus thought.

Silence settled itself among them again.

Occasionally the countess would raise her eyes from the fire and contemplate Erasmus, but each time he met her gaze, she looked away, a great sadness etched on her beautiful face.

"What will we do now?" Hayes asked.

"You, Mr. Hayes," the countess said, "we shall certainly find you a position in the foreign office, if that is what you still desire. I think Sir John Dalrymple will be particularly sensitive to your application."

"And I will go with Brother Norbert to root out all the records of the arts from the archives of the Church of Farrelle," Kehler said, with some satisfaction. He looked over at Norbert. "I expect it will take some little while."

"And when that is done," Brother Norbert said, "I will return to my monastery in the hills. There is a task there I left unfinished. So many spirits that wander still. . . ."

This caused the countess to look up, her gaze thoughtful.

Erasmus felt himself shrug. "Perhaps I will go to Farrow for a while. I don't know. Where does one go after such an experience? Where does one go that memories cannot follow?"

"Forward," the countess answered. "Westward, Halden would have said, traveling with the light. That is what you should do, Erasmus. That is what we all should do—if we can."

Walky took up the reins of the team and looked down once more at his former charge and the countess who stood by to send him off.

"Will I see you again, Walky?" Erasmus asked.

"Perhaps, sir. The world is full of surprises. But I have duties yet and must complete them before my time comes."

Erasmus saw the way the old man glanced at the countess, and with a small bow to his former teacher, he left them alone.

He saw the old man reach down and take her hand. She put a foot on a step and rose up to kiss him tenderly, touching a hand to his cheek. Erasmus was certain there were tears in the old man's eyes as he shook the reins and rolled the carriage forward.

The countess came and stood by Erasmus, watching the carriage disappear down the hill. Dusk appeared beside them, watching as well. He seemed almost to quiver, as though it were Clarendon who left. Then, suddenly, he raced off after the carriage, having apparently made his decision. Who among all of them was most like Randall, after all?

"What will he do now that he does not have Eldrich to serve?" Erasmus said.

"I don't know. It was his life, and when the duties he was left are done, I am afraid poor Walky will be done as well. Try to imagine never having a will of one's own. Having no life that was not in service to some other. It is beyond imagining."

"Yes," Erasmus said softly.

The countess turned to look at him, drawing herself up. Even tired and travel-sore as she was, the countess still seemed almost unnaturally beautiful to him.

They regarded each other a moment, Erasmus searching for something to say.

But then she reached out and touched his arm. "I forgive you, Erasmus. Eldrich put a fear into you in childhood that you could never overcome. I . . . I forgive you."

Erasmus nodded, but before he could speak, she turned and walked away, answering the question he struggled to form.

She went then to Brother Norbert, speaking quietly to him, the hermit nodding solemnly, acquiescing to her request as men invariably did.

The countess took the second carriage and Eldrich's driver and set off at first light, leaving the rest of them wondering if it had all been a dream.

"At least Eldrich is not here to steal our memories away," Kehler said. "Or perhaps unfortunately he is not. I do not know which."

"No," Erasmus said. "We shall have to learn to accommodate them or make peace with them, whatever it is that one does with memories." He looked over at Brother Norbert. "What was it the countess asked of you before she left, Brother? Or can you say?"

Brother Norbert nodded. "When I am done with searching the archives of the church there are two ghosts—the spirits of small children—to whom I might bring peace. We shall see."

"Yes," Erasmus whispered so that none might hear, "but who will bring peace to the living?"

*I do not know why Eldrich chose me to tell his story, or why he chose anyone at all. It was, after all, the practice of the mages to maintain a wall of secrecy around all that they did. But then, Eldrich was the last, and in the end I think he succumbed to the very human desire to be understood, to forge a place in human memory. The common anonymity of death frightened even him.*

Marianne Edden:
*The Last Mage.*

## ～ Epilogue

On midsummer's eve the carriage came to Hyloft manor, making barely a sound as it rolled up the uneven lane. In the circle before the old house it rocked to a stop, and there disembarked a man so small that his weight did not even jiggle the carriage. He straightened his breeches and frock coat carefully and then, from the carriage, retrieved a flat package wrapped in plain paper.

For a moment he stood in the starlight, as though unsure of his intent, but went forward, pausing with a hand raised to knock on the door. He remained thus for some time, then slowly let his hand fall to the package, caressing it.

Bending with the slow motion of an old man, he leaned the package gently beside the door. Again he hesitated, staring down at the package in the faint light, his face in shadow, then made a quick bow, pausing at the bottom of the motion, and rising slowly. Looking back only once he turned and retreated to his carriage, reaching up to grasp the high handle.

"Would you not rather keep it yourself, Walky?" Erasmus said.

Walky turned to find his former charge emerging from the shadow of a hedge.

"Does it not mean more to you? Did she not?"

Walky stared at the silhouette, the emotions on his face hidden, but his posture a riddle of contradictions. "I shall not have the pleasure of it long, Mr. Flattery. Best the portrait go to you, who will treasure it as I have."

Erasmus nodded. "Are you unwell, Walky?"

"Not as any could tell, Mr. Flattery, but I lived to serve the mage. . . . He is gone and so shall I be soon. No, do not express regrets, it was the life I chose. A life few others have lived, I dare say. Do not pity Walky, for it would be wasted sentiment."

Neither man said anything for some moments.

"You are the last magical thing in this world, Mr. Walky," Erasmus said, surprised at the emotion in his voice. "What kind of world will it be without you?"

"The mage was the last magical thing, Mr. Flattery. Not me."

"That is where you are wrong. The mage was hollow in his center. A creature of certain appetites and desires, perhaps of duty. But you—You are good and kind and compassionate. Better you had been the mage, Mr. Walky, then magic would have been of a different character. You would have cast your enchantments on the fields of peasants, and eased the aching of the old, even their aching hearts. No, Walky, you are the last magical thing. I am sure of that."

"Well, sir, I think you're talking a lot of nonsense to please an old man, but I bless you for it all the same." He opened the door, a little embarrassed, Erasmus thought. Placing a foot upon the step, Walky looked back at Erasmus.

"Good-bye to you, sir," he said, his voice coming out as a whisper. "Be at peace, Mr. Flattery. Do you hear? Be at peace."

"And you, Walky."

The old man nodded and climbed up into the high carriage, pulling the door to behind him. His face appeared at the open window, and Erasmus crossed to stand below him.

"Call me your young lion," Erasmus said quickly.

"Sir?"

"Call me your young lion. I want to hear you say it once."

Walky stared down at his former student, his mouth working silently, and then in a whisper. *"Fare thee well, my young lion. Fare thee well. . . ."* This last word swallowed whole.

He reached out the window. Erasmus took the small, tough hand in his own for a moment and then the carriage rolled forward. For a few steps Erasmus clasped the hand, and then he let it go, like a bird into the air.

Walky looked back at him, raising his hand once in the starlight, and then the lightless carriage made its silent way down the lane. A shadow among the shadows. A dream of magic. Gone.